THE EARLY INVESTIGATIONS
of Joanne Kilbourn

THE EARLY INVESTIGATIONS
of Joanne Kilbourn

GAIL
BOWEN

M&S

This omnibus edition published in 2004 by McClelland & Stewart

National Library of Canada Cataloguing in Publication

Bowen, Gail, 1942-
The early investigations of Joanne Kilbourn / Gail Bowen.

Contents: Deadly appearances — Murder at the Mendel —
The wandering soul murders.

ISBN 0-7710-1467-8

I. Title.   II. Title: Deadly appearances.   III. Title: Murder at the
Mendel.   IV. Title: The wandering soul murders.

PS8553.08995E27 2004   C813'.54   C2004-902145-1

We acknowledge the financial support of the Government of Canada
through the Book Publishing Industry Development Program and that of
the Government of Ontario through the Ontario Media Development
Corporation's Ontario Book Initiative. We further acknowledge the
support of the Canada Council for the Arts and the Ontario Arts
Council for our publishing program.

Typeset in Trump Mediaeval by M&S, Toronto
Printed and bound in Canada

This book is printed on 50% post-consumer waste recycled paper.

McClelland & Stewart Ltd.
The Canadian Publishers
481 University Avenue
Toronto, Ontario
M5G 2E9
www.mcclelland.com

1 2 3 4 5   08 07 06 05 04

CONTENTS

Deadly Appearances

CHAPTER

1

For the first seconds after Andy's body slumped onto the searing metal of the truck bed, it seemed as if we were all encircled by a spell that froze us in the terrible moment of his fall. Suspended in time, the political people standing behind the stage, hands wrapped around plastic glasses of warm beer, kept talking politics. Craig and Julie Evanson, the perfect political couple, safely out of public view, were drinking wine coolers from bottles. Andy's family and friends, awkward at finding themselves so publicly in the place of honour, kept sitting, small smiles in place, on the folding chairs that lined the back of the stage. The people out front kept looking expectantly at the empty space behind the podium. Waiting. Waiting.

And then chaos. Everyone wanted to get to Andy.

Including me. The stage was about four and a half feet off the ground. Accessible. I stepped back a few steps, took a little run and threw myself onto the stage floor. It was when I was lying on that scorching metal, shins stinging, wind knocked out of me, chin bruised from the hit I had taken, that I saw Rick Spenser.

There was, and still is, something surreal about that moment: the famous face looming up out of nowhere. He was pulling himself up the portable metal staircase that was propped against the back of the truck bed. His body appeared in stages over the metal floor: head, shoulders and arms, torso, belly, legs, feet. He seemed huge. He was climbing those steps as if his life depended on it, and his face was shiny and red with exertion. The heat on the floor of the stage was unbearable. I could smell it. I remember thinking, very clearly, a big man like that could die in this heat, then I turned and scrambled toward Andy. The metal floor was so hot it burned the palms of my hands.

Over the loud-speaker a woman was saying, "Could a doctor please come up here?" over and over. Her voice was terrible, forlorn and empty of hope. As soon as I saw Andy, I knew there wasn't any point in a doctor.

Andy was in front of me, and I knew he was dead. He looked crumpled – all the sinew and spirit was gone. For the only time since I'd known him, he looked – no other word – insignificant.

The winter after my husband died I had taken a course in emergency cardiac care – something to make me feel less exposed to danger, less at the mercy of the things that could kill you if you weren't ready for them. As I turned Andy over on his back, I could hear the voice of our instructor, very young, very confident – nothing would ever hurt her. "I hope none of you ladies ever have to use this, but if you do, just remember ABC." I was beginning to tremble. *Airway.* I took Andy's chin between my thumb and forefinger and tilted his head back. His flesh felt clammy and flaccid, but the airway was clear. *Breathing.* I put my ear on his mouth, listened, and watched his chest for a sign of breathing. There was nothing. I was talking to myself. I could hear my voice, but it didn't sound like me. "Four quick rescue breaths and then C. *Check circulation."* I bent over Andy and pinched his nostrils shut. "Oh, I'm sorry, Andy. I'm sorry," and I bent my mouth to cover his. ABC – but I never got to C.

There was a smell on his lips and around his mouth. It was familiar, but I couldn't place it. Something ordinary and domestic, but there was an acrid edge to it that made me stop. Without forming the thought, I knew I had smelled danger.

Then I looked toward the podium and saw Rick Spenser filling the glass from the black Thermos. I didn't hesitate. His hands were shaking so badly he could barely hold the glass. Water was splashing down his arms and on his belly, but he must have filled his glass because he raised it to his lips.

Suddenly the world became narrow and focused. All that mattered now was to keep him from drinking that water. I opened my arms and threw myself at Rick Spenser's knees. It was a surprisingly solid hit. He fell hard, face down. He must have stunned himself because for a few moments he was very still.

The next few minutes are a jumble. The ambulance came. Spenser regained consciousness. As the attendants loaded Andy on the stretcher, Spenser sat with his legs stretched in front of him like the fat boy in the Snakes and Ladders game. When I walked over to the podium to pick up Andy's speech portfolio, my foot brushed against his.

In the distance I could hear sirens.

That last day of Andy Boychuk's life had started out to be one of the best. In June he had been selected leader of our provincial party, and we had planned an end-of-summer picnic so that people could eat, play a little ball and shake hands with the new leader of the Official Opposition. Simple, wholesome pleasures. But in politics there is always subtext, even at an old-fashioned picnic, and that brilliant August day had enough subtext for a Bergman movie.

Nomination fights can be intense, and Andy's had been particularly fierce because odds were good that we would form the next government. The prize had been worth having. And for more than a few people in the park that day, watching the leadership slip into someone else's hands had been a cruel blow. Soothing those people, making it possible for them to forgive him for winning, was Andy's first priority at the picnic, but there was another matter too, and this one was going to need skills that weren't taught in Political Science 100.

For years, there had been unanswered questions about Andy Boychuk's domestic life. His wife, Eve, was odd and reclusive. There had been a dozen rumours about her strange behaviour, and now that Andy was leader we had to put those stories to rest.

So behind the homespun pleasures of concession stands selling fresh-baked pies and corn on the cob or chances on quilts and amateur oil paintings, there was a deadly serious purpose. That day we had to begin to lay to rest Andy Boychuk's ghosts. It wasn't going to be easy. I had driven into the park earlier that morning to check things out. Two hard-muscled young women had been stringing a sign across the base of the truck bed we were using as a stage. It said, "Andy Boychuk Appreciation Day," and when I saw it, I crossed my fingers and said, "Let it work. Oh, please, let it be perfect."

For a while it was. The day was flawless: still, blue-skied, hot, and by noon, the fields of summer fallow we were using for parking areas were filled, and we had to ask the farmer who owned them to let us use more. All afternoon the line of cars coming down the hill continued without a break. In the picnic area, the food was hot, the drinks were cold, and the music drifted, pleasant and forgettable, from speakers hung on the trees. Everybody was in a good mood.

Especially Andy. On that August day so full of politics

and sunshine and baseball, he was as happy as I had ever seen him.

I'd watched him play a couple of innings in the slo-pitch tournament, and he'd been sensational. He'd come off the field sweating and dirty and triumphant.

"The man can do no wrong today," he'd said, beaming. "It's never too late, Jo. I could still be a major leaguer."

And I had laughed, too. "Absolutely," I said, "but there are five thousand people here today who want to hear this terrific speech I wrote for you, and –"

"And I have to sacrifice a career with the Jays to your vanity." He grinned and wiped the sweat from his forehead with the back of his hand.

"That's about the way I see it," I said. "Remember that line from your acceptance speech about how it's time to put the common good above individual ambition? Well, your chance is here. There's one bathroom in this entire park that has a functioning hot-water tap, and Dave Micklejohn said that at three-thirty he'll be lurking there with a fresh shirt for you, so you can get up on that stage and give the people something to tell their grandchildren about." I looked at my watch. "You've got five minutes. Forget the Blue Jays. Think of the common good. The bathroom's just over the hill – a green building behind the concession stands."

Andy laughed. "Okay, but you just wait till next year."

"You bet," I said, and I stood and watched as he ran up the hill, a slight figure with the slim hips and easy grace of an athlete. At the top, he stopped to talk to a man. I was too far away to see the man's face, but I would have recognized the powerful boxer's body anywhere. Howard Dowhanuik had been premier of our province for eleven years, leader of the Official Opposition for seven, and my friend for all that time and more. He was the man Andy succeeded in June, and there was something poignant and symbolic about seeing the once and future leaders, silhouetted against the brilliant blue of the big prairie sky. Even from a distance, it was apparent that their talk was serious and emotional, but finally the crisis seemed resolved, and Howard patted Andy's shoulder. Then, in the blink of an eye, Andy disappeared over the top of the hill, and Howard was walking toward me, smiling.

"You look happy," I said.

"I've got every reason to be," he said. "I'm with you. The weather's great. I managed to get over to the stage in time to hear the fiddlers and I got away before those little girls started dancing. What is it that they call themselves?"

"The Tapping Toddlers," I said, "and I doubt if they chose the name. My guess is that the parents who let those kids wear hot-pink satin pants and sequinned bras are the ones who came up with it. Sometimes I don't think we've come very far."

"Sometimes I agree with you." He shrugged. "Come on, Jo. It's too nice a day to despair of the human race. Let's go over and watch the chicken man. I'll buy you an early supper."

I groaned. "I've been eating all day, but I guess the damage is already done. As my grandmother always said, 'In for a penny, in for a pound.'" And so we walked over to the barbecue pit across the road from the stage. A man from the poultry association was grilling five hundred split broilers. Up and down he moved, slapping sauce on the chickens with a paintbrush, reaching across the grill to adjust a piece that didn't seem positioned right, breaking off a burning wing tip with his thick, callused fingers.

Howard's old hawk's face was red from the sun and the heat, but he was rapt as he watched the poultry man's progress.

"Jo, the trouble with politics is that it doesn't leave you time to enjoy the little things. Look at this guy – I'll bet he's cooked two thousand chickens today. He's a real artist. Go ahead and smile, but see, he knows just when to turn those things. That's what I'm going to enjoy now that I'm out of it – the simple pleasures."

"Going to find time to smell the roses, are you?" I said, laughing. "Howard, you're a fraud. Two days ago you told me that anybody who doesn't care about politics is dead from the neck down. I don't think you're quite ready to trade the back rooms for a bag of briquettes."

Across the road, the entertainment had ended and the speeches had begun. The loud-speakers squawked out something indecipherable. In the field in front of the stage, the crowd roared, and the man of simple pleasures was suddenly all politics again.

"Whoever that is onstage has really got them going," he said.

I linked my arm through his. "Are you going to miss all this?" I asked, indicating the scene around us.

"Yeah, of course I am."

"You could change your mind and run again, you know, or just stay around behind the scenes. Andy could use somebody who knows how to keep things from unravelling."

"No, I wasn't cut out to be an éminence grise – lousy fringe benefits."

The man from the poultry association was taking broilers off the grills now, grabbing the tips of the drumsticks between his thumb and index finger and giving his wrist enough of a flick to propel the chickens into an aluminum baking pan he held in his other hand.

"How about you, Jo? Have you thought any more about running? That guy who won Ian's seat in the by-election is about as dynamic as a cow fart."

"Not a chance, Howard. I'm happy right where I am. I think I'm over Ian's death. The kids are great, and I finally have some time to do what I want to do. This year off from teaching is going to be heaven. And, you know, the speech writing I'm doing for Andy is going to fit in perfectly. It'll give me some good examples for my dissertation. If I get it done in time for your birthday, I'll give you the first copy. Want to read a scholarly treatise called 'Saskatchewan Politics: Its Theory and Practice'?"

"God, no. I might find out that I've been doing it wrong all along." He looked at his watch. "Time for the main event. Let's grab a plate of chicken. Incidentally, guess who I strong-armed into giving the warmup speech before Andy comes out."

"His wife?"

Howard winced. "I'm not a miracle worker, Jo. Although Eve is here today. I saw her in that little trailer thing they've got in back of the stage for Andy's family and the entertainment people."

"How did she look?"

"The way she always looks when she gets dragged to one of these things – like someone just beamed her down. Anyway, you're wrong. Eve isn't introducing Andy. Guess again."

"Not Craig Evanson."

Howard pointed at the stage across the road and smiled. "There he is at the podium."

"You underestimate yourself," I said. "You are a miracle worker, especially after that terrible interview last night on Lachlan MacNeil's show. I can't believe Andy isn't more worried about it. I tried to talk to him, you know, but he says people will forget about it in a week, and besides, since everybody knows what MacNeil's like, no one'll take it seriously."

"Julie Evanson's taking it seriously," Howard said grimly. "She tracked me down this morning and told me Andy should either resign or be castrated – I think she felt that as the aggrieved party, Craig should have the option of selecting the punishment that fit the crime."

"Well," I said, "if Craig decides on castration, I might volunteer to hold his coat. Didn't you ever take Andy out behind the barn and tell him the boys and girls of the press can play rough? He should have known better. Craig and Julie had just about gotten over Craig's losing the leadership and what does Andy do? He tells Canadians from coast to coast that if we're elected, Craig had better forget about being deputy premier or attorney general because he's too dumb."

"Be fair, Jo, that shithead MacNeil really drove Andy into a corner. All Andy said was that when we're elected he'll find a job for Craig that's suitable to his talents. And you know as well as I do that Craig isn't the brightest light on the porch."

"Oh, God, Howard, I know. We all know Craig's limited, and I'll even grant you that he shouldn't be deputy premier or A-G. But he's a decent man, and more to the point, he almost won. Andy only beat him by ten votes. That's not much. I wish MacNeil hadn't made Andy run through that list of all the serious jobs and say Craig wasn't up to any of them. And I really wish that Andy hadn't risen to the bait when that twerp asked him to name a job Craig would be capable of handling. Minister of the Family? My dogs could handle that one. No wonder Julie was mad. Speaking of . . . we'd better get over there. Julie's always been able to look at a crowd of five thousand people and know exactly who wasn't there to hear her Craig."

The man from the poultry association opened a metal ice chest, pulled out the last bags of fresh broilers and began laying them on the grills. It was a little after four o'clock. The ballplayers were coming off the diamonds tired and hungry. The poultry man wouldn't be taking any chickens back to the city with him tonight. For a moment Howard was still, watching, absorbed. Then he shrugged and grabbed my hand.

"Let's go, lady," he said. Hand in hand we crossed the road and moved through the crowd toward the stage.

When we got close, Dave Micklejohn ran out to meet us. He had been Andy's executive assistant for as long as I could remember, and his devotion to Andy was as fierce as it was absolute. No one knew how old Dave was – certainly he was past the age suggested for the retirement of civil servants, but he had such energy that his age was irrelevant. He was fussy, condescending and irreplaceable.

That day, as always, he was carrying a clipboard. Also, as always, he was immaculate. He was wearing white, white shorts and a T-shirt imprinted with a picture of Jean-Paul Sartre.

"I like your shirt," I said.

"I tell everyone he's running for us in the south end of the province," he said. "You two were certainly no help. I run my buns off getting that bunch up there at the same time –" he waved at Andy's family and friends, sitting like kindergarten children on folding chairs along the back of the stage "– and you two vanish into thin air."

"Howard wanted to watch his hero, the chicken man," I said. "Anyway, we're here now. Did you find Andy to give him the fresh shirt?"

"Of course," he said, "I'm a Virgo. I know the importance of details."

I reached over and touched his hand. "Dave, don't be mad at us. You've done a wonderful job. How did you ever get Eve to come?"

I could see him thaw. Then, unexpectedly, he looked down, embarrassed. "Well, it wasn't easy. I had to agree to sneak a piece of quartz onto the podium today. She says the electromagnetic field from the crystal will combine with Andy's electrical field to erase negativity and recharge energy stores."

"Oh, God, Dave, no."

He squared his shoulders, and Sartre rippled defiantly on his chest. "She's here, isn't she? And look." He held up a sliver of rose quartz that glittered benignly in the sunlight. "You can put these things in water, you know. Eve says they charge up the people drinking it and bring them into harmony with their environment. Actually, we had quite a nice talk about it."

"Why don't you make Roma a nice cup of water on the rocks?" I pointed to the far end of the stage, where Andy's mother, Roma, was sitting stiffly, as far away as she could get from her daughter-in-law. "She looks like she could use some harmonizing. Actually, what we probably need is a slab of quartz dropped in the water supply for the whole city – take care of all our problems." Beside me, Howard gazed innocently in the direction of the ball diamonds.

Dave snapped the clip on his clipboard. "You don't have to be such a bitch, Jo. In fact, if you could manage to let up a little, I could tell you about our real triumph." He smoothed the crease of his shorts and looked at me. "Rick Spenser's here today."

I was impressed. "What's he doing here? I know this is big stuff for us, but it's penny ante for the networks. Why would those guys at CVT send their top political commentator to cover a little picnic on the prairies?"

"I don't know," said Dave, "but I'm ecstatic. There are a lot of nice visuals here today – all the little kids guessing how many jellybeans are in the jar, and the old geezers throwing horseshoes and reminiscing. How many points do you think all this heartland charm will be worth in the polls, Jo?"

"You'll have to ask Howard. He's the expert."

But Howard was heading behind the stage, where the major players, as they liked to think of themselves, were talking politics and drinking warm beer out of plastic cups. It didn't matter. We couldn't have heard Howard anyway because Craig Evanson had finished, Andy was walking across the stage to the podium, and the crowd was on its feet.

They had waited all afternoon for this, the moment when Andy would stand before them. Now he was here and they were wild – clapping their hands together in a ragged attempt at rhythm and calling his name again and again. "Andy, Andy, Andy." Two distinct syllables, regular as heart-beats until throats grew hoarse and the beat became thready.

We could see Andy clearly now. He was wearing an open-necked shirt the colour of the sky, and when he saw Dave and me, he grinned and waved his baseball cap in the air. The crowd cheered as if he had turned stone to gold. Finally, Andy raised his hands to quiet them, then he turned toward Dave and me and made a drinking gesture.

"Water," I said.

"Taken care of," said Dave, and he ran behind the stage and came back carrying a tray with a glass and a black thermal pitcher. When he went by me, he stopped and pointed to a little hand-lettered sign he'd taped to the side of the Thermos: "FOR THE USE OF ANDY BOYCHUK ONLY. ALL OTHERS DRINK THIS AND DIE."

I laughed. "So much for the brotherhood of the common man."

Dave passed the tray to the woman who was acting as emcee for the entertainment. She was a big woman, wearing a flower-printed dress. I remember thinking all afternoon that she must have been suffering from the heat. She handed Andy the tray with a pretty little flourish, and he took it with a gallant gesture.

I moved to the side of the stage. There was a patch of shade there, and it gave me a clear view of Andy and of the crowd.

They were arranging themselves for the speech – trying to find a cool spot on their beach towels, pouring watery, tepid drinks out of Thermoses, slipping kids a couple of dollars for the amusement booths that had been set up. Afterward, even the police were astounded at how few people had any real memory of what they saw in those last moments. But I saw, and I remembered.

Andy filled his glass from the Thermos, drank the water, all of it, then opened the blue leather folder that contained the speech I'd written for him. It was a sequence I'd watched a hundred times. But this time, instead of sliding his thumbs to the top of the podium, leaning toward the audience and beginning to speak, he turned to look at Dave and me.

He was still smiling, but then something dark and private flickered across his face. He looked perplexed and sad, the way he did when someone asked him a question that revealed real ugliness. Then he turned toward the back of the stage and collapsed. From the time he turned until the time he fell was, I am sure, less than five seconds. It seemed like a lifetime.

As I looked at the empty podium, I knew it was all over. I hugged the portfolio to me. In it was the last speech I would ever write for Andy Boychuk. The solid line of family and friends shattered into dazed groups. Eve Boychuk, Andy's wife, moved from her chair to the portable staircase. She was blocking the stairs, trying to keep the ambulance attendants from taking her husband away.

The August sun was getting low in the sky, and as she stood blocking the stairway, Eve was backlit with golden light. It was a striking picture. She wore a short sundress made of unbleached cotton and she seemed to be all brown limbs – powerful athlete's shoulders, strong arms, long, taut-muscled legs. She looked strong and invulnerable. But her face was dead with disbelief, and her eyes were terrible – vacant and unseeing.

The sirens were getting closer. Dave Micklejohn came up behind Eve, moved her from the staircase, and started giving directions to the ambulance attendants. "Bring him over to the side of the stage," he said, then he turned to me. "Come on, Jo, let's jump down over here and they can lower Andy to us."

And that's what we did. When she saw what we were doing, Eve came over and grabbed Dave's hand, and we all jumped down together. We must have looked like actors from the theatre of the absurd, but it was right that we were the ones who took Andy from the stage that last time.

They hadn't brought the ambulance up to the stage. There were so many people on the grounds, and I guess someone had told them there wasn't any hurry. We wouldn't let the ambulance people take over. They tried, but Dave, who was usually the most courteous of men, snarled at them to get away. As we began carrying Andy toward the ambulance, a woman dressed in blue came over, wordlessly took one corner of the stretcher from Dave and walked along with us.

I had noticed her earlier because she was a genuine beauty. She was, I think, close to sixty, but auburn-haired still, and she had the freckled skin of the natural redhead. As one of the attendants slid Andy's body into the ambulance, she reached her hand out toward the open doors in a gesture so poignant that Dennis Whittaker from our city paper, the *Sun Examiner*, took a picture of her that the paper used on their front page the next day.

We should have counted our lucky stars when we opened the paper and saw that heart-stopping picture. It could have been worse. Seconds after that photo was taken, the nightmare of that afternoon turned another corner.

Eve Boychuk had climbed into the ambulance before the attendants put Andy's body in. She was hunched over, sitting on one of the little jump seats ambulances have so family members can go along to the hospital with their loved ones. The ambulance had begun to pull away when a small, dark figure broke through the crowd and ran after it. She was shouting, but in a language I couldn't understand. It was Andy's mother, Roma Boychuk.

Eighty-three years old, brought from her neat little home in the west end of Saskatoon to watch her son's triumph, and we had forgotten about her. She had lived in Canada for seventy years, but she was still uneasy with English. Ukrainian was the language of her heart, and it was in Ukrainian she was crying out as she tried to stop the ambulance that was carrying her son away.

The scene was like something out of a silent movie: the round little figure in black running across the field, dust swirling around her heavy legs as the sun fell in the sky and the ambulance sped away. But the movie wasn't silent, and you didn't have to know Ukrainian to hear the anguish in her voice.

I didn't recognize the man who ran after her. He was tall and very thin. He looked like the singer James Taylor. The auburn-haired woman and I stood and watched as he reached Roma, enclosed her small body in his arms for a few moments and then, still holding her, walked across the dusty field toward us. When he came close, we could hear that he was saying to her the soft, repetitive nonsense words you use to soothe a child.

She was crying freely now, and her pain hung in the air like vapour. The auburn-haired woman felt it and reached out to Roma. She placed her fingertips under Roma's chin and gently lifted the old woman's face so that Roma could see her. They stood there looking into one another's eyes for perhaps ten seconds – two women united by grief and pain. Then Roma made a terrible feral sound, a hissing growl, the sound of a kicked cat, and she leaned closer to the woman and spat in her face. The man grabbed Roma and I reached for the auburn-haired woman, but she was running across the field toward the parking lot. I started after her, but when I'd run a few steps I was hit by a sense of futility. What was the point? Andy was dead. And so I just stood there as sirens sliced the air and police cars screamed over the hill.

Then someone was holding me. Suddenly my daughter, Mieka, was behind me; her arms, suntanned and strong, were around me.

"Oh, Mummy." She buried her head in my neck the way she had when she was a little girl. Over her shoulder, I could see Howard Dowhanuik with his arms resting on the shoulders of my two sons. They were still in their baseball uniforms, and I remembered they'd had a game before Andy was scheduled to speak.

"So who won?" I asked them. The automatic question. Andy would have approved.

"Us," said Peter, my older son, who was a head taller than I was. He had cried only once since he was a child, but he came running to his sister and me, and wept.

In the west a bar of gold separated sky and land. Over Peter's shoulder, I could see a grove of poplars. Already their leaves were turning, and the golden light caught them and warmed them to the colour of amber.

I closed my eyes and there, in memory, was another day of golden light. My classics professor was standing at her desk while the September sun streamed in the window, and she told us about the myth of the Heliades. Phaeton, she said, shaking her head sadly, had tried to drive the chariot of the sun across heaven, and Zeus had struck him down and turned his sisters into poplar trees. As they wept for their dead brother, the tears of Phaeton's sisters hardened into amber.

As I closed my arms around my son, I knew that my heart had already turned to wood.

CHAPTER

2

At six o'clock the next morning I was walking across the Albert Street bridge, thinking about murder. The city was sullen with heat from the day before, and it was going to be another scorcher. Mist was burning off Wascana Lake, and through the haze I could see the bright sails of windsurfers defying the heat. Already the T-shirts of the joggers I met on the bridge were splotched with sweat, and I could feel the cotton sundress I'd grabbed from Mieka's closet sticking wetly to my back.

The heat was all around me, but it didn't bother me. I was safe in the isolating numbness of aftershock. It was a feeling I was familiar with, and I hugged it to me. This was not my first experience with murder, and I wasn't looking forward to what came after the numbness wore off.

Three years earlier, in an act as senseless as it was brutal, two strangers had killed my husband, Ian. His death changed everything for me. The obvious blows – the loss of a husband and father – had left me dazed and reeling. But it was what Ian's death implied about human existence that almost destroyed me.

Until the December morning when I opened the door and Andy Boychuk was standing there, shivering, telling me there was painful news, I had believed that careful people, people like me, could count on the laws of cause and effect to keep us safe. The absence of motive in Ian's murder, the metaphysical sneer that seemed to be the only explanation for his death, came close to defeating me.

It had been a long climb back, and I thought I had won. I thought I had vanquished the dark forces that had paralyzed me after Ian's murder, but as I stood on the bridge and looked at the sun glaring on the water and smelled the heat coming up from the pavement, I knew nothing was finished. I could feel the darkness rising again, and I was desperately afraid.

The snow was deep the night Ian died. It was the end of December, the week between Christmas and New Year. We always get snow that week, and the day Ian died was the day of the worst blizzard of the winter.

He had driven to the southwest corner of the province just after breakfast. He went because he had lost the toss of a coin. There were two funerals that day: one in the city for the wife of one of the government members and one in Swift Current for an old MLA who'd been elected in the forties. Two funerals, and the night before at a holiday party, Ian and Howard Dowhanuik had had a few drinks and tossed a coin. Ian lost.

We quarrelled about his going. I called him, dripping from the shower, to make him listen to the weather forecast. He dismissed it with an expletive and disappeared into the bathroom. Fifteen minutes later, pale, hung over and angry, he got into the Volvo and drove to Swift Current. That was the last time I saw him alive.

At the trial, they pieced together the last hours of my husband's life. He had spoken well and movingly at the funeral, quoting Tennyson in his eulogy. ("I'm a part of all that I have met . . . /How dull it is to pause, to make an end/To rust unburnished, not to shine in use.") After the service, he went to the church basement and had coffee and sandwiches, talked to some supporters, kissed the widow, filled his Thermos and started for home. It was a little after four in the afternoon.

It must have been the girl who made him stop. I saw her at the trial, of course: a dull-eyed seventeen-year-old with a stiff explosion of platinum hair and a mouth painted a pale, iridescent mauve. Her boyfriend was older, nineteen. He had shoulder-length blond hair and his eyes were goatish, pink-rimmed and vacant.

They didn't look like killers.

The boy and the girl had separate lawyers, but they were alike: passionate, unsure young men who skipped over the death and asked us to address ourselves to the defendants' state of mind on the night in question. The boy's lawyer had a curious way of emphasizing the key word in each sentence, and I, who had written many speeches, knew that if I were to look at his notes I would see those words underlined.

"He was *frustrated*," the boy's lawyer said, his voice squeaking with fervour. "His *television* had broken down. And then his car got a flat tire on the night of the *blizzard*. And he wanted to take his girlfriend to the *party*. When Ian Kilbourn stopped to offer assistance, my client was already agitated, and when Mr. Kilbourn *refused* to drive my client and his girlfriend to the party, my client's *frustration just boiled over*. He had the wrench in his hand anyway, and before he knew it, it just *happened. Frustration, pure and simple.*"

"Fourteen times," the Crown prosecutor said, leaping to her feet. "The pathologist said there were fourteen blows. Mr. Kilbourn's head was pulp. Here, look at the pictures."

When I saw the dark spillage of my husband's head against the snow, the old, logical world shattered for me. It was months before I was able to put the pieces together again, and it was Andy who made me believe there was a foundation on which it would be safe to rebuild.

One evening the September after my husband died, I was in my backyard cutting flowers, and I sensed someone behind me. It was Andy, and there was a look on his face that was hard to read in the half light. As always when he talked with friends, there was no preamble.

"Jo, I've had a hell of a time dealing with what happened to Ian. I know it's been a thousand times worse for you, but today something came back to me, and it's helping. When I was in high school we read *Heart of Darkness* – I guess all the grade twelves read it that year. Anyway, the woman who taught us said that Kurtz possessed a mind that was sane but a soul that was mad. I think those kids who killed Ian must have been like that. Somehow that explains a lot. The world's a rational place, Jo. Anyway," he had said, "that's all I came to say."

Much later, as I thought back to the words, they didn't seem particularly profound, but on that September night I clung to them. In isolating my husband's murderers as mutants, spiritual misfits, Andy had made it possible for me to reclaim the image of a world that made sense. But now the man who had touched my shoulder and turned me from the heart of darkness had been swallowed by the darkness himself.

I turned onto the path that curved around Speaker's Corner. "A mind that was sane, but a soul that was mad," I said. A woman walking by with her basset hound looked at me curiously. I smiled at her. "Just saying my mantra." She tightened her grip on the dog's leash and quickened her steps. I didn't blame her. If I could have managed it, I would have run from me, too.

Considering what was waiting for me at the hospital, perhaps leaving reality behind wasn't such a bad idea. Howard had called at five o'clock that morning sounding tired and worried.

"Jo, I'm at Prairie Hospital – all hell's about to break loose here. How long would it take you to get over here?"

"Howard, I was sleeping. Can't it wait?"

"Would thirty minutes be all right? If you don't want to drive, Dave'll come over and pick you up."

I looked at my clock. I had slept for three hours. Obviously, Dave and Howard hadn't slept at all. They didn't need a prima donna.

"No, I'll walk. I could use the air. Why doesn't Dave meet me in the park and he can fill me in on the way to the hospital."

"Yeah, okay. I'll tell him to meet you at the flowers."

"Howard, the park is full of flowers."

"The red ones. You know, the weird little ones – the ones that bite," he said and hung up.

In the shower, it came to me. The ones that bite were snapdragons; there was a bank of snapdragons on a little hill past the bandstand. Sure enough, when I came over the hill, Dave Micklejohn was waiting. He was still wearing the white shorts and the Sartre T-shirt he'd had on at the picnic. He must have been at the hospital all night.

I put my index finger in the middle of his chest, right on the bridge of Sartre's nose.

"Existence precedes essence," I said.

"Never truer than today," said Dave, straightening his shoulders. "Oh, Jo, this thing just gets worse and worse."

"What now?" I said.

"Well, there's no doubt at all that Andy was murdered. The pathologist is ninety-nine per cent certain Andy ingested potassium cyanide seconds before his death. They think it was in the water that he drank at the podium. You know, the stuff in the black Thermos that I filled myself and then put the little note on for good measure."

I felt a coldness in the pit of my stomach. Cyanide in the water. My instincts had been right.

Dave waited for reassurance. "Oh, Dave, the police will know the note was a joke."

"Well, for the moment they're entertaining that possibility, hence I'm still a free person. You, incidentally, are a hero, Jo. When you decked that bigwig Spenser, you saved his life. If he'd managed to get the water down, there would have been two of them dead instead of . . ." He swallowed and looked toward the marina. The striped windsocks on the poles around the deck of the restaurant hung limp in the hot stillness of the morning. Dave swallowed again.

"Speaking of heroes, Dave, you're not doing too badly yourself," I said, touching his arm gently. "What's happening at the hospital?"

"It's full of media people. Jo, you wouldn't believe the mess and the confusion in that lobby. They've already got a crew setting up a live feed to *Good Morning, Canada*. Andy's murder will be coast to coast by 7:05. Great coverage, kiddo." And then, smiling ruefully, he gave me the final piece of news. Eve Boychuk was insisting that she would take Andy home to their place in Wolf River and handle the burial herself. That was where I came in.

"Jo, for fifteen years we've managed to smooth over the fact that Andy was married to a person who, to put it kindly, is unusual. Now, when we've got every media person in Canada here, Eve is going to throw our leader's body into a bag, pitch him into the back of her half-ton, drive down the

Trans-Canada and bury him in the garden next to her cat."

As we walked across the parking lot to the emergency entrance, we were both laughing. We must have sounded crazy, but the laughter helped. Suddenly, Dave pointed to the emergency room door.

"Well, how about that?"

I looked. There, bigger than life, left arm in a sling, was Rick Spenser. The doctors must have kept him in the hospital overnight for observation. His beautiful cream suit was filthy, and there was a nasty crosshatch of cuts on his forehead, but as a taxi pulled up to the door, his wave was imperious. He settled himself beside the driver, closed the door smartly and was gone.

I said to Dave, "Another myth shattered."

Dave grinned. "You mean our boy Rick in a dirty suit?"

"No, I mean our boy Rick jumping into the front seat of a taxi. A cabbie told me once that he could always spot easterners by the way they head for the back seat, even if they're alone. And there's Rick Spenser, an easterner right to the tip of his Dack's, diving into the front seat like a stubble jumper. A mystery."

"A day for mysteries, my friend," said Dave as he opened the glass door to admitting.

The hospital smell stopped me. Memories. I had come here the morning they brought Ian's body in. I hadn't believed Andy.

Dave was looking at me hard. "Jo, are you all right?"

"No," I said, "but I'm still functioning. Use me while you can."

"In that case, I'll go find Howard and meet the press and you take care of the Lady. That's what Andy used to call her, you know. He'd say, 'Well, Dave, looks like we're going to have to go to the Elstow Sports Day alone. The Lady has declined our invitation.'" He shook his head at the memory.

"They've put her in the conference room. It's just through those doors at the end of the hall. Be firm with her, Jo. Don't let her make Andy look ridiculous. This has to be first class all the way."

He gave me a hug and walked to the foyer, where media people were drinking hospital coffee and checking sound systems and lights. Two men carrying hand-held TV cameras trailed him. I watched as he picked his way carefully over the tangle of cables and wires on the floor and moved a pot of pink azaleas from the reception desk to the table where Howard would be holding the press conference; then, shaking his head, put them back where he'd found them. Virgo all the way.

Then I opened the double doors and walked down the corridor, in search of the Lady.

CHAPTER

3

The room that they'd put Eve in was in the new wing. The corridor I walked down smelled of fresh paint, and the floor was soft with carpet. The names and titles on the doors that opened off the hall made it clear that this was where the power of the hospital, medical and administrative, went to work. When I came to the door marked Conference Room, I took a deep breath, knocked and walked in.

The first thing I noticed was that, by anyone's standards, the room was luxurious. During the election campaign seven years before, the other party had promised a massive program of new health-care facilities. "A hospital for every patient," Howard Dowhanuik had scornfully called their program, but the people had bought it, and we lost the election. Now, seven years of scandals and kickbacks later, the number of hospitals in the province was exactly the same as it had been the day we left office. However, as a sop to the electorate, the government had, the winter before, begun construction on a new wing for the biggest hospital in the capital, Prairie General.

This was their showpiece, their shining rebuttal to nagging questions about available beds and state-of-the-art medical equipment. They would use this as evidence of a promise fulfilled, but we could use it too – as an indictment of a government that starved rural hospitals but emptied out the treasury for the folks in the capital. As I stood in the door of the conference room, I filed away details: the shining oak of the conference table, the deep chairs upholstered in leather the colour of a dove's breast, the handsome pieces of aboriginal art that blazed on the muted grey walls. Andy could get a great ten-minute speech out of this room . . . Then, like a blow to the temple, the correction, the change of tense – Andy could have gotten a great ten-minute speech out of this.

Andy was dead. There wouldn't be any more speeches. But I could do this much for him. I could take care of his wife. She was sitting at the head of the oak table. Her back was to a wall of windows that filled the conference room with the raw light of a city in the grip of a heat wave, but this room was cold – unnaturally cold – and quiet. Through the windows I could see the traffic on the street, but the air in the room was silent and dead.

I walked toward the window and sat in the chair beside her.

"Hello, Eve. How're you doing?"

Her voice was low and strong. "On a scale of one to ten, I'm about a minus five." She tried a smile. "They didn't want me to be alone last night, so I stayed here."

"You're looking fine," I said, and it was true. She was still wearing the unbleached cotton sundress she'd had on at the picnic, but her thick grey hair was brushed smoothly and caught in a barrette at the back, and her makeup was fresh. On the floor beside her was a bag, a large, tooled-leather bag with a shoulder strap, the kind travellers carry. With her deep tan and her Greek sandals and her self-contained, slightly abstracted look, she had the air of a traveller who suddenly finds herself inexplicably in the wrong place.

"Eve." I covered her strong brown hand with my own. "Dave thinks we should talk."

"Sort of widow to widow?" she asked and then she laughed.

"Yeah, kind of like that," I said and wondered if the doctors had given her something. "It's about –"

"It's about Andy's funeral," she said. "Dave told you he's afraid that I'll disgrace you all." She sounded distanced, ironic.

I took a chance. "Yeah, that's about it."

"Did he tell you what I want to do?"

"He said you were thinking about taking Andy home to Wolf River and having a private burial."

"And you don't think I have that right?" Her voice was low and controlled, but there was an edge in it.

"I know you have that right. It's just that Andy meant a lot to a great many people, and I think we should give them the chance to say good-bye."

She looked at me. Her eyes were extraordinary – grey-green with little flecks of yellow, cat's eyes that seemed focused on something behind me that I couldn't see, that I would never see.

"Of course," she said, "a big funeral would be good politics. All those people talking about what Andy believed in, and all of you rededicating yourselves to Andy's principles. By the time we left the cemetery you guys would be way ahead in the polls."

She was right. None of us had illusions about the next election. It was, as they say, a crap shoot. The polls were good for us now, but polls change, and it would be nice to have a cushion. A big, emotional funeral would get a lot of print, and we would use the coverage.

There wasn't a political person in Saskatchewan who

hadn't thought of the impact Andy's funeral could have. What amazed me was that Eve had thought of it. Eve hated politics. We all knew that. And she hated political people. I had known Andy fifteen years, and I could count on one hand the number of times Eve had talked to me and on two hands the number of times I'd seen her in public.

But here she was, sounding as shrewd as a party organizer. She was Protean – changing shape before my eyes – and I was knocked off base. I didn't know where to take the conversation.

Eve did. "Jo, what would you do?" Another surprise. Eve asking advice, looking for a reasonable solution.

Well, I had one. Burying a murdered husband was an area in which I'd had some experience. I tried to keep the relief out of my voice. "I'd do what I did when Ian was killed. I'd ask Dave Micklejohn to arrange everything. I'd show up for the funeral. I'd do the best I could till everything was over and then I'd go home and fall apart."

Eve got up, walked to the windows and looked at the street. The minutes passed. I stored away more details about the room in case I ever wrote another political speech for anyone: the smoky glass of the wet bar tucked discreetly in the corner; the handsome oak sideboard with the circle of crystal decanters gleaming in the sunlight; the spiky beauty of the vase of prairie lilies placed dead centre on the conference table.

Eve turned to face me, picked up her bag, slung it over her shoulder and shrugged. "Okay, let's go find Dave Micklejohn."

I couldn't believe how easy it had been. I had told Dave I was functioning. Apparently, I was functioning pretty well. As I grabbed my purse and headed out the door with Eve, I congratulated myself on a job well done.

The congratulations were premature. I had forgotten what waited for us when we left the new wing and went into the centre block of the hospital. It didn't take long to be reminded. There they were – the *Good Morning, Canada* people and half a dozen others. Howard Dowhanuik and a woman wearing a white medical jacket with a hospital ID picture clipped to the lapel were standing behind a row of microphones. The woman was reading a statement. It was 7:05 and we were going live – coast to coast.

I'd set her up. Eve had trusted me, and I'd led her right into shark-filled waters. It didn't take long for one of the local journalists to recognize her, and the crew turned the cameras on us. Someone stuck a mike in Eve's face and asked her if she had any idea who had murdered her husband. I was furious at the predatory smile on the face of the man who asked the question, and I was furious at myself. But Eve was wonderful. She said she knew people would understand if she didn't say much, she was still shocked. She would help the police in every possible way. Funeral arrangements were in the hands of Andy's friend, David Micklejohn. I looked at Dave, who was standing out of camera range beside the hospital spokesperson. I could see the relief on his face.

I grabbed Eve's arm, pulled her along with me and said, "Let's get out of here. Walk as if you know where we're going." Together we strode purposefully toward the heavy glass doors that opened on the parking lot. After the chill of the conference room, the hot city air was like the blast from one of those automatic hand dryers in a public washroom.

Eve is tall, five foot ten or so, at least a head taller than me. As we came to the fence that divided the doctors' parking lot from the public one, she leaned down and whispered, "Do you know where we're going?" We stopped and looked around. Not twenty feet away was an old maroon Buick – Andy's car. Dave must have driven it to the hospital from the picnic. I pointed it out to Eve, and she rummaged in her purse and pulled out some keys.

"Bingo," she said. We slid into the front seat of that car as coolly as two women driving to the office. Eve slammed her door shut, then put her head on the steering wheel and began to cry great, noisy, racking sobs.

She was entitled. So was I. But it wasn't my turn. Today I was supposed to be the strong one. I sat beside her and played with the paper coffee cups that were lying on the dash. Dave and Andy and I had driven to the picnic in this car together. Just at the edge of town we'd stopped for ice cream and take-out coffee. These were our cups.

Outside in the heat, barelegged women in bright summer dresses were walking to work. It seemed like such an ordinary thing to do that I felt a stab of envy as I watched them. Inside the Buick, Eve wept and I played with the paper cups. One, two, three – one for Dave, one for Andy, one for me.

As suddenly as she had begun, Eve stopped crying. She reached over to the glove compartment and came up with a crushed box of moist towels. We each took a couple and wiped our hands and faces. Then Eve turned to me.

"Joanne, I'm going home. I hate this city, and if Dave Micklejohn is taking care of the funeral, there's nothing for me to do here. I should go and see Carey and tell him his father's dead. We never know how much he understands, but I don't want him to hear about Andy on television." She had not mentioned murder. Her mind was protecting itself more efficiently than mine was. She was devastated but she was coping. As she sat there, pulling a comb through her hair, looking critically at her face in the rearview mirror, she was, I thought, more centred than we had given her credit for being. Maybe I'd been too quick to dismiss all the New Age theories about quartz crystals and cosmic harmony.

However she managed it, Eve was a strong woman and a brave one. Her tender and unpitying reference to her son touched a vulnerability in me, because until that moment

I had forgotten all about him. He must, I thought, be in his late teens now. It had been more than ten years since the accident. I'd seen those flat, factual lines in Andy's biography so often that they didn't register any more.

"Andy and his wife, Eve, have one child, son, Carey, who is learning disabled and lives at the Pines, a special-care facility operated by Wolf River Bible College in Andy's constituency. Both parents visit their son frequently."

Did they? How would I know? I never asked. I thought of all the spring evenings Andy had taken my kids out to the lawn in front of the legislature to play baseball in the pale light of the prairie dusk. And I remembered how, when Mieka had broken her leg skiing last winter and ended up in traction for ten days, Andy hadn't missed a visiting hour. I couldn't remember ever once asking him about his son, or for that matter about his wife.

Andy was the one. We, all of us around him, had dismissed his wife and son in a paragraph and then gotten on to the stuff that really mattered – the next speech or the next meeting. I looked at Andy's widow, and I was bitterly ashamed. I knew what lay ahead of her, the empty months and weeks, but I could only guess at the horror of her next few hours. On impulse, I reached over and touched her hand.

"Eve, let me come with you. I wouldn't mind getting away from the city for a while myself. I can take the bus back later."

"Suit yourself." She shrugged. She'd pulled away again. Well, who could blame her? In fifteen years I'd never attempted to get close to her. I could hardly expect her to embrace me now. She snapped her seat belt on, turned the key in the ignition and pulled out of the parking lot. She didn't say another word till we were out of the city and on the highway.

When she spoke, her voice was small and tight with pain. "Am I going to get over this?"

I tried for the easy answer, but it wouldn't come. When finally I did speak, I told her the truth. There didn't seem to be much point in lying.

"I don't know if you'll get over it, Eve. I haven't."

She turned and gave me a curious little smile, then we both drew back into ourselves.

Outside, the heat shimmered above the fields. Most of the crop was off, and as far as I could see the land was the colour of beaten gold. It was a heartbreakingly beautiful late August day, the kind of day when you know in your bones that the long days of light and warmth are over, and the darkness is coming.

I thought about the cold, white, empty months ahead, and panic rose in my throat. Only yesterday everything had been certain, heavy with promise. And now . . . But if it was bad for me, it was ten thousand times worse for the woman beside me. I turned to ask how she was doing, but the question was stillborn. In an instant, I knew that everything had changed.

On the way out of the city, Eve had driven cautiously and well, but now the little green spear of the speedometer was trembling toward 130 kilometres. She was gripping the steering wheel so hard that the veins that ran from her wrists up her inner arm were rigid; her profile was carved with tension. Even her thick, steel-grey hair seemed charged with wild, kinetic energy. When she turned onto the overpass just west of Belle Plaine the needle on the speedometer moved past 135.

The car and the woman seemed fused. It was as if the little green spear was registering her agony in the numbers on the speedometer. The old Buick was vibrating dangerously.

"For God's sake, Eve, slow down."

She looked at me as if she had forgotten I was there. Her eyes were dull with pain. "I've tried to believe that we can be in charge of our lives, that if we focus on the desire, we can create miracles." Her voice broke. "I don't think that can be true."

I felt the wheels lose traction, and I reached across and grabbed the wheel. The heaviness of the old Buick kept us on the road as we curved around the top of the overpass. Below us was the junction where traffic from the overpass entered the highway. There were a lot of cars down there for a Monday morning.

"Please, Eve, please . . ." My voice sounded wrong – whining, not desperate.

But it did the trick. She shook herself, as if she were coming out of a dream.

"I just lost my focus there for a minute," she said. Her voice came from far away. Then she slowed and drove carefully onto the highway.

Half a kilometre down the road, she pulled the car on the shoulder, stumbled out, bent over in the ditch and retched – terrible, agonizing dry heaves. My legs were shaking so badly I couldn't go to her. I opened my door to the smell of heat and dust and hot asphalt. It smelled terrific. I was alive.

When Eve came back to the car, her face was yellowy grey, but she seemed in control.

"I think it would be better if you drove the rest of the way," she said.

I slid over to the driver's seat, and Eve climbed in and shut the door.

We drove in silence for about ten minutes, then Eve said quietly, "I need you to help me."

"If I can, Eve, anything."

"Food." She opened her hands in a gesture of emptiness. "I don't think I've eaten since yesterday morning. Nobody fed me. I think I need to eat before I see Carey."

I remembered a doctor I knew who said surgeons were always hungry just after they'd lost a patient. Something to do with the need to connect again with the life force, he'd said. I looked at the woman slumped in the passenger seat, and I thought that if ever anyone needed to be connected again with the life force, it was Eve Boychuk.

CHAPTER

4

Disciples is a restaurant on the Trans-Canada Highway just outside Wolf River. It's run by the people from Wolf River Bible College, and whatever you think of their theology, they make the best pastry in the province. If you're serious about food, it's worth the forty-mile drive from the city to sit at their gleaming white Formica tables drinking coffee and eating the pie of the day.

That's what Eve and I did. The pie of the day was raspberry, and when we finished the first piece we ordered another. Two women playing at being ordinary, while the overhead fan stirred the smells of good coffee and fresh baking and on the radio in the kitchen, Debby Boone sang "You Light Up My Life." We didn't talk, but it wasn't an awkward silence, and when I looked at Eve after she'd finished eating, she seemed tired but calm.

"Do you know how long it's been since I ate pie?" she asked. "And I haven't had a cup of coffee in ten years. I try to stay away from toxins."

"I guess we should all be more careful," I said. Even to me, my voice sounded condescending, and Eve, who was unusually sensitive to nuance, caught it.

"Don't patronize me, Joanne. From what I've seen of political people, some cleansing and enlightenment might not be a bad idea." She turned and looked out the window. Across the parking lot from the restaurant was a small motel. In front of it was a sign: "Seek Ye First the Kingdom of God." Remote again, Eve sat and stared at the motel; on the table, her hands were busy making neat little nips around the edge of the place mat.

Finally the silence got to me. "You never really knew us, Eve. You never gave us a chance."

When she turned from the window, her eyes were narrow. "*I* never knew *you*. Listen to yourself, Joanne. That incredible narcissism. You people think the world begins and ends within six blocks of the legislature. I never knew you! Well, none of you ever knew me." Her voice rose. "Oh, you had your opinions – I heard things. Believe me, people always made sure I knew what you all thought. I knew about your contempt. About how you thought I was a liability, an embarrassment. 'Keep her out there in her house in the country, throwing her pots or whatever it is she does. Out of harm's way. Out of our hair. Out of sight, out of mind.'"

One by one people at the tables around us fell silent. Even Christians like a little drama, and the late breakfast crowd at Disciples smelled blood. On the radio, Amy Grant was singing about how much she loved her Lord, and in the booth by the window Eve was giving everybody a morning to remember.

"God damn it, none of you ever took the time to know me. None of you ever tried to understand our marriage." She slid out of the booth, slung her leather bag over her shoulder, then gave me an odd smile. "You never understood me, but you know what's worse? You never understood my husband. He was the centre of your little world, but none of you knew the first thing about Andy Boychuk." She walked toward the door, then turned. "Thanks for breakfast, Joanne. Thanks for driving down with me. Now leave me alone. You people aren't good for me. None of you know shit about anything." She looked hard at me for a moment, then she was gone.

By the time I'd paid the check, she was walking toward the parking lot, her car keys swinging from her hand. I started after her, but I was fresh out of good deeds. I went back into the restaurant, ordered another cup of coffee and checked the bus schedule posted over the cash register. I had two hours to kill until the bus came.

I took a sip of coffee, but I couldn't swallow it. A memory came, and I felt my throat close with pain. Less than twenty-four hours earlier, I'd been eating ice-cream sandwiches at the Milky Way on Osler Street, listening to Andy and Dave argue lazily about whether the Blue Jays had the sand to go all the way this year – good, aimless, hot-weather talk.

I managed to get outside before the tears started. As the door to Disciples slammed shut, Debby Boone's dad was singing "He's Got the Whole World in His Hands."

The sun was climbing in the sky when I turned down the road to the Bible college. The campus had the late-summer stillness that hangs in the air of a college town in the days before students, tanned and reluctant, come back for another year. The smell of pine trees, sharp with memories of cottages and corn roasts, filled the air. In spite of everything, I felt better. Here was a world that still made sense.

To the right I could see a compound of low, flat-roofed buildings that couldn't be anything but World War II military barracks. Once they must have housed the entire school. Now most of them were student residences with names like Bardon Hall and Wymilwood. One was a grocery store called

God's Provisions. That morning there was a hand-lettered sign nailed to the front door: "Closed for the Summer."

In the fifties, the college had come into some money, not an extravagant sum but enough to build a cluster of institutional buildings: smug, bland, closed in on themselves. West of the main road was a little subdivision of bungalows – faculty housing. Over the front doors, burned into pieces of cedar, were the owners' names: "The Epps," "The Wymans."

In the seventies the money had really rolled in: a classroom building, a gymnasium, half a dozen dormitories – all made of cinder blocks with slits for windows – Dachau modern, energy efficient, ugly, utilitarian. The campus was made up of the kind of unexceptional buildings any institution that has to answer to its board of governors would build.

Except – and it was an extraordinary exception – northwest of the main road where it was clearly visible from the highway – where it was, in fact, the first thing anyone driving west from Regina saw – was the new chapel of Wolf River Bible College. It was an amazing structure for an institution that prided itself on cleaving to the traditional values. It looked like a high-tech child's toy – a building made of giant Lego pieces or those intricate metal building sets kids used to play with thirty years ago.

The central building was an octagon, and four lozenge-shaped wings angled off it in an X shape. Everything was there in plain sight: steel beams, trusses, ducts, huge concrete planks, transformers; and everything was painted in primary colours, red, yellow, blue. Only the cross, which soared from the centre of the octagon, was unpainted. In the sunlight it glinted with the soft glow of anodized metal. The chapel was a brazen and innovative building as out of place in the midst of the comfortable mediocrity of the campus as a Mies van der Rohe chair in the middle of a K-Mart. I wanted to get a closer look.

The first thing I discovered was that the building had a name. A sign encased in Lucite pointed the way to the Charlie Appleby Prayer Centre. The construction was recent enough that the area around the chapel hadn't been landscaped. Clumps of earth turned over by machines baked hot and hard in the sun. Someone had thrown down a makeshift path of concrete blocks; and when I looked in the direction of the chapel, I saw a man and a woman walking toward me. The man was pushing a wheelchair, and the woman had a stroller. When they got closer, I realized that I knew the young man. He was Craig and Julie Evanson's son, Mark. Seeing him brought a rush of memories – memories of the time before the leadership race had divided us, and Craig and Julie and Ian and I had been young together.

We had met seventeen years before – the year our party, to everyone's surprise, formed the government. This was the election we weren't supposed to win, and the months that followed were heady times – at least for the men.

The wives saw a lot of one another that first term. It was a time of birthday parties and car pools and earnest discussions about preschools and free schools and French immersion. No one was more earnest than Julie Evanson. She and Craig had one child, Mark, the same age as our daughter, Mieka. He was the centre of Julie's existence. She planned her days around him, and there wasn't an hour in the day when Mark wasn't being instructed or challenged or enriched by his mother. Once, at the deflated end of a birthday party, all the parents began talking about the unthinkable: the death of a child. Julie had been passionate: "Can you imagine if, after all the hours and hours you put in to make them into something really special, it was over just like that?" And she had snapped her fingers defiantly at the disease or the drunk driver or the act of fate that might end her boy's promising life.

Mark Evanson hadn't died. He'd done something worse. He'd turned out to be ordinary. By the time he hit high school it was apparent, even to his mother, that Mark was average, perhaps even a little below average. Betrayed and baffled, Julie floundered for a while. Then, to everyone's amazement, she, who had had only the most perfunctory interest in her husband's professional life, threw herself headlong into advancing Craig's career.

It was, for her husband and son, as if a hurricane had suddenly changed direction. The lives of both men were thrown off course. Craig, who would have been content to be the Member from Regina–Little Flower for the rest of his life, suddenly found himself speaking at strawberry socials and annual meetings all over the province. Julie had decided her husband was going to be the next premier, and the first step was winning the party leadership.

Julie's son's life had taken an even stranger turn. He was confused at first by the sudden withdrawal of his mother's attention and affection. Then Mark linked up with a group of kids from Wolf River Bible College. At sixteen, Mark was born again. At seventeen, he became a husband and, in short order, a father. I'd bumped into Mark and his baby at an outdoor crafts show earlier in the summer. At nineteen, Mark Evanson was a solid, good-looking young man with a solid, good-looking baby. When he said he was happy, I believed him.

Craig and Julie were not happy. If he hadn't loved Julie so completely, losing the leadership to Andy Boychuk would, I think, have been a relief for Craig. He could have accepted defeat gracefully and eased into the life he had wanted all along. Except he did love Julie. Passionately, uncritically, Craig Evanson loved his wife, and her pain at losing gnawed at him. Long after the votes were counted, Craig was haunted by the knowledge that he had failed his wife.

Julie was haunted by demons of her own. Losing seemed to be like a slow poison seeping through her system. She was sullen with those of us who had worked on Andy's campaign, and she was jubilant when, late in June, Andy had answered a question whimsically and had been forced to issue an apology. Before the six o'clock news was over, she was on the telephone. "Well, Jo, what do you think of your blue-eyed boy tonight?" she had asked.

Now summer was almost over, the blue-eyed boy was dead, and Julie's boy was standing in front of me, his face glowing with pleasure.

"Mrs. Kilbourn, what are you doing here? I mean, God loves us all and everybody's welcome at Wolf River, but what are you doing here?" Mark's face was as open and without guilt as a newborn's. He stood on the path, smiling, expectant, waiting for an answer.

"I came down with Mrs. Boychuk – you remember, Andy Boychuk's wife. They're friends of your mum and dad's. I guess you heard what happened to –"

The smile vanished. Mark cut me off. "We heard, but we didn't want C-A-R-E-Y here –" he spelled carefully, then rested his hand on the shoulder of the boy in the wheelchair "– to sense that anything was wrong, so we've been walking him all morning. He loves the new chapel – all the bright colours, I guess."

For the first time, I noticed the boy. I looked into his face. It was hard to imagine him responding to anything. He was dressed neatly, even whimsically, in shorts and a T-shirt that had a picture of Alfred E. Neuman from *MAD* magazine on the front and the words "What, Me Worry?" underneath. He would have been a handsome boy. His head was shaped like his father's, and his hair was the same red-brown, but Carey's head, too heavy for his slender neck, lolled to one side like a flower after a rainstorm. His features were regular but they were slack, and his mouth gaped. A little river of spit ran from his mouth to his chin. Mark reached down and dabbed at it with a Kleenex.

I held Carey's hand and smiled at him, but he didn't respond. When I straightened, I found myself face to face with Lori Evanson. She had stepped out from behind her husband, and she was looking at me with wonder.

"Mrs. Kilbourn, we saw you on television," she said. "Such a terrible thing – an evil thing! You were very brave to save Mr. Spenser's life." Her voice was light and sweet, with a lilting singsong quality, like a child's reciting something she's learned by heart. Lori was holding a baby I knew was her own, but there was a quality about her, a sense that somehow she would never move much past adolescence.

It wasn't her body. Physically, she was mature and beautiful. She looked the way we all wanted to look when we were eighteen. She was wearing a sundress the colour of a cut peach, and her arms and face were golden with tan. Up close, she smelled of suntan lotion and baby powder. Her shoulder-length hair was dark blond and streaked from the sun. She was incredibly lovely but in her eyes, which were as blue as forget-me-nots, there was such vacancy. If the eyes are the windows to the soul, Lori Evanson's soul was spotless.

"We're so glad you're all right. 'Praise the Lord.' That's what Mark said when he heard you were fine." She stopped for a second and looked gravely at her husband, at this man who could say just the right thing; then she directed those incredible eyes at me. "You've always been so good to us – that toaster oven with sandwich grill when we got married, and the cheque for twenty-five dollars when Clay was born. Look, isn't he a precious lamb?" She turned the baby toward me for inspection. The baby was handsome and reassuringly

alert. "So kind," his mother continued. "If ever there's anything we can do for you."

"No thanks, Lori. I was just looking around. Perhaps I'll
go over to the prayer centre. Are visitors allowed?"

Her perfect brow wrinkled. "Gee, Mrs. Kilbourn, I guess
so, but you know, I don't know if anyone ever asked. I mean
we're all, like, very proud of the chapel. It was designed by
Soren Eames in consultation with a prize-winning Regina
architect." Her brow smoothed. "The Charlie Appleby
Prayer Centre seats 2,800 people and is a multipurpose area
that can be converted for other uses. The building also
boasts four radiating modules: a cafeteria, a gymnasium, a
faith life centre and a complex of state-of-the art business
offices." Her innocent blue eyes shone with happiness. She
was on home ground again. I saw the care with which those
vacant blue eyes had been made up – peach eye shadow
blending into mauve and then a soft smudge of grey eye liner
beneath the lower lashes. Suddenly, those perfect eyes
focused on something behind me, and they lit up. I turned
to see what she was looking at.

On the main road that led through the campus, a man
was getting out of a black Porsche. He was dressed like a
university kid – denim work shirt and blue jeans – but even
from this distance it was apparent that he wasn't a kid. He
was tall and boyishly slender but there was something
defeated about the set of his shoulders that suggested this
man's worries went deeper than a conflict in his class
timetable. When he began to walk toward us, I recognized
him. He was the James Taylor look-alike, the one who'd run
after Roma Boychuk to console her after Andy died. Lori
grabbed my hand.

"Here's Soren now. Oh, Mrs. Kilbourn, you have to meet
him. He is so kind and good. He understands everything, and
I mean everything."

But the man who understood everything walked past us with a curt nod for Lori and Mark and not even that for me. Lori's face fell, but she was quick to defend him.

"Mrs. Kilbourn, that is just not like Soren Eames. He is usually so friendly. I think he must be mourning Mr. Boychuk's passing, too."

"I suppose he met Andy when Andy came to visit Carey."

She stood very straight and looked directly into my face. "I don't know about that. All I know is that Mr. Boychuk came to see Soren almost every week, and lately a lot more than that. They were very close."

"Lori, I don't think we should be talking about this – even with Mrs. Kilbourn. When a man talks to his pastor, that's just like when he talks to his doctor. There's a trust there, like an oath."

Lori looked so shattered that I jumped in. "I guess," I said, "that he came to talk about Carey."

Mark was silent. "I guess if you two are going to talk about this, Carey and I better go down to Disciples and get a Popsicle. Lori, I'll see you and Clay at home for lunch." He kissed his son and wife and pushed the wheelchair toward the road to the restaurant.

Lori was solemn. She was attempting to analyze something, and it went against the grain. "Mrs. Kilbourn, please forgive me but I think you're wrong. Mr. Boychuk never really spends – spent much time with Carey. I mean he was like good to him and all that but, you know, Mrs. Boychuk would spend like hours with Carey – watching TV with him and talking to him about the programs and reading to him and telling him about things, but Mr. Boychuk – well, you could tell he, like, loved Carey and everything, but it just seemed real hard for him to stay with him. He'd come in and he'd sit and hold Carey's hand for a little while and then it was like he couldn't take it any more. He'd kiss him and he'd

just leave. No, Mrs. Kilbourn, Mr. Boychuk didn't come for
Carey. Anyway, Soren is the spiritual head of Wolf River
Bible College and all, but he wouldn't have been the one to
like talk to about Carey – that would have been . . ."
Suddenly a laugh as musical as the tinkle of a wind chime.
"Well, of course, it would be Mrs. Manz. She's the matron
for special care – sometimes I can be so dumb." She smiled
shyly, waiting for approval.

I gave it heartily. "Well, thanks, Lori, that's good to know.
It was kind of you to go to so much trouble." We both smiled
– neither of us seeing a barb in a comment that equated
human thought with trouble, and we parted friends.

I didn't make a conscious decision to call on Soren Eames.
It just happened. I'd turned down Lori Evanson's invitation
to have lunch at their trailer and walked down the path that
led to the chapel. Close up, it seemed to change, to reveal
itself. Somehow up close you didn't notice the hard-edged
bravado of the building as much as the simple fact that
everything fit so well.

The Charlie Appleby Prayer Centre was a fitting building
in both senses of the word. The parts fit together with the
cool inevitability of a beautiful and expensive watch. The
result, as I discovered when the front door opened to my
touch, was a building where form and function meshed
smoothly. It was a fitting building in which to worship God.

The heart of the building, the octagon-shaped chapel, was
a beautiful room. No stained glass or groined wood or silky
altar cloths – just a room in which everything was practical
and workable. All eight walls were glass – eight walls of
windows filling the room with natural light. In the centre
of the room was a simple circular altar. Suspended above it
was an unpainted metal cross. Arranged in octagons around
the altar were bright metal pews, covered in sailcloth cushions. The sailcloth was vivid: red, green, yellow, blue. I walked

down the aisle and sat in a pew. From there I could see how pieces of pipe had been joined together to form the cross. It looked functional and heavy. Suddenly, everything caught up with me. Exhaustion and grief and the familiar clutch of panic. There had been other deaths: my grandparents, my best friend from high school, my father, my husband. I had survived, but as I watched the play of light on the cross, I began to tremble.

I sat for perhaps half an hour. There were no tongues of flame. No pressure of an unseen hand on my shoulder. But after a while I felt better – not restored but capable of functioning.

"I am going to make it through this day," I said. There were no thunderbolts, so I picked up my bag and walked.

I don't know which I heard first – the man's voice or the sobbing. But as I stepped outside the chapel, squinting against the harsh midday light, I heard someone in distress. The sound was coming from one of the wings – modules, Lori had called them – that radiated from the chapel like spokes from a wheel. The crying was terrible. It seemed to spring from a pain so pure and so private that I knew there was no help I could offer.

But there was another sound – the sound of a man's voice. At first, I couldn't catch the words, but I didn't need to. The cadences were as familiar to me as my own, and I listened with my heart pounding against my ribs as the sounds shaped themselves into words. "I thought it was the right thing to do, but now I don't know." Then something I couldn't make out, then, "It would have been kinder if I'd used a bullet." The voice was tight with anguish. "Why can't we go back? Oh, God, Soren, why can't we go back?"

Then nothing except the blood singing in my ears and the knowledge that the voice I was listening to was Andy Boychuk's.

I turned and walked to the double doors of the wing where the voice was coming from. When I came to the office marked Soren Eames, I didn't bother to knock. Out of breath and close to hysteria, I opened the door.

There wasn't much to see – a slender man with a receding hairline and on the desk in front of him a portable tape recorder clicking metallically to signal that the tape had ended. I don't know what I'd expected. I was sick with anger and disappointment.

I went over and pulled the tape out of the recorder. I had a hundred like it myself: small, cheap tapes that Andy used, when he was driving, to record an idea or his impression of a meeting or sometimes just the thoughts he had driving late at night across the prairie.

"Where did you get this?" I asked.

Soren Eames's voice was so low I could barely hear it. "He gave it to me."

"What's it supposed to mean? All that about 'the right thing to do' and using a bullet."

Soren Eames looked steadily at me, but he didn't answer.

My voice was shrill in the quiet room. "I asked you a question. Why have you got that tape? What's it all about?"

"It's a private communication." He stood and walked over to me. "I'd be grateful if you'd leave me alone now." His voice was gentle. He took my arm and led me down a corridor, through a door and into the light. For a few seconds, Soren Eames and I stood on the threshold looking into one another's faces with the intensity of lovers. I don't know what we were looking for – clues, I guess, some sort of insight into what had suddenly gone so wrong. Finally, I turned and began to walk down the path toward the highway.

"Mrs. Kilbourn," he called after me, "when you're working through all this, try to remember that you're not the only one. Other people loved Andy, too." It was only later that I realized he had called me by name.

There was one cab waiting outside the Regina bus depot, and I beat out an old lady for it. I'm not proud of that, but there it is. As the cab pulled away, I looked out the rear window. She was standing on the corner shaking her bag at me.

It was two-thirty when the taxi pulled up in front of my house on Eastlake Avenue, less than twenty-four hours since Andy's death. Our dogs greeted me hopefully, and I remembered that I hadn't taken them for their run that morning.

"Sorry, ladies," I said, "it's shower time. You can come up and bark your complaints through the bathroom door." They did. By 2:35 I was in the shower, and by 3:00, clean and cool in a fresh cotton nightgown, I was lying on top of my bedspread fast asleep.

It was late in the afternoon when I woke up. The room was full of shadows, and my son Peter was standing by the bed with a glass of iced tea. He is a handsome boy, dark like his father with the Irish good looks all the Kilbourns have. His sister, Mieka, thinks it's a crime that she looks like me: "blond and bland" are her exact words. She's right, but Peter carries his own burdens. At sixteen, he is as shy as Mieka and my younger boy, Angus, are outgoing. The political life with its endless rooms full of strangers has always been torture for him, yet he has walked into those rooms and offered his hand without grumbling. He is wonderfully kind with our dogs, with his sister and brother and with me. The tea was just the kind of thing he would do.

He sat on the edge of my bed. "Mieka's down there making dinner. It looks kind of gross but it smells okay."

"What's she making?"

"Pork chops something and chocolate mousse."

"Wow."

He smiled. "Right, and Angus and I rented a movie for you. Something with Robin Williams. The guy at 7-Eleven said it's hilarious. And there were a bunch of phone calls for you but Angus took the messages so you'll probably have to wait for people to call back. Anyway, here they are." He handed me some slips of paper and grinned a little. "And that television guy – the one you decked yesterday – Rick Spenser?"

I shuddered.

"Right. Well, a delivery man came with some flowers he sent you." He gave me the thumbs-up sign and closed the door behind him. He had not mentioned the word *murder*. It was a delicacy I was grateful for. I sat on the bed, took a sip of tea and looked through the messages Angus had taken.

There were two surprises: Eve Boychuk and Soren Eames had phoned. I called Eve first. She sounded composed, and asked me to go to the funeral with her. She didn't, she said, know who else to ask. She and Roma Boychuk, Andy's mother, hadn't spoken in years. "And that," she said wearily, "leaves only Carey and, of course, you, Jo." She didn't explain the "of course." I said I would go with her. She said she'd get back to me.

Soren Eames, sounding tentative but friendly, said he just wanted to make sure I'd gotten home safely. I thanked him and told him that the next time he was in the city, I'd be pleased if he'd call me. I hung up, certain I would hear from him again. The lady whom I'd beaten out for the cab at the bus depot didn't call, but I was two for three on my morning encounters. Things were definitely looking up.

There was a call from a detective named Millar Millard of the city police. Detective Millard was out of the office but he would be in touch with me, said a young woman named

Ironstar, who added that one winter she had taken a class in human justice my husband had taught at the university.

And there were phone calls from friends. Ali Sutherland, who had been my doctor and my friend when Ian died, had called to send love and condolences. And there were invitations to dinner from two of the people in this world I would under most circumstances have liked to have dinner with – Howard Dowhanuik and Dave Micklejohn. I turned them both down. They would have talked about Andy's murder, and I couldn't face it. That night, nothing could compare with the prospect of sitting in my cotton nightgown at our kitchen table, eating Mieka's pork chops something and chocolate mousse, then curling up and watching a movie some guy at the 7-Eleven said was hilarious. Safe in my house, I could vanquish the word *murder*.

When I padded downstairs in my nightie and bare feet, I felt virtuous – all those phone calls answered – and I felt hungry. What Mieka was cooking smelled of ginger and garlic. As I entered the kitchen, she was putting a loaf of sourdough bread into the oven to warm, and Angus was chopping vegetables. When Mieka told me to fix myself a drink and check out the dining-room table, I kept walking.

The table was set with the knives and forks reversed – Angus again – but in the centre of the table was a crystal pitcher so exquisitely cut I knew it was Waterford. It was filled with gerbera daisies. Half were that vibrant pink we used to call American beauty, and the others were rosy orange. The late summer sunshine poured in the window, turning the facets of the crystal to fire. It was a centrepiece from a Van Gogh picnic. There was an envelope propped against my water glass. Inside, on hotel stationery, was a note from Rick Spenser: "On November 22, 1963, Aldous Huxley died. His death will always be merely a footnote to the Kennedy assassination. Thank you, my dear Mrs. Kilbourn, for keeping me from becoming a footnote. I have never liked seeing my name in small print." It was signed "RS." I called the hotel and left a message thanking him.

All things considered, it was a happy evening. Mieka's dinner was great, and after we ate I made myself a gin and tonic and plugged in the fan and we all sat and watched the movie. The guy at the 7-Eleven had been right. It was pretty funny. Angus fell asleep on the couch, so when the movie was over, I brought down a blanket and pillow for him, tucked him in, kissed the big kids and went up to bed.

The light from the little brass lamp on the bedside table made a warm pool in the darkness. Under the lamp, a stack of novels in bright dust jackets sat unread and inviting. The bed was turned down and the pillows were fluffed against the headboard. Peter again. Obviously today he was bucking for sainthood. He had my vote.

When I walked toward the bathroom to brush my teeth, I noticed a splash of material on the chair by the window – my dress from the picnic. I picked it up to throw in the laundry hamper. Under it was Andy's blue leather speech portfolio. Printed in gold Gothic type on the cover were the words "Property of Every Ukrainian Mother's Dream." Dave Micklejohn and I had given it to Andy for Christmas, when he'd announced that he was running for the leadership.

When I opened the folder, I expected to see that last speech. What I saw was not my words triple spaced on the familiar buff paper, but a single sheet of dove-grey paper – expensive paper. A third of the way down the page, hand-written in elegant calligraphy, were eight lines of poetry:

O rose, thou art sick.
The invisible worm
That flies in the night,
In the howling storm,

Has found out thy bed
Of crimson joy,
And his dark secret love
Does thy life destroy.

At the top of the page, centred the way they would be on engraved notepaper, someone had drawn the letters *A* and *E*. But they weren't separate; they were linked with little swirls and flowers the way they would be on a wedding invitation.

"His dark secret love/Does thy life destroy." Those had been the last words Andy Boychuk had read before his death, the last image retained on his eye. The warm, familiar room suddenly seemed alien, violated. My hands went slack, and the portfolio slid off my knee to the floor.

That night I dreamed of roses the colour of dried blood and of gold Gothic letters that refused to arrange themselves into coherence. I awoke with my mouth dry and my heart pounding.

"Who killed you, Andy?" I whispered in the dark. "Who killed every Ukrainian mother's dream?"

CHAPTER

5

Inspector Millar Millard had done what he could to make his office human. The fluorescent lights overhead had been disconnected, and the room was lit by a reading lamp on his desk and an old standard lamp in the corner. Along one wall was a bookshelf with some interesting names on the book spines: Dostoevski, Galsworthy, Thomas Mann, C.P. Snow. On either side of the low round table by the window were two chairs, real chairs, overstuffed and comfortable looking. In the middle of the table – a surprisingly domestic touch – was a fat yellow ceramic teapot.

There was a folder on the table in front of one of the chairs; Inspector Millard motioned me to the other one.

"Would you care for tea, Mrs. Kilbourn? Or I could send out for coffee if you prefer."

"Tea would be fine," I said, sinking into the chair.

On the bottom bookshelf were a dozen or so coffee mugs, each with the orange and yellow sunrise logo of *Good Morning, Canada*. They were given as mementos to people who appeared on the show. As I looked across the table at the man pouring tea, I thought I must have watched him earn all those mugs, and a dozen more besides. His face, weary and decent, had flickered across TV screens for twenty years. It was comforting to see him sitting across from me.

He was a tall, courtly man, white-haired and sunburned. His clothes were off the rack: lightweight trousers, not expensive but nice, and a white golf shirt. When he handed me the mug of tea, I noticed that the tips of two of his fingers were missing. The tea was good, and I said so.

"Earl Grey," he said. "I change blends during the day but I like Earl Grey for mornings – a good, no-nonsense tea."

"Yes," I said, and we lapsed into an awkward silence.

"Well," he said finally, picking up the folder, "it's about this business, of course." Across the file in blue marker was the name "Boychuk." "I'll need you to tell me about some things. Why don't you just start at a point you feel is useful, and I'll stop you if I need help following your line of thought. Would it irritate you if I smoked?"

"No, of course, not. I used to smoke myself."

"Everybody's smoking is in the past tense but mine," he said gloomily, opening a fresh pack of Kools. "You deserve praise for quitting."

"Thanks," I said. "It's been a while." If the city police force trained its officers to do the good cop, bad cop procedure, then Millar Millard must have been the prototype for the good cop.

Two hours later I knew he could also be the prototype for the smart cop. I had described that last day hour by hour, minute by minute. I had begun with Dave Micklejohn picking up first me at my house then Andy at the apartment on College Avenue where he stayed when he was in the city, and I had gone through our stop at the Milky Way for ice cream, the time at the picnic, the people we saw, the things we ate and drank. Millar Millard had been gentle and encouraging. After about an hour he had made us a fresh pot of tea, and brought out a box of Peek Freans biscuits, which he arranged carefully on a plate before offering them to me. I began to relax. We were friends, two intelligent people working out a problem together. At least that's what I thought, and that's why what happened came as such a shock.

I had found giving a narrative of that last day painful but bearable until I came to the moment when Andy walked across the stage to the podium. When I remembered how happy and certain he had been in those last minutes, I felt my throat closing. I had to look out the window to keep from breaking down as I told the story of the last minutes of Andy Boychuk's life. When I finished, I turned from the window and looked into the face of my new friend Millar Millard. I guess I expected some sort of commendation. I had, after all, gotten a pat on the head for quitting smoking. This had been worse, but I'd managed to give him a thorough, controlled account of those last awful minutes on the stage. Praiseworthy.

But there was no praise.

Inspector Millar dragged deeply on his cigarette. He had changed. We had changed. I was no longer someone helping the police with their investigation. I had become something else. Millard's blue eyes had lost their weary amiability, and his voice had lost its warmth. He leaned toward me.

"Just two more questions, Mrs. Kilbourn, but I want answers: How did you know there was poison in that water Andy Boychuk drank at the podium?"

I was thrown off base. I babbled a long and aimless story about being in Florida when my children were little and how one day on the beach my daughter had instinctively recoiled from a poisonous man-of-war even though it was as blue as a jewel. "It was as if Mieka just knew that thing was a killer," I finished lamely. "When I bent over to give Andy mouth-to-mouth, I knew the smell on his lips was deadly, and I knew I couldn't let Rick Spenser drink from the glass Andy had drunk from. Call it atavistic, if you will . . ."

"Oh, I will, Mrs. Kilbourn," he said dryly. "I will note in my report that you were obeying a primal response when you tackled Rick Spenser." He stubbed out his cigarette, looked hard at me and said, "Shall we abandon this area for the moment and look at another puzzling aspect of your behaviour that day?" His eyes were the hostile grey of a March sky. "What was it that you took from the podium before the police arrived? There are, I should mention, a dozen witnesses, albeit reluctant ones, who will testify that they saw you remove something from the area in which the murder had been committed."

"I believe they call it the scene of the crime," I said, smiling.

"I believe they do," he said, not smiling.

I took a deep breath, reached into my bag, pulled out Andy's speech portfolio and handed it to Inspector Millard. "This," I said, "is what I removed from the scene of the crime."

It was his turn to be knocked off base. He read the words on the cover aloud: " 'Every Ukrainian Mother's Dream.' " Mrs. Kilbourn, I'm at a loss here. Is this some kind of joke?"

"Yes," I said, "that's exactly what it is – or was. That's Andy Boychuk's speech portfolio. The inscription was a private joke."

His eyes were glacial. "Private between whom and whom?"

"Between Andy and the people who worked for him. The portfolio was a gift to Andy from Dave Micklejohn and me last Christmas. One of the Ukrainian newspapers in the province had run a picture of Andy and used the Ukrainian mother's dream thing as a caption." I hesitated. "It seemed pretty funny at the time . . ."

He lit another Kool and rubbed the area between his eyes. "I'm sure it did. These little whimsies always look a bit tawdry when there's been a murder."

"You have more experience of that than I do, Inspector," I said.

He looked at me wearily. "Mrs. Kilbourn, let's cut the crap. Why did you take the portfolio from the stage that day? You're a clever woman. You knew better than that."

"I guess I wasn't thinking clearly. If you want to dismiss me as hysterical or stupid, go ahead. But there was nothing devious in my taking the portfolio. I had given it to Andy. It contained the last speech I'd ever write for him. He was dead. At that moment I suppose I just thought I was taking something that was mine."

"Mrs. Kilbourn, you amaze me." He shook his head sadly. "Well, let's have a look at the last speech." He opened the portfolio. The poem was still in place. He read it without expression and when he was through, he looked up at me. "William Blake," he said. "'The Sick Rose.'"

"Yes, I know."

"What's it doing here?"

I was angry. I picked up my bag and stood. "I guess that's for you to find out, Inspector. Thanks for the tea." I started toward the door. I think I expected him to stop me. He didn't.

But when I opened the door, he said very quietly, "Any time, Mrs. Kilbourn. And, Mrs. Kilbourn, I'm certain I don't have to tell you this, but we'd appreciate it if you didn't leave the city for a while."

That patronizing "we" ignited something in me. "You seem to forget, Inspector, I have a funeral to go to. I'm not the kind of woman who leaves a friend to go to his grave alone."

It made no sense, but at that moment it was the best exit line I could muster.

The police station was air conditioned, but by the time I got to the street where I'd parked the Volvo, sweat was running down my back. There was a parking ticket on my windshield. Somehow, I wasn't surprised. When I reached into my bag for car keys, I pulled out a sheet of orange paper – the list of school supplies Angus needed before they'd let him through the door to grade eight. That didn't surprise me, either. I wanted a shower, a cold drink with gin in it and a novel in which an inspector of police was first humiliated then killed. But I was not a free agent; I was Angus's mother. I peeled the ticket off the windshield, put a quarter in the meter, crossed the street and went into the Bay.

I like the way stores look in the last days of summer: the stacks of fresh notebooks, the bright new three-ring binders, the crayons sharp with possibilities. I like the "Back to School" signs – cardboard cutouts of shiny red apples and cartoon bookworms suspended above the school supplies. And the "Back to School" clothes cut from heavy fabrics in deep and glowing colours reassuring us that, after a lightweight summer of ice-cream pastels, life is about to begin again in earnest. It's a time of hope, and that morning, in spite of everything, I could feel my spirits rise as I ticked off items on Angus's list.

I saw her by accident. When I was walking toward the boys' department, I happened to look up and spot the televisions, a bank of them, different makes and models and sizes. And on the screen of every one of them was the face of Eve Boychuk. Twenty Eves looking out at me through twenty pairs of unreadable eyes.

I walked over and turned the sound up on one of the TVs. She was amazing – no other word for it. She was reeling from the murder of her husband, but she was opening up her fragile and private world to public scrutiny. Tanned and handsome in a simple blue cotton dress, she was leaning forward, telling the interviewer that she wanted her husband's funeral to be something people would remember all their lives. The camera pulled in for a close-up, and there, in the large appliance section of the Bay, Eve was saying that her "dearest wish" was that her husband's body lie in state in the rotunda of the legislature.

I couldn't believe my ears. Twenty Eves coolly rebuffing the interviewer's timid reminder that lying in state was an honour reserved for premiers and lieutenant governors.

"So many people loved Andy," said all the Eves, "that I'm sure the premier wouldn't be mean enough to deny people the chance to come to the city to say good-bye." Oh, she was smooth. For the first time since his party had booted us out of office seven years before, I felt sorry for the baby-faced ex-linebacker who sat behind the big desk in the premier's office. Eve had flummoxed him.

She had, as it turned out, flummoxed us all. When I walked in the front door of our house, Angus barrelled into me. He was on his way to play baseball, he yelled over his shoulder. I made him come inside to check out his new school supplies.

"Awesome," he said, deadpan. Then on the porch he turned. "Mum, Mr. Micklejohn has called about eighty-three times and he sounds like he's going to cry."

When I picked up the telephone to call Dave, he was already on the line. Not a word about the coincidence of my trying to call him when he was calling me, not a word of greeting. The man who prided himself on taking care of details was starting to crumble. There was no preamble, just, "Jo, something's going on with Eve. I thought she was going to leave everything to me, then this morning, before I'd even had time for my morning ablutions, she was on the phone giving me directions about the funeral. She is intruding in everything from the choice of pallbearers to the food at the reception. 'No perogies, no cabbage rolls.' That's what she says. Can you imagine? Did you catch her act on television this morning? She is not the woman we thought she was."

"Fun is fun till somebody starts to mutate," I said. "Angus has that written on his science notebook."

"Kids," said Dave. "Anyway, what do you think's up with Eve?"

"I think she's showing us she can play the game, too. I think she's showing us that we underestimated her because she wasn't part of our little circle. And don't forget, she's suffering."

"All of us are suffering, dear. But we're professionals. We know how to do things right. I don't think we should have to restructure Andy's funeral as a confidence-building experience for Eve. However, I don't know what options we have. The frame of mind she's in – who knows what she'd do? I need some guidance here, Jo.

"In that case, my advice is to go along with her. Let her give us some general ideas and tell her we'll work them out. We've got the organization. You saw to that."

At the other end of the phone, I could feel Dave preening. He had a right to.

In the last year of his life, Andy Boychuk had the best organization the province had ever seen, and in large part it was due to Dave Micklejohn. We were as attuned to one another as partners in a trapeze act or a good marriage. We knew one another, and we knew Andy. We loved his strengths, but we also knew his weaknesses, and we worked to make sure no one else did. We all had our reasons for working for Andy Boychuk, and we all had our areas of competence, but the working life of each of us was fuelled by one desire: the need to make our guy look good. So strong was that drive that neither Andy's death nor Eve's intrusions stopped us. In those days before the funeral, we kept on going to the Caucus

Office; we kept on working on plans to make sure our guy looked good. "Man makes plans, and God laughs," said Dave Micklejohn sadly, but we kept on. Planning was a way of thumbing our noses at a universe where a bright and decent man could stand up to give a speech and be murdered before our eyes. And so Dave, who had been, among other things, Andy's advance man, advanced the funeral – making sure that the routes from the legislature to the cathedral would be lined with people but not congested, that the cathedral could handle an overflow, that the women who were preparing the lunch had ovens that heated and refrigerators that cooled – making certain, in short, that the final public event of Andy Boychuk's life didn't blow up in all our faces.

Kelly Sobchuk, who had done itinerary, planned the times and places all of us would be the day of the funeral. Lorraine Bellegarde, who had done correspondence, kept track of the memorial donations and flowers and letters that poured into the office first by hundreds and then thousands. Janice Summers, who had been Andy's principal secretary, made certain that out-of-province VIPs and in-province political powers had hotel rooms and schedules and transportation. And there were a half dozen more of us working at a half dozen other jobs efficiently and bleakly.

Every so often a kind of wild gallows humour would erupt. Around five o'clock one steamy afternoon before the funeral, I walked into the offices of the Official Opposition. A bottle of Crown Royal was open on the desk and another was empty in the wastebasket. About five of our people had gathered to hear Lorraine Bellegarde read the mail: a man in Ituna promised to deliver thirty thousand votes for us in the next election if we sent him Andy's clothes, "since I am his identical size and he has no further need for same"; a woman in Stuart Valley had made Andy a pair of slipper socks out of white flannel. She made them, she said, "for all my departeds because I don't like to think of them going over the line with bare feet, but let's call a spade a spade: there's no point in wasting good money on shoes for them." Two men who had seen Eve on television sent proposals of marriage, and one woman who was a cosmetologist from the southwest of the province told Eve she would look ten years younger if she had her hair cut into a "soft bob" and dyed it a colour called Hidden Honey. A stubby sample of human hair – like a paint-brush – was taped to the page. I had a drink and walked out of the building into the heat. I couldn't seem to get into the spirit. There were no more speeches to write, but I couldn't see beyond the day of Andy's funeral. Maybe I didn't want to.

My life between Andy's murder on Sunday afternoon and the Friday morning of his funeral had a shapeless, anarchic quality.

"I'm walking around doing things but none of them seems very real," I said to Dave Micklejohn one sweltering morning when I met him outside the legislature.

"Here," he said, slapping a five-dollar bill into my hand. "Do you want a sense of reality, Jo, dear? Go downtown and get Eve a pair of panty hose for the funeral – taupe, all nylon, no spandex, cotton crotch, queen size – not, you understand, because our Eve is fat but because she is tall." He was joking, but I went. You didn't have to be a psychiatrist to see that he was close to cracking.

There was no pattern at home, either. The boys didn't go back to school till after Labour Day, and Mieka was to start university in Saskatoon in the middle of September, so our lives were ad hoc, listless, like the lives of people who are stuck in a strange city by an airline strike or bad weather.

Part of the sense of strangeness could, I knew, be traced to the fact that on Tuesday, two days after the murder, the kids and I had moved into the granny flat. It was Peter's idea – a way for us all to get away from the heat.

Our house on Eastlake Avenue was built in 1911, and like all old houses it had dozens of cracks and crannies through which winter and summer air passed freely. Air conditioning would have been a waste there. But the granny flat was another matter.

There was a sprawling double garage behind our house, and the previous owner had had a flat built over it for his mother. It was one large room with a kitchenette and a bathroom. She had allergies, so it was sealed tight as a tomb. With a flick of a switch you could have it cool enough to refrigerate a side of beef or hot enough to slow cook it.

The granny flat had been the place where Ian worked on lectures for his human justice class, and on more than one lazy afternoon, a place where we made love. When he died, I moved in the books and notes for my dissertation. Now it was my office, but for me it was more than that. The granny flat was a place where I could mourn or sit staring into space without fear of worrying the children or of being seen to look like a fool.

When Ian had had his office there, he'd panelled the walls in knotty pine and had bookshelves built along one wall. There was a desk, a good leather chair for the desk, a reclining chair for reading, a brown corduroy couch that made up into a hideaway bed, and that was it. The decorating was fifties *Argosy* magazine, but the room had a cottagey feeling I liked.

The Christmas before Ian died I'd ordered a braided rag rug from Quebec as a surprise. It is a joyful splash of colour in that sombre room. The rug and a wall full of photographs Ian's mother sent me after he was killed are the only changes I've made. The pictures are a chronicle of Ian and his brother, Jack, growing up. I don't know what a grief counsellor would say about the hours I spend standing in front of the pictures, but it helps. There is something comforting about the neat and inevitable progression of those young lives: from babies who stare wide-eyed, then beam as they sit, then walk, to boys who hold dogs and play baseball and ride bikes, to young men, faces suddenly serious under strangely dated haircuts, who hold the arms of girls in billowy dresses, and graduate, and receive awards.

I wonder now if Peter didn't believe we all needed the healing power of those pictures when he suggested we carry our sleeping bags into the cool peace of the granny flat until Andy's funeral. Whatever the reason, we moved. And in those still, hot evenings before the funeral, we turned up the air conditioner, ate ice cream from Bertolucci's and worked hard at doing nothing. The boys watched baseball on the portable TV, and they brought the VCR over so they could watch movies when there wasn't a game. Mieka and I read through a stack of old women's magazines she'd bought at a garage sale.

It seemed in that cool apartment we could, for a few hours, seal ourselves off from the hot world of pain and insanity that surrounded us. And it was in those rooms that I decided to write Andy Boychuk's biography.

It was a decision that almost cost me my life.

It began on the morning of the Taber corn. At around seven o'clock, somebody started pounding on the door. When I opened it, Howard Dowhanuik was standing there. Over his shoulder, Santa style, was a gunny sack of corn.

"Jesus, Jo, I thought you guys were all dead. I just about smashed down the front door of the house, and then I remembered this place. What're you all doing up here, anyway?"

"It's cooler for sleeping."

"Well, it's not going to be for long if we stand here with the door open. Aren't you going to invite me in?"

"Howard, would you like to come in?"

"Yeah, I would, and I'd like some coffee. Look, I brought some corn for breakfast. A guy was setting up a stand at a gas station out on Dewdney. He drove in from Alberta this morning – first Taber corn of the season. Let's get some water boiling. I'm starving. Peter, go over to the house and get a pot. Angus and I'll start husking this. C'mon, c'mon. Let's look alive, everybody."

Laughing and grumbling, we began to look alive. The kids had always liked Howard, and since Ian's death, they seemed to treasure his rough kindnesses. They liked to be with him. So did I.

I made coffee. Howard cooked the corn and it was wonderful, indescribably delicate and sweet. Mieka unearthed a half gallon of peach ice cream and a Mieka cheesecake from the deep-freeze. It was an oddly comforting meal, and after Howard left to go to the legislature, I poured myself another cup of coffee and sat back in the reclining chair.

The room was filled with sunshine and the sweet smell of corn and butter. The boys were playing canasta – that summer they'd exhausted the possibilities of every card game but that one. Mieka, barefoot and in her cotton nightie, was sitting in the window seat, a stack of *Ladies' Home Journals* and *Chatelaines* beside her. It was a moment of rare peace.

Mieka's glasses were balanced at the end of her nose. Suddenly she looked over them at me.

"Mum, did you know Margaret Trudeau made her own wedding dress?"

"Good Lord, Mieka, how old is that magazine?"

She flipped it closed and looked at the cover. "June 1971 – five months before I was born."

"Yeah, I remember when you were born, and I also remember that dress. It was a caftan, white, of course, and he had a rose in his lapel. She was so beautiful. Livvy Scobey, who was our MP then, told me Margaret went all over Ottawa talking about how she made all her own clothes. The seams were all crooked and the hems were coming down, Livvy said, but no one had the heart to say anything. Margaret was so young and pretty and, of course, according to Livvy, everyone just felt so sorry for her being married to 'that man.' You know, all the years they were both in Ottawa, Livvy could never bring herself to say his name."

"Oh, Mummy, you guys are awful."

"Not me, Mieka. I thought he *was* terrific. He was terrific. At least, he was terrifically interesting. I suppose now that you're grown up and going to university, I can tell you this. The first time I ever voted, I voted for him."

Mieka twirled her glasses and grinned. "Oh, no. I was counting on you getting a nice cushy job when we get to be government again. But with that kind of skeleton in your closet, I don't know . . . Of course, you do have friends in high places."

"I'm not sure about that any more, Mieka. I'm not so sure about that at all." Suddenly the golden morning was edged in black. I swallowed hard. "Pitch me one of your magazines, would you?"

But she didn't pitch the magazine. She brought it over with a hug. "Are you going to be all right, Mummy?" I hugged her back, but I didn't say anything. I didn't trust my voice; besides, I didn't know the answer.

The magazine she'd brought me had a picture of a very young Natalie Wood on the cover, and inside was a memoir of JFK. The date on the cover was February 1964, a time before the truth had made its cruel revision of Camelot. The article was uncritical and sentimental, and it brought a flood of memories: a grey November day in Toronto, coming out of political science class in the Sidney Smith building and someone saying Kennedy'd been shot and someone else saying they'd shot Johnson, too. Then numbness – walking across Queen's Park with a boy from my class, both of us crying, plodding our way through sodden leaves while old newspapers whipped wetly at our ankles. Then a pub on Yonge Street that smelled of urine but didn't check ID too carefully, and sitting at a table in the back near the television and drinking and drinking but never getting drunk. After that, a weekend of flickering black-and-white images on a television that had come from my grandmother's basement. The vertical was stuck so you always had the top half of the picture on the bottom and the bottom on the top. It had seemed a reasonable enough way to watch what happened in the next few days. Now there was another loss, and I wasn't eighteen any more.

It would be nice to say that the memoir of Kennedy I read that day in the granny flat inspired me to write about Andy. It would be nice, but it wouldn't be true. The decision to write about Andy's life and death came out of a need more jagged and more complex than nostalgia. I was at risk, and I knew it. If I was going to be safe again, I had to prove somehow that life, life with a capital *L*, was a coherent narrative with a beginning, a middle and an end. Somehow I convinced myself that if I understood Andy's life, I could make sense of his death. I had already lost a husband to the abyss. I couldn't lose Andy, too. There had to be logic there – cause and effect. The alternative was unthinkable. And so even before my friend was buried, I was deep in the puzzle of his life.

CHAPTER

6

Andy's funeral was Friday, September 2, in the morning, so people could get away for the Labour Day weekend. "No point," said Dave Micklejohn, "in having it later in the day and ticking people off. Next week they'll be over their grief and all they'll remember is that Andy's funeral loused up the last long weekend of summer." He was right, of course, and we all agreed. But when the telephone rang that morning in the granny flat, I was disoriented. For one thing, it was still dark. I propped myself up on my elbow and grabbed the receiver. Dave Micklejohn was on the other end.

"Wake up, dear. It's show time!"

I looked out the window. "Dave, it's the middle of the night. It's still dark out there."

"Look again, Jo. It's seven a.m. That dark you see is a rainstorm. It's coming down in sheets."

As Dave talked, I got up, picked up the phone and walked to the window. The sky was the colour of pewter, and the rain really was coming down in sheets. There were already pools of standing water in the backyard, and my sad, stunted tomato plants had been flattened.

"Dave, the sky's falling in. What are we going to do?"

"Well, Henny Penny, when it's a funeral you're putting on, it's a little hard to give people a rain check and call it off. Did Kelly get the marching orders to you? You know where you're supposed to be and when?"

"They're right on top of the suit I'm going to wear. Don't worry, I'll be all right. And Dave, I'll buy you a drink afterward."

His voice sounded very far away and old. "There isn't enough liquor in the whole world to help with this. Damn it, Jo, I had such hopes for him . . ."

The receiver clicked down, and I was standing in the still, dark room listening to the sounds of my children sleeping.

I flicked on the coffee machine, walked into the bathroom and stepped under the shower. In an hour and a half the front doors of the legislature would be closed to the public. Twenty minutes after that a limousine would pick me up and take Eve and me to the legislature for her private good-byes to her husband. Why Eve had chosen me for this painful and intimate duty was a mystery, but Eve was full of mysteries. She had asked, and I had agreed. So we two widows would accompany Andy's body from the legislature to Little Flower Cathedral for the funeral mass then to a reception at the parish hall (catered, I had noticed on Kelly's marching orders, by the ladies of St. Basil's Ukrainian Catholic Church – one in the eye for Eve there; I'd bet my last dollar there would be perogies on that table) and finally to Wolf River for a private burial.

I towelled off, put on a robe and poured a cup of coffee, then looked through the rain across the yard to our house. From this angle, it always looked big and foreign. Upstairs on my bed was my outfit for the funeral, my "sad rags," Mieka had said with a small smile when I showed them to her. But she approved. A creamy silk Alfred Sung suit that I'd bought from the "Reduced to Clear" rack at Drache's, a shiny, cream-coloured Italian straw bag and a pair of leather pumps, miraculously the right colour and on sale. I had some good gold jewellery Ian had given me over the years, and the night before, when I tried everything on, I was pleased with how put together I looked. But today the thought of getting dressed or even leaving the granny flat filled me with an exhaustion so complete I wanted to sink down in the nest of sleeping bags with my children and drift back to sleep. I was tired of being responsible. I was tired of being a grownup. I wanted out. The rain continued to fall. The yard would be muddy under my bare feet. But part of being a grownup is knowing that most of the time there aren't too many options. I pulled my robe tight around me, whispered to Peter to remember the dogs and went down the stairs that led to the rainy, pain-filled world.

When the limo from the funeral home pulled up outside my house, I was waiting. The undertaker, a sad-faced young man in a hot-looking wool suit, ran up the walk with a big, black umbrella to shield me. When I slid into the limo, the Alfred Sung was still bandbox fresh. Eve was already in the car. Surprisingly, she was dressed in green, a beautifully cut suit the colour of a new leaf.

She looked my outfit over thoughtfully. "Maybe white would have been better," she said, "but green is supposed to raise the vibrations of the body above the vibrations of pain." She tried to smile. "I don't think it's working." Then without another word, she leaned forward, tapped the driver on the shoulder and told him to go.

The rain was lashing the windows so hard that all I could see was the soft fuzz of the streetlights, still lit although it was almost nine o'clock. The limo was as quiet and set apart as the confessional.

"I like the rain," Eve said, as much, I think, to herself as to me. "It rained on my wedding day, too. Do you know what

my mother-in-law said?" She switched to a burlesque Eastern
European accent. "'Rain good. Means lotsa babies, lotsa
babies for Andrue.' Oh, God." She laughed then choked.
"Lotsa babies."

"Eve." I reached out to her, but she pulled away from me
and pressed her face to the window.

We'd pulled into the circular drive in front of the legislature. Ahead of us, gleaming whitely in the powerful bank of
lights that illuminated the entrance to the legislature, was
the hearse that had come to pick up Andy.

No people – just that silvery hearse and the empty stairs
in the rain. All week, from early morning till mid-evening,
the stairs had been choked with people. The line, patient
and endless, had stretched down Legislative Drive, past the
banks of marigolds and zinnias fading in the baking heat,
out onto Albert Street. Each time I went to the Caucus
Office, I walked beside the line. I was amazed at how many
faces I recognized. People I'd seen at party potlucks or rallies
or picnics – people who, year after year, paid for their mem-
berships and made a pan of brownies for a meeting or
brought their roaster full of cabbage rolls for a dance and felt
as connected to the party as any Cabinet minister. They
were the people who defended the party to their neighbours
and tore it apart at conventions. Political people sometimes
call them the foot soldiers. The soldiers were at home this
morning getting ready for the funeral, and Eve and I were
going to be alone with the leader.

When I looked at those empty stone stairs I felt a spasm
of pain as acute as a blow from a fist. I thought of all the
times I'd seen Andy, always late, pulling on his jacket,
bounding up the stairs to get to the House. And now he was
lying in a box in that building, and it was over, and I'd never
see him again. I couldn't move. I sat there and let the sense
of loss wash over me.

Eve had already climbed out of the limo when the man from the funeral home discreetly tapped at my window. All the way up the stairs he and his colleagues dodged around us with their black umbrellas, trying to keep us dry.

When we opened the doors and stepped into the warmth of the building, everything was still. The premier, in response to one of Eve's televised pleas, had given everyone who worked in the building the day off. Without the knots of tourists and the click of heels on the marble halls, the building was alien, like a house after a family comes back from a long holiday. Until that moment, I hadn't realized how much that building was home for me.

Andy was in the rotunda. There were pots of marigolds and chrysanthemums banked along the far wall, and their smell, acrid and earthy, was reassuringly familiar – a smell to come home to on a wet September day. Except for a commissionaire sitting in the corner reading a newspaper, Andy was alone. His casket was oak, and it gleamed warm and golden like the woodwork around it. The top half was covered with the provincial flag, bright yellow and green with an orange prairie lily blooming at its centre. At the foot of the coffin was a spray of prairie lilies. Three years before, when Ian died, I had counted the panels of the disciples in the altar behind his coffin, and I had been able to shut out reality for a while. But there was nowhere safe to look here. The staircase to the left led up to the opposition offices – our offices. The one to the right was the one Andy and the kids would sit on for pictures when a school group from our constituency came to meet their MLA. He used to do a nice thing with them: after the pictures and refreshments, he'd take them outside and show them how they could use a paper and pencil to make rubbings of the fossils embedded in the limestone walls of the legislature. He had been a good man.

A good man, but not a perfect one. He was reluctant to offend, to make enemies. He didn't want to be the bad guy. Often, too often, when the hard decision was made, one of us was left to enforce it. It was a serious flaw in a human being and a worse one in a politician, but death seems to bring a moratorium on critical thought – at least for a little while. I sat staring at the casket gleaming dully in the soft light. After a while, a terrible sob cut through the silence. I was surprised to realize that the cry was my own.

For me, Andy Boychuk had two funerals. There was the one I went to with the chief mourners, Eve Boychuk and her son, Carey, an event so painfully emotional that it will always exist for me in jagged and surprising flashes of memory. And there is the funeral on videotape I saw rerun many times on television, a coherent ceremony in which all of us seem to move through our parts with a grim composure. On that day, more than most, there was a gap between perception and reality – between the way things seemed to me at the time and the way they were.

Double vision. What the camera shows first is a sullen sky and a street that, except for the police van on the north side, is empty. The white hearse, shiny with rain, and the mourners' car, also white, arrive at the cathedral. Eve and I walk behind as the men from the funeral home carry the casket up the endless stairs. Two women alone, one in white, one in green. Incongruously, there is indoor-outdoor carpeting on the cathedral steps. It is sodden with rain. The honorary pallbearers are inside and dry; the working pallbearers must climb those endless steps slick with water, and the load they carry is a heavy one. I can hear them talking to one another under their breath.

"Shit, I almost fell."

"Watch that one."

"Have you got him?"

Later, I learn that they are not from the funeral home; they are city cops. Eve and I plod after them, the water squishing under our shoes. The camera shows none of this.

When the door to the vestibule is opened, a gust of wind comes out of nowhere and sweeps us inside. Roma Boychuk is there – all in black, of course. She is with an older man, a distant cousin, we learn later. She and her daughter-in-law do not speak. The casket is placed on its carrier, and we stand behind it, waiting. None of this is televised. Instead, the camera picks up the priest and the servers as they process down the middle aisle to meet us. I recognize Father Ulysses Tilley – Mickey to his friends. I'm glad he's the one. He would never have voted for us in a thousand years, but Andy liked him, and I did, too. Across the coffin, Mickey Tilley smiles at me and begins.

"The grace and peace of God our Father and the Lord Jesus Christ be with you."

The casket is sprinkled with holy water. Mickey Tilley has a good voice, an actor's voice that projects without strain. "I bless the body of Andrue with holy water that recalls his baptism." On television, Eve is magnificent, chin high, grey hair coiled regally under the lace mantilla, spine ramrod straight, gloved hands smartly at her sides, every inch the graceful public widow. But up close, I can see the muscles of her athlete's body tensed for flight. As the white pall is spread over the coffin, Eve begins to tremble.

"Consciousness. Energy," she says under her breath.

Finally, Mickey Tilley turns and Eve and I follow him and the coffin up the centre aisle of the church. As we walk, there is a soft babbling and a swishing sound behind me. Mark Evanson is pushing Carey Boychuk behind us. A surprise, at least to me. About halfway up the aisle Carey begins to cry. When I turn, I see Mark calmly stopping to give Carey a hug of reassurance. Eve marches, head high.

The Mass of Resurrection drags on – the confession, the prayers. Beside me, Eve drums her strong fingers on the prayer book. Legs crossed, she swings the toe of her black pump against the kneeler. It makes a small pucking sound. Every so often, she takes a deep breath and sighs audibly. Behind us Carey babbles, and Mark Evanson's low voice whispers reassurances.

There are three readings from the Bible. The camera pulls in for a tight shot of the readers. Dave Micklejohn, solemn and suddenly old, reads from the Book of Joel ("Your old men shall dream dreams, and your young men shall see visions"); a student lector from the Catholic college, her voice break-ing, reads the Epistle; and Father Mickey Tilley reads, well and movingly, the Gospel ("No one who is alive and has faith in me shall ever die").

When Howard Dowhanuik steps to the lectern to deliver the eulogy, he stands, head bowed, for a heart-stoppingly long time. Finally he lifts his head and looks at the congre-gation. In the half light of the cathedral, his impassive hawk's face with its hooded eyes looks almost Oriental. Later, when he embraces me, there is, beneath the light, citrusy smell of his expensive cologne, the smell of Scotch. Up close his eyes are red with weeping or liquor or both. But on television none of this is apparent, and his voice, when he speaks, is deep and assured – the voice of a man accus-tomed to being listened to, a man worth listening to.

Howard's memories of Andy are warm and personal – stories of law school, of campaigning in forty-below weather, of flying through thunderstorms in tiny private planes and finding six people at the meeting.

Andy is so alive in Howard's stories that the people seem

to forget where they are and the cathedral is filled with laughter. When he is finished, his place is taken by an old man from Sweetgrass Reserve, in Andy's constituency. The man wears a baseball cap, a plaid shirt and work pants. He looks like Jimmy Durante. He takes off his glasses, coughs, closes his eyes and begins to sing the honour song in Cree. His voice is strong and pure – a young man's voice. For the first time, Eve seems to connect with what's going on around her. She leans forward in her pew, and when the man is finished and goes to his seat, Eve turns with frank curiosity to watch him.

After he goes, Eve stares straight ahead, and I can almost feel her breaking. The TV camera shows none of this, of course. Her bearing is regal, and when she turns to embrace her son during the kiss of peace, she looks contained and engaged. She is neither. As the bread and wine are brought forward, Eve lapses into lethargy. When the altar and casket are incensed, she smiles a private smile. She takes no part in the communion, and as Mickey Tilley goes through the post-communion prayer ("O Almighty God, may this sacrifice purify the soul of your servant, Andrue"), she drums her fingers and taps her foot. When Father Tilley says, "Grant that once delivered from his sins, Andrue may receive forgiveness and eternal rest," Eve leans forward, head reverently touching the gloved hands that grip the wooden rail ahead of us. When I lean forward, I can hear her desperately repeating her own prayer. "Consciousness. Energy. Consciousness. Energy."

Finally it is over. "May the angels lead you into paradise." Our little party of mourners follows Andy's casket down the centre aisle of Little Flower Cathedral and into the vestibule. This is where our role in the television version ends. The camera pulls away from us and focuses on the faces of the people in the church.

The cameras missed the best part. At first, everything went smoothly. The pallbearers carried the casket smartly toward the door and waited. Roma Boychuk and her cousin took their place near the casket. Mark Evanson pushed Carey's wheelchair beside Roma and stood with his sweet Christian smile, waiting for whatever the Lord directed. Eve and I stood off to the right by a rack of pamphlets from Serena and the Knights of Columbus, waiting, I thought, to thank Father Tilley. I turned my head for a second, and Eve was gone.

It was simple enough. She had pushed past her husband's coffin, her son and her mother-in-law and slipped out the door. Mark and I followed her, but by the time we got out the door, Eve was headed for the street. The rain had stopped pelting down. It was falling in a soft mist – a gentle rain – and Eve was standing in it in the middle of the cathedral stairs, taking her shoes off. Ten minutes before, hair swept into an elegant French braid, face carved with pain, Eve had been the prototype of graceful suffering.

Not any more. She had ripped off her mantilla, and the French braid had come undone. She had tried to stuff the mantilla into her purse, but the bag wouldn't close and the lacy edges of the mantilla hung over its edges. She stood in her stocking feet, arms outstretched, a fashionable leather pump hooked onto the forefinger of each hand. She yelled something to Mark.

"Mark, I just can't . . . Sorry. Take Carey to Wolf River, and I'll meet you at the cemetery." She turned and ran down the steps and along Thirteenth Street. I looked to see if there were any media people there to witness her performance. For once, we were lucky. They were still inside packing up, getting quotes, making head counts. But Mark and I weren't alone.

Three doors open on the cathedral staircase, and the stairs are broad – I would judge about fifty feet across. Mark and I had come out the west door, and we were standing by the railing on the west side of the top step when a woman came out of the east door.

At the picnic she'd worn a dress that was the colour of cornflowers. She wasn't in blue today. She was in full mourning – expensive black from head to toe. But there was no mistaking the still, perfect profile or the dark auburn hair. She was the woman who had walked with us as we carried Andy's stretcher to the ambulance, who had tried to comfort Roma and who had run when Roma spat in her face. She stood and looked around uncertainly in the soft, misty rain. Then she was joined by a man. He put his arm protectively around her shoulder, and together they walked down the stairs and disappeared around the corner. Beside me, Mark watched with the frank curiosity of a child.

"Who was that lady?" he asked.

"I don't know," I said, "but she was at the picnic when Andy – when Mr. Boychuk died. Her picture was in all the papers, but I don't know who she is. I do know the man, though. That was Dave Micklejohn. Your mum and dad know him from politics. Dave Micklejohn was one of Mr. Boychuk's best friends."

While Mark and I stood and watched Dave Micklejohn and the mystery lady disappear into the parking lot, the camera crews and the news people came out of the church. I knew most of the local news people, and they waved or smiled or said they were sorry. They were a nice enough bunch, but they were young, and Andy's funeral was just one of the day's stories for them. It was time to move to the convention centre to interview delegates from the CLC, or to the teacher's club for a feature about how teachers felt about school beginning on Tuesday. The press thought the show was over. But they were wrong. Act Two was just about to begin.

CHAPTER

7

Because it serves the sprawling inner-city parish of the cathedral, Little Flower Hall is bigger than most. Apart from that, it looks like all church halls. A room as big as a gymnasium and about as warm, lined with stacking chairs and heavy tables with collapsible legs, the kind of tables that can be easily set up for banquets or potlucks. At one end of the hall is a stage; at the other is a large kitchen with a long counter open diner-style to the hall, a cloakroom, and off it the bathrooms. The hall was a place for modest wedding dances and parish fiftieth-wedding anniversaries and occasions like this, except I don't think there had ever been an occasion like this.

The ladies of St. Basil's Ukrainian Catholic Church had, they explained, "gone in with" the ladies of Little Flower to put on the funeral lunch. They had planned for five hundred people to come and go. There were three times that many, and the people came but they did not go. They stayed and stayed and stayed. The ladies did their best. Weaving their way through the crowd, they carried black enamel roasting pans filled with cabbage rolls or perogies or turkeys or hams already sliced in the kitchen, and casseroles of scalloped potatoes and chili and macaroni and cheese. But as soon as the women put down the food, it was gone; and at the end, I noticed platters loaded with an unmistakable brand of fried chicken.

I was standing at the end of a line waiting for a cup of tea when Howard Dowhanuik came up behind me.

"I'd give the next two hours of my life for a drink," he said.

I leaned close and whispered, "I'd give the next two hours of your life for a drink, too."

"Jo, you have a cruel tongue," he said but he smiled.

"Hey, this will cheer you up," I said. "The pie eater is here." I pointed to the corner where a man in a red open-necked shirt and too-big pants held up by suspenders was working away at a dinner plate piled high with pie. "The ladies have already been at me about him. They say he has eaten three whole pies in less than half an hour. That must be his fourth."

Howard turned to look at him. "What did you tell the ladies?"

"I told them their pies must be better than St. John's Norway because the pie eater only ate two there, and he left quite a bit of the second one."

"A very political answer. You sure you won't run for Ian's old seat?"

"Positive. You know, Howard, I'm kind of glad he's here. The pie eater, I mean. He came to all Andy's stuff. Do you think he votes for us?"

"Of course, he votes for us. All the slightly bent ones do, and when we're government, they're all there demanding jobs and justice. Speaking of justice, did you notice all the guys in grey windbreakers trying to look inconspicuous? My God, there were cops all over the place. I talked to the police chief on the way over. They had two cops in every pew during the funeral, and cops in the choir loft filming. That must explain some of the low notes the girls from the abbey hit during the hymns. And there's an unmarked van out front filming the comings and –"

He never finished the sentence. A Cabinet minister who had lost his seat in the last election came up and greeted him. Howard sent the man to the dessert table and told him he'd be with him in two minutes. Then he turned to me.

"Jo, I hoped I'd find a quiet minute to tell you this, but no such luck. I'm off to Toronto tonight for a few days. Something's come up. I won't be back till Wednesday – the late flight."

"I'll miss you. Howard, look, why don't you let me pick you up at the airport Wednesday night and bring you back for supper? I can make a pot of chowder, and we can open a bottle of Riesling and catch up on the news. Except it'll have to be an early night. I'm taking Mieka up to Saskatoon on Thursday to get her settled in for school."

Howard turned away for a minute to say hello to an expensively dressed man who looked out of place in the old church hall. "My dentist," said Howard. "Andy's, too, come to think of it. Nice enough guy but a bit of a dandy. Look at that suit. I'll bet it cost him five hundred bucks. Anyway, here's an idea about next week. I have to go up to Saskatoon and do a bit of politicking sometime soon, anyway, and I've got the van. Why don't I drive you and Mieka up? We can get her settled and go somewhere for steaks. I'll buy. Then you can take me down to the river bank and have your way with me in the moonlight."

"Sounds good to me," I said, "especially the part before the moonlight."

He grinned, gave me an awkward hug and walked off to find the Cabinet minister.

I was still smiling when someone came up and touched my elbow. I turned, and Soren Eames was standing in front of me. He was all in black, too, but in his turtleneck and beautifully cut cotton slacks, he looked more like an actor than a mourner. I hadn't noticed before what a handsome man he was. But as everybody's grandmother says, "handsome is as handsome does," and, at that moment, "handsome" wasn't doing much for Soren Eames. He looked ill and harried.

"Mrs. Kilbourn, I need your help. Mark Evanson and I were in the cloakroom getting Carey Boychuk into his coat when Mark's mother came in. She wants Mark to go home with them. She says it's important for everyone here to see they're a family. Forgive me, but I think her concern is less personal than political." I could see the pulse beating in his throat. He took a breath and continued. "Anyway, whatever her reasoning, Mark doesn't want to go with her, but, of course, she won't listen to him. There's no way I can get through to her. She's very negative about me. When I saw you, I thought perhaps she might listen to you because you're –"

"A woman?" I asked.

"No," he said, "I thought she might listen to you because now that Andy's gone, Craig Evanson will run for leader again, and your good opinion of him would carry a lot of weight."

"For someone not involved in politics, you know a lot, Mr. Eames."

"I had a good teacher," he said softly.

He looked about as miserable as I felt.

"All right," I said, "I'll give it a try."

Julie had her back to the door, so she didn't see me come into the cloakroom. She was so intent on her son that I don't think it would have mattered if she had. As always, Julie looked impeccable in a dress that she had, no doubt, sewn herself. It was black with a pattern of pale green leaves and white roses. As she pleaded with her son, the roses on her dress shook as if in a summer storm. But the platinum cap of her hair remained perfect – it always did.

Her voice was low. She was trying not to make a scene, but it was an effort. "Mark, please, let me run through it one more time. Slowly. There are some people coming to the house for drinks, and it would help Daddy if you were there. It's just for a couple of hours, but it's important for you to come. People say things if families aren't together at a time like this."

Mark listened quietly, his hands resting on the handles of Carey's wheelchair. He looked perplexed, as if he were trying to work through the possibilities in his mind.

Finally he said, "I'd like to help Daddy, but I have a job. I have to make sure that Carey is okay. He's my responsibility."

When she was at her cruellest, her most cutting, Julie Evanson had a little trick. She would laugh. I was never sure whether her laughter was intended to lessen the sting of her words or to suggest her disdain. At that moment, when she laughed at her son, there was no doubt. She was laughing to show her contempt for him and his life. It was an ugly sound.

"Mark, you don't have a job. You're just a babysitter." She looked quickly at Carey. "You're a babysitter for a half-wit. Do you know how humiliated I was when you walked up the centre aisle of that church today with your little charge? Everybody we know was there. Can't you at least try to make it up to me? Damn it, we're your family. You owe us something, don't you?"

Mark listened quietly, then he said, "No, Mama, I'm sorry. I'm a family man myself, and I have responsibilities. I'm sorry I disappointed you," and he bent forward and gently did up the zipper on Carey Boychuk's raincoat.

"Can I help you with anything, Mark?" I said. Even to my ears, my voice sounded stilted.

Julie wheeled around and looked at me. Then without a word, she walked past me into the hall, and I knew I'd just moved up another notch on Julie Evanson's enemies list.

But when I looked at Julie's son standing quietly and expectantly, I knew there was no time to worry. I took a deep breath, pasted on a smile and said brightly, "So, Mark, do you need some help?"

His face lit up with its sweet born-again smile. "No, we're just fine, Mrs. Kilbourn, thank you." He thought for a moment. "Well, actually, you could help us with one thing." He leaned forward and whispered confidingly, "You can help us find Soren so we can go home."

I found Soren, then, in one of those small moments that seem significant in retrospect, I saw Rick Spenser.

He was standing with his back to the stage and he was being spoken to by an old woman with savagely cut red hair and lipstick that was a bright fuchsia streak across her face. It was Hilda McCourt, Andy's high-school English teacher. Andy had introduced me to her at the picnic. During the tribute-to-Andy part of the program, she'd given a little talk. It hadn't been the usual "I knew he was marked for great-ness" stuff. She'd given a good, dry and professional account of Andy's strengths and weaknesses as a student, and I had liked her.

I joined them. "Miss McCourt, I don't know if you remem-ber me, but –"

She cut me short. "My memory is excellent, Mrs. Kilbourn, as I was trying to explain to Mr. Spenser here. I was telling him that some time in the past I met him; he insists I'm wrong."

"You know, Miss McCourt, media people are in our living rooms so often that they do seem like acquaintances." From her look, I knew I'd taken the wrong tack, but I blundered on. "A couple of times I've gone up to someone and felt so certain I knew her. Then she's turned out to be someone I'd seen on television."

Hilda McCourt's brown eyes were bright with anger. "Mrs. Kilbourn, if your thought processes are muddled, you have my sympathy. Mine are not. In future, you'd do well not to ascribe your shortcomings to others. I hope you and Mr. Spenser will excuse me if I find more congenial company." And off she clipped on her perilously high heels, leaving Rick Spenser and me face to face.

What was surprising was how attractive he was. He was undeniably a big man. Even the skilful cut of his beige linen suit didn't disguise that. From hard experience I have learned that television is not kind to people whose features are not well defined, but the camera really did not do Rick Spenser justice. On television he looked cherubic and bland; in person, his face was both less innocent and more interesting. He was, I remembered reading somewhere, forty-three, but he looked younger. There was a boyishness about the way he wore his dark blond hair – parted at the side and slicked down, the way mothers and Ivy League academics slick down hair. He wore round glasses of light tortoise-shell, and his eyes behind the lenses were hazel and knowing.

Most of the men I know are politicians or professors – notoriously lousy dressers both – but I recognized that Rick Spenser dressed with elegance. He was six-foot-two or so and at least three hundred pounds, but his clothing was just right. He had style. It was a pleasure to look at him and a pleasure to listen to him. He pronounced words the way someone who loves the possibilities of language does. Even that day in the church hall of Little Flower Cathedral with Hilda McCourt's assault still vibrating in the air, Rick Spenser seemed to savour the words he spoke.

"That's twice you've saved my life in five days. I'm in your debt, Mrs. Kilbourn. She really is a formidable person."

"That's what Andy always said. She was his high-school English teacher, and I think that even after he became leader she intimidated him."

"Not one of those sweet old things who invites the class over for tea and cakes on the Bard's birthday?"

"She seems more the three-fingers-of-gin-for-Dorothy-Parker type to me. But Andy thought highly of her. There was some sort of bad patch in high school that she helped him through . . . I'm sorry, Mr. Spenser, I shouldn't be rambling on. How are you? You look great – no cast on your arm, and that bruise on your forehead looks much less angry."

"I'm fine, and Mrs. Kilbourn – Joanne – I'm not good at this sort of thing, so I'll just say it once. I am deeply grateful to you for saving my life." He reached out one tanned and beautifully manicured hand and touched the top of my hand for a split second, then he withdrew it and smiled. "Now let's hear the gossip about Hilda McCourt."

"I haven't got any, really. I just wish I hadn't hurt her."

"Conscience?"

"Partly. And partly something less admirable. I'm mulling over the idea of writing Andy Boychuk's biography and I don't think alienating Hilda McCourt was the smartest way to begin. She knows a lot, I think."

Rick raised an eyebrow. "A biography?" He reached over and picked something off my suit jacket. "Lint," he said, putting it carefully in an ashtray at the end of the table. When he turned to me, I couldn't read the look on his face. "A biography," he repeated. "Not a bad idea. You certainly have a gripping final chapter. And, if memory serves, some other gripping chapters as well. There was an earlier tragedy, wasn't there?"

"You surprise me, Mr. Spenser."

"I do my homework, Mrs. Kilbourn. Now the accident . . . ?" He looked at me expectantly.

"It's public knowledge. It was about ten years ago. Eve Boychuk was driving. They were all in the car, Andy and Eve and their two children. Their daughter was killed instantly. Carey had terrible head injuries. He'll never be capable of living a normal life. Andy was thrown clear. Eve was injured, but she recovered. Well, I guess a mother could never recover from a horror like that. Anyway, she survived . . ."

Standing in the middle of that hot room filled with smells of turkey and coffee and cigarette smoke and people, I suddenly remembered sitting in my kitchen on a sweet spring day and opening the paper and seeing those pictures: the blackened metal of the car, Eve's eyes, dazed like the eyes of an animal caught in a headlight. Andy standing on the side of the road with the two stretchers . . . and something else. In the background, the swoop of the overpass at Belle Plaine.

"That's where the accident was . . ." I had spoken aloud. Rick Spenser was looking at me curiously. "I'm sorry," I said. "Two pieces of a puzzle just clicked together for me."

"I'm glad," he said. "That is, if you wanted them to fit."

"I don't know if I did, but I guess it's always best to know the truth." Eve's eyes dull with pain as the Buick pulled onto the Belle Plaine overpass. "I've tried to believe that we can be in charge of our lives, that . . . we can create miracles." In that close, hot room, I suddenly felt a chill.

"Are you all right, Joanne?" Rick Spenser's face bent close to mine, concerned.

"I'm fine, just . . . I would like to change the subject, though. How long are you staying in the city?"

He sighed. "I'm here till Sunday night. I couldn't get a flight out because of the holiday weekend. The young woman on the phone assured me they always reserve a few seats for those who might need a flight out for compassionate reasons. Apparently the fact that I was suffering from terminal boredom didn't excite her compassion." He looked so woebegone that I fell into what my daughter calls "the mummy mode."

"Why don't you come over and eat with us tomorrow night? I've promised the kids a barbecue, and I am a serious cook."

He brightened. "I accept, but since the promise of dinner tomorrow will bring to three the number of times you've saved my life, I insist on preparing a meal for you. I, too, am a serious cook, Joanne." He raised a finger to silence any protest. "You'll be doing me a service. Truly. It will give me something to do."

"I'm convinced," I said. "You're on. Now, we're in the book. J. Kilbourn on Eastlake. Give me a call when you're ready to shop and I'll pick you up and take you to Piggly Wiggly."

"Piggly Wiggly?" he said, eyebrows raised.

"Piggly Wiggly," I said. "This isn't Ottawa."

He looked at me hard, then he grinned. "You know, all of a sudden, I don't care that this isn't Ottawa. I really am looking forward to tomorrow night, Joanne."

"Yeah," I said, "me, too," and I meant it.

CHAPTER

8

When I got home after the funeral, there was a note from Mieka saying she'd taken the boys for haircuts. I made myself a pot of tea and a plate of toast, stuck a casserole in the oven for the kids and went upstairs to my bedroom. I turned on the radio to listen to the news, but I never heard it. By six o'clock, I was asleep.

I slept fitfully at first, dreaming dreams that in the strange world of the subconscious had their own peculiar logic. I can remember only fragments of one of those dreams. I was at a wedding and I was dancing with Andy. I could smell the odour of almond paste on his breath, and I tried to warn him not to eat any more wedding cake. I knew he was in jeopardy, but he wouldn't listen to me. Then Rick Spenser and I were in my kitchen and he was making little marzipan doves that carried gossamer strands of spun sugar in their beaks. And then Andy was there, but I don't remember the rest. Finally, I fell into a dreamless sleep and I slept deeply and well.

When I woke up, my bedroom was filled with the pale light of early morning. The digital clock on my radio said 6:00 a.m. I had been asleep for twelve hours.

I went downstairs, let the dogs out, made a pot of coffee and turned on the radio. It was, said the voice of the man buried in the windowless basement room of the glass broadcasting building across the park, going to be a beautiful Labour Day weekend. Bright, warm and breezy – perfect weather for late sailing and football and barbecues.

I showered, pulled on some cotton sweatpants and a T-shirt, stuck my head in Peter's room and asked if he wanted to come with me to take the dogs for a walk around the lake.

Of my three children, Peter is the most restful to be with. Mieka is bubbly and witty. When you are with her, you are, like it or not, drawn into the maelstrom of her exuberance. Angus is the one who questions everything. He is dreamy and stubborn and inventive. When he was six, he came back from Good Friday service at our church and lashed together a broom handle and a piece of two by four. Late that afternoon, I walked into our bedroom and saw him standing in front of the full-length mirror, head lolling to one side, arms gripping his cross. "This is how it must have looked," Angus's image in the mirror said to me. Indeed.

Peter is neither exuberant nor stubborn. He is content just to be. He loves sports, animals, and his family in an order that changes constantly. That morning what I needed more than anything was an hour with his quiet goodness.

When he came down, we put the dogs on their leads and headed toward the lake. The city had that lazy holiday feel to it – light traffic, a few joggers, but generally pretty quiet. There was a breeze from the southwest, and for the first time in a long while, the windsock in the marina showed some life. The little waves on the lake flashed in the sun, and as Peter and I walked along the shore we could hear the water lapping against the rocks. In the sky, some geese were trying out a preliminary V, and my son and I turned to one another and said, "Fall's coming" at exactly the same moment.

By the time we turned up the walk in front of our house, I felt healed enough to start the day. I made pancakes as I do every Saturday, then we went to the Lakeshore Club, also as we do every Saturday. Over the years, the boys have gone through every racquet sport imaginable, and Mieka has graduated from Moms and Moppets to high-impact aerobics, but my routine never varies. Every Saturday morning I put on my never-quite-fashionable bathing suit and swim laps. Then I shower, get dressed and take the kids to McDonald's for lunch. The high life.

Rick Spenser turned out to be an accomplished, considerate, no-nonsense cook. If the meal he prepared for us wasn't the best meal I'd ever eaten, it was certainly in the top ten.

He called just before two and asked me to meet him at the fish counter of the Piggly Wiggly. When I arrived ten minutes later, there he was, a striking figure in rough-weave cotton pants and an open-necked shirt the colour of bark cinnamon. Next to him a woman with a print dress pulled too tight over her small, round, pregnant stomach was looking speculatively at a slab of whitefish. An adolescent boy on yellow roller skates glided up to the counter, filled a clear plastic bag with oysters in the shell and skated toward the front of the store. Rick Spenser didn't see either of them. He was wholly absorbed in something he was pointing to inside a closed glass case.

Behind the counter a bored young woman wearing surgical gloves stood holding a fish.

When I touched Rick on the arm, he didn't even turn toward me.

"Good, you're here," he said. "What do you think of that pickerel? This young woman tells me they were caught last night and flown in from the north this morning."

"From the way the eyes are bulging I'd say she's telling

the truth. I think twenty-four hours ago that pickerel was probably swimming in Lac La Ronge planning her new fall wardrobe."

"What?" He looked puzzled.

"I think the fish looks great, Rick."

"Oh, good." He was still distracted. "That's what I thought, too. Now, do your children like pickerel?"

"I don't think anyone's children like pickerel."

He didn't miss a beat. "We'll get them steaks. Children like steaks." He wrote something in a little pocket note-book, then spoke to the woman behind the counter, who was still holding the fish. "We'll take that one and the third one from the left."

While she was wrapping the fish, he handed me his note-book. "See if there's anything you'd like to add." It was a splendid list: chicken livers, cream, butter, nutmeg, water-cress, baguettes, pickerel, beef tenderloin, new potatoes, fresh dill, walnut oil, blueberries, and at the bottom in tiny letters, "Does J have a garden?"

"How can you add to perfection?" I said, handing the notebook to him, "and, yes, I have a garden."

For the first time since I'd come into the store, he looked at me. "I hope you're going to like me, Joanne."

It was such an intimate and revealing thing to say that I was taken aback. "Of course, I'm sure I will . . ." We both stood there, embarrassed, until Rick had the wit to get us moving.

"Good, that's settled. Now let's leave the Piggly Wiggly behind and get to your place and start cooking."

From the first, we were easy with one another. When we were taking the grocery sacks out of the trunk I said, "Do you like kids?"

He turned and looked hard at me. "Honestly?"

"Honestly."

"I hate them. They scare me."

"Mine won't."

"Well," he said, sighing, balancing the French bread delicately on top of two bags of groceries, "I'm willing to be convinced."

I guess one of the reasons we fell in together so easily was that we shared two passions: food and politics.

Rick had bought an apron that he unwrapped with great ceremony before we began to cook. It was a huge red-and-white striped affair – a butcher's apron. When I laughed, he produced a duplicate – but in a smaller size – for me.

"Jo, you said you were a serious cook, so I thought perhaps we could cook together." He tied my apron at the back, then scrutinized me closely. "I just can't imagine why these would have been on the clearance table. Now let's have a glass of something cold and get started."

"There's some Carta Blanca in the refrigerator."

"You really are perfect," he said. I could feel my neck colouring with pleasure.

We cooked well together. Rick would run through what he had in mind, then, without even discussing it, each of us took a couple of tasks.

There was one odd note. As we stood with the bowl of chicken livers between us, I realized that the recipe for pâté Rick gave me was my own. Not like mine, but mine to the smallest detail. I'd come up with it when I was pregnant with Mieka and I'd had a problem with anemia. Our doctor had prescribed liver, liver and more liver, and the pâté had been one of the ways I'd come up with to make it tolerable. I could close my eyes still and remember standing in that gloomy kitchen in our house on Avenue B and trying out different combinations of herbs and spices till I'd hit upon thyme and allspice. And I could remember Ian's expression when I'd used the last of his Christmas cognac to moisten the pâté. It had been a wonderful addition, but in those days we saw brandy once a year, so I'd switched to cream and melted butter, cholesterol be damned, and that was the way I made pâté to this day. But here was a man who was almost a stranger, and he had my recipe right down to the last cracked peppercorn.

When I spooned the pâté out of the blender bowl into a round little dish, I said to Rick, "This is terribly deflating. All those years believing this was my own invention. Anyway, I'm glad we made it today – it was one of Andy's favourites."

He broke off a heel of bread, spread it with pâté and handed it to me. "Here's to Andy Boychuk," he said with a smile.

"You need one, too," I said. So I broke off the other heel of bread, spread it with pâté and handed it to him. "Here's to Andy Boychuk. Here's to Andy." And very solemnly, we both ate.

For someone who hated children, Rick was thoughtful and generous with them. While we were cooking, he gave Peter money to get a bag of ice cubes and a case of soft drinks, and he threw the ice into an old washtub on the deck so the drinks would keep cold for the kids during supper. And, perhaps even more telling, just before supper, when Angus came in to say we had an hour, tops, to eat and be at the ball diamond because his game had been rescheduled, Rick accepted Angus's need without question. "Really, Joanne, it's all right. Everything's prepared. We just need to get the coals ready. We five can be full and happy and sitting in the dugout in an hour."

"I don't think Angus's coach would be wild about all of us sitting in the dugout, but I can teach you the terminology when we get there. Are you sure you don't mind? We could feed the kids and eat after they leave, you know."

"And miss your son's performance? Never. Let's have another glass of burgundy and get the steaks on. We can come

back for dessert. I think people in Ottawa will be impressed
to hear that I went to a Little League game. You know," he
said happily, "baseball on Labour Day weekend does have a
certain cachet."

And so we went and sat in the bleachers and drank terrible coffee while the baseball mothers around us chanted their
litany for their sons: "Come on, Brandon, buzz like a bee . . .
You got him . . . Hum, baby, hum . . . Bring it in, Brandon,
bring it in!" And the sun slipped down on the horizon and
the sky glowed with streaks of pink and peach and purple.
And I thought about Andy and how much he would have
loved this evening. He would have been down on the field,
volunteering to coach third base, yelling for the kids. I could
feel the anger gathering. He should have been there. God
damn it, he shouldn't be dead. Then the tears started.

Rick didn't say a word, just reached inside his breast
pocket, pulled out a new handkerchief and handed it to me.
I mopped my eyes and blew my nose.

"Sorry."

"Don't be, Joanne. Don't try to hold on. It's been one hell
of a week. Now, look. There's Angus putting that helmet
thing on, so he must be going to get another turn . . ."

The evening ended in muted triumph. In his last turn at
bat, my son hit one out of the park, but the Gulls still lost
thirteen to one. Sort of like winning your poll but losing
the election. We ate our blueberry tart by moonlight. It was
an evening that seemed to flow. Rick and I sat on the deck
with a pot of tea, and the kids drifted in and out of the
house. Mieka came out to ask if there were any sheets and
pillow cases she could take with her when she went to
Saskatoon to start university. Angus came out to talk about
owls. Did we know the burrowing owl was smaller than a
person's hand? Peter came out to thank Rick for a great
meal and to ask me sotto voce if I'd seen his jockstrap. And,

in between, Rick and I sat and drank tea and talked. Or rather, I talked.

There was something cathartic about sitting in the dark with someone I barely knew. As Rick said, it had been one hell of a week. From the minute Andy lifted the glass that killed him, I had done what needed to be done. But now Andy was buried in a pretty little Catholic churchyard a few miles outside Wolf River. I had done the best I could for Andy's wife and child. As a party, we would deal collectively with the question of who would be the next leader. Everything had been taken care of. There was nothing left to do. Tomorrow Andy would have been dead a week. It was time, time to give in, time to rage against the dying of the light.

I didn't bother trying to be brave or strong. In all likelihood, I'd never see Rick again, and if I did, he'd know I wasn't a paragon. I could live with that. So I talked about Andy and the book I wanted to write about him, and every rambling, incoherent memory brought a fresh stab of pain and an awareness of loss. But still, a week after his death, there was one area of pain I couldn't touch in front of a stranger. I wasn't ready yet to ask the question that was at the heart of everything: Who had killed Andy Boychuk?

Rick Spenser was a good listener, and when I stopped talking, we didn't say anything for a while. We sat, two people who'd come too close to the lip of the horror that lies at the edge of our rational lives. Finally, Rick touched my arm, and I turned toward him. In the moonlight, he looked – strange words for such a substantial man – delicate and vulnerable. I wanted him to keep touching me. I wanted to touch him. It had been almost three years since my husband's death, and as Rick's hand rested warm and strong against my arm I felt the remembered stirrings of sexual heat. But after a few seconds he took his hand away, and when he spoke it wasn't about passion.

"Joanne, let me help you with this book. You know all the people, and you're here, but I don't think that will be enough for this job. You've been around politics long enough to know how far the biography of a prairie politician will go in this country if there's not a familiar name attached to it. And I can offer you something more concrete than a name on a dust jacket. I'm not without resources, contacts, file footage. A project like this can be easy or it can be difficult. I have access to the kinds of things that can make it easy. Let me help."

I was astounded, and I said so. Finally, I asked the question that needed answering. "Rick, what's in it for you? I know that's crudely worded, but why would you want to be part of this?"

He shrugged. "I'm not sure that I know myself. But I think it has something to do with discharging a debt."

For me, that was exactly the right answer.

"Rick, let's have a glass of brandy and drink to Andy's book, to *our* book. I have a bottle of something really special that Andy bought for my husband the last Christmas Ian was alive. I've been waiting for an occasion, and I think we are occasion enough. Come on. Let's go over to the granny flat and we'll open that bottle."

"Sounds great, but what in God's name is a granny flat?"

"You're looking at it. It's that apartment on top of the garage. I use it for an office." I reached for his arm. "Come on. It's easier to show you than tell you."

He followed me through the dark garden and up the wooden staircase that led to the little balcony outside the door of the flat.

"Should I carry you over the threshold?" he said.

"I don't think it's that kind of collaboration," I said, turning the key in the lock.

When the door opened, we were met by an arctic blast of cold air. I was annoyed at myself.

"Damn, no one's been in here since the morning of the funeral, and the air conditioner's been on high all that time."

"It's certainly efficient," said Rick, rubbing his hands.

"No more than most. I guess this place is just sealed up so tight it seems that way. Anyway, here's the cognac. Look at the label. Andy was always a generous man. And here are the glasses, but let's take our drinks out on the balcony. It's freezing in here."

Rick poured and we stood on that ridiculous little balcony and looked at one another in the moonlight.

"Here's to Andy Boychuk," he said for the second time that evening.

"To Andy and to sane minds and souls that aren't mad," I said, and I sipped and felt the heat of the cognac spread through my veins.

In the morning I picked him up at his hotel and drove him to the airport. He wouldn't let me get out of the car. "An airport is a grim place to say good-bye," he said and he reached out and traced the lines of my cheekbones with his fingertips. When finally he spoke, his voice was husky. "I'll call you tonight."

He did, and he called many nights afterward. The thing to remember about my relationship with Rick Spenser is that he came at the right time in my life.

CHAPTER

9

The word "bittersweet" is not part of my working vocabulary, but that's the word that seemed to hang in the air that week as my daughter was getting ready to go to university. From the day she was born I had dreaded the day Mieka would go away to school, but suddenly, that September, her going seemed not just inevitable but right.

My relationship with my mother had always been so uneasy that I'd worried about how I'd be with a daughter. Mieka made it easy. From the first day she was level and sunny, and she had grown into a confident and optimistic woman. She has had her share of sadness and often more than her share of responsibility. In the months after Ian died, I had leaned on all the children but, because she was the oldest, I had leaned on her most. On the black days when I would awaken so tired and dispirited that all I could do was turn over in bed and watch the morning light on the wallpaper, it was Mieka, cheery and practical, who would get the boys off to school and run in with a cup of coffee for me before she caught her bus to high school. I'm not proud of that time, but it's there. And Mieka didn't need a rerun.

That September was her time to move into a place of her own and cook and go to classes and do laundry and dream dreams. She had genuinely liked Andy, but she was not yet nineteen, and he had been peripheral to her life. She was sad he was dead, and she was sensitive to my grief, but a new part of her life was going to begin in less than a week, and she was bright with joy.

Because I loved her, I was happy for her. But as I stood and watched my daughter earnestly compare guarantees on toaster ovens and look critically at no-iron sheets, it was hard not to feel a sense of loss – not just of her, but of me.

It had been twenty-eight years since I'd carried my suitcase up to the third floor of the house opposite Victoria College at the University of Toronto. And it was a quarter of a century since I'd invited my seminar group in political science to my flat on Charles Street for dinner, and we'd eaten spaghetti and drunk Italian wine out of fat bottles in straw baskets and argued all night about the meaning of *Last Year at Marienbad* and the philosophy of Ayn Rand. That was the year I met Ian. On our first date he took me to dinner at his logic professor's house in north Toronto. The logic professor, who was smug and reputedly brilliant, was in his late thirties. His wife, whose name was Betsy, was twenty-one, like me, but she already had three little children. Her father had been a mathematician at MIT, and the logic professor had married her when she was sixteen, so he could, he said, "help her grow." Besides the children, Betsy had two cocker spaniels. She called one Professor and one Wife.

It was winter but a beautiful starry night, and Ian and I walked home miles along Yonge Street. I held his arm, and even through his heavy winter coat, I felt a sexual charge. I knew that night I wanted to marry him, but not the rest, not

Betsy's hot domestic world of babies and dogs and casseroles out of the *Good Housekeeping Cookbook*. We would be different, Ian and I – twin stars, separate and brilliant and eternal . . . We would be different . . .

And now it was Mieka's time to turn the key of the door of her first private home, to cook her own suppers for friends, to make her own choices, and I knew how I would miss these two: that daughter of mine, that younger me.

That week wasn't all elegiac. Politics, like nature, abhors a vacuum, and our party had, for ten days, been without a leader. In politics, you do what you have to do. Once when our party was in deep financial waters, I went to a funeral where the best friend of the dead man stood outside the funeral chapel with a fried-chicken bucket and took up a collection for the party. No one was shocked. Even the widow wrote him a handsome cheque before she left for the cemetery. Life goes on.

I was not surprised that the person who came to ask my support was Craig Evanson – "that floppy man," Peter had called him once when he was little, and in our family, the name stuck.

Craig Evanson *was* a floppy man. Tall and shambling, his body was as loose-limbed as his wife's was clockwork tight. I had always liked Craig, and on Wednesday morning, when I came to the door, barefoot and without makeup, and saw him kneeling there talking to my dogs through the screen door, I remembered why.

He was always full of hope, even now when, in my eyes at least, his life had turned out badly. He had wanted three things. I knew this because years before when our children were small, Craig had told me what he wanted. That was the kind of dopey, ingenuous thing he was always doing. He said he wanted to be close to his wife and son, to have friends to talk law with and drink with, and he wanted to serve as the member for Regina–Little Flower till he was sixty-five years old and could retire and write his memoirs. It was, I guess, not much to want from life.

They were modest dreams, but Julie Evanson had undercut them all. Her love for their son, at first so consuming and then so conditional, had driven Mark away in confusion. Her ambition had coarsened Craig's relationship with his friends, and her need to make Craig leader of the party had jeopardized his seat in Little Flower. She had made her husband's name synonymous with all those terms we smirk over: wimpy, spineless, henpecked. She had made him into a joke, but as I saw him with the golden September light behind him, bending to soothe my dogs with his words, it was hard not to feel the old tug of affection.

He was so happy to see me, so grateful to be invited to stay for coffee. And as we sat in the middle of the chaos of Mieka's packing and talked about our children it was like the old easy days. I told him I'd spent a little time with Mark and Lori and had seen their baby, and it was as if someone had thrown a switch inside him. We talked about Mark's gentleness and Lori's beauty and the baby's brightness, and Craig glowed with happiness. Then, suddenly, the switch was shut off.

"You know that Julie thinks Mark has betrayed her," he said.

We sat in awkward silence. Even her name was enough to take the shine from the morning. Finally, he shook himself like an old dog. "Anyway, Jo, I'm here for a reason, and you know what it is. I'm running for leader. If you're committed elsewhere, or you want to wait and see who else announces, that's okay. I just want to be considered."

"You'll be considered." I tried to sound gentle.

"But not for long and not seriously," he said flatly.

"Craig . . ." I tried to find a way to take the sting out of turning him down. "You're such a good constituency man – everybody says you're the best. It's just that you know how tight and how dirty this election's going to be. I think we need someone . . ."

"Smarter." He supplied the word for me.

I didn't say anything.

"God damn it, Jo. After all these years, that hurts. I wish Andy hadn't given that last interview. It just about killed Julie." He looked at his watch. "Well, I should be getting home." He stood up – the floppy man making his exit. "Thanks for the coffee and the talk."

Sad and embarrassed, I walked him to the door. He started to leave, then he turned.

"I can't disappoint her again, Jo."

"I know that, Craig."

"She's given up everything for me," he said simply, then he went down the walk, got in his car and headed home to a marriage that I couldn't even begin to imagine.

The story has a postscript. The next morning, after we finally got everything loaded in Howard's van, I ran into the house to get my sunglasses. The phone was ringing. I was going to leave it. Then I worried that it might be some problem with the boys or maybe with the college kid I'd hired to stay with them while I was in Saskatoon. But it was a woman's voice.

"Don't stand in his way, Jo. Craig might not be tough, but I am." Then her humourless laugh and she hung up. So he had told her.

When I got in the van, Mieka said, "Mummy, you're white as a ghost."

"Nothing, just a nasty telephone call."

"A crank caller?" asked Mieka, all concern.

"No, sweetie. Remember Mark Evanson? Well, it was his mother, Julie." I put on my sunglasses. "I think Julie is about ready to start her own coven."

Mieka smiled, but Howard didn't. "Be careful around her, Jo. She's got a wicked temper."

"I'll be careful, Howard. Now come on, old man, let's get this show on the road."

Mieka, house-proud, didn't want to eat with us. Her new place was a two-storey frame house on Ninth Street. She and her boyfriend had come up earlier in the summer and rented it from a woman who was spending a year in Dublin studying Lady Gregory. It looked perfect to me when we opened the door, and more perfect after we'd spent the afternoon switching furniture around and unpacking Mieka's stuff. But my daughter is not me. She said she wouldn't enjoy dinner when she knew that things "at home" – and she used the word "home" to describe the house on Ninth Street – weren't quite right yet. So she waved Howard and me off, told us to have fun and invited us for a spaghetti dinner the next day before we drove back to Regina.

"So," I said standing on the sidewalk in front of my daughter's new home, "are you ready to take a broken-hearted mother out for dinner?"

"You'll love this place," said Howard.

"I'll bet it has leather menus," I said.

Howard looked off in the distance thoughtfully. "You know, I believe it does."

Howard is not adventurous when it comes to food. Years ago a nouvelle cuisine place opened in town, and Ian and I dragged Howard there between meetings. He'd eaten without complaint, but his despair as he searched the menu for something more substantial than slivers of sole had been palpable. Since then I had let him pick the restaurant, and we always went to places where the beef was cut thick, and the bar Scotch was top of the line.

Tonight, as we drove to the west side, he said, "You'll like this place, Jo. They grow their own vegetables."

"Do they rope their own steers, too?"

Howard snorted. "No wonder Mieka's glad to get rid of you for the evening."

The Hearth did turn out to be a very good restaurant – lots of oak and dark leather and candlelight and a big functioning fireplace, which felt good on a cool September night. The waiter brought the menus, and Howard ordered a double Glenfiddich on the rocks. I ordered vermouth with a twist, and when our drinks arrived, Howard took a long, satisfied pull on his Scotch and settled back in his leather chair.

"Well, how are you doing?" he said.

"Okay, I guess, but I don't want to talk about me, I want to talk about Andy."

"I've got no problem with that."

"You know, the police have that portfolio Andy always used for his speaking notes – the blue leather one with –"

"'Every Ukrainian Mother's Dream' on it in gold." Howard finished the sentence and smiled.

"Millard found a poem in there. It wasn't there earlier, I know, because I checked the speech just before Andy went on the stage. Someone had copied out William Blake's poem 'The Sick Rose' – it's pretty standard stuff, I think, on most freshman English courses. Anyway it was beautifully written in calligraphy – is that redundant? At the top were two letters – initials maybe – *A* and *E*, and they were joined by a bunch of little curlicues like the initials of the bride and groom on a wedding invitation. I can't get those initials out of my mind."

Howard finished his drink and put the empty glass carefully on the centre of his coaster.

The waiter came and asked if we were ready to order.

Howard looked at me hopefully. "They are reputed to do a first-rate Chateaubriand here, but it's a dish for two and I'm always a one. Would Chateaubriand be acceptable?"

"Absolutely."

"Well, then, we'll have that and –" he pointed out a bottle of Bordeaux on the wine list "– a half litre of that."

When the waiter left, he turned back to me. "About the initials – what do you make of them?"

"I guess the most obvious assumption is that they're wedding initials – Andy and Eve. But whoever put that poem in the portfolio killed Andy. I'm sure of it. Do you think Eve Boychuk is capable of murder?" It was the first time I'd said the words aloud, and I felt a shiver of apprehension.

We had chosen a table close to the fireplace. The rosy light turned Howard's drink to fire, and cast flickering shadows across his old hawk's face. He looked like a man to talk to about murder.

"I don't know, Jo. I'm not one of those cynics who says that everyone's capable of murder. There's a threshold there that most of us could never cross. But Eve's had such a hell of a life, I just don't know."

The waiter brought our wine. Howard absently gave it his approval, and the waiter filled our glasses. "You know, Jo, I'm glad we're talking about this. It may ruin our dinner, but since Andy died, I've had more than a few ruined dinners. You see, I think if it weren't for me, Andy would never have met Eve."

The salad arrived and Howard brightened. "Now does this meet with your approval? You will note, recognizable chunks of everything, a good garlicky dressing, and they have the wit here to bring your salad before dinner when you're not too loaded to eat it.

"Anyway, back to the beginning, and the beginning was my thirtieth birthday, April 17, 1963. That was the day I

arrived in Port Durham, Ontario, and that was the day I met
Eve Lorscott."

When he said that name, I felt as if I had lit up a pinball
machine – lights and bells everywhere. "You mean Eve is a
Lorscott – one of the Lorscotts of the Lorscott case? I
remember it from when I was at U of T, but how come no
one ever told me it was Eve?"

Howard speared a piece of tomato and smiled. "Because,
my friend, it was none of your business. Really, Jo, it was no
one's business. After all, Eve hadn't committed a crime, and
she had come out here to make a new beginning, so what
was to be gained?

"Anyway, on April 17, I arrived in Port Durham, and for a
Ukrainian boy from Indian Head it was like landing on the
other side of the moon. Two days before, Ray Lewis had
called me from Toronto. He was my prof at the law school
in Saskatoon, and he'd followed my career a little so he knew
that I'd made a bit of a specialty of the laws governing the
insane. Not a bad preparation for politics, come to think of
it. Anyway, Ray called and said he had a case that he thought
I could be a real help with and, in the process, make a name
for myself in the east. It seemed like a hell of a great idea at
the time.

"Anyway, I was on the first plane out. Ray picked me up
at the airport and drove me to Port Durham. You know, Jo,
I'll remember that drive till the day I die." He sipped his
wine and smiled. "Rural Ontario on an April day. It's hard
to believe the same God that made the prairie made those
gentle hills and the little rivers and the ditches filled with
wildflowers. And those farms –" he shook his head in disbelief. "All those farms with the new paint on the barns and
the fuzzy sheep and fenced-in fields – they looked like
something you'd give a kid to play with. We got into Port

Durham around noon – pretty little place, have you ever been there, Jo?"

"Once, for a weekend with a friend from school."

"Well, Ray took me to the hotel for lunch and filled me in on what I could expect to find at the Lorscott house. Tudor Lorscott, the father, was in Port Durham Hospital. He was badly hacked around the face, neck and groin, but he was going to live. His wife, Madeline, had lost four fingers on the left hand when she tried to stop the attack. The fingers were gone – kaput – but she would be released from hospital later in the week. Nancy Lorscott, the daughter who had, as the papers said, 'wielded the axe,' was in the hospital ward of the Port Durham Correctional Centre, a two-years-less-a-day provincial jail, which also served as a remand centre. Nancy was crazy as a bedbug but physically okay. Eve Lorscott, the younger daughter, the one who had called Ray and asked him to handle things, was waiting for us at the house.

"The 'house' – Ray tossed that word off so casually, but it was wholly inadequate. I was thirty years old but I had never been in a rich man's house – God, Jo, that house made you see why people get the hots for money."

I smiled. Howard had, since I'd known him, lived well, but he always talked as if he had to return his pop bottles to pay for his next meal.

Howard caught my smile and grinned. "I know, I know, Jo, but you should have seen the Lorscott place – another order of things altogether. The house was a beauty – clapboard, I guess, and painted a shade of grey that looked sometimes grey and sometimes – what's that shade of light purple?"

"Lavender?"

"Yeah, lavender. And lilacs. The lilacs were everywhere – great masses of them all around the house – white and purply pink and . . ." He smiled. "Lavender. Gentle – a gentle house for gentle people, but a week before in this gentle house, the twenty-five-year-old daughter had tried to hack her old man's head and nuts off with an ax and, when Mum tried to stop her, had chopped off Mum's fingers."

"Oh, God, Howard, no."

"We rang the bell and, as we were standing there in the sunshine waiting, Ray Lewis said something I've repeated to myself a thousand times. 'Don't let the splendour get to you, kid; when they're scared, they dirty their drawers just like the rest of us.' Words to live by, I guess, but when I stepped into that front hallway, it was hard to believe anybody ever dirtied anything around there. Marty and I had just bought our first house – it was about three blocks from Mieka's new place, close to the Catholic school, of course, for Marty. Anyway, we were fixing it up and we thought it was really special, but next to the Lorscott place it was pathetic – a real dump.

"The housekeeper walked us down a hall as long as a bowling alley. The walls on both sides were hung with discreet pictures of the family – the ancestral line, I guess. I was feeling more and more like the dumb bohunk from the sticks, when I saw yellow police tape blocking off the entrance to a room with a big desk and a globe and a lot of books – the old man's office – the scene, as we say, of the crime. But the housekeeper just marched us right on by and at the end of the hall, she opened a door and we were in the sunroom – the atrium, she called it. In the centre of the room was a bunch of wicker furniture, some chairs with flowery cushions and a round table. Sitting there waiting, as sweet as a little girl at a birthday party, was Eve.

"And here," he said, "is our dinner. Do I get to pick the restaurant from now on?"

"Till the day we die," I said. "That is a beautiful piece of meat."

The Chateaubriand was nicely charred on the outside, pink inside and covered in a good béarnaise sauce made with fresh tarragon. The waiter sliced the beef and arranged it and our vegetables well and without fuss on oval pewter plates.

"You know, whatever you want to say about Eve, and over the years we've all said plenty, she is a beauty. That day she was beautiful enough to stop your heart. She must have been about twenty, and her hair was still black. It didn't turn grey until after the car accident. She wore it kind of fluffed out the way women did in 1963. The housekeeper – Mrs. Cartwright – God, Jo, half the time I can't remember where I parked the car, but I can remember the name of a housekeeper I met for maybe three minutes more than twenty-five years ago. Anyway, Mrs. Cartwright brought us our scones and tea, and everything was very civilized. Eve was cool as a cucumber, pouring the tea, passing the butter, all that stuff, and she told us the history of the house and then, in that same flat little voice, she told us what happened that night."

"How did she deal with it?"

"She made one hell of a witness – every detail, no stumbling, no hysteria. She even put in all the disclaimers, 'and then I believe my sister said,' and, 'then, to the best of my recollection, my father moved rapidly toward the window.' Anyway, she told her little story, and it wasn't very nice. Her sister alleged, to use Eve's word, that the old man had made improper advances to her – Eve's words again – from the time she was a little kid and now she couldn't hold her head up and then, so help me, Jo, Eve kind of giggled the way you do when you're getting near the punch line, and said, 'My sister said if she couldn't hold her head up, my father shouldn't be allowed to, either, so she took this axe and started whacking at his head and his private parts.' Then she laughed, and I swear, Jo, she was surprised when we didn't join in.

"Anyway, apparently when the mother tried to stop Sister Nancy, Sister Nancy chopped her through the fingers."

I swallowed the rest of my wine and filled our glasses. "And Eve saw it all?"

Howard was grim. "And Eve saw it all, but here's the kicker, Jo. She wouldn't let us use any of it. She said, 'Now you know the truth, and that should help you arrange' – that was her word, 'arrange' – 'what they tell you. But what you've heard here must not go out of this room,' and she walked out and left us sitting there, the hired help smelling the pretty flowers."

Howard speared the last of his steak, and the waiter came to remove our plates. Howard asked him to bring us both coffee and B&B, and sat back contentedly.

I was on the edge of my seat. "Well, what happened?"

"Not much. Ray and I tried every tack we could think of, but Eve wouldn't testify. Mum and Pop and Sister Nancy lied through their teeth – said it was an accident, some sort of aberration. Little Nancy had always been delicate, blah, blah, blah, so that was that. Nancy went to a toney sanitarium in upper New York State – the kind of place where you can stash your resident psycho if you've got the money. The Americans are better at understanding that kind of thing than we are. And Mum and Pop went back to the house at the lake and lived happily ever after. Every so often I still see Old Man Lorscott's picture in the *Globe* – appointed to the board of this or that." He shook his head, then looked up. "Jo, do you want to split a piece of cheesecake? They make one with Amaretto here that you would really love."

I groaned. "Howard, if we have cheesecake, that will push the number of calories for this meal into six figures."

"Jo, forget the calories tonight. Yes or no?"

"Yes – now tell me, how did Eve get here?"

"She just came. After the trial I got a cheque signed by Eve

Lorscott. If I hadn't needed the money so much for the new house, I would have framed it, but it was a generous cheque and Marty wanted to fence in the backyard. Anyway, I'd see Ray Lewis at bar association meetings, and the first few times I saw him we'd talk about the Lorscotts and then, you know how it is, we both had other stories. Anyway, the Lorscotts kind of drifted to the back of my mind.

"Then one day, about five years later – I think it must have been 1968, or one of those years when the world was blowing up, I was walking across the university campus. There was a demonstration against the war in Vietnam, and there, marching along together, were Eve Lorscott and Andy Boychuk. They were a striking couple. Andy looked pretty much the way he did when you knew him – longer hair, of course. Eve in 1968 was very different from the woman we know now. Remember how the kids then used to talk about being free? Well, that day Eve was free. She wasn't the wound-up little doll Ray Lewis and I had met in Port Durham, and she wasn't the fragile woman you and I know. She was free and she was very beautiful.

"Andy was in my criminal law class. He waved, came over and introduced Eve. You know, Eve always surprises. I was prepared to play dumb and ignore the connection, but Eve – cool as you please – slipped her hand into mine and said, 'Howard and I have met. In fact, he's the reason I'm here. After all that trouble with Nancy, I needed a place to escape to – and I was sitting there one day, and Saskatchewan just came to mind. I mean whoever would pursue anybody here?' And she beamed and put her arm around Andy's waist and lay her head on his shoulder. They were such a striking couple. Then they got married, and you know the rest. That awful accident . . ." He picked up the little lamp that had a candle burning inside it. "As I said, Eve Boychuk has had one hell of a life."

"I wonder how she survived," I said.

"That's a question for a shrink or a philosopher, Jo. I'm just a washed-up politician; I don't have answers for questions like that."

I reached across the table and squeezed his hand. "Not so washed-up," I said.

The Amaretto cheesecake was as heavenly as Howard promised it would be, but he was subdued as we ate it. When we finished, he leaned across the table and looked at me hard.

"Jo, I guess everyone at that picnic is a suspect. Did you have any special reason for asking about Eve?"

"No – at least no more reason to ask about her than about any of us. And don't forget, there were five thousand people there. I know the police have got the big push on, and I keep hoping I'm going to turn on the radio and hear they've arrested some poor crazy person who killed Andy because he got out of the wrong side of the bed that morning or because God told him to. But we have to face facts. It's been eleven days now, and the police are still coming up empty. What if it's not some anonymous psycho? What if it's somebody we know? What if it's one of us?"

Howard tossed back the last of his drink. "I don't know, Jo. Do you remember that TV show that used to open with the police sergeant saying, 'Be careful out there'? I guess that's all you can do. Be careful."

Mieka, perfect Mieka, had unpacked my suitcase and hung up my skirt and blouse for the next day. She had even thrown my nightgown and robe on the bed.

"Where's the chocolate on my pillow?" I asked.

"You don't deserve one. I'll bet you and Howard ate and drank everything that wasn't nailed down. Where is he, by the way? I thought he might come in for tea."

"Not tonight, little girl. He was a bit tired and I have to get up early tomorrow because I'm going out to see Roma Boychuk."

"Andy's mother?" Mieka said. "Well, don't give her a clear shot at you."

"Mieka, what an awful thing to say. And you don't even know her."

"Oh, but I do. One night I'd had it up to here with you nagging at me about my grades, and I complained to Andy. You know what a nice guy he was. Anyway, that night we had a long talk about mothers."

I was surprised. "When was that?"

"After midterms when I was in grade eleven. Remember when you told me I'd end up scrubbing toilets at the bus station if I didn't pass chemistry?"

"Well, you did pass chemistry."

"With a fifty-three. Anyway, Andy took your side, of course. Said you guys do nag at us because you love us so much. But in the process of defending mothers collectively, he said some pretty interesting things about his own mother."

"Such as?"

"Such as nothing. It's bedtime. You'll be seeing Andy's mother tomorrow. Howard would say I was prejudicing the witness. But you should know" – and she grinned and bent to kiss me good night – "that there are some mothers who devour their young."

CHAPTER

10

Roma Boychuk still lived in the Junction, on the west side of town, in the house Andy grew up in. The west side is where you go if you want used furniture or real Szechuan or twenty minutes of romance. Farther out, toward the railway station, is the area called the Junction. It's a neighbourhood of onion-domed churches and mom-and-pop grocery stores with names like Molynka's or Federko's. The Junction was, Andy said, a great neighbourhood to grow up in. As I walked along the quiet streets where the leaves on the elm trees were already turning yellow, I tried to imagine Andy running along these sidewalks to school, and I tried to remember what I knew about Roma Boychuk.

It wasn't much. Andy had been born when his mother was forty. His father died just before or just after Andy's birth. I don't remember Andy ever speaking of him. Roma doted on her son. I once handed Andy an article about the disproportionately large number of political leaders who were the favoured children of strong, domineering mothers. I had expected him to laugh, but he hadn't.

"They think they're doing you a favour, you know – all that love. But you spend your whole life trying to keep the love coming. That's why so many politicians are so screwed up – and Jo, the demands . . ." His sentence had trailed off.

The fear of his mother's disapproval was something everybody who worked for Andy had to deal with. He always spoke Ukrainian to his mother, and when our party announced a policy that was at odds with his mother's beliefs, Andy would be on the phone with her for hours. I didn't need to understand Ukrainian to know he was explaining, rationalizing, justifying. He would come from these phone calls shamefaced and telling a joke on himself, but he never stopped calling. Once somebody, I think it was Dave Micklejohn, had come back from Saskatoon raving about how generously Roma had welcomed him into her home. Andy had laughed and said, "Just don't cross her or they'll find you at the bottom of the South Saskatchewan with a crochet hook driven through your heart."

I had the address in my notebook, and Howard had given me directions. I didn't need them. I knew the house at once because I recognized the place next door – the home of the Sawchuks, Roma's archenemies. The families had lived next door to one another for sixty years, and they had fought for sixty years.

"Why doesn't somebody move?" I'd asked Andy once.

"And lose their reason for living?" Andy had shrugged. "Jo, if my mother gets a new brooch or if I get my picture in the paper, her pleasure isn't complete until Mrs. Sawchuk – 'that Sawchuk' as my mother calls them all – sees it, and I'll bet it's the same for them. Anyway, the Sawchuks have their revenge. You should see their house."

In truth, the Sawchuks' house was unremarkable except for the colour: a neat, rectangular wooden bungalow painted egg-yolk yellow with green trim. But the lawn in front was spectacular. It had sprouted a bumper crop of lawn ornaments. White plastic lambs whose innards had been hollowed out to hold red geraniums; scale models of wooden airplanes with propellers that hummed in the wind; painted plywood cutouts of little German boys with round pink cheeks and stiff wooden lederhosen; a family of wooden ducks, a mother and the babies; a pair of plywood Percherons that pulled a wooden cart full of petunias past a miniature – perfect in every way – of the egg-yolk and green Sawchuk bungalow.

Compared to the Sawchuks', Roma Boychuk's place, 82 Joicey Street, was a model of restraint. The house was white with red trim. On each side of the walk to the front door was a half an oil barrel painted white. The raw edges of the barrels had been smoothed into scallops, and the barrels were filled with bright red geraniums.

I had told Roma I would be there by ten. It was five past when I knocked on the door, and she was waiting for me. When I called I had told her I was working on a book about Andy's life; she had been interested and pleased.

Less than two weeks before, her only child had died and I expected full mourning, but she was dressed for company. She was a stocky little woman but not fat, and she dressed with the care of a woman who has, all her life, been proud of her looks. Her black skirt was cut carefully to slim the line of her hips, and she had a brooch of china pansies at the neck of her lacy white blouse. Her hair was mauve-rinsed, and she had braided it and twisted it into two knots, one at the nape of her neck and one just above it. She had secured the knots with flowered combs that looked vaguely Japanese. Her cheek, when she placed it in front of my lips for a kiss, was smooth and unlined. "Vaseline every night," Andy told me once when he saw me buying some expensive night cream. "That's what my mother uses, and she has skin like a baby. Of course, she goes to bed looking like a channel swimmer, but she hasn't slept with anyone in forty years, so . . ." And he'd shrugged and laughed.

Roma didn't smell like a channel swimmer; she smelled pleasantly of something masculine and familiar.

"You smell good," I said.

"Old Spice," she said, "the only thing that covers the onions. I make shishliki this morning. I give you some to take when you go." She gestured me into the front room – a place of heavy drapes, heavy furniture covered in plastic slip-covers, and pale, dispirited light. "You'll have coffee," she said, then, brushing aside my offer to help, she left me alone in that gloomy room.

Through the door I could see the kitchen – a room flooded with sunlight and potted plants and good smells. If I had been a friend, I would have sat at the kitchen table and sipped coffee from a thick mug and talked to Roma as she sliced cabbage for soup or twisted dough into circles for poppy-seed bread. But I was company and I sat on the stiff plastic, which kept Roma's living room suite as free of spot or blemish as it had been the day the men from Kozan's loaded it onto the truck and delivered it to Joicey Street. When my eyes grew used to the light, I saw that the room was full of pictures. Half were of the Blessed Virgin and half were of Andy.

Most of the pictures of Andy as an adult I had seen before. They had been in campaign literature or newspaper articles and then we replaced them and forgot them. But Roma hadn't forgotten. She had clipped these pictures of her son and framed them and hung them on her wall next to pictures of the Annunciation or the Sacred Heart. There were pictures of Andy as a child – dozens of them. I walked to the wall by the window to look at these more closely. There was Andy at school, a succession of ever larger Andys sitting, hands folded in front of him, in a series of dim grey class-rooms with the pictures of the Pope and the King and Queen and then the new Queen behind him. There was Andy with his friends, grinning, face bleached almost into nothingness by the sun as he stood with his baseball team; Andy sitting in a canoe, waving at the person who stood behind the camera on the shore of some forgotten northern lake.

There were none of Eve and Andy. None of Eve and Andy and their children.

"You like? I get more." Roma's voice behind me, star-tlingly loud and strong. She set the tray she was carrying on a wooden tea wagon, disappeared and was back almost immediately with a box of photo albums. The one on top had a cover of palest powder-blue satin. In the centre was an oval indentation with a picture of a tired-looking Jesus sur-rounded by little children. Across the top of the album in raised Gothic letters was the legend "My Baptism."

"I get our little lunch while you look at Andrue's pictures for your book," said Roma as she placed the box on the floor beside me. Then, magician-like, she fluttered a lace table-cloth out of nowhere, covered the coffee table and began arranging cups and plates. As I went through the pictures, Roma moved from kitchen to living room, bringing first a pot of coffee and cream and sugar, then a plastic lazy Susan piled high with breads, poppy-seed and zucchini and carrot, then a tray with butter and cheese and dishes of pickles and jams and jellies. And finally another plastic lazy Susan, this one heavy with cookies and squares.

She handed me a dessert plate and a bright paper napkin that said, "No matter where I serve my guests they seem to like my kitchen best," poured our coffee and began her narrative on the albums in the box. She told me about the pictures in "My Baptism" and "My First Communion," then she handed me four fat scrapbooks, each of which was labelled, "My Life in the Church."

"These," she said, "perfect for that book you do on Andrue. Just copy them out."

The scrapbooks were filled with the work Andy had done at school, drawings and poems and essays on subjects like chastity and obedience and piety. *Many* essays on chastity.

"Here," Roma was saying. "Here is the picture for the book – on the front. Andrue with the bishop. This is Andrue's confirmation picture from Saint Athanasius. That bishop dead now, but a good man, very kind and patient with the children."

The bishop did not look kind and patient. He had the bulbous nose and the paunch of a serious drinker. But then pictures often lie.

"You take it," she said. "I have copies. Use it in your book to show Andrue brought up in the church. That baby-murder stuff . . . abortion." She made a spitting sound of derision. "He must have picked it up from that one he married." Again the spitting sound of dismissal. "You write the truth in your book. Andrue did not believe in that stuff. No." And she shoved the confirmation picture in my purse and went to the kitchen for more coffee.

The rest of the morning passed pleasantly enough. Roma wanted to talk about Andy, and I wanted to listen. When I left, she kissed me and gave me an ice-cream pail of lamb shishliki for Mieka.

As I started to walk down Joicey Street, the enemy Sawchuk came running after me.

"So how is she?" He stood, blinking in the sunlight, a barrel-chested man with iron-grey hair and a voice that had ordered a hundred thousand packages of smokes. "What do you make of it?"

"It's a very sad thing," I said.

His eyes were bright with spite. "I suppose she's been carrying on like crazy now that the big shot's been killed off." He laughed a wheezing, sucking kind of laugh that touched a nerve in me.

"Mr. Sawchuk, I hope you're never unlucky enough to lose a child – especially your only child."

His face came alive with malice, and I knew immediately that I'd walked into Sawchuk's trap. He wiped his mouth with a handkerchief before he answered me.

"Is that what she told you? That the big shot was her one and only? Next time, ask her about the girl – the one she threw out."

Suddenly the fun seemed to go out of the situation for him. He sounded distracted, as if his focus had shifted somewhere deep inside himself. "Probably dead now, too, or worse. Such a beauty. The old man, the father, he doted on that girl. Every year he made her a skating rink out back. Hours he'd spend, standing in the cold, holding the hose so the ice would always be smooth for her. She would skate and skate. My wife used to stand by the kitchen window and just watch her. She said it was better than the ice show. She's gone, too, now – my wife." The spite had puffed Sawchuk up. Now he looked depleted – small and old.

"Mr. Sawchuk," I said. But I'd lost him. He was somewhere in the past, standing at the kitchen window with his wife, watching the neighbour girl skate.

"Mr. Sawchuk," I said again.

He looked at me, and suddenly his eyes were as blue and untroubled as the September sky. "Elena," he said. "That was the Boychuk girl's name." He turned, and without another word, he walked away – to his fabulous yard and his empty house.

As I stood waiting for the bus, I was confused and off balance. I had known everything about Andy. And yet I hadn't. A sister. Andy had a sister. But he couldn't have known. He would have mentioned it. He couldn't have known.

But how could he not know?

And behind me, sweet with the singsong of the street chant a little girl's voice.

I am a pretty little Dutch girl
As pretty as pretty can be,
And all the boys on Joicey Street
Are so in love with me.

My boy friend's name is Tony.
He lives in Paris, France.
And all the boys on Joicey Street
Watch me and Tony dance.

CHAPTER

11

Mieka's spaghetti sauce was lighter than mine, but full of fresh basil and very good. Her boyfriend, Greg, joined us for dinner, and he was deferential to Howard, courtly with me and adoring of Mieka. It was a fine party but, as pleasant and courteous and civilized as we all were, it was apparent that Mieka and Greg wanted to be alone. There was a hum of sexual tension in the air as soon as supper was over, and it wasn't coming from our end of the table. When I announced that Howard and I should leave as soon as we did the dishes, Greg was up in a snap, putting the dishes in the sink with one hand and helping me on with my coat with the other.

Howard and I were on Circle Drive and out of the city when I realized I hadn't said any of the tender and wise things I'd planned for nineteen years. I snuffled a bit when we pulled onto the highway, and Howard looked sharply at me.

"Are you okay, Jo?"

"Fine. It's just everything happened so fast, and I think I've been done out of my big scene. Howard . . . I'm going to miss her so much. I can't imagine going back to that house without her." I could feel my throat closing and the tears gathering in my eyes. I seemed to be doing that a lot lately. The skyline of the city faded behind us; ahead the highway was a ribbon in the darkness. Howard turned on the radio, and we listened to a half-hour program on the problem of gridlock in downtown Toronto.

When the lights from the town of Davidson loomed on the horizon, I caught my breath. Andy and I had gone to a bonspiel there last winter. It was the first time I had ever curled, and I loved it. Andy, in an awful, too-big curling sweater, had volunteered to skip our rink. Standing at the end of the ice, shouting encouragement, he had grinned ruefully when my rocks sailed past him into the wall or, inexplicably, stopped halfway down the ice. A good friend.

And someone had killed him. But who? His wife? Poison is a woman's weapon, the mystery novels say. And there was the poem by Blake with its hint of inner corruption. (Eve turning in the door of Disciples the day after the murder and saying, "None of you knew the first thing about Andy Boychuk.") Most damning, those letters *A* and *E* intertwined like the bride's and groom's initials on a wedding invitation.

We passed a gas station. Howard's profile was thrown into sharp relief, and I thought of his terrible story about Eve Lorscott and her tortured family. I was reeling. There had been, as one of my sons had once said tearfully, "just too much day." I didn't want to think any more.

The sky was black and starless between towns. There wasn't even a farmyard in sight. Howard turned off the radio, and the miles slipped by in silence. Finally, he turned and looked at me.

"Are you up to some news, Jo?"

"No, but don't let that hold you back."

He laughed and reached for my hand. "You really are a nice woman. Anyway, no use beating around the bush. I'm going away for a while. When I was in Toronto last week, that old law-school buddy I mentioned asked me to teach a session in criminal law at Osgoode Hall. It's not a real appointment, just a couple of classes to help out a friend. They hired some hot-shot whiz-kid from Montreal, but at the last minute he got a chance at a TV contract interpreting the law as a background man, whatever the hell that is. Anyway, this came up and I took it."

"But that's wonderful. It'll be a good change for you."

"Yeah, I need to get out of Regina. A big part of it is because Andy's gone. Without him in the picture, the possibilities just don't excite me, but there's more . . ."

"I thought there must be," I said. "Is it Marty?" Two years before, Howard's wife, Marty, had left him and moved to Toronto. He never spoke of it, at least to me, but I'd heard rumours – the kinds of things that always seem to float in the wake of someone else's misfortune.

"Yeah," he said. "It's Marty. She's the good Catholic, but I'm the one with the guilt."

"Do you still love her?"

"I don't know. I don't know if love has anything to do with it. But somehow it doesn't seem right to me to pack up thirty years of marriage and say, 'Well, thanks so much, I've got other plans.'"

"How does Marty feel?"

"She says she has a job she likes. She says she has friends. She says politicians make lousy husbands. She says it won't work unless I change. She says a lot of stuff, but it all boils down to the same thing – she thinks it's over."

"And you don't?"

"I don't know. I think I'm too old to change, but that business about politics is just crap. You and Ian had a good marriage."

"Ian and I had a good marriage because we both lived Ian's life." I was surprised at the anger in my voice, and I was surprised at what I'd said. Until that moment I don't think I'd acknowledged how much everything had been for Ian.

"So that's the way it was." Howard's voice was gentle. "You know, Jo, it never seemed like that from the outside."

"It didn't start out that way."

"How did it start out? All the years I knew you and Ian, I guess I always just thought of you as a unit – the Kilbourns. Maybe Marty's right about me. I am obtuse."

"No more than the rest of us when it comes to under-standing what goes on inside other people's marriages. And Ian and I were a unit, so you were right there. It's just that we didn't – I didn't – plan to be part of a unit. Did you ever read D.H. Lawrence?"

"A thousand years ago."

"Well, Ian and I were going to be those fiery twin stars Lawrence talks about, separate and dazzling. And then . . ."

"Ian got into politics," Howard finished for me.

"And I got pregnant. Scratch one star. We were twenty-eight that first election. Mieka was born on E-day, remember?"

Howard laughed. "Sure. I always tell Mieka she showed great wisdom in waiting for the New Jerusalem to be estab-lished before she was born."

"It didn't seem like the New Jerusalem to me. Suddenly I was a mother, and I was married to a twenty-eight-year-old who was attorney-general of the province and who didn't have a clue about how to run the A-G's office."

"Jo, none of us had a clue about anything. All those kids we ran – we figured the young guys could lose their cherries on that first campaign and the next time out, well, maybe we'd get close, and then, well . . ." He reached over and patted my knee awkwardly. "Do you remember the results coming in that night? Did they bring you a TV into the delivery room?"

"Howard!" I groaned.

"Yeah, I guess not. Anyway, when I watched the results that night I just about dirtied my drawers. My God! First of all to win, and then to win and have nothing but kids to form a government." His voice grew serious. "Ian was always so good, Jo. I can count on one hand the number of times he screwed up when he was A-G. And he was smart enough to keep the constituency stuff humming. Except –" he looked at me quickly "– that was because you were there, wasn't it? I'm sorry, Jo. I should've known that."

"Howard, it was too long ago to feel guilt about, and I'm too old to enjoy making you feel guilty. It just happened. The political stuff came my way by default. I liked it. I was good at it, and it was something I could do while I was having kids. Another thing – it really mattered. It was important work. But Howard, Marty knew that, too. She really did. No matter what she says now. We're all revisionists when it comes to our own lives."

"Tell me, Jo." Howard's words were so quiet, I could barely hear him above the hum of the engine and the swish of the miles passing by. "Tell me how Marty was in the old days."

"Let's see. I guess the first time I saw her was a couple of weeks after the election. It was my first outing after Mieka was born, so of course I brought her along. Do you remember? Somebody had the bright idea that we should go out into the rural areas to show off the new team. A bunch of us went to hell and gone out into the country . . ."

"McCallister Valley," he said. "Remembrance Day. I remember. The year it rained right up until Christmas Eve. Damnedest thing I ever saw. Of course, the opposition made a big thing of it. Charlie Pratt was still leader then and he made one hell of a speech in the House. All about God's anger manifesting itself because the people had turned their backs on the one true party, and about how Charlie and his gang would have to build an ark to save the province – metaphorically, of course. The old bastard . . ." He was laughing.

"Anyway," I said, "you and Marty had been to some formal thing in the city, and she hadn't changed."

"And" – Howard's face softened at the memory – "just before we got to McCallister Valley, our car got stuck in the gumbo, and Marty took off her shoes and stockings, jammed a shoe in each coat pocket and walked barefoot through the mud."

"Ian and I were waiting in the hall," I said, picking up the story, "and someone yelled, 'Here's the premier.' I'd never met you, and my heart stopped. The premier and his wife! They threw open the doors to the Elks' Hall, and there you were and there was Marty with the skirt of her evening gown hiked up to her thighs. She was solid mud from the kneecaps down, but she had such a great smile."

We were both laughing. Howard wiped his eyes. "You should have heard her on the way home in the car – but not a peep out of her at the dinner. I'll give her that. She was always the gracious lady in public. Not like . . ."

"Not like Eve."

"No, not like Eve." His voice had a familiar edge of exasperation.

For a while we reminisced about old times, then Howard turned the radio on. We listened to it and gossiped till Howard pulled up in front of the house on Eastlake Avenue. The place was still standing, and I sighed with relief.

"All's well in Jo's universe?" Howard asked.

"No," I said, "but I'll survive. What flight are you taking tomorrow?"

"The 1:30 – gets you into Toronto in time for the rush hour along the 401 – all the charms of metropolitan life Marty's always talking about."

"Need a lift to the airport?" I said.

"Yeah," Howard said, "that would be nice."

"Well," I said.

"Well," he said, gently mocking.

"Well," I said, "I'd better get in there before the boys start flicking the porch light on and off at us."

Howard reached over and covered my hand with his. In the moonlight his face was silvery grey – like an image on black-and-white television. "I'm really going to miss you. Ian was a lucky man."

I leaned over and kissed his cheek. The smell of his body was familiar and comforting – Scotch and lemony after-shave. "I'm going to miss you, too, Marty's a lucky woman. Damn it, everybody's leaving me." I grabbed my bag and ran up the stairs before he could see I was crying.

The kids had managed fine. The house was clean enough. The tuna casserole I'd left for dinner the first night was in the refrigerator next to the freezer container of chili I'd left for the second night. There were two pizza boxes and a half dozen Big Gulp containers in the garbage, but the boys were showered and in bed watching *M*A*S*H* reruns and being civil to one another, so I counted my blessings. I sat on Peter's bed and watched the end of the program with them. When it was over, I filled them in on Mieka's new house, showered and got into my robe. I was careful to look the other way when I passed Mieka's room. I went down-stairs, put on the kettle for tea, changed my mind, pulled out a lemon and some honey and made myself a hot lemon and rum. Just as I poured the hot water into the mug, the phone rang.

Mieka, I thought, or Howard, knowing I was having a hard time. But it wasn't either of them. The voice was male and familiar, but I couldn't place it.

"Joanne, do you use smoked or barbecued salmon in that mousse?"

"Whatever's cheaper."

"What a sensible woman you are. Sorry to call so late, but I'm having people in for breakfast and I'm not a morning person." I still couldn't place that voice. Keep him talking.

"It bakes two hours. You'll be up all night."

"I'm setting the alarm so I can lumber out of bed and grab it out of the oven. Although why I'm going to all this trouble for that preening cow of a minister is beyond me."

That sleepy, intimate voice that curled around words with such affection – "Rick. Rick Spenser. I'm sorry. I just didn't make the connection with your voice for a minute."

"Joanne, I'm the one who should apologize. Damn. I hate people who assume you know who they are. Forgive me for being a narcissistic ass. Let me start again. How was your day?"

"We were on safer ground with the mousse. My day was lousy. I just left my beautiful little girl alone with her new housemate who is also her boyfriend. And Howard Dowhanuik, who is, I guess, my best male friend in the world, just told me he's moving to Toronto to teach a class at Osgoode Hall."

The voice on the other end of the line was suddenly alert and professional. "Is that for public consumption?"

"I don't see why not. Classes start this week, and he's leaving tomorrow. I feel like Little Orphan Annie."

"Then I'm glad I called. I wouldn't dream of trying to fill Mieka's place, but do you think I could try out for temporary status as your best male friend?"

I laughed. "Well, they're not exactly standing in line here."

"I warn you, Joanne. I take my obligations as a friend seriously."

I took Rick at his word, and brought him up to date on everything that had happened since the last time we'd talked. At the end of it all I said, "That business about the sister really threw me. There's something terrible about discovering people's secrets. It's such a violation. If you want out, I'll understand."

"No, no, certainly not." He sounded as if he meant it. "Joanne, if I were there with you, I'd open a vein and become your blood brother, but since I'm in Ottawa, I'll do what our senators do. I'll swear an oath holding onto my testicles."

We both laughed, the balance between us restored. "I think that was the Roman senators, not our guys."

"Well, whoever held onto whatever . . . I, Rick Spenser, do solemnly swear to be friends with Joanne Kilbourn."

"Till death us do part?" I asked, laughing.

"Till death us do part," he repeated, but he didn't sound as if he were laughing.

CHAPTER

12

The next three weeks went by in a haze of activity. Angus hated his grade-eight teacher on sight, but we decided dealing with her would be character-building. Peter made the football team, and I started to research Andy's biography.

We all missed Mieka.

Our routine was the same as ever: a morning run with the dogs, breakfast, school, an early supper, ball, homework, bed. Saturday mornings we went to the Lakeshore Club. I added another fifteen minutes of laps to my time in the pool because I didn't have Mieka to gossip with in the dressing room any more.

Life went on.

Before I opened my eyes on the first morning in October I knew it was raining. The air that came in through my bedroom window smelled of wet leaves and cold. I turned on the bedside lamp, and it made a comforting pool of yellow light in the room. I switched on the radio and a woman's voice, chuckling and ersatz matronly, said it was raining cats and dogs in Regina and Saskatoon. Raining on me and Mieka alike – it seemed like a good sign. I hollered at the boys to hit the showers and went downstairs. The kitchen door had blown open in the night and the floor was wet and cold on my bare feet. I coaxed the dogs out for a run in the rain, turned on the coffee and picked up the telephone. It was 7:00 a.m. If I called right away, I could catch Dave Micklejohn at home. He answered on the first ring.

"Dave, have you eaten yet?"

"No, I was just dropping an egg in to poach."

"Well, don't poach. Let me get the kids fed and off to school and I'll take you out for breakfast."

"Jo, it's so good to hear your voice. How about the club-house at the Par Three in half an hour? There won't be a soul there today, and they make great cinnamon buns."

"Sounds good to me, but make it an hour," I said, but he'd already hung up. Dave hates to use the telephone.

The Par Three clubhouse is the best-kept secret in the south end. It's a queer-looking six-sided building with lots of glass so you have the sense of being on the greens when you eat. It's a mom-and-pop operation – on one side of the build-ing Mom takes greens fees and rents clubs; on the other, Pop runs a little restaurant that offers breakfasts and sandwiches. Mom's and Pop's real names are Edythe and Al. I know this only because they have twin leather belts that have their names burned cowboy style into the backs. Why they bought the Par Three is a mystery. They are people who do nothing to encourage the loyalty or affection of their clientele. However, they have pride in what they do – Edythe's greens are always as perfectly manicured as the flawless ovals of her mauve nails, and Al's baking is the best in the city.

When I pulled in behind the clubhouse, Dave's Bronco, as shiny and red as a Halloween apple, was the only vehicle in the parking lot. Through the window, I could see Dave behind the counter pouring coffee. It didn't surprise me that he was on terms of trust with Al and Edythe. Dave was finicky, too. He handed me a cup as soon as I walked in the door.

"Saw you coming, Jo, and thought you could use some warming." He put his hands on my shoulders, stood back and looked at me critically. "You're looking weary."

"Dave, you always tell all of us that – I'm fine, honestly."

The window over the table Dave directed me to was open and the table was wet with rain but the air smelled so fresh that I left the window open. The rain splashed down on the empty golf course and the sky was grey with clouds, but we were safe in the warmth, and it felt good.

We ate our cinnamon buns and talked small talk – news about my kids, gossip about the leadership convention, which had been set for December. Craig Evanson had announced the day before, and already was the odds-on favourite. Apparently Andy had been right about how long people would remember his dismissive comment about Craig. When we finished eating, Dave brought the coffeepot over from the counter, filled our cups, put it back, sat down again and looked steadily at me.

"Well, Jo, what can I do for you?"

"I don't think it's going to be too hard, Dave. I just need some information. It's about that auburn-haired woman you were talking to after Andy's funeral – you know, the mystery woman that the paper got such a great shot of the day Andy died."

Dave's eyes shifted toward the window. "Look at that bird out there in the parking lot, Jo. Can you tell what it is from here? It looks like a little Hungarian partridge, but it's hard to tell with all that rain."

I didn't say anything.

Dave didn't look at me. He kept his eyes focused on the parking lot where the bird was hopping through the water that was pooling in a little depression near my car.

We sat in silence for a few minutes, sipping our coffee, waiting. Finally, he shrugged. He seemed to have made up his mind about something. "I guess it doesn't make any difference now that Andy's gone. I never could understand why there had to be a big mystery anyway. The woman's name is Lane Appleby. Her husband was Charlie Appleby. They're Winnipeg people. At least, Charlie was from Winnipeg. He died a couple of years ago. A lot of money from real estate, I think, but, of course, people recognize his name from hockey. He used to play for the Montreal Royals, but when he retired, he went to Manitoba, made a bundle and bought the Winnipeg team. He poured about a million dollars into it and got them some slick new uniforms and a new name."

"The Red River Royals," I said.

He looked up, surprised.

"I may not be a jock, Dave, but I am a Canadian."

He smiled. "So you are. Sorry, Jo. Anyway here's the story. Really it's not much. It started during that first election in 1970, just after Andy was first nominated and Howard Dowhanuik was head of the party. Howard called me and said he had some money for Andy's campaign. You know how you have to put a name on all contributions over a certain amount? Well, I can't remember what the amount was back then, but this was over it. I assumed the money was Howard's. Andy had been Howard's student, and Howard had really pressured him to run. So it made sense to think the money came from Howard and he just didn't want others thinking it was favouritism.

"I donated the money in my name and got a really nice letter from Andy after the election – handwritten. Funny thing, but I guess that money I didn't contribute was the beginning of my friendship with him. Well, every year it was the same story. In years that there was no election, I'd just give the money to Andy's constituency association, and when there was an election I'd give the legal limit to the campaign. Andy was always grateful. Then as the years went by and we became friends, it was harder and harder to say anything other than, 'You're welcome – hope it helps.' That's how it was until last year, when Howard stepped down as leader and the race was on.

"Just after he resigned, Howard came over to the Caucus Office. He had a really substantial sum of cash – it was always cash. This time Howard came, not just with the money but with an explanation. He said it was time I knew the score, that I might feel compromised if I believed that he was favouring Andy over the other candidates for the leadership. And then he told me the story of Lane Appleby. That morning in my office Howard was edgier than I ever remember him being. But as he said, from the outset, it had been a queer arrangement. Nothing illegal or immoral or unethical, just peculiar.

"It had started when Andy had been in a class Howard taught. About two months into the term Howard got a call from an old friend in Winnipeg. The guy did Charlie Appleby's legal work and he said Charlie had heard great things about Andy, which was strange, because Andy was, according to Howard, a solid but not exceptional student. Anyway, Charlie wanted to know if he could contribute to Andy's education, anonymously, of course, perhaps through a scholarship. Well, as you would know, that sort of thing has to go through all sorts of official channels, and that wasn't what Appleby's lawyer wanted at all. So Howard, who wanted to help a promising Ukrainian kid and who could see nothing wrong with taking money when there were no strings attached, agreed to set up a couple of ongoing projects that Andy could help with – in return, of course, for a stipend." He shook his head in amusement. "Only academics could come up with that word.

"Anyway, that was the start, and Howard made sure the Appleby money got to Andy through one channel or another till the day Andy died. In fact, about twenty minutes before Andy was murdered, Lane Appleby gave me an envelope of cash for the campaign. That's what I was talking to her about after the funeral. She didn't want to take it back."

"What did the Applebys get out of it?"

"I honestly don't know, Jo. It seems so fishy when I sit here and lay it all out for you. Even my alarm bells are going off. But it happened a little at a time, and Andy never knew. I promise you that. There were never any special favours – never. Not from Andy, not from Howard and not from me. I wish you would just let it go, Jo. I've told you everything you need to know. There's nothing to be gained by digging up the past."

"I can't let it go, Dave. There's been a murder. Our friend was murdered. What if Lane Appleby knows something that could help us find the person who killed Andy? I need to see her, Dave. I need to see a lot of people if I'm going to get to the bottom of this."

He looked old and defeated. "Isn't it bad enough the police are questioning everything about Andy's life? Six times they've been to see me, Jo. Asking about everything from Andy's finances to his toilet habits. Isn't it bad enough they're violating his life? Can't his friends let him rest in peace?"

"That's not fair. Dave, please . . ."

But he wasn't listening. He'd pulled out a pen and a pocket diary and he was scribbling something on a napkin.

"Here, Jo." He slid the napkin over to me, and his face was indescribably sad. "I have a feeling you're going to be very sorry you started this. I hope I'm wrong. I'll pay for the breakfast."

I'd hurt him and I didn't understand why, but as I watched

his jaunty figure trudge through the rain to his Bronco, I felt my throat tighten. When the red truck left the parking lot, the tears started. I sat and looked out the window until Al came over and started ostentatiously wiping the table for lunch. I grabbed the napkin just in time. On it, in Dave's neat, schoolteacher's hand, was:

> Lane Appleby
> 824 Tuxedo Park
> Winnipeg, Man.

There were two telephone numbers. After the second, he had written "her unlisted number – your best bet."

The day after I talked to Dave Micklejohn I drove to Wolf River. I had set up an office in the granny flat the night before. The boys and I ate supper, then I'd spent a quiet, happy evening sharpening pencils and labelling vertical files and notebooks. And I'd made some phone calls. The first was to Ali Sutherland. I hadn't talked to her since the day after Andy died, but I'd been thinking about her open invitation to visit her in Winnipeg from the moment I'd seen Lane Appleby's address. Thanksgiving was in a week and two days, and I decided to call and see if we were welcome. Her voice at the other end of the line was warm and delighted.

"Oh, Jo, the answer to my prayers – a real Thanksgiving with real food and a real family. Oh, God, I sound like something out of a Walt Disney movie, but I thought we were going to end up getting take-out from the deli and calling an escort service. Do those people do just plain friends for family holidays, do you think?"

Even during those black months after Ian died, Ali had been able to make me smile.

"I can't imagine you two without friends," I said.

"Believe. It's been that kind of summer. Mort's been up to his elbows and I think I'm treating half of South Winnipeg. Lord, now I'm whining and you won't come. Call me with a list, Jo. I'll get Mort to shop. We can sit and talk and I'll do all the menial stuff like chopping while you excel. Anything at all, as long as one course is your salmon mousse. No, as long all the courses are your salmon mousse. It'll be like old times – terrific! There goes my beeper – call with the list. Take care of yourself, Jo."

I almost didn't get through to Lane Appleby. Her house-keeper was as protective as a housekeeper in a Gothic novel. Mrs. Appleby was resting and shouldn't be disturbed. I looked at my watch. It was 7:00 p.m. in Winnipeg. "Tell her please that it's Joanne Kilbourn calling about Andy Boychuk." Lane Appleby was on the phone almost immediately, but she did sound as if she should not have been disturbed. Her voice was listless and her responses not entirely coherent. She sounded drugged or drunk. Yes, she knew who I was. Yes, she'd see me at Thanksgiving. I repeated the dates I'd be in Winnipeg four times to make sure they registered with her.

When I hung up, I wondered if in the morning she'd even remember that I had called. But somehow I was going to get to ask my questions. Now I just had to know which ques-tions to ask. I had to find out who knew what about Lane Appleby, and the place to start was Wolf River.

It was time to see Eve again. I needed answers, and I had a feeling Eve had them. She was worth a call.

I also wanted to call Soren Eames. He might know why Lane Appleby had decided to spend millions endowing a chapel in the middle of the constituency where Andy Boychuk had his home, his son and his political base.

When I called Eve, she sounded distracted. Yes, sure, I could come. She'd be in her pottery studio all day. No, it didn't matter when I came, she was just throwing pots – more pots that nobody wanted.

I didn't have to call Soren Eames. He called me. His voice was boyish but edgy. He had meant to call earlier to apologize, but it had been a difficult time. Could I come sometime soon and let him show me through the college? He'd come into the city and drive me down if that would be better for me. He seemed immensely relieved when I said I'd drive down the next day and see him after lunch. His words, before he hung up, made me think that perhaps it was more than just a social call. "This means a lot to me, Mrs. Kilbourn – Joanne. I'm grateful to you – very grateful."

I looked at my daybook for the next couple of weeks. In addition to my big three – Eve Boychuk, Soren Eames and Lane Appleby – I'd pencilled in appointments with the provincial archivist, with the president of Andy's constituency and with eight of the people who'd served in the Cabinet with Andy. Things were shaping up. On a whim, I picked up the telephone and dialled Ottawa. Rick Spenser answered on the first ring. Four for four. This was my lucky night.

"Rick, hi. How did your friend the Cabinet minister like the salmon mousse?"

"She went at it like a pack of jackals and gave me nothing in return but some mouldy rumours that I'd heard before – a waste of your fine recipe and twelve dollars' worth of Lefkowitz Nova Scotia smoked salmon. Joanne, it's good to hear a sane voice."

"You sound beleaguered."

"I am beleaguered. This place is steaming. Record temperatures for October in case you haven't heard, and the humidity is unbelievable. Between the weather and rumours about an election call, people are foaming at the mouth. God, Jo, why do we ever get involved with this stuff? Somewhere civilized people are listening to Ravel string quartets and talking about Proust, and here I am driving all over this town in the heat chasing down some half-wit whose brother-in-law knows somebody who works for an ad agency who says the government has block-booked media time for October and November and the writ will be dropped any minute. God, everybody's gone nuts. The politicians are foaming waiting for the PM to call on the governor general, and we're foaming waiting for something, anything, to happen so we'll finally have a story. Sorry, Jo – referential mania, the Ottawa disease. And oh, God, it *is* hot here. How're things with you? How's the project?"

"Good. I'm cool and organized – sitting in the granny flat with the air conditioner humming quietly and a shelf full of virginal vertical files, a box of fresh paper and a jar of sharp pencils, ready to begin –"

"No word processor, no personal computer – Jo, who would have suspected you were a dinosaur?"

"Anyone who ever saw me dealing with a device that had more than two moving parts. Anyway, dinosaur or not, I think I'm making some headway. Dave Micklejohn told me some stuff that suggests a definite connection between Andy and Lane Appleby – the mystery woman in that picture of Andy's body being put into the ambulance after he was . . . well you know, after . . . Howard says the Applebys have been smoothing Andy's financial path since he was in university, and that seems to be a giant lead to me. I called Winnipeg tonight and Lane Appleby has agreed to see me over the Thanksgiving weekend."

"Thanksgiving? Joanne, that's forever."

"Only for Americans. This is Canada, remember? We have to give thanks before everything freezes on the vine. It's a week from Monday, my friend – October tenth. Life is just moving too quickly for us, I guess. Anyway, between now and then I'm going to see what I can dig up on the Appleby-Boychuk connection. I want to be able to ask the right questions. I'm going to see Eve tomorrow."

His voice was laconic. "How's she doing?"

"Well, to be honest, she sounded a bit out of it on the phone, but even at the best of times, Eve tends to be unfocused."

"And, of course, these are not the best of times."

"No, they most assuredly are not. Not for anyone, I guess. I had a phone call from Soren Eames tonight. Remember him? The mystery pastor? Anyway, he was just about abject when I agreed to go out and see him. I wonder why."

"What's he like, Joanne? What's your sense of him?"

"Well, the only times I've seen him he's been terribly upset. I can't be sure, but I think I saw him for a moment near the ambulance that day at the picnic. He took care of Roma after the ambulance left. Then I saw him in his office at Wolf River the next day. And I talked to him briefly at the reception after the funeral. Emotion-charged times, but even then he was pretty riveting."

"Pretty what? I didn't hear your adjective, Joanne."

"Riveting. He had presence – the kind of person you can feel in a room. He's gorgeous, you know. He looks like James Taylor, the singer – very tall and dark and slim. And he has a sense of drama. He dresses all in black. He's a man you would notice – very sexual."

There was silence at the other end, and I wondered if we'd been cut off.

"Rick, are you there?"

"Yes. I'm here. Sorry . . . Look, I'd better go. I'll call you tomorrow night." His voice was strained, and I found myself smiling when I thought about the reason for his sudden awkwardness. Jealousy – I had gone on too long and too enthusiastically about Soren Eames. Tall, dark, slim, riveting, gorgeous – I had, as we used to say in high school, laid it on with a trowel, and Rick didn't like it because – and I grew warm with the thought – because he was interested in me.

It had been so long since I'd been romantically involved with a man that I'd forgotten the vanities and the vulnerability.

"Rick, it'll be good to talk to you again tomorrow – any time, it's always good."

"Good night, Joanne, and thanks." The connection was broken, and I was alone in the granny flat remembering the interest in Rick's voice, smiling . . .

As I drove along the Trans-Canada to Wolf River I tried to remember the second line of "To Autumn." "Season of mists and mellow fruitfulness" and then something about the maturing sun.

I looked at the scorched fields and the stunted crops – there wouldn't be many farmers in our province reciting odes to the maturing sun this fall. It had rained on and off for a week after Andy's funeral, but the earth had sucked up the moisture without a trace. The rain had come late and the land had been dry. Still, Keats could have made a poem of this morning – brilliant sun, the sky lifting big and blue against the land. It was, I reminded myself as I drove slowly and safely off the Belle Plaine overpass, a good day to be alive.

It was just after nine o'clock when I drove down the lane beside Eve's house and parked in front of the little building she used for her pottery. The neat three-bedroom bungalow that had been the unhappy home of Eve and Andy Boychuk was, I noticed as I drove by, immaculate: the storm windows gleamed hard in the sunlight, the shrubs by the house were wrapped in sackcloth, and the flower beds had been turned over. It was the house of a person who set deadlines and kept them. Eve's studio was a different story. The grass outside was uncut and yellowing, and there was pottery everywhere. Pots and vases covered makeshift trestle tables, and a family of cats stalked each other around bowls and plants stacked in the dying grass. Even to my untrained eyes, all these unsold, unsalable pieces spoke of pathology.

As I stood squinting into the sun, Eve came from a lean-to at the back of the pottery. She looked tense but handsome. Her long grey hair was parted in the middle and fell in heavy braids over her shoulders. Her feet were bare, and she was wearing blue jeans and a denim work shirt so faded they were almost white. She was carrying two blocks of fresh clay wrapped in clean heavy plastic that was looped and tied to make a handle.

The sleeves of her shirt were rolled back, and you could see the muscles of her arms taut with the weight of the clay. She dropped the clay blocks in front of me.

"Jo, carry these inside, would you? I need to get a couple more." I slid my hands through the plastic loops and lifted. The clay didn't move a centimetre, but I could feel my vertebrae creak. Tomorrow I would be forty-six. I didn't plan to celebrate the day in traction.

I left the clay on the ground in front of me. "Sorry, Eve – I'll hold the door for you, but that's my limit."

"Oh, Jo. Those things can't weigh more than forty pounds apiece." She slipped her hands through the loops and carried them easily into her workroom. I followed behind her like a puppy.

Eve's studio was a surprisingly pleasant and functional place. It was square, high-ceilinged and cool. There were windows all around, but set high on the wall. The autumn light poured in through them and turned the dusty air of the studio to a yellowy haze. Beneath the windows were shelves filled with pottery that was finished but unfired. In the centre of the room there were two slab worktables and a potter's wheel. Along one wall was a long table filled with stuff: plastic bleach bottles cut back to hold sponges, gallon ice-cream buckets full of cutting tools and garlic presses and other odds and ends that could press decorations into wet clay. In the corner were a hot plate and an old-fashioned sink.

Eve bent and picked up clay from the potter's wheel – small pieces that hadn't worked out. "It's called reclaiming," she said, but I noticed when she began to wedge the clay that her hands, always so capable, were shaking. "Damn," she said, "sorry, Jo, I'm not good for much today."

"Is there anything I can do to help?"

"No, same old thing," she said vaguely. "Unless . . . Jo, there's a little exercise I do that sometimes brings me down. Do it with me."

I was uneasy. Eve was always quick to sense the moods of others. "Are you worried playing with the loony will make you loony, too? No permanent damage, I guarantee. Come on, Jo, it might even do you some good."

She rummaged around in a box of tapes and with a swift and decisive movement ejected the Hindemith that had been playing when we walked in and replaced it with something that sounded like relaxation music from the dentist's office – waves pounding and a flute. She pulled two chairs side by side and said, "Now just sit and listen. Try to close everything out but the music and my voice.

"Take a deep, cleansing breath – good – now let your hands rest in your lap. Feel the air around them."

On the tape the waves pounded and a sea gull squawked. "Close your eyes . . . Think of all the hands you have known." (Above the waves, the flute notes rose sweet and sad. In the Old Testament the flute is the instrument of death.) "The hands you will never forget . . . your father's hands . . . your mother's hands . . . your grandmother's hands." (Ian's hands warm in mine that first night . . . Mieka's baby hand curled around my finger . . . Peter's hand surprisingly strong when he gripped my hand and led me up the aisle of St. Anselm's for his father's funeral.) "Now think of your hand . . . Think of all the things your hand has done . . . Think of how it learned to lift a spoon . . . grasp a pencil . . . tie a shoelace . . . all the tasks your hand has done." (No flutes now, just the sound of whales singing.) "Working, playing, loving.

"Touch my hand now, Jo." (Her hands are large, strong, the fingertips rough with dried clay.) "Hands are the reaching out of the heart . . . Experience my hand. Grasp it tight . . . now release it . . . The touch is gone, but the imprint will be there forever." (Sea gulls, flutes, the whales singing their death song.) "Forever and ever in your heart."

And we sat in silence, side by side, until the tape was over. Eve looked serene, one hand cupped in the other, palms up, in her lap, her chest rising and falling evenly, her eyes half closed. I was embarrassed. I never seemed to be able to get into these things the way other people could. In the sixties, I was never very good with dope – the magical mystery tour always seemed to leave without me. But the exercise had transformed Eve. When she turned to me her face was wiped clean of pain but her green eyes seemed slightly unfocused, and I wondered, not for the first time, how much dope she had done when she was young. When she spoke, her voice was light and dreamy. "You know, I am so filled with peace that I think I could sleep now if you wouldn't mind . . . Or was there something special . . . ?"

I felt ridiculous, Nancy Drew meets Timothy Leary – but I'd played her game. She owed me at least a turn at mine. "Just one question, Eve. Do you know a woman named Lane Appleby?"

"I don't think so."

"Eve, you must remember her. She was the one who . . ."
I looked at Eve's face. She was almost serene. I couldn't
finish. I couldn't throw those shattering words against the
fragile peace she'd drawn around her – the one who walked
with us to carry Andy's body to the ambulance, the one who
stood motionless when your mother-in-law spat in her face,
the one who endowed the chapel they wheel your vegetable
son into every day of his dim and shapeless life.

"The one who what, Jo?"

I put my arm around her shoulders. "Nothing, Eve. Come
on, let me walk you up to the house."

As I followed Eve into her shining, empty house, I thought
of all the questions I hadn't asked. But one question at least
had been answered. I couldn't prove it in a court of law, and
Inspector Millar Millard would not applaud the process by
which I had arrived at my conclusion, but I was certain that
Eve Boychuk had not killed her husband.

CHAPTER

13

I had told Soren Eames I'd see him early in the afternoon. When I left Eve, it was 10:15 and the morning yawned emptily ahead of me – not enough time to drive to the city, but too much to waste hanging around the Charlie Appleby Prayer Centre.

I decided I'd drive over to Wolf River Bible College and see if I could find Lori and Mark Evanson. Eve had worried me. The meditation or whatever it was had helped temporarily, but no relaxation technique in the world was a match for Eve's demons. Lori and Mark would, I knew, keep an eye on Eve if I asked them. They were limited kids, but they were decent and reliable. Most important, because of Mark's connection with Carey Boychuk, they saw Eve regularly. She would not feel violated by their concern.

When I drove through the main gate of the college, I felt like I'd driven into an old Metro-Goldwyn-Mayer musical. The students were back. They were everywhere and, by some people's criteria, they were an appealing bunch: boys with razor-cut hair and button-down shirts and vivid cor-duroy pants, girls with shining hair and careful makeup and

skirts and sweaters the colours of autumn. Perfect . . . and
yet on this sultry October day, their perfection was jarring.
They had the bright, unreal look of a casting director's idea
of students. There was, I remembered, a dress code at Wolf
River, but this studied perfection went beyond that. I
thought of my own students in their jeans or cutoffs or cords
or dashikis, and of their hair, spiked or crewcut or frizzed or
bleached or removed entirely, but all of them fumbling,
however awkwardly, with an identity. Peter has a phrase
that is both final and withering. "He looks as if his mother
dressed him." The kids at the Bible college looked as if their
mothers dressed them. It was kind of sad.

Lori Evanson wasn't hard to track down. I asked one of the
perfect boys to direct me and, with a flash of flawless teeth,
he did. Lori, he told me, had a new job. She was helping people
"get orientated," and she was working out of the CAP Centre.
I looked blank. He smiled and said carefully, "The Charlie
Appleby Prayer Centre." Poor Charlie – all that endowment
money and he ended up as the first two-thirds of an acronym.

She was in the central reception area, sitting at a table
piled high with student handbooks. On her desk was a sign,
"Please Disturb Me," and there was a picture of a cartoon
turtle with a grin on his face and a happy-face button on
his shell.

When she saw me, her face lit up with pleasure. "Oh, Mrs.
Kilbourn, you are just the person I was supposed to see, and
now here you are. God always hears us." She stopped for
breath and looked at me confidingly. I'd forgotten how compelling that lilting singsong voice could be.

Lori Evanson was a compelling young woman. If the other
college students looked like extras in a movie musical, Lori
was the homecoming queen. Her dark blond hair was swept
back into a thick braid that fell between her shoulder blades
straight as the pendulum on the college clock. The braid was

tied with a broad corded silk ribbon, the same russet red as her angora cardigan and the stripe in her tartan skirt. Her face and neck, still tanned from summer, glowed apricot against her white eyelet blouse. She was beautiful, especially now that this mission to talk to me was about to be accomplished.

"I have a nutrition break in –" She looked carefully at her watch. "Why, my break is right now." Her voice trilled with good fortune. "Let's go to Disciples and – please, Mrs. Kilbourn, let me buy you some pie."

So we walked together through the leafy streets. We made slow progress. Every few feet Lori stopped to welcome someone back or to volunteer news about Mark and Clay. She told me how they'd chosen their son's name. "You know, like in Jesus is the potter and we are the clay," she said matter-of-factly.

Lori Evanson seemed to float in a little globe of uncomplicated and undifferentiated joy. She was as filled with delight at a girlfriend's cute new school bag as she was when a thin, freckled boy told her that since June his cancer had been in remission, or with the news that the pie of the day at Disciples was deep-dish green apple.

When we settled into the booth she chose near the windows, she reached across the table and squeezed both my hands. "I prayed for guidance and here you are."

Suddenly I felt cold and impatient. "What is it, Lori?"

But her vacant lovely eyes continued to look steadily into mine. "I have to ask you something, and I've prayed that my words will be the right words."

"Lori, what is it? Just ask. If I can help, I will."

"Well, here goes . . ." The pleasant, lilting voice rose into the singsong of a child reciting. "Will you support my father-in-law, Craig Evanson, for leader of the party?"

I was astounded. I had been so absorbed with Andy's death that the leadership race just wasn't there for me. Across the table, Lori Evanson looked at me with eyes as guileless as a child's, and I was furious that Julie had put her daughter-in-law up to this. "Damn it, Lori, no! I told your mother-in-law no; I told your father-in-law no; and I'm telling you no. No! I will not support Craig Evanson for leader of the party. How many times do they have to be told, anyway?"

Lori's eyes filled with tears. I could see that each of those startling turquoise irises was encircled – contact lenses. She pulled her braid around and began chewing on the end to keep from crying. I felt like I had kicked a puppy.

"Oh, Mrs. Kilbourn, I'm sorry. It's my fault. Mark's mother's right. I'm stupid. But I wanted to do my part and she said I should ask you and now I've made a mess of everything, and I'm sorry. Please don't be mad at her. It's my fault. I knew I shouldn't ask you. Will you forgive me, Mrs. Kilbourn?" She was crying noisily now, and heads were turning in our direction. This seemed to be my restaurant for scenes.

"Lori, please call me Joanne . . . and of course I forgive you if you'll forgive me." She was nodding energetically, so I kept on. "I just thought it was mean of her to make you do it. Lori, look at me. If you thought it was the wrong thing to do, why didn't you say no?"

She wiped the tears from her face with the back of her hand. "Because I have to trust other people to decide for me." She leaned over confidingly. "You know, Mrs. Kilbourn, I'm not very smart. Soren says most of the time I can decide myself what's right and what's wrong, but if it gets too hard for me, well, I just have to trust the people around me."

"Like who, Lori?"

"Like Mark and his mom and dad and the teachers at the college and, of course, I have to trust Soren."

"Is Soren a good man?"

A look of rapture crossed her face. "Next to Mark, he's the best man I know."

"What exactly does he do? Is he the principal or the head of the church here?"

"He cares for us, Mrs. Kilbourn. He does everything. He preaches and he helps the counsellors and he makes sure everyone's fair and he gets our money for us. Before he came, this was just a little backwater Bible college, but Soren Eames had a vision." (You could almost hear the violins soar on that one.) "Soren has made the college really special. He changes people's lives – kids on drugs and runaways, but really just anybody. He could," she said shyly, "change your life if you'd let him."

"Lori, about the money. Where does Soren get the money for all this? Is there a central church somewhere?"

"We're the church, Mrs. Kilbourn. Soren just goes out in the world and gets the money for us."

"But how does he do it?"

Unexpectedly, she giggled and leaned across the table. "Mark says Soren gets our money by" – and she whispered – "by cuddling up to rich widows."

"The Charlie Appleby Prayer Centre must have taken a lot of cuddling."

"Oh, Mrs. Kilbourn" – she laughed softly – "aren't we awful?" She looked at her watch. "Oh, fudge. I'm late. Thanks for being so understanding. This is my treat."

"Lori, just one thing. Could you and Mark keep an eye on Mrs. Boychuk for me? She's having a hard time." Lori was nodding vigorously again. Grief and adjustment – we were on safe ground. "Please let me know if she gets too sad or . . ." I thought. "If she just isn't herself."

Lori seemed to know what I meant. "A change," she said, nodding gravely. "I should let you know if there's any change in her."

"Yes," I said, "a change. That's the word."

When Soren Eames came out of his office to greet me, he did indeed look like the kind of man rich widows would pay to be cuddled by.

"Black Irish," my grandmother had said the first time I brought Ian to her narrow house on Yorkville Avenue. "Skin like milk, nose like Gregory Peck and broody eyes. You can always spot them. They're passionate men, but often insane." She'd been right, at least in part, about Ian, and Soren Eames had the same dark good looks that my husband had, that my sons have.

I hadn't had a chance to get a good look at Soren Eames until that moment. He was older than I remembered. He was balding; there were hairbreadth lines around his eyes; and he was much too thin. But, romantic as it sounds, you could feel the fire there.

He played on that romantic sense, too. He was all in black again, and he had rolled his sleeves back past the wrist to show off his hands. They were artist's hands, very white, with long, tapered fingers.

He smiled and offered his arm. "Let's walk a little." I would have given odds I was about to go on the widow's tour – the crowded classrooms, the too-small dorms itching for endowment – but he surprised me. We walked away from the college, behind the CAP Centre, over the construction rubble to a hill. As we climbed toward the sun, the air was hot and acrid. It smelled of burning rubber and stubble fires lit by farmers. At the top of the hill was a little windbreak of trees and in front of them a rock, smooth and ancient. Soren Eames gestured me to sit down, and then sat beside me.

Below I could see the whole of Wolf River Bible College. With its neat rows of buildings and lines of yellow aspens, it was, from this distance, as theatrically unreal as the model children who sat in its classrooms and walked across its lawns. Beside me, his profile sharp and oddly youthful in the haze, Soren Eames looked at his vision realized.

It was enough to make me toss my cookies. I had spent too much time around people who cruised from photo opportunity to photo opportunity to tolerate this.

"Very impressive," I said.

"Very impressive, but you're not impressed," Eames said, and I was surprised to hear his voice shake. Normally that vulnerability would have touched me, but not today. There were things I needed to know.

"It's a beautiful setup. Lori Evanson tells me you raised money for most of the new buildings. You must have raised a million dollars."

"More," he said flatly.

"And the Charlie Appleby Prayer Centre," I said. "For the past few months Andy was after me to take twenty minutes to come in off the highway and look at it. He thought it was a really great building."

Eames was silent. I could see his pulse beating in his throat. He swallowed. I wasn't going to be deflected.

"How did you come to know Charlie Appleby?"

"I didn't. It was his wife. She just appeared one day."

"And what happened?"

"Nothing. She came. I told her what we needed. She said, 'Do it, and I'll write the cheque.'"

"Just like that? That's a rather spectacular act of philanthropy, Mr. Eames. A stranger comes in off the street and, with a stroke of her pen, grants your wish. Didn't it seem a little – I don't know – whimsical to you?"

"Widows, especially in those first months after their husbands' deaths, are often a little whimsical, Mrs. Kilbourn. You'll have to accept it on faith as I did. The CAP Centre was a good thing for Lane Appleby. She took quite an interest in it – spent a lot of weekends in Wolf River when it was going up. She's been a good friend to the college, and I'd rather not say anything more about her." He sounded ineffably sad.

The silence fell between us again, and I didn't want it to. I knew there was a missing piece of Andy's life in Wolf River. I didn't know the shape of the piece I was looking for, but I did know that I needed to keep Soren Eames talking.

"Anyway, it's an accomplishment," I said lamely.

"But you question the value of that accomplishment," he said softly.

I turned and looked at him. He was close to forty, and in the harsh morning sun every mark of living showed. But there was such vulnerability in his face, and something else – Fear? Hope?

It struck me suddenly that he was as tired of this aimless circling as I was. He had, after all, telephoned me. He wanted something, too. But neither of us would get anywhere till we cleared the air. I took a deep breath and waded in.

"All right, Mr. Eames –"

"Soren," he corrected gently.

"All right, Soren, I'm mystified. I don't know what I'm doing here. I'm a widow, but I'm not the kind of widow you're interested in. I'm not rich. I can't underwrite anything or give the school an endowment." He winced, but I didn't stop. "I don't know why I'm getting the tour. What possible difference can it make to you what I think of all this?"

I looked into his face. It was hard to believe that this was the Miracle Man of Wolf River. The persona of the confident charismatic was as remote from this shattered man as the moon. When he spoke his voice was almost inaudible, but there was no mistaking his words.

"I wanted you to think well of me, Joanne. I wanted . . ." His voice broke. "I'm sorry. This isn't working out. I'm sorry. I just wanted you not to have contempt for me. We can go back now if you want." As we walked down the hill, the air between us was heavy with things unsaid. Like quarrelling lovers, we walked in silence.

When I pulled up in front of the house on Eastlake Avenue, a woman from a courier service was coming down our walk. I signed a form, took a fat striped envelope from her and went inside. It had been a while since we'd done any house-work. The living room was not a disaster, but it wasn't great. The boys had had lunch in front of the television. They had cleared away the dishes, but the coffee table was dusty with sandwich crumbs, and there were rings from their milk glasses. From talk at dinner lately, I knew the World Series was on. Angus had resurrected his baseball cards, and they were in unassailable piles on the sideboard in the dining room. The afternoon sun blazed through the window and turned the crystal vase Rick had given me to fire, but the daisies I had put in it last week were wilting, and the table it stood on was layered with dust.

I had two hours before the boys came home. I could clean house. If I started right away, things would be shining by supper. Or I could make a pot of tea, head for the granny flat, sit in the cool and read through the stuff Rick had sent.

It was the day before my birthday. My last day as a forty-five-year-old. The choice was easy. While I was waiting for the kettle to boil, I dumped the daisies and went into the backyard with a pair of scissors. I cut a generous bunch of giant marigolds, came back inside and filled the vase with fresh water and arranged the flowers. Their smell, sharp and fall-like, filled with room with other autumns, autumns when the kids were little and they'd go off to school with bunches of marigolds wrapped in waxed paper for their teachers. At that moment the mysteries of Andy Boychuk's life seemed just the antidote I needed for the realities of mine. I made a pot of tea, poured a cup and took it and the courier envelope to the granny flat.

The place was beginning to have a comforting order. I had moved the desk in front of the window overlooking the garden. I worked better when I could see the big house and the shadows of the kids passing by the windows every so often. There had been enough rain in September to brighten the asters and the zinnias and the marigolds, so the garden was pretty to look at. But I couldn't smell it. The windows of the granny flat, energy efficient, satisfaction guaranteed, sealed out dust and the smell of late summer garden alike.

I had come up with a filing system that any professional researcher would laugh at, but that I thought would work for me. I had labelled a vertical file for every year of Andy's life, and into each file I was dumping everything that happened in a particular year, not just to Andy but to the people around him: his family, his friends, his colleagues. When I told Rick Spenser about it, there had been silence. For his research he had devised a computer program with a Byzantine system of cross-references. But I liked my files. We don't live in a vacuum, and my vertical files took that into account.

Finding material was easy. The Caucus Office had boxes of stuff and already the files on Andy's political years were bulging. So when I opened the envelope and a fat package marked "Eve Lorscott Boychuk: Family," slid out, I eyed the 1963 file speculatively.

There was a half-inch-thick stack of clippings on Tudor Lorscott. I scanned them quickly. The usual corporate publicity: head shots of Eve's father looking pleased to be appointed to the board of some company or to be heading up a charity drive. There were notices of business acquisitions by Lorscott Limited – some solid, unspectacular stuff, but a surprising number of gold and nickel mines. Old Tudor was a high roller. And then – bonanza – a feature article from the old *Star Weekly*: "The Lorscott Case – The Family Behind the Headlines." There was not much information beyond what Howard Dowhanuik had told me that night a thousand years ago in Saskatoon, but there was a haunting picture taken, the *Weekly* article noted, greedily licking its chops, less than a week before the murder attempt. It was a colour photo, taken in the living room of the family home in Port Durham – a lovely room, all lemon yellow and ivory, with a glowing abstract over the fireplace and a graceful bowl of iris and tulips and yellow anemone on the glass coffee table. In the forefront of the picture the three Lorscott women sit on a silk-covered love seat behind the coffee table and the spring flowers. Madeline Lorscott, as old as Eve is now, a little heavy in middle age, dark-haired still, worried-looking, is flanked by her daughters, slim young women in smooth, sleeveless A-line dresses with matching pumps, Eve's dress cornflower blue, Nancy's mint green. Their dark hair, like their mother's, is fluffed into bouffants that flip girlishly at shoulder level – the Jackie look. Behind them, leaning over the couch, one heavy-fingered hand resting on (or gripping?) the shoulder of each of his daughters, is Tudor Lorscott. His chin just grazes the top of his wife's hair, and his look is smug, proprietary: "This is mine." Tudor Lorscott, lord of the manor. A man to be envied.

The final photos are fuzzy grey-and-white reprints of wire-service pictures. The newspapers' invariable records of crime and punishment: the crime scene, the arrest, the trial, a sequence as familiar to us now as photos of Shirley Temple and Deanna Durbin were to our parents. Except this is Eve Boychuk's family. The figures on the stretchers being loaded into the ambulance are Eve's father and mother. The tanned, lithe figure in a white turtleneck sweater and capri pants, looking disconcertingly ordinary in the sea of uniforms, is Eve's sister, Nancy. The girl with the dead eyes, raising her hand against the camera as if to ward off a blow, is Eve.

The account of the trial was surprisingly circumspect. Even in a city where a circulation war between the two evening papers was always on the boil, reporters couldn't find much juice in an attempted murder trial where no one would say anything.

But there were pictures and there were captions: a picture of the alleged weapon – a small hatchet, wooden-handled, Nancy Lorscott's old Girl Guide hatchet but fitted with a new steel head with a cutting edge like a razor; a close-up of a bloody Tudor Lorscott as he was wheeled into the hospital. ("How did he look?" asked the *Examiner's* reporter. "He looked," said the reliable source, "as if someone tried to cut off his head and his private parts.")

There was a brief account of the sentencing: the judge's decision that Nancy Lorscott should be committed to the Middlesex Prison for the Criminally Insane (a sentence later commuted to indefinite treatment in a private sanitarium). But of the trial itself, not much beyond a dry recital of the exchange of legalisms between the Crown and the defence, the expert testimony of the expert witnesses, and a running account of what the Lorscott women wore to court.

Of course, there were many pictures of Eve – the only accessible Lorscott during those weeks after the assault. Eve getting out of her car in front of the handsome Victorian hall that served as Port Durham's courtroom building; Eve visiting the hospital where her parents were convalescing; Eve coming out of her dentist's office. And always the same small smile and the same dead eyes.

Eve Lorscott was twenty years old in 1963. Enough trauma there to last a lifetime. But this was not Eve's last trauma.

Nor, if one believed the speculations of the psychiatrist called by Nancy's lawyers, was it her first.

Poor Eve. Poor, poor Eve.

I was trying to find the Eve I knew in the tiny grey face in the newspaper photo when the telephone rang. It was Soren Eames, and he sounded awful. Whatever shreds of pride had impelled him to take me down the hill without accomplishing what he had set out to accomplish were gone. There were no courtly preambles this time.

"Joanne, I have to see you."

And then, when I didn't answer immediately, he apologized.

"I'm sorry for what happened at Wolf River. I'm doing a lot to make myself unhappy these days." His voice trailed off and, for a beat, there was silence on the other end of the line. When he spoke again, his voice sounded better – if not strong at least assured and in control. "Joanne, I'm on a really life-denying trajectory now, and I need to talk. I can be at your place in an hour. Tonight or tomorrow – which?"

The jargon and narcissism ate at me – the life-denying trajectory and the string of sentences starting with "I." When I was a kid there was a game we played at birthday parties. Each child was given five beans, and every time we used the word "I" in a conversation we had to forfeit a bean. Soren Eames struck me as a man who would lose his beans pretty quickly.

Whatever the reason, I said no: no to the next hour, no to the next day. After the darkness of the past month, I wanted a birthday that was sunny and uncomplicated, and I told him so. I would see him, but it would have to wait. We agreed to meet at nine o'clock the morning after my birthday at my house. I was not looking forward to it.

CHAPTER

14

The late afternoon sun filtered through the leaves of the cottonwood tree outside the window of the granny flat and made shadow patterns on my desk: a changing play of light and darkness. It occurred to me that before Soren Eames and I had our meeting it would be wise to find out more about the Miracle Man of Wolf River. It was almost 6:00 p.m. in Ottawa. Rick Spenser would be at his house on River Street pouring Beefeaters into a chilled glass. It would be a pleasure to talk to a happy man.

Rick really did sound glad to hear from me. He was buoyant. It had been a good day. The temperature in Ottawa had finally dropped, and the afternoon had been brisk and bright. Even better for a man who hated campaign travel, it looked as if there would be no federal election call. The government polls were down, and just before Rick left his office for the day, a junior minister had phoned to say the government would wait till spring. Rick was celebrating. He'd stopped at the market and he was in the middle of shredding beets for a pot of borscht "in honour of our friend Andy Boychuk," he said, laughing.

But as soon as I mentioned Soren Eames there was a pause, and when I asked if he'd had trouble finding information on Eames, he sounded sullen.

"I didn't see it as being worth the bother. I asked one of our researchers to look into it, and she came up with a one-page summary of a rather dismal life – nothing we didn't know. If you insist, I'll have her look again."

"Yeah, I insist," I said, laughing.

"So be it," he said, sharply.

Whatever ambivalence he felt about Soren Eames the man, Rick's journalistic instincts weren't dulled. When I mentioned Eames's phone call, the line crackled with interest: What had he said? What had I said? What were my impressions? He congratulated me on my decision to put off seeing Soren until after my birthday. "No use wasting your time on a charlatan, Joanne," he said – a typical Rick line, but he hadn't read it well. There was uneasiness in his voice, and I thought I knew why.

Even when I was young I hadn't been good at boy-girl games. Another woman would have been quick to grab hold of this show of vulnerability. I wasn't.

"Rick, listen. The only reason I'm seeing Soren Eames again is because I think he knows something. There's a connection there."

His answer came from far away. "Good night, Joanne. I'll call you tomorrow night before I go to bed, ten o'clock your time, midnight here. They won't have done the daylight savings thing by then." He sounded fretful.

I laughed. "Rick, it doesn't matter. Call when you're near a phone."

"Ten o'clock," he said again. "And, Joanne, I'll get the research person to send what she comes up with on Eames directly to you. Have a splendid day tomorrow. I wish you that."

The first thing I heard on my forty-sixth birthday was the phone ringing, then my daughter's voice laughing, tuneless, singing a crazy birthday song I'd made up for her when she was little. The kids always screamed and yelled when I started to sing it, but it was as much a part of all their birthdays as the ugly plastic tree loaded with jellybeans that was the invariable birthday centrepiece and the mug with parrots singing "Happy bird day to you" that was always at the birthday kid's place on the table. So much a part of their birthdays but never – until that morning – of mine. That Mieka would sing it to me signalled a change in our relationship. When she finished, she was laughing, and I was crying.

"Oh, Mieka, that was beautiful."

"Mum, that was awful."

"Well, yeah, but beautiful that you phoned me up and sang. Does it sound that bad when I do it?"

"Worse, Mum, worse."

"Mieka, it is so wonderful to hear your voice." And then we were away on a lovely, aimless conversation about the boys ("Tell them I miss them and gently remind them the present for you is under the sleeping bag in Angus's cupboard") and her classes ("The woman who teaches my English class is so much like you – that first day I wanted to follow her home like a puppy") and my growing conviction that Rick Spenser was interested in me ("Well, why wouldn't he be? Except for your singing and your worrying, you're practically a perfect person"). Mother-daughter stuff.

Finally I forced myself to look at the clock. "Mieka, I hate for us to stop, but this is costing you a fortune and we can get caught up when we go to Winnipeg for Thanksgiving. It's only a week from today. I can't believe how quickly the fall is going."

There was no response.

"Mieka?"

Her voice was gentle but firm. "Mum, I'm not going to Winnipeg for Thanksgiving." And then, "Greg's parents have a cottage at Emma Lake, and they've invited me to spend the Thanksgiving weekend with them and Gregory. I really want to do this. I've told them yes, Mum."

No room to negotiate. No need to negotiate. She was grown up. She wanted to spend the weekend with the family of a man she was interested in. Outwardly I was gracious, upbeat, and when I hung up we were both laughing. But inside I was raging. It was, I thought, as I looked at my indisputably forty-six-year-old face in the mirror, one hell of a way to begin a birthday.

It didn't get any better in the next hour. The boys were at each other from the moment they got up. They fought like a pair of six-year-olds over who got to hand me my birthday present, and the truce at breakfast was a fragile one. Peter couldn't find his Latin book, and Angus, for the first time since kindergarten, decided he didn't want to go to school. As I stood on our front porch, shivering in the chill, watching Angus snake up the road toward grade eight, I was not exactly brimming with radiance and peace. When a black Porsche pulled up in front of my house and I saw a slender man in black get out of the driver's seat, I felt like giving up on being forty-six altogether. The man was Soren Eames.

I was still in my robe. I had brushed my teeth, but I hadn't showered. I was in no mood for being on either side of a therapy session. If Soren hadn't already spotted me, I think I would have made it simple and not answered the door, but it was too late. He was coming up the front walk toward me, trying to smile but looking tense. He was carrying a blue box from Birks – the kind you get when you buy a really pricy piece of china or crystal.

He stopped at the bottom of the porch stairs and handed the box to me.

"Many happy returns, Joanne."

I just stood there.

"Aren't you going to open it?"

I started to give the box back.

"No," he said. "Let's go inside. Please. Once you open the box, I think you'll understand some things."

He followed me into the house. I went through to the kitchen, poured us both some coffee and joined him in the living room.

The blue box was on the coffee table between us. Soren leaned over and pushed it toward me.

"Please, Joanne."

I think I knew as soon as I pulled back the tissue paper and saw the little ceramic figure inside. I had seen it before. In fact, one blistering Canada Day weekend I had bought it at a craft fair in the southwest corner of the province. It was the work of a local artist, and it was a lovely, witty piece – a cabbage, perfect in every detail, unfolding its top leaves like a flower. Rising from the heart of the cabbage is a woman with the broad hips and heavy breasts of the Ukraine. She is wearing a brown peasant's dress, and a bright kerchief covers her hair. Her face, with its sweep of Slavic cheekbones and bright blue eyes, is uncannily like Roma Boychuk's. The woman's arms are raised toward heaven, and in her hands, solemn and handsome, is a baby boy. The piece is called "Ukrainian Genesis," and as soon as Andy Boychuk saw it that July day he had to have it.

I did the purchasing. Andy paid me later. When you're in politics and you go to a show where all the work is by local artists, it's prudent not to single one artist out and stiff the rest. Andy had loved that piece. I would have sworn it hadn't left his desk since the day he bought it. Except "Ukrainian

Genesis" had left his desk. Somewhere along the line he had given it to Soren Eames; and now Soren Eames was giving it to me.

"How?" I asked.

"It was a gift, a gift to commemorate a special time for me. It was a wonderful gesture."

I could feel my safe world shifting, and I didn't want it to. I grabbed a handhold. "Andy was full of wonderful gestures. He was a generous man. He gave things to a lot of people."

Soren Eames leaned across the table and looked into my face. His voice was soft, almost diffident, but his gaze was steady. "I loved him, Joanne."

I felt oppressed, as if something were pressing me down. I didn't want to hear this. I didn't want to know.

"A lot of people loved Andy," I said and I turned and looked out the window.

Soren Eames half stood and leaned toward me. His hand touched my cheek and turned my face. "Look at me, Joanne. You're not a simple woman. You know what I'm talking about here. I didn't love Andy like a lot of people. It was more for us – a great deal more. He was my lover, and I was his."

Free fall. The old, safe world gave way. I heard my voice, pleading, stupid. "Who knew? Were you careful?" The political questions. Andy was dead. This man was destroyed by grief, but the political instinct was always alive and kicking. There are a hundred jokes about the referential mania of political people: the husband of a woman running for the House of Commons is killed in a car accident and her opponent bitterly dismisses the new widow's loss as "a great break for her"; a campaign manager tells his workers to make sure all their supporters in the senior citizens' homes vote in the advance poll so that, no matter what, the party won't have lost a vote. And me, right in there with the best or worst of them, treating this fragile man as a political problem, not a suffering human being.

His face was so close to me that I could see the faint blue-black of the beard growing beneath his skin, and I could smell his aftershave, light, woodsy – familiar.

Surprised, I said, "You smell like Andy. Did you always use that cologne? Or . . ."

"I changed after," he said. "Stupid – as if it could change anything." He flinched, and the pain on his face was as sharp as if he had been stabbed.

It all changed for me in that moment. Not Paul on the road to Damascus, exactly, but the shock of recognition was there.

"I did that, too," I said, "after my husband died. At night, before I went to bed, I'd rub his aftershave into my body so that when I woke up in the night . . ."

"You could pretend that he was still there," he finished for me.

"Something like that."

We sat in silence, wrapped in our separate memories. Finally, I wanted to talk.

"I'm sorry," I said.

"For what?"

"I don't know, just . . . Soren, come into the kitchen and let me get some fresh coffee and we'll start again."

He stood up and smiled. "Is being invited into the kitchen a mark of friendship?"

"Yeah, I guess it is."

"Then I accept with pleasure. I need a friend."

We sat at the kitchen table. The sky was threatening. The yard was heavy with leaves from the cottonwood tree, sodden and disintegrating. It was a thoroughly dismal day. Soren Eames was oblivious to the weather. For a long time his eyes didn't shift from the window, but I think he was seeing a different landscape.

He had brought the little baba figure into the kitchen, and as we sat, his fingers traced her lines, like a man playing with worry beads.

Finally, he began to speak. His voice was warm and intimate.

"Joanne, I wish we could stop the movie right here. It's a good frame – the respectable matron and the closet gay reach out to one another over their friend's death. But it's more complex than that. Not long after we met, Andy told me you were one of the few people in his life he trusted. That's going to have to be good enough for me because" – he swallowed hard – "I have to trust somebody."

He was wearing a bomber jacket of buttery, smooth cowhide. As he spoke, he reached into an inside pocket and pulled out an envelope. It was of good quality paper, dove grey. On the front, in elegant and familiar calligraphy, was the name Soren Eames. There was no address. My hands began to shake.

"Hand delivered?" I asked in a bright, artificial voice.

He nodded. "Apparently. It was in my mail slot at the college. It's a fairly public place. Open it."

I turned the envelope to open it. On the back flap were the letters *A* and *E* intertwined the way they are on a wedding invitation, the way they were on the copy of "The Sick Rose" someone had placed in Andy's portfolio the day he was killed. My hands were shaking so badly I could barely pull the enclosure from the envelope.

I recognized it immediately. It was a pre-election brochure of Andy's. I had written the copy. General stuff: a careful biography, a few platitudes and a couple of soaring, meaningless slogans. No one ever reads the words, anyway. But the pictures were extraordinary. They'd been taken by a young man who had wandered into the Caucus Office early in the summer. His name was Colin Grant, and that day he was wearing cheap runners, cutoffs and a Georgia O'Keeffe sweatshirt. He had a Leica slung around his neck.

"What you want," he had said as he struck a match on Dave Micklejohn's no-smoking sign, "is subtext not substance."

We hired him that day, and he hadn't disappointed. His pictures were extraordinary. He could do magic things with light, and the photo on the front of the brochure Soren was holding was one of his best – in part, because it violated all the conventional wisdom about how you show your candidate.

Andy's back was to the camera. Coatless, hands out-stretched, he was plunging into the crowd at a rally in Victoria Park. We saw the people from his angle: hands reaching out to him, touching him, faces raised to his.

It was a scene all of us who'd been involved in politics had seen a hundred times. But Colin Grant had played with the light to show what seemed to happen when Andy walked through a crowd. The sun was behind Andy, so that while his shape was dark, the faces in the crowd were illuminated by a light that seemed to come from him. In truth, he could do that to a crowd. It was, I thought, a great photo. But in the brochure Soren Eames handed me, someone had scrawled a word in dark lipstick over Andy's back and head. The word was "Faggot."

"I think we should begin at the beginning," I said, my voice shaking. And he did – with the night he and Andy became lovers. He told his story with such restraint, but every so often his voice would be soft with joy at the simple pleasure of saying his lover's name or remembering a moment of intimacy. His voice was full of wonder when he described the night he and Andy walked at dusk to the prayer centre. "I wasn't his first lover, but he was mine . . . Oh, Joanne, that first time he touched me, I thought, 'This is what it feels like to bloom' – as if I were unfolding under his hands until the dark centre of what I was came into the light. I haven't had a particularly happy life, but that night everything changed for me – for us both. It wasn't a casual intimacy for either of us, Jo. I want you to know that. Andy would want you to know that. There hadn't been anyone before for me, and there had just been one other for him – just one, but he ended that when we fell in love.

"Andy was a person of such honour. That first night we wanted each other so much, but he didn't begin with me until he'd broken off with the other man." He picked up the brochure. "Joanne, this obscenity doesn't make sense because no one knew. We were so careful. For both of us, there were so many other people involved. You, for example – Andy knew how much you'd given to his leadership campaign, and if this had come out . . . Well, you can imagine. Professionally, it would have been the end for me, of course. The good people at Wolf River think my Porsche is kind of flamboyant and daring, but a gay pastor?" He shrugged and smiled sadly. "However, it was Eve we felt we had to protect the most. There hadn't been anything between them for years, but I think Andy would have endured anything rather than cause her to suffer. He said she had suffered enough. She didn't know about us – about me. I'm certain of that. But I always had the sense that she knew the truth about Andy, and I think she knew about the first one."

"Who was he?"

"Andy was a man of honour, you know that, Jo. I never knew the first man's name. I do know they were together for a long time – for years. Andy was terribly shaken about severing their relationship."

Soren looked close to breaking. But I had to press him. "Could it have been him, Soren? Could it have been that first man who killed Andy?"

He didn't answer. He was watching the cold rain falling on the leaves. Finally, he turned to me.

"Jo, what am I going to do about all this?" He tapped the brochure.

"About all this? I don't think you have much choice. I think you have to go to the police. Soren, everything's connected." I pointed to the initials on the envelope. "It's not the first time I've seen that design. It was on a poem someone put in Andy's speech folder the day he was killed."

He looked dazed. I knew how he felt. There had, I thought, been too many shocks.

"Soren, are you all right?"

He held the ceramic cabbage up to the light and turned it gently. "Jo, it's not the first time I've seen those letters, either. I've been trying to remember exactly where I saw them before. I know it was at Andy's house in the city. We were looking through some of his old English texts one day, and I saw those initials drawn together that way a couple of times."

"Did you say anything?"

"I always hated to bring up the subject of Eve."

"So you assumed the *E* and *A* were Eve and Andy?"

"It seemed logical. Who else would it be? And that's one reason I don't want to go to the police. It was always so important to Andy that Eve be protected – I want to do that for him. And, Jo, I don't want people to know about Andy. I don't want anything to hurt him."

His eyes were full of tears. I reached over and touched his hand. "Soren, he wouldn't want anything to hurt you."

He looked up and started to say something. Just then the phone rang. It was Ali Sutherland, breathless, between patients, calling to wish me a happy birthday.

"We are counting the days till Thanksgiving," she said. "Guess what I bought? China with turkeys on it – ten place settings. It's your birthday present but we get to use it first. You'll love it, Jo – a little border of fruits and vegetables and everything – god-awful but right up your alley. There goes my other phone – one of us will meet you at the train – happy birthday!"

When I hung up, Soren was zipping his bomber jacket. "I've taken up too much of your time today. I'll call you in a few days and let you know what I decide about the police." He touched my cheek with his fingertips. "Thanks for listening. It was good just to say his name." He smiled. "And, Joanne, many, many happy returns."

"For you, too," I said. I walked him to the door and watched him go down the front steps.

"Soren, I'm glad Andy had you."

He bounded up the stairs like a boy, kissed me on the cheek and gave me a smile of indescribable sweetness.

"Thank you. Jo, you can't know how much that means to me." He ran down the walk, jumped into the Porsche and took off. Just as he turned the corner the rain turned to snow, huge wet flakes that fell heavily on everything, and I thought, "I'll call him tonight and see if he got home all right." But I never did.

The postman came with a fistful of birthday cards, and a note of thanks from Eve in her curiously schoolgirlish handwriting. There was a Creeds box with a pretty striped silk scarf from Howard Dowhanuik. (A memory – Howard coming to me the Christmas after Marty left. "Jo, what do I get all the women in the office? Booze seems a little crude." And me: "Well, Howard, you can never go wrong with a scarf." Indeed.) There was a first-edition James Beard cookbook from my old friend Nina Love, and a handsome book on Frida Kahlo from Nina's daughter, Sally. I looped the silk scarf around my neck, put the James Beard and the Kahlo books on the kitchen table and sat down and looked through my birthday cards.

Then I went upstairs to shower. I stood under the hot water and thought about Soren Eames and Andy.

How could I not have known? That was the thought that kept floating to the top of my consciousness. I shampooed my hair and soaped myself. How could I not have known? I had known Andy for seventeen years. For ten of the years we'd been close, and for two we had been as close as a man and woman working together can be. But it had never crossed my mind. How did I feel about it? Angry. Not angry at it, but angry at Andy for not telling me. Not trusting me – but why would he? Why should he? I turned the cold water down and the shower beat down on me hot and steamy. Why should he tell? Whose life was it anyway?

I went into my room and pulled on jogging pants and a sweatshirt and my old hightops, went downstairs, put the dogs on their leashes, slipped on a slicker I'd bought Peter to wear to football games and headed for the creek. It was still snowing. In October. "Go for it, prairies," I said as the snow fell steadily, covering the dead leaves. There was no one in the park, so I unhooked the leashes and let the dogs run. Everywhere their feet touched they left a mark.

"A life in translation." That's what a gay friend of mine had called it. His name was Carlyle Wise, and he ran a small art gallery in a heritage house he had restored. He had waited until he was forty to come out, and the only time I heard bitterness in his voice was when he talked about his first forty years. "All that deceit," he had said. "All that energy wasted translating your life into something other people will accept. You're always a foreigner."

The dogs had run down the river bank and were swimming downstream – two sleek golden heads cutting through the grey water.

After he came out, Carlyle Wise had established himself as a kind of informal crisis centre for young men troubled by their homosexuality. Several times a year, one of the hospitals' psychiatric wards would call him, and he would go down and collect a boy who had attempted suicide, bring him home, arrange for counselling, cook for him, get him started in classes or a job and give him a home until he was ready to start life on his own.

"As I hit my dotage I am reduced to being the Queen Mother of the gay community," he would say with a laugh. "But you know, Jo, it's a relief. As Popeye used to say, 'I yam what I yam.'"

Andy had never made it that far. When he died, he was still leading a life in translation, still protecting the secrets of his private world. Somehow that made his death even harder to bear.

The dogs, worried to see me sitting so long on a park bench, came out of the river shaking the wet off, then nuzzled my raincoat. We walked home together through the wet snow. The house was cold and dark. I turned on lights and the furnace, towelled off the dogs and rummaged through the freezer for something good for lunch. I found a container of clam chowder and a loaf of Mieka's sourdough bread, put them both in the oven to warm and took another hot shower. I ate my lunch at the kitchen table wearing an old flannel robe and a pair of fuzzy slippers I'd always loved. At forty-six, you take your comfort where you find it.

After lunch I made myself a cup of tea, opened a new scribbler and wrote two questions: Who knew about Andy and the first man? Who knew about Andy and Soren? I listed the possibilities. (1) Eve. If she knew about the first man, it would explain her outburst at Disciples the day after Andy was killed. (2) Howard Dowhanuik. He had been Andy's teacher and friend and the leader of his party. Would Andy have told him so he could weigh the possibilities of trouble ahead? There was a chance he knew about Soren. Andy was, as Soren said, an honourable man. He might have felt he owed Howard that. (3) Dave Micklejohn. He might know

everything. That would explain his outburst at the Par
Three. In the early days Andy had stayed with him when the
session was on. He was Andy's oldest friend and probably
the closest. (4) Craig Evanson. He and Andy had been in law
school together, then in the legislature together all those
years. Would he have heard rumours? But he would have told
his wife, and Julie Evanson would never have kept quiet
about it when Craig and Andy were contesting the leadership. (5) Mr. X. The first man obviously knew there was a
new man. Did he know it was Soren Eames?

I looked at my list – a good beginning. I picked up James
Beard, went upstairs, curled up with his recipe for honey
squash pie and fell into a sound and dreamless sleep.

When I woke it was three o'clock. I felt better. A man
from the florist came with a dozen creamy long-stemmed
roses from Rick Spenser. My neighbour, Barbara Bryant,
brought over a box wrapped in pink paper. Inside was a
flowered flannelette nightie. Every year for fifteen years we
had given one another a nightie for our birthdays. The first
year mine, I remembered, had been black with a lot of lace;
now it was long-sleeved flannelette with a granny collar.
Milestones.

The boys came home from school cheerful and full of
themselves. They had made dinner reservations at Joe T's, a
favourite restaurant of theirs and mine. Peter quietly suggested that if I wanted a pre-dinner drink, I have it at home.
They had saved enough for either dinner and a drink or
dinner and dessert, and Joe T's cheesecake was famous. I had
my pre-dinner drink at home.

We went to the restaurant, ate a lot and laughed a lot.
When we came home, Dave Micklejohn was waiting on the
porch with a wicked-looking chocolate cake, a bottle of
California champagne and an apology. The kids made a fire
and we sat and watched a ball game, and between innings we

talked about school and ball and politics. Andy's name, of course, came up, and Dave seemed able to talk about him easily and affectionately. The world was starting to piece itself back together, and I was grateful.

A little before 10:00 p.m. the phone rang. On the other end was Rick Spenser. It was good to hear his voice.

"How was your day?" He sounded in high spirits.

"On balance, my day was just fine. Yours must have been wonderful. You sound manic."

"I am exuberant. I'm talking to you. How was your day really, Jo?"

"Really, it was good – very happy. Now let's leave the subject of my birthday." And so we did. We talked about the kids and James Beard's passion for butter, and I told him a crazy story I'd read in a tabloid about how, from beyond the grave, James Beard had written a health-food cookbook. Rick loved that story and matched it with one about the prime minister, and that led to his final wonderful piece of news. He would be free to join us in Winnipeg for Thanksgiving.

I was glowing when I hung up. By the time I said good-night to Dave, let the dogs out one last time, turned out the lights and locked the doors, I felt the fragments of the good old life knitting themselves together again. Maturity, I thought, as I walked up the stairs. Forty-six wasn't going to be so bad after all. When I walked past Mieka's room I opened the bedroom door and said, "Coping," in a declaiming theatrical voice. It was a joke we had when the world fell apart. It was a measure of how good I felt that when I pulled Mieka's door closed, I was smiling.

CHAPTER

15

I had put the dogs on their leashes for their morning run when the phone rang. It was a little before nine o'clock. At first, I thought it was a crank call – for a few long seconds there was background noise, but no one spoke. Then a terrible, unrecognizable voice said:

"Jo, they say I killed him."

"What? Who?" The dogs were going crazy at the front door. Always when their leads were on, it was time to go. I shouted above the racket, "I'm sorry, I can't hear you. Who is this?"

"It's Eve, Jo. Eve Boychuk. Oh, Jo, they say I killed him." Her voice was rising with hysteria.

"Eve, stay calm. Where are you?"

"At the police station in the city. They came and got me this morning. I hadn't even . . . Oh, God, Jo. I can't deal with this." She was almost incoherent.

"Eve, do you know where you are? Ask someone if you're on Smith Street."

I could hear the muffled noise that happens when someone has a hand over the receiver, then she was back on the line. "Yes, Smith Street. Oh, Jo, please."

"I'll be there in ten minutes." When I hung up I noticed how badly I was shaking. Not a good day to drive. I called a cab. Five minutes later, as I slid into the back seat of the taxi, I could hear my dogs barking in the house, still angry.

The new police station was all glass and concrete – "state-of-the-art," as our local paper invariably said. I had been there with Angus's class in the spring, not long after it opened. A nice young constable had shown us around, fingerprinted the kids and talked to them sensibly about drugs and never being afraid of the police and always trusting them when they were in trouble.

Well, I was in trouble now. At the front desk a woman with a round face and granny glasses was waiting for me. Her identification card said "Special Constable Doris Ironstar." She filled out a temporary identification card for me and led me down a corridor and into a small room. There, sitting alone at a square metal table, was Eve. She looked almost catatonic, but as soon as she saw me, she ran across the room and embraced me. She was covered in blood, and the smell was so strong I almost retched. I turned and looked at Constable Ironstar.

"My God, what have you done to her?"

"I'll get the inspector," she said and left.

Eve was sobbing and embracing me. She was a strong woman and it took me a minute to pry myself loose. She was wearing the unbleached cotton dress she had worn the day Andy died, and she was barelegged. Her dress and her legs and hands were caked with blood, but I couldn't see where it was coming from.

"Eve, where are you hurt?"

But the only answer she gave was a low guttural sound. She crooned my name and said the words "no" and "oh" over and over.

Finally my old friend Inspector Millar Millard came in.

"Can't you at least get her a doctor?" I said. "She could be bleeding to death."

The inspector looked at me wearily. "There's a doctor on her way from City Hospital, but the blood isn't coming from Mrs. Boychuk; it came from him."

Now I could feel the hysteria rising in my throat. "Is everyone here crazy? Andy's been dead for a month. How can that be his blood?"

When he bent to calm me, I saw that the good Inspector Millard, the one who gave me tea and biscuits, was back. His voice was weary but kind. "Mrs. Kilbourn, the blood didn't come from Mrs. Boychuk's husband. It seems we have another murder here."

I looked up. Millar Millard was watching me, waiting.

"Mrs. Kilbourn, that blood on your friend came from a man named Soren Eames. Mrs. Boychuk is being held in connection with his murder."

I felt as if I had turned to ice. The inspector continued.

"We had a call this morning from" – he checked the notes on his clipboard – "from a girl named Kelly Evanson . . ."

"Lori Evanson." I corrected automatically.

He smiled and pencilled in the change on his report. "Early this morning Lori Evanson found Soren Eames dead in his office at Wolf River Bible College. Someone had beaten him rather savagely with an axe. We have the weapon. We're checking it out, of course, but it seems to be pretty standard issue, the kind of axe kids use in Boy Scouts. You have children, Mrs. Kilbourn. I'll bet you've had an axe just like it in your house at one time or another. Not that I'm suggesting a connection there," he said, tapping his cigarette package on the corner of the table. He looked again at his notes. "When Lori Evanson walked into the office this morning, Mrs. Boychuk was standing over the body with the axe in her hands."

All on their own, my legs had begun to tremble uncontrollably. I looked down at them. Somewhere in the distance the inspector's voice, patient and gravelly, was talking about physical evidence.

A tiny young woman in a trenchcoat came in carrying a medical bag. She went not to Eve, but to me. She slid her fingers around my wrist, positioned her face close to mine.

"Shock," she said, still holding my wrist in her hand. Then there was a swab and a pinprick sensation at the crease of my elbow, and I felt warm and weary. "You'll be all right now. You're Joanne Kilbourn, aren't you? Well, Joanne, someone will get you some tea. Plenty of sugar," she said over her shoulder. "Hang in there, Joanne," and then, smooth as silk, she moved along. "Now, Eve, what you need is a hot bath and a chance to get all this muck off. The inspector tells me there is a shower here, and some fresh clothes, but just let me give you a little something to bring you down a bit. There. Now that should keep the bad stuff away for a while." She motioned to Constable Ironstar. "I think it's time we took Eve to the shower; we can sit outside and talk to her as the water runs. Come on, Eve, let's go." She took Eve's hand in hers, and the two of them walked out of the room as coolly as if they were at a pyjama party.

Constable Ironstar picked up the medical bag and followed them. She looked edgy. Tranquillized or not, Eve was an unknown quantity. As soon as Constable Ironstar shut the door behind her, the inspector leaned forward in his seat.

"Are you all right now, Mrs. Kilbourn?"

"Yes, I think so. I'm sorry, it was . . ."

"A shock. I know. It always is – especially the smell. We would have given Eve a chance to clean up if things had worked out. We've had personnel problems here today, a death."

A piece slid in place. A staff sergeant had been killed earlier in the week. I'd read in the paper that the funeral was this morning. "I'm sorry about your colleague, Inspector," I said.

Unexpectedly, he smiled. "Thank you, Mrs. Kilbourn. That's a kind thought. Now." He sighed regretfully. "I guess we have to concentrate on this other matter. Mrs. Boychuk needs a lawyer. Normally, people make the call themselves or give us a name and we make the call for them. But Mrs. Boychuk couldn't seem to get much beyond you this morning. I wonder if you could suggest someone."

"Craig Evanson," I said, then wondered where that suggestion came from.

"Is he in the book?"

"Yes, his office is on Broad Street. Just be sure to tell him what it's about. He'll come."

"Thank you, Mrs. Kilbourn. I'll call him myself." He stood up. "I'll have someone bring you some tea." He closed the door behind him.

In a few minutes Doris Ironstar came with a pot of tea and some cookies on a plate. The cookies looked homemade.

"Police issue?" I said.

"Out of my lunchbox," she said. "My boyfriend made them. They're good. You look as if you could use a little nourishment."

I felt tears come to my eyes. "I'm sorry," I said, "I seem to be right on the edge this morning."

"Drink the tea and eat the cookies," said Special Constable Ironstar, and she gave me a small smile as she went out the door.

Then Craig Evanson stuck his head in. "I'll be back. I'm just going to see about Eve," he said, and was gone.

I drank my tea and ate my cookies, gingersnaps with lots of molasses. Constable Ironstar's boyfriend was no slouch. I felt better.

In a few minutes a little party trooped down the hall past my door – the inspector, the doctor from the hospital, Craig Evanson, Eve. When she saw me, Eve started into the room toward me. She was clean and dressed in what appeared to be pyjamas. Her hair was damp but neatly combed and she had a grey army blanket around her shoulders. She had the slightly punchy look of an exhausted child. Craig and the young doctor guided her into the hallway and down the corridor, and Eve gave me a little wave.

The inspector came in and sat down with me. "Mr. Evanson wants to talk to his client privately. We'll be taking her to the correctional centre later. You can leave any time. If you wait a little, I'll have someone drive you." As if on cue, a dozen policemen in dress uniform marched by the door.

"I feel as if I'm in a Fellini movie," I said.

The inspector smiled and said, "I often have that feeling myself. Anyway, you can walk out of this movie whenever you're ready."

I looked at him. I felt as tired and sad as he sounded.

"No, Inspector, I'm afraid you're wrong. I don't think I can walk out of this movie. I think there are some things I have to tell you."

Two hours later, a police car delivered me to the house on Eastlake Avenue. When I went to stand up after my interview with Millar Millard, my legs had turned to rubber. I'd been glad of the ride.

When I walked in the front door, Peter and Angus were home for lunch. They were sitting in front of the TV eating Kraft Dinner. The news of Soren Eames's murder had become public. When I sat on the floor beside them, the television was showing Eve and me walking across the parking lot of the hospital the morning we drove to Wolf River. I hadn't realized the network had filmed us, but there we were. Eve, tall and elegant, and me, short and matronly. Mutt and Jeff. There were other pieces of file footage: the funeral, of course, and the dedication of the Charlie Appleby Prayer Centre. There was Soren Eames, wired with excitement, talking passionately and sensitively about the design of the building, then a sweeping shot of the dignitaries sitting in chairs on the hard-packed dirt in front of the centre. The premier was there, looking, as always, boyishly hyperactive (too much sugar, Angus once said knowledgeably), and Lane Appleby, sitting not far from Eve and Andy, then a quick shot of Andy and Soren Eames together at the microphone: two handsome men in young middle age, squinting in the pale, cold sun of an April morning. When everything came out, that shot of Soren and Andy would be on the front page of every newspaper in Canada.

Then pictures of the body being taken out of the CAP Centre and loaded into an ambulance. Suddenly, I couldn't handle it: Soren, blinking in the sunlight, talking about form and function in architecture, and Soren, an anonymous bulk under a red blanket, wrapped in darkness forever. My knees began to tremble again, and I turned off the television, went to the liquor cabinet and pulled out a bottle of Hennessey's. I poured myself a generous shot and walked into the kitchen.

As I took the first sip, the phone rang. It was Howard Dowhanuik calling from Toronto. His news was grim. Already the Toronto media were having a field day with Soren's murder. They'd dug up the Lorscott case, and one of the city TV stations had sent a crew to Port Durham to get Eve's father's response to the charges against his daughter. The old man had smashed in the television cameras and chased the reporters off his property. Apparently, Eve was going to be spared nothing.

Howard's assessment was brutal: "Thanksgiving came early for the shitheads of the press this year. They aren't going to have to scramble for this one. No, this one is going to jump into their word processors all by itself."

It seemed as good a time as any to ask my question. "Howard, there's more here and I think you must know about it."

"What kind of more, Jo?" His voice on the other end of the line was suddenly wary.

"Andy was a homosexual. He and Soren Eames were lovers."

There was a sigh. "Jesus, no. I didn't know that. Not about Andy and Eames."

I pressed him. "But you did know about Andy."
Silence.

"You knew, didn't you? Answer me." I could hear my voice, shrill and demanding.

Then Howard's voice, defeated. "Yeah. I knew, Jo."

"How long? When did you find out?"

"From the beginning, at least from the political beginning. Andy told me the first time I asked him to run for us."

"Damn it, Howard, why didn't you tell me?"

There was anger in his voice. "Because, Jo, there was no Goddamn reason in the world for you to know. Because it wasn't any of your Goddamn business, any more than it was Andy's business how often you and Ian got it off in bed. Andy did the right thing by telling me, but it was nobody's business but his and mine."

"And Eve's," I said meanly.

"Yes, and Eve's."

"Howard, did you know any of the men?"

There was a beat of hesitation. "No, I didn't – not for sure. There was one I saw just for a second, that first year Andy was elected."

"What was he like?"

"Oh, for God's sake, Jo, it's been almost twenty years . . . Tall and thin, I think. I just saw him for a second and he was . . ."

"He was what, Howard?"

"Naked. He was naked, Joanne. We were in Toronto for a conference. I went to Andy's hotel room early. While we were talking at the door, the other guy came out of the bathroom. I guess he didn't hear me at the door."

"And what happened?"

"I gave Andy hell for not being careful and for balling around, and he said it wasn't like that – that this guy was 'the one and only.' Funny choice of words, but that's what he said . . . Jo, I'm sorry I barked at you. This is a hell of a mess. Look, do you want me to come out there? Does Eve have a lawyer?"

"I suggested they call Craig Evanson. He'll be good with her – gentle. Howard, I'd love for you to come, but really, there's nothing you could do but hold my hand."

"Not the worst fate I can think of."

"The big city's turning you into a smooth talker."

"I mean it, Jo."

"I know you do. You're a good soul, Howard. Look, I'll call you if I need you."

"Don't wait for that – just call."

"Okay. Hey, take care of yourself. Stay away from the painted ladies down there."

"Oh, Jo, I miss you," and then "shit," and he hung up. I sat there for a minute wondering. Then I went into the kitchen and ate some of the boys' leftover Kraft Dinner while I sipped my Hennessey's. It's not a bad combination on a day when the world falls apart.

When the phone rang again, I was in the granny flat sorting through files, looking for places where Andy and Soren might have been together or, more to the point, might have been seen together. The voice on the line was male, young and tentative.

"Mrs. Kilbourn, this is Mark Evanson. The memorial service for Soren Eames will be held on Thursday at the CAP Centre, at ten o'clock in the morning." He hung up.

"Well," I said to the empty room, "I can wear the outfit I wore to Andy's funeral. There'll be a different crowd for this one." And then I repeated Howard's farewell expletive and went back to my files.

I should have been able to predict that Rick would come to Soren Eames's memorial service. The funeral was the climactic coda of the tragedy of the summer, and as his news director said, Rick did have a unique connection with the story. The prospect of his coming was the one small bright spot in the darkness of that day, especially because he was going to stay with us. It made sense. He hated hotels. The granny flat was self-contained, and except for my files and boxes, it was empty. Despite everything, when I hung up after Rick's call, I felt my spirits lifting. It had been a while since I'd had something to look forward to, someone to get ready for.

He was due on the late afternoon flight on Wednesday, and I woke up that morning with the sense of anticipation that a day filled with small and pleasant errands brings. It was a grey and misty day, cool and magic. The snow that had fallen the morning of my birthday was gone, and it really seemed like harvest time. After breakfast I drove down to the valley for late summer vegetables: carrots, Brussels sprouts, squash, potatoes. There was a stand near the highway selling fruit from British Columbia, and I bought a basket of Delicious apples for us, then drove back and bought another basket for Rick. I stopped in Lumsden at the one butcher I know who can cut a perfect crown roast of pork and then, on impulse, I drove to the correctional centre to leave a note for Eve. Even with the extra drive to the correctional centre, I was home well before lunch.

I made a good molassesy Indian pudding, and by the time Angus came home for lunch the house smelled the way a house is supposed to smell in the week before Thanksgiving. Before Angus went back to school, he helped me put sheets on the hide-a-bed in the granny flat and clean towels in the bathroom.

"Now what else?" I asked him, looking around.

"Some of those orange things along the fence in that mug there – a guy would like that." We filled Ian's pewter beer mug with Chinese lanterns and dried grass. Angus was right, it did look like the kind of thing a guy would like. When he went to school, I took the phone off the hook, set the table with our best cut-work tablecloth and the good silver, prepared the vegetables, made a quick trip to the liquor store for Rick's brand of gin, and ran up my bill at the florist's by buying two pots of fat bronze chrysanthemums and a bunch of creamy cosmos for the Waterford vase Rick had given me. Peter came home from school, filled the wood box and set a fire in the fireplace. I showered, dressed in a dark outfit of clingy silk that made me look glamorous and thin, then changed into a skirt and sweater that made me feel comfortable and drove to the airport to pick up Rick.

I had forgotten how big he was – tall and heavy. *Maclean's* said he was the only TV journalist who was larger than life when you saw him in person. "He doesn't disappoint" – that's what the article about him said, and it was right. He certainly didn't disappoint me that afternoon when I saw him standing by the luggage carousel in our bleak new airport.

He was all in brown, tweed and cashmere and silk. His dark blond hair was freshly barbered, and when he reached out to embrace me he smelled of good cologne, Scotch from the plane and something else.

"Deli," he said extending a shiny shopping bag already beginning to darken with grease. "You said you couldn't get good deli here, so there's pastrami and salami, and with my luggage, in a box which, in theory, is insulated, there's a cheesecake from the Red Panzer. Happy Thanksgiving, Joanne."

It was one of the all-time great evenings. The meal was very good, and afterward we had coffee and brandy and went to Taylor Field to Peter's football game. Under the lights of the stadium the players in their crayon-bright uniforms looked theatrical and unreal.

"I feel like I'm in the middle of a Debbie Reynolds–Donald O'Connor musical," Rick said and smiled. His breath was frosty in the fresh, cold air.

"I always feel like that at these things," I said. "I always find myself hoping I'll be homecoming queen and get to go to the harvest dance with the captain of the football team."

"Were you ever homecoming queen?" he asked, looking at me gravely.

"Nope," I said. "Never went out with the captain of the football team, never even went to a harvest dance."

"Thank God." He laughed.

Peter's team won, and we drove some of the kids home. As they climbed into the car they were exuberant. It was good to drive through the moonlit streets and hear their new deep voices cracking with excitement. At home, the boys went to bed, Rick lit the fire and we sat in front of it drinking tea and brandy and talking about everything and nothing: Mieka's classes, Margaret Laurence's novels, why politicians didn't read more, and finally, when the sounds from upstairs died down and I knew the boys were sleeping,

I told Rick about the relationship between Andy and Soren Eames. He was silent for a long while, then he said quietly, "Those things never end happily," and stood up. "Time for bed, my homecoming queen."

I walked out on the deck with him. The sky had cleared, and the night was full of stars, pinpoints of light in the darkness. I had left the lights on in the granny flat, and they glowed warm and inviting across the yard. Rick took both my hands in his and looked down at me.

"Thank you for a perfect night," he said. Then he walked heavily across the yard. I watched him climb the stairs, watched as he tried the door then shrugged and turned toward me. "Key?" he said.

"Damn," I said. "Sorry – in the window box – there's a little plastic bag, taped to the side."

He reached in, then raised his hand in the darkness. "Triumph," he said, and he opened the door and disappeared inside.

I stood for a few minutes in the fresh cool air, watching his huge silhouette moving in the square of light from across the yard. Then I called in my dogs, and because I was at peace with the world when we went upstairs, I let them sleep at the bottom of my bed.

The day of Soren Eames's memorial service was heart-breakingly lovely – a late Indian summer day, all blue skies and hazy autumn light. Rick and I drove to Wolf River right after breakfast. His TV crew was taping some background material when we arrived, and he excused himself and went over and talked to them. I was standing in the sunlight, warm in my white suit, when Inspector Millard tapped me on the shoulder.

"Hello, Mrs. Kilbourn."

"Inspector? I'm surprised to see you here. Did you know Soren Eames?"

He lit a cigarette and shook his head. "No, I'm just kind of looking around."

"But surely when you have Eve in custody . . ." My voice trailed off.

"Well, you never know."

"Never know what?"

He shrugged and started to walk away. "See you in church, Mrs. Kilbourn." But then he turned. "The other day in my office you said you were writing a book about Andy Boychuk – I don't suppose you've changed your mind."

"No, I haven't. In fact, I'm more committed than ever. I don't think Eve Boychuk killed her husband, Inspector, and I don't think she killed Soren Eames." It was the first time I'd said the words aloud, and they sounded right.

He took a drag on his cigarette, threw it on the ground and crushed it with his toe. It was only half smoked.

"Mrs. Kilbourn, do your friends, the police, a favour, would you? Exercise prudence in this research of yours." He pulled a package of Kools out of his breast pocket and took one out. He looked hard at me. "That's a very attractive suit you have on. The perfect thing for this occasion." Then he walked off, leaving me standing in the sunlight, speechless in my perfect suit.

I went over to talk to Rick, but he was taping – or almost. Just as I came up, the cameraman signalled Rick to move. "The way the light hits you where you're standing, it looks like you've got the fucking cross burning on the top of your head."

Rick smiled and shook his head at me, but he moved and started again. As I walked to the entrance of the CAP Centre, I could hear Rick's voice, professionally solemn.

"Six months ago, Soren Eames stood on this spot in triumph. He had personally raised $5.5 million, and the prayer centre behind me had become a reality. He could not have known then that –"

A construction truck went by, blasting its horn. Someone who appeared to be in charge yelled, "Okay, that's it, close it down while we silence our pal with the Tonka over there."

Rick gave me a little wave, and I walked over and leaned against a pile of rocks, carefully arranged by size and colour. There was going to be a rock garden outside the chapel. Soren Eames had told me that the day we walked up the hill.

It really was warm. I could feel the sweat start under my arms.

Rick began again. "Six months ago, Soren Eames stood on this spot in triumph. . . ."

I turned and walked into the cool building.

Soren Eames's memorial service broke my heart. The administration of the college had brought in a grief counsellor to help the students deal with Soren's death. She had suggested that they would recover from their loss more quickly if they had a hand in planning the service. It was a sensible recommendation and a terrible one.

Because they were children who had little experience of death, they hadn't learned the tricks of ceremony and tradition the middle-aged use to mute emotion. After the funeral, Mark Evanson, his young face swollen from crying, told me, "We wanted it to be special for Soren – not something out of a book. We wanted to say good-bye to him in our own voices." The service was full of touches that collapsed the space between us and our grief. The coffin was covered with a flawless piece of white lace that Soren had brought back with him from Dublin the summer before. Placed carefully in the centre was a child's Bible. The president of the student association told us that Soren's grandfather had brought it to the hospital the day Soren was born.

There was a program. The school choir sang a ragged selection of songs that Soren had liked – some solid gospel hymns but also, surprisingly, two show tunes, "Somewhere" from *West Side Story* and a Stephen Sondheim song called "Not While I'm Around."

Between selections, students came forward with memories of special moments, special kindnesses. Finally, there was a tape of Soren's speech at the dedication of the CAP Centre. When his voice, full of music and hope, began, the sobbing in that silent room cut straight to the bone. Beside me, Rick Spenser shuddered.

At the end, Lori Evanson, a small figure in black, stepped to the front and in her sweet, tuneful voice sang "Amazing Grace."

Then her husband came and stood beside her and said very simply, "John 15 will help us now. 'The light shines in the darkness and the darkness has not overcome it.'" And it was over.

Rick and I didn't find much to say to one another on the drive to the city. I could feel a knot of tension in my shoulders and the beginning of a headache, so I decided to go to the Lakeshore Club for a swim.

When I told Rick, he smiled. "That seems like an inspired idea."

"Inspired enough for you to join me?"

He looked horrified. "God, no." Then, seeing my face, he added more kindly, "Do you swim often?"

"Every Saturday morning. We all do. Well, we all do something at the Lakeshore Club. It's our one invariable routine."

He smiled. "Routine is comforting, isn't it?"

"Yeah," I said, "it is. Now where would you like to be taken?"

I dropped him off at his network's local studio. Then I drove to the Lakeshore Club. An hour later, damp-haired but relaxed, I decided to drive to the correctional centre to see Eve.

The guard, a tall, pretty redhead whose name, according to her identification tag, was Terry Shaw, told me Eve hadn't talked all day but she seemed "engaged," so they weren't concerned. As we turned the corner to the hospital block, Terry Shaw said, "She's in the craft area doing a little project we got her started on. You can watch her through the glass if you like."

Eve was sitting at a table near the observation window, bent over, drawing the wattles on the head of a construction-paper turkey. The table was littered with turkeys, and they were cleverly done, proud, handsome birds with bright and malevolent eyes. As she worked, Eve's thick grey hair fell forward, blocking her face from my eyes. I stood and watched her for a few minutes. When it was time to leave, I tapped on the glass and waved. She looked up at me distractedly, like a woman called from an important task by something foolish. Then, without acknowledging me, she smiled and went back to her turkeys.

Dinner was a casual and comfortable meal. It was warm enough to eat on the deck, so while Rick went to the store for beer, I put a cloth on the table and set out plates of pastrami and salami and trays of bread and mustards and fat kosher dills. Like the man who brought it, the Red Panzer's cheesecake did not disappoint. It was every bit as good as I remembered.

The train for Winnipeg left early, before 7:00 a.m., so the boys brought our packed suitcases down to the front hall and we made an early night of it. When I was locking up, I looked over to the granny flat. In the square of light in the darkness I could see Rick Spenser on the telephone. After the jagged emotions of the morning it was a comforting sight.

CHAPTER

16

I had worried that Rick Spenser would feel like an outsider, or worse, put a tear in the seamless intimacy that always sprang up when I was with Ali Sutherland and her husband, Morton Lee. But as soon as Rick walked over, hand outstretched, to greet Ali in the Winnipeg train station, it seemed as if they belonged together. Ali is a big woman, tall, heavy and always brilliantly fashionable. As she and Rick stood under the dome of the old Victorian station, they looked like travellers from a huge and handsome race.

From the moment Rick opened the door of Ali and Mort's brick bungalow in Tuxedo Park, he was at home. The work worlds of Rick and the two doctors might have been disparate, but their private lives were fired by the same loves: art, opera and the passionate enjoyment of food.

Two hours after we arrived, Rick Spenser was in the kitchen pressing a square of butter into a rectangle of dough for puff pastry, sipping an icy martini and fighting with Mort about whether the duet from *The Pearl Fishers* was the most perfect piece of music ever written. The evening was full of good talk and easy laughter. Even Peter forgot his shyness and told stories about a boy from school named Gumby who seemed to have achieved mythic stature among the grade elevens. That night as I slid between the soft flannelette sheets in the front guest room, I said aloud, "I'm going to stay here forever," and I fell asleep, smiling.

Saturday morning, Morton Lee pushed himself back from the breakfast table and said, "Here's what Ali and I are going to do this morning. We're going to take Peter and Angus and anyone else who wants to come downtown to the greatest toy store in western Canada." Seeing Peter's polite display of enthusiasm, Mort thumped himself on the head theatrically and said, "Did I say toy store? What I meant, of course, was toys for jocks – a store that has every kind of ball the mind of the jock can conceive of and all the equipment you need to play anything, plus cards: baseball cards, football cards, hockey cards. Everything." Then Peter's enthusiasm was real.

Rick sipped his coffee. "Well, I'm a cook not a jock so I'll make dinner tonight. I have the menu planned and it is, to use Peter's word, dynamite."

As I slid behind the wheel of Ali's Volvo, I knew I had left behind a happy house.

Tuxedo Park Road, where Lane Appleby lived, was just a five-minute drive from Ali and Mort's. It was a street of tall trees, wide, deep lots and houses that glowed with the sheen of money. The Appleby house had the tallest trees, the widest, deepest lot and the most discreet glow. When I lifted the door knocker, I was glad Ali's shiny Volvo was parked out front. Even borrowed glory is better than no glory at all.

Lane Appleby's housekeeper answered the door. She was a square Scot with faded red hair and pale, freckled skin. She was no more welcoming in person than she had been on the telephone. In fact, she made no attempt to disguise the fact that she was not glad to see me. The day was cool, but she didn't invite me in.

"Mrs. Appleby is resting. You'll have to come back at a more convenient time." She turned and began to shut the door.

I edged my purse into the space that was still open. "This is the time we agreed to. I'm certain if you'll just speak with Mrs. Appleby . . ."

"I'm certain" – she pronounced it "sairtin" – "she would prefer another time," she said and began to push the door shut again.

I stuck my head past her into the house and called, "Lane Appleby, this is Joanne Kilbourn here to see you." From inside the house I heard a voice husky and petulant. "Come." I shot the Scot a look of triumph as I flashed past her into the front hall. Ahead was a foyer as big as my living room and a staircase that circled up to the second floor, but we turned left and walked through the dining room into a small room off it that opened onto the garden. I had been on enough tours of houses of this age to know what the room had been – a ladies' sitting room, a place where women could wait out the time until the gentlemen came back from their brandy and cigars.

The room had been restored with taste and intelligence. All the elaborate detail of the woodwork had been left but everything, walls and woodwork, had been painted a soft yellow. There were three flowery love seats, just the right size for female confidences, turned toward one another in front of the window, a pretty grandmother's clock in the corner, and in front of the fireplace, which glowed with warmth on this cold October morning, was a round table, set for coffee. On either side of the table was a wing chair covered in something silky and embroidered with bright, exotic birds. Lane Appleby was sitting in the chair facing the door.

The whole scene was so obviously one of welcome that I

was baffled at the housekeeper's hostility. But when Lane Appleby stood to greet me, I understood. The lady of the house was as drunk as a monkey.

She reached across the table to take my hand and fell, laughing, back into her chair. I would have guessed her age at fifty-five but a great fifty-five: trim, athletic body, good skin, skilful makeup and a terrific haircut. When she smiled, the years melted away and you could see the girl she must have been, flirtatious, with that confidence lovely women often have, that way of saying, without saying, we both know this beauty thing is just silly, but let's enjoy it.

Her voice was husky and pleasant. Next to her was an ashtray, full, and a half-empty pack of Camels. She'd earned the gravel in that voice. She picked up the coffeepot, aimed it at my cup, splashed the tablecloth and laughed.

"Well, maybe you'd better take care of yourself," she said. Then without self-consciousness, she reached beside her to pick up a bottle of brandy and poured a generous slug into her own cup. That time she didn't spill a drop. After she took a sip she sat back and looked at me. Her eyes were as unfocused as a baby's and about as comprehending. She had lost the reason I was there.

"I'm Andy Boychuk's friend, Joanne Kilbourn," I said.

As soon as I mentioned Andy's name, a flash of pain crossed her face. She took another slug of her drink, stood up and said very formally, "Mrs. Kilbourn, I'm not well today. I wonder if you would do me the favour of coming another time," and she moved unsteadily toward the door. The side of the coffee table caught her leg, and she started to fall. I caught her before she hit the grandmother clock. She crumpled against me and leaned her head on my shoulder, like a football player who'd taken a punishing tackle.

"I'd like to go upstairs to bed now," she said. There was nothing to do but take her there.

We walked through the dining room, past a magnificent table that would seat sixteen easily. Somehow, I doubted that Lane Appleby needed to seat sixteen often any more. When we came into the entrance hall, I looked around for the housekeeper.

"Gone," said Lane Appleby, "gone for the turkey," and she leaned even more heavily against me. Ahead, the stairs curved perilously toward the second floor. I adjusted my grip on her and took a deep breath, and we started up. It was a long trip. Lining the wall beside the staircase were pictures of Lane. As we went, she gave me a running commentary. The first one was black and white, a professionally posed picture of her in a figure-skating outfit.

"Nineteen forty-six," she said, "the year I met Charlie. I was in the Ice Capades, but that picture's a fake. I was never a star, just in the chorus . . . Not really good enough but, as you can see, cute as a button."

"You still are," I said, and meant it.

She laughed her throaty laugh. "Well, I think they would have canned me, but I beat them to it . . . Married the boss." We moved up two steps toward the next picture – this one a wedding photo, palely tinted. I'd seen Charlie Appleby's picture in the paper a hundred times, mostly with his hockey team. He was a big, rough-looking man, twenty years older than his pretty bride, but in the photo with Lane on their wedding day, plainly adoring.

That look of adoration never changed. The pictures by the staircase traced a life of rare and singular pleasures. Lane, laughing, struggles under the weight of the Stanley Cup while Charlie, the man who takes care of his wife, reaches to steady it. Lane, fifties-chic in a dark mink coat and a close-fitting feathered hat, smiles up into the face of a very young Lester Pearson while Charlie beams. Lane and Charlie, tanned and vital, drink cool drinks, piled high with fruit, at Montego

Bay; Lane and Charlie, brilliant in their bright ski clothes, stand silhouetted against the blue skies of Stowe, Vermont.

Finally, there is one of Lane by herself. Handsome still, but clearly growing older, she sits alone in the photographer's studio.

"That's the last one I'll get done," she said. "Damn depressing. If I had the nerve, I'd take them all down. Depressing, watching yourself grow old." She turned and made a sweeping gesture with her hand and almost pulled us down the staircase. I strengthened my hold on her and dragged her along the hall to her room.

She didn't put up a struggle. She sat at her dresser while I turned down her bedspread, then she lay on top of her sheets and fell instantly asleep. I was looking for some sort of cover for her when I found the picture – the picture that I had felt all along must exist somewhere. It was in a silver oval frame. A little girl of about six or seven in a white confirmation dress, her hair corkscrew tight in ringlets, stands on the stairs of a church. Beside her, a bishop, paunchy, bulbous-nosed, looks unsmilingly into the camera.

I put a blanket over the woman sleeping on the bed and slipped the picture into my bag.

Then I walked down the stairs, through Lane's life, from the drunken, lonely woman passed out on the bed, to the widow, the wife, the bride, the shining figure skater. Somehow, I thought, as I opened the front door and stepped into the fresh air, Lane Appleby's life seemed better when you looked at it backward.

Barbara Bryant answered on the first ring. "Jo, this is uncharacteristically sentimental of you. Or are you calling to see if the dogs are lonely?"

It was tonic to hear her voice. "No, I trust you to keep them reassured, but I need a favour, Barb. Would you mind

going next door to the granny flat and getting a picture that's
in a file there and sending it to me here?"

"As that odious toad across the street says, 'No problem.'"

"Great. The key is in the window box."

"Trust you, Jo. Never the obvious."

"Well, you won't have any trouble finding it, anyway. The
picture I want is in a vertical file marked 1950. It's Andy's
first communion picture. You can't miss it."

"Jo, speaking of the granny flat, there were some guys
out there today from –" There was a crash and a howl. Then
Barbara's voice again, good-natured and resigned. "Sam just
fell off his rocking horse. Have a great Thanksgiving. Sam
and I'll drive the picture out to the airport right now. The
ride will take his mind off his injuries. The picture should
be there by late this afternoon."

"Barbara, thanks, I'll do it for you someday. And happy
Thanksgiving."

I drove straight to Lane Appleby's from the airport. I had
the two pictures in my purse, and they confirmed what I
had felt from the moment Roma Boychuk spit in Lane's
face the day Andy died. I knew that if I called Lane would put
me off, and I was growing bored with her self-indulgence.
Two good men had died, a broken woman I felt was innocent was in the correctional centre, and that might not be
the end of it. I wasn't sure where this piece fit, but I knew
that at this point I couldn't afford to set anything aside out
of delicacy.

She answered the door herself. That was the first surprise.
She was sober. That was the second surprise.

"Lane, I'm coming in," I said. "I have something to give
you."

She must have felt like hell, but she gave me a smile and
threw open the door. She led me through the dining room

to her little sitting room. There was a fire warm and welcoming in the grate and a fresh bowl of freesias in the centre of the table.

"This time really is drink time," she said. She was pale but she was game. When she alluded to the adventure of the morning she tried another smile. "I think we have almost everything. I'm having tea, if you'd like that?"

"Tea would be fine."

Her hands were shaking when she poured but this time she hit the cup. "Mrs. Kilbourn – Joanne – I'd like to explain about this morning."

"Lane, believe me, that's the least of my concerns. Since Andy's death and then Soren's, things seem to be spinning out of control. I need your help. I can't force you to get involved, but I can tell you that if you know anything about any of this I think you have an obligation to tell someone." I fished into my bag, pulled out the two photos and set them side by side on the table. The frames of both pictures were silver. Hers was oval, chased with a little flowery pattern; his was plain silver, heavier and square. But the church steps in the pictures were the same and the bishop was the same, although clearly younger in Lane's communion picture. Andy had joked once or twice about being the child of his mother's withered loins. Roma must have been much younger when Lane was born.

Lane's reaction surprised me. She took my theft of her picture without comment, but there was a sharp intake of her breath as she saw the picture of Andy. When she picked it up to look at it more closely, the light from the fire warmed the picture's silver frame.

It was, I thought, the right moment to ask my question. "Lane, Andy was your brother, wasn't he?"

She looked up, surprised. The look on her face was the same as the look on Eve's face the day in Disciples when she told me I didn't know the first thing about Andy. Lane leaned toward me. I could smell tobacco and perfume. Her voice was husky.

"I'm afraid you're wrong, Nancy Drew. Andy Boychuk was my son."

It was a familiar story: the pretty young girl and the favourite uncle – Roma's brother. "I thought," said Lane, "that when she found out she'd be on my side, that she would kill him, but it was me she wanted to kill." She raised her voice in an uncanny imitation of her mother's. "'Slut. Whore. It's always the girl's fault, Elena. My brother Sid is a good man. You threw yourself at him. Scum. Streetwalker.'" Lane laughed throatily. "Mother love. She took the baby, of course. 'The innocent baby, may he never know his mother, the whore.' Well, you get the idea."

She lit a Camel and inhaled deeply. "Charlie knew, but not until years after we were married. Oh, God, the guilt. And when I finally told him, he was so sweet. He said, 'Well, Lane, what d'ya want to do?'

"I had this great scheme, straight out of a Bette Davis movie. I was going to go to Andy and tell him he wasn't the son of some little babba out by the railroad tracks. He was Lane and Charlie Appleby's son. The son of rich people who could do anything for him. And, of course, he would fall down on his knees at this amazing news." She laughed. "And my mother would see the error of her ways and repent. Or she'd die. And either way we'd all live happily ever after."

The ash fell off her cigarette onto the perfect carpet. She didn't miss a beat. "But I made the mistake of asking Charlie what he thought I should do." Her eyes grew dreamy. "Do you know what he said? He said, 'Lane, honey, let the guy be and let you be. If you want to do something monetarily, we'll find a way to do it incognito. Enough money to smooth the way without upsetting the apple cart.'" That's what Charlie thought was best and that's what he did – we did. Charlie's lawyer knew Howard Dowhanuik, and he handled it from the time Andy was eighteen. And it was always" – she smiled sadly – "incognito."

"But you saw Andy," I said. "You were at the picnic that day and at the dedication of the prayer centre in Wolf River. I saw you on the tapes."

"After Charlie died I couldn't stay away. I had no one. I have no one. I told Howard Dowhanuik, and he suggested I do something at the Pines where Andy's little boy lives. He said that would give me 'legitimate access' to Andy. I don't know what Howard had in mind, but I was too old to be a candy striper, so I asked Soren Eames what I could do for the college."

"And the CAP Centre was born," I said.

"The Charlie Appleby Prayer Centre was born," she corrected gently. "And that's my involvement." Her cigarette was still burning in the ashtray, but she lit another. "Now," she said, "I have a question for you." Her voice broke. "Who's doing these things? It isn't Eve. I'm as certain of that as I am that I was never Barbara Ann Scott. What kind of monster is loose out there?"

When I pulled up in front of the pretty doorway of the house in Tuxedo Park, Peter and Angus were throwing a football around on the lawn with Morton Lee. Collectively, they were wearing enough equipment to get a CFL team through the season. Mort was a generous shopper.

It was just before dusk, the time in autumn when suddenly the light fades, the temperature dips and I'm glad I have a place to go home to. When I opened the door, the house smelled of roast beef and pies browning. Somewhere

Jussi Björling was singing "O Mimi, tu piu non torni" from *La Bohème*. Rick strode down the hall. He was wearing a huge butcher's apron and he looked agitated.

"Damn. I thought you were Mort," and then realizing what he'd said, "Jo, I'm sorry, it's just that . . ."

"You wanted him to hear the Björling-Merrill duet from *The Pearl Fishers* – I have this record, too. Go get him." And so Mort came in, face flushed with cold and exertion, and we three stood and listened to "Au font du temple Saint," and I thought, Rick was right. It was the most perfect piece of music that's ever been written. Then we drank Bordeaux and ate roast beef and Yorkshire pudding and Mort played Ravel's *Quartet in F* and argued that yes, *The Pearl Fishers* was beautiful, but . . .

In that civilized house it was easy to forget Eve sitting in a prison hospital cutting out turkeys with cruel little eyes, and Lane Appleby running her perfectly manicured finger around the frame of the picture of her dead son. It was even possible to forget for a while the monster who was loose out there just waiting.

Sunday was damp, but Thanksgiving Day was bright and cool.

"Last chance for the zoo," Mort said, "Next week it'll be too cold. Jo, throw that salmon mousse of yours into the oven and let's go. If we're going to eat half the stuff that's cooking around here, we'll need to work off a few calories."

At the zoo, Ali and I trailed behind, talking, while Rick and Mort walked with the boys. I hadn't thought this would be Rick's kind of outing. In fact, I had doubted he would come. But here he was in his heavy Aran Isle sweater, larger than life and as happy as I'd seen him. He was knowledgeable and he was fun. He made connections between the animals and political people: a huge, lugubrious female baboon was our ex-Minister of Energy; a sleepy, moth-eaten old lion who sprang across his cage in a single bound when someone pelted him with a pebble was, Rick said to me solemnly, "Your ex-Premier, Howard Dowhanuik."

"What about them?" Angus asked, pointing to some zebras chasing one another skittishly in an open field.

"Glad you asked," said Rick. "They're the press gallery. In Ottawa, as in the zebra world, young males not mature enough or aggressive enough to claim a group for themselves or lead a herd live in bachelor groups." And then, while we were still laughing, he added seriously, "The lion is their principal enemy."

Dinner was a splendid affair. The table looked like a cover of *Gourmet*. Mort found just the right Moselle to serve with the salmon mousse; the meal from roast turkey to pumpkin pie was as traditional as it was perfect. There was a sense of family at that table, and when Mort drove Rick to the airport to catch the flight to Ottawa, we all felt a sense of loss. It was as if the circle had been broken.

Ali and I went into the kitchen, cleared a place at her oak table, poured coffee and split the last of the pumpkin pie. As we ate, we talked about old times. They hadn't been good old times, especially at the beginning, but with Ali's support and love they had become good times and I was, I thought, a happy woman. And it was me, past and present, Ali talked about as we sat in her handsome kitchen with the light dying outside and the good smells of a holiday dinner still hanging in the air.

Her face was serious as she looked at me. "You know, Jo, I think you've really put it together this time. When I heard about Andy, I worried that maybe you weren't strong enough yet to handle another trauma, but here you sit looking wonderful and full of energy, and with a remarkable man in the picture. As your doctor, I'm proud, and as your friend, I'm delighted." She reached across the table and squeezed my hand. "You're made of good stuff, lady, really good stuff."

I hugged those words to myself all the way to Regina.

CHAPTER

17

The next morning I woke up in my own bed in the house on Eastlake Avenue. The room was full of light, and as I lay there, I could hear in the distance the mournful cries of geese flying south. I got out of bed, opened the window and curled up in the window seat to watch. The air that came into the room was fresh and cold and smelled of the north. I hugged my knees for warmth and looked out. There were no clouds. The sky was a clear, hard blue. It was a flawless October day.

Suddenly the air was black with geese, hundreds, then thousands of them. Their cries filled the room and, like a tuning fork, a part of me that I had forgotten resonated, responding. It was a pure and shining moment – one of the best and one of the last.

That day it all began to fall apart and, for a while, it looked as if all the king's horses and all the king's men wouldn't be able to put it together again.

Nothing seemed wrong at the beginning. When the dogs and I came back from our morning walk, there was a Canada

Messenger truck in front of our house. Two men were
unloading boxes. I'd been expecting them. Before we left for
Winnipeg, a woman from Supply and Services called and
told me there was still a lot of Andy's stuff ("Boychuk-
related material," she had called it) in a storeroom at the legislature, and they needed the space. They didn't want to
distress Mrs. Boychuk further. (Yes, I thought, the permanently bewildered should be spared something.) Dave
Micklejohn had suggested I was working on a book and . . .
Here it was. The machinery of government had been kicked
into high gear to clean out a storeroom, and I wasn't ready.

I signed the invoice and said I'd pay the driver and his
helper if they'd carry the boxes up to my office in the granny
flat. I hadn't been in there since I went to Winnipeg, and it
was cold. I turned on the heat and paid the men, then I went
to the house to warm up. I made a couple of phone calls, so
it was after ten by the time I got to the office. I was feeling
edgy and frustrated. I hate days that fritter themselves away;
this seemed to be shaping up as one of them. And to add to
my frustration, there was a fine dusting of pollen over everything: the boxes from the Caucus Office, the desk, window-
sills, files. Obviously, the pollen had settled into the heating
system all summer long, and when I'd turned on the heat, it
had blown out. I tried to ignore the pollen and started to
unpack a box of files, but it was getting into everything. I
filled a bucket with hot soapy water and washed everything
down. By the time I was ready to unpack the government
boxes, it was noon, and Angus was home for lunch. As I
turned on "The Flintstones" and poured tomato soup into
his bowl, I gave myself a little pep talk. "You've learned to
handle the big stuff, now don't let the little stuff eat at you."

After Angus went back to school I decided to celebrate my
resolve. I unwrapped a basket of dried fruit Craig Evanson
had sent for Thanksgiving and took it to the granny flat. An

incentive. But I didn't need one. Once I started going through the boxes, the afternoon flew by. There was a huge box of clippings, arranged, of course, by subject, not by year. Getting all the material refiled was too daunting a job for that afternoon, so I opened another box. It was full of gifts, the kinds of things all politicians acquire in the course of a career: a provincial crest made from bits of broken bottles set into a concrete block; a pair of pillowcases with Andy's and Eve's faces drawn on with liquid embroidery; a stack of amateur oil paintings of prairie scenes, garish sunsets and grain elevators that bulged and tilted against turquoise skies; a metal lunch box with Andy's initials. The potash workers at Lanigan had given it to him at the beginning of August so he could "go to work on those bastards in the next election."

Junk, but hard to deal with if you remembered the day the junk was presented and the look on the face of the presenter and how you laughed about it on the way back to the city.

Of course, some of it wasn't junk. I was sitting looking at the weaving in a lovely and intricate Métis belt and eating the last of the sugared figs when the boys came racing up the steps to the granny flat. They looked winsome – always a trouble sign.

Peter began. "Since it's almost dinnertime and since I don't think you've had time to cook . . ."

Angus finished the preamble. "And since we all love pizza and since we have a two-for-one coupon for that new pizza place, why don't we . . . ?"

"Order Chinese food?" I suggested.

"Oh, Mum," said Angus, "you never used to say dumb stuff like that when Mieka was here."

"Sorry," I said. "Pizza it is, but I insist on anchovies."

"On one quarter only?" said Angus.

"Half," I said.

"A third," he said, beaming.

"Fair enough" I said. "But this place better give double cheese."

That night I woke up with a terrible cramping in my stomach. When I turned on the light and sat up to look at the clock, a wave of nausea hit me. I ran to the bathroom and sat on the edge of the tub, shivering and reading an old *Chatelaine*. Finally, I pulled on a robe, went to the kitchen and poured some milk into a saucepan to warm. The dogs were nuzzling me worriedly. In our house, people didn't come downstairs in the middle of the night and sit huddled over the kitchen table. But the warm milk helped, and after a while the dogs and I went upstairs and I slept until morning.

I keep a little daybook by my bed. That morning I wrote in one word – "sick" – but then I got up, showered and felt better. I called the correctional centre to check on Eve, phoned Patterson, New Jersey, to see why the Mets jacket I'd ordered six weeks ago for Peter's birthday hadn't come yet, made a pot of tea, took it to the granny flat and began on the files. At lunch I had some soup with Angus, and by the time Rick called that afternoon, I felt so much better I didn't even mention my bout the night before. The boys weren't sick. I decided it had been the anchovies on my third of the pizza that made me ill. Rick sounded up, buoyed still by Thanksgiving and excited about the stuff the Caucus Office had sent.

"Stick with it, Jo. How I envy you that granny flat. Right now, I'd give six bottles of Beefeater to have the kind of quiet you have there. That's what we need – a place where we can lay out all the material and then just look at it in peace until the answers start to emerge. And they will emerge. Trust me."

The strength of his assurance got me through the rest of the afternoon. I had dinner with the boys, showered, and by

8:30 was in bed with a new unauthorized biography of the PM, good gossipy stuff. I fell asleep still grinning about some of the revelations. No wonder he hadn't called an election at the end of summer. I woke up in the night with another attack, the same thing but worse – nausea, cramping and this time diarrhea. Again I went downstairs and made myself warm milk. This time I took a couple of yogurt pills, which I had bought at a health-food store, to counter the diarrhea. I fell into bed exhausted, but I slept. The next morning in my daybook I wrote the word "sick," followed by the symptoms.

It was a significant moment. I had begun to track this illness, whatever it was. Without realizing it, I had moved across that fine line that separates the world of the well with all its dear and familiar preoccupations to the world of the sick where the only real concern is the sickness itself.

That first week I continued to function, to keep up at least the appearance of business as usual. I went to the correctional centre to visit Eve, who seemed to be sliding away; to Craig Evanson's office to drink tea and talk about Eve's defence; around town to do family errands; to the granny flat to unpack and sort and file. Saturday morning the kids and I even made it to the Lakeshore Club, but I spent most of my time sitting on the edge of the pool shaking. And, last thing at night, every night, I talked to Rick Spenser, whose voice, warm and full of concern, was increasingly becoming my reason for getting through the days. As long as I could keep up the rounds of ordinary domestic routine, nothing was wrong.

By the second week it was becoming harder to pretend. The evidence of my daybook was there every morning in black and white: the word "sick" followed by a growing list of symptoms – diarrhea and cramps and nausea, but also a cold, clammy feeling and, something new, a taste of metal in my mouth that for the first time in my life made eating a chore to be endured.

That second week I played a game with myself – if it's not better tomorrow, I'll call the doctor – but I never did. By the weekend I was frightened and exhausted. I didn't even bother to take my bathing suit to the club. I sat in the coffee shop and watched the boys playing tennis through the glass. The morning seemed endless, and when finally we did get home, I noticed the boys exchanging worried looks. To escape, I told them I had to work. I went to the granny flat, shut the door and collapsed on the couch for most of the afternoon. Peter brought me a tray at suppertime. He was seventeen years old, but he looked close to tears. He remembered the bad time after Ian died, too. I felt so guilty that I followed him to the house like a whipped dog.

"Okay, you guys, if you want to pamper me, go to it," I said and I went upstairs, showered and crawled into bed. In the night the cramps and nausea hit me in waves. I got up and went and sat in the bathroom. But the memory of Peter coming to the granny flat with the tray fired something in me. I heard my voice, frightened but defiant. "I am not going to let this happen again. I am not going to give in." Finally, I went back to bed and slept until morning.

Sunday was cold and sleety. The boys volunteered to stay home from church, and I was too weak to fight them. I stayed in bed most of the day and slept through the night. Monday morning I awoke feeling better – not completely well, but well enough to make some plans.

Hallowe'en was a week away. I decided to treat myself. Andy's old administrative assistant, Rosemary Vickert, had opened a store a couple of weeks before. She'd sent me an announcement. The store was called Seasons, and it sold everything I could want for celebrating a holiday. I dressed with more than usual care, and noticed with a certain grim pleasure that the Black Watch tartan skirt that had been snug around the waist at Thanksgiving was now not just comfortable but loose.

"Today I declare myself not only well but thin," I said as I ran my finger around the waistband.

Rosie's store was in a strip mall, the same strip mall where Ali Sutherland had once had her partnership. I parked as far away as possible from Ali's office. Today I was well. I had no need of doctors.

Seasons was a wonderful store. Rosie was downtown on an errand but her partner was cheerful and unobtrusive and I found some great stuff, a Hallowe'en wreath with orange ribbons and little black cats for Mieka's door, a spooky ghost windsock for our front porch and some cards for friends. I was standing by the cash register when I spotted a pumpkin suit in size two or thereabouts. On impulse I decided to buy it for Clay Evanson, Lori and Mark's little guy. I'd just put the suit on the counter when Rosemary Vickert came in the door. When she saw me, her face lit up, but as quickly as it had come, the joy was gone.

"My God, Jo, what's the matter with you? You look like hell."

"I've had the flu, but I'm better now."

"The hell you are," she said. "How much weight have you lost?" She reached up and felt my forehead. "You feel like you've got a chill."

"I'm better," I repeated numbly.

"Take a look, lady," she said and spun me around so that we were both looking in the mirror over a display case by the door. Suspended from the ceiling were dozens of rubber skeletons. Rosie swept them aside so I could see myself.

It was a shock. Rosemary, pink with wellness, was looking over my shoulder into the mirror. But she wasn't looking at herself. She was looking at a yellow-skinned woman with dry, chapped lips and sunken eyes. She was looking at me.

"What does the doctor say?" asked Rosie, looking over my shoulder at my mirror image.

"I haven't been," I said.

"Well, we're going now," she said. "Do you want to get taken to a doc in a box or do you want to see if someone at Ali's old place can look at you?"

I didn't say anything.

"Jo," she said, "we're not negotiating whether you are going. We're negotiating who you are going to see. Whether is off the table. Now who will it be? Somebody at the Medi-centre or someone from Ali's?"

"Ali's," I said numbly, looking at my feet. I knew I'd been defeated.

"There's nothing wrong with you," the slim woman in the medical coat and the impossibly high heels said, smiling as she came into the examining room. "I can't see anything. I've made an appointment with a gastroenterologist just in case, but my guess is you won't need it. No harm in having an appointment, though. Those guys have waiting lists that are yea long." She swung herself up on a stool at the side of the examining table. "Mrs. Kilbourn, I had a quick look at your records. I noticed you had a pretty bad time after your husband died and you know that was only a couple of years ago."

"Three," I said numbly. "It'll be three years in December."

She looked at me kindly. "You've been under an incredible amount of stress, you know. I read the papers, and it seems to me you've been right at the centre of Andy Boychuk's murder – terrible in itself. It must have opened a lot of old wounds for you."

"You're saying this is all in my head."

"I'm saying we can't rule that out, Mrs. Kilbourn. As you

well know, the body often has its own way of coping with stress. Now this is what I think we should do. I'm going to prescribe something to help you over this rough spot – very short term. Sometimes that's all it takes, you know – a tranquillizer to unknot the knots and let your body get in touch with its own wisdom. Why don't we try that, and then if things don't sort themselves out, you can keep the appointment with the gastroenterologist. His name is Dr. Philip Lee. He's a bit brusque, but he's good."

"I know his brother, Mort."

She looked mischievous. "Well, Mort got all the charm in that family, but they're both brilliant." She stood and smoothed her skirt. "I want to see you in a month – even if you're okay."

I walked into the waiting room, clutching my prescription for Valium and the slip of paper with the time and date of my appointment with Dr. Philip Lee. Rosemary Vickert looked up expectantly.

"Nothing wrong with me," I said. "It's all in my head." I tried to laugh, but the sound that came out was jagged and forlorn.

Rosie jumped up and put her arms around my shoulder. "C'mon, Jo, let's go someplace and have a sinful lunch. You can pay – punishment for scaring the . . ." She gave a sidelong glance at the doctor's office. "For scaring the fecal matter out of me."

I took a Valium with lunch, went home and slept through the afternoon. That night I went to Peter's football game, came home, got into bed with the unauthorized biography of the PM and slept through the night.

The next morning in my daybook I wrote a tentative "Better" followed by a string of question marks. I had breakfast with the kids, took the dogs for their run, changed my clothes, grabbed the little pumpkin suit I'd bought for Clay

Evanson and drove to Wolf River. I took a deep breath when I pulled onto the overpass. "So far, so good," I said aloud and then something went wrong in my chest muscles. I couldn't move the air in and out of my lungs. I took a series of gulping breaths. I managed to keep the car on the overpass and get onto the highway. I pulled over onto the shoulder at almost exactly the same spot where Eve and I had stopped six weeks before.

There was a paper bag from a take-out place on the dash-board. I held it over my mouth and nose and breathed deeply. The bag smelled of stale grease and salt, but after a while, my breathing became regular again. I sat by the side of the road for a few minutes, frightened and angry. Then I said loudly, "I'm not giving in to this, you know," put the car in gear and finished the drive to Wolf River.

For once, Lori Evanson was not immaculate. I had stopped in at Disciples for a cup of coffee and was told that Lori was home and ill. When she opened the door of the trailer she and Mark and Clay lived in, she certainly looked ill and, without her careful makeup, very young. She invited me in, turned off the soap opera she was watching, made a futile stab at picking up the toys that were everywhere in the sunny living room, then collapsed on the couch.

Clay's eyes had been drawn by the bright colours of the bag from Seasons, and he grabbed at it.

"Oh, Clay, no." Lori's sweet singsong voice sounded weary.

"It's all right, Lori. It's a present for him."

Like a child, she was off the couch and over to where Clay was, helping him open the bag.

When she saw the pumpkin suit, she began at once to pull it over his little T-shirt and jeans.

"Oh, Clay, you are going to be such a cute little Mr. Pumpkin." She sat back on her heels and looked up at me solemnly. Her eyes were as round and full of wonder as the eyes of her son. "How can I ever thank you?"

"It's just a Hallowe'en costume, Lori. My kids are all grown up now – at least past the pumpkin stage. This was fun for me, and Clay really does look great."

"Then I'll just get up and give you a hug." She was smiling when she reached her arms out to me but something she saw in my face killed the smile. My chest felt tight, as if something were squeezing it. Lori's eyes were filled with concern. "Why, Mrs. Kilbourn, you're sick. You look so very sick. What's wrong with you?"

"Nothing, it's all in my head, Lori. I went to the doctor yesterday and she said it was just stress: Andy's death and then Soren's and then Eve – Mrs. Boychuk – getting arrested. I guess it's just been too much." My chest felt like it was caught in a vise. I tasted metal then my mouth filled with saliva. "It's all in my head," I said again lamely.

Lori looked at me and burst into tears. Clay, who was twirling in front of the window in his pumpkin costume, stopped and ran over to see what was wrong with his mother. Lori was sobbing brokenly, but between her sobs there were odd little fragments of self-accusation. "I've hurt you," "It's all my fault," and "If I hadn't done it, Mrs. Boychuk wouldn't have . . ."

I went to her. When I bent to put my arms around her, the vise tightened on my chest. It felt as if my heart were skipping beats. I broke out in a clammy, cold sweat.

"Lori, why don't you get us some tea, please." I sounded sharp, but she got up and went into the kitchen.

I could hear her filling the kettle, still sniffling, getting down cups.

I sat and said under my breath, "You are not sick. It's in your head, in your head." My hands were shaking but I managed to pull the bottle of Valium out of my purse and get a small, pale green pill into my mouth before Lori came back.

It helped – or at least it seemed to. Lori gave Clay some juice in a plastic glass that had a picture of Big Bird on it, and she poured our tea into blue and green striped mugs. I put three teaspoonfuls of sugar into the tea, and when I took a sip, the metal taste left my mouth. I really did begin to feel better. I tried to sound kind but firm.

"Now, what's all this about Mrs. Boychuk's problems being your fault?"

Lori was holding her mug in both hands, and she looked as if she were about to cry again. I remembered when she'd asked me to support her father-in-law. ("Mrs. Kilbourn, I'm not very smart. Sometimes I just have to trust the smart people to tell me what to do.")

Well, I was smart people. "Lori, what's all this about? Begin at the beginning and no tears. This is too important."

She took a great hiccuping gulp of air, mopped at her eyes and began.

"Well, the beginning, I guess was . . ." She hesitated. ". . . was the phone call I got the morning they found Soren passed away. But it was before he died. This person told me to call Mrs. Boychuk to make sure she was at Soren Eames's office by 7:30 a.m. It was very early but it was important. So I called Mrs. Boychuk and told her, and she asked, 'Is it about Carey? Is he all right?' and I said it was something else altogether, and she said, 'What's it about?' and I said just what my – the person told me to say, which was 'You'll just have to trust me, Eve or Mrs. Boychuk.'"

"That's what you said? 'Eve or Mrs. Boychuk'?"

"That's what the person told me to say, Mrs. Kilbourn." She looked at me confidingly. "And it worked because she said she would go, and then" – her lower lip began to quiver –

"and then after I got to work, I went over to the CAP Centre like I always do with some coffee and muffins for Soren, for his breakfast, you know, and there he was passed away and Mrs. Boychuk was all bloody and . . ." The scene was playing again in her mind, and she was beginning to hyperventilate.

"Easy, Lori, easy. Take a big breath . . . and another one . . . Better now?"

She nodded.

The vise was squeezing my chest again, but I got the words out. "You've done all the hard part, now I just need to know one other thing."

"Yes?" She was steeling herself for the next question.

My heart was pounding in my chest. "Lori, who told you to phone Eve? Who told you to get her to Soren's office that morning?"

There was silence in the sunny room. I could hear Clay Evanson in the kitchen opening drawers and talking to himself in a low baby voice.

"Lori?" I sounded strong, like the old Jo.

"Yes, Mrs. Kilbourn?"

"I have to know who called you that morning."

She looked at me craftily. "Promise you won't tell?"

"I can't promise that, Lori, you know that. This is too important for games," I said sternly.

She took a breath, licked her lips and out it came. "The person who told me to phone was my mother-in-law, Mrs. Julie Evanson." Then she sat back and looked at me expectantly.

I was stunned. "But why? Did Julie give you any explanation?"

"Just that if Mrs. Boychuk was in Soren's office that morning, he could help her."

"Help her what, Lori?"

"I didn't ask, Mrs. Kilbourn. I didn't ask because Mrs. Evanson scares me. She's never liked me because I was p.g. when Mark married me."

I must have looked puzzled.

"I was p.g. – pregnant," she whispered. "And Mrs. Evanson has, you know, held it against me, so when she asked me to do this . . ." Her face was clouding over again. "She promised me it would be okay, that Soren would help Mrs. Boychuk. But it wasn't okay and then after when I wanted to go to the police she yelled at me and said I was stupid, which I know, and that Mr. Evanson, my father-in-law, would never become leader if this came out and if he didn't it would be my fault. Mrs. Evanson may be a witch, but Mr. Evanson has always been so good to me, and I wouldn't betray him for anything. I knew it was wrong not to tell, but what could I do? And then when I saw you so sick from worrying . . . I hope it was right to tell you."

I felt so tired I didn't think I could move out of the chair. But I stood up and held my arms out to her. She came and laid her head on my shoulder. She was Mieka's size. It felt good to hold her. Her hair smelled like apples.

"You did the right thing, Lori. You didn't betray anybody. Mrs. Evanson was the one who did the betraying. I'll make it all right with Craig – I promise. Now go in there and wash your face and bundle up your little guy and take him for a walk in the leaves. It'll do you both good."

Her lovely face shone with gratitude. Someone had taken the burden away. Someone had taken over. She looked better already.

I drove to the Evanson house on Gardner Crescent. All the way to the city, my chest muscles ached and my heart banged against the hollow of my rib cage. But I wasn't sick.

The doctor had told me. It was all in my head. I pounded on the front door.

"Come on, Julie. Come on out here and deal with your mess."

She was wearing a flowered silk dress, the colour of raspberries, and her hair was a smooth platinum cap.

"I was just going out," she said, and then an honest outburst, "Joanne, you look like . . ."

"I know, I look like hell. Let me in, Julie. You're not going anywhere."

The dining-room table was covered in photographer's contact sheets. I picked one up. Some of Craig, some of both of them.

"Picking the official photo for the new leader?" I asked. "What's your stand on justice, Julie? Are you for it or against it? How about the family? How about the dim and trusting? In favour of giving them full employment doing your dirty work?"

"You'd better leave, Joanne. You're hysterical."

"No, Julie, I'm not. I'm just sick of people dying and people being hurt." A spasm of nausea hit me, and the metal taste came into my mouth, then the saliva. "What's your game, Julie? Why did you set Eve up? Why did you have your daughter-in-law, who is as innocent as she is slow, call Eve and tell her to go to Soren's office the morning he was murdered?"

Julie had gone pale under her makeup. Her hands were clenched into fists.

"That's family business, Joanne."

"That's where you're wrong. It's police business, and I'm going to drive down there now and tell them to pile into a cop car, turn on the sirens and come and get you, Julie. They'll be so interested. Cops are funny that way. They wait and wait, and then finally they look at all the evidence" – I shook the contact sheets in her face – "and they figure, well, what's her connection here? How is the wife of this guy who wants to be premier involved? What the hell is going on? That's what they do, Julie. Take my word for it."

She grabbed me by the wrists and brought her face close to mine. Her breath smelled of coffee.

"Send the police here," she said, "and I'll tell them your beloved Andy Boychuk was a fag."

For a moment, my eyes lost their focus. Julie's face blurred; I blinked, and she became clear again.

"What did you say?" My voice sounded small and frightened.

She pushed her advantage. "You heard me, I said Andy was a faggot. You know, Joanne" – She moved her face so close to mine our noses almost touched – "a pansy, a fruit, a fairy, a ho-mo-sex-u-al." She enunciated each syllable of the word.

"I'll tell them myself," I said and I shook my wrists loose from her grasp and headed for the door. "After I tell them about how you set up Eve Boychuk."

It worked. I'd called her bluff, and she gave in.

"Jo, wait. Hear my side."

I turned the doorknob.

"Not for me, but for Craig. I know you still like him."

I walked into the living room and sank into a chair by the window. Across the road the trees on the creek bank were bronze and gold in the October light. It seemed impossible that there could be such beauty out there, while in here . . .

"All right, Julie, let's hear your side."

Julie's story was weird enough to be credible and unsettling. Early on the morning that Soren Eames's body was discovered, the phone had rung. She'd answered it "in this room here," she said, gesturing to the living room. It was a man's voice on the other end. He identified himself as a supporter of Craig Evanson, and he said he'd come upon some information that could clinch the nomination for Craig. The man was, Julie told me, very knowledgeable about their campaign. His estimate of the number of delegates supporting Craig was just about the same as Julie's. What the man knew and what Julie knew was that Craig didn't have enough votes for a first-ballot win, and it didn't seem likely that he'd be the one who would pick up votes on the next ballots. "You and I know," the man had said, "that it isn't going to work for him unless you can get some of the Boychuk loyalists to support him." Julie looked at me. "He mentioned your name, Joanne, and Dave Micklejohn's, and he said to me, 'You know who the others are' and of course, I did. He said the only way 'to pry you people loose' – that was the phrase he used – was to get someone you trusted to ask you to support Craig, and the person he named was Eve. He said that if I could get Eve into Soren Eames's office within the hour, Eames would give Eve some information that would guarantee she'd do what she was told about the election."

"What did you say?" I asked.

"It was all so bizarre, and it was early, before seven, I think, but I remember I said, 'What's the information?' He didn't say anything for a while, and then he kind of laughed and said, 'Well, there's no reason why you shouldn't know. Soren Eames has information that will prove that Andy Boychuk was involved in a sordid homosexual liaison at the time of his death. Eames has agreed to keep quiet if Eve can get the people around her to support Craig Evanson.'"

"Did that make sense to you, Julie?"

"I told you, it was early in the morning, Jo, and face it, he was saying what I wanted to hear. After I'd called Lori, I thought about it. And it did make sense. Eames could have wanted to help Craig out of loyalty to Mark and Lori. And, you know, some of those fundamentalist churches really hate homosexuals. If Soren had come upon that kind of information, he might have felt he had to use it.

"Anyway, I called Lori. Joanne, you'll have to believe me. I didn't mean to hurt Eve. But . . ." And then the old Julie was back, defiant and shrill. "It's not my fault Eve went crazy and killed him." She looked at me. "Are you going to the police?"

"Not this minute, but I suggest you do." I stood and started for the door. "Julie, do you remember anything at all about the man on the phone? Even a general impression?"

She looked thoughtful. "I don't know. He was agitated, and that 'sordid homosexual liaison' thing seemed overdone."

"Yes," I agreed, "it sounds that way to me, too." My hand was on the doorknob again. "Well, Julie, I'll be seeing you."

"Joanne?" Her voice was small and tentative.

I turned wearily, prepared for a last-ditch appeal that would keep me from exposing her to the police.

"Julie, what is it?"

She looked around then lowered her voice. "It's someone we know, Joanne."

"Who?"

"The man on the phone. He'd muffled his voice, but I still knew it. And he knew so much about our campaign and so much about all of us – about Andy's people. It's someone close to us, Jo. It has to be someone we know."

CHAPTER

18

Where to begin? I sat in the granny flat and thought about what I had to go on. The muffled voice on Julie's telephone; Howard Dowhanuik's voice, exasperated and embarrassed: "For God's sake, Jo, it's been almost twenty years. Andy said it was his one and only." I stared at the vertical files and finally I picked up four and put them on my desk. I chose 1961, 1962, 1963 and 1964 – Andy's high-school years, the years of sexual awakening. It seemed as good a place as any to start.

There wasn't much in the files. Some photos of Andy receiving awards from the Knights of Columbus for essays on chastity and obedience. Roma had given me those. Four years of *Intra Muros*, the yearbook of E.T. Russell High School in Saskatoon. Four years of photos of Andy with his class, with the debating team, with the track team. Four years of end-of-the-year messages. "I'll never forget you," "To a great guy," from girls named Barbara Ann and Gloria and Sharon, and joking insults from people who signed off, "Just kidding, your great!!!" Remembering my own yearbook, I shook my head, smiled and started to shut the cover

of *Intra Muros*. In the corner, tiny and feathery, was some
writing that had been obscured by my thumb. I bent to look
at it more closely. "Forever, E." I looked again at the cover:
1964, grade twelve, graduation year. I looked at the signatures in the other years of *Intra Muros*. Nothing. I went back
to 1964. There were forty-five people in the graduating class.
Counting surnames and given names, in Andy's class alone
there were twenty-three people with the initial E. Those had
been big years for Elizabeths and Edwards.

There was a group photo of the class. Andy's teacher
looked like an original – hair frizzed out to shoulder length,
hoop earrings, gypsy scarf, dirndl skirt – but even in the
halftones of an old school photo she had an air of great vital-
ity. I looked at the bottom of the page. Of course, Hilda
McCourt. The one with the dazzling red hair and the sharp
tongue who'd been onstage the day Andy was murdered and
who'd been so angry with me when I underestimated her
memory at the lunch after the funeral.

She lived, I knew, in Saskatoon. Andy used to take her out
for dinner every so often when he was up there. I thought of
Saskatoon, and I remembered hugging Lori that morning and
the smell of apples in her hair. Then I thought how good it
would be to hold my own daughter, and I picked up the
phone and dialled information. Five minutes later, I had
arranged to meet Hilda McCourt the next day before noon.

When Rick phoned that night, we talked for close to an
hour. Like me, he sensed that the pieces were there if only
we could see the pattern. I didn't mention my illness. There
was no point because it wasn't there. It wasn't real. All in
my head.

The next morning, when I went to get dressed, the first two
skirts I tried on hung on me. When the waistband of the
third skirt gaped, too, I went into Mieka's room, found a

wide belt and belted the skirt tight. Sort of like Scotch-taping a drooping hem, but I was starting to simplify.

It was a mild day, but I was freezing. I put on a heavy sweater and then, when that wasn't enough, I went to the basement and dug out my winter coat. The phone rang as I was about to go out the door. It was Dr. Philip Lee's office, and they'd had a cancellation for the next day, late afternoon. Was I interested? If I left Saskatoon after lunch I'd make it easily. As soon as I hung up, I was hit with a knot of abdominal cramps. Just my body's way of saying I had made a good decision, I thought, as I waited till the cramping stopped. I made a few arrangements with the boys, picked up my car keys, slung my purse over my shoulder and went out the door. It wasn't quite 8:30 a.m. With luck, I'd have had my talk with Hilda McCourt and be at Mieka's by noon.

About an hour out of the city, the cramping hit again, and the diarrhea. I was lucky. There was a gas station with a garage – a real garage, the kind where men in coveralls come to watch other men in coveralls peer into the bowels of vehicles. There was a smell of oil and gasoline and something else – an artificial pine smell that must have come from the display of cardboard deodorant pine trees by the cash register.

When I came from the bathroom, the man in the station looked up at me curiously.

"You all right, lady?"

"Fine thanks . . . Just the aftermath of the flu."

"It's going around," he said sagely, and then, surprisingly, "There's coffee, but let me get you some tea. I had that flu and it's a bitch. The tea will settle you, so you can get to . . . I suppose you're going to Saskatoon."

I nodded.

"Two more hours. If you feel as crappy as I did, you'll need something. Put lotsa sugar in it for energy."

The tea got me to Davidson, a little more than halfway. Again, there was the cramping, like a fist tightening in my lower stomach, then I broke out in a cold sweat. I pulled into the parking lot behind a hotel and shook. Then I went into the hotel coffee shop, which was almost empty at this time of morning and still smelled of stale beer from the pub across the hall.

There were cardboard cutouts of pumpkins and skeletons on the mirror behind the counter, and a young albino girl with her back to me was taping orange and black crepe paper around the mirror's edge. On the radio, a woman who said she was a witch was taking calls on a phone-in show. The girl never said a word. She blinked at me incuriously through her white lashes while I gave her my order, set the soup down carefully in front of me, brought a glass of water and a cellophane-wrapped package of crackers and went back to taping her crepe paper. On the radio, the witch was explaining the witch's alphabet.

The soup and the fresh air seemed to do the trick. By the time I got to Hilda McCourt's neat little house on Avenue B, I felt better. When I rang the doorbell, Hilda came around the side of the house from the backyard. The October sunlight was kind to her. She looked her age – eighty, give or take a year – but she looked great. She was wearing lime-green coveralls and a lime-green and cerise cotton shirt. Both had labels from a designer who had dominated the youth market for the past couple of years. She had covered her brilliantly dyed red hair with a scarf, and a slash of lipstick – cerise to match her blouse – was feathered across her lips. Her smile when she greeted me was as open and vital as the smile on her face when she posed with Class 12-A, E.T. Russell H.S. (1964).

"Come around back with me. I'm just about through turning over my garden for the winter. Carpe diem. We may not get many more days like this. I'm going overseas for a short holiday next week, and I want to leave everything shipshape."

"It looks shipshape to me already," I said when we came into the backyard. Orange plastic garbage bags full of leaves were neatly lined up against the garage, shrubs were tied with sacking, rosebushes were covered in dirt, and the flower beds had all been turned over.

"Just this last bit of the vegetable garden to go," she said, "and then we can go in and have a glass of sherry." She picked up her shovel. "Why don't you sit down on one of those lawn chairs and get some sun? You look a little green. What is it, that god-awful flu that's going the rounds?"

"Something like that."

Hilda McCourt wasn't a woman who felt she had to amuse a guest. As soon as she saw I was settled, she went back to her digging. She worked with energy and efficiency, and as I watched her, I had a memory of how good it had felt when my body had worked that way, strong and obedient. I wondered if it ever would again, and I shuddered in the warm sunlight.

"That's it," she said finally. "I leave that for the devil," she said, pointing to an unbroken piece about three feet square at the corner of her vegetable garden. "Have you heard of the devil's half-acre? There are a hundred names for it in folklore – all wonderful, all nonsense, of course, but a nice idea still. A little gesture of conciliation to the dark powers. I even have an incantation I use when I sow my seeds: This is for me. This is for my neighbour. This is for the devil. It's American, but before that from Buckinghamshire and before that – who knows? Probably our ancestors were saying it when they were still painting themselves blue. Anyway, it's good to feel connected with what went before." She took off her gardening gloves, undid the scarf and shook her head.

Her hair, improbably orange, fuzzed out around her head. It seemed to have an energy of its own. "Come on." She reached out a hand to help me up. "By the looks of you, you could use a real drink. I have a bottle of Glenlivet an old student brought me at Thanksgiving. The sun must be over the yardarm somewhere."

She sat me down in a little glassed-in porch that over-looked her garden. "Why don't you put your feet up – lie down on that lounge there while I get our drinks."

It was a fine and individual room. Along one wall there was a trestle table filled with blooming plants: hydrangea, azalea and hibiscus. Across from it was an old horsehair chaise longue covered in a bright afghan. At the foot was a television set; at the head, a table with a good reading lamp and a pile of best sellers. The walls were covered with pic-tures of pilots and aviators, dashing young men in bomber jackets or RCAF uniforms or – in the most recent ones – the red coveralls and white silk scarfs of the Snowbirds.

"Heroes," said Hilda McCourt as she came into the room. She was carrying a tray with a bottle of Glenlivet, an ice bucket, glasses and a round of Gouda cheese. With one hand, she pulled out a little nesting table from the corner, and she set the tray on it. "Now, here's our lunch. I don't share the old country passion for drinking whisky neat, but there's no need to dilute good Scotch with water."

She poured us each a stiff drink over ice, then she reached into the back pocket of her overalls, pulled out a Swiss army knife and cut us each a wedge of Gouda. We lifted our glasses.

"To heroes," she said.

"To heroes," I agreed. The Scotch was smooth and warming. I felt the bands that had been enclosing my chest relax a little.

Hilda leaned across the table to look at me. "You look better," she said. "Now, what's all this about?"

"Andy Boychuk," I said.

"Andy was a hero of mine," she said simply.

"Me, too," I said, and I was surprised to feel my eyes fill with tears. I took another sip of Scotch. "Miss McCourt, this isn't going to be easy for either of us, but I have to ask some questions, and I think it's best if I come right out with them."

"That's always the best plan of attack." She took a thin slice of Gouda and peeled the red wax from it. Her army knife gleamed sharp and lethal in the sunlight.

"When Andy was in high school, was there ever any unpleasantness?"

Her clever old eyes looked up at me, alert to a threat to her hero.

I continued. "Anything involving another boy? I don't mean bullying."

"You mean, of course, something sexual," she said, and then, hostile, defending her hero: "What? Has some tabloid got hold of something?"

"It's more serious than that."

She sat back, plunged the knife into the wedge of Gouda and cut again. "Yes, I guess I knew it must be serious for you to come here." She finished her drink and poured another. "To answer the question you pose, Mrs. Kilbourn, yes, there was some unpleasantness, but it was an isolated incident. Over the years, I have decided to disregard it. Teachers see a lot, and that kind of thing happens more than you can know.

"Generally, it doesn't amount to much at that age. The hormones are racing, you know. Sometimes they just boil over. I never worried about Andy. He was always so masculine." She turned and looked out the window, and I knew there was more.

"But you did worry about the other one," I said, "the partner."

"Yes, I did worry about the other one. He was . . ." She turned her hands palms up. "He was different, tall but very delicate and slender, a poetic boy. Now what was his name? It was something unfortunate. A name to plague a boy, but I can't call it to mind now. It'll come to me. Is it important?"

"I think it may be a matter of life and death," I said. "But it'll be in the yearbook."

"I don't think so. He came right at the end of the year." She shook her head with frustration. "I can't remember the boy's name, but I can close my eyes and remember that desk in home room – right in front of me, empty all year, of course, until this poor, sad boy was transferred to Russell. I was furious, too, that that kind of rumour had to attach itself to Andy so close to the end of high school. A blameless record – absolutely blameless."

She looked at my glass. "Damn, you're empty. I'm not much of a hostess, am I? But I can do this for you." She splashed the Glenlivet into my glass. "And one other useful thing: I can go to the board office. They keep records for years. I've looked up students before, for reunions and some-times just out of idle curiosity. Nothing simpler. Are you planning to drive back to Regina today?"

"No, I'm staying with my daughter tonight. She's going to school here." A spasm hit me in the stomach, and the metal taste came in my mouth.

"I think that's a wise decision, Mrs. Kilbourn. You're looking tired. Does your daughter live far from here? You don't look well at all."

"Not far," I said, standing up. "If I could just use your bathroom."

When I came back, Hilda McCourt was standing by the front door wearing her jacket.

"I'll drive you," she said, holding my coat for me.

"I'll make it," I said sliding my arms into my coat, trying to look capable. "It's not far at all."

"That's a blessing," she said. "Now what's your daughter's number? I'll call you when I get back from the board office. Take care of yourself, Mrs. Kilbourn."

I felt strange when I pulled up in front of Mieka's house on Ninth Street, weak and heavy-limbed. I reached into my purse and pulled out my makeup bag. I rubbed blush across my cheekbones and drew a fresh lipstick mouth over my own. "Putting on my face," as the old ladies always say. I didn't look in the mirror – I was feeling rotten enough already.

I had hoped my visit would be a surprise, and it was. From the length of time it took Mieka and Greg to answer the door and from the way they looked when they finally did, it was apparent that they had been making love.

Mieka opened the door, blinking in the sunlight, looking rosy and happy and vague. Greg was behind her, his arms wrapped protectively around her. She tried to smile.

"Oh, Mummy. I wish you'd called ahead."

I walked past them into the hall. I was trembling. That was a new symptom. "I thought you'd be baking bread or something," I said and kept walking toward the kitchen. There'd be a chair in the kitchen.

"I baked bread this morning," she said, following me. Amazingly, she had – half a dozen loaves of crusty dark bread were sitting on racks.

"Oh, Mieka," I said and slumped into a kitchen chair. The nausea hit like a breaker, and then another spasm, wave after wave. I was crouched in my chair like an animal. My mouth filled with the taste of nails and then saliva. Finally, unforgivably, in the middle of that kitchen that smelled warmly of yeast and fresh baked bread, I vomited.

They were both there at once. She, wrapping her arms around me as the spasms hit and I retched and retched; he, wrapping his arms around her.

"I'm all right, Mieka," I said at last, sitting up.

"I know, Mum, I know," my daughter said in a voice weary, resigned, determined, a voice I remembered from the time after her father died, and I had cracked into a thousand pieces.

"Damn it, Mieka, don't patronize me." I moved to get loose from her grasp. And there in the mirror above the sink I saw it, a tableau. Call it Paradise Lost or Mother Comes to Call: a young dark-haired man, his face still tanned from summer; a girl with ashy blond hair and an oversized university sweatshirt. Handsome people, but looking frightened of the grotesque burden in their arms: a woman with dark ash-blond hair and wild eyes and hectic makeup, circles of colour on her white cheeks and a slash of lipstick smeared across her mouth. Old womanish, clownish – me. The vise tightened around my chest and then, merciful and tender, the blackness came.

I awoke in an unfamiliar room, in a strange bed that still, in its soft flannelette sheets, held the smell of sex. Of course, they wouldn't have had time to change the sheets. And outside the room, voices young and deep and urgent.

"Mieka, I know you love her. I'm going to love her, too, but you could smell the Scotch a mile away. Babe, if that's the problem, we need to help her. I'm not saying we don't. I'm saying face it."

And then my daughter's voice, strong, defending me. "She's not a drunk, Greg. Even at the worst, she didn't go that route. She's been through so much and she wasn't over that horror show about Daddy. Nobody could come through what's happened to her without some sort of reaction. They would have had to peel me off the walls of my rubber room. But she's not a drunk. It has to be something else."

Good old Mieka, defender of embarrassing mothers. I curled up and went to sleep and dreamed strange dreams: Rick Spenser in Mieka's kitchen making bread, pulling points of dough from a long, thin baguette. Soren Eames at the kitchen table with Andy, laughing and saying to Rick, "Now don't forget a seed for you and a seed for me and one for the master," and then the bell on the stove ringing and ringing and then floating up through consciousness to the knowledge that the phone was ringing. I picked it up.

"Joanne Kilbourn speaking."

On the other end, husky-voiced and excited, was Hilda McCourt. "Well, Mrs. Kilbourn, may I call you Joanne? I feel we're into an adventure together, so let's use first names."

"Fine, Hilda. What did you find out?" My voice sounded a hundred years old.

"Nothing, absolutely nothing. Someone sliced through the microfiche."

I felt a prickle of excitement. "Someone did what?"

"Sliced through the microfiche. The board transferred all their school records to microfiche a couple of years ago. Joanne, do you know what microfiche are?"

"Those films that you scoot through a projector and then you see your document on a screen?"

She laughed. "Well, that'll do. Apparently someone scooted the grade twelve records of E.T. Russell High School through the blade of a knife."

"When?"

"The people at the board don't know. Employees are in and out of there all the time. You're supposed to sign in and out, but they're quite lax. These aren't precious documents or even particularly confidential ones. Twenty-five-year-old school records have pretty well done whatever damage they're going to do."

"I suppose you're right," I said. I felt deflated, and I guess I sounded weary.

"Are you all right?" The surprisingly young voice was alert, concerned.

"Well, I'm going to disembowel the next person who asks me that, but, yeah, I think I'm okay, just disappointed. I think that boy's name could help us."

The us I meant was Rick Spenser and me, but Hilda McCourt, my co-adventurer, picked up the reference happily.

"I agree, Joanne, I believe it can help us, but don't despair. I have an excellent memory, and I expect that name will surface. Now give me your Regina number so I can call you as soon as it does."

I gave her the number.

"We'll get to the bottom of this," she said, "never fear, and when we do I still have almost half that bottle of Glenlivet left for our celebration."

I shuddered. "Almost half!" I thanked her, lay back in bed and drifted off to sleep.

When I woke it was dark. I looked at my watch: five o'clock. I listened for street sounds. Almost none; it must, I reasoned, be morning – 5:00 a.m. in the morning, as Lori Evanson would say. I felt weak but purged, and better. My overnight bag was at the foot of the bed. I pulled out clean clothes, tiptoed down the hall and showered and changed. I wrote Mieka and Greg a note, thanking them, explaining I was much better, apologizing without sounding pitiful, and crept downstairs. They were asleep on the living-room floor with their arms curled around one another: the title of a novel, *The Young in One Another's Arms*.

If I could remember the title of a Canadian novel, I must be all right. I looked again into the living room at my daughter's dark blond hair fanned out against the crook of that unnervingly male arm, said a prayer, took a deep breath and walked out the door.

Except for a stop halfway home for take-out coffee and a foil-wrapped Denver, I drove straight through. I was home in time to give the boys lunch and answer Mieka's anxious phone call. Yes, I was better, yes, I had a doctor's appointment that afternoon, yes, it was a specialist, highly recommended, Morton Lee's brother, and yes, I would call as soon as I knew anything.

When I hung up, I didn't even bother going upstairs to get a blanket. I grabbed my coat and, like a transient in a bus station, I covered myself with it and fell asleep where I was.

CHAPTER

19

The gastroenterologist's office was the top floor of a medical building so old it had an elevator operator. The waiting room was oddly comforting although it took me a while to understand why. There were the usual stacks of magazines with cover stories about things that had once seemed important and pages soft with use, and there was the standard office furniture, Naugahyde and steel tubing. But there wasn't that heart-stopping medical feeling, and as the receptionist, a young Chinese woman, exotic as a forties' movie villain, raised a perfectly manicured hand and flicked a lighter into flame, I recognized why. The whole place smelled of cigarette smoke. No signs from the cancer society. No cute cartoons. There were ashtrays, and people were using them. I closed my eyes and that smell, acrid and familiar, mixed with the alien smell of things plunged into sterile baths and ripped from sterile wrappings, carried me back to doctors' waiting rooms when I was young, and to doctors who measured and weighed and made jokes about school and husbands and the future.

When I stood to follow the receptionist into the examining room, I felt my stomach cramp, but safe in the smoky air, I said, "Nothing bad can happen here."

The beautiful Chinese woman raised a perfectly waxed eyebrow and, in the flat accents of small-town Saskatchewan, said, "Well, I wouldn't go that far." Then she turned and glided out of the room on her stiletto heels.

The examining room had a spectacular view of the city, and as I stood and watched the late afternoon traffic, I heard in the next room a man's voice talking on the telephone about some property he had bought. I heard the name "Little Bear Lake" and then, after a while, the word "developer." The conversation was heated. Someone hadn't checked something and now the building couldn't start "till spring if ever," I heard the voice say. Then something muffled and finally, very distinct and loud, "You can tell those rubes I'll drag them into the tall grass on this one." A phone slammed down, then the door to the examining room opened and Dr. Philip Lee walked in.

Physically he was as unlike his brother, Mort, as it was possible to be. Mort was a teddy bear of a man – "A Panda bear," Ali said once, "after all, the man was born in Hong Kong and half the family's still there." But there was nothing cuddly about Dr. Philip Lee. He was tall, balding and scholarly looking. He bowed slightly toward me.

"I apologize, Mrs. Kilbourn, for the delay – a consultation."

"Well," I said, sitting on the examining table, "if the developers fall through, you can always build yourself a cottage. Little Bear Lake is beautiful, especially in the spring."

He looked at me sharply and nodded. "Mrs. Kilbourn, in your estimation, what seems to be the trouble?"

I went through the whole dismal history, starting with the first attack in the middle of the night after the boys and I ordered pizza and ending with my performance at Mieka's the day before. I finished by saying, "I have no opinion – I'm the patient. In the other doctor's opinion, the problem is stress. It's all in my head."

Dr. Philip Lee gave me a wintery smile. "That is, of course, one possibility, but let's eliminate the more interesting possibilities of the body first."

The physical examination he gave me was gruelling, "from mouth to anus" as he told me gravely when he began. After it was over, I dressed and the receptionist led me into the doctor's office.

"I see nothing," he said, lighting a Marlboro and inhaling deeply. "We must, of course, await the test results, but everything appears to be entirely normal."

"So you agree that there's nothing wrong with me."

"At this point, I would agree with my colleague that there appears to be no physical cause for your symptoms."

"It's all in my head, then."

"That possibility cannot be ruled out," he said judiciously. "I'm going to write you a prescription for a little nostrum of my own. You are extremely tense and you appear not to be eating well."

"What's in this little cure of yours?"

"Something to relax you and some vitamins. Since you are not a medical person, the names would mean nothing to you."

I shredded Dr. Philip Lee's prescription into the old brass ashtray in the lobby of the medical building. On the way home I stopped at a strip mall and bought a quart of milk, some dark rum and a dozen eggs. "Just what the doctor ordered," I said, lifting my glass in a kitchen filled with the good smell of rum and eggnog, "something to relax the patient."

The doctor called four days later. I was in the granny flat sorting through some of the early press clippings about Andy. He attempted to be genial, and I had a strong suspicion that

Dr. Philip Lee had talked to his brother in Winnipeg, "the one with the charm." He was certainly trying harder.

The test results were negative.

"Good," I said, "wonderful news."

Had the prescription helped?

"Absolutely," I said.

Then I was feeling better?

"Right as rain," I said, but I had to hang up because a spasm hit and I doubled over with pain.

Pain – that was one of the new constants in my life. The other one was fear. Entry after entry in my daybook began with the single word "sick," and then the symptoms: "cramps, diarrhea, metallic taste in the mouth, have to spit all the time." The last words were underscored in exasperation. And there were the symptoms that couldn't be neatly categorized: the increasingly frequent times when I had problems getting air in and out of my lungs; the sense that there was a band of steel wrapped around my chest; the strange and terrifying tricks my heart was playing, pounding when I was sitting idle at my desk in the granny flat, skipping beats when I did something as simple as walk across the room.

The pretty young woman with the curly hair who was one of the family practitioners in Ali Sutherland's old practice made an appointment for me with a cardiologist. The cardiologist taped disks to me and hooked me up to a machine.

"Good news," she said, smiling, "nothing is wrong. Perhaps a short-term use of tranquillizers?"

Craig Evanson called me one morning to ask me to go to the correctional centre and visit Eve, and I promised I would go soon. He had thrown himself into Eve's case with a passion that surprised me. The floppy man had been superseded by a tense, driven stranger. "The shrink who pops in and out of there is worried about her, Jo. He says she's shutting down. The way he explained it to me was it's like closing off rooms in a house. First you close the public rooms and then the guest rooms, until you box yourself into one little room. The problem is Eve's run out of rooms to shut down."

I knew how Eve felt. I was running out of rooms to shut down, too. Except for the boys, I stopped seeing people. November had settled in grey with misery. The easy, communal times when you stand out on the front lawn and visit with neighbours and people riding by on bikes or pushing babies in strollers were gone till spring. The focus of life had turned indoors, and indoors it was easy to say no to people. Everyone was understanding. The leadership convention was set for December fifth, so there were phone calls soliciting support and phone calls asking me to help write rules for the rules committee or to chair the balloting committee or to buy a ticket to the leader's dance. I told everyone the same thing. I'd been ill, and on doctor's orders I was resting and recuperating and getting back my strength. "And besides" I would add, clinching it, "I'm working on a biography of Andy."

For a few weeks Mieka called every day, but after I'd relayed my passing grades from Philip Lee and the cardiologist, she followed my lead and wrote off the episode in her kitchen as an understandable if unendearing reaction to stress.

I did the best I could with the boys. I sat down for breakfast with them in the morning, had lunch ready at noon, sat around for an hour or so with them at dinner time, took them to the Lakeshore Club on Saturday mornings. But children get used to most things, and the boys simply grew used to my being sick. They were kind always, but they had lives of their own: school and friends and football and hockey.

And, I had to admit, precedent was against me. They had seen this pattern after their father's death. Then as now, I was short-tempered and withdrawn. Then as now, the granny flat had become my refuge.

One windy day I drove out to see Eve. We sat in the pale sunlight of the visiting area in the hospital wing, two women who had been defeated, and played a listless game of double solitaire. The irony of our choice of game struck me on the way home, and I had to pull over because when I laughed, I started the bands tightening in my chest again.

Yes, I understood about shutting down rooms. By the second week in November, I had pretty well shut down all the rooms but one: the big room over the garage where I could close out the world, my clean, well-lighted place. Except keeping it clean had become a burden. Every so often the heating ducts would gather their strength and belch out a fresh dusting of summer pollen, and I would have to fill a bucket with hot sudsy water and scrub everything down.

One day when I was carrying the pail my legs began to twitch uncontrollably, the way an eyelid sometimes twitches spasmodically, for no reason. I had to sit down with my bucket until the twitching stopped. That night in bed the twitching started again. The next morning I added twitching to my list of symptoms.

Twitching and double vision. I had begun to have difficulty reading. The first time it happened I'd been reading some photocopies of old newspapers. The print was small and pale, so when my vision blurred, I wrote it off to eyestrain. I was still doing that, still looking for a reasonable excuse, still searching out a logical explanation for my symptoms, but the careful list of symptoms in my daybook was defining a profile that couldn't be ignored. I was either sick or crazy. I was also terrified.

I said that sickness and fear were the two constants of my life. There was a third – Rick Spenser. Every night, wherever he was, he would call, and we would talk. We had gone beyond the Andy book, he and I. In fact, he rarely mentioned the book any more. He was more interested in me and in my days. What was I doing? Who had I seen? How did I feel? I am not a vain woman but with every call it became increasingly clear that Rick Spenser was as attracted to me as powerfully as I was to him.

Sometimes late in the evening when I sat in front of the television and saw his face, round and clever and knowing, my heart would pound and, sitting in my old jogging pants and sweatshirt, I would feel like a fool: a forty-six-year-old housewife watching her heartthrob, a newsroom groupie, but ten minutes later the phone would ring and it would be him. How was I? What was I up to? Who had I been talking to? And, always, had I seen him on the news? How had he done? Had he been clear, witty, insightful?

This Rick Spenser, the vulnerable man behind the persona, touched something in me. Often when I would hang up the phone, I would feel as intimately connected to him as I would have if we'd made love. And so Rick became the third constant in my life, one of the few fixed stars that lit up the darkness of those early winter weeks. And that was the pattern until Remembrance Day.

The call came early on the morning of November eleventh. It couldn't have been much past six. It was Craig Evanson, sounding strained to the point of breaking. The correctional centre had called him a few minutes before. Somehow in the night Eve had gotten hold of a surgical knife and slashed her wrists. The morning nurse had found her. Crafty Eve had been lying with her blanket pulled up to her chin, innocent as a sleeping child. But the nurse noticed a stain in the middle of the blanket and, when she bent to look at it more closely, she saw that the stain was spreading. She pulled back the blanket, and there was Eve, covered in blood, still clutching the knife and near death. Eve was alive, and she was in the hospital wing of the correctional centre.

That whole morning had a dreamlike, surreal quality. It was still dark, and light snow was falling on the empty streets. The stores and office buildings were lit, but when we pulled onto the Ring Road, there wasn't another car in sight.

"Do you have the feeling we're the last two people left on earth?" Craig asked.

His voice came from a place I didn't ever want to go, and his words made my heart pound. There didn't seem to be much logic left in the universe. I would not have been surprised if I had turned in my seat and found that Craig had vanished, just as I would not have been surprised to go home and see a charred and smoking ruin where twenty minutes before my home and children had been. I didn't answer him. I didn't trust my voice.

The process of being admitted to the correctional centre was, by now, grimly routine. We drove up to the gate and waited as the harsh orange security lights swept the exercise yard and shone into our faces, leaching them of colour, turning them into death masks. The guard, enveloped in a yellow slicker, checked our names against a list, and somewhere somebody activated something that opened the electric gates.

Inside it was the familiar rite of passage: doors unlocking to reveal other locked doors, which opened to reveal still more locked doors. A Chinese puzzle.

The guard took us through double doors at the end of Eve's old ward. As we passed Eve's old bed, I noticed that the mattress was gone, and just the bare frame of the bed was left.

"That'll teach her," I said aloud, and Craig looked at me sharply. Eve was in a small room lit by a powerful overhead light. "Does the light have to shine right into her face that way?" I asked.

The nurse who was standing at the head of Eve's bed stopped writing on his clipboard and gave me a warm and surprisingly human smile. He was wearing a poppy, too.

"It's regulations, but they don't notice it or, if they do, they don't mind. Some of them, afterward, even convert. They remember the light of heaven shining down upon them."

Eve looked past caring. She was hooked to tubes that put things into her and took things out of her, and she was connected to machines that measured the beat of her life. Something out of a sci-fi movie – "The Mechanical Woman – only her face is human."

Human, but not Eve. Not gallant Eve who tried to transcend cruelty and betrayal and death with crystals and colour therapy and a cleansing diet. Poor, poor Eve.

Her wrists were heavily bandaged. I reached down and carefully took her hand and held it between my own, warming it. ("Think of all the hands you have known. Your father's hands . . . your mother's hands . . . Experience my hand. Grasp it tight . . . now release it. The touch is gone, but the imprint will be there forever. Forever and ever in your heart.")

After a while, I felt Craig Evanson touch my shoulder. "I think it's time to go, Joanne." Then he took my hand from Eve's, but he didn't let go.

When the guard came to lead us out of the prison, Craig Evanson and I followed him, hand in hand, like children in a fairy-tale.

CHAPTER

20

"Double solitaire," I said.

Craig turned the key in the ignition and looked at me.

"Double solitaire. The last time Eve and I were together that's what we played." My legs began to tremble. "Oh, God, Craig, when is this going to end?"

He reached over and gave me an awkward hug. "I don't know, Jo. I just don't know."

We sat for a while, isolated, thinking our own thoughts. It began to snow, and the banks of orange security lights turned the snow orange.

Finally, Craig said, "I don't know about you, but I need a drink."

I looked at the clock on the dashboard. "Craig, it's not even nine o'clock yet."

"Fine," he said absently as he backed out of the parking spot, "we'll go to the Dewdney Club. I've belonged to that place for twenty years. If they can't find me a bottle of whisky on a holiday morning, I'll break every window in the place."

I looked at him in amazement. "Whatever you say, Craig."

After the harsh realities of the correctional centre, the elegance of the Dewdney Club seemed like another dimension. There was a fire in the fireplace and in the background, discreetly, Glenn Gould played Bach. Craig led me to a table for two by the fire, took my coat, then disappeared. When he came back he was carrying a bottle of Seagram's, and a waiter was dancing around him trying to intercept him.

"Mr. Evanson, I'm certain I can make you a drink you'll find quite palatable."

"I find this palatable, Tony," said Craig, brandishing the bottle.

The breakfast on the sideboard was the kind you see only in magazines and men's clubs: grapefruit halves sectioned and dusted with brown sugar; silver chafing dishes of sausage and bacon and kippers; hash browns and toast and oatmeal kept warm in warming trays; eggs scrambled fresh in a copper pan.

"Do you want food, Jo?" Craig asked.

"Maybe some coffee to put the rye in."

Craig laughed, but there was no fun in the laughter.

"A lady doesn't drink liquor before noon. That's what" – a flash of pain crossed his face – "that's what the lady in my life always says."

I thought of Julie, guilty of God knows what, but not a lady to drink before noon. I sipped my coffee. The rye was smooth, and it felt good to be by the fire, but I couldn't get warm.

Across from me, Craig had filled his water glass with whisky. He raised it. "To you, Jo. A good person."

I lifted my cup, to return the toast.

"No, don't," he said, holding up his hand to stop my toast. "At the moment, I would welcome a lightning bolt to blast me and mine out of existence."

When I spoke, my voice sounded unused and rusty. "You didn't make the phone call that morning, Craig."

"I might as well have. She did it for me." He drained the glass. His voice broke. "Sweet Christ, she did it for me."

The ambiguity hung in the air. She did what for him? The phone call? Or something unspeakably worse? I felt a spasm in my bowels.

"Craig, I'm sick. I need to go home."

He didn't seem to hear me. "I found out by accident, you know. I found out this morning. When the correctional centre phoned the house, it was Lori who answered. Julie's gone to her mother's for the long weekend – said she was exhausted from everything she was doing for me." He laughed his new hollow laugh. "Everything – that covers a multitude of sins, doesn't it?" He looked at the bottle speculatively, but he didn't touch it.

"Anyway, I thought with Julie away it was a good time for Mark and his family to come home. Lori answered the phone. I was still sleeping. The clerk at the correctional centre didn't ask if the Mrs. Evanson he was talking to was my wife. Lori was hysterical when she heard about Eve. Jo, you know how sweet she is, but she's a very limited girl, and she has that fundamentalist guilt to deal with. She's taking all this on her shoulders. She told me the sequence of events before Soren Eames's body was discovered – including" – he looked at his knees – "including that abysmal phone call from Julie about her anonymous caller. If," he said softly, "there was an anonymous caller."

I felt a cold sweat breaking out on my skin, and my heart began to race. "Craig, could I go home now – please?"

"Right, Jo, of course." He went to the cloakroom and came back with my coat.

We drove up Albert Street in silence. As we came to the bridge across the creek, the air was filled with the sound of gunfire. Terrible, pounding shots that made my head hurt and the marrow in my bones ache. One upon another they came – shots fired across the creek from cannons pulled into position in front of the legislature, shots to mark the eleventh hour of the eleventh day of the eleventh month. Remembrance Day, the day they turned the swords into ploughshares.

Craig walked me to the door of my house. I didn't ask him in. As I started to go, he put his hand on my arm and turned me so he could see my face.

"Joanne, are you okay?"

I looked at him. The tall, floppy man shivering in the thin November snow, his future shadowed, the delicate fabric of his marriage ripped apart, his wife guilty of unknown cruelties and crimes in the name of love.

"Nope. I'm not okay, Craig, and you're not okay. And Eve's not okay, and Julie's not okay. Okay is a concept gone from the universe." I felt hysteria rising in my throat. "I'm sorry, Craig."

As soon as I closed the front door I began to shudder, and my mouth filled with saliva.

In the hall mirror I saw my face, yellow and covered with a sheen of sweat. I could feel my heart beating in my chest. It was the worst attack yet. I bent double and closed my eyes. Worried, the dogs began to nuzzle me and lick my face. I pushed them away. Upstairs, the boys were yelling. I didn't even take my coat off. I walked out the back door and went across the yard to the granny flat.

I had to hold onto the rail to pull myself up the stairs. When I opened the door, the phone was ringing. It was Rick. A report about Eve's suicide attempt had come to the newsroom. When I started to tell him about what had happened that morning, my voice was jagged, shrill.

"Rick, we've got to do something. There are things you don't know. Someone's doing this to her. She's innocent. I know it." Then I broke down completely. I couldn't go on.

Rick's voice was calm, almost professionally reassuring. He sounded like a social worker on the business end of a suicide hot line. "Joanne, where are you now?"

"The granny flat. I couldn't face the boys. I'd rather they think I don't care about them than let them see me like this again."

"Stay where you are. Just curl up on that absurd hide-a-bed thing you stuck me on and spend a weekend in bed, away from the noise of the house and the boys."

"But Rick, we have to save Eve. She's innocent. Someone is doing this to her. Someone has driven her to this."

When he answered me there was a new tone in his voice, something unpleasant and patronizing. "Joanne, listen carefully. There is no 'someone.' Eve drove herself to suicide just as she drove herself to murder. There's a pattern there, a history. You know that yourself. The police have the right person. Now just rest."

"You think I'm crazy." My voice was shrewish, accusing.

He sounded exasperated. "I think you've been through a great deal."

"And cracked under the strain. I have a history, too, don't forget. Well, I'm not crazy. Someone is out to get Eve. I know it."

"No one said you had cracked. The consensus of the doctors seems to be that you're exhausted. Nobody could fault you for that."

"I don't need you telling me I'm crazy. Now listen, Rick." I heard my voice, triumphant, crazy. "I'm pulling the jack for this phone right out of the wall. Now try to get to me." Then I was alone in the empty room, a room so quiet I could hear my heartbeat.

I don't know how long I sat there, shaking and exhausted. A queer phrase kept floating through my mind. "You've got to get your bearings." But bearings had to do with navigation when you were lost, and I wasn't lost. I was safe in my granny flat. "A room of one's own," Virginia Woolf had said. Well, this room was my own. Joanne Kilbourn's room. The walls were lined with pictures of my dead husband and the floor was littered with cartons and files that contained the record in words and pictures of the life of my dead friend, Andy Boychuk. My daughter had crocheted the bright afghan on the bed the summer she'd broken her leg. On the desk, dusty now but still heartbreakingly beautiful, was the crystal pitcher Rick had given me. It was filled with branches of Russian olive I'd cut by the creek. The olive berries were pale in the grey half light of November.

In front of the window, as familiar to me as the lines of my own face, was my desk. On it, next to a picture of Mieka and Peter and Angus, soaked to the skin, laughing, giving the dogs a bath, was that other emblem of motherly pride, the ceramic cabbage I had bought for Andy, which Andy had given to Soren and Soren had given to me – a sequence out of a child's book. The leaves curl back, to reveal the tiny figure inside, her face hard with triumph as she offers up her naked son to the world – Ukrainian genesis.

At the edge of the desk was the phone; its cord, unplugged from the jack, hung lame and useless. Impotent. No one could get at me through that.

My place, a room where I could get my bearings. A room where I could be safe. And then, across the window, the quick shadow of a man and the door opened and the room was filled with fresh, cold air and the dark outline of my son's body.

His voice was deep, a man's voice, but he sounded frightened. "Mum, are you all right? You looked like you had fallen asleep sitting up. Were you sleeping? You look kind of weird."

"I'm fine, Peter, just . . . I don't know. Just working."

He looked at my empty desk and then, quickly, into my face.

"Mum, Mieka just called. She wondered how you'd feel about Angus and me going up there for the weekend. I could have a look at the campus and maybe do a bit of Christmas shopping."

The band was tightening around my chest, and my mouth filled with the taste of metal. The bottom of my feet pricked oddly as if something inside my legs were short-circuiting.

"Mum?" Peter's face had the familiar look of worry.

"Sorry, Pete. It sounds great. How are you going to get there?"

He looked at his feet. "Mieka suggested we come up on the 5:30 bus."

My voice was terrible. Falsely hearty. Mum the pal. "It sounds great, Pete. By all means, you guys take the 5:30."

"You're sure, Mum?"

"I'm sure, Peter . . . But one problem, money. I haven't got any, and today's a holiday."

"Barbara, next door, says she'll lend us some till Monday."

"You went to Barbara before you came to me?"

"Mum, I knew you didn't have any money. You didn't have any last night to pay for the paper. Remember, we talked about it?" His voice trailed away. "I didn't want to make a problem for you."

"No problem, Peter." That terrible voice again. I turned from him and picked up a folder. "You guys come over when you're ready, and I'll drive you to the bus station. Pete, could you make a sandwich or something for both of you? I'm a little shaky today."

The adult look again – worried, tentative. "Mum, we don't have to go – really."

I tried to smile. "Peter, I want you to go – really. Now get out of here so I can get some work done."

I watched him walk across the yard toward the house. The footprints he left in the snow seemed much too big.

I parked the car opposite the bus station and sat there, shaking with cold and something else, until the bus pulled out. As it disappeared up Broad Street, a swirl of snow curled behind it and a picture came into my mind, clear in every detail, of a blinding snowstorm and the bus sliding off the road and bursting into flames. "They'll be killed, and I'll be alone forever," I said to the empty car. It was five minutes before I trusted my hand to put the key in the ignition and five more before I dared to turn it.

The house was cold and dark when I got home. I made myself a hot lemon rum and drank it at the kitchen table, looking into the evening. When it was finished, I made another one, called the dogs and walked across the backyard to the granny flat. I plugged in the phone so I could talk to the boys if they called me from Mieka's house, covered myself with the afghan and fell into a fitful sleep.

I dreamed crazy things. I was looking for my sons on the bus, and it was filled with people I knew. Andy was there, pinning bright poppies to Eve's bandaged wrists. "This is for me. This is for you, and this," he said, driving a third poppy into her vein, "is for the devil." And then his face became Rick Spenser's face, leaning confidentially toward Eve, whose poppies were suddenly pulsing with bright blood. "There's a pattern here, Eve." And then I was Eve. I was the one with the bandaged wrists and the poppies blooming blood.

And then the snow that had swirled around me, blinding me, suddenly cleared, and I could see the front of the bus. Terry Shaw was there with my sons, who were handcuffed together, and the prison security system was ringing and ringing, and when I finally came awake, the telephone was ringing, shrill and insistent.

A woman's voice – reassuring, familiar. "Oh, good – there you are. Well, the boys are safe. I haven't killed them yet."

"Who is this?"

"Mummy, it's Mieka. Did I wake you up? You sound like you're on the planet Org. Did you hear me? I said the boys are here, safe and sound. Angus is in the shower and Peter's building a fire. Greg's making popcorn. It's a regular Disney movie here – a festival of wholesome family fun."

My voice was tight and falsely bright. "Great, good. Have fun." And then, "Thank you, Mieka. I love you. I have to go now." I hung up quickly because I could feel the tears coming. She didn't need them. I reached down and unplugged the phone. Then I changed my mind. Peter was building a fire, Mieka said. The house was old. There could be a crack in the firewall and they could all burn to death, and I wouldn't know. No, I'd have to take my chances on that phone. I plugged it in. The bottoms of my feet began to do their odd new trick – electric pins and needles.

"The world's a rational place, Joanne." That's what Andy had said that September night, nine months after Ian died. "The world's a rational place," I said to the darkness outside. The band around my chest tightened. The darkness outside knew better, and I knew better, too. "Andy, my friend, you were wrong." I poured brandy into a snifter. "The world is not a rational place."

I watched my reflection in the window, lifting the glass, drinking, and I wondered if there'd been enough time for him to find that out before he died.

CHAPTER

21

Sitting in the granny flat, looking into the November night, I knew all my protections were gone. Since we had come up here, my dogs and me, the snow had stopped falling. My backyard was a smooth expanse of white, shining in the light from the house.

Crisp and even, but not deep. I knew how thin that layer of snow was. If you stepped on it, your foot would break through to the leaves, under there, decaying, wet and black, on the cold ground. You weren't safe on that snow.

But you were never safe. Across the yard my house, a place where rational people had once planned their lives, stood in darkness. A spasm hit my bowels, then another. I doubled over, hugged my knees and rocked back and forth, back and forth, making a sound that was sometimes keening and sometimes a growl. Back and forth, back and forth until, sometime toward morning, the sky grew lighter and I slept.

I woke up in the chair, cold and disoriented. The room was full of light. My head was pounding; my mouth was dry; and the telephone was ringing.

The voice on the other end was male and pleasantly accented.

"May I speak with Ian Kilbourn, please?"

I thought, I must be careful here. I must sound sane. I mustn't give anything away.

"My husband's dead."

An intake of breath on the other end of the line and then, "I'm so very sorry, Mrs. Kilbourn. Forgive me for disturbing you at this sad time."

"No, it's . . . He's been dead a long time. I was just surprised to hear you ask for him." My heart was pounding.

"Mrs. Kilbourn, I think, then, that I should speak with you. My name is Helke de Vries, and I've just purchased Homefree Insect Pest Control Service."

"I don't need an exterminator."

"Mrs. Kilbourn, I'm not a salesman, but you're correct about not needing an exterminator, because you already have one – me. Allow me, please, to explain. I spent yesterday going over invoices – familiarizing myself with the business. I'm looking at our records for services rendered to you, and I think there must be some mistake –"

"My mistake?"

"Please, allow me to finish. It is not money. All your bills have been paid promptly – in advance, in point of fact. You have done nothing wrong, but I'm concerned that we have. Are you there, Mrs. Kilbourn?"

"Yes. Please, tell me what you want. I'm not feeling at all well today."

"It's the carpenter ants in your addition. Perhaps if you'd just allow me to read you our instructions."

I was so tired I could barely speak. "Read them, do whatever you want."

"The service is to be provided to a residence at 433 Eastlake Avenue – that is your home?"

"Yes."

"In the backyard, over the garage, there is a self-contained apartment unit, 150 square feet, accessible through a door that opens off a small balcony."

"Yes."

"The key is in a plastic bag taped to the inside of a window box to the left of the door to the unit."

"No . . ." My voice was barely a whisper.

Helke de Vries sounded uncomfortable but determined. "Spraying program for carpenter ants to begin Saturday, October 8, 9:30 a.m. and continue weekly – that is under-lined in red, Mrs. Kilbourn – until notice to discontinue. Payment, cash in advance. In the space marked client, there is the name Ian Kilbourn. Then there's something hand-written in red pen – 'Under no circumstances is anyone else in the family to know of the spraying program. The wife and kids are Save the Whales environmentalist types. Trouble.' That last word is in capital letters and underlined."

I felt like Alice after she walked through the looking glass. I picked up a pen and wrote "pest control" on the notepad in front of me.

"Mr. de Vries, could you give me the name of what you've been using?" I was trembling.

"Certainly. We have used an organophosphate spray and a methyl carbonate. In my opinion, we have used them too often, but today is Saturday, time for another treatment, so I thought I would check. Do you wish me to continue, Mrs. Kilbourn? We are paid, in cash, until after Christmas."

"No, Mr. de Vries, I do not wish you to continue."

"Then I should refund your money."

"It isn't my money. Who paid you?"

"The bill was paid in cash, and no receipt was given. The previous owners of the business assumed Mr. Kilbourn was paying."

"Keep the money." I was beginning to see light. "I need to know more. Would any of that stuff, the organophosphate or the methyl whatever it is, leave a residue?"

"The organophosphates would leave a yellow dusting."

"Would it look like pollen?"

"Yes, an excellent description – like pollen."

"Then stop it."

"Your instructions, then, Mrs. Kilbourn, are to discontinue spraying until further notice?"

"No, Mr. de Vries, my instructions are to discontinue spraying until hell freezes over."

There was a long silence, then laughter. "Another excellent description – thank you, Mrs. Kilbourn."

"Oh, thank you, Mr. de Vries. Thank you."

When I hung up, my body was trembling and sweating and pounding and cramping. I felt worse than I'd ever felt in my life, and better. Someone was trying to kill me. I should have been terrified. I should have been hiding under the bed. But all I felt was relief. The darkness wasn't coming from me; it was outside. Out there, where it could be stopped.

I opened the door of the granny flat and stepped onto the porch. It was going to be a cold day. The sky was high and grey, and the sun was pale. I took deep breaths of cold air that knifed at my chest. The dogs ran past me down the steps and chased each other around the yard in the snow.

My stomach was empty, my mouth was dry, and I was trembling with cold and excitement, but I went straight to the phone and called Ali.

"Ali, good news. I'm not crazy. Somebody's trying to kill me."

Her voice was warm and encouraging, but it was her professional voice, guarded, holding back. "Jo, why don't you turn this tape back to the beginning and let me follow along."

I told her about Helke de Vries's phone call, and his revelations. Ali listened without comment. When I finished, her
questions were professional. She asked me to repeat the
names of the insecticides the exterminators used, to tell
her the size of the granny flat in square feet and to describe
the kind of ventilation the room had.

"Jo, I'm going to have to check this out in one of my
college texts. I haven't studied pharmacology for fifteen
years. I'll call you back as soon as I can. Stay where you are.
You're not in the –"

"No, I'm out of there. I left the door open. I'm never going
in there again. Ali . . ." I began to cry. "Oh, Ali, hurry."

She called back in five minutes.

"Well, you have Mort to thank for this. He has the
Oriental passion for order: a place for everything and everything in its place. Anyway, tell me if this sounds familiar.
I'm going to read from the section on insecticides in a
book called *The Pharmacological Basis of Therapeutics*,
Goodmand and Gilman – the G-men, we used to call them
in med school. Here's the clinical profile of exposure to
organophosphates. 'Respiratory effects consist of tightness in
the chest and wheezing respiration due to the combination
of bronchi-constriction and increased bronchial secretion.
Gastrointestinal symptoms occur earliest after ingestion and
include anorexia, nausea and vomiting, abdominal cramps
and diarrhea, localized sweating, fatigability and generalized
weakness, involuntary twitchings.'"

My voice was small and frightened. "I've got all of them,
Ali. Is it too late? Can you do anything?"

"Yes, I can, or my brother-in-law can until I get there.
When was the last time you were in the granny flat?"

"Most of yesterday and all last night."

She swore softly. "Nothing for it but do the best we can. Go
take a hot, soapy shower, wash your hair and your fingernails,

and by the time you're out of there, Phil will be pounding at the front door."

"A house call?" I said.

"It'll do him good," she snapped. "Now into the shower. I'll be there tonight. Mort and I will drive down this afternoon."

I began to cry again. "Oh, Ali, you're so good."

"Jo, don't. Mort bought himself a new BMW last week, and he's been dying to get it on the highway. It's a six-hour drive. We'll be there by ten o'clock. Don't fuss. In fact, it wouldn't be the worst idea in the world if you spent a couple of days in bed. If you want to nap, do it. I still have a key from the last time I was there. Now, go get your shower, do what Phil tells you, and I'll see you later."

I made the shower as hot as I could stand it, soaped my body with some antibacterial soap the kids had for zits and scrubbed at my skin until it hurt.

By the time I was dry and in my robe, Dr. Philip Lee was at the front door, scowling.

"It was good of you to come to the house," I said.

"My sister-in-law is a very persuasive woman," he said. And then he smiled. "Well, what the hell, eh?"

While he examined me, he asked about the granny flat, the same questions Ali had asked. How big was it? How was it ventilated? How often had the extermination people sprayed? What did they use?

"Organophosphates." He repeated my answer as he pressed down on my abdomen with his graceful hands. "Do you know what they used organophosphates for in Germany before the Second World War? They were active ingredients in nerve gases. Your granny flat was a little gas chamber for you, Mrs. Kilbourn. Amazing, eh?"

"Amazing," I agreed weakly.

"Well," he said after I'd pulled the covers over me, "you're going to live. I would put you in a hospital if my brother and sister-in-law weren't coming. But you need a neurologist and a psychiatrist and" – he snapped his long, tobacco-stained fingers – "presto, they appear . . . More house calls." He grinned. "Ali says you're a nice woman, Mrs. Kilbourn. You're certainly a lucky one. I'm going to prescribe atropine sulphate – perhaps you know it by its other name, bella-donna. You take it orally, every four hours. Set your alarm. The timing is important. The atropine should relieve your symptoms. My brother might wish to prescribe something to reverse the muscular weakness, but I'll leave that to him. I'll call in your prescription for you, and the drug store will deliver it."

He started to walk out of the room but turned in the doorway. He looked at his feet like a bashful boy in a movie, then shrugged.

"Could I look at it, Mrs. Kilbourn?"

I didn't understand.

"Your gas chamber," he said.

"Absolutely, be my guest. What the hell, eh?" I said and sank down into the warmth of my bed.

I waited for the prescription, and after it arrived, I took the phone off the hook, curled up and went to sleep. There were things I had to do: call the police, call the kids, call Rick. But the phone calls would have to wait. I needed sleep. I awoke around five o'clock, made myself a bowl of chicken noodle soup and ate it with some crackers, then I fell asleep again.

When I woke, it was just before ten. The national news was coming on.

I turned on the TV in my bedroom and put the phone on the hook. Sometimes Rick called as soon as his report was over, and suddenly I wanted very much to talk to him. I wasn't crazy. I was a woman with a future again, a woman a man could think about loving, a woman who could think about having a man as part of her future.

And not just any man. I lay back on the pillows piled against the headboard of my bed and remembered. I remembered how his smile started in one corner of his mouth and spread, slow and knowing, until his face was transformed. And I remembered how his hair, dark blond like mine, fell forward when he bent his head to look down at me, and how he had sat on the bleachers with me in the twilight, and cooked with me and laughed with me and worked with me. And I remembered how he'd fit so smoothly into all our lives at Thanksgiving, and I thought, when Ali and Mort come, I'll invite them for the holidays here with us, with my children and me, with Rick.

The phone rang and at just that minute his face filled the television screen. I picked up the receiver, but my eyes never left Rick's image. He was still wearing his poppy. He must have rushed to the studio and grabbed yesterday's jacket, with its poppy and its day-old creases, from the dressing room before going on the air.

I strained to listen to the television, but in my ear there was a woman's voice, familiar and old: "And I thought, well, I'll put all these books I brought back from overseas away until after Christmas when I can have a really good look at them. So it was while I was trying to find some space in that little garage of mine that . . ."

Rick was saying something about a group in the prime minister's party meeting at a cottage in the Eastern Townships to talk about challenging the PM's leadership before the next election.

The voice went on in my ear: "And that's when I found the box. I can't imagine why it didn't surface before."

Rick was taking a hard line against those who were plotting against the prime minister. "It is a question not just of party solidarity but of fundamental decency," he said. "Decency has been a commodity in short supply during the life of this government, but in the dying days perhaps it is not too much to hope . . ."

"At any rate, our little mystery is solved," said the woman's voice.

"Hilda McCourt," I said, suddenly making the connection.

"Yes, Joanne, it's Hilda. I'm sorry, I should have identified myself. Egotism seems to be as much a part of getting old as creaks and flatulence. Anyway, it is I, and the box I unearthed in the garage contained all my old grade books from E.T. Russell. It was the easiest thing in the world. I looked up grade twelve and found Boychuk, Andrue Peter – that's Andrue with a *ue*, as I'm sure you know." Angus had left an old spelling test on my night table. I picked up my pen and wrote, "Boychuk, Andrue Peter" in a clear space at the top of the paper.

"The boy with the unfortunate name, as I had remembered, came late in the year. His name is added at the bottom of the roll. The name is Primrose. Eric Spenser Primrose."

I wrote the name beneath Andy's and circled the initials of their given names, Andrue and Eric.

"You see it, don't you, Joanne?" Hilda McCourt was saying. "That delicate boy, Eric Spenser Primrose, grew up to be Rick Spenser. Isn't that a shocker? When I saw him after Andy's funeral I knew there was something in Rick Spenser's face that I recognized, but of course, I was upset. I remember you offering the explanation that I was just responding to the familiarity of celebrity. I didn't care for that explanation, Joanne, and I was right not to. They can get grey or bald or even fat but I always remember my students' faces. Still" – she laughed – "Eric Primrose being Rick Spenser strained even my powers. The last place one would think to look for a thin boy is in a fat man. Anyway, there's our mystery solved."

On the TV screen, Rick's face dissolved and was replaced

by a commercial for camera film. A handsome family was getting ready for Christmas. Words came on the screen: "For the times of your life."

Hilda's voice sounded in my ear. "And you can't blame him for dropping the 'Primrose.' The jokes would have plagued him forever, and he suffered so with them. Memories are coming back to me now. Our grade twelve curriculum, for example. We used to do William Blake's 'The Sick Rose.' Do you know it, Joanne?"

I said the lines mechanically in a voice that sounded like Lori Evanson's.

> O rose, thou art sick.
> The invisible worm
> That flies in the night,
> In the howling storm,
>
> Has found out thy bed
> Of crimson joy,
> And his dark secret love
> Does thy life destroy.

"You must have had a good teacher," Hilda McCourt said admiringly. "Well, you can imagine what high-school children did with that poem and an effeminate boy named Primrose."

On the screen, the president of the United States boarded Air Force One and went somewhere.

"Yes," I said, "I can imagine."

"Joanne, this has been a shock for you, hasn't it? But no harm done. I assure you, Eric behaved very handsomely when I confronted him with it, if 'confronted' isn't too strong a word. He said he was upset that day, but he always finds it difficult to be reminded of those times. That's understandable, I think. Adolescence must have been a painful time for him."

"When did you talk to Rick?"

"Early this afternoon. I called him just before lunch."

On the television, there were pictures of a benefit production of a Broadway musical. The choreographer had died of AIDS the week before. "One more reminder," said the announcer. The prime minister and his family, bundled into handsome fall sportswear, were going to Harrington Lake for the long weekend. Everybody was on the move. I reached over and turned them all off, vanquished them.

"Joanne, are you all right?"

"Yes, I'm all right, Hilda – just assimilating," I said and wondered at my choice of words.

"Good. Eric suggested that I shouldn't tell you. He said you'd been under a great deal of stress."

"Yes," I repeated dully, "a great deal of stress. Hilda, I'm grateful for your help – truly. I have to go. I have things to do."

I didn't give her a chance to respond. I hung up the receiver and sat staring at the television set as if I could conjure up his face, make him materialize from the hidden electronic dots.

"You bastard," I said to the empty screen. Despite the atropine, my heart was pounding. "You murderous son of a bitch." I stood up and grabbed my robe. There was something I had to see.

At the bottom of the stairs, Peter's snow boots lay abandoned. I shoved my bare feet into them and grabbed a ski jacket from a coat hook in the entranceway. It was an old one of Mieka's, ripped under the arms and heavy with buttons and pins from rock groups that, by now, had disbanded and gone their separate ways. I put the ski jacket on over my nightgown and walked out the back door and across the yard to the garage.

The door to the granny flat was still open. It had been open all day. My legs were trembling, but I climbed the stairs. I knew what I wanted.

It was in the vertical files for the current year, in a box marked "August 28." No other reference was necessary. I slipped it out of its box, checked the label and slid it into the VCR. My hands were trembling. I had had the tape for weeks. A woman I knew in the newsroom at CNRC-TV had given it to me when she heard about the book I was writing, but until that moment, I hadn't been able to face looking at it.

I hit the play button and it was August again. There were crowd shots. I recognized a few people, sweating and happy, and with a start, I saw the man from the poultry association brushing barbecue sauce on chicken halves that were just beginning to sputter and smoke.

I hit the fast-forward button. There was the makeshift stage, empty still. There was Dave Micklejohn, bringing Roma on stage. And there was Eve, looking the way she always did in public, strained and anxious, ready to bolt. Then Dave leaned toward her and whispered something, and she smiled.

In that moment, Eve Boychuk's face was transformed. She was both carefree and lovely. There couldn't have been more than a handful of such times in her life, and now her face was waxy white as she lay beneath stiff hospital sheets, her wrists blooming blood. "Eric Primrose, you bastard, you'll pay for this, you'll pay for doing this to her," I said, and my breath made little clouds in the cold air of the granny flat.

On the television, the big woman who would hand Andy the black Thermos of water appeared at the top of the portable staircase at the back of the truck, and in the cold, dead room, I stopped breathing. She picked her way carefully through the snakes of wires from the sound system and finally, safely across the stage, she put the leather speech folder on the podium.

He always did that, handed the speech to someone who'd be onstage before him, so he could bound on boyish, spontaneous. There she was, putting the folder down so carefully, right where we had told her. Inside was the sheet of paper, grey as a dove's breast, and on it the Blake poem, and at the top of the page, two letters, *A* and *E*, curled together like the initials of a husband and wife on a Victorian headstone. *A* and *E*, Andy and Eric. But Andy hadn't seen that – not yet.

My teeth were chattering. In the yard, my dogs were barking, but I was transfixed. Craig Evanson was on the screen, introducing Andy. Another victim, but I didn't want to see him. I pushed the fast-forward button. There was a blur then Andy was there, suntanned, so slight in his blue jeans and cotton shirt as he walked across the stage to his death. He was laughing. Then he took off his baseball cap and waved it. Graceful, doomed, he was, in that moment, the last of the boys of summer. In the cold moonlight in the yard, my dogs were barking frantically, but I was lost in the eternal summer of Andy's last picnic.

Then he turned from the podium and the woman in the flowered dress handed him the tray and on the tray were the black Thermos and the glass. I couldn't watch it. I closed my eyes, and when I opened them again I saw myself on the TV screen kneeling by Andy, twenty pounds heavier, and so strong and capable. I had forgotten I was like that. I pulled the hem of my nightgown around my knees for warmth. Rick Spenser was on the screen, his back to the podium, shakily raising the glass to his lips. Then there was a blur. In the next shot, I was wrapped around his knees, and he was coming down hard.

In the yard the dogs were frenzied, yelping and growling. On the tape, Andy and Rick were lying on a metal truck bed under the August sun. Then Rick was talking, but not on television. He was in the doorway of the granny flat, his bulk blocking out the moonlight. I could smell fear, but he didn't sound afraid. He sounded like he knew he was going to win.

"I have always detested ad hockery, Joanne."

"What?" My voice was barely audible.

"You had an excellent education. You know the meaning of the term 'ad hoc,' and this whole affair has reeked of it. Everything cobbled together on the spot. You know, I'm not a monster. It's never been a question of calibrating the attacks against you. I've just had to do the best I could. Improvising, although I've always shrunk from improvising."

He moved closer, and I could see his face in the moonlight. He didn't look like a maniac, but he was saying terrible things.

"It's working, though, Joanne, and that, of course, is the test, isn't it. There are no loose ends. Certainly there's nothing to connect me with this place tonight. I've discovered there's an advantage to dealing with women. There's always such a miasma of hysteria around them that you can get away" – he smiled a little sadly – "well, with almost anything. You're not quite as dramatic as Eve, but still, no one would be surprised if you walked down the stairs and into the garage. I think it would be a very logical way for a despondent woman to die, asleep in her own car with the motor running.

"I talked to Mieka yesterday. I told her I feared you were heading for another breakdown. Do you know what she said? She said, 'That would just kill her. She's such a good mother. I think she'd rather die than let us see her like that again.' Your own daughter, Joanne." He shrugged and gave me his professional smile, amused at the vagaries of the world. "Look at yourself. You've even dressed for the part – a crazy woman in a nightgown, a ripped ski jacket, a man's snow boots and bare legs," he said, bending closer and shaking his head.

"You were wearing a poppy," I said.

"What?" I had thrown him the wrong line, and he was at a loss. "What did you say?"

Underneath my nightgown I could feel my knees knocking together, but my voice sounded okay. "Half an hour ago on your special report on the news, three million people saw you wearing a poppy on the day after Remembrance Day. A man as fastidious as you . . . Someone's sure to put it together. Some smart young cop or some assistant producer you've been snotty with. Maybe even some hick out here in the prairies. Most of us know about the magic of video-taping by now."

I had no plan. I watched his face in the flickering light from the VCR. There seemed to be something tentative in his smile.

Ad hockery. "It's just a matter of time now, Eric," I said. He flinched from the name as if it were a blow. I'd scored a hit. "They're going to catch you, Eric, and then everyone will know. Not just that you're a murderer – that still has a certain Nietzschean appeal." I was shaking uncontrollably. "Or even that you're gay." My voice quavered. "That still has a certain cachet. But they'll find those old pictures, you know." In the silvery light, I could see a fine line of saliva between his lips. It was now or never. "Little Eric Primrose, the fairy boy. They'll find those old pictures, and they'll have a field day. Rick Spenser, the erudite friend of people who matter, is really little Eric Primrose. Little Eric, the delicate fairy boy who dreamed of weddings and lace and who connected his initial to his beloved's with little curlicues and flowers. Just like a girl. O rose thou art sick. Blake will be in the headlines, Eric."

As I talked, I stood and walked toward him, and he backed

away as if I were exerting some kind of physical force. I had a vague idea that I might back him out the door and knock him over the balcony, like in the movies, but I was too sick and too terrified to focus on any plan.

Ad hockery. I had to keep talking. His chest was heaving, and there was an animal smell in the room. I didn't know whether it was coming from him or me. He seemed mesmerized. The crueller the cut, the more intent he became.

"Poor Andy, having you in his life. But, you know, he did find real love with Soren Eames. He and Soren were equals. Soren told me once that when Andy touched him for the first time, he knew what it felt like to bloom. To bloom, Eric. It must have been so good for them both."

He was going to break.

"I don't blame Andy for falling out of love with you. Not just because you're fat, but because you're a fake."

He braced himself against the desk. His fingertips touched the base of the crystal pitcher he had given me. His hand curled around the handle, then he raised it like a club above his head. Moonlight streamed through the open door and caught the curve of the pitcher. He looked as if he were holding a club of pale fire.

My eyes lost their focus. I blinked, then I blinked again. Standing on the balcony, just behind Rick, was Ali Sutherland.

She was a shade less than six feet tall, and heavy. She seemed like a match for him. She was looking straight at me. It was hard to read her expression in the half light, but she nodded her head slightly, and I took that as a sign of agreement and encouragement. I took a deep breath.

"Are you going to kill me with that? That would bring the total to three, wouldn't it? Four, if you want to count Eve, who's as good as dead, lying on her back, counting the cracks in the ceiling. Five, if you want to count her son – that beautiful bright boy who's a vegetable now, his sister dead." Then suddenly I knew. "Because that day, before Eve got behind the wheel of the car, you made sure she knew, didn't you? Didn't you?"

He nodded, raised the pitcher higher and took a step toward me.

I moved toward him and I put my face so close to his I could smell his breath. And then very low, I said, "Why didn't you just kill yourself, Eric?"

He spit his answer at me. "Because, bitch, I wasn't the one who deserved to die."

Behind Rick's shoulder Ali Sutherland looked at me levelly, then I saw the slightest nod of her head, almost imperceptible. I thought, she's going to make her move.

Ali's voice and her hand came at the same time. "You must be so tired of all this, Rick," she said, and she reached from behind him and took the crystal pitcher. And then, very calm and unhurried, she led Rick out the door, put the vase in the window box, took Rick's arm and, murmuring reassurances, led him carefully down the stairs. I stood on the little balcony and watched them cross the yard and go into my house, two large and handsome people, silvery in the moonlight, visitors from another country, going home.

I went into the granny flat, called the police and turned off the television. Then I went to the balcony, took the pitcher out of the cold dirt in the window box, sat on the top step and waited until I heard the sirens. The crystal vase was safe. I used the hem of my nightgown to rub the dirt from the deep lines of its pattern. I rubbed until I thought they'd have enough time to take him. I rubbed until it was safe again.

When I went in the house, Ali was making tea. Beside her was a tumbler of Scotch – neat.

"The tea's for you," she said. "There must be quite a chemical soup in you at the moment. I don't think alcohol would be a smart move." She turned her back to me, swirled boiling water in the teapot. "Mort went to the police station with Rick. Mort really liked him, you know. I guess we all did." She poured out the water and carefully measured tea into the pot. Suddenly, the kitchen smelled of oranges and spices.

"Does any of this make sense to you?" I asked.

Ali looked into my face. "Rick talked to me while we were waiting for the police. He wanted me to understand, I think. He and Andy were lovers for over twenty-five years. Then in the spring Andy suddenly left him. Rick hated Soren Eames for taking Andy away from him, but he hated Andy even more for leaving him. And so, he contrived to kill them."

"His dark secret love/Does thy life destroy," I said.

Ali looked concerned. "Perhaps you're not ready to deal with this, Jo."

"Maybe not," I said, "but one more thing. Why would Rick drink the water from Andy's glass if he didn't want to die?"

"Subterfuge?" said Ali. "You were a lucky break for him, but if you hadn't happened along, he could simply have pretended to drink. You told me there were five thousand people in the park that day. There would have been one credulous soul prepared to swear that Rick was innocent because he'd lifted that glass."

"Smoke and mirrors," I said.

"Time for tea." Ali put her drink, the teapot and a cup on a little tray and walked into the living room. I followed her. When she sat on the couch, I curled up against her warm bulk and cried like a baby. She held me in her arms and rocked me until I fell asleep.

CHAPTER

22

Writing this account was Ali's idea. "Get it out," she said, sitting on my bed one morning before she drove back to Winnipeg. "Give it shape then move along. You don't need an analyst any more; you just need rest and a little time to evaluate. Besides," she said, brightening, "a journal will give you something to do while you're cooling your heels in all those specialists' waiting rooms." After the initial rounds, I ended up with just one specialist, a neurologist, a gentle man with a crewcut who explained in terms a lay person would understand what had happened to me. The pesticides had blocked the enzyme that governs the transmission of nerve impulses, so my nervous system was in a constant state of stimulation. That, directly or indirectly, caused all my symptoms.

"So what do I do now?" I had asked him.

"Well, stay away from organophosphates for a start," he said seriously, then smiled. "Sorry, that was stupid. From what Ali tells me, I gather you didn't exactly bring this upon yourself. Anyway, I'm not planning anything heroic here – some B-12 shots, a prescription for oral B complex, some good food, lots of rest and an exercise regime. The CFL season's over, and there's a guy I know who's a trainer for the Riders. He can help you with the exercising – muscle-strengthening stuff, some leg raising with weights, hamstring lifts. He'll turn you into a jock, Mrs. Kilbourn. The only thing wrong with him is that he's a Barry Manilow fan. He plays one tape after another."

And that's my life: vitamin shots, eating, resting, jock stuff and writing this. Ali says I should give myself over to inva-lidism for a while. And introspection. "But don't let it go on too long," she said. "Watch out for the Magic Mountain syndrome – taking your pulse every thirty minutes and checking out your BMs. New Year's Eve seems a nice sym-bolic time to move along, but until then let the world dance without you."

And so I do. The leadership convention came and went without me. The party elected a radical young farmer from the southwest of the province. He won't win the election for us, but in the long run he may be what we needed all along. Craig Evanson nominated him. Julie was not there.

Christmas is two weeks away, and although I have a nice stack of invitations for holiday parties, I am not taking part in what Ian used to grimly call "the mulled wine and salmo-nella season." Mieka and Greg will be home next week, and Ali and Mort will arrive on Christmas Eve. Mort made reser-vations for Christmas dinner at a splendid old hotel down-town. This will be the first year since I was married that I haven't cooked a turkey. Somehow that seems significant.

Peter and Angus are doing most of the cooking around here, so we've been through the take-out list a couple of times. For the first week or so after the "incident in the granny flat," as my friend Millar Millard calls it, the boys were unnervingly solicitous, but we're back in our familiar grooves now. They come, singly or together, and throw themselves on the bed to pass along the news or gripe about each other, and I ask them why they can't get along better and complain about no one recognizing my need for peace and quiet. We're all relieved to pick up the old roles and the old lines.

I find it odd to be an outsider. Everything I know about other people comes from Christmas cards. In the normal course of things, I'd pick them out of the mailbox, rip them open and glance at the signatures, but this year I'm reading the cards carefully, looking not just for news but for subtext.

There are some beside me now that I keep coming back to. There is a lithograph of Osgoode Hall in Toronto from Howard Dowhanuik. The card came tucked inside a silk scarf. He is staying in Toronto for the holidays but will be back early in the new year. Not a word about Marty.

Terry Shaw from the correctional centre writes a note of thanks for a small gift I sent and says that she is "not hopeful about Eve's chances of psychological recovery but after all this is the season for miracles."

Hilda McCourt's card is hand-done, a brass rubbing from the tomb of the Venerable Bede ("Something I did for some special friends when I was overseas"). With her card, she encloses a letter in which she details the contributions "gays" (her word, carefully chosen) have made to the arts and asking me not to be embittered by "one tortured boy."

Lori and Mark Evanson's card is a conventional and pretty nativity scene. Inside, behind a cutout oval, is a picture of Mark and Lori and their son, Clay. Mark stands behind a chair with his hand on his wife's shoulder. Clay is on his mother's knee with his face turned toward her. As she looks down into her son's face, Lori Evanson's look, dim, radiant and trusting, seems to me eerily like that of the Madonna on the front of her card.

There is one final card, a large and handsome one on which a grey dove with an olive branch flies against a pale grey sky. Inside in raised letters is a printed message:

Peace on Earth. Goodwill to All.

A Holiday wish from
Homefree Insect Pest Control Services
The Name Says It All.

Murder at the Mendel

CHAPTER

1

If I hadn't gone back to change my shoes, it would have been me instead of Izaak Levin who found them dying. But halfway to the Loves' cottage I started worrying that shoes with heels would make me too tall to dance with, and by the time I got back to the Loves', Izaak was standing in their doorway with the dazed look of a man on the edge of shock. When I pushed past him into the cottage, I saw why.

I was fifteen years old, and I had never seen a dead man, but I knew Desmond Love was dead. He was sitting in his place at the dining-room table, but his head lolled back on his neck as if something critical had come loose, and his mouth hung open as if he were sleeping or screaming. His wife, Nina, was in the chair across from him. She was always full of grace, and she had fallen so that her head rested against the curve of her arm as it lay on the table. She was beautiful, but her skin was waxen, and I could hear the rattle of her breathing in that quiet room. My friend Sally was lying on the floor. She had vomited; she was pale and her breathing was laboured, but I knew she wouldn't die. She was thirteen years old, and you don't die when you're thirteen.

It was Nina I went to. My relationship with my own mother had never been easy, and Nina had been my refuge for as long as I could remember. I took her in my arms and began to cry and call her name. Izaak Levin was still standing in the doorway, but seeing me with Nina seemed to jolt him back to reality.

"Joanne, you have to get your father. We need a doctor here," he said.

My legs felt heavy, the way they do in a dream when you try to run and you can't, but somehow I got to our cottage and brought my father. He was a methodical and reassuring man, and as I watched him taking pulses, looking into pupils, checking breathing, I felt better.

"What happened?" he asked Izaak Levin.

Izaak shook his head. When he spoke, his voice was dead with disbelief. "I don't know. I took the boat over to town for a drink before dinner. When I got back, I found them like this." He pointed to a half-filled martini pitcher on the table. At Sally's place there was a glass with an inch of soft drink in the bottom. "He must have put it in the drinks. I guess he decided it wasn't worth going on, and he wanted to take them with him."

There was no need to explain the pronouns. My father and I knew what he meant. At the beginning of the summer Desmond Love had suffered a stroke that had slurred his speech, paralyzed his right side and, most seriously, stilled his hand. He was forty years old, a bold and innovative maker of art and a handsome and immensely physical man. It was believable that, in his rage at the ravages of the stroke, he would kill himself, and so I stored away Izaak's explanation. I stored it away in the same place I stored the other memories of that night: the animal sound of retching Nina made after my father forced the ipecac into her mouth. The silence broken only by a loon's cry as my father and Izaak carried the Loves, one by one, down to the motorboat at the dock. The blaze of the sunset on the lake as my father wrapped Nina and Sally in the blankets they kept in the boat for picnics. The terrible emptiness in Desmond Love's eyes as they looked at the September sky.

And then my father, standing in the boat, looking at me on the dock, "Joanne, you're old enough to know the truth here: Sally will be all right, but Des is dead and I'm not sure about Nina's chances. It'll be better for you later if you don't ride in this boat tonight." His voice was steady, but there were tears in his eyes. Desmond Love had been his best friend since they were boys. "I want you to go back home and wait for me. Just tell your mother there's been an emergency. Don't tell her . . ."

"The truth." I finished the sentence for him. The truth would make my mother start drinking. So would a lie. It never took much.

"Don't let Nina die," I said in an odd, strangled voice.

"I'll do all I can," he said, and then the quiet of the night was shattered by the roar of the outboard motor; the air was filled with the smell of gasoline, and the boat, low in the water from its terrible cargo, began to move across the lake into the brilliant gold of the sunset. It was the summer of 1958, and I was alone on the dock, waiting.

★ ★ ★

Thirty-two years later I was walking across the bridge that links the university community to the city of Saskatoon. It was the night of the winter solstice. The sky was high and starless, and there was a bone-chilling wind blowing down the South Saskatchewan River from the north. I was on my way to the opening of an exhibition of the work of Sally Love.

As soon as I turned onto Spadina Crescent, I could see the

bright letters of her name on the silk banners suspended over the entrance to the Mendel Gallery: Sally Love. Sally Love. Sally Love. There was something festive and celebratory about those paint-box colours, but as I got closer I saw there were other signs, too, and some of them weren't so pretty. These signs were mounted on stakes held by people whose faces shone with zeal, and their crude lettering seemed to pulse with indignation: "Filth Belongs in Toilets Not on Walls," "Jail Pornographers," "No Room for Love Here" and one that said simply, "Bitch."

A crowd had gathered. Some people were attempting a counterattack, and every so often a voice, thin and self-conscious in the winter air, would raise itself in a tentative defence: "What about freedom of the arts?" "We're not a police state yet!" "The only real obscenity is censorship."

A TV crew had set up under the lights of the entrance and they were interviewing a soft-looking man in a green tuque with the Hilltops logo and a nylon ski jacket that said "Silver Broom: Saskatoon '90." The man was one of our city councillors, and as I walked up I could hear his spiritless baritone spinning out the clichés for the ten o'clock news: "Community standards . . . public property . . . our children's innocence . . . privacy of the home . . ." The councillor's name was Hank Mewhort, and years before I had been at a political fundraiser where he had dressed as a leprechaun to deliver the financial appeal. As I walked carefully around the camera crew, Hank's sanctimonious bleat followed me. I had liked him better as a leprechaun.

When I handed my invitation to a commissionaire posted at the entrance, he checked my name off on a list and opened the gallery door for me. As I started through, I felt a sharp blow in the middle of my back. I turned and found myself facing a fresh-faced woman with a sweet and vacant smile. She was grasping her sign so the shaft was in front of her like a broadsword. She came at me again, but then, very quickly, a city cop grabbed her from behind and led her off into the night. She was still smiling. Her sign lay on the concrete in front of me, its message carefully spelled out in indelible marker the colour of dried blood: "The Wages of Sin is Death." I shuddered and pulled my coat tight around me.

Inside, all was light and airiness and civility. People dressed in holiday evening clothes greeted one another in the reverent tones Canadians use at cultural events. A Douglas fir, its boughs luminous with yellow silk bows, filled the air with the smell of Christmas. In front of the tree was an easel with a handsome poster announcing the Sally Love exhibition. Propped discreetly against it was a small placard stating that Erotobiography was in Gallery III at the rear of the building and that patrons must be eighteen years of age to be admitted.

Very prim. Very innocent. But this small addendum to Sally's show had eclipsed everything else. To the left of the Douglas fir, a wall plastered with newspaper clippings told the story: Erotobiography consisted of seven pictures Sally Love had painted to record her sexual experiences.

All the pictures were explicit, but the one that had caused the furor was a fresco. A fresco, the local paper noted sternly, is permanent. The colour in a fresco does not rest on the surface; it sinks into and becomes part of the wall. And what Sally Love had chosen to sink into the wall of the publicly owned Mendel Gallery was a painting of the sexual parts of all the people with whom she had been intimate. Erotobiography. According to the newspaper, there were one hundred individual entries, and a handful of the genitalia were female. Nonetheless, community standards being what they are, the work was known by everyone as the Penis Painting.

The exhibition that was opening that night was a large one. Several of the pictures on loan from major galleries throughout North America had been heralded as altering the direction of contemporary art; many of the paintings had been praised for their psychological insights or their technical virtuosity. None of that seemed to matter much. It was the penises that had prompted the people outside to leave their warm living rooms and clutch the shafts of picket signs in their mittened hands. It was the penises the handsome men and women exchanging soft words in the foyer had come to see. As I walked toward the wing where Nina Love and I had agreed to meet, I was smiling. I had to admit that I wanted to see the penises, too. The rest was just foreplay.

The south wing of the Mendel Gallery is a conservatory, a place where you can find green and flowering things even when the temperature sticks at forty below for weeks on end. When I stepped through the door, the moisture and the warmth and the fragrance enveloped me, and for a moment I stood there and let the cold and the tension flow out of my body. Nina Love was sitting on a bench in front of a blazing display of amaryllis, azalea and bird of paradise. She had a compact cupped in her hand, and her attention was wholly focused on her reflection. It was, I thought sadly, becoming her characteristic gesture.

That night as I was getting ready for Sally's opening, I'd heard the actress Diane Keaton answer a radio interviewer's question about how she faced aging. "You have to be very brave," she'd said, and I'd thought of Nina. Much as I cared for her I had to admit that Nina Love wasn't being very brave about growing older.

Until Thanksgiving, when she had come to Saskatoon to help care for her granddaughter, Nina and I had kept in touch mostly through letters and phone calls. I'd seen her only on those rare occasions when I was in Toronto to check on my mother.

Illusions were easy at a distance. I was discovering that up close they were harder to sustain. Nina had aged physically, of course, although I suspected the process had been smoothed somewhat by a surgeon's skill. There were feathery lines in the skin around her dark eyes, a slight sag in the soft skin beneath her jawline. But that seemed to me as inconsequential as it was inevitable. She was still an extraordinarily beautiful woman.

The problem wasn't with Nina's beauty; it was with how much of herself she seemed to have invested in her beauty. I couldn't be with her long without noticing how often her hand smoothed the skin of her neck or how, when she passed a store window, she would seek out her reflection with anxious eyes.

That night at the Mendel as I watched her bending closer to the mirror in her cupped hand, I felt a pang. But Nina had spent a lot of years assuring me that I had value. Now it was my turn. I walked over and sat down beside her.

"You're perfect," I said, and she was. From the smooth line of her dark hair to her dress – high-necked, long-sleeved, meticulously cut from some material that shimmered green and purple and gold in the half light – to her silky stockings and shining kid pumps, Nina Love was as flawless as money and sustained effort could make a woman.

She snapped the compact shut and laughed. "Jo, I can always count on you. You've always been my biggest fan. That's why I was so worried when you were late." Then her face grew serious. "Wasn't that terrifying out there?"

Our knees were almost touching, but I still had to lean toward Nina to hear her. Sally always said that her mother's soft, breathy voice was a trick to get everyone to pay attention to nothing but her. Trick or not, as I listened to Nina that winter evening, I felt the sense of homecoming I always felt when I walked through a door and found her waiting.

At that moment, she was looking at me critically. "You seem to be a little the worse for wear."

"Well, I walked over, and as my grandfather used to say, it's colder than a witch's teat out there. Then I had an encounter with someone exercising her democratic right to jab me in the back with her picket sign."

"Those creatures out there aren't human," she said. "It's been a nightmare for us. Stuart's phone rings at all hours of the day and night. I'm afraid to take the mail out of the mailbox. Even Taylor is being hurt. Yesterday, a little boy at play school told Taylor her mother should be tied up and thrown in the river."

"Oh, no, what did Taylor do?"

"She told the boy that at least *her* mother didn't have a mustache."

I could feel the corners of my mouth begin to twitch. "A mustache?"

"According to Taylor, the boy's mother needs a shave," Nina said dryly. "But, Jo, I'm afraid I'm beyond laughing at any of this. I really wonder what can be going through Sally's mind. First she leaves her husband and child, then she makes a piece of art that outrages everyone and puts Stuart in a terrible position professionally."

"Nina, I don't think you're being fair, at least not about the painting. I don't know much about these things, but from what I read Sally's a hot ticket in the art world now. That fresco must be worth a king's ransom."

"Oh, you're right about that, and of course that's what makes Stuart's position so difficult. He's the director, and the director's duty is to acquire the best. But he also has a board to deal with and a community to appease. Sally could have painted anything else and people would have been all over the place being grateful to her and to Stuart. As they should be. She's an incredible artist. But she has to have her joke. And so she gives the Mendel a gift that could destroy it. Jo, that fresco of Sally's is a real Trojan horse." Nina reached behind her and pulled a faded bloom from an azalea. "I guess I don't have much sense of proportion about this. It's been so terrible for Stuart and, of course, for Taylor."

"But at least they have you, dear," I said. "I'm sure Stuart would have broken into a million pieces if you hadn't been there to make a home for Taylor and for him. You didn't see him in those first weeks after Sally left. He was like a ghost walker. She was the centre of his life . . ."

Nina's face was impassive. "She's always the centre of everybody's life, isn't she? Right from the beginning . . ."

But she didn't finish the sentence. Stuart Lachlan had come into the conservatory.

"Look, there he is at the door. Doesn't he look fine?" she said.

Stu did, indeed, look fine. As I'd told Nina, his suffering after Sally left had been so intense it seemed to mark him physically. But tonight he looked better – tentative, like a man coming back from a long illness, but immaculate again, as he was in the days when he and Sally were together.

He was a handsome man in his late forties, dark-eyed, dark-haired, with the taut body of a swimmer who never misses a day doing laps. He was wearing a dinner jacket and a surprising and beautiful tie and cummerbund of flowered silk. When he leaned over to kiss me, his cheek was smooth, and he smelled of expensive aftershave.

"Merry Christmas, Jo. With everything else that's been going on, the birthday of the Prince of Peace seems to have been lost in the shuffle. But it's good to be able to wish you joy in person. Your coming here to teach was the second best thing to happen this year."

"I don't have to ask you what the first was. Nina's obviously taking wonderful care of you. You look great, Stu, truly."

"Well, the tie and the cummerbund are Nina's gift. Cosmopolitan and unorthodox, like me, she says." He laughed, but he looked at me eagerly, waiting for his compliment.

I smiled past him at Nina, the shameless flatterer. "She's right, as usual. Do you have time to sit with us for a minute?"

"No, I'm afraid it's time for me to make my little talk and get this opening underway. I just came in to get Nina." Then, flawlessly mannered as always, he offered an arm to each of us. "And of course to escort you, Jo."

It had been a long time since I'd needed an escort, but when we walked into the foyer, I was glad Stuart was there for Nina. The picketers had come through the door. They couldn't have been there long because nothing was happening. They had the punchy look of game show contestants who've won the big prize but aren't sure how to get offstage. The people in evening dress were eying them warily, but everything was calm. Then the TV cameras came inside, and the temperature rose. Someone pushed someone else, and little brush fires of violence seemed to break out all over the room. A woman in an exquisite lace evening gown grabbed a picket sign from a young man and threw it to the floor and stomped on it. The young man bent to pull the sign out from under her and knocked her off balance. When she fell, a man who seemed to be her husband took a swing at the young picketer. Then another man swung at the husband and connected. I heard the unmistakable dull crunch of fist hitting bone, and the husband was down. Then the police were all around and it was over.

The lady in lace and her husband were escorted to a police car; the protesters were shepherded outside, and the TV crews started to pack up. Stuart stood beside me, frozen, like a man in shock. Nina tightened her grip on his arm and said in her soft, compelling voice, "Stuart, it's up to you to put things right here; you can still set the tone for the evening.

Now go talk to those TV people before they go. Put things in perspective for them. Then give one of those witty talks you give, and show the board you're in charge."

It was as if someone had flicked a switch in him. He squared his shoulders, straightened his beautiful tie and headed for the cameras.

Nina and I stood together and watched. The show was worth watching. Stu moved into the bright lights at the front of the foyer with the élan of a model in an ad for expensive Scotch, and the speech he made was impressive, full of references to the civilizing power of art, a gallery's need always to go for the best whenever the best presents itself, a director's obligation to exercise his professional judgement and the community's obligation to support that judgement.

Stuart's face was flushed with the joy that comes when you know that, at a significant moment in your life, you're putting the words together right, that what you're feeling and what you're saying are one and the same. And the icing on the cake was that there were cameras grinding away, recording everything for posterity – or at least for the ten o'clock news.

And then, in just the way that the hour of enchantment ends in fairy tales, the heavy glass doors of the gallery opened and Sally Love walked in. One of the news people spotted her and called out, "Sally's here." And that was that. The crowd turned; the cameras swung around to capture her image, and as quickly as they had begun, Stuart's fifteen minutes of fame were over.

There was always an element of the theatrical about Sally. Part of it, of course, was just that she was so physically striking. She was her father's daughter in every way. She had Desmond Love's talent for making art, and she had his looks – the blond hair that seemed to radiate a wild electric energy of its own, the eyes blue as a larkspur flower, the wide and generous mouth, the long-boned animal grace. And like Des, Sally was always the focal point of whatever room she found herself in. The picture always rearranged itself so that Sally was in the foreground, and that night all of us in the gallery foyer found ourselves suddenly peripheral, background figures in yet another portrait of Sally.

She walked straight to where Stuart was standing with the microphone. She had just come back from New Mexico, and she was wearing a Navajo blanket coat that glowed with the colours of the desert: purple, turquoise, orange, blue. She slipped it off and handed it to Stu. He took it wordlessly. Suddenly he was redundant, no longer the champion of freedom of the arts, just a man holding his wife's coat, waiting for his instructions.

Sally was wearing an outfit a Navajo woman might have worn to dance in: soft boots of pale leather, an ankle-length red cotton skirt belted with silver and turquoise and a black velvet shirt open at the neck to show more silver and turquoise at her throat. Her heavy blond hair was parted in the centre and tied, just above each ear, in a butterfly-shaped knot, and she touched one of the butterflies as she leaned forward to kiss her husband's cheek.

"The traditional hairstyle of unmarried women," she said huskily into the microphone. "With all the hassles this exhibit is causing Stu, I thought I'd better start looking for a new man." Then she grinned wickedly. "Number one hundred and one."

There was a burst of nervous laughter. Sally leaned closer to the microphone. "You know, the people outside are having a great time: they're singing hymns and throwing snowballs. Lots of fun. A couple of people even threw snowballs at me. I think they wanted me to stay out there with them. But I wanted to be in here with you. This is our night. We always say that one of the purposes of art is celebration.

Well, let's celebrate." She turned and looked into her husband's face. "Stu?"

Despite himself, Stuart Lachlan smiled, and Sally seized the moment. She slid her arm through her husband's and said, "The director and I are going to find a drink. Why don't you guys join us?" And she led him smoothly out of the foyer toward the exhibition.

Beside me, Nina smoothed the shimmering line of her dress. There was a flicker of anger in her face, but when she spoke, her words were mild.

"Quite a performance," she said.

I had to agree. In the forty-five years since I'd tiptoed into Nina Love's room to look at her new baby daughter, I'd seen many of Sally Love's performances, but even by Sally's standards, this had been a star turn.

CHAPTER

2

It was a lovely party. This was a major show and the gallery had pulled out all the stops. As we walked among the paintings, two men from the caterers circulated carrying silver trays of tiny tourtieres, so hot the juices were bubbling through the top crust, and fluted paper cups holding crab-meat quiches shaped into perfect hearts. In the middle of the main gallery there was a serving table with a round of Cheddar as big as a wagon wheel and platters piled high with grapes and melon slices and strawberries. And there was a bar.

I was watching the bartender grate nutmeg on top of a bowl of eggnog when I heard a familiar voice.

"I know you like strong drink, Joanne. I'll ask Tony to make a Christmas Comfort for you. It's a drink that's out of fashion now but you'll like it."

I turned and found myself face to face with Hilda McCourt, a woman I had met the year before when a man who was dear to both of us had died violently. In the time since, our friendship had become one of the pleasures of my life. She was more than eighty years old and she looked every minute of it, but she always looked great. She was as slender as a high-school girl, and that night she was wearing an outfit a high-school girl would wear: a kind of combat suit made out of some shiny green fabric, very fashionable, and her hair dyed brilliant red was tied back with a swatch of the same material.

"Well, Joanne?" she asked.

"I trust you implicitly," I said, smiling.

"A Christmas Comfort for Mrs. Kilbourn, please, Tony, and another for me. He's an old student," she said as Tony went off to get the ingredients. He warmed a brandy snifter over a fondue pot he had bubbling on his worktable, filled the glass three-quarters full of Southern Comfort, added a slice of lemon and a little boiling water and then warmed the glass again.

"Drink it quickly now, while it's hot," said Hilda.

"There must be three ounces of liquor in that thing. I'll be under the table."

"Don't be foolish," Hilda said impatiently. "Just keep moving and eating." When she shook her head, I noticed that she had tiny golden Christmas tree balls hanging from her earlobes. She took my arm and led me toward the pictures.

"Now, what do you think of all this brouhaha about the fresco?" she asked.

"I haven't seen it yet, but I'm sure it's extraordinary. Everything Sally does is extraordinary."

"I hear ambivalence in your voice."

"Sorry," I said. "I guess when you've had the kind of history Sally and I've had, it takes a while to get rid of the ambivalence."

Hilda raised her eyebrows. "A tale for another time?" she asked.

I smiled. "For another time. Hey, speaking of tales, the one that's unfolding here tonight's pretty engrossing. Those people outside aren't going to be satisfied until someone comes here with a brush and paints over Erotobiography. I wonder what the board's going to do?"

"I can answer that," said Hilda. "The board is going to give Sally a splendid dinner to thank her for her generosity and they're going to issue a statement of support for Stuart Lachlan and then they're going to renew his contract for another five years."

"You sound very certain."

"I am very certain. I'm on the board. I've known most of the other members for years. They're decent people and they're reasonable. A lot of them are from the business community. They may not know a Picasso from a Pollock but they do understand art as investment. That fresco of Sally's is going to be worth a million dollars in five years. The board won't want to be remembered as the fools who threw a bucket of paint on a million dollars." Suddenly, her face broke into a smile. "Here's the artist now."

Sally slid her arm around my waist, but her attention was directed toward Hilda. "Miss McCourt, it's wonderful to see you again. People tell me you've been my champion in all this."

Hilda McCourt beamed with pleasure. "I was happy to do it. It's always a pleasure to nudge people into acting in a civilized way. They generally want to, you know."

Sally seemed surprised. "Do they?" she said. Then she shrugged. "If you say so. Anyway, besides thanking you, I wondered if you two would let me trail around with you for a while. There's a picture here I want to see with Jo."

Hilda looked at her watch. "I think you and Joanne had better look without me. I still have choir practice to get to tonight. We're doing Charpentier's 'Midnight Mass' for Christmas. A bit of a warhorse, but a splendid piece, and I think the Southern Comfort has prepared my voice nicely."

Sally leaned forward and kissed Hilda's cheek. "Thank you again for your heroic efforts. I know Erotobiography is troubling for some people."

"Oh, I've had lovers myself," said Hilda McCourt. "Many of them," and she turned and walked across the shining parquet of the gallery floor. Her step was as light as a young girl's.

I looked at Sally. "I'll bet she has had lovers," I said. "And I'll bet she'd need a bigger wall than you have to mount her memoirs of them all."

"Right," Sally said, and she laughed. But then there was an awkward moment. I had told Hilda McCourt that Sally and I had a history. Like many histories, ours had been scarred by wounded pride and estrangement. Since I'd come to Saskatoon in July to teach at the university, Sally and I had moved carefully to establish a friendship. After thirty years of separation, it hadn't been easy, and Sally hadn't made it easier when she had suddenly left her husband and child for an affair with a student in Santa Fe.

This was the first time we had been alone together since she'd come back from New Mexico, and she seemed tense, waiting, I guess, for my reaction. In my heart, I thought what she had done was wrong, but at forty-seven I didn't rush to judgement with the old sureness any more. And I had learned the value of a friend. I turned to her and smiled.

"Now, where's this painting I can't see without you?" I said.

She looked relieved. "In Gallery II – right through that doorway."

The gallery was only yards away, but our progress was slow. People kept coming up to Sally, ostensibly to congratulate her, but really just to see her up close. She was as she always was with people, kind enough but absent. Not many of the clichés about artists were true of Sally, but one of them was: her work was the only reality for her.

"So," she said finally. "Here it is. On loan from the Art
Institute of Chicago. What do you think?"

It was a painting of three people at a round picnic table:
two adolescent girls in bathing suits and a middle-aged man
in an open-necked khaki shirt. The man was handsome in a
world-weary Arthur Miller way, and he was wholly absorbed
in his newspaper. The girls were wholly absorbed in him.
As they looked at him, their faces were filled with pubescent longing.

"Wow," I said. "Izaak Levin and us. That last summer at
the lake. The hours we spent in the boathouse writing those
steamy stories about his lips pressing themselves against our
waiting mouths and about how it would feel to have him –
what was that phrase we loved – lower his tortured body
onto ours. Even now, my hands get sweaty remembering it.
All that unrequited lust." I stepped closer to the painting.
"It really is a wonderful painting, two young virgins looking
for . . . What were we looking for, anyway?"

"Someone to make us stop being virgins," Sally said dryly.
Then she shrugged. "And fame. Izaak was the toast of New
York City in those days. Remember when he was a panelist
on that TV show where they tried to guess people's jobs?"
Suddenly she smiled. "Izaak's in Erotobiography, you know."

Amazingly, I felt a pang. It had been more than thirty
years, but still, it had been Sally who won the prize. She'd
been the one to live out the fantasy.

"Come on," she said. "I'll show you which one's his." She
grinned mischievously. "Actually, maybe you could get him
to show you himself. He just walked in."

"You're kidding," I said, but she wasn't. There he was
across the room. Thinner, greyer, but still immensely appealing, still unmistakably the man I dreamed of through the
sultry days and starry nights of that summer.

He came right over to us. Sally beamed, pleased with herself.

"Izaak, here's an old admirer," she said. "The other girl in the picture – Joanne Ellard, except now it's Joanne Kilbourn."

Izaak Levin looked into my face. His expression was pleasant but bemused. It was apparent that the only memories he had of me were connected with a piece of art Sally had made. He gestured toward it. "I've enjoyed this picture many times over the years. It's a pleasure to see that you've aged as gracefully as it has."

I could feel the blood rushing to my face. I stood there dumbly, looking down at my feet like a fifteen-year-old.

"Has your life turned out happily?" he asked.

"For the most part, very happily," I said. My voice sounded strong and normal, so I continued. "It's wonderful to see you again. Did you come up for the opening?"

He looked surprised. "I live here. This has been my home since Sally and I came back in the sixties. Didn't she ever mention it?"

"Izaak's my agent, among other things," said Sally, and then she moved closer to him and touched his arm. "Incidentally, speaking of being my agent, I ran into these people in Santa Fe who bought *The Blue Horses* from you last summer. You'd better chase down the cheque because I never got it."

Her words seemed to knock Izaak Levin off base. He flushed and shook himself loose from her. "And the implication is . . . ?" he asked acidly.

"For God's sake, Izaak, the implication is nothing. I don't suspect you of financing a love nest in Miami. I've been travelling so much. I just thought the cheque must be stuck in a hotel mail slot somewhere. It's no big deal. Just track it down, that's all." She grabbed my arm. "Come on, Jo, let's go look at the filthy pictures."

There was a lineup for the Erotobiography exhibit, but we didn't wait in line. Everyone recognized Sally, and no one

seemed to mind being pushed aside. People flattened themselves against the walls to allow us safe passage. It was very
Canadian – the artist as minor royalty. And as if she were
royalty, Sally's entrance into the room transformed the
sleekly clothed art lovers from their everyday selves into
people who talked in muted voices and used significant
words: "life-affirming," "celebration," "mutability," "vari-
ability," "transcendence."

"Balls," said Sally as she moved toward the painting just
inside the door. "They have to be the hardest thing to draw.
Now look at this." The painting she pointed to was of an
intimate encounter. The woman, clearly Sally Love, sat
naked in a kind of grove while a young man knelt before her,
performing an act of cunnilingus. It was a beautiful work:
the colours were pure and vibrant, and the lines were all
curved grace. Sally reached out unself-consciously and
traced the lines of her own painted genitals with a forefinger:
"Look how lovely a woman is – all those shapes opening up,
moistening. There are so many possibilities there, but balls
are balls – small, hard, bounding around in their crepey skin
like avocado pits or ball bearings. Just from a technical
standpoint, they were a problem – I mean to make them
individual." She looked thoughtful. "Cocks, on the other
hand, were easy. Anyway, come see."

They were three deep in front of the fresco, but the sea
parted for Sally and me, and in a minute we were standing
in front of it. The first thing that struck me was the size. It
consumed a wall about ten feet by thirty feet – huge. And
Sally had played with scale too – some of the genitals were so
large they were unrecognizable as parts of the body; they
looked like lunar landscapes, all craters and folds and folli-
cles. Some were tiny, as contained and as carefully rendered
as a Fabergé egg. The second arresting feature of the fresco
was its colour. The genitalia seemed to be floating in space,

suspended in a sky of celestial blue. I looked at those fleshly clouds and I thought how impermanent they seemed against the big blue sky, the blue that had been there before they came into being and would be there long after they were dust. People had been made miserable, yearning for those genitals; lives had been warped or enriched by them; they had made dreams become flesh and solitudes join, but isolated that way . . .

"The perspective is pretty annihilating," I said. "I don't mean in a technical sense, lust in human terms. All the agonies we go through about those little pieces of us. They look so bizarre floating up there."

Sally looked at me with real interest. "You're the first one who's picked up on that."

"And the other thing," I said, my lip suddenly curving with laughter. "Oh, God, Sally, they are funny. Did you ever see Mr. Potato Head, that toy the kids have where they give you a plastic potato and a box full of detachable parts, so you can cobble together a funny face? Well, that's what the little ones look like to me – things you'd stick into Mr. Potato Head."

"Or Mrs. Potato Head," said Sally, grinning. "Oh, Jo, what a Philistine you are. But it is so good to be with you. Sometimes I feel as if . . ."

But she never finished. A man in a leather bomber jacket had come up to us. He was slight, fine-featured and deeply tanned. He had a leather bag the colour of maple cream fudge slung over his shoulder.

"Sally, it's transcendent," he said. His voice was soft with the lazy vowels of the American South. "But, you know, pure creation isn't enough any more. Idle art is the devil's plaything. That's the new orthodoxy. We have to put Erotobiography into a socio-political context. Be a good girl and tell me what all these dinks are saying about our social structure." He patted my hand. "You can play, too. But I get to go first. And I want to know about that wonderful pinky one at the top, second from the left."

Sally bent over and looked at the stitching on his over-the-shoulder bag. "I'll tell you that if you'll tell me where you got this. Jo, look at the needlework on this leather. Incidentally, this is Hugh Rankin-Carter; he's an art critic and an old friend."

We talked for a little while, but it was clear I was out of my league with Rankin-Carter. Besides, I was beginning to feel the effects of my Christmas Comfort, so when there was a break in the conversation, I said, "Sal, I'm going to let you two look for social context. I'm going to get something to eat."

Sally put her hand on my arm. "Don't just wander off on me, Jo. Please. At least let's make some arrangements to get together. I was going for a workout at Maggie's tomorrow. Do you want to meet me there? I'll even buy lunch."

"Sounds great," I said.

"Eleven-thirty okay with you?" she asked over her shoulder as Hugh Rankin-Carter pulled her along after him. "I'll meet you in the lobby."

A voice behind me, pleasantly husky, said, "I find it hard to believe that anyone who looks like that needs a workout."

The voice belonged to a small woman in a high-necked grey silk dress. She looked to be in her late thirties with the kind of classic good looks that grow on you: ginger hair cut boy-short, pale skin with a dusting of freckles across the nose and grey, knowing eyes. She was smiling.

I smiled back. "I think it's because she works out when she doesn't need to that she looks the way she does."

"Right," she said. "Sally Love's always been good at taking care of herself." She extended her hand. "I'm Clea

Poole. Sally and I have a gallery together – womanswork on Fourteenth Street."

"Of course," I said. "That old stone lion on your front lawn is terrific, and I love the wreath you've got around his neck for the holidays."

"Around her neck," Clea said. "It's a female lion. Anyway, sometime you should beard the lion in her den and come in and look around. We have a wonderful eco-feminist exhibition on now, Joanne – very gender affirming."

"You know my name," I said, surprised.

"Right," she said. "I know a lot of things about you. You're the other girl creaming her jeans over Izaak Levin in the lake painting."

I could feel my face grow warm. "It's a little unnerving to have your teenage lust out there for all the world to see."

"That's what Sally does – she captures the private moment."

"And makes it public?" I said.

"And makes it art," she corrected me gently. "You should be flattered."

"I guess I am," I said. "Not many people get to hang in the Art Institute of Chicago."

"Right," she said. "You're between a Georgia O'Keeffe cow skull and a Mary Cassatt mother and child."

"Great placement."

"Yes," she said seriously, "it is a great placement. Sally's the only Canadian woman artist they have."

"Another gold star for Sally."

"Right," said Clea. Then she looked at me with real interest. "I'll bet it was tough being friends with someone who got all the gold stars."

I felt myself bristling. "She didn't get them all," I said. "I've had a couple myself."

Clea Poole looked amused, and I laughed.

"Yeah," I agreed, "it was tough. I was one of those blobby ordinary little girls. Even when Sally was a beanpole of a kid, everything lit up when she walked into a room. She's always had that extra wattage."

Clea pointed across the room. Sally and Hugh Rankin-Carter were still together in front of the fresco, but they weren't alone any more. The private talk had become public. An earnest young man with a microphone was asking Sally questions, and a crowd had gathered, hushed, listening.

Clea shrugged. "As you say, extra wattage."

From across the room, a woman called Clea Poole's name. She waved, then turned to me. "I've got to get back to her. I said I wouldn't be long. But I had to meet you, Joanne. No matter how much drifting apart there was, you've always been a major player in Sally's life."

Puzzled that she knew so much about Sally and me, I watched Clea as she started to walk across the room. When she had gone a few steps, she suddenly turned.

"I'll bet Sally's tickled pink that you two are friends again," she said. I think she intended the comment to be sharp and ironic, but her tone was wistful. As she disappeared into the crush of the crowd, I thought there wasn't much doubt about the identity of the major player in Clea Poole's life.

Suddenly, I was tired of the emotional crosscurrents. I'd had enough of the art world for one evening. But there was one more drama to be played out.

The crowd in front of Erotobiography had changed. Stuart Lachlan was standing there now, and nose to nose with him was a young woman with a hand-held TV camera. Neither of them looked very happy, but the crowd watching them sure was. Stuart said something, and as the woman responded, she put down her camera and began to punch him in the chest with her forefinger. Sally, standing a little to the side, was watching the scene intently. Finally, she looked across at me. When she caught my eye, she raised two fingers to her temple in the suicide gesture I had seen her use a hundred times at school when someone was droning on too long in chapel. I smiled, and when she grinned back, I felt a rush of pleasure. As Clea Poole would say, I was tickled pink.

Despite all the Southern Comfort I'd drunk at the opening, when I crawled into bed that night, I couldn't sleep. At 2:00 a.m., wondering if Janis Joplin had had the same problem, I gave up and went downstairs. I decided on herb tea, filled the kettle and sat down at the kitchen table. The shoe box of pictures I'd hauled out that night to show my sons was still at my place. "Capezio," said the legend on the box. I remembered those shoes, soft leather dancer's shoes that had cost me a month's allowance and promised to make me graceful. The shoes had lied, and I'd pitched them out before I'd graduated from high school, but the pictures were still there.

I'd been surprised that the boys had been interested. My sons were teenagers, and knowing Sally Love wasn't exactly like knowing Darryl Strawberry before the Dodgers gave him his $20.5 million contract. But apparently being childhood friends with a woman who'd covered a wall in the Mendel Gallery with penises had a certain cachet, and after dinner that night the kids and I had had fun looking at old snapshots. There had been the usual dismissive comments about mothers in bathing suits and guys with nerd haircuts, but the pictures of Sally at thirteen had inspired reverence in my thirteen-year-old, Angus.

"Oh, she was awesome," he said, "truly awesome."

"She still is," Peter, who is eighteen, had said quietly.

In those early morning hours as I sifted idly through the pictures I realized how right the boys were. Sally had always been awesome. But the picture that stopped me wasn't one of Sally. It was one of the three of us: Sally and Nina and me. I hadn't remembered it existed. It wasn't an exceptional picture, just a faded black-and-white summer picture taken by an amateur photographer. We were in a rowboat. Sally and I were rowing, and Nina was sitting in the front. We were all smiling, waving at whoever was standing on the dock taking our picture.

"Nina and Us," it said in my handwriting on the back of the photo. And now, after thirty years of wounds and alienation and unfinished business, we were together again. It was, I thought as I went over to take the kettle off the burner, enough to make you believe in the workings of cosmic justice.

CHAPTER

3

The next morning I awoke to the smell of coffee perking and bacon frying. In the kitchen my son Peter and Johnny Mathis were singing "Santa Claus Is Coming to Town." I rolled over and looked at the clock. I still had fifteen minutes before I had to get up. So I burrowed down in the warmth of my double bed and thought about my kids and Christmas.

The holidays hadn't been an easy time for my family. Four years earlier, my husband, Ian, had died in the week between Christmas and New Year's, and the year before this one I had spent the holidays recovering from an attempt to kill me that had almost succeeded. Not exactly material for a remake of *It's a Wonderful Life*.

But we had begun a new life in a new city, and I was optimistic. My sons and I had been in the house we'd rented on Osler Street since July. In the sixties, when it had been built, houses like this one had been called split-level ranchers. It was a solid house on a well-treed lot near the university. A Milton scholar who was spending a sabbatical year in England had built it himself, and apparently he had an affection for generous spaces and sunlight. In the months since we'd moved in, I'd thanked this man I'd never met a hundred times. His house had smoothed a rocky passage for me.

There were a handful of logical reasons why the move to Saskatoon, a hundred and fifty miles north of my home in Regina, had been a good idea. My two oldest children were enrolled at the university here, and the political science department had offered me a chance to teach a senior class in the contemporary politics of our province. The fact that the appointment was for one year only was, oddly enough, a plus. No commitments, no committee work, so I had time to finish the biography of the man who had been my friend and the leader of our party. Logic. But the real explanation for our coming couldn't be calibrated on a scale of reason. The year before we moved, bad things had happened in our old house, and in my bones, I had known we had to get out for a while.

As I sat listening to the cheerful, tuneless voice of my son, I smiled. This Christmas on Osler Street was going to be a good Christmas. I rolled over and pulled the blankets close. It didn't get much better than this. But as Gracie Slick used to say, "No matter how big or how soft your bed is, you still have to get out of it." It was December twenty-second, and I had things to do.

Half an hour later, when I went down to the kitchen, showered and dressed for a run, Peter was slipping eggs out of the frying pan onto a plate, and his brother was feeding his toast crusts to our dogs.

"Perfect timing," said Peter. "Two more minutes in the pan and they would have been what Dad used to call whore's eggs, black lace around the edges and hard as a rock at the centre."

"Whenever did Dad say that?" I asked.

"At the fishing camp up in Manitoba when we'd go there

with the guys. He told me not to say it in front of you because you'd think it was crude."

"Well," I said, looking at the eggs on my plate, "he was right about that. But it's a moot point. These eggs are perfect, Peter. You do know, don't you, that I've already bought all your Christmas presents?"

Peter poured me a cup of coffee. "I want to borrow your car tonight. Christy and I are going to *The Nutcracker* and it's going to be tough for us to make a grand entrance if we drive up in the king of junkers." He sat down opposite me. "One of those presents you got me wouldn't happen to be a new car, would it?"

"Nope," I said, spearing a piece of bacon, "no new car, but you can have the Volvo as soon as I'm through with it today. In the spirit of the holiday, I'll even throw in a coupon I've got for a free car wash and wax."

"Careful, Mum, those coupons don't grow on trees. When will you be finished, anyway?"

"Let's see. First, I'm going to take the dogs down to the river bank and run off this terrific breakfast. Then I'm getting a ski rack put on the car to carry the secret skis we're all getting for Christmas for our secret ski holiday at Greenwater. Then I'm going to meet Sally Love and humiliate myself at the gym. Then probably I'll come home and collapse. You can have the car by one o'clock."

"That'll be okay. Angus wants me to take him Christmas shopping. He can go to the car wash with me and vacuum out the back seat. It's really gross. He's still got Halloween candy back there."

"A mark of maturity, being able to hold on to candy for almost two months," I said to my youngest son.

He reached over and took a piece of bacon off my plate. "Oh, you couldn't eat the stuff that's back there. Most of it's got dog hair on it."

I shuddered. "I don't think I want to know about this. Let's talk about something else. How much Christmas shopping have you got left to do?"

Angus smiled innocently. "All of it."

I moved my plate toward him. "Here, have another piece of bacon. You need it more than I do."

I rinsed my dishes and put them in the dishwasher. The dogs were by the door looking at me anxiously.

"Anyone want to go for a walk?" I asked as I did every morning. As soon as I opened the drawer to get their leashes they went crazy with pleasure. They did that every morning, too. None of us liked surprises.

The morning passed happily. It was a grey day, but the dogs didn't mind, and neither did I. Along the river, there were lots of clear spaces where the brush had kept the snow off the path. It was a good day for the dogs and me to run and feel the fresh air knife at our lungs. When I stopped to look at the South Saskatchewan curling toward Lake Winnipeg, the river's cold beauty made my breath catch in my throat.

The man at the garage got the ski racks on first crack, and when I went to pay him, he smiled and said it was a Christmas present for a new customer. As I pulled into the parking lot across from Maggie's, I was filled with seasonal optimism about the human condition. It really was the time for peace on earth and good will toward one another.

Two hours later, I knew I'd peaked too soon.

The seventies gave us earth colours and macramé and places like Maggie's: private clubs where women could work out or learn about Oriental art or sit over plates piled with sprouts and talk about sisterhood. People didn't talk about sisterhood at Maggie's any more, but the food was still good, and the exercise classes were the best in the city.

Sally was sprawled over a chair in the lobby when I came in. She was wearing boots, blue jeans, a man's shirt and an

old woollen jacket that looked vaguely military. Her long
blond hair was loosely knotted at the nape of her neck. Over
her shoulder she had slung an exquisite leather bag – the
same bag that had hung over Hugh Rankin-Carter's shoulder the night before.

I leaned forward and traced a line in the stitchery. "Did
Hugh Rankin-Carter earn a spot on the Wall of Fame?" I
asked.

Sally grinned. "Not on my wall," she said, standing up.
"He was pretty taken with Stuart, though. God, speaking of
Stu, guess what I caught him doing last night at the gallery?
Measuring his penis – the one on the wall. For comparative
purposes, I guess," she said mildly. "Listen, class doesn't
start until noon. Shall we go to the coffee shop and get in a
little goof and gossip time?"

"Absolutely," I said.

The coffee shop at Maggie's was deserted. By the cash register a cardboard Mrs. Santa held up an announcement that
the restaurant would be closing at noon for the staff
Christmas party. The manager gave us a drop-dead look when
we came in. She didn't warm to us when we refused menus
and ordered a pot of Earl Grey and a bottle of mineral water.

She was back almost immediately with our order, as if to
impress us with the importance of moving along quickly.
But Sally wasn't in a mood to be hurried. As the woman
stood behind her, Sally fished around in the new leather bag
and pulled out a bottle opener and a package of rice cakes.

"Allergies." She shrugged, looking at the manager. The
woman turned on her heel and left us alone.

"I'd forgotten about your allergies," I said, "or maybe I just
thought you'd left them behind somewhere."

"No, I'm worse than ever. The world seems to get more
dangerous every year."

I shuddered, and Sally looked at me curiously.

"No use worrying about it," she said. "I just have to be careful." She ripped the cellophane from her rice cakes. Her nails were unpolished, and her hands looked strong and capable. "Anyway, it could be worse. This doctor I saw in Santa Fe told me about a patient of his who was allergic to semen. Died on her wedding night. She started going into acute anaphylactic reaction: wheezing, gasping for air. Her husband just thought she was having this incredible orgasm, and he kept pumping away like crazy – super stud."

She held out a rice cake to me. "Here, eat. These things are guaranteed to make you live forever."

"Or make it seem like forever," I said, grimly. "God, poor woman . . . poor man. How did they figure out what happened?"

"Apparently she had a history of allergies, and Jo, when the ambulance came, the husband was sitting stark naked on the side of the bed with his weapon still smoking."

For a beat, we just looked at each other and then we both burst out laughing.

"Oh, Sal," I said, "it's so good to be together again. Now that we're in the same city, maybe we can make up for all the years we lost."

Sally reached across and patted my hand. "We'll make up for them, Jo, but not in Saskatoon. I'm not going to stick around here too much longer."

I was surprised at the sense of loss I felt, but I tried to sound philosophical. "Considering the welcome you got at the gallery last night, I can't say that I blame you."

Sally took a long sip of her mineral water. "Oddly enough I'd decided to leave before all this happened. When I approached Stu about doing the Erotobiography, I told him I wanted it to be a kind of parting gift for the city. You know I've lived here on and off for twenty-five years."

"At the moment, I don't think this city deserves a parting gift," I said.

"I've done some good work here. You know, Jo, it's going to be tough leaving. I've owned that studio on the river bank since I was twenty. Anyway, it's time. That last year I was with Stu, I made such bad art. Everything just turned grey: me, my work, the world. I wish I could buy back everything I did that year and burn it. It's so choked. You can't breathe when you look at it." She shook her head in disgust.

"I never should have married him. Stu's a nice guy and all, but he's such a stiff. I must have been crazy."

"You have Taylor," I said.

Her face brightened. "Yes, I have Taylor, and since I left Stu and that house, I'm making some decent art again. The pieces seem to be falling into place. Did you ever see that gallery I own on Fourteenth Street?"

"All the time. In fact, just last night I was telling Clea Poole how much I admire the lady lion with the Christmas wreath you've got out front."

Sally raised an eyebrow. "The lion's about the only thing worth admiring at womanswork now. The place is an embarrassment – all that seventies clitoral epiphany stuff. Clea's really lost her judgement. Anyway, there'll be something new there soon. There's a new owner."

"A new owner?" I repeated.

"Yeah, a surgeon. I got a call while I was in Santa Fe from the real estate people. They were desperate to track me down. This woman I've sold it to wants the gallery as a Christmas present for her husband. Cash. No dickering. I stopped off to sign the papers on my way in from the airport last night."

"What about Clea?" I asked. "Doesn't she have to agree to the sale?"

Sally looked puzzled for a minute. "Why? She just manages the place. I'm the owner. Anyway, it'll be good for Clea – get her out of her warm little cocoon and give her a chance to see what's happening in the big bad art world. Don't look at me like that, Jo. I've been carrying Clea Poole for twenty years. If the good doctor hadn't come along, I probably would have carried her for another twenty. But this offer came out of nowhere. It really seemed like a sign that the time had come to make some changes."

"A providential nudge?" I asked.

Sally grinned. "Yeah, that's it – a providential nudge."

"Well," I said, "Robertson Davies says it's spiritual suicide to ignore these pushes from fate."

"Sounds good to me," Sally said. "I wish Robertson Davies, whoever he is, would tell Clea I sold the gallery. When she hears about womanswork, I'd rather he was in the line of fire than me." She stood up and stretched lazily. "But that's this afternoon's problem. Right now, let's get into the gym and do it, Jo. You never know when you're going to meet the man with the smoking gun."

When Maggie's had opened, much had been made of the fact that the woman who designed the building had muted the light in the changing rooms "to forgive what we perceive as the imperfections of our bodies." As I inched my leotard on, I thought how humane that architect had been. And then I looked at Sally Love.

Naked, forty-five years old, Sally's body still didn't need forgiving. She was tanned golden everywhere, perfect everywhere. No stretch marks. No sags. No cellulite. Perfect. She pulled up her body suit and turned to me.

"Ready?" she asked.

"As I'll ever be," I said.

"So," she said, "let's get in there and shuffle it around a bit."

As soon as I walked into the gym, I knew we'd be doing more than shuffling it around. The room was filled with women whose bodies were like Sally's: sleek, hard-muscled, shining in spandex. And they all seemed younger than either of us by at least a decade.

The instructor, a tiny redhead in peppermint-striped cotton, slid a tape into her ghetto blaster and said, "This is a super-fit class, but if you can't cut it, all I ask is that you women keep moving. By the way, my name is Charlene."

I leaned across to Sally and whispered, "Did you ever notice how many aerobics instructors are named Charlene? I think it's kind of menacing."

Sally grinned and started to say something, but then the music soared and we were away.

By the time we came to the last song, an aerobic "Joy to the World," I was slick with sweat and exhausted, but Sally was glowing. On the wall of the gym were signs: "If It's the Last Dance, Dance Backwards," "You Can't Turn Back the Clock, But You Can Rewind It." As I watched Sally high kicking to the beat of the music, her blond hair tied back in a ponytail and her face set in concentration, I thought that she didn't need any inspirational signs. All on her own, she'd discovered a way to make time stand still.

When we finished our floor exercises, Sally stayed behind to do some relaxation technique she'd picked up in Santa Fe. That's how it happened that I was the first one to see Clea Poole.

She was sitting on a bench in the changing room, with her back ramrod straight and her hands folded in her lap. She was wearing a handsome grey wool coat. All around her, young women were peeling off brightly coloured body suits, laughing, gossiping; Clea in her cloth coat was set apart, a moth among the butterflies.

When I went over and said hello to her, she looked at me with dead uncomprehending eyes.

"Are you all right?" I asked.

She didn't answer.

I knelt beside her and touched her hand. "I'm Joanne Kilbourn. Remember? Sally's friend."

She pulled her hand from mine. "I remember," she said thickly. "Where's Sally?"

"She'll be along soon," I said. I waited, but Clea didn't seem to have anything to say, so I opened my locker, picked up my towel and went off to shower. When I came back, Clea was still there, sitting, waiting. She had the look of someone who would wait forever.

Sally had apparently gone straight to the showers. When she finally came in, her hair was dark with water and she had a blue towel wrapped sarong-like around her. Clea Poole jumped up and ran over to her. It seemed to take Sally a moment to focus on the situation.

"Clea, what are you doing here?"

Clea Poole's voice was tight with anger. "Where else would I be? This morning a total stranger walked into womanswork – our gallery, Sally, the one we built up together – and she told me she'd be bringing her husband around Christmas Eve to see his present." Her composure was breaking. "This person had a big red satin ribbon with her and she asked me if as a favour I'd mind tying it across the door when I closed up Christmas Eve. Sally, do you hear me? She wanted me to tie a ribbon on the front door of womanswork because you sold it to her. You sold it without telling me, Sally. Our gallery is a fucking gift for a fucking husband."

"Clea, I didn't want it to be like this. I'm sorry, truly I am, but things just happened too fast."

Clea Poole had begun to cry. As the tears spilled onto her cheeks, she wiped at them with the sleeve of her coat.

"Remember our dream about a gallery where women from all over the west could come? What am I going to do if I don't have . . ." The end of her sentence dissolved in a sob.

Sally's voice sounded tired and sad. "You're going to do what everyone else in the world does. You're going to cope. Look, Clea, it really is time for a change of direction. Nobody does all that vaginal stuff any more."

"Including you?" sobbed Clea.

"Oh, Mouse." Sally reached out to comfort Clea. The blue towel that had been wrapped around her body fell to the floor. Confronted with Sally's nakedness, Clea Poole's face grew soft. Then she bent down, picked up the blue towel and draped it over Sally's shoulders.

"I don't want you to be cold," she said simply.

It was a terrible and intimate moment. For a split second the two women stood connected but apart, then Sally enclosed Clea in her arms.

It was a ludicrous coupling: the small woman in the drab wool coat clung ferociously to Sally's naked body, as if somehow by an act of will she could penetrate that amazing Amazon beauty.

The changing room was silent except for Clea Poole's muffled sobs and Sally's voice, gentle and weary. "There, there, Mouse. It'll be all right. You'll see. It's just been a shock for you. Let me get dressed, and we'll find some place to have a quiet drink and we can talk." Her eyes swept the changing room, so carefully designed to forgive human imperfection. The air was heavy with the tension that comes after a public scene. On the pastel benches, women were hooking bras, pulling on stockings, zipping boots – trying not to be there.

Sally smiled ruefully across at me. "Thanks for coming, Jo. Let's not wait so long for the next time."

As I drove home through the snowy city streets, I couldn't shake the image of Clea Poole clinging to Sally. It

was a disturbing picture. Then as I turned from Spadina
Crescent onto the University Bridge my car hit an ice patch
and, for a heart-stopping ten seconds, it spun lazily toward
the oncoming traffic, until I gained control again. By the
time I pulled into the driveway in front of my house I could
feel the pins-and-needles pricks of anxiety on my skin, and I
was beginning to think that maybe Sally was right. Maybe
the world did get more dangerous every year.

The fear started to melt the moment I walked in the front
door. The tree lights were plugged in, there was Christmas
music on the radio, and my daughter, Mieka, was sitting at
the dining-room table behind piles of boxes and wrapping
paper and ribbons. She was wearing a green knit sweater
with a bright pattern of elves and Santas, and her dark blond
hair was tied back with a red ribbon. She was twenty years
old and had been living with her boyfriend, Greg, in a place
of their own for a year and a half, but in that moment she
looked twelve, and I felt a surge of happiness that she was
home and it was Christmas.

"Help," she said, "I'm three days behind in my everything."

I sat down beside her and picked up a box. "For whom?
From whom?" I asked.

"For you. From me. No peeking. Now choose some nice
motherly paper. Something sedate." She looked at me. "Are
you okay? You look a little wiped out."

"I had a rather unsettling morning," I said, and I told her
about the scene in the changing room.

When I finished, Mieka ran the edge of the scissors along
a length of silver ribbon. It curled professionally and she
looked thoughtful. "It sounds as if Clea/Mouse was talking
about more than art. Is Sally a lesbian?"

"I don't think so . . . I think she's just someone who likes
sex with an interesting partner."

"Or partners," Mieka said. She picked up a piece of red

tissue and began to wrap some baseball cards for Angus. "I went over to the Mendel this morning."

"Sally's show is turning us into a city of art lovers," I said. "So what did you think?"

"Well, the crazies were out in force. A woman stopped me on my way in from the parking lot and asked me if I was a virgin. She was pushing her dog around in a shopping cart."

"Poor dog," I said. "And poor you. Was the show worth the trip through the parking lot?"

Mieka looked up, and her eyes were shining. "Oh, Mum, it was wonderful. That fresco is the most amazing art I've ever seen. But the thing that's really dynamite is the painting of you and Sally. Of course, I had to tell everyone that was my mother up there."

"Did that impress them?"

"Stopped them dead in their tracks." Then she looked thoughtful. "The guide at the gallery told me Sally moved heaven and earth to get that painting on loan. He said that she was absolutely insistent that the lake picture be part of the exhibition so the other girl in the painting could see it." Mieka turned to me. "Did you know about it before last night?"

"No, it was a surprise. I think Sally wanted to see my reaction."

"She really must care a lot about you to go to all that trouble."

"You know," I said, "I think she does."

Mieka picked up a marker and drew paw prints on the red tissue wrapping Angus's baseball cards. She held the package up for my approval.

"Nice," I said. "The dogs are lucky to have you to wrap for them."

She smiled and handed me a box. "And I'm lucky to have you to wrap for me. It all comes around."

"Yeah," I said, "I guess it does."

For a few minutes we worked along in silence, listening to the radio. It was Mieka who spoke first.

"Mum, what happened with you and Sally? You were like sisters when you were little. You told me that yourself. But on the way back from the Mendel today, it hit me that, until you and the boys moved up here last summer, the only time I'd seen Sally was at Daddy's funeral. I remember that because afterwards, back at our house, I went upstairs and Sally and Nina were in my room fighting."

"I'd forgotten that Sally came to your dad's funeral," I said. "Of course, that day was pretty much a blur for me, I certainly don't remember a fight between Nina and Sally. What was it about?"

"I don't know," Mieka said. "It didn't matter to me. The reason I'd come upstairs in the first place was because I was starting to lose it. But I do remember hearing Nina tell Sally she should leave because all she ever did was hurt you."

"What did Sally say?"

"Nothing. I think she just left."

I picked up an Eaton's box. "What kind of paper for this one?"

"That's a pair of driving gloves for Pete – to go with the new car you're not getting him. Something manly."

I held up some shiny paper covered in toy soldiers. "Enough testosterone in this one?"

She grinned and started making a bow. "Mum, I didn't mean to pry before, when I asked you about Sally. You don't have to talk about it if you don't want to."

"Except," I said, "I think I do want to talk about it. Seeing that lake picture last night has brought back a lot of memories." I reached over and touched her hand. "Mieka, let's take a break and get some tea. I could use a daughter right now."

We sat at the table in front of the glass doors that opened onto the deck from the kitchen. The backyard was brilliant with sunshine, and at the bird feeder, sparrows were pecking through the new snow at the last of the sunflower seeds and suet I'd put out that morning.

"I don't know where to begin," I said. "Maybe when Sally's father died. That's when everything went wrong."

"September, 1958," Mieka said quietly. "The date was in the catalogue I picked up at Sally's show this morning. They had a nice little tribute to him."

"Right," I said, "except they glossed over a few things, like the way he died. Mieka, Des didn't just die. He committed suicide, and he . . . he tried to take Nina and Sally with him."

I could hear Mieka's sharp intake of breath. "He tried to kill his own wife and child?" The elves and Santas on her sweater were rising and falling rapidly. A man who could murder his family was a long way from Mieka's safe and sunny world. "He must have been a monster," she said finally.

"No," I said, "he wasn't a monster. In fact, until he got sick, he was one of the most terrific people I ever knew. I used to love just being in the same room with him. Living was so much fun for him. He was so interested in everything; he could be as passionate about the right way to cook corn on the cob as he was about the way Sally built her sand castles or the way he made art.

"Then he had this massive stroke and everything changed. He used to love to swim. When I close my eyes, I can still see him running down the hill from the cottage and diving off the end of the dock into the lake. He never hesitated. Suddenly he couldn't even walk without help. He'd been a great storyteller, and of course that was gone, too. After the stroke it was painful to watch him try to form a word. He was dependent on Nina and Sally for everything. He couldn't even feed himself properly. And, of course, worst of all, he couldn't paint. For a man who had lived every day as intensely as Des had, I guess the future just looked . . ."

"Unacceptable?" asked Mieka in a high, strained voice. "So unacceptable that he decided to kill two innocent people?"

"But he didn't kill them, Miek. My father saved Nina when he gave her the ipecac, and Sally had saved her own life by throwing up. They lived. Although for a while, I don't think they much wanted to. You know, for a time, I didn't want to. People talk about their world being turned upside-down. That was how it felt for me. As if suddenly everything had come loose from its moorings.

"That was the worst September. It rained and rained, and I was so alone and so scared. My father had to deal with everything: the police, the funeral, Nina and Sally at the hospital, his own patients. I never saw him. I remember when he came up to my room to get me for the funeral, there was a split second when I didn't recognize him. It wasn't so much that he'd aged as that life seemed to have seeped out of him. He didn't have his heart attack until that next August, but I think your grandfather started to die when Desmond Love died."

"And my grandmother was drinking," Mieka said, a statement not a question.

"Yeah, she was drinking a lot that summer, and the 'tragedy at the lake,' as the papers called it, really propelled her into the major leagues. I felt as if I didn't have anybody. Nina had always been there before, but she was in the hospital for weeks after Des died."

Mieka looked puzzled. "I thought you said she was okay."

"Physically she was, but she didn't seem to recover the way she was supposed to. I kept asking my father when I could see her and he kept saying soon, she just needed rest. I guess I believed him because I wanted to. Then one night,

I overheard my parents fighting. Your grandmother had never liked Nina and she was screaming that Nina was faking her grief, playing on my father's sympathy and my gullibility to keep us from seeing how things really had been at the lake. For once, my father didn't just let her rant. He told her that Nina had suffered a complete breakdown and he told her – oh, God, Mieka, it's been thirty years but I still feel sick when I think of this – my father said that morning when he'd gone by Nina's room on his rounds, she'd been crouched naked in the corner, tearing at her own flesh with her fingernails – like an animal in a trap, that's the phrase he used."

Across from me, Mieka winced. "It's hard to imagine. Nina's always so controlled."

"I know. Anyway, after that they were careful not to leave her alone, but I guess they didn't think Sally was in any danger. I don't know how else it could have happened, because one day Sally just walked out of the hospital. They found her with Izaak Levin."

"The man in the picture with you and Sally," Mieka said. "His name was in the show catalogue, too."

"He used to come to the cottage for a few weeks every summer. I was about to say he was a friend of Des Love's, but that wasn't the connection. Izaak was Nina's friend first. In fact, he was the one who introduced Nina to Des Love. Nina's an American, you know, from New York, and Izaak knew her there. Anyway, once Sally got to Izaak's place, she refused to leave. When my father tried to get her to come home to our house, she became hysterical. She said she was never going back to the house on Russell Hill Road. She was going to leave the city and never come back. And, of course, that's exactly what she did."

Mieka looked at me. "Sally was what? Thirteen? Why would any mother let a thirteen-year-old child move in with someone else?"

"For one thing the arrangement Nina and Izaak worked out was supposed to be temporary – just until Nina got better. There was a school of the arts for gifted children in New York, and they enrolled Sally there. She was supposed to come back at Christmas."

"Except she didn't come back at Christmas," Mieka said.

"She never came back," I said. "She never phoned. She never wrote. She just cut us all off as if we'd never existed. I must have written her a hundred letters that first year, but I never heard a word from her. Nobody did, not even Nina. She told me that Izaak kept her informed about Sally's progress, but she never heard a word from her own daughter."

Mieka looked puzzled. "Why would Nina let the situation go on? Can you imagine letting me just walk out of your life when I was thirteen?"

I smiled at her. "I can't imagine letting you walk out of my life ever. But that's us. Nina and Sally always had difficulties. When I think about it now, a lot of it was Des. He loved Sally so much and, of course, he was her teacher as well as her father. I think sometimes Nina must have felt excluded."

"All the same, Sally was Nina's daughter," Mieka said.

"It was a bad time for everybody," I said. "And in bad times, people don't always think clearly. It must have been hard for Nina to know what was best for Sally, because no one could really understand why she'd turned against us. My dad's explanation was that Sally was so filled with rage at Des for leaving her that her feelings for everyone and every place connected with him were tainted."

Mieka looked thoughtful. "That makes sense to me. Don't forget, Mum, she was only a kid. Thirteen – the same age as Angus is now. That's pretty young to think things through."

"Oh, Mieka, I know. But then the next year, when your grandfather died, Sally didn't even come to the funeral. Izaak

Levin came, but he said Sally refused to come to Toronto. He had to leave her with his sister in New York. For a long time I found it hard to forgive her for that. My dad would have done anything for Sally, and she must have known how much I needed her. If I hadn't had Nina, I don't know if I could have made it."

Mieka's face was sad, "Did you ever hear Sally's side of the story?"

"No, I never did. When sally and I finally got together again last summer, we were both pretty careful not to bring up the past. But I'm beginning to wonder now if that wasn't a mistake. There's a part of me that's still mad at her, you know. And that's not fair to either of us."

"Talk to her," Mieka said simply.

I stood up. "Well, doctor, if the therapy session's over, we'd better get back to our wrapping. But come here and let me give you a hug first – for being so smart. I'll throw in dinner, too, if you want. I think I've got a pan of lasagna in the freezer."

She stood up and stretched. "Sounds good. I'll consider it a professional fee. And, Mum, don't forget to hear Sally's side of things. I think after all this time, it may finally be her turn."

CHAPTER

4

On the morning before Christmas I was pouring myself a second cup of coffee and thinking about making French toast for breakfast when the phone rang. Until the night of Sally's opening, I hadn't heard that low, gravelly voice for thirty years, but I knew who it was immediately. You don't forget anything about a man you dreamed about through the heat-shimmering days and moonlit nights of your sixteenth summer.

Izaak Levin's invitation had the polish that only practice brings. "Joanne, forgive the early morning call please, but in all the excitement the other night I didn't have a chance to make an arrangement to see you again. I know this is Christmas Eve, and I'm sure you have plans, but I thought perhaps between Christmas and New Year's we could have dinner together and share our remembrance of things past."

"That sounds wonderful," I said, "but my kids and I are going to Greenwater to ski that week. Can I have a rain check?"

"Of course," he said. "I'll call early in the new year. I won't let you slip away again . . ."

As I hung up, I could feel my face flush. There was a mirror on the wall above the phone, and I gave myself a hard, critical look. My hair was the same ashy blond it had always been, but now it took more than lemon juice and sunshine to keep it that way. There were fine lines in the skin around my eyes, and my face was fuller than it had been when I was young, but, on the whole, I was comfortable enough with what I saw. "Not Sally Love, but not bad," I said to my reflection. "Izaak Levin would be a fool to pass you up this time." When the phone rang again, I was still smiling.

The smile didn't last long. Sally was on the line, sounding edgy but in control.

"Jo, somebody just called to tell me there was a fire last night at womanswork. I should go down and see how bad the damage is. Would you come with me?" There was silence for a moment and when she spoke again, her voice had lost its authority. "I really could use some company, Jo. Can you meet me there in half an hour?"

"I'll be there," I said.

I went upstairs, dressed in a heavy wool sweater and jeans, woke Peter to tell him I'd be back before lunch, started out the door, then came back and made Peter come downstairs. "In case of a fire," I said, vulnerable again.

When I backed the car out of the garage, it was snowing, theatrical lacy flakes that drifted steadily through the December air and made the city look like a scene from an old Andy Williams Christmas special. It was a little after eight-thirty, and the traffic was light as I drove across the bridge toward the centre of the city.

Fourteenth Street was a pretty street of pre-war houses, restored and fitted out as offices for architects and fast-track law firms; womanswork was in the middle of the block. What I remembered was a two-storey grey clapboard building, simple and elegant. It wasn't elegant any more, but as I looked through the smoky, snowy haze at what had once been Sally's gallery, I was struck by the fact that even the ruins of the building had a certain perverse beauty. Water from the fire hoses had frozen in fantastic patterns against the charred skeleton, and snow had begun to layer itself on the burned wood. When I squinted against the smoke, the gallery looked like a Christmas gingerbread house.

It didn't take long to spot Sally. She was standing in what had once been the front door to the gallery talking to a firefighter. She was wearing the Navajo blanket coat she'd worn the night of the opening, and its purple, turquoise, orange and blue were a splash of brilliance in the grey. She came over as soon as she saw me.

"Arson," she said. "At least that's what they think. I'm supposed to come up with a list of my enemies. Maybe I should just give them the Saskatoon phone book and a pin." She sounded as strong and defiant as ever, but when she raked her hand through her hair, I noticed her fingers were trembling. Up close, her face looked drawn despite its tan. There was a smudge of soot under her cheekbone. I reached out and rubbed it with my mitt.

She smiled. "Oh, God, Jo, I feel awful. I need a five-mile run or a stiff drink."

I looked at my watch. "It's nine o'clock straight up. I think the sun must be over the yardarm somewhere. Come on, let's get out of here."

As we started toward our cars, I heard a shout behind us. It was the young firefighter Sally had been talking to. He ran up and handed something to her.

"I thought maybe this might have some sentimental meaning for you," he said.

Suddenly the wind picked up, and as the three of us stood looking down at what he had brought, the snow swirled around us. It was a porcelain doll, obviously old. Not much was left of her clothes, and her hair had been burned so that only a scorched frizz shot out around her face. But her face was intact, and her eyes, as fiercely blue as Sally's own, looked up defiantly out of the sooty porcelain.

Sally slid the doll through the opening between the top buttons of her coat so that it rested against her chest, then she leaned over and kissed the firefighter on the cheek.

"Thanks," she said, and she started to walk across the lawn toward the street. I looked at the young man standing in the snow, transfixed. Sally was old enough to be his mother, but the look on his face wasn't the kind of look a man has after his mother kisses him.

"Dream on," I said under my breath, and then I put my hands in my pockets and ran through the snow to catch up with Sally.

She wanted to go back to her studio on the river bank. I said I'd follow her. The streets were clogged with snow and last-minute shoppers, so it was after nine-thirty when I pulled up behind Sally in front of her place on Saskatchewan Crescent.

She called it a studio, but really it was a one-storey bungalow on a fashionable street of pricey older houses. Years before, Sally had torn down walls and opened the house up with windows and a skylight so that her work area would look out on the river.

When we opened the front door, the house was cold and the air smelled of paint and turpentine and being closed up. There was a tarp thrown down in the centre of the room, and it was covered with containers of paint: tins, buckets, plastic ice-cream pails, jam jars. There were canvases stacked against a wall and a trestle table with brushes and boxes of pencils and rags and lengths of wood and steel that looked like rulers but were unmarked. In the corner farthest from the window were a hot plate, a couple of open suitcases and a sleeping bag.

"*La vie bohème,*" I said.

Sally looked around as if she were seeing the room for the first time. "I guess it is a little depressing," she said, "but my living here is just temporary. Although," she said gloomily, "with this fire, I'm probably going to be stuck here till fucking forever. You know, Jo, I don't even know if womanswork was still mine last night. There was a possession date on the papers I signed, but who pays attention to stuff like that?"

"Well," I said, "I'll guarantee there's a surgeon in town who's paying a lot of attention to stuff like that at this very minute. A burned-out building isn't much of a Christmas present. Anyway, I think the first order of business is to call your lawyer and your insurance agent."

The phone was in the corner by the sleeping bag. Sally dropped to her knees and swept aside a pile of clothes that covered her answering machine.

"Jo, look at this. I was working last night and I always just turn off the phone and leave the machine on. I plugged the phone back in when I went to bed but I didn't check my messages." Over the red light signalling that there had been a call was a little window with digital numbers recording the number of messages received. The number in the window was sixty-two.

"It must be a mistake," I said.

Sally hit the play button. "Let's see," she said.

A computerized voice announced the date and time of the first message: December 23, 9:05 p.m. Then Stuart Lachlan's voice, tight and strained, was telling Sally that Christmas dinner would be served at two o'clock, but if she wanted to come and see Taylor's presents, she was welcome at one-thirty.

"You're a wild man, Stu," said Sally, and she pushed herself up off the sleeping bag and walked across the room to the table where she'd thrown her coat. She picked up the porcelain doll and started checking solvents on her work-table. The computer voice announced call number two at 9:30 P.M. With a start, I recognized Izaak Levin's voice, but there was none of that easy charm I'd heard an hour before. He was telling Sally he had to talk to her immediately. His voice sounded urgent. Five minutes later, when he called back with the same message, he sounded menacing. The fourth call came at 10:03. It was Clea Poole; her voice was husky, heavy with emotion, again apologizing – she tried to laugh at that word – for the scene at Maggie's. But she immediately began to replay the scene, and she was cut off in mid-sentence when the time for her message ran out. She called again, within seconds, picking up where she had left off. Throughout the night, her litany of betrayal and longing had continued. In all, there were fifty-nine calls from Clea. Sometimes the interval between calls was half an hour; sometimes there were three or four calls in a row. At the end, her voice, dead from pain and exhaustion, was as void of emotion as the mechanical computer voice that announced the time of her calls.

All the while Clea talked, Sally worked on the doll, cleaning its face and body, dabbing at its burned frizz of hair with some kind of cream and then taking a scarf that she had obviously brought back from Santa Fe and cutting it into a sarong and turban. When the machine clicked, signalling there were no more messages, Sally turned toward me and held up the porcelain doll. With her frizz of hair shining from the cream and her Carmen Miranda outfit, she looked sensational.

"What do you think?" Sally asked.

"I think you saved the doll. Saving Clea Poole is going to be harder. Sally, she needs help, and so do you. I think you should take that tape to the police."

Sally shook her head impatiently. "I can't do it, Jo."

"For God's sake, why not? I wouldn't be surprised if Clea set the fire herself. She's clearly over the edge."

"Who pushed her?" asked Sally. "Damn, I don't even know what made me sell womanswork. I don't need the money. It was just some symbolic thing – good-bye to all that. Case closed. Now Clea's frying her brain about it."

She reached over and switched on the radio. The Christmas weather forecast was snow and more snow. Sally listened for a moment, then she said quietly, "Jo, you can't push somebody over the side of a cliff and then be surprised when they fall. I won't take the tape to the cops. It's not that I don't think you're right about Clea. Burning down a building she loved is just the kind of thing she'd do. She's big on symbolism. You know she used to have the most beautiful hair. It was a coppery red colour and long. She hadn't cut it since she was a kid. Anyway, when I married Stu, Clea had a kind of breakdown, and she hacked off her hair and mailed it to us at the house."

"Oh, Sally, how awful. Poor Clea. I can't imagine that kind of mourning. It can't have been much fun for you and Stu, either."

Sally shook her head. "No, it wasn't. And there were phone calls then, too. Hundreds of them. Just like these. Stu was going to go to the police, but I told him not to. I took Clea to the desert with me for a couple of weeks. When we came back, she was okay again.

"Anyway, the buildings of Saskatoon are safe. Clea's a one-trick pony, and she's done her trick. I'm not going to turn her in to the police. But I'm not going to stay here and dry her tears, either. As soon as the holidays are over, I'm going to take my daughter and go someplace hot where nobody knows me."

I was astounded.

"Take Taylor? Where did that come from? I thought you and Stu had agreed to leave Taylor with him. At least that's what Nina told me."

"That was the arrangement before Nina came into the picture. Don't look at me like that, Jo. Let's just say I've changed my mind. I want to show you something." She took a framed drawing off the wall by the trestle table and handed it to me.

It was a picture drawn on paper with felt pens. In it a row of hula dancers with spiky eyelashes and corkscrew shoulder-length curls bumped grass skirts against one another. It was indisputably a child's picture, but even I could see evidence of real skill and something that went beyond skill.

When I looked up, Sally was still focused on the drawing. Her face was soft with love and pride. "Look at that, Jo. It's exciting all over. There's something interesting going on everywhere on that paper. You'll have to take my word for it. It's an exceptional picture for a child of four. If it weren't, if all her pictures weren't so good, I'd tell Nina to take a hike and I'd leave Taylor with Stu."

Mother love. I didn't know what to say, and so I said nothing. My silence spurred her into uncharacteristic self-justification.

"It would be immoral to leave her in that house, Jo. I know I can't expect you to understand, but if Taylor is going to make art, she can't have someone standing around telling her what it means all the time. You know what Stu used to do? He'd come over here when I was working and give me all these insights about my work and then sit back and wait for praise – like a dog bringing me a dead bird." Her voice dropped into a deadly imitation of Stuart Lachlan's. "'You see, don't you, Sally, that your art invites judgements that are sexually dimorphic: women judge its complex inter-relationships; men look to its statement.'"

In spite of myself, I laughed. "God, you and Nina, you're both so good at mimicking. I was always afraid you did imitations of me behind my back."

Sally smiled. "I'd never mock you, Jo, and Nina thinks you walk on water. Of course, she'd never make fun of her Stuart, either. She's right. He's a good person. It's just – he's dangerous to be around when you're working. He'd wall Taylor in with words, Jo, and the art she made would get more airless and miserly till he choked her off altogether."

"Have you told him?" I asked.

"I thought I'd tell him tomorrow."

"On Christmas Day! Come on, Sally."

"Okay, Jo, you win. But soon. I don't like putting things off. Now come on, get out of here. I'm all right now, and it's the day before the big event – you must have a million things to do. Here," she said, and she handed me the porcelain doll, "souvenir of your morning."

I took the doll, put on my coat and boots and walked to the door. When I opened it, the winter light hit Sally full in the face. She looked tired and somehow forlorn.

Stuart Lachlan didn't know that his estranged wife planned to take their daughter. If he had, I would have suspected him of staging the paean to family life that my kids and I walked into that Christmas Eve. On the front lawn of the Lachlan house on Spadina Crescent, there were three snow people: a father, a mother and a little snow girl. They all had pink scarves, and the snow lady had a pink hat and purse; the snow girl was holding up a sign: "Merry Christmas from Taylor."

Taylor herself opened the door to us. She was dressed like a child in a Christmas catalogue, all velvet and lace. Her hair, which was blond and thick, like Sally's, had been smoothed into a sleek French braid. Taylor's hair may have

been like her mother's, but her face, fine-boned, dark-eyed
and grave, was Stuart Lachlan's. She thanked us for the gifts
we had brought, placed them carefully on a sea chest that
was covered with a piece of Christmas needlepoint and disappeared down the hall.

"I'll bet you a vat of bath oil that she's forgotten all about
us," said Mieka.

"No, that was your trick," I said. "All those kids in snow-
suits, melting in the front hall when you went upstairs for a
pee and forgot about them. Taylor seems to have better long-
term memory than you had."

"A tuna fish sandwich has better long-term memory than
Mieka has," said Peter as he hung up his coat and walked
into the living room.

Angus followed him, looking around. "Deadly," he said,
and he was right. Royal Doulton Santas gleamed, expensive
and untouchable, behind the glass of a curio case; teak
camels, big as rocking horses, strolled behind intricately
carved wise men carrying gold, frankincense and myrrh to
the baby king. On the mantel above the fireplace, real holly
filled pink Depression-ware pitchers, and antique wooden
blocks spelled out the names of the people in that household
for Santa: Taylor, Daddy, Nina, and then, a little apart, Sally.

Mieka and I took off our things and followed the boys into
the living room.

"You know," I said, "every year I promise myself we're
going to have a living room that looks like this for Christmas,
and every year I end up hauling out the same old decorations.
The only thing I ever seem to change is the poinsettias."

"I like the way our living room looks," said Peter, "but if
you want something different, one of the guys in my biology
lab showed me a battery-operated Santa Claus he got at the
Passion Pit. Mum, you should see the stuff that Santa can
do, and just with four double-A batteries."

I was just about to ask for details when I heard Stuart Lachlan's voice behind me.

"Oh, good, you've made yourselves at home." He was standing in the living-room doorway. Beside him, her hand gripping his, Taylor smiled tentatively. Stu came in and kissed my cheek.

"Sorry we weren't here to greet you, but we had a little problem in the kitchen. Nina's taking care of it."

"Then," I said, smiling back at him, "it's taken care of. There's never been a problem yet that Nina couldn't vanquish."

As if on cue, Nina appeared in the doorway, flushed and laughing. "Jo has always been my one-girl fan club."

"No longer a girl," I said, "but still a fan. Nina, you look beautiful." And she did, although it was a risky look. Her hair was smoothed into a French braid, not as long as Taylor's, but I could see the intent had been to suggest relationship, and Nina's dress was the same dusky rose as her granddaughter's. It was a stunning outfit. The dress itself was very plain, high-necked and long-sleeved, but over the dress, she had a white organdy apron, full in the skirt, fitted in the bodice and gently flaring over each shoulder. Stunning, but a bit self-consciously domestic.

As she had been all my life, Nina was quick to read my expression. "I know, Jo, the apron is a tad too lady-of-the-manor, but an hour ago the roof of Taylor's gingerbread house slid to the floor and smashed, so I just made a replacement."

Not in that outfit, I thought, but it was such an innocent subterfuge, and Nina looked so happy, I couldn't help smiling. "It's a beautiful dress, Ni, and I notice it matches your granddaughter's. Pink must be the colour of choice on Spadina Crescent this Christmas."

"It's Taylor's favourite," said her grandmother simply.

"Now, Stuart, why don't you get us drinks." She touched the little girl's shoulder. "And Taylor and I will get our special cookies."

Stuart came back with a tray full of soft drinks for the children and a bottle of Courvoisier for the adults. When Angus saw the soft drinks, he was jubilant.

"Great," he exclaimed. "None of that crappy eggnog. Everywhere you go people give you that stuff, and it's so gross."

When Nina appeared in the doorway with a cut-glass bowl of eggnog, Peter turned to his brother. "Way to go, Angus," he said.

"I can dress him up, but I can't take him anywhere," I said, laughing. Taylor came in, carefully balancing a plate of cookies.

"Why?" she asked, and in the set of her mouth I could see the girl who had told a classmate to lay off Sally because *his* mother had a mustache. "Why can't you take him anywhere?"

"Because he always acts silly," I said. "Those cookies are beautiful, Taylor. How did you make the ones with the little stars cut out on top?"

Gravely and in great detail Taylor gave me the recipe, then she told me how she and her grandmother had made the candy-cane cookies, twisting pink and white together, and the gingerbread Santas with the red sugar hats and the beards white with icing. As she explained, her dark eyes never left my face, just as Stuart's eyes never left your face when he was trying to make you understand something.

"These cookies really take me back," I said to Nina, "especially the jam-jams with the little stars. You must have spent a hundred hours making those with me when I was little."

"You always dropped the cookie dough on the floor at least four times," said Nina. "All those dirty little cookies."

"But always miraculously perfect when they came out of the oven. How did you do that Nina, smoke and mirrors?"

"No," she said, laughing, "more domestic than that. I always had an extra batch of dough in the refrigerator. I still do. Sometimes grown-ups have to intervene, you know, for everybody's good." She turned her perfect heart-shaped face to me and smiled conspiratorially. "While we're being nostalgic, come upstairs with me and let me show you what I'm giving Taylor for Christmas."

When we came to the guest room that Nina was using during her visit, I was surprised to see her take down a key from the molding over the door.

"A bit Gothic novel, I know," she said, "but I'm a believer in Christmas secrets. Now you close your eyes, too. I want to see your face when you see Taylor's present." She led me into the room. "All right, Jo, you can look now."

When I opened my eyes, I was back forty years in the brick house Sally and Nina and Desmond Love had lived in on Russell Hill Road in Toronto. On Nina's night table, faces carefully painted into expressions of gentility, were those emblems of nineteenth-century womanhood, Meg, Jo, Amy, Beth, and Marmee from Louisa May Alcott's *Little Women*. An American dollmaker had produced the dolls in the late 1940s. The woman's name was Madame Alexander, and the dolls had become famous. Nina had gone to New York especially to buy a set for Sally's fifth birthday.

"I see you replaced Amy," I said.

"Yes," said Nina, straightening the ribbon on the Marmee doll's hair.

A memory. A room full of little girls in party dresses and patent leather shoes, clustered around the dolls, watching. And Nina with that same gesture. "You see, this is Marmee, the mother doll. She's a mother like me, and these are her girls. This one with the brown eyes and the strawberry blond hair is Meg. She's the oldest, and this one with the brown hair and the plaid rickrack on her petticoat is Jo – she likes to read, like our Jo does, and this is Amy, she's Marmee's little artist, like you, Sally, and she has beautiful blond hair just like . . ."

But Sally wasn't listening any more. Her face dark with fury, she grabbed the Amy doll by the ankles and smashed her china face against the edge of the table. Her voice had been shrill with hysteria. "She is not me. I am my own Sally Love," and she'd hurtled blindly past all her birthday guests and out of the room.

In this room, now, Nina was talking. "Yes. I replaced her, and she cost a small fortune, but Taylor's worth it. She's such a bright little girl, and she's like you were, Jo; she wants to learn. It's fun to do things for her. She's going to grow up to be a beautiful and gracious woman."

"Like her grandmother," I said.

Nina's face shone with happiness. "Thank you, Jo. That means a lot. Everyone needs to feel valued. I haven't had enough of that feeling lately." She shrugged. "But no self-pity. It's Christmas. And I have wonderful things to look forward to in the new year." She took both my hands in hers. "Come on, let's sit down for a minute. I have some news."

We sat down facing one another on the edge of her bed. I could smell the light flowery scent of her perfume. Always the same perfume – Joy. "A woman's perfume is her signature, Jo." That's what she'd told me. The glow from the lamp on the night table enclosed us in a pool of yellow light, shutting out the darkness.

"Stuart's asked me to move here permanently," she said. "When I came, we'd agreed to try the arrangement until Sally came to her senses, but I think we all know that's not going to happen. Stuart thinks Taylor needs a mother or at least someone to take the place of a mother in her life. Jo, it took me three seconds to give him my answer. I've put my house in Toronto on the market. It looks as if you and Stuart are stuck with me."

I felt my heart sink. "That's great news," I said weakly.

Puzzled, Nina looked at me. "I thought you'd be thrilled, Jo. I know I was, at the thought that after all these years, you and I'd be in the same city again, able to pick up the phone and meet for lunch or tea or go for a walk."

"I am thrilled," I said. "One of the best Christmas gifts I could have would be having you here permanently. It's just . . . has anyone thought about what Sally might want in all of this?"

"Sally always thinks enough about Sally for all of us," Nina said sharply. "Damn it, Jo, she made her decision when she walked out on Stuart and Taylor. She didn't go alone you know. She went with a student of hers, a boy of seventeen. It didn't last, of course. Do you know the joke that went around the gallery? 'Someone told Sally Love it was time she thought about having another child. So she went out and had herself a seventeen-year-old boy.' You should have seen Stuart's face the first time he heard that. He came home looking like a whipped dog. No, Jo, we haven't given much thought to Sally in all this, or perhaps I can put it more acceptably, we've given her about as much thought as she gave us." Her face, usually so expressive, was a mask.

I reached out to embrace her, and she turned away. "Nina, don't," I said. "Don't be angry at me."

She took my hands in hers again. "I could never be angry at you, Jo."

"And don't be angry at Sally. She wants what's best for Taylor, too. And she has her own worries right now. Did you hear her gallery burned down last night?"

"Of course. It was all over this evening's paper. Stu thinks it must have been some sort of retaliation for Erotobio-graphy. Sally's always chosen to live on the edge, Jo. And if you live on the edge, you have to accept consequences. I'm just glad she's out of this house. It wouldn't have been much of a Christmas for Taylor being stalked by a lunatic." She stood up and smoothed her hair. "I don't want to talk about this any more. Come on, let's go downstairs. We have one last Christmas Eve surprise."

We came back to a scene of perfect holiday harmony. The boys and Stu were sprawled on the floor in front of the fireplace looking at baseball cards, and Mieka and Taylor were sitting side by side at the coffee table, drawing butterflies.

It was Nina who broke the spell.

"All right, Taylor," she said. "Time to come into the dining room for the big moment."

"The next event calls for champagne," Stuart said, filling five glasses and splashing two more. "Now you Kilbourns stand right there in front of the French doors, and I'll go back into the dining room and let you know when we're ready."

The kids and I stood obediently, with that self-conscious air of celebration that comes when you're holding a glass of champagne. Someone turned off the lights; the doors to the dining room were flung open, and we were confronted with the extravagance of the Lachlan family Christmas tree.

It was a plantation pine, full and ceiling high; its fragrant, soft needles had the fresh green of new growth, but every-thing else was pink. There were dozens of dusty pink velvet bows tied to the branches, and each of them held a shining pink globe. And there were candles, pink, lit candles that sputtered a fatal hairbreadth away from pine needles, and there were pink roses, real ones suspended from the pine branches in tiny vials of water that glistened in the candle-light. Beside the tree, Stu and Nina and Taylor stood, hands linked. "We wish you a merry Christmas," they sang in their thin, unprofessional voices, and I felt a sense of dread so knife-sharp it sent the room spinning.

"Steady," Peter said, and I felt his arm around my shoulder. The moment passed, and in seconds, we were all drinking champagne and exclaiming over the tree.

Twenty minutes later, Taylor's stocking hung with care and the last holiday embraces exchanged, the children and I were walking along the river bank toward the Cathedral of St. John the Divine. The church was packed, and we had to sit on a bench at the back. Beside us Mary, Joseph and a real baby sat waiting for their cue. I knew the girl playing Mary. She had borrowed our tape recorder at the beginning of school and gone out to the dump to do a project on all the reusable things people throw out. The local TV station had heard about it, and I'd seen her on the evening news, standing on a mountain of garbage, swatting at flies and telling us that time was running out for the environment. A real firebrand. At the front of the church a boy in a white surplice and Reeboks started to sing "Once in Royal David's City" and Mary stood up, adjusted her baby, shook Joseph's comforting arm off her shoulder and strode up the centre aisle. A Mary for our times.

It was a good service. Hilda McCourt had been right about the beauty of Charpentier's "Midnight Mass" for Christmas, and as we left St. John the Divine's, I felt happy and at peace. The anxiety that had been gnawing at me since Nina told me about her plans to move to Saskatoon was gone. That night when, stockings filled and breakfast table set, I finally crawled into bed, I fell into an easy sleep.

But not an untroubled one. Sometime in that night I dreamed a terrible dream. I was in Stuart Lachlan's house, and Sally was there with me. There was a Christmas tree with candles, and Sally was lighting them, very carelessly

thrusting a lighted taper in among the branches. I kept pleading with her to be careful, but she just laughed and said, "It's
not my problem." With the terrible inevitability of a dream,
the tree caught fire, and as I looked through the burning
branches, I could see Nina's face. My legs were leaden, but
finally, blinded by smoke, I pushed through the fire to get to
her. Then we were outside somewhere and I was holding
Nina, but it was dark and I was frantic because I couldn't see
if she was all right. Finally, I put her down in the snow,
crouched beside her and lit a match. But the face on the
woman in the snow wasn't Nina's. It was Sally's. Her clothes
had burned away, and her wonderful blond hair was just a
charred frizz around her face, but her open eyes were still
bright with defiance. And that was a strange thing because I
knew she was dead.

CHAPTER

5

When I opened my eyes Christmas morning, the porcelain doll Sally had given me was on my nightstand looking back at me. I must have left it there when I'd gone to wash my hair after I got back from womanswork. That morning as I looked into the doll's bright, unseeing eyes, it seemed as if my dream of fire and death had been carried over into the waking world, and I was uneasy. But after I'd showered and dressed, I felt better. It had, after all, been only a dream.

When I went downstairs, the kids were sitting in the living room trying to be cool about the fact that there were presents under the tree and it was Christmas morning. As soon as he saw me, Angus called out the name on the first present, and in the usual amazingly short time, the room was filled with empty boxes and wrapping paper and ribbons and it was over for another year.

Around noon, I called Sally's studio. There was no answer, and I felt edgy. But when Nina called early in the afternoon to wish us happiness, she said Sally was sitting in their living room, and I stopped worrying. We ate around five. Peter's girlfriend, Christy, had spent the day with us, and when we came in from cleaning up the kitchen, the boys were already taking down the tree.

"Oh," Christy said, "it seems so soon."

"We're leaving after breakfast tomorrow. There won't be anybody here to look at it," Peter said, and he began wrapping the lights around a cone of newspaper. "A woman on *Good Morning, Canada* showed how to do this," he said. "It's supposed to keep them from getting tangled."

"I've certainly tangled enough in my time," I said.

He smiled. "It's because you don't watch enough television." Then he looked up. "It was a great Christmas wasn't it, Christy?"

I looked at her standing in the doorway. She was wearing a Christmas sweatshirt under a pair of red overalls, and she was flushed with happiness. I expected her to answer him with her usual headlong rush of superlatives, but she looked at me and said simply, "It was the best Christmas I ever had," and I could see why Peter was beginning to care so much for her.

"Pete," I said, "be a good guy and show Christy and me how to make those paper cones. I hate it when you kids know more than I do."

The next morning as we started for Greenwater everybody was in a rotten mood. Mieka and Greg had almost cancelled because Greg was coming down with a cold; Peter was angry because, at the last minute, Christy had decided to go to Minneapolis with friends instead of coming north with us. Angus was worrying about the dogs languishing at the vet's, and I was worrying because everybody was so miserable. To top it all off, the weather had warmed up dramatically.

When I went out to the car for a last-minute check, Pete was clicking the new skis into the rooftop carrier.

"I wonder if we're even going to need these," he said gloomily.

I looked around. The sun was shining hard, and patches of snow on our front lawn were already fragile, melting, blue under white.

"Of course we'll need them," I said. "This is Saskatchewan. We'll need skis, and before the week's out, we'll need raincoats, and we'll probably even wish we'd brought our bathing suits along." I ruffled his hair. "This is God's country. Have a little faith, kid."

He was just beginning to smile when Angus came barrelling through the front door saying Sally was on the phone.

As I went inside, I felt oddly relieved. I picked up the receiver.

"So," I said, "how was your Christmas?"

"It was a real jingle bell," she said. "How long have you got?"

"The kids are packing up the car. About five minutes."

"Okay, in five minutes. First, I didn't take your advice. Couldn't wait to break the news to Stu that I wanted to take Taylor. I told him right after we ate. Lousy timing in that mausoleum with that tree straight out of decorator hell." Her voice dropped. "Honestly, Jo, what did you think of that tree?"

"I thought it was a little excessive."

On the other end of the phone, she mimicked my words. "'A little excessive.' Oh, yes, indeed. Anyway, I should have waited till Stu was alone because there was Nina giving him massive infusions of backbone and making subtle remarks about the problems I bring on myself because of my questionable lifestyle and my odd friends."

"Come on, Sal," I said. "Be fair here. There *are* problems, and Nina's stepped right into the middle of them. She's doing the best she can."

For a minute Sally's irony vanished. "Jesus, Jo, are you ever going to wake up to that woman?" Then she laughed. "Okay, okay, I withdraw that. I don't want you mad at me, too. You're the only sane person I know. Clea seems to be in deep waters again. Last night Stu caught her in the bushes in front of his house with a video camera whirring away. I think I'm going to have to do something about her, after all."

"Sally, be careful. Clea sounds as if she's beyond a woman-to-woman chat; you might just do her more harm than good. She needs professional help."

"Who doesn't?" Sally said grimly. "Maybe we can find a shrink who'll give us a group rate. I could use a little understanding myself. I'm beginning to think the world has declared open season on Sally Love. I haven't finished telling you about my Christmas. The battle with Stu and Nina was just for openers. When I came back to the studio, there was this box on my doorstep – all wrapped in shiny paper, very pretty and Christmassy. So I took it inside and opened it – it was full of used sanitary napkins. There was a note saying that since I seemed to like filth . . . well, you get the idea."

"Oh, Sally, no!"

"Look, let's be grateful. It didn't explode or bite. Hold on, there's more. I took my little prezzy out to the trash, and when I came back in, Izaak was slumped against my front door, full of the Christmas spirit and about a quart of Scotch. He spent last night here, passed out on my sleeping bag. But I wasn't lonely because Clea was lurking around out front all night with her Brownie." She was laughing, but it sounded awful to me.

"Sally, why don't you give yourself a break. Go to a hotel for a few days, or better yet, we're going to be out of this house in twenty minutes. Come and stay here away from everything. You can take care of whatever business you have to deal with during the day and get some peace at night. The dogs are already at the kennel, so you won't even have them to bug you. And we're both past the stage where a sleeping bag is an adventure. Wouldn't it be nice to sleep in a real bed?"

"Would it ever," she said wearily. "You've got yourself a houseguest. Leave the keys in the mailbox."

"They'll be there," I said. "Have fun. And I'm sorry about your Christmas. Next year will be better."

"Promise?" she said.

"Promise," I said, and hung up.

As soon as we arrived in Greenwater, the cloud that had been hanging over us seemed to vanish. Greg's cold didn't materialize. Peter and Angus snapped out of their funks, and the temperature dipped. The skies were clear; the sun shining through the tree branches made antler patterns on the snow, and the ski trails were hard packed and fast.

Every morning we woke to birdsong, the smell of last night's fire and the bite of northern cold. Our days developed a pattern. As soon as we cleaned up after breakfast, we'd cross-country ski. When we got tired, we'd hike the nature trails and Angus would read the small metal plates that told us what we were seeing: beaver dams, aspen stands, places where carpenter ants had made their intricate inlay on tree trunks and fallen branches.

"Think of a world without decay," he would read in his serious, declaiming voice. "Think of it. Every animal that died and every tree that fell would lie there forever. Decay is essential to the recycling of energy and nutrients through successive generations of organisms."

At noon, we'd go back to the cabin, and Mieka and I would make a fire and the boys would make soup in the old white and blue enamelled cooking pot. After lunch, we'd dry our boots in front of the fire and argue lazily about whether we'd ski in the afternoon or skate or just take the binoculars and a bag of peanuts and look for squirrels and birds.

We'd eat early, and by seven o'clock I'd be in my room working on my book about Andy Boychuk and trying to block out the sounds of the kids laughing and fighting over cards or Monopoly. By ten o'clock we'd all be in bed. The good life.

Until the last day of the old year, the day we left Greenwater, I felt immune to the ugly things that life sometimes coughs up. Then the immunity ended.

I'd given my two guys and Mieka's Greg new hockey sticks and Oilers jerseys for Christmas, and the morning before we left they headed off to the little inlet down the hill from our cabin for one last game of shinny. After Mieka and I had checked the cabin to make sure everything was packed, we went down to the lake to watch. It was good to stand breathing in the piny air and listening to the sounds of skates slicing the ice and Angus's running commentary on the game:

"A perfect pass from Harris to Angus Kilbourn – right to his stick, deked the defenceman. Peter Kilbourn's not looking happy. It's back to Harris. He's shooting for the corner. It's a blistering slapshot but it's not enough – Angus Kilbourn's in there . . ."

Mieka turned to me. She was wearing a new Arctic parka Greg had given her for Christmas, and her cheeks were pink with cold. My daughter had always despaired of her looks, but that morning she was beautiful.

"Mum," she said, "let's take one last walk on the lake. These guys are their own best audience."

We walked onto the ice, past the wood huts of the ice fishers, toward the centre of the lake. It was a long walk and when we finally turned and looked back toward the inlet where the boys were skating, their orange and blue jerseys were just scraps of colour in the grey sweep of land and lake and sky. They seemed so far away and vulnerable that I shivered and pulled my jacket tight around me.

"Cold?" Mieka asked.

"No, it's just . . . I don't know . . . usually the sun's out and the sky's blue and everything's like a postcard, but when it's grey like this, the lake scares me."

Mieka widened her eyes in exasperation. "The ice is about three feet thick here. We're perfectly safe."

"It's not that. It's just . . ." I smiled at her. "You're lucky you're sensible like your dad. Good gene selection. Come on, let's change the subject. It was a great holiday, wasn't it? And, Miek, I really enjoy Greg. He fits in so well."

Mieka smiled and looked toward the far shore. We were silent for a while, then she turned to me and took a deep breath. "Mum, I'm glad you like him. That makes my news a little easier."

Pregnant, I thought, looking at her bright, secret eyes. My mind raced – a wedding, of course. But why 'of course'? Women didn't bolt to the altar any more, but still, a baby. A new life . . .

"I'm quitting school to set up a catering business with Greg," she said.

"What?" I asked stupidly.

"A catering business. They're renovating the Old Court House, and there's a great space on the main floor – central, very posh, perfect location for what we're planning. Here's our idea – we're going to specialize in catering for businesses. We come to your offices or your boardroom and when you break for lunch or supper we serve you a really fine meal. No waiting. No wasting time. Everything fresh – supplies will be key. We'll pay for the best. Everything freshly prepared – we'll do the *mise en place* in the main kitchen and bring everything with us. Then when you're having a glass of wine –

good wine, we'll have a nice wine list – we'll cook for you, everything *à la minute,* and everything served by people who care about food. The place I'm after is the old small claims court – I'm going to call the place Judgements."

"No, you're not," I said harshly. "You're not calling it anything. You're going back to university next week."

She looked at me levelly. "Thanks for hearing me out."

"Mieka," I said, "I'm sorry. It was a shock – even the French – you got forty-three in French last semester. Where did all this fluency come from?"

She bit her lip and looked across the lake.

I started again. "Opening a catering business isn't something ordinary people do. It's something you talk about doing, like writing a novel or living on a Greek island. The food business is brutal, Miek. There was an article in the *Globe and Mail* last week that said for every two restaurants that open, three close."

She took a breath and turned to me. Her voice was controlled and it was determined. "Mum, I'm not opening a restaurant. Now come on. I have our business plan at the cabin: feasibility study, marketing surveys, projected financial statements – the works. We figure we can open the doors on Judgements for a hundred thousand dollars."

"Mieka – a hundred thousand! You've got to be crazy. Where are you going to get that kind of money?"

"Some of it we'll get from a bank – the way everybody else does. They're not keen about financing upscale catering businesses. The bank people I've talked to say they're too risky – capital intensive, labour intensive – you're right about that. But Judgements is going to work. Greg's uncle is going to arrange for a line of credit and Greg has a twenty-five-thousand-dollar inheritance from his grandfather that we're going to use." She took a deep breath. "Now, I guess you know what I'm going to ask you for . . ."

"Your money for university," I said.

"The money you and Dad put away for my future," she corrected gently.

"I'm not going to give it to you. Mieka, you got a thirty-two in Economics last semester. How in the name of God do you expect to run a business?"

She looked at me hard. "Do you realize that's twice you've mentioned my grades in the last five minutes? But maybe you're right. Maybe there's a clue in those numbers. Maybe the fact that, except when you beat it into me, I've gotten terrible grades should tell us both something. I'm not a student, Mum. I don't like to learn from books. I like to do things with my hands. And you know what? I'm good at what I like to do. Be happy for me." She laughed. "Lend me money. Give me my money. Daddy had enough set aside to get me through grad school. I know that. Well, I don't want grad school, and they won't want me, but I do want a chance at my business."

"No," I said.

"And that's it?" she said in a small, tight voice.

"Damn it, Miek. What am I supposed to say when I see you walking away from any possibility of a decent future? What did Greg's mother say when he told her he was quitting university?"

"He's not quitting."

I could feel the anger rising in my throat. "Well, that's just great. The girl quits school to put the guy through school. Mieka, I've seen this movie a hundred times."

"No, Mum, you have not seen this movie a hundred times. I'm not working at a dumb job to put my husband through med school. I'm an equal partner in a business. Greg is finishing his admin degree so when the time comes we'll know how to expand our business. We've made some good decisions here. Now you make a good decision. Face the fact that I'm just not university material."

I touched the sleeve of her jacket. "Mieka, please, you're not stupid."

She pulled up the hood of her parka and knotted it carefully under her chin. Suddenly her profile was alien. I didn't know her any more. When she spoke, her voice was patient and remote.

"Mum, I never thought I was stupid. I was just never good at school." She turned toward me and shrugged. "I was just never you."

For a few moments we stood there. Finally, wordless, we walked toward the cabin. For the first time in our lives, my daughter and I didn't seem to have much to say to each other.

When we got back, the boys were sitting at the kitchen table drying the blades of their skates, and the cabin had the cheerless feeling of a place that was about to be abandoned. It didn't take the kids long to pick up on the tension between Mieka and me. Even Angus didn't put up a fight when we started toward the cars. We all knew the holiday was over.

When Greg and Mieka's Audi got to the top of the hill, I waved. Greg turned and waved back but Mieka stared straight ahead, and in a moment the car disappeared and she was gone.

Beside me, Peter said, "I'll drive the first hour. Angus can bag out in the back seat. He was up half the night with that stupid game he bought himself for Christmas."

Peter and Mieka had always been close, and I could tell by the set of his jaw how upset he was.

"You're a good guy, Pete," I said.

He looked at me wearily. "Mieka's a good guy, too, Mum. Hang on to that thought."

At the edge of the park we stopped for gas. There was a rack full of Saskatoon papers by the cash register. Councillor Hank Mewhort was on the front page under a headline that said, "Vigil at the Mendel." He was holding a candle and, in the darkness, the play of light and shadow on his face made him look like a slightly cracked cherub. I bought a paper.

The story wasn't encouraging. There had been vigils in front of the gallery every night since Christmas. There were the usual interviews with people talking about pornography and community values, but things seemed to be turning ugly. The night before someone had hung an effigy of Sally from a tree in front of the gallery, and the crowd had pulled the effigy down and burned it.

It was a disturbing image. I closed the paper and looked out the car window. When the pine trees gave way to the white fields and bare trees of the open prairie, my eyelids grew heavy.

The radio was on and a man with a gentle, sad voice was talking about the dangers of genetic engineering in poultry. "So many species endangered," he said, "a virus could wipe out one of these new super breeds or some genetic problem . . . important to keep some of the original breeds as a safe-guard . . . so vulnerable . . . the world's more dangerous now . . . could die so easily . . ."

And then a man was laughing and Stuart Lachlan was saying, "Of course, it would have been better if Sally died," and I awoke with a start to the sun hot in my face and Stuart Lachlan's voice on the radio.

" . . . realized instinctively that didactic art is trivial art and that the burden of dogma will always crush the artist's spirit."

"What is this, Pete?" I asked.

"Some arts show. Hey, you must trust my highway driving more these days. You were asleep for almost two hours. That's Stuart Lachlan talking about some book he's written about Sally. He just about put me under, too."

"You would have been on the edge of your chair if Sally were a quarterback."

He grinned. "Yeah, right, Mum."

Outside, the sky was grey, heavy with snow. In the car, Stuart Lachlan's voice droned on, patient, professionally exact.

"What people don't understand is that as a maker of art, Sally's always been a loner. She claims to be uncomfortable with movements and schools and labels. She says, 'When I'm in the studio I'm just a painter,' yet for all her disclaimers Sally Love has always been on the cutting edge of change in the art world. How do we explain that?" he asked rhetorically.

Out of nowhere, a hawk swooped across the highway and picked up a small animal from the ditch beside the road. It was a heart-stoppingly clean movement.

"Gotcha," I said.

"The explanation is simple," Stu said. "As a painter, Sally Love has always been self-conscious in the best sense of the word. She is acutely conscious of the people and places around her, and she has always managed to get herself into situations where she has been able to make significant art."

"And out of situations where she was unable to make significant art," the interviewer said flatly.

Stuart laughed, but his voice was tight. "Yes," he agreed, "and out of situations where she was unable to make significant art."

The interviewer thanked Stu; the music came up. I poured two cups of coffee from the Thermos and handed one to Peter.

"Peter," I said, "was I dreaming or did Stu say something about Sally dying?"

He looked at me quickly. "Yeah, it was at the beginning – something about the critic's art and how it's always better if the person you're writing about is dead. What he said was – now this isn't exact, but it's close – 'If they're dead, they

can't embarrass the writer by destroying all his theories.'
And then, Mum, he said something so shitty. He said, 'Of
course, as far as my critical appraisal of Sally's work is concerned it would have been better if Sally died.' I mean, isn't
that a little parasitic?"

"Parasites live off live tissues. It's saprophytes that eat
dead things." Angus's voice came loud and disoriented from
the back seat.

I turned to look at him. He was thirteen – not an easy age,
and there were times when he was not an easy kid.

"I see the reports of your death were greatly exaggerated,"
I said.

"What?" he asked, rubbing his eyes.

"You slept for over two hours. I'm glad to see you're
alive." I touched Peter on the hand. "We'd better put this
conversation on hold for a while. We can talk more about
Stuart and Sally when we get home."

But it was a long time before we did. Things happened.

Sally's Porsche was still in the driveway when we pulled up
at our house late in the afternoon. She came out to help us
carry in our luggage, and when it was all inside, she sat down
at the kitchen table. She didn't seem in a hurry to leave.

I went over and gave her a hug. "Make yourself comfortable," I said. "I've got some unfinished family business to
take care of. It won't take long."

She smiled. "I'm not going anywhere."

I picked up the kitchen phone and dialled Mieka's
number. Greg answered. When I asked for my daughter, he
sounded the same as he always did, laconic but pleasant. At
least he wasn't mad at me.

"Sorry, Jo. Mieka's in the tub, soaking."

"Safe from mothers who rail at her about her life," I said.

"For the time being, I guess she is," he said gently.

"Greg, I'm sorry. I shouldn't be involving you. It's between Mieka and me. It's just I love her so much and I worry. Have her call me, would you?"

"I'll do my best."

"Thanks," I said. "Damn it, why isn't anything ever simple?"

He laughed. "Well, you know what Woody Allen says. 'Life is full of anxiety, trouble and misery, and it's over too soon.' I'll have her call you, Jo."

I hung up and sat down opposite Sally at the kitchen table. Through the sliding doors to the deck, I could see the backyard. A pair of juncos were fighting at the bird feeder.

"Everything okay now?" Sally asked.

"Mieka's boyfriend gave me a Woody Allen line. 'Life is full of anxiety, trouble and misery, and it's over too soon.'"

Sally looked thoughtful. "I'll drink to that," she said.

"You know," I said, "I think I will, too. What'll we have?"

"Bourbon," she said, leaning back in her chair. "Bourbon's good when you're talking about life." She was wearing a hound's-tooth skirt and a cashmere sweater the colour of Devon cream. It matched the bag she had talked Hugh Rankin-Carter into parting with the night of the opening. Her hair was looped back in a gold barrette, and the last sunlight of the day fell full on her face. She looked relaxed and at peace.

I came back and set our drinks down on the table. Sally picked up hers.

"So what's up with Mieka?" she asked.

"She wants to quit school and open a catering business."

"Is she any good?"

"As a cook? Terrific! And she's always been a good manager. It's just that her quitting school scares me."

"Does it scare her?"

"Not a bit, but still . . ."

"There is no 'but still.' Mieka's what? Twenty? Let her alone. Nobody likes a control freak. Think where I'd he if I'd let Nina choose a life for me." She winced. "No, don't think where I'd be. But look at me. A daughter any mother would be proud to tell her friends about. Now come on, let go. Let Mieka be Mieka. Let's drink to that and let's drink to the new year."

I smiled and lifted my glass. "To Mieka and to letting go. Happy New Year, Sally. I can tell just by looking at you, it's going to be wonderful. You look terrific."

"That's because, despite Councillor Mewhort and his campfires in front of the Mendel, things are working out. Stu's relented about Taylor. She's coming to live with me after her school has its midwinter break in February. I've called a friend in Vancouver to start looking around for a place for us – on the ocean and near a good school. Meanwhile Taylor and I are going to spend some time getting to know each other. Nina's idea. She says we really haven't spent much time together – which is true – and she says there's still too much ugliness about the Erotobiography to have Taylor move in with me, which is also true. There were a couple more incidents when you were away."

"Clea Poole?"

"Among others. A lot of people wrote to me. Half of them wanted me to make the city a better place by leaving, and the other half just wanted me to make them. My studio got broken into twice; someone put sugar in my gas tank, and I got some more Christmas presents."

"Oh, Sally, no."

"Nothing I couldn't handle, and the important thing is I'm getting Taylor."

I took another sip of my drink. "That really surprises me. I thought Stu would haul you into the tall grass over that one. What did you do? Sell your soul to the devil?"

Sally finished her drink and gave me an odd little smile. "No, to a mouse. I sold my soul to a mouse. Look, Jo, you must have a million things to do. I'd better get out of here. Thanks for the drink and for giving me a week in a real bed."

"Want to prolong the pleasures of the season and come for dinner tomorrow night? It's steak au poivre."

She slid her bag over her shoulder and stood up. "One of my favourites, but I think I'll pass this time. I'm going to spend the first day of the new year at the studio working. Even the crazies will have plans for tomorrow, so I might actually get something done."

I walked her to her car. She reached into the glove compartment and pulled out a package the size of a book. It was wrapped in brown paper, and for a minute I thought it must be a gift for the use of the house.

She handed it to me. "Jo, put this somewhere safe, would you? I don't seem to have any safe places any more. Just stick it up high where Angus won't get curious about it. And don't you get curious about it, either."

I raised my eyebrows. "What is it? A bomb?"

"No, nothing like that." Suddenly she grinned. "It's my insurance policy. If you lose it, I'm dead."

When I went in the house, the phone was ringing. It was Mieka, sounding friendly enough. She and Greg were spending New Year's Eve with friends but they'd be over, as planned, for dinner with us New Year's Day. She didn't say she had reconsidered her decision about school. She didn't say she realized I was right. She didn't say she was counting her blessings that I was her mother. All the same, she was coming to dinner. It was a start.

I spent the last night of the old year doing laundry and listening to the radio. Peter had picked up the dogs at the kennel, delivered them to our house, then gone off to a black-tie dinner at the Bessborough Hotel, so it was just

Angus and me. We had pancakes for supper, then he disappeared into the den and started calling all his friends, comparing holidays, getting caught up on what he'd missed.

About ten, I put the last load into the washing machine and went upstairs to check on Angus. The television was blaring. Dick Clark was standing in front of a room full of people in party clothes and paper hats sweating under the TV lights and trying to look as if they were having the time of their lives. Angus was curled up on the couch, sleeping the sleep of the just. I turned down the television, covered him with an afghan and went into the kitchen to make a pot of tea.

New Year's Eve at mid-life.

I let out the dogs for a final run and sat down at the kitchen table. It was a magic night. The sky was bright with stars, and the moonlight made the snow glitter. A party night. Even the dogs seemed to be in a giddy mood; they chased each other through the snow like puppies.

I thought of how happy my kids were, or at least how happy they would be if I let them, and I thought about how well the biography I was writing was going. With luck, by next New Year's Eve it would be in the bookstores and I'd be safe in a tenure-track position in some nice but not too demanding university. And I thought of Sally sitting in the chair across from me that afternoon telling me how she and Stu and Nina had reconciled their differences over Taylor. It seemed as if everyone was, as we used to say in the sixties, in a good space.

"All in all, not a bad year. Maybe the worst is over," I said as I opened the back door to call the dogs in.

They wouldn't come. The backyard was deep, and the dogs were at the farthest corner, at the gate that opened on the back alley. They were barking at something. Going crazy. Kids, I thought, out late for New Year's Eve.

"Sadie, Rose." I called the dogs' names in the voice that let them know I meant business. "Come on, get in here." They wouldn't come. There were stairs leading from the deck to the garden. I went halfway down and called again. Next door there was a party. A woman screamed, then laughed. I went the rest of the way down the stairs and started walking along the path to the gate. I was wearing runners, not great for walking in deep snow, and my feet were getting wet and cold.

"Damn," I said, "get in here. I've had enough." My voice sounded thin and vulnerable, but the dogs didn't take pity on me. They just stood there barking.

The woman at the gate didn't make any attempt to leave when she saw me. She was rooted in the snow with her video camera pointed at me, recording me as I walked toward her. I could see her face clearly in the light from my neighbour's garage. I could also see that she was wearing only a light jacket – not enough for December thirty-first in Saskatchewan. Suddenly, I was bone-tired.

"Clea," I said. "It's New Year's Eve. Time to wipe the slate clean and look ahead. Why don't you go home and get a good night's sleep. Everything will look better tomorrow."

"I'm not finished," she said dully.

"Not finished what?" I asked.

"Filming the history of womanswork," she said. "It should be recorded. All of it. Where it began. The women who helped." She waved a finger as if to chastise me. "The woman who didn't help. The record should be set straight. The gallery was a significant experiment. It deserves a memorial."

Seeing me talking to Clea apparently made her seem less of a threat to the dogs. They left us and went to the back door and waited. Without them, I wasn't so brave.

"Clea," I said, "if you need a cab, I'll go and call one for you. Otherwise, I'll just say good night. It's been a long day, and I'm tired."

She didn't say a word, just turned and walked down the alley.

I was shivering with cold and fear when I got in the house. I went straight to the kitchen. The package Sally had given me, her insurance policy, was still sitting on the kitchen table. I took it downstairs to the laundry room and hid it up high in a basket the kids had given me a hundred years ago for my sewing. No one, including me, ever went near it. I pulled my warmest sweats out of the dryer, walked down the hall to the bathroom and took a hot shower.

When I went upstairs to the kitchen, the tea in the pot was cold, but the Jack Daniel's bottle was still on the counter. I dumped the tea, made myself a bourbon and water, went down to the den and sat beside my sleeping son.

Five minutes to midnight in New York City. It was raining in Times Square, but nobody seemed to care. Slickers soaked, hair pasted against their faces by the rain, the tourists mugged for the TV cameras. At the bottom of the screen, the digital clock moved inexorably toward the new year. I took a deep pull on my drink and moved closer to Angus. The electronic apple in Times Square had started to fall – in the east, there were just seconds till midnight.

"Five, four, three, two, one," the crowd in New York chanted. Beside me, my son stirred in his sleep. "Happy New Year," screamed the people in Times Square. And in the room with me, the phone was ringing. I leaned across Angus to pick up the receiver.

"Happy New Year," I said.

"Not yet," said the voice on the other end. "There's still an hour left."

"Clea, please, leave it alone. Leave me alone."

There was silence on the other end of the phone.

"All right," I said, "if you've got nothing to say, I'm hanging up. I'm too old for pranks."

"This isn't a prank. This is my life." Her husky voice cracked with emotion. "This is my life. I need to talk to somebody about what to do next."

"I barely know you."

"But you know Sally."

For Clea Poole apparently that was recommendation enough. I closed my eyes and remembered Clea as she had been the night of Sally's opening: delicate, carefully groomed, buoyant about the work she was showing at the gallery.

"All right, Clea," I said wearily. "But not tonight."

"Tomorrow, then. Here at the Mendel. I'm working in the education gallery on an installation. I'm going to work through the night. I don't want to go back to my house. Holidays aren't good times when you're alone."

"No," I agreed, "they're not."

"I'll tell the security man to let you in," she said, and the line went dead.

On television, Dick Clark was saying, "Remember if you're driving tonight, make that one for the road a coffee." I turned off the TV, went upstairs and poured myself another Jack Daniel's. I wasn't driving anywhere.

The next morning as I walked across the bridge to the gallery I was tired and on edge. Peter had come home very late – not too late for an eighteen-year-old on New Year's Eve, but too late for a mother who can't fall asleep till she knows her kids are safe. And I wasn't looking forward to spending the first morning of the new year with Clea Poole.

The banners for Sally's show were still up at the gallery. A solitary picket was out front. The others had drifted away during the holidays, but this one was vigilant. Sally called him the Righteous Protester, and every day he had a new sign. Today's said, "Whatsoever a Man Soweth That Shall He Also Reap."

I waved to him as I ran up the steps to the gallery, but he didn't wave back. I waited five minutes in the cold before anyone came in answer to the security buzzer. The guard who finally opened the door was young enough to be my son. On the breast pocket of his uniform, his name was embroidered: Kyle. He seemed surprised to see me. Clea Poole, he said, had not left a message that I was to be admitted; if I insisted on coming in and looking for her, he would have to accompany me.

As we walked down the cool, quiet corridor toward the education gallery, I was furious. In all likelihood, Clea was safe at home in bed. To make matters worse, Kyle was dogging me in a way that suggested that if he left me alone, I would do unspeakable damage.

Outside the education gallery, he suddenly became human. As he pulled open the door, he grinned and made a sweeping gesture of presentation.

"Here we are. Hang on to your hat."

The room we were in was large and, except for one corner, dimly lit. In the area of full light, a naked woman lay on an operating table. Clea Poole was standing over her, drawing a scalpel carefully along the lower part of the woman's stomach. When Kyle called her name, Clea looked up.

"You can go," she said to Kyle. "Joanne is here to talk to me."

"Go ahead and look," Kyle said. "She won't bite."

The figure on the operating table seemed to be made of some sort of soft plastic. She was lifelike, but if she had had a life, it had been a hard one. She was covered with neatly stitched surgical incisions. There wasn't much of her that hadn't been cut open and sewn up: her eyelids, the hairline between her ear and her temple, her nose, her jawline, her breasts, the sides of her thighs.

"Good Lord," I said, "what's it supposed to be?"

"She's a scalpel junkie," Clea said. "An emblem of how society obsesses women with body image."

A half-moon line on the figure's lower stomach gaped open, and Clea removed a piece of foam and stuck it absent-mindedly in the back pocket of her jeans.

"She's part of a triptych," Clea said, although I hadn't asked. "It's an installation by an artist Izaak Levin is interested in. I'm just doing menial work, carrying out the artist's plans." She laughed. "No one better qualified than me for that. The junkie will be suspended from the ceiling. That," she said, pointing to a double bed in the corner, "will be brought over and put underneath her."

Half the bed was traditionally bridal, soft-looking, inviting, covered with a satiny white duvet. At the head of that part of the bed was a pillow embroidered "His." The other half of the bed was bare, just a frame covered with the kind of barbed wire used in electric fences to keep cattle confined. In the half light of the gallery, the wire hummed and sparked blue. The pillow on that side of the bed said "Hers."

"The camera will be moved over, too," Clea said, pointing to the ceiling where, unheeded, a video camera whirred. "They're going to tape people's reactions to the junkie. The third part of the concept is a coffin. They're delivering it at the end of the week."

Clea's voice was curiously detached, the voice of a person who'd lost interest in her own life. Across the room the red light of the emergency exit glowed invitingly.

"'Skin-deep,' that's the name of the installation," she said, walking back to the operating table. She picked up a darning needle and threaded it expertly with catgut. "They tell us all we're good for is being caretakers of our surfaces. We've lost all the ground we gained in the seventies, you know. We've been battered, ghettoized by the sexual hierarchy."

She began stitching the incision on the woman's stomach. She sewed mechanically and well, and as she sewed she talked listlessly about women and art and Sally.

"History is repeating itself," she said. "We have to reclaim our own terrain. It's important that she's with other women now. Not women like you. She's a catalyst. She used to know what the male power machine did to women. She knew we had to get past male critics and dealers and collectors and create a nonjudgemental environment where women could show their work. She was wearing a T-shirt the first time I saw her. She was the most beautiful creature I'd ever seen. The womanswork gallery was her idea. China painting, performance art, soft sculpture, murals, needlework, body art – we did it all. It was the best time of my life. The only time of my life. I thought it meant the same thing to her, but it didn't. 'Time to move along,' that's what she says. It's my life, but it's just a blip on the screen for her, like neo-expressionism or post mod. Time to move along. Time to let go." When she stopped sewing and looked at me, her eyes were filled with tears. "She knows I can't let go. Letting go is for people who know they won't fall."

"Clea, how can I help?" I asked. "What do you expect me to do?"

"What do I expect you to do?" she repeated. "I expect you to stop turning her against me. I've thought about this, Joanne. It's no coincidence that Sally decided to sell our gallery shortly after you came back on the scene. You're one of those women who's been co-opted by the system. You don't care about other women."

I tried to keep the anger out of my voice. "Clea," I said, "that is so untrue and so unfair. I've never tried to undermine your relationship with Sally."

She finished sewing the incision, knotted the thread and snipped the catgut with her scalpel.

"I don't believe you," she said flatly. "If I were you, I'd get out of here now, Joanne. You're making things worse. Cut your losses. Isn't that what people like you do when you're in a no-win situation?" The tears were streaming down her face, but she didn't seem to notice them. "Is loss-cutting a skill you're born with?" she asked, her voice thick with pain. "I need to know this, Joanne. Is it too late for me to learn how to cut my losses? Have I missed the deadline?"

I stepped toward her, but she raised her hand as if to ward off a blow.

There was nothing I could do. "Good-bye, Clea," I said. "Get some help. Please, for all our sakes, get some help."

At the door, I turned and looked. Clea was standing behind her operating table watching me with dead eyes. In her hand, the scalpel glinted lethal and bright.

It was good to step outside into the sunshine of an ordinary day. It was even a relief to see the Righteous Protester making his lonely rounds. Bizarre as he was, he at least seemed connected to a recognizable world.

As I stood looking at the deserted street in front of the gallery, I started to shake. The encounter with Clea had disturbed me more than I realized. I didn't make a conscious decision to cross Spadina Crescent and walk up the block to Stuart Lachlan's house. Reflexively, I did what I had done a thousand times when life overwhelmed me. I went to Nina.

She came to the door herself. As always, she was immaculate. Her dark hair was brushed into a smooth page boy, her makeup was fresh, and she was wearing a black knit skirt, a white silk blouse and an elegant cardigan, black with a pattern of stylized Siamese cats worked in white.

When she saw me, her face was radiant. "Oh, Jo, come in out of the cold and visit. This is the best surprise, especially because I have a surprise for you, too. Let me take your coat and then we'll go and see an old friend."

I followed her into the living room. "Now, look," she said. "How's this for bringing back the memories?"

In front of her was the drop-leaf desk she'd had in the sitting room of her Toronto house. She was right. It did bring back memories.

They weren't all pleasant. The desk was Chinese Chippendale, lacquered black with gilt trim. Nina used to keep a lacquerware water jar on it. Painted fish swam on that jar – perfect, serene in their ordered, watery world. When my mother was at her worst, I would come to Nina and she would tell me to sit at that desk and try to close out everything but the smooth passage of the bright fish as they swam around and around the jar. It always worked. That desk had been my refuge, and Nina had been my rock. None of my mother's dark hints about Nina's character or my blindness to her faults could erode that.

Behind me, Nina, her voice vibrant and affectionate, said, "We've weathered a lot of storms at this desk, haven't we, Jo? I'm leaving it to you in my will."

I felt a chill. I put my arm around her shoulders and breathed in the familiar fragrance of her perfume.

"Well, when you leave, I'm going, too. My world would be a desolate place without you."

She laughed. "Don't break out the crepe, yet. I'm not planning to leave the party for a long time."

We brought coffee and some still-warm banana bread into the living room and sat at a small table near the front window. There was a bouquet of white tulips on the table, and the sun bathed them in wintery light. This bright and civilized room seemed light-years removed from Clea Poole's dark and pain-filled world, but it was of Clea we talked as the good smells of coffee and fresh baking surrounded us and the crystal purity of one of the Brandenburg Concertos floated in from another room.

I told Nina everything, and as I talked I realized how much Clea had scared me. "She's in the middle of a terrible breakdown," I said, "and she's unreachable. I think all the things she does – phoning Sally fifty times a night, stalking us with her camera, working on that extraordinary exhibition – I think all those things seem logical to her, and what terrifies me is that I don't know what might seem logical to her next. I think she's reached the point where she's capable of anything. She's even made some oblique threats to me."

Nina frowned. "Jo, I'll give you the same advice someone should give Sally. Stay away from Clea Poole. Stuart's had some dealings with her in the past, and he thinks she could be violent. If she sees you as a rival, God knows what she'll do. Sally's used to dealing with people like that, but you're not. Be careful, Jo. Please, be careful."

"Nina's right," said a man's voice behind us. "I can attest to the fact that Clea Poole is a nasty enemy." I looked up and there was Stuart Lachlan. I wondered how long he'd been standing there. I had expected the prospect of Taylor's leaving to devastate him, but he looked fine. He was wearing a black and white pullover that was obviously the masculine version of the cardigan Nina was wearing, and as he bent to embrace me, I thought I smelled the kind of lemony fragrance she liked on him. She was having an influence.

He sat down beside her on the love seat and looked at me earnestly. "I'm serious, Jo. When Sally and I were first married, Clea did some amazing things."

"Sally told me about the hair incident."

He winced. "You know, then. Clea's been better for so long, I guess we all thought that breakdown was an isolated thing. In fact, I arranged for her to do that work on the installation at the gallery. Usually a student would do that, but Clea seemed desperate for diversion."

"Stu, I just came from the Mendel, and Clea didn't look diverted to me. She looked like somebody who shouldn't be spending her days and nights working with surgical instruments."

Nina shuddered. "I'm sure Stuart will look in first thing tomorrow, Jo. Now could we please talk about something pleasant? I don't think we've even said Happy New Year to one another."

I smiled. "Happy New Year – I hope it's a wonderful year for you both. You deserve it. Stu, that was such a generous arrangement about Taylor that you worked out with Sally. And, Nina, you deserve praise, too. I know how much being with Taylor day to day means to you. Not many people could have been so selfless."

They looked at one another quickly, then Nina reached across the table and patted my hand. "Jo, if it were anyone but you, we'd take the praise and run, but you deserve the truth. Sally will never take Taylor. Stuart and I feel the idea of being a mother and mentor is just a flirtation for her. She's between partners, and for Sally that always means a drop in creative energy. As soon as there's a new relationship, she'll be back painting fifteen hours a day, and she'll forget all about her daughter." Nina leaned forward and touched the petals of the flowers in front of her. "Mark my words, when the tulips bloom in the flower beds out front, Taylor will still be in this house."

In the background the Brandenburg soared. Stu and Nina sat side by side, quietly waiting for me to say something. I hadn't noticed until that moment how much they were alike physically: the same dark hair, the same fine features, the same intensity as they waited for reassurance.

I couldn't give it to them. "There's nothing in the world I wouldn't do for you, Nina. And, Stu, you know I want you to be happy, but I think you're wrong about this. Sally is very serious about having Taylor live with her. She told me last night she's been looking for a house in Vancouver – something near a good school for Taylor. As painful as it is, I think you have to be realistic. Sally plans to take her daughter with her in February."

They looked quickly at each other, but neither said anything. When I stood up to leave, they both followed me to the hall. It wasn't until Stuart was helping me on with my parka that he finally spoke.

"She may not have that chance, you know. Events sometimes intervene."

I kissed Nina on the cheek and grasped Stu's hand. "Don't count on it, Stu, just please don't count on it."

CHAPTER

6

I slept for a couple of hours when I got home, and by the time I finished lunch, I felt ready to start the new year. I spent the afternoon curled up by the fireplace reading an exposé of our current prime minister by his ex-chef. When I was finished, I was glad I did my own cooking. Around four, Mieka and Greg arrived with the news that there was a blizzard on the way, and the RCMP were telling everybody to stay off the roads. By the time Peter brought Christy over, the snow had started, the wind had picked up, and I sent Angus down to wash another load of sheets in case everyone stayed the night.

Dinner was an easy, happy meal, and afterwards it was good to sit in the candlelight, finishing off the Beaujolais and watching the storm gathering power outside. Safe. We were safe at home. We had finished cleaning up and the kids had gone downstairs to watch the last of the Bowl games when the phone rang.

At first I didn't recognize the voice.

"Jo, I'm in trouble. Big trouble. I just got to the gallery and . . ."

I could hear sirens. They were so faint I couldn't tell, at first, if they were coming from the TV downstairs or the phone. The doubt didn't linger.

"Oh, God, the cops are here," she said. "I'm just going to stick where I am, Jo, at the Mendel. I already said that, didn't I? Jo, she's dead. Clea's dead."

"Do you have a lawyer, Sally? Someone I can call?" On the other end of the line there was silence and then a click as the receiver was replaced.

My parka and boots were by the kitchen door. I started down to the family room to tell the kids where I was going, then changed my mind. I didn't have time for explanations. I left a note on the table, picked up my car keys and headed for the garage. As I walked through the breezeway, I heard the crowd in Pasadena roar. It sounded like a touchdown.

When I pulled the Volvo out of the driveway, I leaned forward automatically to turn on the radio. Pete had left it tuned to a soft rock station, and a woman named Brie, who sounded too young to be out after dark, was saying her station was going to get us through the blizzard by playing the songs of summer. As I pulled onto Clarence Avenue, the snow had become a dense and dizzying vortex that looked capable of sucking me through the windshield, and Eddie Cochran was singing that there ain't no cure for the summertime blues.

There was also no visibility. I inched along using the streetlights as reference points until I came to the intersection of Clarence and College, just before the University Bridge. As I pulled onto the bridge, Brie said the Lovin' Spoonful were going to do their classic "Summer in the City"; a hundred feet beneath me was the South Saskatchewan River, killingly cold but frozen only in parts because of the runoff from the power station. To my right, the guardrails that kept me from plunging over the top were an incandescent fuzz, but I couldn't see in front of me – in fact, I didn't know where in front of me was. Suddenly, I became convinced that I'd drifted out of my lane. I turned off the radio and rolled down my window so I could hear any car that might be about to drive head-on into mine. I could hear the wind keening along the river, but there were no sounds of cars. "I'm the only car on the bridge," I said aloud. That should have made me feel better, but it didn't.

When I turned off the bridge onto Spadina Crescent I could see the Mendel's orange security lights. The word *security* had never seemed sweeter or more ironic. The front of the gallery was brightly lit. Sally's Porsche was there. So was a police car, and two more were just pulling up. I could see an officer sealing off the entrance to the gallery with tape. It didn't seem likely he was going to invite me in.

Frustrated, I rested my forehead against the steering wheel. I thought of Sally surrounded by police in that room with the scalpel junkie and the electric bed. And then I thought of the red glow of the exit sign over the emergency door in the education gallery. They might not have blocked that door off yet. It was certainly worth a shot. I drove past the gallery and parked on the side street north of the grounds. I covered my face with a scarf and started off across the lawn to the gallery. It was slow going. My legs ached from the effort of plodding through the heavy snow, but I held an image of Sally in my mind and kept trudging. Finally I could see the outline of the door to the education gallery, and I began to run toward it.

There was a little stand of bushes beside the door, and the snow had drifted deeply in front of it. When I climbed through the snowdrift, my foot caught on something and I fell face down in the snow. But not wholly in the snow. My legs were on top of something. When I reached my right arm out to see what it was, I touched the silky smoothness of a down-filled coat. It felt like the padding in a coffin. I moved my hand up, and under the snow my fingers touched the contours of a human face. When I sat up, I could see the orange glare of the security lights reflected in his eyes.

I had never seen him up close, but I would have known his face anywhere.

It was the Righteous Protester.

Suddenly I began to shake. I pushed myself up and ran toward the door. I pounded it, shouting for help, screaming for Sally. Desperate, I tried the knob. The door opened easily, and in a minute, I stepped from the cold into the hot craziness of a nightmare.

There was a smell in the room. Something familiar, the smell of meat cooking. It took my eyes a few moments to adjust themselves to the half light and then to take in the scene.

Clea had made real progress on the installation since morning. The scalpel junkie had had her last surgery and was suspended from the ceiling on wires, like a marionette. Beneath her was the bridal bed. There weren't any blue sparks coming off the wires. Someone had turned off the power. But there was a figure on the bed. Clea Poole was lying face down on the barbed wire. She was naked. When I saw her, I knew where the meat smell was coming from. The hooks from the barbed wire must have embedded themselves in her skin; until the power had been turned off, Clea had been slowly cooking. I closed my eyes. I didn't want to see any more. The room swayed around me. In a minute I felt an arm around my shoulders, and I heard a familiar voice, choked but recognizable.

"I knew you'd come," Sally said. Those were the only words she had time for. Suddenly we weren't alone any more. Two policemen had come over: a young man who looked the way Burt Reynolds must have looked when he was twenty,

and a heavier man. They seemed to have just arrived; their
cheeks were still pink with cold. They were both very
young, and despite their uniforms and their heavy regulation
winter boots, it soon became apparent that nothing in the
police college had prepared them for this.

The Burt Reynolds officer looked up at the scalpel junkie
and said in a tone of awe, "Jesus Christ, it must have been
some sort of cult thing – a ritual murder or something." His
partner didn't reply. He had taken one look at Clea and bent
double with the dry heaves.

"There's another man outside in the snow," I said in a
voice I didn't recognize.

The heavy cop straightened up, squared his shoulders and
walked to the exit door. "I'll check it out," he said, and I
thought how grateful he would be to fill his lungs with cold
fresh air and have a chance to redeem himself.

The Burt Reynolds officer turned to us and said in carefully measured tones, "I think the inspector is going to be
pretty interested in talking to you."

Sally watched him walk across the room.

"You know, I've never had a cop," she said.

"You'll have the whole Saskatoon force to choose from
before this is over," I said, and I looked around that scene from
hell and thought I had never said a stupider thing in my life.

In fairness, there didn't seem to be much to say. Sally and
I lapsed into silence until Inspector Mary Ross McCourt
came over and introduced herself. She didn't look like a cop.
She was about average height, not good looking, but carefully groomed. Her hair was bleached an improbable white
blond, and her makeup was dramatic, red 1940s lipstick,
scarlet fingernails, but her eyes behind the bright blue eye
shadow were intelligent and knowing. I had the sense, as my
grandmother used to say, that not much got by her.

Inspector McCourt quickly established two things: in

response to my question, she said that, yes, she was the niece of my old friend Hilda. But it was clear from her manner that I was not to presume that friendship with her aunt put us on social terms.

The Burt Reynolds constable brought her a chair, but Mary Ross McCourt did not sit down. She stood with her hands resting on the chair back and looked at Sally and me. Psychological advantage to the inspector.

"Under normal circumstances," she said, "we'd go downtown, but those streets are lethal. It would be unconscionable to ask you to drive on them." She looked hard at Sally and me. "I'm sure you agree that there's been enough death for one night."

Sally and I exchanged glances: two schoolgirls in the principal's office struggling with the etiquette of whether to answer a rhetorical statement. We didn't say anything. But we didn't stay silent. I had a question of my own, and it wasn't rhetorical.

"How did she die?" I asked.

Mary Ross McCourt sighed. "The pathologist's initial judgement is a bullet through the heart. About here," she said, tapping the centre of her own chest with a scarlet-tipped finger. "Now, Ms. Love, I wonder if you'd be kind enough to move out of earshot while I talk to Mrs. Kilbourn."

Sally picked up her chair and carried it over to the area behind the scalpel junkie. Inspector McCourt moved her chair a little closer to mine but she still didn't sit down. Up close, her hair was as blond and fluffy as Barbie's, but she didn't sound like a Barbie.

"Mrs. Kilbourn," she said, "I want you to tell me about your life in the last few hours. Don't edit. Everything is significant."

I couldn't seem to stop talking – shock, I guess, or aftershock. Mary Ross McCourt listened impassively, like a psychoanalyst in the movies. All the while I rattled on about preparing and eating the dinner with my children and driving through the blizzard, the crime site experts moved purposefully around us dusting surfaces for fingerprints; taking photographs; putting evidence in what looked like heavy plastic freezer bags; drawing floor plans. Across the room, prim as a schoolgirl, Sally sat in the shadow of the scalpel junkie. The scene was as surreal as a Salvador Dali landscape.

When I finished, the inspector thanked me and suggested I stay in touch with the police. Then her professionalism broke. She took a step closer to me. Suddenly the eyes behind the bright blue shadow were glacial, and her voice was low with fury.

"This is a terrible, terrible crime," she said. "Whoever did this will never know another peaceful moment this side of the grave." For the first time that night, Mary Ross McCourt reminded me of her aunt.

The inspector took her chair over to where Sally was sitting, and I was interested to see that she established the same relationship with Sally as she had had with me: questioner standing, witness sitting. Then they brought in the Righteous Protester and some new cops came to take Clea's body and I lost interest in police procedures.

I followed along as they carried the bodies toward the front door. At first, the scene outside seemed like an instant replay of the night Erotobiography opened. The blizzard had stopped, and some hardy souls had braved the snow to come and gawk. The media people were there, too, adjusting equipment, waiting. But there were differences. This time the centre of attention wasn't Sally Love; it was the two blanket-covered shapes on the stretchers being loaded into twin ambulances. And this time the target of the crowd's moral outrage wasn't art but murder.

I was standing in the foyer, watching the ambulances pull

away, when Sally came up beside me. She couldn't have been
with Mary Ross McCourt ten minutes.

I was surprised. "You certainly got off lightly," I said.

Sally shrugged. "I didn't have much to say. Jo, I haven't got
an alibi. I was working all day in the studio. I didn't go out. I
didn't see anybody until I ran into one of the merry pranksters
in my driveway after Clea called. He was hunkered down
behind the Porsche – probably giving me a flat tire."

"In the middle of a blizzard?" I asked.

"Jo, these guys are on a holy mission. Snow doesn't mean
diddly to them."

"I hope you told Inspector McCourt," I said. "Sal, that
could be important. Did you notice anything about him
that could help the police find him?"

"Sure," she said, "he hates art, he hates me, and he was
wearing a ski mask. That should narrow it down for them.
But I got my revenge. I stole his tuque."

"What did Inspector McCourt say?" I asked.

"About the hat?"

"No, about the whole thing?"

Sally shrugged. "What could she say? She did her best
Katharine Hepburn imitation of the public official who
means business, then she just gave up – probably told me
what she told you: 'Don't leave town. Keep in touch.' Now
come on. Let's get out of here. My bravado is failing fast."

"We still have the rest of that bottle of Jack Daniel's at my
house," I said. "Bourbon's good for bravado – actually I could
use a little bravado myself. Let's go."

My kids greeted us at the door, white-faced and concerned. The local TV station had interrupted the Rose Bowl
festivities to show the bodies of Clea Poole and the Righteous Protester being loaded into ambulances, and there had
been a shot of Sally and me running for her car. Pete helped
us off with our coats, and Greg, without being asked,

brought us each a stiff drink. I was liking him better by the moment. I gave the kids an abbreviated account of what we knew, assured them that we were okay and told them they could get back to what they had been doing. Sally and I needed to talk.

We took our drinks downstairs to the family room. There was a fire, and Sally sprawled on a rocker near the fireplace. I curled up on the couch in front of it.

"I can't get warm," Sally said.

"Here," I said, handing her an afghan. "Mieka made this for me the year she broke her leg skiing."

Sally wrapped it around her shoulders. "I wonder if Taylor will ever want to make an afghan for her notorious mother."

"Sure," I said. "Notorious mothers are the best kind."

Sally smiled and lifted her glass. "To mothers," she said. Then her smile faded. "And to Clea Poole, may she rest in peace."

We drank, and Sally said thoughtfully, "You know, Jo, I'm glad she's dead. She was my – what was that bird the old sailor had hung around his neck in the poem?"

"An albatross," I said.

"Right. Clea was my albatross. She wanted me to carry her around forever. She would have done anything for me; you know, she did some terrible things. She had no morality when it came to me."

Instinctively, I looked over my shoulder to see if anyone had heard her. "Sally, you can say that to me, but I'd be careful not to say it to anyone else. Clea didn't put a bullet through her own heart and throw herself down on that bed because she was in a snit. Somebody murdered her, and until the police find out who did, you're going to have to watch what you say."

The fire was dying down, and I got up and put on another log. Behind me, Sally said, "I wonder who they think killed her? The nakedness makes it look like some kind of sex thing."

I shuddered. "You mean fun and games that got out of hand?" I asked. "Is that a possibility? You've known her all these years. Were there other connections, another relationship that might have gone sour?"

"All her relationships turned sour," Sally said flatly. "This city is filled with her failed relationships. Those baby cops we saw tonight are going to learn a lot about life before they're through with Clea." She stood up and stretched her arms above her head. "I've got to make tracks, Jo. That car of mine is fairly noticeable, and it's only a matter of time before the media people start beating down your door."

"Sal, stay here. The roads are terrible. I can open out this couch for you."

"No," Sally said. "The best thing for me right now is work. Take my mind off things. I'm going to go to the studio, take a bath, crack open my Christmas Courvoisier and make some art."

I walked her upstairs and stood in the entrance hall as she put on her boots and parka. At the door, she turned and hugged me.

"Thanks for everything. I'm not sure I could have made it if you hadn't been there." She smiled. "People can always count on Jo, can't they?" she said, and then she walked down our front path and vanished into the night.

I woke up early the next morning, anxious and restless. When I went down to make coffee, the sky was beginning to lighten, and I looked out on a white world. New snow was everywhere. The tracks I had made New Year's Eve when I'd gone to the bottom of the garden and found Clea waiting were gone. Clea's tracks would be gone, too – all her tracks, everywhere, filled in with snow as if she had never been.

I went out and picked up the morning paper from my mailbox. The double homicide had beaten out the blizzard in the headlines. Pictures of Clea and the Righteous Protester were on the front page. She was graduating from university, and he was standing in front of the Mendel with his placard and his Bible. I threw the paper unread on the breakfast table, went upstairs, showered and dressed. I still felt lousy, so I came downstairs, picked up the keys to the Volvo and headed out, figuring that maybe a drive would help.

Inevitably, I guess, I was drawn to the gallery. In the first light of morning, it looked quite festive. The bright yellow of the banners with Sally's name was matched by the bright yellow crime scene tape; there were police around the front entrance, and on the lawn, police dogs were pawing at the snow. Other people had decided to take in the murder scene, too, and traffic was slow. I was inching along when I looked across the road and saw Stuart Lachlan out on his front lawn. His house was close enough that I had a clear view of what he was doing. Bundled against the cold, he was repairing one of Taylor's snow people. Someone had knocked off an arm and caved in its side. Stu was methodically repairing the damage. In the doorway, I could see Nina's neat figure, watching.

I drove past the gallery and made a U turn. I pulled over to the curb in front of number seventeen and rolled down my window. Stuart came over immediately and leaned in. When she saw me, Nina ran out, too, and stood shivering behind him. She was immaculate as always but she looked tired and old, and I realized what a toll all this was taking on her.

"I guess there's no point asking if you heard about Clea," I said. "I couldn't sleep, either. But I didn't think of making a snowman as therapy."

Stu looked at me gravely. "It's not therapy, Jo. It was vandalism. I didn't want Taylor to wake up and see her snow

lady wrecked. Nina was out here trying to repair it first, but
. . . there are things a man has to do."

I looked to see if he was joking. He wasn't. "You're a good
father, Stu," I said, and meant it. "Anyway, I'm glad to see
you're up and about. You're both okay, aren't you?"

Stu shook his head and laughed humourlessly. "Couldn't
be better. Have you read your morning paper? The media
are making certain connections between the murders and
Erotobiography. Of course, Sally's being discovered at the
scene of the crime didn't help matters. On the radio this
morning there was a not exactly veiled suggestion that if I
hadn't been so anxious to push my wife's pornography, two
more people would be greeting the dawn today. And the
gallery's a disaster – police everywhere. Tracking dogs
sniffing the galleries. Doors left open. Temperature control
all shot to hell. I was over there this morning pleading with
the police to let me move some paintings into the vault
until they're through." He raked his hand through his thin-
ning hair. "If I'd known there was going to be such chaos, I
wouldn't have . . ."

"You wouldn't have what, Stuart?" Nina's voice sounded
small and frightened.

He gave her an odd look. "I wouldn't have been so eager
to accept Sally's offer to donate Erotobiography to the
Mendel. What did you think I was going to say, Nina?"
There was an ugly edge to his voice. The spoor of murder
and suspicion was already changing everything.

"I don't know," she said vaguely, "something else." And
then she asked the painful question, the one we'd all backed
away from.

"Who do they think did it, Joanne? Is Sally a suspect?"

"I don't think they've gotten that far yet," I said. "Listen,
I didn't tell you, but I was there at the gallery last night. I . . .
I was the one who found the Righteous Protester."

I could hear Nina's intake of breath. She looked quickly at Stu. In the hypercharged atmosphere of that morning, I could see the fear in her eyes.

"I know," I said. "It's terrifying, all of it, but, Nina, they'll find out who really committed the murders. The police inspector who interviewed us last night looked as if she could see through walls. When she gets this case put together, she'll know Sally was just in the wrong place at the wrong time."

"Thank God," said Stu.

"Yes," I agreed. "Thank God. Stu, you'd better get Nina back inside. It's too cold to be out with just a sweater. I'll talk to you later. Ni, don't worry. Everything's going to be all right. It really is."

As I turned onto the University Bridge, I wondered if my assurances had sounded as hollow to Nina's ears as they had to mine. I looked back at Stuart Lachlan's house. Stu and Nina were standing on the front lawn watching me, and Taylor had come out and joined them. Behind them, in exactly the same grouping – Daddy on the left, Mummy on the right and the little girl safe between them – was Taylor's family of snow people. As Angus would say, "Deadly."

I drove straight to my office at the university and worked for a couple of hours. I made up a syllabus for each of my classes, checked some handouts and read over my lecture notes for the first day – busywork to make me believe I was in charge of my world.

It was a little after noon when I went home to the hollow feeling of an empty house. There was an empty ice-cream pail on the counter in the kitchen, and when I put it under the sink to keep kitchen scraps in, I noticed two burrito wrappings in the garbage. Wherever they were, Peter and Angus were well fed.

I found their note on the kitchen table. They'd gone tobogganing at Cranberry Flats with some of Peter's friends from the university. They'd be home for supper. I could imagine how pleased Pete would be to have Angus along. I made myself a sandwich, then I peeled a bag of onions and threw them in the processor to slice for onion soup. Homemade soup would taste pretty good after an afternoon tobogganing.

I was just cleaning up when the phone rang. It was Sally. Her gun was missing.

"What gun?" I said. "For God's sake, what kind of person owns a gun?"

"A person like me who works alone at night in a house that sometimes has a couple of hundred thousand dollars' worth of art lying around. God damn it, Jo, don't yell at me. Stu bought the gun for me the first year we were married, and it was a good idea. That studio of mine is right on the river bank. Anyone could break in. And someone has. Remember I told you I had two break-ins over Christmas? Well, both times whoever was there left things behind: more used sanitary napkins, a bag of kitty litter, also used, and some stuff that's too disgusting to talk about. But the point is, because they were leaving things, I never checked to see if things were missing. The paintings were okay, and that's about all that's of interest there."

"Except your gun," I said.

"Yes, except my gun," she repeated. "And according to the police, it appears to have been the same kind as the one that did the job on Clea and poor old Righteous Protester."

"How do they know?"

"The same way they knew to look for a gun at my house in the first place. From the registration. God, Jo, it looks like I've really managed to get myself up shit creek."

The realization seemed to hit us both at the same time, but I was the one who put it into words.

"Sally, I think we're going to have to stop talking about what you've managed to do to yourself. Too many things are going wrong for you. The police show up at the gallery as soon as you discover Clea's body; your gun, apparently the same kind as the one that committed the murders, suddenly disappears. I think there's somebody else involved here."

Her voice on the other end of the line was small and sad. "Yeah, I think you're right, Jo. And you know what else? I think whoever wants me up shit creek is doing everything they can to make sure I don't have a paddle."

CHAPTER

7

When I read the paper's lead story the morning of Clea's funeral I could feel my throat closing. The police had started to give the media details about their investigation, and there weren't many arrows pointing away from Sally and me. There was one item of hard news: Kyle, the museum guard, told the police that minutes before they arrived, the burglar alarm had gone off in the delivery area at the back of the gallery. When he went out to investigate, he saw a figure running down the hill toward the river bank. The snow was so heavy that he couldn't give the police a description, couldn't in fact tell for certain whether the runner had been male or female. Kyle had given chase but when he heard the siren from the police car, he returned to the gallery. The only thing that seemed to be missing from the gallery was the film from the video camera suspended over the bridal bed.

A mystery runner and an empty camera: it wasn't much.

The human interest angle was more fertile ground. From the beginning, the local paper couldn't seem to get enough of Clea and Sally. The morning after the murder, the obituary column had carried the details of Clea's funeral: services were to be conducted at the University Women's Centre by a woman named Vivian Ludlow from the radical feminist community. She taught a course called Human Justice, and I knew her slightly from the university. Interment was at a cemetery on the east side of the city. While men were welcome at the interment, they would not be permitted to attend the funeral service.

The paper managed to repeat the details of the funeral arrangements in most of the stories about Clea's life and death. Those few lines always gave a titillating but not libellous spin to their stories. Clea's association with Sally at womanswork; the arson that destroyed their gallery; the public outcry against the bisexual imagery of Erotobiography: all were suddenly set against a dark feminist world, a world where men were not welcome. It was hot stuff.

The Righteous Protester wasn't hot stuff. Even on the day of his funeral, he only rated a column and a half on page three. His name was Reg Helms, and as I read his obituary, I was struck again with how sad and stunted his life had been: a childless marriage to a woman who had died the year before of cancer, no friends to speak of, and a dead-end clerical job with a company called Peter's Pumpkin Seeds. Reg Helms was a great writer of letters to the newspaper; and every talk-show host in town recognized his voice. His preoccupation was our disintegrating society, and it was a theme he played with variations. Sometimes it was Quebec that was destroying the country, sometimes ethnic groups or Aboriginal peoples, but the subject that really warmed his heart was sexual permissiveness. Sally's show had been a holy mission for him. He had been fifty-four years old when he died.

The facts of Reg Helms's life had become as familiar to me as my own, but today there was something different. There was a final paragraph that laid out the medical details of his death. Helms had died of a bullet in the carotid artery.

The pathologist said death had come swiftly; nonetheless, there had been a second shot. Police theorized that when Reg Helms had raised his hand to his shattered throat, his murderer had fired again. The second bullet had struck Helms's watch. He had died at 6:21 on Tuesday, January first. His watch had recorded hour, minute, day and date. Cosmic timekeeping.

As soon as I saw the numbers, I felt a rush of excitement. Sally's phone call had come at ten to seven, and she had told me she'd just arrived at the gallery. I'd left home immediately. Under ordinary circumstances, I could have been at the gallery in ten minutes, but the blizzard and the walk across the lawn outside the gallery had slowed me. It would have been after seven when I found Reg Helms's body. At 6:21 I'd been at home with my kids cleaning up after dinner, getting ready to watch the end of the Rose Bowl game. I had an alibi. And if there was justice, Sally would have one, too.

She answered the phone on the first ring. When I told her about the story in the paper, she was restrained.

"It's great for you, Jo. Really, I'm happy and relieved that you're off the hook. It was awful knowing I'd involved you in all this. But it's no out for me. I don't know what time I got to the gallery. I don't even wear a watch. If you say I called you at ten to seven, then I must have gotten to the Mendel at about a quarter to. I called you as soon as I saw Clea."

"But, Sal, don't you see, I can tell the police that. I can swear to it."

"It's not enough. My best friend swearing that I told her I'd just arrived at the scene of a crime and found a body – it's just too thin, Jo. The cops would blow that alibi out of the water in about eleven seconds. I need more than that. I've been sitting here figuring out times. Let's say I got to the Mendel at 6:45. The roads were bad so it took me about ten minutes to drive there. That puts me out in front of my house at 6:35. And I must have been out there five minutes or so having my altercation with the guy in the ski mask." She laughed. "That probably happened around 6:30, so he'd be the one to give me the alibi. Do you think I can count on him?"

"Stranger things have happened," I said.

"No," Sally said, "stranger things than that have not happened. Face it, Jo. Nothing's changed. I'm still up the creek."

As I went upstairs to dress for the funeral, the relief I'd felt earlier was gone. Sally was right. Nothing had changed. She was still up the creek. And she still didn't have a paddle.

When Sally came in to have a cup of coffee before we went to the funeral, the paper was lying on the kitchen table. She picked it up and started reading aloud. There were signed messages of condolence from a local women's art co-operative and the Daughters of Bilitis. There was also a full-page ad from one of the fundamentalist churches containing a number of first-person accounts from men who described themselves as victims of pornography. All of them described exemplary boyhoods that ended abruptly when they were exposed to pornographic pictures and began to masturbate their way down the slippery slope to damnation.

When she had read the final confession, Sally slapped the paper down on the table.

"God, these guys are amazing. The old monkey-see-monkey-do theory of art and sex. Didn't the mums who taught these good boys ever tell them to keep their hands above the sheets?"

Angus, sitting opposite her, tried to look suave, as if he had conversations about masturbation at the breakfast table every day.

Sally seemed to dawdle over her coffee. I was the one who finally stood up and said it was time to go.

"My first all-girl funeral," Sally said to Angus as she zipped up her parka. He gave her a look that made me realize he was growing up.

It was a brilliant January morning, so cold there were sun dogs in the sky. We didn't talk much as we walked the few blocks to the campus. Classes started the next day, so there were students around with winter tans and new knapsacks and bags from the bookstore. On the signpost outside the University Women's Centre was an old poster with a picture of Paul McCartney and the word HELP in block letters above his head. Someone had drawn a balloon around it and given Paul some additional dialogue. "HELP – I'm old and boring," Paul said.

"No one can accuse Clea of that one any more," said Sally, and there was an edge to her voice that I should have picked up on, but didn't. In retrospect, it would have been better if Sally had not gone to the funeral. From the minute we walked up the steps to the women's centre, she was edgy and combative, and there was nothing inside that building to chill her out.

The women's centre was hot, and it had that egg-salad smell that seems to linger in all public buildings that serve short-order food. It was a pretty barren place: some posters on reproductive choice and date rape on the walls, and chairs arranged in semicircles with an aisle up the middle. By the time we arrived, almost all the chairs were full. Even so, the sister Sally sat next to ostentatiously got up and moved to the back of the room, and there was a nasty hissing sound from the people in the row behind us.

"Cows," Sally said under her breath. "So fucking self-righteous, so fucking precious about the place for women's art, but not one of them had the decency to ask if they could use my work on their little card here. Look at this." She tapped the front of the memorial card with one of her long, blunt fingers. It was a reproduction of a painting Sally had done in the early seventies: an adolescent girl sat legs apart, naked in front of the mirror over her dressing table. Her look, as she sat absorbed in the mystery of her body, was both radiant and fearful. The girl was Clea Poole.

"Not that I mind," Sally was saying, "but these women are always whining about being used by the power structure, you'd think one of them might understand the laws of copyright."

I started to say something, but at that moment, two women began to sing a cappella and the casket was brought in. It was covered in a quilt with a clitoral pattern, peach and ivory. All the pallbearers were women, and it stirred something in me to see them, strong and handsome, carrying a sister. When the singing ended, there was silence, then a thin woman in designer blue jeans and a white silk blouse came out of the front row, laid a hand on the casket and began to speak.

The thing you noticed first about Vivian Ludlow was her hair. She was younger than me, perhaps forty, but her hair was white, and she wore it shoulder length and extravagantly curled. It was very attractive. She was very attractive: good skin, no makeup, a full-lipped, sensitive mouth. She made no effort to raise her voice, yet she commanded that room.

"Like all of you here today, Clea Poole lived a life of risk and confrontation and inherent subversiveness," she began. "To be a woman is to live every day with the knowledge that the personal is political. It is to risk everything and to gain everything. It is to know the radically transgressive power of gender, but it is also to experience the moment of incarnation as self becomes flesh."

Beside me, Sally's voice was low with disgust. "They

think they invented it, you know. Clea made me go to a meeting once, and at the end the speaker jumped on the table and invited us all to have a peek at her uterus."

In spite of everything, I started to laugh. No one else was laughing. At the front, Vivian Ludlow was asking Clea's friends not to turn their eyes from the broken woman she was at the last because to do that was to devalue the purpose of Clea's life. Every eye in the place was on us now, and Sally was gazing back defiantly. Around us little brush fires of hostility were breaking out. At the front, Vivian Ludlow had moved to a safer topic, Clea's delight in Christmas, and I felt myself relax.

"Remember," Vivian Ludlow said softly, "how every year as the holidays began, Clea would make each of her friends a gingerbread house, small, perfectly crafted with love, an exquisite work by woman for woman, a reminder throughout that family time that we are family, too."

There was sobbing in the room. Beside me, Sally said in disgust, "And all she ever asked in return was that you crawl into the little gingerbread house with her and live happily ever after."

"Sal, for God's sake, shut up," I whispered. "You're going to get us lynched."

She glared at me, but she lapsed into silence until the pallbearers brought the casket down the aisle. On the way out, the other mourners gave us a wide berth, and as we left the women's centre and stepped into the brilliant January sunshine, I thought we were home free.

I was wrong. There was an old bus parked across the street from the centre, and as Sally and I stood on the steps, people began pouring out of it. They knew what they were doing. As they hit the street, a woman gave each of them a sign, and they crossed toward us. The messages on the signs were

Biblical, but the selections showed a distinct bias toward Old Testament retribution; verses about sin and punishment and death seemed to be the favourites.

"The revenge of the Righteous Protester," Sally said mildly, and she waved to them. They didn't wave back. Councillor Hank Mewhort was leading them. He was still wearing his "Silver Broom: Saskatoon '90" ski jacket, but the old green Hilltops tuque had been replaced by a tweed cap with ear flaps. The hat was an improvement, but the face under it was still smug and mean. He started to say something to Sally, but suddenly his jaw dropped and he fell silent. I turned to see what had stopped him.

Behind us, the doors of the women's centre had opened and the pallbearers were bringing out the casket. When I saw them, I knew why Hank Mewhort had frozen in his tracks. The pallbearers had changed their clothing. During the service, they had been wearing street clothes; now they were all in black – combat boots, skintight pants, leather jackets – and they were wearing gorilla masks, big toothy ones, the kind you pull right over your head.

Beside me, Sally snorted. "Just what this party needed, the Guerrilla Girls."

"What?" I said. The world was getting too complex for me.

"It's a political thing some women who make art in New York started. I guess these dopey souls think they're the road company. It's supposed to be a protest against tokenism and chauvinism and sexism and paternalism – all the isms. It's ridiculous, but of course Clea thought it was swell."

As the Guerrilla Girls loaded the casket into the hearse, Councillor Mewhort's friends stood dumbstruck. They looked as if they had seen the beast with seven horns and ten heads from Revelation. When the hearse pulled away, the Guerrilla Girls raised their leather-jacketed arms in a solemn salute.

Beside me Sally said, "Makes you proud to be a woman, doesn't it?"

One of the Guerrilla Girls heard her and she gave Sally the finger. Sally went over to her and ripped the mask from her face.

"I should have guessed you wouldn't miss out on this one, Anya," she said. "Look, why don't you do the art world a favour. Find some nice guy, settle down and forget about painting."

One of the other Guerrilla Girls reached toward Sally and shoved her.

"Cat fight," yelled Councillor Mewhort from the sidewalk. A Guerrilla Girl ran down the stairs and grabbed him by the collar. Then the fight was on. I didn't wait to see who won. It's hard to care about who wins a fight between moralists who want people to be struck down and feminists who wear animal heads to celebrate womanhood. Hank Mewhort had fallen to the sidewalk, and there were three Guerrilla Girls on top of him. Sally was trying to pull them away when I came up behind her, grabbed her by the arm and dragged her toward College Drive. I thought I heard a man's voice yell thanks at our retreating backs.

"Why were you trying to save him?" I asked.

"Three against one," said Sally. "Even if you're an asshole, those aren't fair odds."

I gave her shoulder a squeeze. Then without another word, we walked home.

The story has an addendum. That night after I'd driven home half of Angus's basketball team, I dug out my lecture notes for the next day and opened a bottle of Tuborg. Angus was having a shower, and Peter and Christy were downstairs studying. I went into the living room, put on an old recording of Dennis Brain playing the Mozart horn concertos and started to look over my introductory lecture. I had crossed out a couple of references that were no longer current and added a few that were when I heard someone at the front door. I looked out the window and saw Sally's Porsche at the curb.

It was a bitter night, and when I opened the door Sally walked past me into the house. She was carrying a packing case.

"Here," she said, leaning it against the wall, "this is for you. I'm sorry about this morning. I'm not much good when I feel cornered."

"I remember," I said.

She grinned. "Right. Anyway, open your present."

I started to wrestle with the box.

"I'll do it," she said. She bent over the box, and with a few strong, sure movements, she had it open and was holding the painting that had been inside.

"Let's take it into the light and see what you think," she said.

The picture took my breath away. Part of it, I guess, was seeing a piece of art that had a six-figure value casually propped against my kitchen wall, but the real impact came from the subject matter.

The scene was a tea party in the clearing down by the water at the Loves' summer cottage. The picture was suffused with summer light, that soft incandescence that comes when heat turns rain to mist. In the foreground there was a round table covered with a snowy cloth. On either side of the table was a wooden chair painted dark green. Nina Love was in one of the chairs. The eyelet sundress she was wearing was the colour of new ferns, and her skin was translucent. The light seemed to come through her flesh the way it comes through fine china. She was in profile, and the dark curve of her hair seemed to balance exactly the pale line of her features: yin and yang. Across the table from her sat a girl of fifteen, very tanned in a two-piece bathing suit that did nothing to hide a soft layer of baby fat. The girl's braided hair was bleached fair by the sun. Her expression as she watched Nina's graceful hands tilt the Limoges teapot was rapt – and familiar. The girl's face was my own thirty-two years before, and it glowed with admiration and love.

The woman and the girl bending toward one another over the luminous white cloth seemed enclosed in a private world. In the distance beyond them, the lake, blue as cobalt, lapped the shore.

There were other figures in the picture, and I knew them, too. Under the water, enclosed in a kind of bubble, were a man and a young girl. I could recognize the slope of Desmond Love's shoulders and the sweep of his daughter's blond hair as she bent over the fantastic sand castle they were building together in their little world under the waves.

Sally had been watching my face. Finally she said laconically, "Well?"

"It's incredible. I don't know what to say. The colours are wonderful – they seem to shimmer. And the way you've remembered us – not just the way we looked, but the way those days felt endless and hot . . ."

"And innocent," said Sally.

"Yes," I agreed, "and innocent. Sal, no one's ever given me a gift like this. I don't know what to say."

She smiled and made a gesture of dismissal.

"Does it have a title?" I asked.

"*Perfect Circles*," Sally said.

"Yeah, I guess that's right, isn't it. You and Des in one circle and then Nina and me. God, I'd forgotten how I idolized her. It must have been awful for her to have this fat little girl hanging on her all the time."

"She loved it," said Sally. "She loved your need." And then she looked at me oddly. "I'm not being fair. Nina loved you, Jo. She still does. The one good thing I've ever been able to say about my mother is that she loves you."

"And you, Sal, if you'd let her."

For an answer she shrugged. "Anyway, if you ever decide to take up art, don't paint over this one. It's the only picture I ever did of Nina. She's so beautiful I can almost forgive her. Anyway, those were good summers."

"I can close my eyes still and see you and Des coming down the hill from the cottage with all the stuff you used to make your sand castles: shovels and trowels and spatulas and palette knives and sprinklers to keep the sand moist, and things to use as moulds and shapers. It always looked like you were going to work."

Sally smiled sadly. "We were. Des was a wonderful teacher. He was a wonderful artist. He was a wonderful father . . ." Her voice broke.

I looked up, surprised. "Hey, can I buy you a beer?"

"Sure," she said.

I went to the fridge and pulled out a cold Tuborg.

Sally checked the label carefully. "This one's okay. I won't spaz out on you." She snapped the cap off and held the bottle toward me. "To old times."

"To old times," I said.

For a while we were both silent. Then I said, "That picture brings so much back. You know, a couple of weeks ago Mieka asked me what happened between us, and when I tried to tell her, I thought I didn't really understand it myself."

"You were Nina's friend," she said simply.

"That's not fair," I said. "You were the one who went away. After Des died and you went away to New York to that art school, you vanished from my life."

"Is that what Nina told you?" Sally shook her head in

disbelief. "Jo, there was no art school. I never went to any school after I left Bishop Lambeth's."

"Come on. You were thirteen. You had to go school. That was the whole reason Nina let you move down there with Izaak Levin."

Sally roared. "Trust Nina to obey the letter if not the spirit of the truth. I guess I was at a school of the arts, except there was only one teacher, Izaak, and one pupil – me."

"What did you do?"

She took a long swallow of her Tuborg and set the bottle down in front of her.

"Well, the first year after Des died, I was pretty wrecked so we travelled most of the time – just drove around the U.S.A. in Izaak's shiny yellow convertible, seeing the sights, staying in motels."

"Sal, I don't believe a word of this. Why would a famous man like Izaak give up a year of his life to drive a thirteen-year-old girl around?"

She gave me a mocking smile.

"Sally, no. I know you said that you slept with him but . . . God, you were still a child. That's a pathology."

"Not such a child, Jo. It was a fair exchange. He got to have sex to his heart's content with a hot, young girl, and I got to see the U.S.A. in his Chevrolet. It worked out."

"How did you live?"

"Well, Izaak didn't have to work in burger joints to support us. He had quite a reputation in those days, and every so often he'd just sit down and make some phone calls. Then he'd go to some junior college or ladies' group, talk about art, pick up his cheque and we'd move along. He tried to make it interesting for me. You know, Vermont when the leaves changed and warm places in the winter. Once he did a class in San Luis Obispo for a month or so." She smiled at the memory. "Oh, Jo, we stayed at this motel that had fantasy rooms – a real fifties place – the court of Louis, jungle land, the wild west, that kind of thing." She shook her head and smiled. "Anyway, after a year we went to New York and Izaak wrote and went on TV and taught a bit, and I began to make art.

"I painted and we went to galleries and we fucked, and that was my school of the arts." She laughed. "Not a bad preparation, when you get right down to it, I guess. Anyway, that went on till I was about twenty. Things were getting ugly in the States – Johnson, Vietnam, all that stuff. Izaak said he'd stuck it out through McCarthy, but he'd had enough. We came to Saskatchewan for the Summer Art Colony at Emma Lake and we never went back."

"Sally, I'm incredulous. Where was Nina in all of this?"

She stood up. "Recovering from the tragic death of her husband," she said coldly. "Look, Jo, I've got to motor. I'm glad you like the painting."

I put my coat and boots on and followed her out to her car. I wanted the closeness to continue a little longer. As we walked down the driveway, our breath rose in ice fog around us. At the curb, the Porsche gleamed white in the moonlight, but as we got close to it, I noticed there was something wrong with the way it was positioned. It didn't take long to discover why. Someone had slashed the tires. Sally and I went around and checked them out. They had all been attacked, and whoever had done the slashing had done it over and over again. I felt a coldness in the pit of my stomach, and it didn't have anything to do with the weather.

"Sal, let's go back in and call the police," I said.

She looked into the heavens. "Full moon tonight – Looney-Tunes time. The cops are going to be busy chasing down people whose eyeteeth have started to grow. They won't get to us for hours." She hugged herself against the cold. "So, Jo, it looks like you're going to have to ask me for a sleepover."

"Done," I said. And we trudged through the snow to the warmth of the house.

CHAPTER

8

On the tenth of January I finished my class on populist politics and the Saskatchewan election of '82 and walked across campus to my office in the arts building. From habit, I slowed up in front of the room where English 250 met. Mieka had been taking that class before Christmas, and it had always given me a nice feeling to walk by and see her sitting at her desk by the window, chewing the end of her pen, looking thoughtful. The desk by the window was empty now; Mieka hadn't come back to university after the break. During the hours in which she should have been learning about Alice Munro and Sinclair Ross, she was stripping woodwork at the Old Court House and talking to suppliers. Her decision didn't please me much.

When I walked through my office door, the phone was ringing. It was Sally, and what she had to say didn't please me much, either.

"Jo, do you have any free time this afternoon?" She was silent for a beat. "There's news."

"I have to pick up Angus's skates over on Main Street –

the sharpener's near the Broadway Café. I can meet you there in fifteen minutes."

"The Broadway'll be fine. I'm at Izaak's now just around the corner."

"Sal, is the news good?"

When she answered, she sounded infinitely weary. "Is it ever?" she asked.

It was a grey, sleety day, and the only parking place I could find was three blocks from the restaurant. By the time I walked through the front door, I was chilled to the bone and apprehensive, but the Broadway Café was a welcoming place for the cold and the lonely. It looked the way I imagined the café looked in Hemingway's story "A Clean, Well-Lighted Place": a shining counter with stools down one side of the room; dark wooden booths upholstered in wine-coloured leather down the other. The walls were covered with mirrors and blowups of pictures of old movie stars. Sally was sitting in a back booth under a palely tinted Fred Astaire.

When she saw me, she smiled wanly. "They found my gun," she said without preamble. "Some kids were tobogganing down by the river and they found a gun and took it to the police. They say it's the one that did the murders."

The waitress came over and poured coffee for us. When she left, I turned to Sally.

"Okay, start at the beginning."

Her hair was loose around her shoulders, and she ran her hands through it in a gesture of frustration. "Tell me where the beginning is, Jo, because I don't know any more. Do you know how often I've been down to the cop shop? But until this morning I thought it was all going to go away. It seemed as if everything was in limbo. Nothing got better, but nothing got worse, either. Well, now something has gotten worse. And, Jo, nothing's gotten better: the police haven't found the tape that was in the video camera at the gallery the night Clea was killed. They haven't even got a sniff about who it was Kyle chased down the river bank. And I still don't have an alibi."

"Have the police stopped looking for the man in the ski mask?" I asked.

"Mary Ross McCourt says they haven't, but now that they've got the gun, I wonder how hard they're going to look. There are just too many pieces falling into place."

Sally took a sip of coffee and closed her eyes. She looked exhausted.

"Are you okay?" I asked.

"Just great," she said. "I've got the police breathing down my neck from nine to five, and when they go off duty, the merry pranksters are in there cranking up the action."

"Oh, no, I thought that would be over by now," I said.

"Well, you thought wrong," she said flatly. "It's still, as they say, a happening thing. Most of it's just head games: eggs frozen on the windshield in the morning, sugar in the gas tank, lipstick love letters on the windows of my studio. But it's getting to me. I'm giving up. Tomorrow, I'm moving into an apartment in the Park Towers, you know the ones, downtown by the Bessborough. Stu has a friend in the penthouse who's in Florida for the winter. This guy likes to think of himself as a patron of the arts, so he didn't mind me using his place."

"Probably gets off on the idea of the notorious Sally Love sleeping in his bed," I said.

For the first time that afternoon she laughed. "Probably. But it's nice, and there's a swimming pool for Taylor when she visits. Anyway, I should give you my number there." She wrote it down on a napkin and handed it to me with a sigh. "God, I wish this was all over. But it will be soon. And when I can get working again, I'll be okay. Good old Stu found me some studio space at the university. I've already moved my stuff in."

"Sounds like Stu's turned chivalrous now that you're a lady in distress."

"Well, it might be something a little less – is the word *altruistic*? – anyway, a little more selfish than chivalry. Stu's got this book on my art coming out in the spring, and I think he's worried I'm not going to like it. He's already puffing out his chest and talking about how art thrives on diverse critical approaches . . ."

"Which means?" I asked.

"Which means that what he's written is a crock and he's terrified I'm going to blow the whistle on him."

"But you wouldn't," I said.

"Jo, this is serious. It isn't personal. It's not about me. It's about what I do. If it's stupid, I'll have to say so."

"Well," I said, "for everyone's sake, let's hope it isn't stupid."

"Right," she said, standing up and pulling on her coat. "Let's hope it isn't stupid. And let's hope that guy who was trying to give me a flat the night of the murder decides he'll give me an alibi if I give him his tuque back, and let's hope my terrorists get frostbite or writer's cramp and leave me alone." She shrugged. "Hey, let's go crazy and wish for it all. Maybe for once life will work out."

I followed her toward the front of the restaurant. Halfway to the cash register Sally stopped and looked up at a picture on the wall. It was an old poster advertising *The Misfits* with Clark Gable, Marilyn Monroe and Montgomery Clift.

"All dead," said Sally.

"But we remember them," I said, "through their movies."

She gave me the old mocking Sally smile. "That doesn't make them any less dead," she said.

I picked up Angus's skates and headed to Ninth Street and my car. When I looked at the house I'd parked in front of, it seemed familiar. It was a pleasant unexceptional place: two-storey, white clapboard. With a start, I realized it was Izaak Levin's house. I'd looked him up in the book after I saw him the night of Sally's opening. I'd even driven by. I told myself I might need to know where he lived for future reference.

There hadn't been any need for future reference. When I'd spoken to him the morning after Sally's opening, Izaak Levin had promised to call in the new year, and he had – twice. The first time, I had already arranged to have dinner with an old political friend. The second time Izaak called was after Sally had told me what had happened between them in the months after Des died. It took real restraint to keep from banging the receiver down and blowing out his eardrum.

I was just about to pull away when Izaak's front door opened and a woman in a black mink coat came hurrying out. She had her head down, but I knew the coat and I knew the woman. It was Nina Love. She didn't see me. She turned and walked toward a car I recognized immediately as Stu's Mercedes. I watched the licence plate as she drove up the street. ARTS 1 it said. So it wasn't Stu's car; it was the car that had belonged to Sally when she and Stu were together. His was the twin of this one, but his licence read ARTS 2. "Grounds enough for divorce in those licence plates alone," Sally said blandly when she told me about them.

There was no mistaking the car or the woman. I turned off the ignition and walked up the front path to Izaak Levin's house. He answered the door almost immediately. It was apparent when he opened the door that he had expected to see Nina again. He even looked past me, to see if she was still there.

"She's gone," I said, "but I'm here. May I come in?"

Without a word, he stood aside, and I walked past him. He was holding a manila envelope. It was sealed. When he saw me looking at the envelope, he shoved it into the drawer of a little table in the entrance hall. Not very trusting.

"Well," he said finally, "this is a welcome surprise. The last time we talked, I thought I discerned a chill. Come in and sit down. Can I get you something? A drink perhaps, or there's fresh coffee."

"Coffee would be fine," I said as I followed him into the living room. If I'd known what was waiting for me there, I would have chosen the drink. When I looked around Izaak Levin's living room, I knew I was at an exhibition curated by an obsessive. I was standing in the middle of a gallery of Sally Love – of art made not by her, but about her. Sally in all her ages, all her moods, seen by different eyes, transmuted into art by a hundred pairs of hands working with differing techniques in different media.

The walls were filled with paintings of her, and the floor was stacked with more. To get my bearings, I sat in the first chair I came to. Propped against the wall beside me, a sepia Sally, all halftones except for the brilliant red of her mouth, licked a sensuous upper lip; next to it, a pastel Sally's virginal profile glowed in a spring garden; on the coffee table in front of me a ceramic Sally holding a cat sprawled on a rocker. Sally was everywhere in that room, and even I knew the art was wonderful. But the effect was not wonderful; it was eerie, like the rooms you see on TV after a psychopath has committed a crime.

When Izaak came in from the kitchen carrying a tray with coffee and a bottle of brandy, I jumped.

He smiled. "Maybe you should have a little of this in your coffee," he said, holding up the bottle.

"No, thanks," I said, "I'm just a little overwhelmed by your collection. How did it come about?"

He handed me my coffee. "Sally did the first one herself –
that one over the mantelpiece, the one where she's sitting
on the hood of the old Chevy. It was a kind of joke. When
she first came to study with me, I called her an academy of
one. Someone told her that when artists are admitted to
the American Academy in New York, they have to give the
academy a self-portrait. Sally painted that picture for my
birthday. She was fourteen. The others just came over the
years. Sally is such an exceptional subject; people who make
art are drawn to her."

I put down my cup and walked over to look more closely
at Sally's self-portrait. It would have been easy to dismiss
that picture because, at first glance, it seemed so stereotyp-
ical: a fifties magazine ad for a soft drink or suntan lotion.
A pretty girl wearing a halter top and shorts hugged one
knee and extended the other leg along the hood of a yellow
convertible – a glamorous pose, sex with a ponytail. But
Sally had used colour to create light in an odd and disturbing way. The car glowed magically surreal – it was a car to
take you anywhere, and the hot pink stucco of the motel
behind the girl panted with lurid life. Sally herself was a
cutout, a conventional calendar girl without life or dimension, an object in someone else's world of highways and
clandestine sex.

I turned and looked at Izaak Levin. "And what did you
make of that picture when she gave it to you?"

He looked at me quizzically. "Do you mean as a piece of
art?"

"No," I said, reaching over and pouring a little brandy into
my coffee cup, "as a young girl's self-assessment. What would
you think was going on in the mind and heart of a fourteen-
year-old who saw herself like that?" The image of the woman
that child had become floated up and lodged in my mind

("Maybe for once life will work out"), and I was surprised at the rage in my voice. "You understand, I'm not asking you this as an art critic, I'm asking you as a human being."

He was silent.

"I'm waiting," I said.

His glass still had a couple of ounces of brandy in it, and he drank them down and shuddered. "How much," he said finally, "do you know about Sally and me?"

"Everything, I guess."

"Joanne, no one knows everything." His voice was so soft I had to lean forward to hear it. A private voice.

"Sally told me you were lovers," I said, "and that it started when she was thirteen."

"And you're appalled."

"Yes. I'm appalled. Thirteen! My God, Izaak. You were what? Forty? Her father had just died. Didn't certain patterns suggest themselves to you?"

I thought he was a weakling who would be devastated by someone else knowing the truth about what he had done. He wasn't. He looked at me steadily.

"The circumstances were unusual. Joanne, don't judge us yet. How much do you remember about the time after Des Love died?"

"The time immediately after? Everything. I don't think you remember, but I was there that night. Sally and I were going to a birthday dance across the lake. Nina was going to take us across as soon as you got back with the boat. Anyway, I went back to our cottage to change my shoes, and that made me late getting to the Loves'. But I was there just after you found them. I'll remember every second of that night till the day I die."

He pulled a cigarette from a fresh pack of Camels and placed it between his lips. He didn't light it.

"I remembered a girl being there," he said. "I didn't know it was you. So you've carried your own burden of memory all these years."

"Yes," I said, "I have, and what made it worse was I lost Sally, too. After that night I didn't see her again for years. They wouldn't let me see her in the hospital. And then – well, she was supposed to be away at school."

"But she wasn't," Izaak finished for me. He lit his cigarette and splashed more brandy in his glass. He was, I realized, well on his way to being drunk. "And now, Joanne," he said, "I'm going to try to mute your hostility. Are you mutable?"

"Try me," I said.

He laughed thinly. "Well, as they say, it was a dark and stormy night – the night after Des's funeral, to be precise. Owing to circumstances, the funeral had been particularly grisly, and I was sitting in my living room trying to get drunk. I lived not far from the Wellesley Hospital, which, of course, was where they had taken Des's family. There was a knock at the door, and when I opened it, Sally was there. She was in terrible shape. She hadn't been discharged. She had just put on her coat and walked out.

"'I won't go back to that house,' she said, 'and I won't go back to her.' She was soaked to the skin, and I went upstairs to run a hot bath and get her some dry clothes. When I came down, the bottle of whisky on the coffee table – a bottle which, incidentally, I had just nicely started – was just about empty. Fortunately, Sally's stomach rebelled. I got her upstairs to the bathroom in time, but while she was retching into the toilet bowl, somehow her jaw locked open – I suppose like a hinge that's pushed back too far.

"At any rate, there I was with a drunken thirteen-year-old, no relation to me, in a hospital gown and in need of help. I started to call a cab so I could get her to an emergency ward somewhere, but the idea of going back to the hospital made her wild. She started clawing at the phone and at me and making the most godawful sounds. So I slapped her – the movie cure for hysteria." He dragged gratefully on the Camel. "Luckily, the slap unlocked the jaw. I undressed her, put her in the tub and went out in the hall and sat on the floor outside the bathroom door listening until she came out, and I knew she was safe." He smiled to himself. "Or as safe as any of us ever are."

I was stunned. "Sally made it sound like such a lark – an adventure," I said weakly.

He picked up the ceramic figure of Sally with the cat and ran his forefinger along the curve of Sally's body. "She was a very wounded girl. That first year was a time of convalescence for her."

"With you as doctor. Where was Nina in all of this?"

He shrugged. "Where is she ever? Taking care of Nina." He looked hard at me. "I can see I have just made your hostility less mutable. So be it. To answer your question, Nina was enthusiastically in favour of dumping Sally on my doorstep. Sally and I went to Nina's hospital room together to ask. It took Nina an excruciating one-tenth of a millisecond to accede to our request."

He pronounced his words with exaggerated care. I knew the alcohol was beginning to blunt his responses, but I couldn't let the slur against Nina go unanswered.

"Be fair, Izaak. Nina had just endured a situation that went beyond nightmare."

"Our nightmares arise out of our deepest fears and longings," he said gently. "And no matter what, Sally was her daughter."

"And you," I said, fighting tears, "were the man Nina chose to act as a father for her child. In loco parentis – isn't that the phrase? Damn it, Izaak, you can't shift the blame for what you did to Nina. You were the one who took advantage.

You were the one who violated the trust." I picked up my coat and started to leave.

He followed me to the front hall. For the first time that day I noticed that he was limping, and at some not very admirable level, I was glad. I was glad he had hurt himself. The phone rang and he went to answer it. I couldn't hear much of what he said. I heard the phrases, "That won't be necessary, the need is past," and then he lowered his voice and I couldn't make out the words, but I could hear that he was speaking. The drawer to the table in the entrance hall was open a little. I pulled it out and picked up the manila envelope. I could still hear Izaak Levin's voice in the kitchen, low, indistinct. I shook the envelope the way children do on Christmas morning with their packages and then decided the hell with it. I ripped the flap back a little. Not far, just enough to see that inside was a roll of bills that would choke a horse.

I put the envelope back and carefully shut the drawer. When I got in the car, I was surprised to see I was shaking – coffee or guilt, I didn't know which. I sat there for a minute, taking deep breaths, calming down. Finally, I put the key in the ignition. But before I pulled out into the street, I took one last look at Izaak Levin's house. He was standing in the doorway, elegant, worldly as ever in his tweed jacket and horn-rimmed glasses. In one hand he had the brandy bottle, but he used the other to give me a mocking salute.

CHAPTER

9

As I stopped for the light at Broadway, I was trying to work it all out. What had Nina been doing at Izaak Levin's? They had known one another for years, but their relationship was hardly cordial. And where had the money come from? Nina had told me that Izaak had chronic money problems, but the roll of bills I had seen in that envelope went well beyond what you kept around in case the paperboy came to collect. Sally had been there earlier, but if she had taken the money over as part of a business transaction, why was it in cash? And why did Izaak still have the envelope in his hand, unopened, half an hour after she left? Questions. I looked at my watch. There was time before Angus came home from school to stop by Nina's and get some answers.

The light changed and I pulled into the intersection. Across the street I could see Angus's mecca: 7 Eleven, Home of the Big Gulp. As I pulled onto Broadway, I felt rather than saw a car coming toward me. By the time I turned to look at it, I only had time to know three things for certain: the car coming at me was big, it was green, and it wasn't going to stop.

The next thing I knew I was lying on my back in a room that smelled of medicine, and a black man with a gentle voice was asking me if I knew my name. When I told him, he nodded approvingly. "And what did you have for breakfast today, Jo?" I knew that, too. "And the day of the week?" Right again. He looked pleased. Obviously, I was a promising student. I also knew the names of the prime minister and of the premier of my province. Head of the class.

"Well, you're salvageable," he said with a smile. "We're going to patch you up a bit now," and then I felt a pinprick in my arm, and I drifted off. I remember an elevator and a room where Debussy was playing, and there was a bright light over my head and the same gentle voice that had asked me to name the prime minister was saying something about garlic. And then a woman was saying, "Joanne, Joanne, time to wake up. Come on, Joanne, take a deep breath. Get the oxygen in." Then I was in a bed and Mieka's Greg was standing over me.

Panicked, I fought my way back to consciousness. "Is Mieka okay? And the boys?"

He held my hand. "Everybody's okay, including you. You were in a car accident."

"Nobody was . . . ?" I asked.

"Nobody was hurt but you and the Volvo. You're going to be fine."

I felt a rush of relief and gratitude. "Greg, thank you. Thank you for everything."

"Jo, I didn't do anything."

I smiled at him. "You're here. I'm here." And then an inspiration. "Hey, Greg, remember what Woody Allen says? 'Eighty per cent of success is showing up.'"

He laughed, and safe again, I felt my limbs grow heavy and I drifted off to sleep.

To sleep and to dream. I was walking down a corridor in

the hospital, looking for the way out. But the corridors were arranged oddly, like a maze. I knew I was going in circles and I could feel the gathering of panic. Then I came to a big double door marked AUTHORIZED PERSONNEL ONLY. I pushed the door open. There was a vast room, empty except for an eight-sided desk in the middle. In the centre of the desk was a well, and Izaak Levin was seated there. "I can't find my way," I said. "Right or left?" he said. "What?" I said. "Conscious or unconscious," he said irritably. "Left," I said. "You'll be sorry," he said. But I'd already started through the doors at the left. I knew at once that I was in the old wing of the building, the one that no one used any more. All along the corridors the doors to rooms were open. The patients' rooms were empty. The medical rooms had things in them that I remembered from my father's office thirty years before. Finally I came to the sunroom that had been in the Wellesley Hospital when my father was on staff there. The room was filled with the furniture that I recognized at once as coming from the Loves' old cottage. Nina was there, wearing her black mink coat, but she must have been a nurse because she was pouring medicine into glasses. She didn't see me. And then Sally was there, not Sally as she was now, but Sally at fourteen in her nightgown. She was pushing a gurney, very purposefully. There was a body on it covered with a green sheet.

When she saw Nina, she hissed at me urgently, "Jo, you should have turned right. You can still get out, but you'll have to leave her behind." I turned to tell Nina where I was going but she was in another room counting money. Then Sally and I ran along the corridors of the abandoned wing till we came to the part of the building that was still used. I could feel my apprehension lighten. "You can look now," Sally said, pointing to the figure on the gurney. I didn't want to, but I knew I had to. I grabbed the corner of the sheet and pulled it back in one quick gesture. There on the stretcher was Woody Allen. He sat up and rubbed the bridge of his nose. "Eighty per cent of life consists of just showing up, Jo," he said.

I started to laugh, and when I woke up I was laughing and Mieka was there laughing and looking worried at the same time.

"Well," she said, "no need to ask you if you're glad to be back from the jaws of death. It looks like you were having a lot of fun in there." Then she hugged me. "Mum, we were so scared."

"I know," I said.

She started to cry. "I love you."

"I love you, too," I said. "So how's the catering business coming?"

She told me. And after a while Peter came and told me about a summer job possibility with a veterinarian down in the southwest of the province. Then Angus came and told me that three guys from the Oilers were going to be in the mall signing autographs on Saturday and if he donated fifty dollars to the Hockey Oldtimers he could have breakfast with them. And then a nurse said a plastic surgeon wanted to check my forehead and anyway I'd had enough visitors for one day. She shooed the kids away. Then after the doctor left, she came back and tucked me in for the night.

I couldn't sleep. I lay there listening to hospital sounds. Then the lights were turned down in the hall and I was alone in the half light. At first, when I saw Sally in the doorway, I thought I was dreaming. She put her finger to her lips, then moved quickly toward the head of the bed where she couldn't be seen by anyone passing by.

When she leaned over to give me a hug, I could smell the cold fresh air on her. She looked at the cuts on my face critically.

"How bad are they?" she asked.

"Not bad at all," I said, "except for the one on my forehead, and it's manageable. A plastic surgeon was just in here. He said that I'll be 'scarred but not disfigured' – that's a direct quote. He also said I'm lucky I have bangs because they'll cover the scar."

Sally shook her head. "Good news all around, eh?"

"Right. Oh, Sally, it's so good to see you. But how did you ever get by the nurse?"

She opened her coat. There was a picture ID pinned to her blouse. "I flashed this at her. Said I was a specialist from St. Paul's."

I laughed. "Where'd you get it?"

"One of Stu's loonier ideas a couple of years ago. Everyone with access to the vaults at the Mendel had to have an ID. Anyway, for once something Stu did actually worked out. It came in handy tonight." Suddenly, she was serious. "I had to see you, Jo. When Mieka called to tell me you were okay, I was so relieved, and then I just started to shake."

"That's about how I felt," I said. "It's not much fun to see how easily it can all end."

She sat down carefully on the bed beside me. In the shadowy light, her face looked both older and younger. "But you can't think about that," she said. "You can't think about how quickly it can be over, or you'll be too paralyzed to live. There's no point in being afraid of dying. It's going to happen. What we should be scared of is blowing the here and now."

"Carpe diem?" I asked.

She raised her eyebrows questioningly.

"Seize the day," I said.

"Seize the day," she repeated softly. "That's it. Because nobody knows how many days we have. I've never thought much about any of this stuff before. I've always just done what I wanted to do – made art. But Taylor's changed everything.

Jo, she is so talented. She is going to be so good. And she needs a good teacher. She needs me to do for her what Des did for me. Keep her from getting dicked around."

She stood up and walked over to the window. I could see her profile as she looked down at the lights of the city. "I'm not going to wait any more. Lately I've let everybody but me call the shots – the police, Stu, Nina, even the merry pranksters. But that's over. I'm getting on with it. I'm going to Vancouver tomorrow morning. My lawyer says since I haven't been charged with anything, the police here can't stop me. I'm going to look for a house for Taylor and me." She turned to face me. "You're sure it's okay with you if I leave."

"I'm sure."

"Do you want me to leave you the keys to my car? Mieka says the Volvo's done for."

"Are you sure you trust me to drive after today?"

She smiled. "I trust you. And since you're being so brave, I'll bring you a present. What's B.C. got that you want?"

"Pussy willows – the fat kind. I want an armful."

She sighed. "You know, Jo, sometimes you're just too wholesome for words." Then she bent down and kissed my forehead. "Did I ever tell you I love you?"

I felt a lump in my throat. "No, but now that you have, I may get you to put it in writing." For a moment I couldn't speak. Then I said, "I love you, too, Sally."

She grinned. "Good. Look, Jo, I've got to motor. I'll call you from Vancouver and tell you all about the boys on the beach." She gave my foot a squeeze and she was gone. Five minutes later I fell asleep. Despite the bruises, stitches and bandages, I was smiling.

I awakened the next morning to the smell of coffee and the sounds of carts loaded with breakfast trays being rolled along the hall. When I swung my legs over the side of the bed and sat up, I felt lightheaded, but I was determined to make it to the bathroom. There was a mirror above the sink and when I saw my face, I wished I'd stayed in bed. My forehead was hidden by a surgical bandage, both my eyes were black, and there was bruising across my cheekbones.

"You've never been at your best in the morning," I said to my reflection, then I hobbled to the safety of bed.

Breakfast was a lukewarm boiled egg, toast and margarine, dry cereal with room-temperature milk and a glass of Quench. Still, I was alive. Being ugly, being fed a meal prepared by the dieticians from hell didn't change that. I was alive, and as I sat watching the political panel on *Good Morning, Canada* I was happy.

Nina was my first visitor of the day. She came by just after breakfast, bringing the novel that was at the top of the *New York Times* best-seller list and a pink azalea, heavy with blooms. When she saw my face, I could see her muscles tense. She didn't like sickness. It was, I knew, an effort of will for her to come into a hospital. She embraced me affectionately, but I noticed that when she sat down, she pulled the visitor's chair well away from the bed.

We talked a little about the accident, and then Nina told me that Sally had flown to Vancouver that morning. She didn't try to hide her anger.

"This is why she drives people crazy. All these spur of the moment decisions as if no one exists in the world but Sally Love. She had promised to take Taylor up to the university and show her the studio today."

"Was Taylor upset?" I asked.

Nina hesitated. "Well, no. Sally called her and seemed to explain things to Taylor's satisfaction, but that's not the point."

"What is the point then, Ni? If Taylor's happy and Sally's happy, why does it matter?" I spoke more sharply than I intended to, and Nina looked surprised and wounded.

"You don't think I have a right to involve myself?"

"No, Ni, of course you have a right to be involved. It's just I don't think you're being fair to Sally. She came by here last night, and I think I understand why she felt she needed to go to Vancouver. This hasn't been the greatest time for her, you know."

"But it's been great for the rest of us?" Nina asked icily.

My head was starting to ache. "I know it's been hard for everyone." I took a deep breath. "Nina, there's something I need to ask you about. In fact, I was on my way to talk to you when I had the accident."

She stiffened. I tried to choose words that weren't threatening. "Yesterday afternoon I had an errand over on Broadway. I was parked in front of Izaak Levin's house. I saw you coming out of there, and after you left, I went in and talked to him."

At first, it seemed as if she hadn't heard me. She was wearing a heavy silver bracelet of linked Siamese cats. While I was talking, the catch had sprung open and she seemed, for a while, to be wholly absorbed in the problem of fastening it again. Finally, she looked up.

"What did he tell you?" she asked.

"Just things about the past," I said.

She seemed to relax. "I wouldn't believe everything Izaak Levin tells you, Jo. He's not a very nice man."

I could feel a pressure behind my right eye. "Damn it, Nina, if he wasn't very nice why did you let your thirteen-year-old daughter move in with him?"

She was alert again. "So that's it. Do you think it was easy for me? You were there, Jo. You remember how it was. She didn't want any part of me. Your father said it was because I reminded her of what she had lost in Des. He urged me to let her go." She reached out and covered my hand with her own. Her hand was cool and smooth, and I thought how often that hand had reached out to reassure me.

"I had you, Jo," she said. "And that made all the difference. It was a fair exchange. Your mother didn't want you,
and Sally didn't want me. I had to come up with a solution
that was right for everyone. It wasn't easy; you know that.
You saw how much Sally's defection hurt me. But it had
to happen."

I looked at her perfect heart-shaped face. "Ni, how can
someone who looks as fragile as you do be so strong?"

She looked pleased. "Do you know that old Chinese
proverb: 'The sparrow is small, but it contains all the vital
organs of the elephant'?" She stood up and started to put her
coat on. "I think you've had enough for one day. You look a
little weary. Next time, let's leave the past in the past, and
talk about all the things convalescent women are supposed
to talk about."

"Such as?"

Her smile was impish. "Such as Easter bonnets and where
hemlines are going to be in the spring and the best place in
town to get a bikini wax."

My head was pounding. "That sounds so good, and we'll
do it next time, I promise. But there's one more thing, and I
have to know this. Nina, did you give Izaak some money yesterday – a lot of money in a manila envelope?"

The cat bracelet slipped from her wrist and clattered
noisily onto the floor. For a beat, we both looked at it in
horror, as if it were a living thing. Nina bent to pick it up.
She fastened it carefully, then she looked at me. I couldn't
read the expression on her face, but her tone was urgent.

"Jo, you must promise me that what I tell you won't leave
this room. The money was from Stuart. I was just the messenger. He'd die if he knew you'd found out. No one must
know about this. If it gets out, it will destroy Stuart, and he
and Taylor have suffered so much already." She had tears in
her eyes.

"My God, Nina, what has Stuart done?"

"He wrote a book, Jo. That's all he did, but he's so anxious about its reception that he struck a kind of bargain with Izaak. Izaak agreed to give favourable attention to the book in print and send copies to his colleagues in the art world along with a flattering letter."

Suddenly I was so tired I could barely hold my head up. All I wanted to do was sleep. But I had shaken out the bag of tricks and I had to stay there until all the surprises were accounted for.

"And what did Stu agree to do for Izaak?" I asked.

"You know the answer to that already, Jo. You saw it yesterday afternoon. In exchange for friendly consideration, Stuart agreed to extricate Izaak from his latest financial crisis."

"This doesn't make sense, Nina. If the book's so bad, there'll be other reviews. Stuart can't buy off everybody."

"The book's brilliant, Jo, but you know how these things are. Izaak's always been considered the expert on Sally's work. People will take their lead from him. A good response is crucial. Stuart's going to be fifty years old this summer. He sees this book as his chance to make his mark professionally." She sat on the bed in the same place where her daughter had sat twelve hours earlier. "Jo, please don't say anything. Stuart's been wounded enough. If this came out . . ."

"He'd be a laughingstock," I said.

She winced. "Or worse. Please, Jo."

I sighed. "I won't say anything, Nina. You've asked me not to, and that's all I need." Suddenly I was exhausted. "But I think you're right. I think I should sleep now."

She plumped up my pillows and smoothed my sheet. Then she blew me a kiss and moved quietly out of the room. This time, when I fell asleep I wasn't smiling.

When I woke up, there was a small green wicker basket on the nightstand. Inside was a bagel with cream cheese and lox, a bottle of soda, a century pear and a piece of wicked-looking chocolate cake. There was a white silk bow on the basket and a card. "Judgements," the card said. Mieka's name and a phone number were printed in the lower right-hand corner. On the back she had scrawled, "Eat and be well. Love, M." I ate and felt better.

Hilda McCourt came by just as the one o'clock news came on the radio. She was wearing a skiing outfit, lime green and cerise, very Scandinavian in design. It looked expensive enough for Aspen. Her bright red hair was tucked under a lime-green ski cap, and her cheeks were rosy from the cold. In that room that smelled of disinfectant and medicine, she was bright with health. She pulled up a chair by my bed, sat down and bent close to look at my face.

"It could have been a great deal worse," she said thoughtfully. "I've had your name put on the prayer roster at the cathedral. We're thanking God for your deliverance, not praying for your recovery."

"I've been doing some thanksgiving myself," I said.

"I expect you have," she said. "Well, let's get on with life. Shall I bring you up to date on the gallery's celebration for Sally Love?"

"You're going to have to do more than bring me up to date on it," I said. "I didn't even know it was happening."

She looked puzzled. "I stopped by your house last week and left some information with your younger son."

"Angus?" I said. "He's the black hole of messages."

"I'll bear that in mind next time," she said. "At any rate, the affair for Sally is going to be on February fourteenth. I couldn't resist the Eros-love-Valentine connection, and, of course, we had to speed things up because Sally told me she and her daughter are leaving town. It's going to be a glittering evening, Joanne. Black tie, of course, with a sit-down dinner prepared by a first-rate caterer."

"I suppose you already have a caterer," I said.

"Yes, all that's been taken care of. Did you have someone in mind?"

"Maybe for next time," I said, smiling.

"Well, as I said, there'll be dinner. But here's the treat, and it was Sally's idea. She's agreed to let us auction off the preliminary sketches for the sexual parts in the fresco in Erotobiography. It's a wonderful tie-in with Valentine's Day. And an auction will be a feather in the cap for the gallery, not to mention a solid moneymaker. We've already had some nibbles from the national media interested in a Valentine story with a twist. Stuart is thrilled with all the attention."

"Hilda, how long have you known Stu?"

She looked surprised. "He was my pupil when he was in high school, and, of course, I knew his parents."

"What do you think of him?"

"That's an odd question," she said, "but I presume not an idle one, so I'll be candid. I think Stuart Lachlan is a pleasant but weak man. He's good company but not the man you'd want with you in a foxhole. Do you want to hear more?"

"Yes," I said, "I think I do."

"I'll give you a little family history, then. Stuart was an only child. His parents were wealthy, at least by Saskatoon standards, and his mother doted on him. I bristle at those who blame all their difficulties in life on their mothers, but in Stuart's case it would be justified. Caroline Lachlan protected her son so rigorously that she emasculated him.

"I remember when he was in grade eleven he received a poor mark on an essay. Caroline came up to the school to castigate me. She told me that Stuart's understanding of the play was deeper than mine and she was taking his paper up to the chairman of the drama department at the university to have it 'assessed by a qualified person.'"

"Did she do it?"

"Of course. That night when I was at home, my phone rang. Gordon Barnes was chairman of the drama department in those days. He was a dear man, but he did not suffer fools gladly, even rich ones. When I picked up the phone, he was on the other end. 'The mark is not altered,' he boomed, and that was the end of it."

I laughed. "Poor Stu."

"Indeed," said Hilda. She leaned a little closer. "And Joanne, do you know the title of the play that Stuart's mother thought he had done such a bang-up job on?"

I shook my head.

"*Oedipus Rex.*"

We both laughed, and then Hilda grew serious. "It is funny in the telling. But when you think of what Stuart became, the story's not so funny. Graham Greene has a splendid line in *The Power and The Glory*: 'There is always one moment in childhood when the door opens and lets the future in.' I wonder if that was Stuart's moment?" Her eyes looked sad. "I don't think Stuart ever had a chance to develop any moral muscle. Caroline was always there, running inter-ference, and her son became a man who has no ability to deal with adversity because he never had to. You saw him when Sally left him. He just about destroyed himself with liquor. Luckily for everyone, Sally's mother came along and Stuart had someone to lean on again. She's much the same type as Caroline, you know."

I thought I'd misheard her. "Nina and Stu's mother? Oh, no, Hilda, you're wrong there. Nina has her faults, but . . ." Pain stabbed the place behind my stitches. It was the first time I'd ever articulated a criticism of Nina.

Hilda looked at me curiously. "I'm always willing to be convinced, but not at this moment. Right now, I want to talk about you. How long are they keeping you in here?"

"The doctors say a few more days. They also say I can teach on Monday. The way my face looks, I may wear a mask. The plastic surgeon says no makeup till all the cuts are healed. I hope I look a little less horrifying by the night of Sally's party."

"You'll be fine. You're in good health. You'll heal quickly." She stood up. "Now, if there's anything at all I can do to help, let me know. And when you're up to snuff again, you can help me. I need a fresh eye to help me shop. I'm having a terrible time finding a dress for Sally's gala. Everything seems too trendy. I like a sense of fun in daytime clothes, but when I get an evening gown, I want to get one I can wear for years."

She zipped up her ski jacket and disappeared down the hall – more than eighty years old and determined to find a party dress she could really get some mileage out of.

Two days later I was discharged from the hospital. The cuts in my forehead would be a long time healing, but the bruises under my eyes were fading, and the cuts on my cheek were distinctly better. Most importantly, I felt fine. Mieka had continued with what she called her "test runs"; three times a day something freshly prepared and tasty would arrive in the distinctive green Judgements wicker basket. There was a half bottle of wine with dinner. It was food to get well for, and I did.

On the day I was discharged, a package came to me by courier from Vancouver. Inside was a bubble-gum pink sweatshirt, with *I LOVE JO* written across the chest in sequins and bugle beads. In Sally's surprisingly precise hand there was a note: "Now you've got it in writing. Get well soon. Love and XXX, S."

I wore the sweatshirt home from the hospital. As Peter pulled into the driveway, I could see the dogs waiting at the front window. Inside, Angus had a bed made up for me on the couch in the den, and the morning paper was open at the TV page. As I pulled the afghan around my chin and settled in to watch the local news, the dogs came in and nuzzled curiously at the hospital smells on my clothes. When they satisfied themselves that the old familiar smell of me was there after all, they relaxed, curled up on the floor beside me and fell asleep. I was home.

CHAPTER

10

In the next two weeks it seemed that life had gone back to normal. I taught my classes on Monday, and when my students did not run screaming from the classroom at the sight of my face, I was encouraged enough to try again on Tuesday. That worked, too, and by Wednesday, it seemed as if I'd never been away. The only lingering effects from the accident seemed to be that I tired quickly and that I was afraid to drive a car.

That first week, Peter drove me out to the auto graveyard in the North Industrial Park, and I saw the Volvo. The driver's side was mashed in, and the motor had been badly damaged. It was a write-off. As I stood looking at the car, once as familiar to me as my own face, now alien and abandoned in the snow, the man in charge of the yard came over.

"Any other car and you would have bought it, lady. I hope you know that."

I looked at him. Then I looked at my valiant Volvo. For the first time since the accident, I burst into tears.

Peter made me stop at the car dealerships on the way home and pick up some brochures.

"Therapy," he said. "You have to get back on that horse. If you're nervous about driving Sally's Porsche, get a car of your own."

But I didn't. That January I looked at a lot of brochures and went to a lot of showrooms. Somehow nothing I saw seemed quite right. By the end of the month I still hadn't driven a car.

Sally was coming back the afternoon of February first. That morning, Peter looked at me sternly when I came down to breakfast.

"The least you could do is take Sally's car around the block to make sure it turns over," he said. "It's been pretty cold. I don't think a dead battery would be much of a home-coming present for her after she was decent enough to leave you her car."

"Browbeating me into doing the brave thing, are you?" I asked.

He grinned. "Something like that. Just drive it around the corner, Mum. They came and cleaned our street this morning so it's clear sailing. You know, it really is time you got behind the wheel again."

"Okay," I said, "you win. After I take the dogs for their run, I'll drive Sally's car around the block."

"Promise?" he asked.

"Promise," I said.

When the dogs and I came up the driveway after their walk, I patted the Porsche on the hood. "Your turn now. I'll run in and get the keys and we'll go for a spin. Nothing to it."

But as I slid into the driver's seat, I was overwhelmed with anxiety. I felt frightened and clumsy. I dropped the keys on the floor, and it seemed like an omen.

When I bent down to pick them up, I saw the tuque. It was under the passenger seat, and it was dirty and wet. It looked like any of a dozen wool hats that my kids or their friends had abandoned on the car floor over the years. Except this hat didn't belong to my kids. I pulled it out and looked at it carefully. A green tuque with the logo of the Saskatoon Hilltops. Like the hat Councillor Hank Mewhort had been wearing the night of Sally's opening. But not like the one he'd been wearing at Clea Poole's funeral. That day he'd been wearing a tweed cap with ear flaps.

The hat in my hand was the tuque Sally had ripped off the head of the man who was lingering around the Porsche the night Clea was killed. I was certain of it. She must have thrown it on the seat when she drove to the gallery. In the inevitable progress of tuques in cars, it had worked its way onto the floor and out of sight.

"Out of sight, out of mind, until today," I said as I went into the kitchen and picked up the city phone book. "But, Councillor Mewhort, today your chickens have come home to roost."

The woman who answered the telephone at his office in City Hall told me I was in luck. Friday morning was the time the councillor reserved for drop-in visits from his constituents.

Half an hour later, I dropped in.

His office surprised me. I thought a man whose daily business was hand-to-hand combat with sin in Saskatoon would work in a room furnished with flaming swords and thunderbolts. Hank Mewhort's office was ordinary: a nice old oak desk, clear except for a telephone and a desk set; an empty bookshelf; a wall filled with the plaques from organizations I didn't want to know the names of, and a large and ugly ficus plant.

Councillor Mewhort was sitting at his desk. Stripped of his troops and his placards, he looked ordinary, too. He was wearing a shirt and tie and a powder-blue cardigan that had

Christmas present written all over it. His pale hair was carefully combed, and his face was pink and innocent. When he saw me he rose and held out his hand.

I didn't take it, and I didn't sit down when he motioned to the chair across from him.

"I'm a friend of Sally Love's," I said, "and I have something for you." I dropped the tuque on his empty desk, and for a moment it lay there between us, alive with possibilities.

I think I expected a scene – a denial or threats and accusations – but for the longest time there was silence as Hank Mewhort looked down at the hat.

Finally, he spoke. "You won't believe this, but I'm glad you're here. Ever since Miss Love pulled those creatures off me after the funeral, I've known I had to come forward. They had the time of Reg's death in the paper that same day, you know, 6:21. I cut the story out of the newspaper." He opened his desk drawer, pulled out the story and handed it to me. Proof of good intentions.

"Sally Love was in her house at 6:21," he said. "I could see her through the front window. She was painting. She didn't come out until later. By the time our disagreement was over, it was 6:35. I looked at the clock in my car." He looked at me steadily. His pale eyes were as guileless as a choirboy's. "I believe in doing the right thing," he said.

"Now's your chance," I said.

He walked over and took his Siwash sweater off the coat rack.

"Right," he said. "Now's my chance."

I walked to the police station on Fourth Avenue with him, and I waited with him in the reception area until Mary Ross McCourt was free to see him.

"Councillor Mewhort has information that proves Sally couldn't have killed Reg Helms," I said when Inspector McCourt came out to get us.

She raised her carefully plucked eyebrows and looked hard at him.

"True?" she asked.

"True," he said.

I watched as he followed her down the corridor and into her office. Then I sighed with relief. The wheels of justice were starting to grind.

Five hours later I was sitting at the kitchen table marking thirty-five papers on the failure of Meech Lake when the dogs started going crazy. I went to the front door and there was Sally with her arms filled with pussy willows.

I helped Sally off with her coat and took the pussy willows from her. Then we walked into the kitchen together.

"I have news," I said.

Sally smiled. "It must be pretty hot. You look like the cat that swallowed the canary."

"I feel like the cat that swallowed the canary. Sal, I found the man you had the fight with the night of the murder. And he's already been downtown and told Mary Ross McCourt his story. You're off the hook."

Sally collapsed onto the kitchen chair. "Oh, my God, Jo, this is so wonderful. I can't believe it. Is it really over? Is it really over at last?" She jumped up and hugged me. "Who was it?" she said. "Who did it turn out to be?"

"Elvis," I said. "Back from the dead to give you an alibi. Sit down and I'll tell you the whole story."

When I finished, Sally looked serious. "Who would have believed it? Councillor Hank Mewhort, the leader of the pack. Anyway, I'm in the clear. How can I ever thank you, Jo?"

"Be happy," I said. "Now let's have some coffee and talk about ordinary things. You can fill me in on Vancouver."

I made the coffee and we sat at the kitchen table in the middle of my Meech Lake papers and looked at pictures

Sally had taken of her new house in Vancouver. It was beautiful: very West Coast, surrounded by trees, lots of glass and exposed beams and dazzling views. She was filled with homeowner's pride, and as she talked she drew quick floor plans of the rooms on the cover page of one of my essays.

"Here," she said. "Here's where the door is, but we'll knock that out so Taylor can have a really spectacular bedroom. And that deck can be extended clear around the house, so you can sit there any hour of the day and feel the sun on your face. It'll be like living in a clearing in the forest." Then she stopped drawing and looked at me. "Jo, I am so happy," she said simply. Then she bent over her sketches again.

The night of February fourteenth was a Valentine itself: mild, still, moonlit, a night for lovers. It was a little after six when the taxi dropped me in front of the gallery. Everything was quiet. The invited guests wouldn't be arriving for an hour and a half. I was there early to help.

The first voice I heard that morning had been Hilda McCourt's. "Joanne, I'm taking advantage of our friendship to ask a favour. That fine young woman who's been looking after this appreciation with me just telephoned to say she has the flu. Everything is in the hands of the professionals, but as you know even professionals need a nudge now and then. Do you know Nicolas Poussin's work? Seventeenth-century French?"

"No," I said, "I don't think I do."

"Well, you should," she said. "He was the greatest of all classical painters. His motto was '*Je n'ai rien négligé*' – I overlook nothing. When it comes to this celebration of Sally Love's generosity, I think we should emulate Poussin. Come early tonight, would you, and help me keep everybody up to the mark? After all she's done for the artistic community of this city, Sally Love deserves a perfect evening."

When I saw the gallery that night, I thought of Nicolas Poussin. *"Je n'ai rien négligé"* – every detail was perfect. The bright banners bearing Sally's name were still hanging along the portico, but they were interspersed now with vertical chains of hearts, very stylized, very contemporary. In the reception area a string quartet played Ravel, and porcelain vases filled with roses perfumed the air with the sweet promise of June.

Hilda McCourt came out of the tea lounge to meet me. She had found her classic evening gown: a Chinese dress of red silk shot through with gold, form-fitting and secured from throat to ankle by elaborate frogs. She was wearing a pair of milky jade earrings that fell almost to her shoulders. When I complimented her on them, she smiled.

"They came from a friend," she said. "He was a missionary in China, but a great lover of beauty."

"I can see that," I said.

I was surprised to see her blush at the compliment, but she was quick to seize the initiative again.

"You look lovely, Joanne. Just as I predicted, your face has healed nicely, and that dress was a wise choice. Lipstick red is wonderfully vibrant on ash blondes. There's a lesson there. After forty, women should stick with true colours; pastels wash us out. Now come along. Let's get a peek at those studies that are going up for auction."

The drawings were on display in the Mendel salon. They were mounted simply, and to me at least they were a surprise. In their final form, painted in the fresco, the sexual parts had seemed spontaneous, fleshly imaginings. But here I could see the work behind the flash and the wit. The preliminary sketches showed process. Each of the genitalia was drawn in pen on a kind of grid of faint pencil lines. At the top of each page in a neat pencilled hand were notes on scale and proportion. I looked at the complex relationships of angles and circles and marvelled at the effort it must have taken for Sally to teach herself the principles of geometry she needed for her work. The studies were designated by number only.

Hilda and I went through quickly. Every so often, we'd stop at a particularly interesting one and speculate about the identity of the owner.

"Tempted to bid on any?" I asked.

"Oh, yes," she said. "Either number twenty-three or fifty-seven would add an interesting dimension to my bedroom. Now come along, we'd better check on the caterers. They've done wonders in Gallery III. If the food is as good as the ambience, we're home free."

The caterers had set up round tables throughout the room. Each table was covered by a red and white quilt of the wedding-ring pattern; in the centre a scented red candle in a hurricane lamp cast a soft glow.

I bent to look at the stitching on a quilt.

"Hand done," I said to Hilda McCourt. "It's exquisite. The whole room is exquisite."

"Here comes the man you should praise," she said as a tall, heavy-set blond man moved carefully among the tables toward us. He looked like a man who cared about the pleasures of the senses. The chain from his gold pocket watch gleamed dully against a cashmere vest the colour of claret, and his moonlike face arranged itself easily into a smile.

"Stephen Orchard," he said, "from Earthly Delights Catering."

"I've always loved your company's name," I said, "and the food, of course. It's always good news for me when I see one of your trucks parked outside a party I've been invited to."

He beamed. "Would you like a look at what you'll be eating tonight?" He picked up a stiff menu card from the table nearest us and handed it to me.

Barbecued British Columbia salmon
Consommé Madrilene
Rolled veal stuffed with watercress
Wild rice La Ronge
Fiddleheads
Tomatoes à la Provençal
Sorbet Saskatoon
Coeurs à la crème fraîche

"Perfect," I said, handing the menu back to him. Then a thought struck me. "Someone did tell you about Sally's allergies, didn't they?"

He adjusted the fold of a linen napkin. "Her husband was most conscientious. And really it's no big deal. I don't use nuts for parties this size; you'd be amazed how common that allergy is. And everything else Mr. Lachlan mentioned is simply a basis of sound cooking: organically grown ingredients, no additives, no preservatives." He smiled. "We're all growing wiser about what we put in our bodies."

"Yes," I said, "we are." I started to say more, but I felt a hand touch my elbow. I turned. It was Kyle, the gallery guard. He was wearing what must have been his dress uniform, navy blue and vaguely military.

He didn't look very cheerful. "You're not going to believe this," he said. "There are a bunch of ladies out there in ape masks."

"I believe it," I said. "They call themselves the Guerrilla Girls. They protest the way women are treated in the art world."

Kyle nodded sagely, but Hilda McCourt looked baffled.

"Why would they protest an event to honour Sally?" she asked.

"She isn't exactly in tune with them philosophically," I said. "She thinks all they care about is numbers, not quality.

Sally believes that if you have talent, you'll make your way
to the top. Of course, in her case that's been true."

Hilda McCourt shook her head sadly. "The solipsism of
the gifted. They truly can't understand that we are not all
created equal. Still, whatever Sally's philosophical differences with them might be, I don't feel we can ignore a
protest by other women artists."

"If that's all it was, I'd agree," I said, "but it's more complicated than that. Sally and I got into a scuffle with this
bunch after Clea Poole's funeral, and it was scary. People in
masks are scary. And, Hilda, I don't think these women are
interested in making a political statement. The real Guerrilla
Girls, in New York, are legitimate social critics. Even Sally
says they're principled. But I don't like what I've seen of these
women. They frighten me. I don't like anonymity. I like to
know who I'm dealing with. I don't think we owe anything
to people who won't show their faces. I'd be a lot happier if
they were out of here."

Hilda looked thoughtful. "We may just be giving them
grist for their mill if we throw them out. I think we should
see them."

"You're the boss." I shrugged and smiled at Kyle. "I guess
the decision's made. We have to go see some guerrillas about
a lady."

They were in the reception area, a dozen of them, wearing
the outfits they had worn the day of Clea Poole's funeral:
boots that came to their knees, skintight black pants, bomber
jackets, big, toothy gorilla masks. Two of them were wearing
gorilla hands, and the rest wore gloves. Gorillas or not, they
were Canadians in an art gallery, so they were behaving
themselves, waiting to deal with someone in authority.

Hilda McCourt was that somebody.

It was a compelling scene: the commanding eighty-year-
old with the brilliant hair and the extravagant Chinese dress

and the twelve dark figures towering over her, listening intently.

Hilda McCourt's voice was the voice of the classroom: "Why don't you tell me what you want, and I'll see how much I can accommodate you."

"We want to poster this event," one of them said, stepping forward. She handed me some of the posters she'd been holding. I looked at them quickly. They were nicely done, black and white with bold graphics. One showed a loonie with a large bite out of it; the bite represented the income lost to a Canadian artist if she happened to be a woman. Another was a list of the ten top galleries in Canada; a number beside each indicated the number of one-person exhibitions Canadian women had had at that gallery. The numbers were not impressive. Nor were the numbers on a third poster, which showed the proportion of women to men as art critics on newspapers or as directors or curators of art museums. At the bottom of each poster was the imprint: "A Public Service Message from the Guerrilla Girls: Conscience of the Art World."

I handed the posters to Hilda McCourt. "I don't see anything wrong with these," I said. "In fact, people should know this. They could put them over on that wall where the gallery's stuck all those newspaper stories about Erotobiography."

"All right," said a small figure in the back, "that's one. The next thing is we want to go to Sally's party – to represent all the women who've never had a dinner to celebrate their accomplishments."

"Or even an exhibit," said another Guerrilla Girl.

"Or even a fucking chance," said a third.

"Give us a chance," said another. "Two, four, six, eight. Empowerment now; women won't wait. Three, five, seven, nine. They've had their chance; now I want mine. Power! Now!" Their voices, muffled by the heavy masks, rose in a chorus. Their bodies began to sway rhythmically. A stocky woman at the end leaned too close to a porcelain vase filled with roses, and it fell to the floor and smashed.

Suddenly the room was silent.

"That was English soft paste porcelain, more than a hundred years old," Hilda McCourt said mildly. "A piece of great charm and vigour. Pieces like that always seem proof of our civility." She took a step toward the Guerrilla Girls. "You may certainly display your posters, but you are not welcome at this celebration. Joanne, I think we should check on the Chablis for dinner. Stephen Orchard wondered if he should bring over another case, just to be on the safe side."

I followed her across the room, but at the doorway I turned and looked back. The twelve women in the toothy masks were still standing there, staring at the broken roses and the delicate shards of blue and white and gilt. They looked like something left over from an old Ernie Kovacs TV show.

We checked the Chablis and decided that since there were three other wines being served, drinks before dinner and liqueurs afterwards, people would just have to make do. By the time we told a janitor about the broken vase and reassured Stephen Orchard, the first invited guests had arrived. Soon the gallery was filled with the scent of expensive perfumes, the rustle of evening clothes and the sounds of people laughing and calling to one another in greeting. The string quartet switched from Ravel to Cole Porter, and the evening had begun.

It seemed that everyone wore red. Nina wore a dress I remembered from the sixties, a slim, sculptured Balenciaga evening gown of velvet as lustrously red as a spring tulip. She had worn that dress to the rehearsal dinner the night before my wedding. She had been lovely then and she was lovely now. Now, as then, her dark hair was swept back, and there were pearls at her throat and earlobes. But tonight she looked worn, and I felt a pang when I thought of how little I had seen her since I'd come out of the hospital. There'd been a lot going on in my life, but obviously the past few weeks had been troubling ones for Nina, and I should have been there to help her.

Stuart wore a red tie and cummerbund with his tux. He was in an odd mood – jumpy and overly solicitous with Nina and me until Sally came in, when he walked away from us without a backward glance.

Not many people would have blamed him. In one of those ironies that revealed she was Nina's daughter after all, Sally had chosen something from the sixties, too. But where Nina had chosen a classic gown that paid homage to the timelessness of good design, Sally's outfit was pure costume, a sexy joke that raised a finger to people who took fashion seriously. She was wearing a one-piece jumpsuit, white lace appliquéd on some sort of stretchy net with matching leggings. There wasn't much lace in the jumpsuit, but there was a lot of net and a lot of Sally. Later she told me her outfit was a Rudi Gernreich, and I smiled at the memories of see-through blouses, topless bathing suits and promises of revolution.

From the moment she came in, Stuart was all over Sally – leaving his arm around her shoulders after the initial greeting, bending his face close to hers when she talked, stroking her hair with his hand. Finally, laughing, she shook him off, the way a woman shakes off a drunk at a party. But Stuart Lachlan wasn't drunk, and he wouldn't be shaken off. When Sally started in the direction of the bar, he followed her, still trying somehow to get his hands on her. It was as if he was afraid to leave her alone. Nina and I watched the scene in silence.

"Whatever do you make of that display, Ni?" I asked. But she didn't answer; she just watched the space where they had been with an expression I couldn't fathom.

And then there was another tableau. Kyle, the gallery guard, had approached Izaak Levin. They were across the room, and I couldn't hear their conversation, but when Izaak limped toward us, Kyle watched him thoughtfully.

When Izaak Levin joined us, I was amazed at the change in him. I hadn't seen him since the day of the accident, five weeks ago, but he looked twenty years older. He skin had a greyish cast and he seemed distinctly unwell. Selling his integrity was apparently taking its toll. We had just started talking when an old friend from the political days came over, full of excitement, to introduce me to her new husband. By the time I turned back to Izaak, he and Nina had moved to the side of the room. He was whispering something in her ear and he had his hand on her arm. When finally he walked away, Nina scrubbed at the place where his hand had rested as if she had been touched by something loathsome.

Loathsome or not, when it came time for dinner, Izaak Levin was seated at Sally's right, and on his right was Nina. I was at their table, and we were an uncomfortable grouping. Stuart was on Sally's left, and I was beside him. Next to me was Hugh Rankin-Carter, the art critic. On his left was Hilda McCourt. She'd positioned herself beside the only person I'd never met at our table, a woman named Annie Christensen, who had parlayed a smart marriage and a genius for mathematics into a substantial fortune. She was known as a generous supporter of the arts, and it was no accident that, boy-girl seating be damned, Hilda had put her at the table with the star of the evening.

The meal was magnificent, but dinner was not a pleasant affair. Hugh Rankin-Carter was a man with real power in the art world, and Annie Christensen was a philanthropist with deep pockets; the fact that both were seated at our table was apparently too much for Izaak and Stu. A tense rivalry, part professional, part sexual, seemed to spring up between them.

Whatever his faults, Izaak Levin had always been a witty and self-effacing man, but that night he told pointless repetitive stories whose sole purpose seemed to be to lament the brilliant career he'd given up for Sally and to celebrate his influence on her art. Not to be outdone, Stu quoted long passages of analysis from his book.

Sally sat between them looking trapped and miserable. She was patient longer than I would have thought possible, but finally she turned on Stu. At first she kept her voice low.

"Okay, Stu, that's enough. You're boring the tits off everybody. Now be still, and listen to me for a minute. You might actually learn something. No matter what that ridiculous book of yours says, I'm not some sort of holy innocent the great god of art drips paint through. I actually know what I'm doing." Her voice rose with anger. "I told you last night I can't believe you could have lived with me five years without understanding one single thing about what I do. Damn it, Stu, if I could put what I see into words, why would I paint it?" She shook her head in exasperation, and when she spoke again, her voice was weary. "Look, the best thing to do with that book is junk it. If it doesn't come out, nobody will be the wiser, but if you actually let that stuff get published, everybody is going to know you're . . ."

"Dumb as shit." Hugh Rankin-Carter smiled as he finished the sentence for her.

Izaak Levin poured himself a glass of wine and laughed. "Not bad, Hughie," he said.

Sally looked at him with anger. "You're no better, Izaak. All that whining about how you sacrificed your career for mine. Tell me, when was the last time you earned a dime that wasn't connected to me?"

In one of those terrible moments that happen at parties, the room was suddenly quiet, and Sally's words, bell clear, hung in the air.

Izaak's face sagged. Across the table, I was surprised to see a flicker of pleasure cross Nina Love's face.

A woman I recognized from Clea's funeral had been moving from group to group taking pictures. She came over to our table.

"Not now, Anya," Sally said, but the woman kept snapping away until Sally flared and told her to get lost.

The rolled veal arrived, savoury and tender enough to cut with a fork, but the misery continued at our table. Stuart sat silent, his face a mask carved by humiliation. Izaak Levin drifted into the self-pitying phase of drunkenness, talking incoherently about how Sally could never begin to understand all the things he had done to protect her. Finally, he lurched off to the men's room. When he came back, his fly was undone and Sally, with a savage look, bent over and zipped him up.

"It's over, Izaak. No use advertising any more."

In my two brief encounters with him, Hugh Rankin-Carter had struck me more as gadfly than peacemaker, but the crosscurrents at our table became so menacing that even he tried to pour oil on the troubled waters. After Sally's outburst, Hugh leaned across to Nina and asked her to tell him about the early fifties when Des Love had scandalized Toronto the Good with his bold and sensual paintings.

Nina was a gifted storyteller but that night she told one story remotely and badly, and when Sally corrected her on a detail, Nina excused herself and left the table. As she moved behind Sally's chair, a flashbulb went off in her face, and I saw her freeze as if she'd been shot.

Only Hilda McCourt and Annie Christensen seemed immune to the tensions. They ate with gusto and chatted happily about art and theatre. I envied them, and I was relieved when the table was cleared and the only course left was dessert. Stephen Orchard was known for the dramatic presentation of dessert at the parties he catered.

Certainly, no one in the room that night would ever forget the arrival of his coeurs à la crème fraîche. The lights were extinguished, leaving the room illuminated only by the candles blazing in hurricane lamps at the centre of each table. The string quartet struck up "My Funny Valentine," and a half-dozen red heart-shaped spotlights focused on the entrance to the tea salon. Through the door came a procession of waiters carrying silver trays. As the waiters moved to the tables, the spotlights swept the room. It was a knockout.

Our waiter swooped dramatically in front of Sally, picked up the first dessert and began to serve. There were eight glass plates on the tray; at the centre of each plate was a creamy heart surrounded by strawberry sauce. When we all had one, Hugh Rankin-Carter leaned across to me.

"Tacky but effective," he said.

It happened just at that moment. The spotlights were turned off, but in the darkness we could see figures running. They moved quickly, blowing out the candles that were the only light in the room. Soon the room was in total darkness, but not before everyone in it had had a good look at the Guerrilla Girls in action.

Afterwards, we learned that most people thought they were part of the entertainment. Whatever the explanation, no one was particularly upset. For a few seconds there was nervous laughter, then people lit the candles at their tables, and it was over.

Except it wasn't over. The Guerrilla Girls had left a large red envelope on each table, and you could hear the intake of breath around the room as people opened them. Sally ripped open ours, looked quickly at the poster that was inside, then handed it to me. She looked shaken but defiant.

"Jo, we should have pounded them into the ground when we had the chance."

I looked at the poster. It was black and white, like the others, but this one had an illustration, a blowup of what must have been a police photo of Clea Poole the night she was murdered. She was naked, lying face down on the barbed wire bridal bed. Underneath in heavy black letters were the words, "Remembering a martyr to women's art on Valentine's Day."

I shuddered, but I tried to match Sally's tone. "There'll be other chances," I said.

Hugh Rankin-Carter took the poster by two fingers, shook his head in disgust and dropped it in a leather bag that was the twin of the one he'd given Sally the night of the opening.

"Pathetic," he said. "But if they want recognition, I'll write a column about them. And I'll be sure to mention that the one who reached in front of me has apparently taken a philosophical stand against deodorant." He turned to Sally. "Don't let them ruin your party, Sal. My grandfather always said, 'Life is uncertain, eat dessert first.' Now, be a good girl and eat your coeur before it melts."

Sally grinned at him and stuck her spoon into the centre of her perfect heart. She swallowed the first bite, then waved her spoon at Hugh.

"Yum," she said.

She was right. I began eating my dessert and listening to the conversation between Hilda McCourt and Annie Christensen. I don't know when I knew something was wrong. At some point, I looked over and saw that Sally had pushed her chair back from the table. There was an odd stricken look on her face. Then she reached down as if she were searching for something on the floor. When she sat up, her eyes were wide with fear. She braced herself against the table as if she were afraid of falling.

I started toward her.

"Sal?" I said.

"I need my bag," she said. "I'm having a reaction to something in the food."

I dived under the table. It was hard to see in the darkness. Stu was already under there raking the floor with his hands. Sally's purse wasn't there.

"Somebody get a doctor," I said, and I went over to Sally. She was slumped in her chair, and her breathing was laboured. She looked at me in terror.

"I can't get air in," she said.

I stroked her cheek. "It'll be all right," I said. "They're getting a doctor."

The gallery had set up a microphone for people to make thank-you speeches at the end of dinner, and as if on cue, I heard the soft American voice of Hugh Rankin-Carter asking if there was a doctor in the house.

There were seven medical doctors in the room that night: three urologists, the plastic surgeon who had sewn my face up after the accident, a proctologist and two psychiatrists. A few drops of epinephrine would have saved Sally's life, but there was no epinephrine in that room. Sally's evening bag with the emergency supply she always carried with her had disappeared, and none of the doctors had come to the party prepared to meet death. I could hear one of them calling for an ambulance; she was very specific in her instructions about the epinephrine, but it didn't matter, because by the time the ambulance attendants ran into the room, Sally was dead.

She died slowly and in mortal terror. She deserved better.

Izaak Levin was luckier. His death was quick. When the ambulance attendants began loading Sally's body on their stretcher, Izaak made a little crying sound and fell to the floor. The doctors tried CPR. They struggled over him for what seemed to me to be a painfully long time, but nothing worked.

"Heart," one of the doctors said laconically as he stood up and turned away from Izaak's body. "He just wasn't salvageable."

Ours was the last table the police let go. The people at our table were interviewed separately and then together, but the police seemed less interested in our relationship with Sally than in the Guerrilla Girls, and we were questioned again and again about the sequence of events that began with the second dousing of the lights and the entrance of the Guerrilla Girls and ended with Sally's death. Finally, they told us we were free to leave.

It was one-thirty in the morning. Mary Ross McCourt offered to take her aunt home, and Hilda followed her gratefully. It was the first time I had ever seen her appear old and helpless. Annie Christensen and Hugh Rankin-Carter left together. They were staying at the same hotel, and as they left I heard Annie invite Hugh to join her in the bar for a nightcap. No one wanted to be alone.

When the police gave us permission to go, I walked over and put my arms around Nina. She held tight to me, and then she looked at me hard.

"You're all the daughter I have now," she said.

People, including me, laugh at the phrase, "I thought my heart would break," but that night as I looked into Nina's eyes, I knew it could happen. When she kissed my cheek, I could smell the familiar scent of Joy. Always that perfume had meant I was safe, home free. That night, the magic didn't seem to work. As I watched Nina take Stuart Lachlan's arm and lead him gently out of the room, I knew that none of us would ever be safe again.

I couldn't leave the room without looking around one last time. The police hadn't let the people from Stephen Orchard's catering company clear the tables. The candles had, of course, guttered and burned out long ago, but the coeurs à la crème fraîche were still there, and that is my last memory of that night: three hundred creamy hearts dissolving into red.

CHAPTER

11

It was a little after 2:00 a.m. when Peter and I pulled into the driveway on Osler Street. As soon as the police told me I could go, I'd called home. Pete had answered on the first ring. Every light in our house was blazing. It wasn't a night for shadows or dark corners. Mieka and Greg were waiting for me at the front door; Angus was in his room with the dogs. As soon as he heard my voice, Angus came running down the hall. He threw his arms around me and buried his face in my neck.

"This really sucks," he said. "This really, really sucks."

I tried to think of something I could say that would make it better, but there wasn't anything. I pulled him close, and we walked into the living room together. When I sat down on the couch, Angus curled up against me the way he used to when he was little. We were both shivering. Mieka came in with an afghan and covered us both.

The afghan was the one Sally had pulled around her the night Clea Poole died. A flash of memory. Sally in a rare moment of doubt, seeking reassurance. "Do you think Taylor will ever make one of these for her notorious mother?" And me, reassuring, "Sure, notorious mothers are the best kind."

Mieka and Greg stayed at the house that night. It was nice of them, but it didn't make any difference. Every time I closed my eyes I saw Sally as she had been in those last seconds, her lovely face frozen in the primal panic of an animal at the moment of death. Anything was better than that. I went downstairs and sat in the chair by the window in my dark living room. Across the street I could see the familiar shapes of the neighbours' houses. I looked at them and thought about nothing. When the sky began to lighten and the first cars started to drive along the street, I went into the kitchen and made coffee. I poured myself a cup, but somehow the mug slipped from my hand. It clattered noisily across the floor, leaving a dark spoor in its wake. I picked up a cloth, but when I knelt to clean up the mess, I started to sob. I started, and I couldn't stop. Barefoot, shivering in my thin cotton nightie, I sat on the kitchen floor and cried until I felt an arm around my shoulders, and my daughter led me upstairs to bed. She stayed with me till I fell asleep.

I didn't sleep long, but when I woke up I felt better. I showered and pulled on jeans and a sweatshirt. When I went downstairs, the kids were sitting around the kitchen table and Mieka was making French toast.

"Your favourite," she said, "so you have to have some."

"I will, later," I said. "Honestly. Right now all I want is some coffee."

I'd just taken a sip when the phone rang. Mieka answered it, then turned to me.

"For you. Shall I ask him to call back?"

I shook my head and took the receiver. It was Hugh Rankin-Carter.

"Joanne, I've found out some things I'd rather you heard from me than . . . well, than from others. Would you like to meet me somewhere? Or I could come there if it's better for you."

"Why don't you come here?" I said. "My daughter's just making French toast. If you haven't already had breakfast, you could eat with us."

"I'll be there as soon as I can get a cab," he said.

He was at our front door in fifteen minutes. As I helped him off with his coat, I noticed that he had shaved and was wearing a fresh shirt. He still looked like hell. I caught a glimpse of my face in the hall mirror. I looked like hell, too.

We went into the kitchen and I introduced the kids to Hugh. The boys said hello and excused themselves. Peter had a class. Angus asked if he could go back to bed. It seemed as good a thing to do as any. When they left, Mieka turned to us.

"Two orders of French toast?" she asked.

"Sounds delightful," Hugh said.

"Nothing for me," I said.

"You have to eat," Hugh said curtly. He smiled at Mieka. "I'll bet Joanne can be tempted." He turned to me. "Didn't your mother ever tell you about keeping your strength up in a crisis?"

"My mother limited herself to telling me I'd ruined her life."

He raised his eyebrows. "Ah, the search for the mother. That explains Nina. Sally was always baffled at how close you and her mother were."

"They were very different women," I said. "I don't think they were ever very fair in their assessments of each other."

"From what I've seen of Nina Love, Sally was more than fair," Hugh said. He sipped his coffee. "Joanne, about last night. I'm afraid I have something in the nature of a revelation. After I had my drink with Annie Christensen, I went down to the police station. The boys and girls in blue were amazingly forthcoming. You'd be touched to see how people welcome me when I tell them I'm from a Toronto newspaper. Anyway, the first thing I learned is of forensic interest. Sally died of food-induced anaphylactic reaction. Her coeur à la crème fraîche was covered in powdered almonds."

I felt my throat start to close. "Stephen Orchard knew she couldn't eat almonds," I said weakly.

"Stephen Orchard didn't put them there, Joanne. The police found a little plastic bag in the pocket of the jacket Izaak Levin was wearing when he died. It had been emptied, but there were traces of something that the police, with their flair for language, are at the moment calling 'potential almond residue.'"

I picked up my coffee cup, but my hands were shaking so badly I could barely get it to my lips.

"There's more," Hugh said. "They found Sally's purse with the epinephrine kit. It was in the gallery cloakroom. Jo, the purse was in the pocket of Izaak Levin's overcoat."

"So he killed her," I said.

"It looks that way," said Hugh. "Either that or, after all his rude comments about my lifestyle, old Izaak's turned out to be a cross-dresser."

Despite everything, I laughed.

Mieka brought over two plates of French toast. "I'll leave you two alone now. Shout if you need me."

"Thanks," I said. "For everything." I took a bite of French toast. "Good," I said. "It really is. You were right about eating, Hugh."

He smiled and put maple syrup on his French toast. "So what do you think?"

"I don't know," I said. "I don't know if I even care. All those questions last night about the Guerrilla Girls. I guess they're off the hook now."

"I don't think they're off the hook at all," Hugh said. "I'm a visual arts editor, not a crime reporter, but I had the distinct impression last night that the police aren't fond of coincidence. You know, Jo, the Guerrilla Girls did turn out the lights, and they were running around that room. Who knows what they did in the dark. They could have been working with Izaak Levin."

"Yes," I agreed, "they could have been working with him, or it could have been the other way round."

Hugh went over, picked up the coffeepot and filled our cups. "You've lost me," he said.

"I guess it's possible," I said, "that the Guerrilla Girls could have set Izaak Levin up. You know, Hugh, in all the confusion after the lights went out it wouldn't have been hard to slip something as small as an empty plastic baggie into a jacket pocket. The Guerrilla Girl who came to our table was standing right between Izaak and Nina. I remember that clearly. And it certainly would have been easy for her to grab Sally's purse. It was slung over the back of her chair all evening. You must have noticed it – one of those antique evening bags with a chain so you can carry it over your shoulder."

Suddenly I was so weary I could barely move. "Why are we doing this?" I asked. "It doesn't matter. It doesn't change anything. We can sit here till doomsday and nothing we figure out is going to change the past twenty-four hours."

Hugh looked as weary as I felt. He stood up. "I think it's time to go," he said.

He called a cab, and when it came, I walked him to the front door.

"Take care of yourself," he said. "Thank your daughter for the breakfast."

"Come back again," I said.

"Every time I'm in Saskatoon." Then he smiled. "Be sure to wear that shirt next time. It's a little Dolly Parton but very cute. I'll bet your kids got it for you."

I didn't remember what I was wearing. I looked down: bubble-gum pink with sequins saying *I LOVE JO*. I leaned forward and kissed his cheek.

"You lose your bet," I said. "It wasn't from my kids. It was a present from a friend."

It didn't take me long to decide to go to Nina's. I was exhausted, but I couldn't get clear of what she had said to me the night before. "You're all the daughter I have now." It was my duty to tell her about Izaak Levin. As strained as her relationship with Sally had been, this would be a shock. I had to be there to help her deal with it.

I went up and changed into my best black skirt and sweater and called a cab. All the way to Spadina Crescent, the cab driver kept up a running commentary on Sally's murder. I couldn't seem to work up the energy to tell him to stop. Traffic near the gallery was heavy. The prospect of seeing the building where four shocking deaths had occurred really brought out the citizens. Apparently, Stuart Lachlan's address was still secret because the only cars in front of number seventeen were Stu's matched Mercedes. The family of snow people had been revised a little by thaws and storms but they were still perky. A banner, white with big red letters and a border of hearts, stretched from the father to the daughter. HAPPY VALENTINE'S FROM TAYLOR LOVE LACHLAN, it said.

I took a deep breath before I lifted the brass door knocker. Nina answered the door. She was wearing a white cashmere dress that I didn't remember, very chic, very flattering. An antique gold locket gleamed at her neck, and in her ears were tiny hoops of chased gold. She took both my hands in hers and pulled me gently inside.

"I'm so glad it's you, Jo," she said in her low breathy voice. "I need help and I was debating with myself about whether it was too early to call you."

"It could never be too early, Ni," I said.

She helped me off with my coat and then, hand in hand, we walked into the living room.

I don't know what I expected. Neither Nina nor Stuart Lachlan was the keening or rending garments type, but everything was so serene, so life as usual. Mozart was on the CD player; there were bowls of shaggy white chrysanthemums on the mantel and coffee table, and the air smelled of coffee and fresh baking.

I turned to Nina. "You know I'd do anything for you, Ni, but it certainly looks as if everything's in hand."

"Looks can be deceiving," she said. She made a sweeping gesture toward the Chinese Chippendale desk. "Really, I've just begun."

I looked over at the desk. There was an open telephone book on it and a notepad with notations in Nina's neat backhand.

"I'm just trying to think of everything that needs to be done and match up the chore list with the names of the local people. I don't know this city well enough to make an informed decision myself, but I thought I could make some preliminary lists for Stuart to choose from. This is going to be a trying day for him."

"For all of us," I said.

"Of course," she agreed. "We're all the walking wounded today."

"Ni, I have more news. Could we sit down?"

She drew me over to the couch. "I'm sorry, Jo. You'll have to forgive me. It's just that there's so much . . ."

"I'm afraid I'm going to add to it, dear. The police have completed some of their investigation, and they have some ideas about what might have happened last night." I moved closer to her and told her about Izaak and the almonds and the epinephrine. She listened with her back ramrod straight and her hands cupping one another loosely, like a woman waiting to have her photograph taken. Her calm unnerved me.

"Nina, did you understand what I said? The police think Izaak was the one."

"Yes," she said, "I heard you."

In the kitchen there was the treble pinging sound of an oven timer. Nina stood up and gave me a shaky smile.

"Currant scones," she said, "Stuart's favourite. I'm going to fix a tray for him and take it upstairs. I'll bring us something, too, Jo. Please, just be patient and make yourself comfortable."

It was a tall order. I walked over to Nina's desk. The telephone book was open to funeral homes. I shuddered and walked through the dining room to the bay window that overlooked the backyard. Nina's evening dress, tulip red, and Stu's tuxedo were out there, hanging side by side on the clothesline. Even before smoking had become the great social sin, Nina had hated the lingering smell of cigarettes. She always hung her clothes out to air after she had been somewhere where people smoked. There had been smoking last night. And there had been murder.

For a while, my mind drifted. White think. Then I felt someone beside me. I looked down and Taylor Love Lachlan was there. Her blond hair was smoothed back behind an *Alice in Wonderland* black velvet bow, and she was wearing a Black Watch tartan skirt and a white blouse. She was silent, intent on what she saw through the window.

"Look," she said finally, "when the wind blows, Nina's dress and Daddy's suit look like they're dancing on the clothesline."

I smiled and gave her shoulder a squeeze.

"Sally died, you know," she said conversationally. "I was asleep, but when I woke up, Daddy told me Sally had gone to heaven."

I didn't know what to say. I stood there, numb, looking into the yard, my hand resting on Taylor's shoulder. The wind had picked up, and Taylor was right. Nina's dress and Stu's tuxedo looked as if they were dancing. Inexplicably, I felt a clutch of panic.

But suddenly behind me there was Nina's voice, warm, reassuring. "Come and eat something, you two." And I felt safe again. She was sitting at the dining-room table in a pose I'd seen a thousand times: a tray set with the thinnest cups, a teapot, plates, linen napkins, something still warm from the oven for tea.

Izaak Levin was not mentioned again that morning. As Nina talked quietly about the kinds of birds that would come to their bird feeder when the great migrations north began, I saw that she was trying to protect Taylor and Stuart by enclosing them in a world of familiar pleasures. There was no place for Sally's murderer at that table, and so we talked of birds and gardens and Stuart's summer home at Stay Away Lake, a hundred miles north of the city. Stuart wanted to go there after everything was settled, Nina said in her soft voice. He loved the house at Stay Away Lake. His family had owned it since before he was born, and everything was exactly as it had been half a century ago.

"He needs that now," said Nina. "So much has changed."

"So much has changed." I repeated those words to myself as I started the long walk to Osler Street. I didn't even make it to the bridge before the tears started. I didn't care. I stood and looked down at the river and cried. When I was finished, I took a deep breath, squared my shoulders and started to walk again. The sky was overcast but the air was fresh, and when I turned up the back alley toward our house, I was feeling in control. My neighbour was out in her backyard taking sheets off the line. The sheets were frozen, and she had to wrestle with them to get them folded and in her laundry hamper. I thought of Nina's evening dress and Stuart's tuxedo dancing against the grey February sky. And then out of nowhere, a poem, something we used to write in autograph books when I was in grade school:

> I love you. I love you. I love you almighty.
> I wish your pyjamas were next to my nightie.
> Now don't get excited.
> Now don't lose your head.
> I mean on the clothesline and not in the bed.

When I walked across our backyard, I couldn't tell if I was laughing or crying.

Angus was sitting in the den watching a kids' show that he'd outgrown years ago. He was wearing a T-shirt he'd bought himself at the joke shop in the mall. On the front a cartoon rooster with a huge beak and a macho leer was strutting on a beach filled with hens; underneath it said, "Chicks Dig Big Peckers."

I gestured toward the TV. "Anything new in Mr. Dressup's world?"

"Nope, everything's just the same." Then he looked up at me. I could see he'd been crying, but he tried a smile. "Nothing ever changes on Mr. Dressup. You know that, Mum. That's why I'm watching."

At three o'clock I went over and gave my senior class a reading assignment. There was a message on my desk to call Izaak Levin. I shuddered when I noticed the message was dated the day before.

When I got home, Angus met me at the door. "I'm going down to the Y to shoot baskets with James if it's okay."

"It's okay," I said. "Supper's at five-thirty."

"What are we having?"

"Takeout, your choice."

"Fish and chips?"

"Sounds good to me," I said. "I could use a load of grease right now."

He smiled. "Right. Oh, I almost forgot, Sally's mother came over with some flowers," he said. "They're in the living room."

On the coffee table was the Japanese porcelain bowl with the painted swimming fish. Serene. Beautiful. Nina had filled it with white anemone, and there was a note card with a line written in her neat backhand propped up against it. "Remembering and cherishing, N."

I sighed and went to the phone. She answered on the first ring, and when she heard my voice, her relief was evident.

"Jo, thank heavens it's you. I'm feeling very alone right now. Stuart's been drinking all day. He's so withdrawn I can't reach him. And I think the reality of her mother's death is starting to hit Taylor. She's just clinging to me. I haven't been able to get anything done. You said this morning that if there was anything you could do, I should ask. Well, I'm asking."

"I'm here," I said.

"Someone needs to go to the funeral home and make some decisions. And a curious thing. A priest came to the house this afternoon. He said Sally was a parishioner of his. That's a surprise, at least to me. At any rate, he'll do the funeral, but he needs to talk to someone from the family." Her voice broke. "Jo, there is no one from the family. I'm all alone."

"I'll go, Nina," I said. "Just give me the names and addresses."

"Thank you, Jo. I knew I could count on you."

When I hung up the phone, I felt about as wretched as I could remember. I put my face in my hands and leaned against the telephone table. After a while, I felt a tap on my shoulder. I looked up. Peter was standing there.

"I have to go and pick out the coffin," I said.

"You'll need a ride," he said simply.

I was glad I had him with me. The people at the funeral home were kind and helpful, but making funeral arrangements was a lousy job. After we finished, Pete dropped me off at St. Thomas More Chapel.

I had called Father Gary Ariano before dinner and told him I'd meet him at eight o'clock. The college bells were chiming when I walked in the front door, and Father Ariano was waiting for me. He was a dark-haired, athletic man in early middle age, very intense. He was wearing blue jeans and a sweatshirt from Loyola University. He held out his hand in greeting, and I followed him up two flights of stairs through a door marked "Private" into the priests' common room. It was a comfortable room, with an outsize aquarium, a wall of windows that looked out onto the campus and a generously stocked bar.

"What'll it be?" asked Father Ariano.

"Bourbon, please, and ice."

Father Ariano opened a Blue for himself and poured a generous splash of Old Grand-Dad over ice for me. We sat down on a couch in front of the windows. It was a foggy night, and below us the lights of the campus glowed, otherworldly.

I didn't know where to begin but after we'd had a few minutes to grow easy with one another, Father Ariano began for me.

"Sally told me once that the only good things about the Catholic church were its art collection and its funerals."

"And yet she was a regular communicant?" I asked.

"She was," he said. "She came most often on weekdays. There's a mass around five, and sometimes we'd go out for a sandwich after or she'd come up here and we'd talk."

"It's hard to think of Sally as devout," I said.

"I think Sally would have called herself interested rather than devout. The nature of faith and the faithful interested her. She was a very bright woman."

"Not just a holy innocent the great god of art dripped paint through," I said.

He smiled. "That sounds like a direct quote from our friend Sally. People always underestimated her. Stuart Lachlan certainly did. He put her in a terrible position when he wrote that book. It was an incredible breach of trust."

"Not the first in her life," I said.

He looked at me oddly. "No," he said, "not the first and not the only. But don't get me started on that. Look, I guess we'd better discuss the details for the funeral."

"Right," I said.

Father Ariano was, as they say, a godsend: factual, presenting options, suggesting choices. When we'd finished, I stood up.

"Thanks," I said. "I guess that's it."

Father Ariano looked at me. "Except for one thing."

I waited.

He squeezed his right hand together, crushing his beer can. "Except," he said, "that this is the shits. It really is the shits."

"That's what my son said, too."

"Smart kid," he said, standing. "Come on, follow me, I'll show you the chapel."

We went down the stairs to the main floor, but instead of going toward the front doors, we turned down a wide and brightly lit hall. On one side were pictures of the priests who had been heads of the order. On the other were clothing racks, the kind you see in department stores. Arranged on each rack, seemingly by ecclesiastical season and size, were dozens of clerical vestments.

"This is where we robe," Father Ariano said casually, "and here," he said, as we walked through some double doors, "is where we go to work."

The air in the chapel was cool and smelled of candle wax, furniture polish and, lingeringly, of wet wool. The chapel was uncluttered and attractive: white painted walls and plain blond pews arranged in a semicircle to face the gleaming wooden cross suspended from the ceiling above the altar. It looked like any of a dozen chapels I'd seen that were designed for the university community at worship. But on the north wall was a mural, and it was to the mural that Gary Ariano directed my attention when we came through the doors.

"There's our prize," he said.

From a distance the mural was conventionally pretty: a prairie field on a summer's day with Christ at the centre performing the miracle of the loaves and fishes. I wasn't much interested.

"The colours are lovely," I said dismissively.

Gary Ariano said, "Go closer. Get a good look."

Up close, the mural glowed with apocalyptic light. Dark storm clouds in the corner menaced the perfect blue of the sky; under the crowds that circled the field where Jesus stood, the earth was cracking open, and arms shaking their fists at God thrust themselves through wounds in the earth.

"That just about reflects my world view at the moment," I said.

"I knew you'd like it," said Gary Ariano dryly, as we turned and walked out of the chapel and back into the world.

CHAPTER

12

Sally's funeral was set for Monday afternoon, the first day of the university's February break. The administration had introduced the break a quarter of a century before because the university had the highest suicide rate in the country. The students still called it Dead Week. The period between Friday night when I walked home through the darkness from my meeting with Father Gary Ariano to the morning of the funeral was a blur for me: arranging for musicians, choosing the proper spray of flowers for the coffin, the right arrangements for the tall copper vases the college chapel provided, talking to Mieka about food for the reception afterwards – busywork, but anything beat thinking about Sally.

And anything was better than thinking about Izaak Levin. I couldn't get my mind around the fact that the brilliant man Sally and I had dreamed over that hot, starry summer was a killer. Looking at my reflection in the hall mirror, I saw the same woman I always saw, but I felt like Saint Bartholomew, flayed alive. In desperation, I grabbed my gym bag and went to Maggie's. The aerobics class was in the same gym Sally and I had been in before Christmas, and she was everywhere in that room for me, face set in concentration, body slick with sweat, invulnerable. Halfway through the workout, I couldn't take the memories any more, and I ran to the dressing room and wept.

I talked to Nina many times that weekend but I saw her only once, when Mieka and I went Saturday morning to take Taylor shopping for an outfit she could wear to the services on Monday.

We pulled up in front of the Lachlans' at nine o'clock. Stuart met us at the door. He looked, as the Irish say, like a man who has spent the night asleep in his own grave, but he helped Taylor on with her coat and walked us out to the road.

When he saw Mieka waiting in her car, Stu looked at me. "Haven't you replaced your car yet, Joanne?"

I shook my head. "No," I said, "there doesn't seem to have been any time."

Stu fumbled in his pocket and produced a set of keys. "Here," he said, pointing to the two silvery Mercedes in his driveway. "Take one of them. I'm not going anywhere, and even Nina can't drive them both at once. Jo, she told me you're handling everything for us. Keep the car as long as you want. Keep it forever."

Taylor had already climbed into the front seat of Stuart's car, so I went to tell Mieka I didn't need a ride after all. When I slid into the driver's seat, I smiled at Taylor.

"Okay, miss, let's go look at some dresses." It wasn't until I pulled into a parking place at the mall that it hit me. For the first time since the accident, I had driven a car again.

I was still driving the Mercedes when I pulled up in front of St. Thomas More Chapel an hour before Sally's funeral. I'd come early because I wanted to make sure everything was perfect.

As I walked into the hushed coolness of the chapel it seemed as if everything was as it should be. A screen was in

place to the side of the altar. Hugh Rankin-Carter was giving
the eulogy, and he wanted to show some of Sally's work as
he talked about her life. The college's copper urns had been
replaced by two of Nina's most beautiful lacquerware water
jars, and they were filled with orchids. The mass cards with
the reproduction of *Perfect Circles*, Sally's painting of us that
last summer at the lake, were piled neatly on a table by the
door. "*Je n'ai rien négligé.*" Me and Nicolas Poussin.

During the funeral, my children and I sat under the mural
of the prairie Jesus performing the miracle of the loaves and
fishes. He was wearing a white robe, and His arm was raised
in benediction. I tried to keep my eyes on that sign of blessing, but I kept seeing other things: Taylor, looking like a
Parisian schoolgirl in her black double-breasted coat and
beret, pulling back from her father and grandmother as they
walked up the centre aisle. Stuart stumbling and Nina reaching to steady him as they took their places in the front pew.
Hugh Rankin-Carter at the lectern, unrecognizable for a
moment in a dark business suit, his face broken by anguish.
Hilda McCourt, back ramrod straight, saying good-bye to
another free spirit. And in front of the altar, inescapable, the
plain pine box that held all that was left of Sally's grace and
laughter and beauty.

We had taken two cars to the chapel. Taylor was going to
our house with my kids right after the funeral. She said she
didn't want to see them put Sally under the snow. I didn't,
either, but I was an adult; I didn't have any options.

As I drove to the cemetery, I was glad to be alone. Nina
had asked me to ride with them, but at the funeral Stuart
had broken down completely, and I knew if I had to spend
any time with him, I'd go over the edge, too.

Prospect Cemetery was on the river south of the city. The
road into it was narrow, overgrown with bushes. In the

summer the bushes became a dense and primitive place where city kids would drink beer and make love. But as I looked at that windswept hill, bleak as a moor, it was impossible to believe in a world of pleasure and hot coupling.

There were only a handful of us at the graveside: Father Ariano, Nina, Stuart, Hugh Rankin-Carter, Hilda McCourt and me. I didn't react when they lowered Sally's casket into the ground. I think by then I had entered a place in my mind that was beyond reaction.

Nina had invited me to come back to their house for a drink. As I pulled onto Spadina Crescent, I wondered if I should have been so quick to say I'd come. I didn't remember the drive from the cemetery at all, and when I looked at the art gallery I felt a stab of panic. It seemed unfamiliar, changed from the place I knew. Disoriented and frightened, I tried to grasp what was different, and then suddenly I knew.

The banners were gone. They had taken down the yellow banners that had celebrated Sally's name against the winter sky since the week before Christmas. In one of her books, Virginia Woolf says something about how we experience the death of someone we love not at their funeral but when we come upon a pair of their old shoes. I hadn't come upon Sally's old shoes in the portico of the gallery, but for emotional impact, the missing banners were close enough. I pulled into the parking lot, put my head on the steering wheel and wept.

On the dashboard in front of me was the mass card from Sally's funeral. Hugh Rankin-Carter had chosen the epigraph. It was from Jacques Lipchitz, the great sculptor. "All my life as an artist I have asked myself: what pushes me continually to make art. The answer is simple. Art is our unique way of fighting death and achieving immortality. And in this continuity of art, of creation and denial of death, we find God."

Tuesday morning was Izaak Levin's memorial service. I wore the same black wool suit I had worn the day before to Sally's funeral. Dead Week.

Izaak's service was at a small performance studio in the old fine arts building. Whoever had chosen the venue had made a wise choice. Not many people came to say good-bye to a man who was alleged to have killed four people. That morning as I had rummaged through my dresser for a pair of black panty hose, I had come up with a dozen reasons I shouldn't go.

A dozen reasons not to, and just one that compelled me to go, but it overrode all the rest. I was there for Sally. I had a sense that she wanted me there, and so I was there.

Someone had taken pains with Izaak Levin's memorial service. There was a good jazz quartet playing fifties progressive jazz: "Round Midnight," "Joyspring" and some tunes I recognized from the album *Kind of Blue* by Miles Davis. Between numbers, three men who looked like contemporaries of Izaak's read from his art criticism.

There was no coffin. Izaak Levin had been cremated as soon as the coroner released his body.

I didn't know any of the people in that room, but one woman held my attention, mostly, I think, because she seemed like such an unlikely mourner. She was a small, square woman in her sixties, nicely but not fashionably dressed in a royal blue crepe dress. Her jet-black hair was upswept, and her face still had traces of plump prettiness. When the service was over, she shook hands with the musicians and the men who had read. Then she turned and walked toward me.

As she held out her hand, she smiled.

"I'm Ellie Levin, Izaak's sister, and I wanted to thank you for coming."

"I'm Joanne Kilbourn," I said. "I knew your brother many years ago in Toronto and I was a friend of Sally Love's."

She flinched but she looked at me steadily. "I was a friend of Sally's, too. I didn't see her often enough, but I loved to be with her. She always made me laugh. She made Izaak laugh, too. He used to say she'd lead him to an early grave, but he worshipped her."

Now it was my turn to flinch, but I reached out and touched her hand. "I know he worshipped her," I said. I grasped for something else to say. "Miss Levin, I'm truly sorry his life ended so unhappily."

She covered my hand with her own. "So, do you think he did what they said?"

The question took me by surprise, and so did my answer.

"No," I said, "I don't. They have all that evidence against him, but I just don't believe it."

"You don't believe it because it's not true," she said flatly. "He was my brother for sixty-five years. I knew his limits. He was no killer. He was a gambler, and like a lot of smart people he wasn't smart about money. You would have been a fool to cosign a loan with him, but killing? Never. Izaak Levin was no killer."

I didn't know what to say, so I said nothing. In the background, I could hear the sounds of the musicians packing up: instrument cases shutting, plans being made for lunch. I wondered if they knew how lucky they were to be part of the normal world.

For a moment Ellie Levin seemed to be lost in her thoughts. Finally she said, "He was in a lot of trouble when he died."

"Money trouble?" I asked.

"Worse," she said. "In-over-your-head trouble. It started with money. Before Christmas it was money. He called me Christmas Eve and told me he was seriously in need of cash."

"Did you give it to him?"

"Do I look crazy? I'm not a wealthy woman, Joanne. All I have is my home and some bonds our parents left me. I've always been firm with Izaak about money. I had to be. I was saving for our old age. I always figured somehow we'd end up together at the end of our lives, and I wanted things to be nice."

For a moment, I thought she was going to break, but she took a deep breath and went on.

"I talked to him two more times before . . . before the end. It was after New Year's Day, but I don't remember the days. Who remembers days when it's just ordinary life going on? Anyway, the first time, Izaak was on top of the world. 'No more money worries. I'll be your banker from now on, Ellie.' That's what he said. Of course, I tried to get him to tell me the particulars, but he just laughed.

"He wasn't laughing the last time he called. He sounded screwed up tight and frightened. This time when he wouldn't tell me what was going on, I didn't take no for an answer. I kept at him. I badgered him until finally he hung up on me. But I didn't give up even then. I phoned him back. He sounded so tired it broke my heart, but I was scared, too. I pleaded with him. I told him I'd keep calling him until he confided in me. Finally, he said, 'You always were persistent. But you know, sometimes it's safer not to know. I found out something I wasn't supposed to know, and now I'm out past Jackson's Point, Ellie. I'm way past Jackson's Point.'" She looked at me, waiting.

"I'm sorry," I said. "I don't understand."

"It was a place we weren't supposed to swim past when we were kids. Every summer there were stories about kids who swam past Jackson's Point and got caught in the weeds and were never seen again. Anyway, for Izaak and me, Jackson's Point became a way of saying we were in over our heads." Suddenly her eyes were filled with tears. "So I should have listened, right? Miss Practical saving for the future while the weeds are pulling my brother under."

"Have you told the police this?"

"Oh, yes," she said, "they were very patient. They heard me out and they asked me if I thought Izaak was involved in blackmail. When I said that's exactly what I was afraid of, they pounced. All the more proof of his guilt, they said. If Izaak knew he was going to be exposed, he might have killed Sally so she'd never know what he'd done." She looked directly at me, and there was a flash in her eyes that was very like her brother's. When she spoke again, her tone was like his, too: sardonic, mocking. "So," she said, "does that make sense to you? To kill someone you love so they won't think less of you?"

Her question was still in my ears as I walked across the snowy lawn in front of the fine arts building. There were other questions, too. If there was blackmail, who had been the target? Stuart Lachlan? If Stuart was the one, what was he being blackmailed about? How was Clea Poole involved? She and Izaak had little use for one another. Sally had told me that, but they both loved Sally. Had they discovered something condemning about Stuart Lachlan and decided . . . Decided what? And the one question that suddenly loomed over everything. If Izaak hadn't committed the murders who had? Who had killed Sally Love?

As I turned onto the street where I'd parked, my head was pounding. I was tired. I couldn't seem to work out any of the permutations and combinations, and I didn't want to. I wanted to go home and stand under the shower until all the horrors were washed away.

But the horrors were just beginning.

There was a traffic ticket on the window of the Mercedes. Except when I got closer I saw that it wasn't a traffic ticket.

It was an envelope, square, creamy, good quality. I opened it. Inside on a square of matching paper a message was printed in careful block letters: I SAW YOU KILL SALLY LOVE.

My first thought was that the note was some kind of bizarre sendoff for Izaak. But Izaak was dead. Twenty minutes earlier, the small mahogany box that held his earthly remains had been sitting on a table in the fine arts building. He was beyond messages. And the envelope hadn't been delivered to the funeral. It had been stuck on the windshield of my car.

Except it wasn't my car. The silvery Mercedes with the characteristic ARTS licence plate didn't belong to me. It belonged to Stuart Lachlan. The accusation of murder hadn't been directed at me; it was directed at Stuart Lachlan. I got into the car. My hands were shaking so badly I had trouble getting the key in the ignition.

I started to drive to Spadina Crescent. Then I thought about the nature of my evidence: an anonymous letter, a sister's belief that someone other than her brother was a killer. Why was I so ready to believe Stuart Lachlan was capable of murder? We had never been close, but I had liked him well enough. I'd been a guest in his home. I was his dead wife's oldest friend.

Things had gone very wrong for Stuart in the past months. There was no denying that, but Stu was a civilized man, and civilized people don't commit murder when things go wrong. As I turned onto my street, I thanked my lucky stars that I hadn't jeopardized my relationship with Stu and Taylor by levelling hysterical accusations at him. I'd always considered my two best qualities loyalty and common sense and I didn't seem to be exhibiting either. What I needed was rest and a chance to put things like an anonymous accusation into perspective.

Angus was running out the front door when I got home. "I left you a note. James asked me to sleep over. His parents are taking us to the Globetrotters and his mom says it'll be late so if it's okay with you I'll stay there. I know it's a school night, but I thought maybe for the Globetrotters, you could bend your rules."

I was glad to see him excited about something again. "For the Globetrotters, I'll bend," I said. "Have you got money?"

"Their treat," he said happily. "Thanks, Mum. I'll get my stuff after school."

"If I don't connect with you then, have a good time."

"Right," he said as he kissed the air near my face and ran out the door. He was back in a second.

"You'll be all right alone, won't you?" he asked.

"Absolutely," I said.

"It's all over, isn't it?" he said.

"Yeah," I said, "it's all over."

"It's all over," I repeated, as I stepped under the shower. But in my bones I knew that it wasn't over, and I was filled with apprehension.

It was when I was zipping my blue jeans that I remembered the package Sally Love had left at my house the night we came back from skiing at Greenwater. "My insurance policy," she'd called it. "If you lose it, I'm dead. And don't get curious."

Well, I hadn't lost it, but suddenly I was curious. The myth of Pandora's box didn't scare me. I couldn't imagine loosing any more evils on mankind than the horrors we'd already seen. I pulled on the sweater Nina had given me for Christmas. The pattern was an elaborate and brilliant patchwork of colours. Nina said it had taken her most of the month of November to finish it. Just putting it on made me feel close to her.

The package wrapped in brown paper was right where I had left it, in my sewing basket. I tore the wrapping off and found a videotape.

"Surprises," I said as I walked down the hall to our family room. *Young Frankenstein* was in the VCR. Angus and I had watched it together the night before. I pushed eject, then I put in Sally's tape, sat back in the rocking chair and watched.

For the first seconds I thought that somehow I'd erased the tape. The screen was filled with grey static, but then I saw a long shot of Stuart Lachlan's house. There was no sound, and the quality of the video wasn't very good. There was a close-up of Taylor's family of snow people, the father, the mother and the little snow girl with her sign – "Merry Christmas from Taylor." Home movies. The camera lingered a little on the snow people and then it moved down the flagstone walk past the stand of pine trees at the corner of the house and around to the backyard. Somehow the movement seemed purposeful, as if the person behind the camera had a plan in mind. There was a quick establishing shot of the backyard and then we were looking through a window. I recognized the room immediately. There was a wall of books and family pictures, a cabinet filled with Royal Doulton figurines and, over the mantel of the fireplace, a portrait of Sally and Taylor. The room was Stuart Lachlan's study at the back of the house.

There were people in the shot, and at first I couldn't make any sense of what they were doing. The quality of the film wasn't good – grey and grainy and unfocused. But then the focus was adjusted and I saw. There were two figures, a man and a woman. Both were naked. The man was on the floor on all fours in a position of submission. Behind him the woman raised what looked like a pony whip and brought it down on his back. He flinched but he didn't move. She raised the whip again. And again and again. Finally the whipping stopped. He rolled over and she lowered herself onto his erect penis.

I didn't watch any more. I didn't have to. I'd seen enough. The man on the floor was Stuart Lachlan, and the woman who first beat him and then guided him into her body was Nina Love. My heart was pounding, and the blood was singing in my ears, but I didn't hesitate. I knew what I had to do. I pushed the eject button and threw the tape into my bag. I went upstairs, put on my ski jacket and boots, got into the Mercedes and drove to Stuart Lachlan's house.

CHAPTER

13

By the time I turned off the University Bridge the place behind the scar on my forehead was aching so badly I thought I was going to have to pull over. I could hear my mother's voice: "Nina may have fooled you, Joanne, but she never fooled me. She never fooled me."

"Shut up," I said, "just shut up. Let me work this out." The tape was terrible, but I couldn't let my horror over the video of Nina blind me to the significance of the tape itself. I had no doubt about the identity of the person who had held the camera. After all, I'd been in her sights myself New Year's Eve. Clea Poole had been everywhere with her video camera during those last days of the old year – "Mouse and her faithful Brownie," Sally had called her.

The tape was the missing piece in so many puzzles. Its existence explained Stu's sudden change of heart about Taylor's custody. ("Sally, did you sell your soul to the devil?" I had asked, and she had laughed. "No, to a mouse.") The tape was the explanation for the envelope of money Nina had taken to Izaak Levin's – not as an advance on a favourable book review, as Stuart Lachlan had told Nina, but

to keep a humiliating image of himself buried. He had succeeded; Stu's sexual practices were not a matter of public
record. But increasingly it looked as if a worse image of him
was about to emerge: the image of a man who had cold-
bloodedly murdered three people because they stood in the
way of how he believed his life should be lived.

I had no plan when I rang the doorbell of the Lachlan
house on Spadina Crescent. Somehow I had to warn Nina so
we could get Taylor out before . . . Before what? I didn't
know. My mind was numb. I couldn't seem to think beyond
the next moment. No one came to the door.

"Please, please, please," I said, as I rang the bell again, but
there was only silence and the sound of the blood singing in
my ears. I followed Clea Poole's route to the backyard: down
by the stone wall, past the stand of pine trees, along the
snowy flagstone walk.

I banged at the back door. I think I knew there'd be no
answer. I pulled the keys to the Mercedes out of my bag.
They were on a chain with other keys. I tried one that
looked like a house key, and first time lucky, the kitchen
door opened and I was inside.

On the round oak table by the window were the remains
of breakfast: three juice glasses, a half-empty milk glass,
three porridge bowls. I wondered if Goldilocks had felt as
scared as I did. I called Nina's name, then Taylor's. Finally,
tentatively, hoping there would be no answer, I called for
Stuart. There was nothing but silence. As I moved through
the house, I felt a coldness in the pit of my stomach. The
living and dining rooms were immaculate, but in the bed-
rooms the beds were unmade, and drawers and cupboard
doors gaped. It looked as if they had left in a hurry.

I left Stuart's study till the last. I don't know what I was
afraid of – a scarlet letter marking the place on the rug where
Stu and Nina had performed their strange act of love? I had

to steel myself to open the door, but there was nothing there. An innocent room filled with books and family pictures, a display case where Stuart's mother's collection of Royal Doulton ladies smiled and poured tea and bowed to one another, and over the mantel the portrait of Sally and Taylor, mother and daughter.

On the desk there was a telephone with an answering machine. I pressed the button to hear the message they had recorded for callers. No clues to where they had gone there; it was the same message I'd heard a dozen times over the winter. "This is Stuart Lachlan. Nina and Taylor and I are unable to come to the phone right now, but if you'll leave your name . . ."

I pushed the button again. "This is Stuart Lachlan. Nina and Taylor and I . . ." I pulled open Stuart's desk drawer. Shoved inside, not hidden, was a square envelope, the twin of the one I'd found on the Mercedes. I opened it. There was a note: THE CAMERA SAW WHAT YOU DID. There was also part of a photographer's contact sheet with eight proofs of pictures on it. I recognized them immediately as the ones the woman Anya had taken the night of the dinner. THE CAMERA SAW WHAT YOU DID. The camera saw, but I couldn't. The proof of Stuart's guilt was in my hand, but I couldn't see it. The pictures were so small I couldn't make out anything beyond the identity of the people at the table. Sally was in all of them: sitting between Stu and Izaak and looking miserable; leaning across Stu to say something to me; looking up at the camera as Nina stood behind her; scowling at Izaak as Stu leaned across her plate. I looked at that last picture again. It had to be the one. I couldn't make out what Stu was doing, but I thought I could see his hand close to Sally's plate.

"You're a killer, Stu." I tried the words aloud. They sounded right. "Well, you're not going to win this time, Stuart. I'm going to find you, and I'm going to make sure you pay." I picked up the phone book and found the number of the city police. On the other end of the line, the man's voice told me Inspector Mary Ross McCourt was unavailable, could he help. I thought of what would happen next. The search for Stuart and Nina. The media announcements. Nina's private life suddenly becoming public knowledge. I imagined Nina somewhere answering the door, and strange men in uniforms surrounding her, questioning her. What Stuart had done was not her fault. She loved him. I remembered the videotape. The thought of strangers sitting in a dimly lit room in police headquarters watching Nina's nakedness made my stomach turn.

"Can anyone else help you?" the voice on the other end of the line asked.

"No," I said, "no one can help me," and I hung up. There was a personal telephone directory on the desk. How did you list your own summer house? I was halfway through the alphabet when I thought about S for Stay Away Lake.

The phone rang a dozen times before it was picked up. The voice on the other end was Nina's. It seemed like a good omen. I hadn't thought where to begin, but I knew I had to keep her from reacting in case she wasn't alone.

"Nina, it's Jo. Is Stuart there with you?"

"No, he's out taking Taylor for a walk down by the lake, but I can get him. Joanne, is something wrong?"

"Yes, Ni, something's wrong. Something's terribly wrong. You have to get Taylor and come back to the city right away."

"Is there a problem with your family?"

"No, my family's fine. Ni, please get back here."

"Joanne, we just got unpacked. Stuart's exhausted. I can't ask him to turn around and drive back to the city. He needs time to heal."

"Fuck Stuart," I said. "Nina, you and Taylor have to get out of there. I know I'm not making sense. Too much has happened. It looks like Izaak Levin isn't the murderer after all. Ni, prepare yourself for some terrible news. I think Stuart is deeply implicated in the murders. You have to get out of there."

The silence on the other end of the line lasted so long I was afraid that Stuart had come into the room. But finally Nina answered me.

"Joanne, come and get me. Come and get us both. If Stuart has done what you say he did, I'm afraid of what will happen if I try to leave. Please, Jo. I've never asked much of you, but I'm asking this. Please, please come and get us."

The area behind my scar was throbbing. A steady beat of pain. I closed my eyes, and the image of Nina was there, lovely, loving, caring about me when no one else did. The one constant in my life.

"Of course," I said, "Ni, just hold on. I'll be right there."

"Do you know the way?"

"I can find it."

"If you start now, you'll be here before dark. Taylor and I will be at the dock waiting for you. Don't worry about driving across the lake. I know it's been warm, but the man at the crossing says the ice is safe. We'll be waiting."

It was a three-hour drive from the city to the Lachlan cottage on the island at Stay Away Lake. Three hours to think about the unthinkable. Sally's death was the perfect solution for Stu: no more problems about custody; no more threats to blow him out of the water over the stupid book he'd written. With Sally dead, Stu had it all. But he wasn't going to get it. When I saw the turnoff sign, I was filled with relief. It was almost over.

I looked at the lake. The ice was the colour of pewter, but there were dark places, too. There are often wonderful legends about these northern lakes, but the story of how Stay Away Lake got its name was not appealing. Local people said that at the turn of the century a madman lived on the island where the Lachlans later built their cottage. He killed anyone who came near the island and he dumped their bodies in the water – a dozen in all, they said, before finally he turned his rifle on himself. The legend was that at night you could hear the voices of his victims calling up their warning from the lake bottom: "Stay away. Stay away. Stay away."

The old man at the landing was not as sanguine about the ice as Nina had been. "It's been warm and the ice is punky," he said. "If I was you, I'd leave my car doors open, in case I had to make a quick getaway out there."

So I drove with the doors of the Mercedes open, and thought about the lost souls a few feet beneath me in the weedy darkness, crying out their warnings.

Finally, I made out the point where the Lachlans had built their cottage and I saw Nina and Taylor, two small figures in bright ski clothes standing on the dock in front of the boathouse.

I stopped the car at the far end of the dock. I didn't like the look of the ice closer to shore. Taylor ran out to meet me.

"Your car doors are open," she said. "We watched you drive across, and your doors were open all the way. Did you forget?"

"It's just the way you drive on ice," I said, "to be safe."

"You wouldn't want to go through," she said sagely. "You'd hurt all the fish down on the bottom waiting for spring."

"I was careful," I said. "No one got hurt. I promise."

Nina hadn't moved. She was still standing in front of the boathouse. Taylor and I walked to her. I didn't like the way Nina looked; she was composed but very pale. Her ski jacket was a brilliant blue. When she'd bought it, she'd asked me if the style was too young for her. That day, as she'd stood in the Ski Shoppe slender and glowing with happiness, I'd said, "Nothing will ever be too young for you." I couldn't have said that now.

"Are you ready?" I asked her.

Her eyes widened. It seemed as if she had just noticed I was there.

"No," she said in a low, flat voice, "I'm not ready."

"Nina, we have to go."

She raised her hand as if she were warding something off. "I have to look at him. I have to tell him that I know what he did. I have to finish it."

She turned and went into the boathouse. I followed her. It was dark in there and cold. The air smelled of fish and dampness, but intermingled with the lake smells was the scent of Nina's perfume. When she opened the door on the other side, a shaft of pale light came toward me, but she was in darkness.

"Ni, I'm coming with you," I said.

When she answered, her voice was terrible.

"No, Jo. This is private. Just for me alone. Please, go and stay with Taylor. She'll be frightened. I'll be back. I can't just walk away from him." She stepped outside and pulled the door shut after her.

I walked through the boathouse. Taylor was waiting at the end of the dock. She had the mass card from Sally's funeral in her hand. I'd left it on the dash of the Mercedes. I came and looked over her shoulder at the picture on the front: Sally's present to me. "Hang on to it, it's the only picture I ever did of Nina. She's so beautiful I could almost forgive her." Beside me, Taylor traced the perfect circle that enclosed Sally and Desmond Love.

"Did Nina put them there?" she asked.

"What?" I said stupidly.

Her voice was small and patient. "Did Nina put Sally and my grandfather under the water?"

I looked at the picture. Sally's golden head bent toward Desmond Love's – they had never needed anyone else.

Daughter and father, absorbed, happy, complete, as together they built sand castles in the perfect circle of their private world.

In that moment I knew.

"Get in the car, and no matter what happens, stay there. I'll be back for you. I promise. Just stay there."

I ran through the boathouse. The scent of Joy lingered like a memory. I was halfway up the hill when I heard the first shot. It sounded dry and inconsequential, and then I heard the second.

At the top of the hill, the lights from the cottage shone yellow and welcoming in the dusk. A place to come home to.

When I got to the door I was overwhelmed with a sense of déjà vu so violent it was physical. Another cottage. Another night. Thirty-two years before. And I had stood there looking past Izaak Levin into the cottage, and I had seen . . .

I had seen exactly what Nina Love had planned that I would see. Hilda McCourt had quoted Graham Greene: "There is always one moment in childhood when the door opens and lets the future in."

That had been my moment. If I hadn't gone back to my cottage for my shoes, I would have been the one who walked in and found them. But it was Izaak who found them. I was late. She had taken a risk with that poison. My father said that another half hour would have tipped the balance. But, of course, I would never have made Nina wait another half hour. She knew I would come. She knew she could count on me to make her plan work. And it had worked. Des was dead. Sally had been so shattered she was easily disposed of, and Nina was rich and free of an invalid husband and a daughter who would always be her rival. She had taken a risk, but she knew the risk was minimal because she had me.

And now she had taken another risk. I knew she was behind that door waiting, waiting for me to come in, so the performance could begin. She knew she could count on me. Whatever story she told me, I would believe. I would swear to.

I almost walked away, but then I thought of Sally and Des and Izaak and Clea and the Righteous Protester – debts waiting to be discharged. I reached out and turned the doorknob.

Stu was lying face down on the floor. Nina spun around when she heard me. The gun was still in her hand.

"Oh, thank God, Jo, it was terrible, he pulled the gun. You were right, it was Stuart all along."

I was crying. I couldn't recognize my voice. "No, Nina, not Stuart. It wasn't Stuart. And it wasn't Izaak and it wasn't Des. It was you, Nina. It was you. I loved you, and it was you. All these years. It was you."

I looked at her and I saw that imperceptibly she had raised the gun. It was pointed at me now.

"It had to be done, Jo." She shook her head in a gesture of impatience I'd seen a thousand times. "Jo, I had to . . . Sometimes people have to act. Otherwise lives would just go off course." She moved closer. The gun was still pointed at me. "I wish you hadn't stopped being loyal, Jo." She raised the gun.

In that pleasant cottagey room, there was the scent of Joy, and other smells, not flowery, not pleasant: the smells of death and of fear. The smell of death was Stuart's, but the fear was mine.

Suddenly, behind me, there was a small voice. Clear and clearly frightened.

"Are you going to kill us all, Nina?" Taylor asked.

Nina shifted her gaze for a moment, and I moved toward her and smashed at her hand. She looked quickly at me, astounded, as if the ground had suddenly opened beneath her feet.

The gun was still in her hand, but it was pointed toward the floor now. Nina couldn't seem to take her eyes from Taylor's face. She began backing away from her granddaughter, past Stuart into the living room. Finally, when her back was against the big plate-glass window that looked out on the woods, she stopped. On the other side of the window the aspens shivered in the pink-gold light of the dropping sun.

There were no last words. Nina looked quickly at me, then at Taylor. Then she turned to face the aspens and raised the gun to her temple – the barrel touched her temple at just the point where the dark curve of her hair hit the flawless plane of her cheek. Yin and yang.

I didn't go to her. I turned and put my arm around Taylor's shoulder, and after forty-seven years I walked out on Nina Love. By the time Taylor and I got to the dock, the sun was low, and the ice glowed with the cool colours of a northern winter: white, purple, blue, grey. But across the lake, in the west, the sky was the most incredible shade of pink.

I pointed to it as we got into the car. "Your favourite colour," I said.

"Not any more," she said.

In that moment, there was an inflection in Taylor's voice that sounded just like her mother's. We looked at each other and then, without another word, we drove across the fragile ice to the safety of the shore.

CHAPTER

14

Taylor is with us now. She came home with me that night and she never left. There was, in fact, nowhere else for her to go. Stuart and Sally were both only children. Stu had an old aunt in a nursing home somewhere in Ontario, but Sally had no one. Nina had seen to that.

The morning after she came, Taylor and I walked over to the campus together. It was a pretty day, and we bought hot chocolate from a machine and took it outside so we could watch the squirrels. I told her that our family wanted her to live with us, and we wondered how she felt. For a while she didn't say anything. Then she looked at me.

"Is it taken care of?" she asked.

"It can be," I said.

"Good," she said and that was the end of it. She hasn't brought up the subject since. My old friend Ali Sutherland, who's a psychiatrist, flew in from Winnipeg to talk to her. She said Taylor is doing as well as any child could after what Ali called "an appalling and crushing series of traumas." Indeed. What Taylor needs, says Ali, is counselling, reassurance and routine – constant reinforcement of the knowledge that everything in her new home is fixed and permanent. "Forever," Ali had added for emphasis.

And so we do our best. So far, our best seems to be good enough. Taylor is beginning to trust us. The rest will, I hope, come later.

The final murder investigation was swift and decisive, and that helped. I didn't have to produce the tape of Stuart and Nina, and that helped, too. The day after I got back from Stay Away Lake, the police discovered a tape that made mine irrelevant. This tape had been in the video camera above the bridal bed at the gallery, and it showed Nina killing Clea Poole. "Murder as performance art," Hugh Rankin-Carter said when he called to see how I was taking this latest blow. I was glad they found the tape. I didn't want there to be any doubts.

Now there weren't.

This final unassailable proof of Nina's guilt was discovered under circumstances that make me believe in cosmic justice or at least in cosmic jokes. When the police searched Izaak Levin's house, they found a key stuck to the back of the self-portrait Sally had painted for Izaak when she was fourteen. The key was to a safety-deposit box Izaak had rented under the name Desmond Love. The tape was there, and with it was a long and incoherent letter addressed to Sally. When the police sorted through all the justifications and mea culpas, the history of the tape and the role it played in Sally's death became clear.

The night Clea Poole was murdered, Izaak Levin went to the gallery to check on the installation Clea was working on. The young woman who had created the piece was a talented conceptual artist whom Izaak was thinking of taking on as a client. He had told several people at the gallery that the installation had to be executed perfectly and that he was concerned that Clea Poole was too sick to do the job right.

When he arrived, Clea was dead and the video camera was whirring away above the bed. Sally had made no secret about the disintegration of her relationship with Clea, and Izaak had assumed Sally was the murderer. To protect the woman he had loved for thirty years, he ripped the tape out and took it home for safekeeping. If he hadn't given in to his curiosity, Sally might have lived. But when Izaak looked at the tape, two things came together for him: his own financial need and the knowledge that he had hard proof Nina Love was guilty of murder. The blackmail began, and the chain of circumstances that ended in Sally's death and his own was set in motion.

Izaak had to die. He threatened not only Nina's freedom but also the family life she had so carefully crafted after she came to Saskatoon. As long as he lived, Nina's happiness hung by a thread. But Izaak Levin wasn't the only threat.

Nina had always seen Sally as her rival: first with Desmond Love, then with Stuart Lachlan and Taylor. As Sally's plans for taking her daughter with her to Vancouver took shape, Nina's plan to kill Sally took shape. It was Anya the photographer who showed how the murder was done. When the proofs on the contact sheet were enlarged, the police saw what Anya had seen: Sally's evening bag slung over the back of her chair seconds before Nina passed by but missing after she left. After Nina went to the cloakroom and slipped Sally's bag with the epinephrine into the pocket of Izaak Levin's coat, she came back to the table and put the powdered almonds on Sally's dessert. Izaak was so drunk it would have been easy for her to slip the empty bag into his pocket.

Nina never had to put the next part of her plan into effect. She never had to kill Izaak Levin. He died all on his own. It was the one lucky break she had. But Nina Love had never relied on luck. When the police opened the locked door of her room in the Lachlan house, they found enough prescription drugs to kill ten men. All the drugs were perfectly legal, the kind of medications a charming woman with a flair for acting could get a doctor to prescribe for her. The kind of drugs that could easily and fatally be slipped into a shot of whisky and offered to a drunk in a state of shock.

We'll never know, but as Mary Ross McCourt said, the one thing we know for certain is that Nina Love would not have allowed Izaak Levin to leave the Mendel Gallery alive that night. And so it's over.

Hilda McCourt came by today with a brochure for Shakespeare on the Saskatchewan. This summer they'll be doing *Twelfth Night*, and Hilda wants to take the kids. When she was leaving she looked into the living room. Angus was putting the finishing touches on a diorama for his biology project, and Taylor was drawing the morpheus butterfly that's going to be the star of the show.

For a moment, Hilda watched them without comment, then she touched my arm.

"I used to tell my students that at the end of a satisfying piece of fiction there is always something lost but there's also something gained. Try not to lose sight of that, Joanne."

I watched as Hilda got into her old Austin Healey and drove off. What I have lost still overwhelms me: Izaak, Stuart, Sally, Nina. Me. Or at least that part of me that believed the magic of life could be found in Nina and her world of eyelet dresses and dappled sunlight on the tea table and mist hanging heavy on the lake. All of this is gone, and much of it is, I know, past recovery.

But as I stand here on this, the first day of spring, watching my new daughter transform the blank page of an ordinary school notebook into the electric-blue flash of an Amazon butterfly, I repeat Hilda's words like a mantra. Something was lost, but something was gained. Something was lost but something was gained.

The Wandering Soul Murders

CHAPTER

1

When my daughter, Mieka, found the woman's body in the garbage can behind Old City Hall, she called the police and then she called me. I got there first. The sun was glinting off the glass face of the McCallum-Hill Building as I pulled into the alley behind Mieka's catering shop. It was a little after eight o'clock on a lush Thursday morning in May. It was garbage day, and as I passed the chi-chi pasta place at the corner of Mieka's block, the air smelled heavily of last night's cannelloni warming in the sun.

It wasn't hard to spot the dead woman. Her body was jack-knifed over the edge of the can as if she was reaching inside to retrieve something. But the angle of her body made it apparent that whatever she was looking for wasn't going to be found in this world. Mieka was standing in the shadows behind her. She seemed composed, but when she put her arms around me, I could feel her shaking.

"Come inside," I said.

"I don't want to leave her out here alone," Mieka said, and there was a tone to her voice that made me realize I'd be wise to go along with her.

Without a word, we stepped closer to the garbage can. It was a large one, industrial-size. I looked over the edge. I could see a sweep of black hair and two arms, limp as a doll's, hanging from the armholes of a fluorescent pink tank top. The space Mieka was leasing for her shop was being renovated, and the can was half filled with plaster and construction materials. The plaster underneath the body was stained dark with blood.

I stepped back and looked at Mieka.

"It's the woman who was helping with your cleaning, isn't it?" I asked.

Mieka nodded. "Her name's Bernice Morin." She pointed toward the lower half of the body. "Why would someone do that to her?" she asked.

"I guess they figured killing her didn't debase her enough," I said.

Mieka was gnawing at her lower lip. I felt like gnawing, too, because whoever had murdered Bernice Morin hadn't been content just to take her life. As an extra touch, they had pulled her blue jeans around her ankles, leaving her naked from the waist down. She looked as though she was about to be spanked or sodomized. Sickened at the things we do to one another, I turned away, but not before I saw the tattoo on her left buttock. It was in the shape of a teddy bear.

"My God," I said. "How old was she?"

"Seventeen," said Mieka. "Still teddy bear age."

And then the alley was filled with police, and a seventeen-year-old girl with a teddy bear tattoo became the City of Regina's latest unsolved homicide. I stood and watched as the crime scene people measured and photographed and bagged. And I listened as Mieka told her story to a man who had the sad basset eyes of the actor Donald Sutherland and who introduced himself as Inspector Tom Zaba.

Mieka's story wasn't much. Bernice Morin had been

cleaning for her under the city's fine-option program. It was a way people without money could work off unpaid fines for traffic tickets or minor misdemeanours. The building in which Mieka was leasing space was city property, so she had been eligible to get someone from the program. Mieka told the inspector that Bernice Morin had been working at the shop for a week. No one had visited her, and there had been no phone calls that Mieka knew about. Bernice hadn't appeared to be upset or frightened about anything, but Mieka said they hadn't spent much time together. She had been in and out, dealing with glaziers and carpenters, and Bernice wasn't much of a talker.

When the inspector asked her when she had last seen Bernice Morin alive, Mieka's jaw clenched. "Yesterday," she said, "about four-thirty. My fiancé's mother brought his grandfather by to take me out to their golf club to arrange for our wedding reception. I told Bernice I was coming back, but then Lorraine, my fiancé's mother, decided we should all stay out at the club for dinner. If I'd come back . . ." Mieka's voice trailed off. She was looking down at her hands as if she'd never seen them before.

Inspector Zaba took a step toward her. "Keep your focus, Miss Kilbourn. You were at the country club. Did you call Bernice Morin to tell her you'd be delayed?"

Mieka seemed wholly absorbed in her fingers, but her voice was strong. "I called a little before six and asked Bernice if she'd mind locking up when she left."

"And your premises were locked when you arrived this morning at . . . ?"

"At around seven-thirty. I'm an early riser. And, no, the shop wasn't locked. The front door was closed, but the dead-bolt wasn't on, and the back door, the one that opens onto the alley, was open. There was a pigeon flying around in the store. And there were bird droppings on the counter."

Inspector Zaba looked at Mieka expectantly.

Mieka shrugged. "I chased the pigeon around for a while until it finally flew out, then I cleaned up and I brought the dirty rags out here to the garbage. That's when I found Bernice. I went inside and phoned you and then I called my mother."

A female constable came outside and told Inspector Zaba that there was a phone call for Mieka. He nodded and told Mieka she could take it, but when she went into the building, he followed her.

I stayed behind, and that's when I heard two of the younger cops talking. One of them apparently knew Bernice pretty well.

"She was a veteran," he said. "On the streets for as long as I was in vice, and that was three years. She was from up north; she used to be one of that punk Darren Wolfe's girls."

The other man looked at him. "Another Little Flower homicide?"

"Looks like," said the first cop. "The bare bum's right. The face didn't seem mutilated, but maybe they'll pick up something downtown."

The young cops moved over to the garbage can and started bagging hunks of bloody plaster. They didn't seem to feel like talking any more. I didn't blame them.

When Mieka came out, it was apparent that the brutal reality of the murder had hit her. Her skin was waxy, covered with a light sheen of sweat. I didn't like the way she looked, and apparently Inspector Zaba didn't, either.

He came over to me and lowered his voice to a rasp. "I think we know what we've got here, Mrs. Kilbourn, and your daughter looks like she's had enough. Get her out of here. We've got all we need from her for the moment."

Grateful, I started to walk away, but I couldn't leave without asking. "What do you think you've got?" I said.

Inspector Tom Zaba had a face that would have been transformed by a smile, but I had the sense he didn't smile often.

"An object lesson," he said. "In the past year, we've had four of these murders." He looked thoughtfully at Bernice Morin's body and then at me. When he spoke, his voice was patient, the voice of a teacher explaining a situation to an unpromising student. "We've got some common denominators in these cases, Mrs. Kilbourn. One, all the victims were hustlers who'd gone independent. Two, all the girls walked out on pimps who don't believe in free enterprise. Three, the faces of all the victims were mutilated. Four, all the dead girls were found with the lower halves of their bodies exposed." He raised his eyebrows. "You don't have to be a shrink or a cop to get the message, do you?"

I looked at Bernice Morin's body. Her legs were strong and slender. She must have been a woman who moved with grace. I felt a coldness in the pit of my stomach.

"No," I said, "you don't have to be a shrink or a cop to get the message."

Victoria Park looks like every other inner-city park in every other small city in Canada: a large and handsome memorial to the war dead surrounded by a square block of hard-tracked grass with benches where people can sit and look at statues of politicians or at flower beds planted with petunias and marigolds, the cheap and the hardy, downtown survivors.

Mieka and I sat on a bench in front of Sir John A. Macdonald. It was a little after nine, and we had the park pretty much to ourselves. In three hours, the Mr. Tube Steak vendors would be filling the air with the smell of steaming wieners and sauerkraut, and the workers would spill out of the offices around Victoria Park and sit on the grass in their short-sleeved shirts and pastel spring dresses and turn their pale spring faces to the sun. But that was in the future. The only people in the park now were the sad ones with trembling hands and desperate eyes who had nowhere else to go.

And us. We sat side by side, not saying anything for a few minutes, then Mieka started to talk. Her voice was high and strained. "I only ever really talked to her once, Mummy, and it was here. One morning we came over here so Bernice could have a smoke. We talked about her tattoos. She was so proud of them. She had a snake that curled around here." Mieka traced a circle around the firm flesh of her upper arm. "Bernice was wearing a tank top that day, and she caught me staring at the snake. I was embarrassed, so I mumbled something complimentary. Then she just opened up. Told me she'd gotten the snake done down in Montana, and she thought it was so hot, she'd had a rose done on the other arm. She said all the people she hung with thought the snake and the rose were the best, but that was because they hadn't seen her private tattoo.

"Then she did something strange. We were sitting over there by the swings. Bernice looked around to make sure we were alone, then she turned away from me and hiked up her tank top. On her back was a picture of unicorns dancing.

"I knew it was an honour that she was showing me the tattoo, and I knew I should say something, but I just choked. Finally, Bernice pulled her shirt back down and laughed. 'Knocked you out, eh?' she said. Then she said she wanted me to see her back so I'd know she wasn't just somebody who did cleaning.

"I didn't mean to ignore her, Mum. You know I'd never be mean deliberately, but I guess I was just so busy I didn't pay much attention to her . . ."

I put my arm around my daughter's shoulder and pulled

her toward me. "It's okay, Miek," I said. "It's okay." But I knew it wasn't, and so did Mieka.

Her eyes were filled with sadness. "I haven't told you about the unicorns. Bernice dreamed about them one night after her boyfriend beat her up. The next morning she made the drawing, then she took the bus up north to a tattoo artist she knew who could do the design right. She said it took three hours and it just about killed her, especially the parts on her shoulder blades, but she said the unicorns were so beautiful they were worth it."

"Let's go home, baby," I said.

She shook me off. "Do you know what she told me, Mummy? She said she liked unicorns because they were the only animal that refused to go on the ark with Noah, and that's why they're extinct. She said her boyfriend told her it was because they were so dumb, but Bernice said she thought it was because they were too proud to get intimidated." Mieka's face was crumpling in pain. "That's what she said, Mummy. Unicorns died out because they were too proud to get intimidated."

Finally the tears came, and I took my daughter home. She slept most of the morning, but when I came back after picking up my youngest child, Taylor, from nursery school, Mieka was sitting at the kitchen table and there was a plate of sandwiches in front of her.

"Peanut butter and jelly for Taylor and salmon for us," Mieka said. She bent down and gave Taylor a quick hug. "Sound good to you, kiddo?"

Taylor beamed. "Look," she said, "I made you something, too. I did it at school." It was a painting. In the centre of the page, a baby lamb nuzzled its mother and a chick cracked the top of an egg. The rest of the page was alive with red tulips. They were everywhere: bursting through the grass on the ground and the clouds in the sky. A corona of them shot out in a halo of red around the yellow sun. On the top, in the careful printing of the nursery school teacher, were the words "NEW LIFE."

I tapped the words with my fingertip. "Life will go on, you know," I said, looking at Mieka.

She smiled and said quietly, "I know. It's just hard to think that it won't go on for Bernice. Seventeen is too young."

"Too young for what?" asked Taylor.

"Too young to miss the spring," Mieka said, turning away. "Now, come on, T., what's the drink of choice with peanut butter and jelly?"

After lunch, Mieka said she had some errands she should do, and she'd feel better if she was busy. Taylor and I drove to the nursery to buy bedding plants. It felt good to stand in the sunshine, picking up boxes of new plants, smelling damp earth and looking at fresh green shoots. As we drove home, Taylor was still curling her tongue around the names: sugar daddies, double mixed pinks, sweet rocket, bachelor's-button, black-eyed Susans. By the time we pulled into the driveway her lids were heavy and she came in, curled up on the couch and fell asleep. I covered her with a blanket, poured a cup of coffee and dialled the number of a friend of mine from the old days before my husband died.

Jill Osiowy was director of news at NationTV now, but when I met her, in 1971, she'd just been hired as a press officer by our provincial government. It was her first job, and she was very young. We were all young. My husband was twenty-eight when he was elected to the House that year, and when we formed the government, he became the youngest attorney general in the country.

In those days, Jill's hair was an explosion of shoulder-length red curls, and she wore Earth shoes and hand-embroidered denim work shirts. She was smart and earnest, and her face shone with the faith that she could change the future. By the time we lost in 1982, Jill's hair was sleek as the silk shirts and meticulously tailored suits she bought in Toronto twice a year; she was still smart and she was still earnest, but she'd had some bruising encounters with political realities, and the glow had dimmed a little.

She had used the first years after the government changed to go back to school. She got two graduate degrees in journalism, taught for a while at Ryerson in Toronto, then came back to Regina and her first love, TV news.

That afternoon, when she heard my voice, Jill gave a throaty whoop. "Well, la-di-da, you're back in town. I'd heard rumours but since you never actually phoned me, I didn't want to believe them."

"Believe them," I said. "And as susceptible to guilt as I am, you can't guilt me on this because we've only been back in Regina two weeks. We're not even unpacked yet."

"Okay," she said, "I'll come over and help you unpack. That'll guilt you."

"Right now?" I asked.

"Sure. I'm just poring over our anemic budget trying to find some money that didn't get spent. Depressing work for the first five-star day we've had this month."

"Come over then. It'd be great to see you. But listen, I was calling for another reason, too. Have you heard anything about a case called the Little Flower murders?"

Jill whistled, "I've heard a lot. One of our investigative units is putting together a feature on it. I can bring over some of their tapes if you like." She was quiet for a beat. "What's your interest in this, Jo?"

"I'll tell you when you get here. Listen, I bought a new house. Same neighbourhood as I lived in before I moved to

Saskatoon, but over on Regina Avenue." I gave her the address. "Twenty minutes?"

"Fifteen," she said. "I've been cooped up here long enough. I'm starting to wilt."

When I saw her coming up the front walk, she didn't look like a woman who was wilting. She looked sensational, and I was conscious of the fact that I hadn't changed since I'd grabbed my blue jeans and an old Mets T-shirt out of the clean laundry when Mieka had called that morning. Jill's red hair was cut in a short bob, and she was wearing an orangey-gold T-shirt, an oversize unbleached cotton jacket, short in the front and long in the back, and matching pants. On the lapel of her jacket she had pinned a brilliant silk sunflower.

"You look like a van Gogh picnic," I said, hugging her. "Where did you get that outfit?"

"Value Village," she said. "It's all second-hand."

"How come when I wear Value Village it looks like Value Village?"

"Because you're too conservative, Jo. You've got to force yourself to walk by the polyester pantsuits." She stepped past me into the front hall and looked around. "My God, this isn't a polyester pantsuit kind of house. You must be doing all right."

"Well, I am doing all right," I said, "but not this all right. Come on, let me give you the grand tour, and I'll tell you about it."

Even after two weeks, I felt a thrill when I walked around our new home. It was a beautiful house, thirty years old, solid, with big sunny rooms and lots of Laura Ashley wallpaper and oak floors and gleaming woodwork. I loved being a tour guide and Jill was a wonderful companion: enthusiastic, flattering and funny. When we walked out in the backyard and she saw the pool glittering in the sun, she said, "This really is sublime." Then our dogs came out of the house and ran down the hill. Sadie, the collie, stopped dead at the edge of the pool, but Rose, the golden retriever, jumped in and began doing laps.

"Not so sublime," I said.

Jill grimaced. "Does that happen often?"

"She's getting used to it," I said. "We're down to about fourteen times a day."

"This is why I have cats," Jill said.

"Lou and Murray are still alive?" I said, surprised.

"They're planning their joint birthday celebration even as we speak," Jill said. "They'll be thirteen July 29."

"Come on," I said, "let's go in and get a beer and you can tell me all about it. Are cat years the same as dog years? Are Lou and Murray really going to be ninety, or just thirteen?"

"You're mocking us," Jill said, "so I'm not going to tell you. Let's hear your family's news."

We went into the kitchen. Jill found a couple of beer glasses while I opened the beer.

"You did hear, didn't you," I said, "that I've adopted a little girl? Her name is Taylor, and she's five. She was my friend Sally Love's daughter."

Jill's eyes looked sad. "I heard about Sally, of course. That was such a tragedy."

"Yeah," I said. "I don't think any of us are over it yet. Anyway, there was no one to take Taylor, so I did. It seems to be working out. The kids are really good with her, and I think Taylor's beginning to feel that we're her family."

"She's lucky to have you," Jill said. "Not every kid gets Gaia, the Earth Mother."

"Well, thanks," I said, "I think."

We brought out two bottles of Great West and sat at the picnic table and watched Rose do her patient laps. It was a perfect day, still and sunny and warm. Jill turned to me. "This is what my mother and her friends used to do when I was growing up," she said. "Twenty-fourth of May weekend they'd hit the backyards and start working on their tans. My mother used to call it her summer project."

"Do you want to go back to that?" I asked.

"Lord, no," she said. "Now tell me about the house."

"Actually it was Sally's lawyer's idea. When I was making the arrangements to adopt Taylor, he asked me if I was going to have to renovate my old house for an extra child. In fact, I'd planned to. Nothing very elaborate, but Taylor's inherited her mother's talent for making art."

"Not a bad inheritance," Jill said.

"Not bad at all. It's amazing to see. You read about gifted children, but to actually live with a little kid who has this incredible talent is something else again. Anyway, I told Sally's lawyer I wanted to add on a room where Taylor could paint. He just about patted me on the head. 'Good, good,' he said, 'we mustn't ignore the fact that in cases like these the concept of life expectations comes into play.'"

Jill shook her head. "Ugh, lawyer talk. What are life expectations?"

"According to this guy it's a term the law uses to describe what Taylor could have expected her life to be like given her parents' earning power and position in the community. Sally and Stuart Lachlan were both wealthy people – so the lawyer said Taylor could have reasonably expected to grow up with pretty much everything she wanted."

"I don't like the sound of that," Jill said thoughtfully.

"Neither did I," I said, "but in this particular case it simply meant investing a little money from Taylor's trust fund in the place she was going to live. At first I was going to put it toward the new addition, but then this house came on the market. I'd gotten a pretty good advance for that biography I wrote about Andy Boychuk, and you know what a slump real estate's in here. With what I got for our old house and the advance, this place really didn't cost much more than the renovations would have."

"And this is so spiffy," Jill said.

"Right," I said, "and this is so spiffy. Can I get you another beer?"

"No, I've got a meeting at four o'clock with the vice-president of finance. He's coming out from head office, and I need to smell hard-working and underfunded." She looked at her watch. "If we're going to look at the Little Flower tape, we'd better do it now. You never did tell me why you're interested."

I tried to keep the emotion out of my voice. "This morning Mieka found a body in the garbage can outside the place she's going to have her catering business. It was a woman who had done some cleaning for her – actually it was a girl, seventeen. I overheard one of the cops say it looked like another Little Flower murder."

Jill's body was tense with interest. "Was the face mutilated?"

"I couldn't see her face," I said. "But whoever killed her had pulled her slacks and panties down around her ankles."

"Bastard." Jill spit the word into the fine May afternoon.

Her face was ashen as we walked into the house. Neither of us said a word as Jill put the tape in the VCR and the first pictures filled the screen. They were sickening. Reflexively, I closed my eyes. When I opened them, the images on the screen were even worse. The camera had pulled in for a tight shot of the inside of a commercial garbage bin. There were two girls lying on some garbage in the bin. They looked as if they had been folded in two and dropped in. Both girls were naked from the waist down, and each of them had long hair that fell in a dark pillow behind her head. They would have looked like children hiding if it weren't for their unnatural stillness and for the hideous distortion violence had made of their faces. The features were unrecognizable; eyes, nose and lips had run together into a charred, melted mass.

Beside me, Jill said quietly, "Their names were Debbie and Donna Lavallee. They were twins."

The camera panned the grey sky and dirty snow of a city alley in late winter. Then it focused on the next victim. Her pants had been removed, too. She was splayed over the rim of an oil can so that the edge hit her vaginal area.

"Michele Macdonald," Jill said. "Be grateful you can't see her face."

The dirty snow and grey skies were gone in the next pictures. It was spring, and the sky was bright as the camera zoomed in on the industrial garbage can. This girl's body was leaning into the can the way Bernice Morin's had been. When the camera positioned itself over her shoulder and focused down, I could see that she'd worn her blonde hair in a ponytail.

"Two years ago she was a cheerleader at Holy Name," Jill said. "Her name was Cindy Duchek."

I sat there stunned. I felt as if I had been kicked in the stomach. Finally, I said, "Where did the name Little Flower murders come from?"

"The bodies of the girls in that first picture, the Lavallee twins, were found behind Little Flower Church."

"Kind of a variation on the baby left on the cathedral doorstep," I said.

Jill looked at me hard. "Are you all right?"

"I don't know," I said. "It's the worst thing I've ever seen. How old were they?"

"They were all fifteen."

I thought of Mieka at fifteen. The biggest problems in her life had been the shape of her nose and her algebra marks. "How does it happen?" I said. "How does a young girl get to the point where life on the street is an option?"

Jill looked weary. "You know, Jo, the street isn't a last resort for these kids. For a lot of them, it's a step up. When they meet that guy with the Camaro and he tells them he loves them and promises to take care of them, it must sound like they've died and gone to heaven."

"And the next step is . . ."

"And the next step is three-inch heels, fuck-me pants and their own little corner on Broad Street." Jill's voice was bitter. "And it just keeps getting better. I'm sorry, Jo. This Little Flower thing really gets to me. No one seems to care about those girls. I don't mean the cops aren't investigating. They are. But there hasn't exactly been a public outcry to find the killers."

"Because the girls are prostitutes?" I asked.

"Because people think they're garbage," Jill said. "And nice people are always relieved when someone else takes out the garbage. What was that term your lawyer friend came up with? Life expectations? Well, the life expectations for these girls are zero. Zip. Nothing. And once their lives kick into high gear, the odds start going down."

She stood up, and the contrast between the bright sunflower on her jacket and the despair in her eyes was pretty hard to take.

We were silent as we walked through the house. At the front door Jill turned to me. "I'm glad you're back in town, Jo. Hey, tell Mieka congratulations for me, would you? I saw her engagement announcement in the paper. I hope what happened this morning doesn't cast too long a shadow on all the happy times ahead."

"I hope you get your wish," I said.

But she didn't.

CHAPTER

2

Mieka was too quiet during dinner. After we'd put the dishes in the dishwasher, she started down the hall to her room. I didn't want her to be alone, and I went after her.

"Why don't we go out on the deck and watch the kids for a while?" I said. "Your brother and Camilo are showing Taylor how to take care of baseball equipment. We've already missed how to sand a bat."

Mieka shook her head. "Taylor will be the hottest rookie in Little League," she said, as she followed me out the back door. Angus and his friend Camilo were kneeling on the deck oiling their gloves. Taylor was between them, watching intently.

I touched Angus on the shoulder. "Maybe if you didn't use quite so much Vaseline, you'd get over your fielding problems," I said. He looked up at me, pained, and Taylor moved a little closer to him. It seemed like a good sign that she was already on his side, and I wasn't surprised when she decided to go to 7-Eleven with the boys instead of staying home with Mieka and me.

After they left, I turned to Mieka. "Feel like taking the dogs for a walk?" I asked.

"Your solution for everything," she said. "A shower or a walk. And I'm already clean. Sure, let's go."

It was a beautiful evening, and we followed the bicycle path all the way out to Mieka's old high school on Royal Road. As we walked around the grounds, we could hear the lazy whoosh of the sprinklers watering the new geraniums and the sounds of kids playing Frisbee.

Bernice Morin's death and the tapes of the Little Flower victims were fresh wounds, but the problem that dogged me as we walked around the old high school was five months old.

That morning when Mieka had called and asked me to come down to the shop was the first time she had turned to me since January. The rupture had begun when she dropped out of school in Saskatoon and used the fund her father and I had set up for university to buy a catering business called Judgements. Despite my predictions, Judgements had caught on like wildfire, and when the chance came to open a sister business in Regina, Mieka hadn't missed a beat. She drew up estimates on how much it would cost to lease and renovate space in Old City Hall, then she went to her fiancé's mother, Lorraine Harris, and borrowed the money. It wasn't until the papers were signed that she told me what she'd done. I'd been furious: furious at Mieka for getting in over her head and furious at Lorraine Harris for letting her get in over her head. And something else: I was jealous, jealous that Mieka had gone to Greg's mother rather than coming to me.

We loved each other too much to risk a no-holds-barred confrontation, but there had been some troubled weeks. Then, when we came back to Regina, I'd asked Mieka to move home. It seemed like a good idea all around. With two new businesses and a September wedding, Mieka's life was pressing in on her. I thought being with me and the kids and having the details of day-to-day living taken care of would help her deal with the demands of the summer. For me, of course, it meant a chance to get our relationship back to the old closeness. The perfect solution to everybody's problems. But, like a lot of perfect solutions, this one hadn't worked.

Mieka had changed. She was a woman and, in many respects, a stranger. In my more honest moments, I knew it was wrong to want her to be the sweet, pliable girl she had been at eighteen. Twenty times a day, I repeated C.P. Snow's line that the love between a parent and a child is the only love that must grow toward separation. Every morning I woke up determined to be open and reasonable, and every night I went to bed knowing I had been neither. My only justification was that I believed I was right. In my heart, I felt my daughter had chosen the wrong path.

That night, as I looked at Mieka's profile, so familiar and so dear, somehow being right didn't seem important any more.

As if she had read my mind, Mieka turned. "Was John Lennon the one who said, 'There's nothing like death to put life in perspective'?"

I smiled at her. "I don't know, but whoever said it, it's a good thought."

Her eyes filled with tears. "I'm sorry things have been bad between us, Mummy."

That was when I started to cry. "Oh, Miek, I'm sorry, too. All I ever wanted was what was best for you."

Mieka reached in her pocket, pulled out a Kleenex and handed it to me. "Peace offering," she said. Then she smiled. "Do you remember that time Peter decided to take up wrestling?"

"Some of my darkest hours as a mother."

"But you let him. I remember you went to all his matches."

"Including the one where your brother got knocked unconscious. I'm still proud of the fact that I didn't jump in the ring that night and cradle him in my arms."

Mieka took my hand. "That must have been hard for you. You're not exactly deficient in the motherly instincts department, you know."

I turned to look at her. "I take it you'd like me to work on suppressing those instincts for a while."

"Yeah, Mum, I would." Her voice was strong and determined. "I want my chance. I know I may get flattened, but I have to try."

I gave her hand a squeeze. "One good thing about me," I said, "I always know when I'm licked."

Mieka smiled. "Don't think of it as being licked. Think of it as accepting the inevitable gracefully."

"Same thing, eh?" I said.

Her smile grew broader. "Oh, yeah," she said, "it's the same thing, but this way you get to look like a good guy."

We walked home arm in arm, like chums in a 1940s movie, and as we settled into our old pattern of comfortable, aimless talk, I was filled with gratitude.

When Mieka hesitated at the back gate of our yard, my first thought was that she wanted to tell me she was grateful, too. But as I watched her square her shoulders and take a deep breath, I knew that whatever was coming was not happy talk. When there was bad news, Mieka never wasted time in preamble.

"Christy Sinclair came into Judgements yesterday," she said. "I wasn't going to mention it because I knew it would upset you, but considering everything else that's happened . . ." She shrugged her shoulders.

"What did she want?" I asked.

"She wanted to know where Peter was."

"Did you tell her?"

"Yes, I did," Mieka said. "She made it sound so urgent, and there were other people there. Bernice, and Greg's mother, and poor Blaine was waiting outside in the car. It just seemed easier to tell her."

"Damn," I said, "I'd hoped Christy was out of your brother's life – out of all our lives."

"Maybe she is," Mieka said wearily. "Christy has always been unpredictable."

"I wish that's all she was," I said. "Her problem's more serious than that. I think it's a pathology, and it scares me."

Mieka was silent. Suddenly the magic had gone from the evening. The light faded, the wind came up, and someone on a bicycle yelled at the dogs. If you believed in omens, the signs accompanying Christy Sinclair's re-entry into our lives didn't bode well.

When Peter had begun dating her before Christmas, we had all been ecstatic. He was nineteen years old and painfully shy. There had never been a girlfriend. Christy was exuberant and outgoing – just the ticket, it seemed. She was his biology lab instructor, and when it turned out that she was not twenty-one, as she had told Pete at first, but twenty-five, I took a deep breath and tried not to let it worry me. But as the winter wore on, other things started to.

Christy's lie about her age had not been an aberration. She lied about everything: where she'd eaten lunch; the names of the people with whom she had spent the weekend; the way her superiors in the biology department assessed her work performance. That winter I had been teaching political science at the university where Christy was working. She must have known the lies she told about her daily life would come to light, but it didn't seem to alarm her. In an odd way, it seemed to make her more reckless. As the winter wore on, her lies became more transparent, more vulnerable to disclosure. It was a frightening thing to witness.

There was another thing. I had been touched at first by how much Christy liked us, but it began to appear that her need to be part of our family was obsessive. She wanted to be at our house all the time, and when she was there, she wanted to be with me. She was an educated and capable woman, but she followed me around with the dogged determination of a tired child. I tried to understand, to sympathize with whatever privation had brought about this immense need, but the truth was Christy Sinclair got under my skin. When I was with her, I itched to get away; when I got away, I felt guilty because I knew how much being with me mattered to her.

As the winter wore on, it became clear that I wasn't the only one Christy was making miserable. She was crowding Peter, too. Night after night, I could hear her, pressing him for a permanent commitment. Peter was, in many ways, a very young nineteen-year-old. I was almost certain that Christy was the first woman with whom he'd been intimate. He was an innocent kid. My husband used to say that innocence is just a step away from crippling stupidity. He was warning me, not Peter, but my son's unquestioning acceptance of people made him vulnerable, too. Peter wasn't stupid, but it wouldn't have taken much for Christy to convince him that a sexual relationship needed to be legitimized.

By Easter, Christy seemed to be a permanent part of our lives; she was the problem without a solution. Then one day Peter came home and told me he had taken a job at a vet clinic in Swift Current until the fall semester started. It seemed too good to be true.

"What about Christy?" I asked.

"It's over," he said, and he'd looked so miserable that I hadn't pressed the matter. I never did find out what had happened between them. I didn't care. It was finished, and I was grateful. These days when Pete called to talk he sounded relaxed and hopeful. Now, just a little over a month after he'd set us free, it seemed as if we might become entangled again.

"Stay away, Christy," I said to the warm spring night. "Just please stay away."

When I walked into the house, the phone was ringing. The old ones used to say that if you mentioned the name of an enemy, you conjured him up. Christy Sinclair wasn't my enemy, but when I heard her low, husky voice on the phone, I felt a superstitious chill. If I hadn't said her name aloud, perhaps she wouldn't have materialized.

As always, she rushed in headlong. "Oh, Jo, it's wonderful to hear your voice again. Guess what? Pete and I are back together."

I held my breath. There was still the chance that she was lying, still the possibility that this was just another case where Christy had crossed the line between what she wanted and what was true. But when she spoke again, I knew she hadn't crossed the line.

"Pete says Greg's family is throwing a big engagement party at their cottage, Friday – a kickoff for the Victoria Day weekend. He suggested that I ride down with you and the kids. He won't be able to get there from Swift Current till around seven. Jo, are you still there? Is that all right with you?"

I felt numb. It was all beginning again.

"Yes," I said, "if that's what Pete wants, it's fine with me."

"Great," she said. "What time should I come over?"

"Around four, I guess. I thought we'd leave as soon as Angus got back from school."

"Great. Four o'clock tomorrow. I'm counting the minutes."

I walked down the hall to Mieka's room and knocked on the door. She was sitting on her bed reading a bride's magazine, and when she saw me, she laughed and hid the magazine behind her back.

"My name is Ditzi with an *i*," she said in the singsong cadence of a TV mall stomper. "Oh, Mum, I can't believe I'm reading this. But since I am, what do you think of that one?" She pointed to a dress that was all ruffles and lace. "It has a hoop sewn into the skirt."

"I guess it would be all right if you were marrying Rhett Butler," I said, sitting down next to her. "Whatever would you do with something like that afterwards?"

Mieka raised an eyebrow. "Frankly, my dear," she said, "I wouldn't give a damn."

It was good to see her laugh, but as I told her about Christy's phone call, her face fell.

"Poor Peter. What are we going to do, Mum?"

"Nothing," I said. "Remember what you said about the wrestling? It's his life. We'll be nice to Christy and hope for the best."

But at four o'clock the next day, as I watched Christy Sinclair get out of her car, I knew that being nice and hoping for the best were going to be hard.

Even her red Volkswagen convertible brought back memories. At the end of her relationship with Peter, I had felt my heart sink every time the Volks had pulled into our driveway. But I tried to be positive. Christy looked great. She always did. She wasn't a beautiful woman, but she had a lively androgynous charm – slim hips, flat chest, dark curly hair cut boy short. And she always dressed the part. Christy was estranged from her family, but she said they always made sure she had the best of everything. Today, for a trip to the country she looked like she'd stepped out of an L.L. Bean ad: sneakers, white cotton overalls and a blue-and-white striped shirt. As soon as she saw me standing in the doorway, she ran up and threw her arms around me. She smelled good, of cotton and English soap and sunshine.

"I've missed this family," she said, her voice breaking. Then she stood back and looked at me. "And I've missed you most of all, Jo." She smiled.

It was hard not to respond to that smile. Christy's best feature was her mouth; it was large, mobile, expressive. Theodore Roethke wrote a poem where he talks about a young girl's sidelong pickerel smile; Christy Sinclair's smile was like that – whimsical, sly and knowing.

"We had some good times," I said. It seemed a neutral enough statement.

"Right," she said, and this time there was no mistaking the mocking line of her mouth. "Good times, Jo." She reached over and picked up a suitcase and threw it into the trunk of my car. "And we're going to have more."

Her words were defiant, but there was a vulnerability in her voice that hadn't been there before. She sounded almost desperate, and I was grateful when the kids came barrelling out of the house. In the flurry of bags being stowed in the car and the greetings and last-minute instructions to the girl next door who was going to take care of the dogs, I didn't have to weigh the words I would say to Christy.

Apparently, though, she'd already thought of what she wanted to say to me. As the solid homes of College Avenue gave way to the strip malls and fast-food restaurants of Park Street, Christy turned to me.

"What's the date of Mieka's wedding?" she asked.

"It's the Saturday of Labour Day weekend."

"Maybe Peter and I can make it a double wedding," Christy said, and I felt a chill.

From the back seat Angus's voice broke with adolescent exasperation. "Pete's just a kid. He can't get married."

Christy shrugged and smiled her knowing smile, but Taylor had heard a word that interested her. "Samantha at my school says that when her sister got married, their poodle wore a wedding suit and carried the rings down the aisle on a little pillow."

Angus snorted. "Great idea, T. Can you imagine our dogs in a church?"

"They could have dresses," Taylor said resolutely, "dresses for a wedding."

Angus was mollifying. "Well, yeah, maybe if they had dresses, it would be okay." Then he exploded in laughter again.

Between the dogs in their bridesmaids' dresses and Christy's suggestion about a double wedding, there didn't seem to be much left to say. As we pulled onto the Trans-Canada east of the city, we settled into a silence that if it wasn't companionable was at least endurable.

It had been a wet spring. The fields were green with the new crop, and the sloughs were filled with water. On that gentle afternoon, the drive to the Qu'Appelle Valley was a pretty one, and as we travelled along the ribbon-flat highway, I was soothed into daydreaming. Just before Edenwold, the air outside the car was split with a high-pitched whooping.

Beside me, Christy was excited. "Oh, Jo, look over there in that field – those are tundra swans. You have to pull over to let the kids see."

To the left was a slough, and it was white with birds. There must have been thousands of them. The air was alive with their mournful cries and the beating of their powerful wings.

I pulled over on the shoulder, and Christy and I and the kids ran over and doubled back along the fence.

Taylor was tagging along behind Christy. "Where are they going?" Taylor shouted, raising her voice so she could be heard above the racket.

"The Arctic Circle," Christy shouted back, and she turned and took Taylor's hand. "They spend the winter in Texas and they fly north for the summer. They're a little off their migration path."

Taylor stopped in her tracks. "If they're lost, how will they find their way?"

In the brilliant May sunshine Christy looked young and defenceless. "Instinct," she said, "and luck. If they're smart and they're lucky, they'll make it."

I liked her better in that moment than I had in weeks. As she stood by the fence and watched that prairie slough filled with swans, it seemed as if the mask had dropped and the woman who lived behind that complex repertory of roles Christy played had revealed herself. I had said to Mieka that all we could do was wait and hope for the best. Maybe there really was a best. I was reluctant to make the moment end.

"I guess we'd better go," I said finally. "They're expecting us for supper."

As we passed Balgonie, I noticed that it was close to five o'clock, and I reached over and switched on the car radio for the news. Bernice Morin's murder was the lead story. The announcer's voice was young, nasal and relentlessly upbeat. "Regina police announced a possible break in the Bernice Morin case. A witness has come forward with the information that at seven-thirty on the night of the murder, he heard a cry in the alley behind Old City Hall. When he looked down the alley, he saw a jogger running south. The jogger is described as five feet seven, slender, wearing grey sweatpants and a hooded grey sweatshirt. Police ask that anyone having –"

Beside me, Christy reached over and savagely turned the radio off.

I was surprised that she wasn't interested. "You met her," I said. "Mieka said she was in the store Tuesday afternoon when you came in."

I noticed a tightening in the muscles of Christy's neck. She didn't say anything.

"She was so young," I said. "She had all her life ahead of her."

"She was just a hooker," Christy said coldly.

I was so angry I wanted to shake her, but she cut me off. She turned her back to me and stayed that way, looking out the window of the passenger seat, till we got to the Harrises. I could hear her breathing, tense and unhappy, but she didn't say a word. As far as I was concerned, that was fine. An hour after she'd come back into our lives, I'd already had enough of Christy Sinclair.

By the time the highway started its slow descent into the Qu'Appelle Valley I'd decided that letting my son get the wind knocked out of him in the wrestling ring was one matter; standing by while he entered into a serious relationship with a cruel and angry young woman was another. As soon as I had a chance, I was going to talk to Peter about Christy.

Once I'd made the decision I felt better; when I saw the rolling hills of the Qu'Appelle I felt better yet. I had been to the valley a thousand times, but it had never lost its power to quicken my pulse. We turned off the highway and drove up the narrow winding roads until we passed a sign that said we were entering Standing Buffalo Indian Reserve. Below, Echo Lake glittered, and on the other side of the water, the hills rose green with spring.

It wasn't long till we drove out of reserve land, and the ubiquitous signs of cottage country thrust themselves up along the road: "Heart's Eze," "The Pines," "Dunrovin." Through the trees I could see the bright outlines of the cottages hugging the hills overlooking the lake. At the crest of the highest hill we came to a discreet cedar sign that said, "Eden."

"This is it," I said to the kids. "We are about to enter the Garden of Eden. And you guys always say I never take you anywhere."

Hedges of caragana protected what was behind from public view. We drove through the gate and along a road narrowed by bushes and wildflowers. At the turn, we came to a clearing; below was the summer cottage of the family of the late Alisdair Harris.

Except it wasn't a cottage; it was a country home, a handsome old dowager of a house of gleaming white clapboard with verandas on both storeys and gingerbread trim. At the side of the house, a pool, its water an improbable turquoise, shimmered in the late afternoon sun. White wrought-iron chairs and tables, already set for dinner, ringed the manicured green of the lawn around the pool.

The air smelled of fresh-cut grass, and in the distance I could hear the song of the valley's birds. It really was Eden, or as close to Eden as I expected to come on this side of the grave.

"No snakes in this paradise," I said.

"Good," said Taylor. "I'm scared of snakes."

"I'm not," said Angus. "Anyway, the only kind of snakes around here are garter snakes, and they never hurt anybody. You've got nothing to worry about, T."

But Angus was wrong, and I was wrong, too. In that serene and perfect world, there was a serpent waiting. Before the night was over, it would glide silently across our lives, leaving behind its dark gifts of death and evil, changing us all forever.

CHAPTER

3

When he saw that there was a tennis court behind the house, Angus rolled down his window.

"Look out, Toto, we're not in Kansas any more," he said.

Beside him, Taylor laughed appreciatively. I would have bet my last dollar she'd never heard of the Wizard of Oz, but it didn't matter. Angus was her brother now, and she was determined to be his best audience.

Greg and Mieka had driven out to the lake earlier in the day, and as soon as we pulled up, Mieka came running out of the house to greet us. She hugged me, scooped up Taylor for a kiss, and gave her brother's shoulders a squeeze. Then she turned to Christy, who was standing apart from us in the driveway.

"You're sharing a room with me," she said. "Just let me grab some of my family's twenty thousand bags and I'll show you where you can freshen up."

With Mieka's welcome, some of the misery seemed to leave Christy's face, and I could feel my body relax. When Mieka was around, life had a way of working out, and I smiled gratefully at her.

She grinned. "Dinner's at six-thirty, you guys – my mother-in-law-to-be is a stickler for punctuality."

We carried our bags into the house, and Christy disappeared upstairs with Mieka. Taylor and I were sharing a room, and Angus was in what Mieka had described as the male wing of the house.

"My new family believes in propriety," Mieka had said, deadpan. "Men on one side, women on the other; don't embarrass me with any midnight creeping."

I closed the door and looked gratefully around our room. It had a spectacular view of the hills and the lake. Everything in it was the palest shade of pink.

"Look," I said to Taylor, "your favourite colour."

"Do you think Mieka picked the pink room for me?"

"Absolutely," I said. "Now, why don't you hit the bathroom and get some of the dust off, and we'll get ready for supper. I could smell the barbecue when we pulled up."

I had just finished braiding Taylor's hair when there was a knock at the bedroom door. I went, expecting Angus, shocked into courtesy by the splendour of his surroundings. But when I opened the door it wasn't my son who was standing there, it was Christy Sinclair.

She didn't wait to be asked in. She walked past me and sat down on the bed. She was still wearing the overalls and striped shirt she'd had on in the car, but she'd splashed water on her face, and her hair curled damply at the temples. Christy never wore makeup. Her good looks were the kind that didn't need help, and that afternoon, as she smoothed her hair nervously and tried a tentative smile, I was puzzled again at her mystery.

Anyone who walked into that room would have been struck by the sum of Christy Sinclair's blessings. Physically, she had great charm; moreover, she was bright and educated and privileged. But somewhere, buried in her psyche, was a dark kink that distorted her perceptions and subverted her life.

I went over and sat beside her on the bed. My presence seemed to encourage her. She moved closer.

"I'm sorry about that business in the car, Jo," she said. "I know that kind of language is totally unacceptable to you."

I was horrified. "Christy, this isn't a problem of diction. It wasn't your language that upset me. It was the way you dismissed Bernice Morin. Whatever Bernice's life was like, her death was a terrible thing."

What I said seemed a statement of the obvious, but my words hit Christy like a blow. The smile faded, and when she spoke her voice trembled.

"Understand one thing, Joanne. Your death would be a terrible thing. Mieka's death would be a terrible thing. But when girls like Bernice die, it's just biological destiny. They're born with a gene that makes them self-destruct. They're all the same – antisocial, impulsive. They take risks that people like you and Mieka wouldn't. They never learn. They just keep taking risks, and sooner or later their luck runs out."

I felt cold. "Luck had nothing to do with it, Christy. Bernice Morin was murdered. She didn't self-destruct."

Christy's voice was weary. "It was her fault, Jo. Believe me, I know. I've done a lot of reading on genetic profiles. These girls are born with a gene for self-destruction. Nobody can change what's going to happen to them. Whatever girls like Bernice do, the disease is in them. It's just a matter of time."

"I refuse to believe that," I said.

"That doesn't make it any less true," she said quietly. Then she did a surprising thing. She reached down and pulled off the wide silver band she always wore around her wrist and held it out to me.

"You always said you admired this, Jo. I'd like you to have it."

I didn't want the bracelet. At that moment, I didn't want anything that would connect me to Christy Sinclair. But as I looked at the smooth circle of silver on the palm of her hand, I didn't know how to refuse. I took it. When I slipped it on my wrist, it was still warm from her body.

The bracelet was engraved with Celtic lettering, and I read the words aloud: "Wandering Soul Pray For Me."

Christy smiled. "I will," she said. She touched the silver band with her forefinger. "I love this bracelet, Jo, but I love you more. I didn't want you to go on thinking I was a bad person."

I moved closer to her. "Oh, Christy, I never thought you were bad. I've never felt as if I knew you at all. If you could just –"

I never finished the sentence. There was a knock at the door. Taylor came running out of the bathroom to answer it, and the moment was lost. Christy stood up and moved toward the doorway; she looked at the man who was standing there, then turned to me.

"Thank you for taking the bracelet, Jo. People aren't always what they seem, you know."

I went over to say goodbye, but she was gone.

"That's the worst introduction I've ever had," said the man in the doorway, "so I'll try to make up for it." He was holding a drink and he offered it to me. "Vodka and tonic with a twist. Your daughter said that's what you like on a hot day."

I took a long swallow from the drink. "God bless Mieka," I said. "It's turning into a vodka kind of afternoon."

He laughed. "I'm having one of those afternoons myself. I'll keep you company. Incidentally, I'm Greg's uncle, Keith Harris."

"I've seen you on television a thousand times," I said. "You're much nicer looking in person."

"So are you," he said. "But I have a more politically correct compliment for you. I read a review copy of your book on Andy Boychuk. It's the most intelligent biography I've read in ten years. You're going to be on the best-seller list."

"Kind words and a cold drink. Keith, I really am glad to meet you at last. And the kids were so worried we wouldn't get along."

Keith raised his eyebrows. "I tried to reassure Greg," he said, "but I think he and Mieka were convinced that the moment you and I met, we'd lock horns."

The talk of locked horns caught Taylor's attention. She was too young for metaphor. She moved between us and looked up expectantly.

"This is my daughter Taylor," I said. "Taylor, this is Mr. Harris. He's Greg's uncle."

Keith dropped to his knees to be eye level with Taylor. I saw her look with interest at his tanned and balding head. So did Keith.

"No horns," he said. "Although your mother might have been surprised to discover that, too. When people talk about locking horns with somebody they just mean they don't get along very well."

"Why wouldn't you and Jo get along?" Taylor asked.

"Because our politics are different," he said. "I work for one party, and your mother works for another party. Not much of a reason to fight, when you come right down to it."

But Taylor was not interested in politics. "We saw a field of swans," she said. "When we were in the car, we saw a field of swans. They were resting on their way home to the Arctic Circle. That's north," she added helpfully.

"Sounds better than my afternoon," he said. "I spent the last hour on the phone talking to . . . Well, never mind who I was talking to. It's boring. I can't offer you any swans, but if you and your mother come outside, I can show you the hill where once a long time ago a man saw a million buffalo coming down to the water."

Taylor looked up at him, dark eyes keen with interest. "A million buffalo," she said. "I wish I'd seen that."

He smiled at her. "I wish I had, too," he said, and with the easy camaraderie of people who've known each other for years, the three of us started toward the lake.

Angus caught up with us when we were halfway down the hill. He was running and his face shone with sweat and excitement. "There are frogs down there. Little ones –"

"No," I said.

"No to what?"

"No, you can't ask Mieka for a jar. No, you can't capture them and sell them. No, you can't take any back to the city and give them to your friends."

"I'm not a kid, Mum," he said. "Come on, Taylor. Let's go down to the lake and look at frogs. But don't get your hopes up. We already heard the answer about taking one home. See you, Mr. Harris," he said.

We watched them run toward the lake. "You've met my son?" I asked.

Keith nodded. "When I was getting ice, Angus was in the kitchen looking for . . ." He trailed off innocently.

"For a jar," I said.

"I've been in politics all my life, Joanne. I'm not walking into that one. Now, come on, and I'll show you where Peter Hourie saw that amazing sight. If you'd like, that is."

"I'd like," I said.

We walked down to the shore and looked up at the hill. "It was right over there," he said. "Hourie had just started building up Fort Qu'Appelle, and he was camped out here with some of his men. They looked over there and the buffalo were coming down to the water. Hourie and his group stayed here twenty-four hours, and the buffalo never stopped coming. They really did estimate there were a million animals in that herd. It must have sounded like the end of the world."

For the next half-hour we sat on the grass, talking about everything and nothing: the buffalo hunts, politics, friendships. Taylor and Angus, absorbed in the mysteries of the shore, were wading contentedly in the water that lapped the stony beach. The smell of barbecue and the sounds of music drifted down from the house. Finally, sun-warmed and at peace, I lay on the grass and closed my eyes.

"Happy?" Keith asked.

"God's in Her Heaven. All's right with the world," I murmured.

I'd almost drifted off to sleep when I heard Mieka's voice. "Here we were, worried sick that you two were going to kill each other and all you've done is put one another to sleep."

I sat up, rubbed my eyes and looked at Keith.

He shrugged. "Vodka and sunshine. A lethal combination."

Mieka shook her head. "Time to straighten up, Keith. Your dad's car just pulled in. Lorraine says he'll want to see you as soon as he gets settled."

"I'll be right up," Keith said, and he sounded weary and sad.

"Troubles?" I asked.

"My father," Keith said. "Blaine had a cerebral hemorrhage at Easter. It's hard to be with him now. For seventy-five years he was one man, and now he's another. The worst thing is he knows. He knows everything."

Keith stood up and held his hand out to me. "Do you want to come up to the house and meet Blaine? He's always enjoyed the company of intelligent women."

"I'd be honoured," I said. Then we called the kids and walked up the hill.

Keith's father was sitting in a wheelchair by the pool. Even the ravages of his illness hadn't eroded Blaine Harris's dignity. He was wearing golf clothes, expensive and well-cut, and he was beautifully groomed. But there were surprising notes: his white hair was so long it had been combed into a ponytail, and he was wearing not golf shoes but moccasins, soft and intricately beaded. He looked like a man on the verge of embracing another lifestyle.

When he saw his son, Blaine Harris raised his left hand in greeting, and garbled sounds escaped his throat. Keith went to him and kissed the top of his head.

His tone with his father was warm and matter of fact. "Blaine, this is Mieka's mother, Joanne. She teaches political science at the university and she's written a pretty fair book about Andy Boychuk."

Blaine made muffled noises that even I recognized as disapproval.

Keith looked at me. "My father's politics are somewhat to the right of mine." He turned back to his father. "Blaine, it's a wonderful book. We can start reading it tonight if you like."

Blaine made a swooping gesture toward me with his good arm. "Pancakes," he said.

Beside me, Taylor, recognizing another practitioner of the non sequitur, laughed appreciatively.

Keith patted his father's hand. "Yes, Dad, Joanne's book deals with campaigns, mostly the provincial ones."

The old man made a growling sound in the back of his throat.

Keith shook his head. "Yeah, Dad, I know it's awful when all the words are in there and they just won't come out. But what the hell, eh? You've got me. Now come on, it's time to eat."

It was a fine spring meal: barbecued lamb, the first tender shoots of asparagus, carrots, new potatoes, strawberry shortcake.

We sat outside at the tables around the pool I'd noticed earlier. I was surprised to see that Mieka had asked Christy to sit with Greg and her. Christy had changed clothes; she was wearing a white dress that looked cool and elegant. When Lorraine Harris joined them, I noticed she was wearing white, too. Midway through the meal, Greg and Mieka left to greet some latecomers, and as Lorraine and Christy bent toward one another, deep in conversation, I thought they looked like a scene from *The Great Gatsby*: handsome women in dazzling white, insulated by their money against the sordid and the wretched.

The kids and I sat with Keith and his father. Eating was a torturous process for Blaine Harris. He had the use of his left arm, but as he lifted his fork from his plate to his mouth, the signals sometimes got scrambled. His hand would stop, and Blaine would look at the fork hanging in midair as if it were an apparition. It was agony to watch, but Keith eased the situation. He was quick and unobtrusive when his father needed help, but he didn't hover, and he kept the conversation light.

To celebrate Greg's and Mieka's engagement, there were going to be fireworks later. Keith told the kids that when he'd been in Macau for the Chinese New Year in February, the fireworks had been loud enough to blow his eardrums out. He said the streets had been filled with people from Hong Kong because firecrackers were illegal there.

"And they're not illegal in Macau?" Angus asked approvingly.

"Nothing's illegal in Macau," he said. "The restaurants serve endangered species in the soup."

Angus shuddered.

"To build up your blood for the cold winter months," Keith said.

"Jo makes us take vitamin C," Taylor said.

"Probably a more responsible move environmentally," Keith said.

When Keith took his father into the house to rest before the fireworks, Angus turned to me. "Mr. Harris is a really neat guy, you know."

"Meaning?"

Angus grinned. "Meaning, I think it's about time you had a man in your life."

"Thanks, Angus, I'll take that under advisement."

"You wouldn't not go out with him because of politics, would you?"

"Nope," I said, "but it would be a problem. Keith is a good friend of the prime minister's, you know. In fact, a lot of people think Keith was the one who got him in as leader."

Angus grimaced. "Well, we all make mistakes."

"Yeah," I said, "but that one was a lulu."

Angus laughed. "I still think he's a nice guy."

I looked at the house. "There he is," I said, "bringing me coffee and brandy."

"Then we're out of here," said Angus. "Come on, T. Let's see if we can find a radio and catch the baseball game." He gave me the high sign. "Be nice to him, Mum."

I was. When I took my first sip of brandy, I leaned back in my chair. "What a perfect night," I said.

" 'Calm was the even and clear was the sky, and the new-budding flowers did spring,' " Keith said.

"Dryden," I said, " 'An Evening's Love.' "

Keith Harris looked at me in amazement. "There's not another woman in Canada who would have known that."

"No," I agreed, "there isn't. You're in luck. It's a magic night."

"You wouldn't have a spell that would keep Lorraine away, would you?" Keith said. "She's about to swoop. We're going to be organized for some after-dinner fun, I can tell by the glint in her eyes."

Then in a cloud of Chanel, Lorraine Harris was upon us. She embraced her brother-in-law, then she turned and bent to kiss the air by my cheek. Out of nowhere, a poem from childhood floated to the top of my consciousness:

> I do not like you, Dr. Fell.
> The reason why I cannot tell.
> But this I know and I know well.
> I do not like you, Dr. Fell.

I do not like you, Lorraine Harris, I thought. But what I said was, "You look wonderful, Lorraine. That's a beautiful suit."

"Sharkskin," she said. She sat down on the arm of Keith's chair and balanced her clipboard on her knee. She was tanned, and the setting sun warmed her skin to the colour of dark honey and made her grey eyes startling. She was a stunning woman, and her most striking feature was her hair. In defiance of all the rules about how women should wear their hair after forty, Lorraine's grey hair was almost waist length. That night she had clasped it at the back with a silver barrette, and as she talked, she reached back and pulled the length of her hair over her shoulder. The effect was riveting.

"How do you two feel about croquet?" she asked.

I smiled at her. "I haven't played croquet in thirty-five years, but I think it's a terrific idea."

Keith sighed. "If Jo's in, I'm in."

Lorraine's grey eyes narrowed. "So you two are getting along, after all," she said. "There'll be some raised eyebrows about that."

"Not any eyebrows that matter," Keith said mildly.

Lorraine looked at him quickly, then she pulled part of a deck of cards out of her jacket pocket and held it out to me. "Choose one, Joanne."

I pulled out a jack of diamonds.

"All you have to do is find the other people who have jacks," she said, "that'll be your team."

Keith reached over and took the cards from her. He sorted through it and pulled out a jack of clubs. "That's me on your team, Jo." Then he found the other two jacks. "That's one for Angus and one for Taylor. Get the word out, Lorraine. The Jacks are the team to beat."

A flicker of annoyance crossed her face. "It's supposed to be random," she said as she wrote our names down on her list, "an icebreaker. But obviously you two have already broken the ice."

She finished writing and stood. "Come up to the tent in about twenty minutes and see who you're supposed to play." Then her face softened, and she smiled at someone behind me. "You have to be Peter," she said. "I made Mieka show me your picture when Greg said you were going to be a groomsman."

I turned and there was my oldest son. For a split second he looked unfamiliar. He seemed taller, his face was sunburned, and he had a new and terrible haircut. I thought he looked sensational.

I jumped up and threw my arms around him. "I'm not going to let you go back to Swift Current," I said. "I've decided I don't believe in kids having independent lives."

Angus was sitting on the ground trying to get an old portable radio to work. "I think Pete probably figured that one out the night you called him three times because you thought he sounded weird."

Peter looked at his brother. "Actually, Mum was right." He turned to me. "I wasn't going to say anything until you could see that I was still alive, but that time you called a cow had just kicked me in the head."

I shot Angus a look of triumph. "Okay, okay," he said, scraping at the batteries of the radio with his Swiss Army knife. "You win. You're psychotic, Mum."

"Thank you," I said, "and the word is psychic."

Peter introduced himself to Lorraine and Keith, then Taylor asked to hear the story of the cow. It was a good story, and Pete told it well. We were all still laughing when Christy came down from the house. She touched Pete on the shoulder, and as he turned I saw the light go out of his face.

Christy saw it, too, and despite our history I felt a rush of sympathy for her. In the months they were together, I don't think Christy ever really understood what she wanted from Peter. But that night at the lake she knew. She wanted him to be in love with her, and when she saw his face, she knew he wasn't. It was a bad moment, and I was glad when Peter took her hands in his.

"You look beautiful, Christy," he said. "You really do. That dress is a knockout."

In fact, it was a simple dress, white, scoop-necked and short-sleeved. A dress for a summer party. And she was wearing shoes for a summer party, white Capezio flats of the softest leather. Taylor couldn't take her eyes off them. Finally, she knelt on the grass and touched one. "Dancing shoes," she said.

Peter slid his arm around Christy's shoulder. "Would you like to dance? I don't know what they've got planned here tonight, but I can hear music somewhere."

"I'd love to dance," she said, and there was such longing in her voice that I turned away, embarrassed.

It was almost eight-thirty. The sun had moved low in the sky, and a swath of golden light swept from the west lawn to the lake. As Peter and Christy walked to the house, they followed that path of light. They looked like the happily-ever-after picture at the end of a fairy tale.

On the ground beside me, Angus gave the portable radio one last adjustment with his knife. Suddenly the radio blared to life, and a man's voice, disjointed and unnaturally loud, cut through the night. ". . . that was found by children in a stair-well two blocks from the murder site may be the weapon used in the stabbing death of seventeen-year-old Bernice Morin. Tonight, the provincial lab is analyzing blood found on the scalpel to see if it matches the blood type of the victim. As well, pathologists are attempting to correlate a number of small nicks in the cutting edge of the surgical scalpel with the wounds inflicted on . . ." The radio fell silent.

As soon as she heard the words, Christy broke away from Peter and turned to face us. For a terrible moment, she stood frozen, staring at the radio, her eyes wide with horror. Then she turned and ran toward the house. Peter went after her. He got to the veranda just as she slammed the door. He hesitated, then he opened the door and disappeared into the darkness of the house.

Lorraine Harris sat looking thoughtfully at the spot on the lawn where Christy had acted out her curious tableau. Then she shook herself out of her reverie and checked her watch.

"Time to get the croquet started before we lose the light," she said. "I'll put Peter and his fiancé on the same team."

"His friend," I said, "they're not engaged."

"Well, his friend told me they were engaged," Lorraine said. She wrote the names on her list. "Keith, you might as well bring your crew along now. It's getting late. People can pick their own teams."

She stood, and we followed her as she strode up the hill and into the house. I started to go inside, too, then I stopped. "Remember the wrestling," I said under my breath, "let them be. They're not children. They'll work it out."

A striped tent had been set up on the west lawn. It was filled with people and laughter. There was a well-stocked bar set up on one side; beside it, on a small table, an orchard of fruit floated in a crystal bowl of punch. In the centre of the tent, Lorraine Harris stood with her clipboard arranging teams, setting up games. There was a master list on a flip chart beside her. I checked the list.

"We're playing the Deuces," I said to Keith.

The Deuces turned out to be the rest of Greg's grooms-men, four young men with the flawless good looks that come with a lifetime of solid nutrition and expensive ortho-donture. The game wasn't as one-sided as I'd feared. When it was over, we hadn't distinguished ourselves, but the Deuces hadn't blown our doors out, and as we walked to the tent we were happy. Inside, the noise level had risen, and the level in the liquor bottles had fallen.

From the talk in the tent it was apparent that croquet had caught on. There were challenges and counter-challenges. On the flip chart someone had written the names of the winners of the first games and the matches for the second set.

Keith checked the chart. "Losers' tournament starts at seven-thirty tomorrow morning," he said.

I snapped open two bottles of Heineken and handed one to Keith. "I've already forgotten what you just said. Now, come on, let's find the kids and get ready for the fireworks."

"Jo, I promised my dad I'd sit up on the veranda with him and watch. Do you mind?"

"Of course not," I said. "I'm going to see if Peter and Christy will come down and watch with us from the dock. I can't figure out what's going on there, but whatever it is, she and Peter might find it easier to be away from strangers."

Keith and I walked to the house together. Blaine Harris was already on the veranda waiting. The woman who had served our dinner was with him, tucking a blanket around his legs, but when Blaine saw his son, he shook the woman off.

Keith called to his father, then he turned to me. "I'll find you after the fireworks. I'll bring that bottle of brandy, take the chill off our bones."

"I'll be waiting," I said.

Keith bent and kissed my cheek, and from the veranda, the old man growled in disapproval.

"His bark is worse than his bite," Keith said mildly. Then he kissed me again.

When I knocked on Peter's door, he opened it so quickly I thought he must have been on his way out.

"How are you doing?" I asked.

"I'm okay," he said.

"And Christy?"

"She's out on the lake," he said. "Canoeing. She said even when she was a kid, she did that when she was upset. It calmed her down."

"Where did she find a place to canoe in Estevan?" I said. "That's pretty arid country down there."

Peter shrugged, "You know Christy. Anyway, if you want, you can ask her when she gets back. She says she has to talk to you. It's urgent."

I stepped close to him. "What's going on, Peter?"

He gave me an awkward pat on the shoulder. "I don't know, Mum. I thought I did, but now I'm not sure."

"Whatever it is, Peter, I'm on your side."

"I know," he said softly. He looked very young and very troubled. In that moment, I knew that, this time, having me on his side wasn't going to be enough.

The kids and I walked to the dock alone. Just as we arrived, Mieka came and dragged her brother off to the beach, where Greg and his friends had lit a bonfire and set up the drinks.

"You look like you could use some company that isn't Angus," she said. "Mum, you and the kids are welcome, too, but Greg swears the dock is the place to be because you get the best view of the lake. That's where he always sat when he was little." She shook her head. "I can't believe Lorraine got everybody to set off their fireworks for our party instead of waiting till Monday night."

"She's a very persuasive woman," I said. "But I'm with her on this. I think your engagement's more important than a dead Queen's birthday."

Taylor grabbed my hand and gave it a yank. "Jo, come on. Don't talk any more, let's go."

We agreed to sit at the end of the dock. I'd brought blankets, and as Taylor curled up against me, I pulled a blanket around her and we looked at the lake. There were boats out there, lazily circling, waiting for the fireworks. I thought I could pick out Christy in her white party dress, but the canoe was so far away I couldn't be sure. The fishy-bait smell of the lake brought memories of other lakes, other summers, and I let my mind float. I could feel Taylor getting heavier in my arms.

"You're falling asleep, T.," Angus said.

She started. "No, I'm not."

"Just resting her eyes, Angus," I said. "Remember, that's what you used to say."

"Right, Mum," he said. "Want me to tell you one of the stories I heard at scout camp last year, T.?"

"Oh, yeah," she said.

"Not too scary," I said. "I want to sleep tonight."

So Angus told all the old stories: the babysitter and the anonymous calls, the kids parked in lovers' lane when the ghost of her first boyfriend comes and bangs on the roof of the car. And Taylor and I screamed and giggled and then somewhere around the lake a cottager put his tuba to his lips and played "God Save the Queen," and the fireworks began.

Greg had told us the Victoria Day ritual was as old as the

cottages. The anthem, then one by one, the cottages set off their fireworks from the beach until the lake had been ringed with rockets.

This year it was the Harris's turn to begin. Greg had set up a rocket in the sand. As he knelt to light it, I could hear Mieka's voice, "Be careful. Be careful. Get back." And I thought she was her mother's daughter after all.

There was a small flash of light, and then the rocket went screaming up into the dark night; it hung there in space for a heartbeat, then it shattered into a shower of brilliant sparks, gold, green, pink.

"Coloured stars," Taylor said, and her eyes were wide with wonder. They kept getting wider. The Harrises were presenting an impressive array of fireworks. When the last stars from the last rocket fell to the ground, Greg came over to the dock with a packet of sparklers. As the moonlight hit his face, I looked for traces of Keith's side of the family in him, but I couldn't see any.

Greg Harris had his mother's colouring and her grey eyes but, curiously, not her good looks. The week before, he'd called the tux rental place from our house, and I'd heard him say, "I'm just an ordinary-looking guy, so nothing too Ralph Lauren." He was right. He was ordinary looking. He was also kind and bright and funny, and crazy about Mieka. Every time I looked at him, I counted my blessings.

As he handed the sparklers to Angus and went through the warnings, I counted my blessings again.

"Best part coming up, Angus. You're in charge. Watch your eyes, and don't light Taylor on fire." Greg grinned at me. "How'd I do, Jo? Cover all the bases."

I smiled at him. "You always do," I said.

We stood and watched as Angus, newly mature, lit the sparklers carefully and handed them to Taylor. She had never seen a sparkler, and her face was solemn as she wrote her name in letters that glowed and vanished in the dark summer night. And then there was a whooshing sound and the fireworks from the next cottage began, sputtering, climbing to the stars and exploding.

"I'd better get back to the party," Greg said. "From the sound of things they need a moral centre over there." He gave me a quick hug. "Have fun, Jo. If you need anything, holler."

For an hour the rockets soared and coloured lights rained down on the lake. When I saw a man jump from the dock next to ours onto the beach, I said to the kids, "Last one. Greg says the last family always has to buy the most expensive stuff for the grand finale."

Taylor, already punchy from excitement and tiredness, leaned forward expectantly. But nothing happened. Then I heard a man's voice, very faint.

"Help," he said. "Someone help me. There's been an accident."

I looked toward the beach. Peter and Mieka were standing by the bonfire, their faces ruddy from the heat and reflected flames. They hadn't heard a thing. People had started dancing, and the music must have drowned out the man's voice.

"Take your sister up to the house and get some help," I said to Angus. Then I ran along the dock, jumped onto the rocky shore and moved toward the voice in the darkness.

The man was still holding the rocket that was going to be the grand finale, but it didn't look as if he'd be setting it off that night. He seemed to be on the verge of shock.

"She's drowned. I just got here from the city. I got tied up at the office." He pointed to the pilings under the dock. "There's a girl down there. I think she's dead."

"Call an ambulance," I said. "I'll do CPR until someone comes. Go on," I said.

I went over to the pilings and pulled the woman's body to the beach. Then I knelt on the rocks, leaned forward and tried to breathe life into the limp body of Christy Sinclair. I'd completed four cycles of compressions and ventilations when one of Greg's friends came and relieved me. I'd talked to him earlier in the tent. He'd said he was an intern, and this was his first night away from the hospital in two weeks. We spelled each other off for what seemed like hours. Finally, he rocked back on his heels and said, "We lost her."

For the first time, I looked up. The guests from the engagement party were huddled in silent knots along the length of the dock. Greg and Peter were directly above me. Mieka was behind her brother, with her arms locked around his waist as if she was holding him back. But Peter didn't look as if he was going anywhere. He seemed frozen, and his face as he looked at Christy showed disbelief. I moved toward Christy. One of her Capezios had fallen off. She had always been immaculate, and it didn't seem right to let people see her with one foot bare and her white party dress sodden and weedy. I leaned forward and took off the other shoe and laid it beside her body. Then I wiped a flume of weeds from the skirt of her dress. She was so still. The animation that had always illuminated her face was gone. The stillness changed her, made her look as if, already, she had become the citizen of a far-off land. But her mouth hadn't changed; it had curved into its familiar sardonic line. Christy Sinclair was greeting death with her sidelong pickerel smile.

CHAPTER

4

The RCMP officer who was first on the scene after we discovered Christy Sinclair's body was a round-faced constable
named Kequahtooway. He wasn't much older than the
young men and women at the party, but he took charge
easily. The first thing he did was call headquarters for rein-
forcements. It was a prudent move. There were sixty-three
people at that party, and one of them was dead. The second
thing Constable Kequahtooway did was try to bring some
order to the chaos.

Less than an hour earlier, Mieka's and Greg's friends,
handsome in their summer pastels, had been careless and
confident. Nothing would ever hurt them. Christy's death
had made them all vulnerable. Now, dazed and disoriented,
they turned for reassurance to a young Indian man wearing
the uniform of the RCMP and the traditional braids of his
people. It was a scene that would have surprised everybody's
grandparents.

Constable Kequahtooway blocked off the area where
Christy had been found, then he set up a place for questioning in the tent. It had been half an hour since I'd sent Angus

up to the house with Taylor; suddenly, I needed to know that they were safe. As soon as I turned down the hall on the main floor of the house, I ran into Keith Harris.

"My God, what's happening?" he said. "We were watching the fireworks. Everything seemed fine, and then the police car pulled up. As soon as he saw it, my father just went crazy." As if on cue, a howling noise came from Blaine Harris's room at the end of the hall. Keith winced. "He's been like this ever since the police came. Jo, what's going on?"

"Peter's friend Christy was in some sort of accident down on the beach. Nobody knows what happened, but, Keith . . . Christy didn't make it. She's dead." It was the first time I had said the words, and I shuddered at their finality. "I still can't believe it," I said.

Keith reached out and touched my cheek. "I'm so sorry," he said. He looked toward his father's room. "I've got to find a doctor for Blaine. He can't go on like this. I'll be right back. As soon as I get my dad taken care of, I'll find you, and we can talk."

"I'd like that," I said.

Keith took me in his arms. It was the briefest of embraces, but that night it was good to be close to another human being, good to have an ally against the things that go bump in the night.

The room Taylor and I were sharing was next door to Lorraine's room, or what was normally Lorraine's room. She'd put Blaine Harris in there because it was on the main floor. As I walked down the hall toward the room, I could hear the sounds he was making. He sounded furious. There was an edge of frustration in his cries, and I thought of the inchoate fury of my kids when they were very young and didn't have the words to tell me what they wanted. Just as I opened the door to our room, the old man managed to form a word.

"Killdeer," he said, and as he pronounced the word, his voice was as loud and as penetrating as the bird's call.

Taylor was sleeping, and Angus was sitting in a chair by the window.

"Scrunch over and make room for me," I said.

I squeezed in beside him and pulled him close. "How are you doing?" I asked.

"Okay, I guess. Greg came by and told me that it was Christy down there. He said he'd stay with me, but I told him Mieka probably needed him more than I did."

He looked up at me. "I didn't like Christy, Mum. She was always pulling stuff with Pete, and what she said in the car about getting married gave me the creeps."

"Me, too," I said.

"All the same . . ." His voice cracked, and he started again. "All the same, now that she's dead, I feel like a real butt head."

For a moment we sat in silence, absorbed in our thoughts. Finally, I leaned toward my youngest son. "I fed like a butt head, too. Listen, Angus, I haven't got many answers about this, but I do know it's normal to feel rotten when someone dies and we haven't treated her as well as we should have. You and I are going to feel bad about Christy for a long time. There's no way around that. But there's one thing we have to hang on to here. It wasn't our fault that Christy died. It was an accident.

"Now, come on, it's late. You should try to get some sleep. I'll walk you to your room, or would you rather stay here?"

"I'd better go to my own room," he said. "Pete's in there with me, you know. He might want to talk."

He looked at me, and we both smiled. Pete had never been much of a talker.

"He'll be glad you're there, anyway," I said.

I checked Taylor. She was sleeping deeply.

"Come on," I said. "Let's get you settled. At least over there, you won't have to listen to Greg's poor grandfather."

"What's the matter with him, Mum?"

"I think he's frustrated," I said. "I think he's mad because he has something important on his mind, and he can't talk any more."

After I got Angus settled, I went outside. It seemed as if there were as many police as there were guests. There were uniforms everywhere. I walked to the tent and looked in. Peter was there, sitting across the table from a young woman in an RCMP uniform. I went and sat at one of the wrought-iron tables that had been set out around the pool for dinner. If I couldn't help my son, I could at least be somewhere he could see me.

I was sitting there feeling powerless and sad when Greg came and sat across from me. The lights from the tent leached the colour from his cheeks and knifed lines in the planes of his face. He looked twenty years older than he had when he'd come to the dock to bring the kids their sparklers.

"Thanks for checking on Angus," I said.

He shrugged. "I wanted to do something." He looked at me. "You know what I've been thinking about?"

"Woody Allen," I said.

He smiled. Greg's passion for Woody Allen was a family joke. When his relationship with Mieka started to get serious, Greg had come over one snowy Friday night with an armload of videos. "I think it's time you met God," he had said as he loaded *Annie Hall* into our VCR.

That weekend we had a Woody Allen festival, and Greg, smart enough to know he sounded like a groupie in a Woody movie, explained every frame of every movie. After that, Woody had become a part of all our lives. We teased Greg about him, but it had been terrific for all of us to have a touchstone to share with the man Mieka loved.

That terrible night at the lake Woody seemed to work his magic once again. At the mention of his name, Greg seemed to relax. "For once you're wrong, Jo. I wasn't thinking of Woody, but now that you mention him . . . Do you know what he said about death? 'I'm not afraid of death. I just don't want to be there when it happens.'"

"Woody and the rest of the thinking population," I said.

"Right." Greg picked up a matchbook someone had left behind, took out a match and lit it. He watched it flame, then burn out. His young face was stricken. "What I was thinking about was Christy. Jo, they found the boat she was in – it was almost in the middle of the lake. It was the red canoe my mother gave me for my sixteenth birthday. There was a half-empty bottle of rye in it. And, Jo, there was an empty pill bottle in the boat, too. My mother sometimes takes these tranquilizers, and Christy must have found the bottle in Mum's bathroom cupboard. Anyway, it was empty. The police aren't saying anything, of course, but from the questions they were asking me, I think they're treating this as a suicide."

I thought of Christy's face in the moments after Peter came, when she knew that whatever future they had together wouldn't include love.

"Oh, God, poor Christy," I said. Then I thought of my son. "Greg, does Peter know?"

He shook his head. "I don't think so. I had to go down and identify the boat and my mother's pills. I just overheard things. I'm sure the police aren't telling people yet." He pushed himself back from the table. "I'd better see how Mieka's doing. This has been a pretty awful night for her, too."

"She's lucky she has you," I said.

He smiled. "That goes both ways, you know."

After he left, I felt myself slump. When Constable Kequahtooway came over and slid into the chair Greg had been sitting in, it took an effort of will to look up. "P. Kequahtooway," his badge said. I had heard one of the other cops call him Perry.

Up close, Perry Kequahtooway looked very young, but he was assured and he was thorough. I didn't find his questions painful; I had already moved into that zone of blunted emotion that comes when I know the worst has happened. I was able to replay the scenes of the evening pretty much without emotion: the time Christy had arrived at our house; the drive down; when I had seen her; when I hadn't seen her. Constable Kequahtooway took it all down without comment. Then he looked at me and asked a question I wasn't prepared for. "Did you know that Christy Sinclair listed you as next of kin on the emergency card in her wallet?"

I was dumfounded. "That doesn't make sense," I said. "I'm just the mother of a boy she was going out with. She has family in Estevan. They sent her money regularly. I mean she said they did, and they must have. Christy's only income was what she earned as a teaching assistant – there's no way she could have afforded the life she lived on a graduate student's stipend." I realized I was talking more to myself than to him. When I looked up, he was waiting patiently.

"And the name of the people in Estevan is Sinclair?" he asked.

"I guess so," I said weakly. "At least that's what Christy said."

"But you didn't believe her?" Constable Kequahtooway asked.

"She was a complicated young woman," I said.

Constable Perry Kequahtooway looked at me patiently. "Tell me about it," he said.

"There's not much to tell," I said, "except that sometimes Christy had her own perception of reality."

"She told lies," he said softly.

I nodded. Behind him, I could see Peter coming out of the tent, alone.

"Can I go to see my son now?" I asked.

Constable Kequahtooway looked surprised. "Of course, Mrs. Kilbourn."

"Did you tell him that Christy committed suicide?" I asked.

Suddenly, he was tense. "What makes you think she did?"

"Greg Harris told me about the empty pill bottle in the bottom of the canoe."

"An empty pill bottle doesn't make a suicide, Mrs. Kilbourn. I'd appreciate it if you kept your theories to yourself. I really would. We don't want to muddy the waters here."

I caught up with Peter at the front door to the house.

"How about some coffee?" I said. "It's getting cold out there. Or tea?"

He shook his head. "Nothing, thanks. I think I'd like to walk, though."

He started toward the road, and I followed.

"The beach is pretty crowded, with the police and everybody," he said.

We stopped at a hairpin turn in the road and walked toward a jut of land that overlooked the lake. Beneath us we could see the police checking the beach. The red canoe had been pulled up on shore.

I touched his arm. "Peter, I know this is a bad time to ask, but the police say that Christy had a card in her wallet that listed me as her next of kin. Do you know anything about it?"

There was a full moon that night. In the pale light, my son seemed alien, not just older but metamorphosed, as if Christy's death had changed him into a different man.

"She was so fucked up," he said in a voice tight with pain. "She was so fucking fucked up."

Then he began to cry. I put my arms around him and held him as he sobbed out his grief. Finally, he wiped his eyes with the sleeve of his sweater. "We'd better get back," he said.

For a few minutes we walked in silence, then Peter stopped. "I wanted her out of my life, and now she is," he said. It sounded as if he was speaking more to himself than to me.

"Peter, can you talk about it? What happened with you two tonight?"

"I don't know, Mum. Everything seemed all right. All·we were doing was going up to the house to dance, remember? It was all so quick. Christy said she'd talked to you about us getting married the same day Mieka and Greg did, and I said okay. Then that radio Angus was playing with came on, and Christy just bugged out. I went after her, but when I finally found out what room she was in, she wouldn't let me in. I know you'll find this hard to understand, but it didn't really worry me when Christy wouldn't talk to me."

"Why?"

He raked his hand through his hair. "She did it all the time. She never needed a reason. Once she told me it was a compulsion – that she had to keep testing me to see how far she could go before I'd stop loving her."

I ran my forefinger over the lettering on the bracelet Christy had given me. "Did she get to that point tonight?"

"She got past that point a long time ago," he said bleakly.

"Then what in the name of God were you doing back together?" I asked.

He put his head down and started walking faster.

"Peter, please, I know you don't want to talk about this, but we have to. This isn't *The Brady Bunch*. This is real. A young woman died tonight. If you didn't care about her, what was she doing here talking about marriage?"

Suddenly the answer was there, and I wondered if I'd been waiting for flaming letters in the sky.

"She was pregnant," I said.

He nodded. "We would have gotten married. That wasn't what upset her."

I felt as if I'd been kicked in the stomach. "What then? What made her decide to . . ."

"Decide to what, Mum?"

I could see the pulse beating in Peter's neck. He didn't need to hear speculations about Christy's death tonight. "Nothing, Pete. You look exhausted. What time did you get up this morning, anyway?"

"Five-thirty," he said. "Animals are early risers." For a beat he was silent, then he turned to me. "I wish I was back there now. I wish it was still this morning and none of this had happened."

I slid my arm around my son's waist, and together we started toward the house. We didn't say anything. There was nothing left to say.

When we got back, the house and grounds were still brilliantly lit. It would have been easy to believe there was still a celebration going on. But as I walked through the silent house I knew the party was over. Suddenly, I was so weary I had to force myself to turn the knob of the door to my room. Taylor had kicked off her bedclothes. I tucked her in, then I went over to my bed and collapsed. I didn't even turn down the bedspread.

That night was a troubled one for Blaine Harris, and that meant it was a troubled one for me. For hours, Keith's father seemed to drift in and out of anguish. Close to morning, I heard muffled voices on the other side of the wall, and the old man's voice was finally stilled. I couldn't sleep.

Every time I closed my eyes, Christy was there. The last time he saw her alive, Christy had told Peter she had to talk to me, that it was urgent. Why would she tell him that if she'd planned to take her own life? It didn't make sense.

When it was light enough to read the hands on my watch, I decided to give up. During the night Mieka had come in and crawled into bed with Taylor. As I walked to the bathroom, I stopped and looked at them. They were curled together spoon fashion, rosy, seeking out animal warmth in the time of trouble. It was instinct.

I showered and pulled on a fresh cotton dress and sandals. It was still cool, and I took a sweater out of my bag and walked to the kitchen to make coffee. In the half-light of dawn the kitchen was a ghostly place and shiningly perfect, although I knew the couple who worked for Lorraine Harris had made sandwiches and hot drinks for everyone late in the evening.

I found coffee in the cupboard, and as I waited for it to brew, I wandered into the sunroom next to the kitchen. Lorraine had set up an office in one corner of the room; a pretty rolltop desk faced the windows, and a small filing cabinet was tucked discreetly in the corner. There were two pictures on the desk. In one, Lorraine, elegant in black, her extravagant hair smoothed in a chignon, sat at a head table beaming up at a man giving a speech. I recognized some of the other people at the banquet. Like Lorraine, they were wheelers and dealers in the business community, people I knew because I had seen their pictures on the financial pages of the newspaper. The man who was speaking seemed familiar, but I couldn't place him. He must have been a major player in Lorraine's life, because he was in the second picture, too. This one was informal, a holiday picture, someplace where there were palm trees and white sand. In this photo, Lorraine and the man were wearing cruise clothes and they were both deeply tanned. The man was reaching out to touch a spray of flame-coloured hibiscus in Lorraine's hair. He looked smug and proprietorial, and I was glad it wasn't my hair he was touching.

I went to the kitchen, poured a mug of coffee and took it down to the dock. The sky was overcast, and mist was rising like smoke from the lake. I had the sense that I was the only person in the world. The morning had the cool menace of an Alex Colville painting. Across the lake was the hill where Peter Hourie and his men had seen the buffalo. A million buffalo. All dead now. Murdered into near extinction. Out of nowhere a phrase came into my mind – "too proud or too dumb to live" – and I thought of Bernice Morin sprawled over the garbage can outside Mieka's store and of Christy, her generous mouth frozen in a death grin. Two young women dead.

Through the grey mist I could see the yellow police tape marking off the beach where Christy had died. To the south, on the other side of the dock, more police tape marked off the beach where hours before young people had danced and laughed, privileged, enviable.

Suddenly I had the sense that I wasn't alone. I turned and behind me was Keith Harris. He was wearing a pale blue sport shirt. A shirt for a Saturday morning, except this wasn't going to be a day for golf and sun and gin and tonic in the clubhouse. His face was haggard.

"I looked for you last night," he said, "but I saw you were with your family. I didn't want to intrude. Did you get any sleep?"

"Not much," I said.

"Of course, your room's next to Blaine's. I'm sorry, Jo. That must have been the last thing you needed."

"He sounded so angry," I said. "My kids used to sound like that when they were little and they couldn't figure out how to get from point A to point B."

Keith sighed. "Most of the time I just deal with the situations that come up. Straightforward stuff, problem and solution. Then, every so often, like last night, I get a glimpse of what it must be like for him. That's when I go crazy."

"How long has he been like this?"

"Since Easter Sunday. I was with him when it happened. We were golfing. My dad had a putter in his hand, and suddenly he gave me this odd, preoccupied look and said, 'I don't know what to do with this.' I thought he was kidding and I made some joke. But he didn't laugh. He just stood there looking baffled.

"One of the other members of our foursome was a doctor. He knew right away. I went to the hospital with them, and I asked the neurologist to let me stay while they did the CAT scan. I don't think I've ever been so scared. There was this picture of my father's brain; on it, I could see a dark stain about the size of a robin's egg. That was the hemorrhage, and as I watched, the stain started spreading. And the neurologist said, very coolly: 'He just lost speech,' and then the stain elongated and spread, and he said, 'That was mobility. If it keeps augmenting there won't be much left.' And I looked at him, and I said, 'That's my father you're writing off, asshole,' and I walked out of the room."

Keith had been looking away from me, toward the lake. Suddenly he faced me. "Jo, I'm sorry. Sometimes, I think Blaine's becoming an obsession with me. I should be thinking about you. Do they know anything more about what happened last night?"

I shook my head. "I had a long talk with Constable Kequahtooway, but I think it's too early for them to know much for sure."

"Greg said he told you about the police finding that empty pill bottle in the canoe. You knew Christy Sinclair, Jo. Does that add up? Would she have committed suicide?"

"If you'd asked me yesterday, I would have said no. But now I'm not so sure. In the last twenty-four hours of her life, something went terribly wrong for Christy. I don't know what kinds of things she was dealing with. Except . . ." I stopped.

"Except what?" Keith said gently.

Suddenly, I was tired of secrets. I wanted somebody else to share the burden. "Christy was pregnant, Keith."

He looked stricken. "Poor Peter," he said, "to lose a child." It was such an odd thing to say, but somehow it was exactly right. I was feeling that loss, too.

When the wind came up, we walked to the house hand in hand. Keith brought coffee out, and we sat at one of the tables near the pool and talked about life and loss.

When Taylor came running out of the house, the mood shifted from the elegiac. She had chosen her own clothes from the suitcase; they were mismatched, and her blonde hair was tangled from sleep, but she was hotly eager to get the day underway. No one had told her about Christy.

She jumped on my lap and put her arms around me.

"And good morning to you, too," I said. "This is a great way to begin the day."

She looked around. "Can I go and get Angus?" she said.

"Let him sleep for a while, T.," I said. "He was up pretty late. Why don't you draw him a picture?"

Keith handed her a pen. "Sorry, I don't have paper," he said.

"I know where there's some," I said. I went into the tent. Lorraine's clipboard was still on the card table. I ripped a sheet from the pad where she'd written the names of the teams for croquet. I brought the paper out and handed it to Taylor.

"There's writing on it," Taylor said.

"Use the other side," I said. "Angus will be proud of how you're conserving trees."

She sat and drew, and Keith and I watched her.

When I'd finished my coffee, I stood up. "I'd better go see what's happening here. If there's anything I can do, I'll stay, but if not, I'm going back to the city. I'm sure Lorraine would be relieved to have everyone out right about now."

He smiled. "I think I'd better stick around till tomorrow. Blaine shouldn't be moved when he's like this. Besides, Lorraine has a touching belief that men are useful in a crisis. I'll call you as soon as I get back in the city."

I gave him my number, then I tapped Taylor on the shoulder.

"Come on, T. It's time to boogie."

Taylor handed me her drawing. "Here, for Angus," she said. It was a page full of frogs. "Since he can't take any real ones home with him," she explained.

"Great," I said. I looked at it again. "It really is great, Taylor." I showed it to Keith, and we walked to the house. When I got to my room, I slipped the picture into my bag and forgot about it.

The couple who worked for Lorraine Harris were busy in the kitchen making breakfast. I could smell the good aromas of bacon and toast and waffles. Some of the young people from the party were already eating. They were over the first shock, but as I looked at them, I knew it would be a long time before they recovered. Their voices, so exuberant the night before, were muted; even their gestures seemed careful and controlled, as if they were afraid of drawing attention to themselves.

Keith and I filled plates for ourselves and for Taylor. After we'd eaten, I poured a glass of juice and went up to check on Peter. I knocked at his door.

"It's okay. Come on in," he said.

He'd showered and dressed, but he looked terrible.

I handed him the juice. "They have breakfast downstairs," I said. "Can I bring you something?"

He took a tentative sip. "Thanks, Mum. I think I'll be doing pretty well if I manage to get this down."

"Pete, I think as soon as you're up to it, we should go back to the city. This place is a nightmare for everybody right now. If we went home, you could sit out in the sunshine with the dogs and be by yourself for a while."

Peter went to the corner, picked up the clothes he'd been wearing the night before and shoved them in his knapsack. "I'm ready when you are," he said.

After everyone had eaten, it didn't take us long to get organized. Mieka decided to stay at the lake with the Harrises. She said they needed her, and she was right. The doctor who came to check on Blaine had been alarmed about the deterioration in his condition. Greg wanted to stay with his grandfather, and Mieka wanted to be with Greg.

Peter said he'd feel better if he drove, and Angus volunteered to go with him. So just Taylor and I were riding in the Volvo for the trip back. As I started up the driveway, a yellow Buick hurtled out of the garage behind the house and turned onto the driveway. I had to brake to keep from hitting it. I don't think Lorraine Harris even saw me, but I saw her. She was wearing her horn-rimmed glasses, and her grey hair was loose. She disappeared over the hill in a split second, but as I drove carefully around one of the hairpin turns on the reserve road, I saw the buttercup-yellow Buick on the other side of the valley. Lorraine was really tearing up the highway. I thought she must be desperate to put miles between herself and the disaster she left behind.

It was the Saturday morning of a holiday weekend, and traffic on the highway into the city was light. When we passed Edenwold, I saw that the tundra swans had gone. Moved on north. I thought of Christy standing by the fence in the brilliant May sunshine: "If they're smart and lucky, they'll make it." Maybe, I thought. Maybe.

We were in Regina by ten-fifteen. As we drove through the city streets, we could see people in their front yards putting in bedding plants, visiting. The months of grey isolation were over; it was time to get reacquainted with the neighbours.

"How would you like to do that today?" I said to Taylor, pointing to a girl helping her mother garden.

She frowned. "I thought maybe we could get my new bike today, since we came back early. Maybe Angus could teach me how to ride it."

I hadn't told her about Christy yet, and I was dreading it. Taylor had already seen too much death in her young life. I remembered Angus's guilt and confusion about Christy the night before. Giving his sister bike-riding lessons might be just the distraction he needed.

"What do you say we go right now? Then we can come home and surprise the boys."

When we came back from the bike shop, Peter's car was in the driveway. Angus shook his head in amazement when he saw the bike. "Oh, T., a pink two-wheeler?" But he helped her buckle on her helmet and lifted her onto the seat. I ran inside and got the camera and snapped away as Taylor, proud in the bike seat, wobbled onto the sidewalk.

When I went to the house to get another roll of film, the phone was ringing.

Jill Osiowy sounded excited. "Something interesting's come up in the Little Flower murders, Jo."

I sank into the chair by the phone. I didn't want to hear what Jill was going to tell me. I didn't want to hear anything more about young women who had died before they'd even started to live.

"Listen to this," she said. "The cops have decided that Bernice Morin's death wasn't one of the Little Flower murders. The face wasn't mutilated, and the weapon was wrong. The other girls were stabbed with heavy knives, the kind you buy in a sporting goods store if you're going hunting. The scalpel that killed Bernice came from a medical supply house. It's the kind they use in hospitals and labs. I'll tell you the details later, but here's the scary part. The cops think Bernice's murder was a copy-cat killing. Think about that for a minute, Jo. There's somebody out there who figured if he made Bernice's death look like another Little Flower murder, the police would just kind of wink and look the other way. The perfect crime."

Suddenly, Jill noticed that I hadn't said anything. "Jo, what's the matter? Have you lost interest in these girls, too?" She sounded angry, and I felt a lump come to my throat.

"Don't be mad," I said. "It's not that I don't care. It's just . . . Jill, we've had a tragedy ourselves. Peter's friend Christy Sinclair died last night out at the lake. I'm doing my best to keep everybody, including me, from falling apart. I don't think I can take in another thing."

Jill's voice was soft with concern. "Jo, I'm sorry. How awful. Is there anything I can do? If you want company, I can be over there in ten minutes."

"Maybe later on tonight," I said. "Right now, I think we're better off on our own. Everybody's pretty fragile."

"I can imagine," she said. "Look, if you need me, call. You know, sometimes the best thing to do is just go through the motions."

And that's what the kids and I did. We went through the motions. All things considered, we didn't do badly. We had lunch, and the kids rode bikes most of the afternoon. No one broke a bone, and they were still speaking to one another when they came in for dinner. Peter curled up on the couch and watched the Mets-Dodgers game, and I put in bedding plants. I had just finished planting the last of the geraniums in the front garden when the police car pulled up.

I recognized Constable Perry Kequahtooway, but I didn't remember seeing the woman who was with him. She was a small brunette with a tense body and clever eyes. Perry Kequahtooway introduced her as Officer Kelly Miner.

"I wonder if we could step inside for a moment, Mrs. Kilbourn?" she said. "We're still puzzled about Christy Sinclair's next of kin situation."

They followed me in, and we sat down at the kitchen table.

Constable Kequahtooway spoke first. His voice was as gentle as his manner, but he got right to the point.

"We keep coming back to you, Mrs. Kilbourn. Everywhere we check – her employment records, her university insurance policy, even the form she filled out when she had some outpatient surgery in Saskatoon last February – every place we look, Christy Sinclair listed you as her next of kin."

I started to say something, but he held his hand up to stop me. "There's more. The Saskatoon police just checked out Christy Sinclair's condominium. Were you ever there?"

I shook my head. "She always came to our place."

"It's in Lawson Heights," Officer Miner said, "very posh. But the point is that there were pictures of you and Christy all over the place." She was watching my face carefully.

"Christmas pictures," I said.

"For the most part," she agreed.

"They'd have to be," I said. "Peter and Christy only dated for a few months, and Christmas was the only time we were taking pictures. But we took pictures of everybody during the holidays. There were pictures of Christy with all the people in our family."

"Not in her home," Officer Miner said. "And there weren't any indications of the Estevan connection you mentioned, either. No address book or envelopes with an Estevan address. We've checked in Estevan, too. No Sinclairs. No one by that name in the area. We're trying a picture ID down there, but so far no luck."

I looked at them both wearily. "What's your point?"

Officer Miner looked at me steadily. "Easy on there, Mrs. Kilbourn. There are no accusations being made here. This is an information session. We're just letting you know that, no matter how you saw the relationship, Christy Sinclair apparently chose you to be the most important person in her life."

Unexpectedly, I felt my eyes fill with tears. "It's too late now to do anything about that, isn't it?"

Officer Kequahtooway lowered his gaze and coughed. "Actually, Mrs. Kilbourn, it isn't too late. There are a number of details that have to be attended to, funeral arrangements, that kind of thing. You have no legal responsibility. I should make that clear. But there are other kinds of responsibility."

"Yes," I agreed, "there are."

Officer Miner stood to leave, and Constable Kequahtooway and I followed her to the front door. But when she started down the front walk, he didn't follow.

Instead, he turned and said, "Mrs. Kilbourn, this is unofficial, but I think when we get the final reports from pathology, we're going to find out that Christy Sinclair's death was a suicide."

I leaned against the doorjamb. "I kept hoping it wouldn't be," I said. "That makes everything a thousand times worse."

"It always does," Perry Kequahtooway said softly. Then he looked at me. "Sometimes people find comfort in searching out the truth about the life of a person who's passed on."

"You mean investigating?" I said. "But you'll be doing that."

Constable Kequahtooway shrugged. "That's right, we will, but sometimes people like you can get to a different kind of truth than the police do. It's just a thought, Mrs. Kilbourn. But I think, in the long run, it might comfort you and Peter to find out why you mattered so much to Christy Sinclair."

When he started down the steps, I touched his arm. "Constable, what does your last name mean? We had a friend years ago named Kequahtooway, and I know the name is significant."

He squinted into the sun, and then, unexpectedly, he grinned.

"In Ojibway," he said, "it means he who interprets. You know, the guy who tries to help people understand."

CHAPTER

5

On Victoria Day, when I went to the mailbox to get the morning paper, Regina Avenue was as empty as a street in a summer dream. I went in, made coffee and looked out at the backyard. Peter was in the pool swimming, and Sadie and Rose, our dogs, were sitting on the grass watching.

I went out and knelt by the edge of the pool.

"How's it going this morning?" I asked.

Peter swam to the edge of the water and looked up at me.

"It's been better," he said, and I could hear his father in the weary bravado of his voice.

"I know the feeling," I said.

His face was a mask. "I didn't go after her, Mum. When she said she was going out on the lake, I was relieved. I was going to have a whole hour where I didn't have to worry about her. So I didn't go after her, and she died. How am I going to live with that?"

"I don't know, Peter," I said. "But for starters, you can see that what you did was pretty normal. You thought about yourself. You wanted some breathing space, and when the chance came, you took it. Mother Teresa may not have done what you did, but most people, including me, would have. Look, I'm not saying that it was right to let Christy go when she was that upset, but we don't carry a crystal ball around with us. You didn't know what Christy was going to do, and you're certainly not responsible for what she did."

"Mum, listen to yourself. You don't even believe what you're saying. You know I didn't have to be in the boat with her. You know it's not that simple because you're the one who told me it's never simple – that we're always responsible for what we do and what we don't do. You've been drumming that into me for nineteen years, you can't expect me to just walk away now."

He pulled himself up on the side of the pool. His body, still pale from winter, was as graceful as his father's had been.

"I'm seeing Daddy everywhere in you today," I said.

He raked his hair with his fingers. "That's not bad, is it?"

"Not bad at all," I said. "Come on inside, and I'll get us some breakfast."

Taylor and Angus were already at the breakfast table having cereal. Taylor was unnaturally quiet. The night before when I had told her about Christy's death she had listened attentively, then gone off to her room to draw. When I went in to say goodnight, she was asleep, and the bedspread was covered with pictures of swans.

While Peter went upstairs to dry off and change, I poured us all juice and started batter for pancakes.

"Anybody want to take the dogs for a walk after breakfast?" I asked.

"Samantha's mum is taking us for a ride on the bike path," Taylor said.

"Are you up for that, T.?" I asked. "You just started yesterday."

"Samantha's mum has never ridden a bike in her life, but she says today's the day."

"Good for her," I said. "Angus, how about you?"

He wiped his mouth on the back of his hand. "I'm playing arena ball as soon as I'm through here, then I'm coming home to make a cake."

"A cake," I said, trying to keep the surprise out of my voice.

"Alison next door made this cake, and it was great. She says it's a real no-brainer."

"A no-brainer?" I asked.

He looked at me kindly. "Easy? Any dummy can do it?"

"Right," I said.

After breakfast, Peter and I put the dogs on their leashes and walked them downtown to Victoria Park. The walk to the park was a family tradition on the twenty-fourth of May weekend, one of those small ceremonies whose only justification was that we did it every year. My husband, Ian, used to say it was our way of making sure that Good Queen Vic, the fertility goddess, would smile on our garden.

It was the first really hot day of the year, and the streets were coming to life with people riding bikes or jogging or pushing babies in strollers. There was a regatta on Wascana Lake, and from the bridge we could see the bright sails of the skiffs waiting for wind.

Peter and I didn't say much. We never did. We sat on the bench in front of the statue of Sir John A. Macdonald and listened to the chimes the multicultural community had donated to the park play "Edelweiss." Four days earlier I had sat on this same bench with Mieka, reeling from the shock of the death of another young woman. It was not a pattern I was happy about repeating.

Finally I said to Peter, "Do you remember Constable Kequahtooway? He was the first one there the night of the accident."

Peter nodded.

"Well," I went on, "he says that taking care of the details of Christy's funeral and finding out more about her might help us accept what's happened."

"Face it," Peter said angrily. "Nothing's going to help."

He leaned back on the bench and raised his face to the sun. The chimes finished "Edelweiss" and started on "The Blue Bells of Scotland." When "Blue Bells" was finished, Peter leaned forward and looked across the park.

"That doesn't mean we shouldn't try to do the right things for Christy," he said. "But it's not going to be easy. Sometimes I wonder if she ever told me the truth about anything."

"Maybe that's what she wanted to tell me that last night," I said.

Peter shook his head. "You never give up, do you?"

"That's what your dad used to tell me. He didn't see it as a particularly admirable trait." I shrugged. "Anyway, the truth must be somewhere. I guess the place to start is Christy's family. The Estevan angle doesn't seem to be true, but she must have somebody. It's terrible to think of her people out there not knowing. How would you feel about calling some of Chris's friends in Saskatoon and seeing if she ever mentioned anything about her family?" I looked at him. "Nothing's come back to you, has it? I mean something she said that might help the police."

"Mum, she said so many things . . ." He leaned forward and put his arms around the neck of our golden retriever. The dogs had always been his consolation. In a minute he stood up.

"We'd better get back," he said. "I think what I'll do is drive up to Saskatoon. If I leave now, I can be there after lunch. It'll be easier for me to talk about Christy face to face. I'm hopeless on the phone."

"I know," I said, picking up Rose's leash. "I've talked to you on the phone for nineteen years."

As soon as we got to the house, Peter filled a Thermos with coffee and headed north. I was watching Angus line up the ingredients for his cake when the phone rang.

The man's voice was brusquely authoritative. "Joanne Kilbourn? This is the pathology department at Pasqua Hospital. We're ready to release Christy Sinclair's body and we need a signature." He hesitated, and when he spoke again he sounded almost human. "You'd better make some arrangements for a pickup."

I watched Angus carefully break three eggs into a cup, then I went upstairs and opened my closet door. I looked at the bright cotton skirts and blouses and wondered what you were supposed to wear when you signed for a body. I picked the dress closest to me, a grey cotton shirtwaist. As I left the house I caught my reflection in the hall mirror. I looked a hundred years old, which was about half as old as I felt.

What happened at the hospital was either Keystone Kops or cosmic justice working itself out. It began when I saw the picket line blocking the entrance. There was a nurses' strike in our province. Under normal circumstances I would have walked twenty miles before I crossed a picket line, but these were not normal circumstances.

A blonde woman, X-ray thin and carrying a picket sign, stood between me and the front steps of the hospital.

"I don't want to do this," I said to her, "but there's been a death."

"I'm sorry," she said and she lowered her sign. It said, "The Only Good Tory Is a Suppository."

The hospital was quiet. The administration had dismissed as many patients as possible before the strike. "To stream-line the operation," they had said. There was one harried-looking woman sitting in a reception area designed for four.

"Pathology," I said to her.

"Top floor," she said without looking at me.

When I got off the elevator, I was struck by how pleasantly domestic the pathology department seemed. There were plants everywhere. To the left of the elevator was a floor-to-ceiling window that filled the area with warm spring sunshine; to the right there was an area that looked like a nursing station. On the counter a huge azalea bloomed unseen by anyone but me. The nursing station was empty.

I walked to the window and looked out. Beneath me was Queensbury Downs, the racetrack, seductive as a sure thing in the May sunshine. Trainers were taking horses through their paces, and I could see the lines of the horses' powerful muscles as they moved around the track. I felt myself relaxing.

There was a cough behind me. When I turned, I saw a woman standing behind the counter. She was wearing street clothes, not a uniform, and she seemed as harried as the woman downstairs had been.

"Well?" she said, and her voice was flat and uninterested.

"Joanne Kilbourn for Christy Sinclair," I said.

"Right," she said. She turned, took a file from a rack on the wall and placed it on the counter between us. The name "Sinclair" was written in bright green felt pen across the top of the folder.

"Everything's ready for your signature," she said and opened the file. Behind her a phone rang. She answered it, looked even more harried, then ran down the hall. I picked up the form on the top. I thought I could sign it and have it ready when she came back. Cheerful as pathology was, I didn't want to stick around.

Underneath the release form was a typewritten report labelled "Autopsy Findings." I pushed it away from me. Then I looked at the bulletin board behind the nurses' station. Someone had tacked up a computer printout; the letters were large, mock-Gothic: "We speak for the dead to protect the living."

Good enough. I pulled the autopsy report toward me and began reading. The first page confirmed what Perry Kequahtooway said it would confirm: Christy Sinclair's death was a result of a deadly combination of alcohol and tranquilizers. The drug names and the strength of the pills didn't mean anything to me; obviously whatever Chris had taken had been enough to do the job. As I turned to the next page, I was surprised to see that my hands were shaking.

I found what I was looking for on page three. The typewriter pathology used had a worn ribbon, and the report was dotted with vowels whose imprint was so vague their identity could only be guessed at. Moreover, the report was written in the language of medicine, and I was a layperson. But I had given birth to three children, and there were certain things I knew. I knew, for example, that any woman whose reproductive system had been as badly scarred by repeated non-clinical abortion procedures as Christy Sinclair's had been was unlikely to sustain a pregnancy. I looked at that hard medical language again. No mention of a fetus, no mention of any physiological changes that would indicate pregnancy. There was no baby. I was flooded with relief and then, almost immediately, I was overcome by a sense of loss.

I replaced the first page, and that's when I saw it. About a third of the way down the page under the heading "Identifying Marks" was a single entry: "left buttock, tattoo, 3 cm, bear-shaped, not recent."

I felt my head swim. The harried woman came back. I signed the form and pushed it toward her without a word. I stood up and started to leave. She called after me. "You should make some arrangements to have her taken to a funeral home," she said. "You can use my phone, if you like."

She was, I knew, trying to be kind, and I walked into the nursing station.

"Just pick one and dial," she said pointing to her desk pad. Under the plastic were the business cards of all the funeral homes in town. Easy reference. I picked the one nearest our house and made my call. The woman went through the doors marked "No Admittance." I picked up the phone again and called long distance information.

Constable Perry Kequahtooway didn't sound surprised to hear from me, and he didn't chide me for reading a confidential file. When I told him about the teddy bear tattoos on the buttocks of two girls dead within a week, he whistled softly. "Now I wonder what that means?" he said in his gentle voice.

As I drove along the expressway, I repeated the question to myself. By the time I walked in the front door of my house, I still hadn't come up with an answer.

Taylor was sitting at the kitchen table eating cake. Her face was dirty except for the places where tears had run down her cheeks. A half-dozen *Sesame Street* Band-Aids were plastered on her knee. Angus was across from her.

When Taylor saw me, she said, "I wiped out."

"So I see," I said.

"I put the Band-Aids on myself."

"Right," I said. "Taylor, did you clean the cut out before you put on the Band-Aids?"

"No time," she said.

"Finish your cake and we'll make time," I said.

"I told you," Angus said wearily.

Cleaning Taylor's knee and disinfecting it was a trauma for us both. When we were through, we collapsed on the couch in the family room. Taylor snuffled noisily beside me, and I pulled her close. I looked at the sun shimmering on the brilliant blue of the pool and tried to block out the ugliness of the medical profile the coroner's words had drawn.

Christy Sinclair had had so many abortions she was sterile. There had never been a baby. Beside me Taylor sang a tuneless song and finally drifted off to sleep. Not long afterwards, I followed her.

When I woke up, Mieka was there with Greg.

"Phone call from the uncle," she said, "wanting to take you out for dinner. I accepted for you. Greg and I will take the kids to McDonald's and the movies so you can make a night of it." She looked at me. "I think we all deserve a night off, Mummy."

I looked at them groggily. "I don't think so, Miek. I'd be rotten company tonight."

Greg came and sat by me on the couch. "It'd do you good, Jo. You've had a hell of a time the last few days. We all have. Anyway, don't decide right now. Let's all have a swim. It's gorgeous out there. If you don't feel better after that, I'll call my uncle and tell him Mieka the Matchmaker will go out for dinner with him, and you can come to McDonald's with me and the kids."

By the time I came out of the pool, I'd decided against McDonald's. The mindless rhythm of swimming had always relaxed me. By seven o'clock, my heart still felt leaden, but I was ready. Mieka had suggested I find something sensational to wear. I didn't have anything sensational, but I did have a cotton dress that was the colour of cornflowers. Every time I wore it, good things happened.

As I met Keith at the front door, I hoped good things were going to happen again.

"No car?" I said.

"This place is in walking distance," he said. "Actually, it's my house. Our housekeeper got some food together and left. The rest of the evening is going to be a clumsy seduction scene. You can bolt out the door whenever you want."

"I'll let you know," I said.

The streets were quiet, and the air was sweet with the scent of flowering trees: chokecherry, lilac, crabapple.

At the corner of Albert Street there was a cherry tree in full bloom. We stopped under it and looked up into branches heavy with rosy blossoms, thin as silk.

"I feel like I'm standing in the middle of a Chinese water-colour," Keith said.

Just then a gust of wind came and the cherry blossoms drifted down on us, pink and fragrant.

I reached over and brushed the petals from his shirt. "Is this part of the seduction?" I asked.

He smiled. "Is it working?"

Suddenly I felt awkward. "Keith, it's been years since I've done this. There hasn't been anybody for me since Ian died."

He shrugged. "I'm not a teenager. I'm fifty-three years old. I've learned how to wait."

Keith lived in a two-storey apartment house on College Avenue. It was white stucco with a red tile roof, vaguely Spanish and immaculately kept up.

"Second floor," Keith said and we walked up an oak stair-case, opened the front door and went in. It was a comfort-able-looking apartment, airy and cool, with chairs and couches that looked as if they were meant to be sat in, gleaming hardwood floors covered here and there with hooked rugs, and a scarred pine table set for two in front of doors that opened onto the balcony.

Keith looked at me. "I'm not a cook," he said, "but don't worry. My housekeeper says everything's ready. I just have to follow her instructions about what to heat up and what to leave alone. Dead simple, she says."

"My youngest son would call it a no-brainer."

He grinned. "He'd be right. Would you like a drink first?"

"Gin and tonic would be great," I said. "It's been a rotten day."

Keith brought the drink. "Do you want to talk about it?" he asked.

I shook my head.

"In that case," he said, "why don't you have a look around while I follow my instructions."

"Need help?" I asked.

"Relax," he said. "Have a look at the art. It's my one extravagance. All Saskatchewan, you'll notice."

"So I see," I said. On the coffee table a Joe Fafard ceramic bull, testicles glowing like jewels between his flanks, sat proudly beside clay six-quart baskets filled with brightly glazed vegetables: potatoes, carrots, tomatoes.

"Victor Cicansky," I said looking at the vegetables. "My dream is to have a kitchen filled with these some day." On the walls an Ernest Lindner watercolour of a peeling birch hung next to a brilliantly coloured blanket painting by Bob Boyer. Over the mantel was a magically realistic painting of a horse, so black it seemed blue, leaping into the arc of the prairie sky. Underneath was a title plate: " 'Poundmaker Pegasus' by Sally Love (1947–1991)." Sally was Taylor's mother. I was standing looking at the painting, remembering, when Keith came, slipped his hand under my elbow and said, "Come on, I'll show you the rest of the place."

He led me into a room that looked like a working office. There was a desk that Keith said had belonged to his father covered with files and papers, shelves of books and a wall full of political pictures. I moved closer to the pictures. They were all there, my chamber of villains, the men and women I had spent much of my adult life trying to turn out of office. Blaine Harris was in some of the pictures; Keith was in all of them, smiling with presidents and prime ministers and premiers. All the pictures were inscribed affectionately and fulsomely.

In the lair of the enemy, I thought.

Keith touched my arm. "Was this a mistake?" he asked.

"No, not a mistake," I said. "Just a reminder. What is your status these days, anyway? I remember hearing that you came back to Saskatchewan because you wanted time away from Ottawa. Is it just a summer holiday or a permanent thing?"

He shrugged. "It depends, I guess."

"On what?"

"I don't know. Just stuff. Come on, let's get out of here. It's killing the mood. Besides, I'm hungry."

"Me, too," I said. "Would it be rude to ask what we're having?"

"Probably," he said, "but you're with a friend, so you get an answer. Cold lake trout, some sort of green salad, cornbread and Chablis." He dropped a disc into the CD player, and the room was filled with the shimmering sounds of the Goldberg Variations. Keith held out his hand to me. "And Glenn Gould is going to play until we decide we've had enough."

"Which will be never," I said.

"Which will be never," he agreed.

We brought the food to the table, and he lifted his glass to me.

"To music," he said.

I sipped my wine. "Good," I said. I tasted the fish. "In fact, more than good. Everything's wonderful. Do you know this is only the second seduction meal of my life? When I was sixteen, the boy across the street invited me for dinner. His parents had left him alone overnight for the first time. I guess the temptation was too much. He made the most romantic evening – vodka and orange juice and candlelight and his mother's tuna fish casserole and, of course, music.

Guess what he played during dinner?"

"'Bolero,'" Keith said.

"That was later," I said. "During dinner he played 'Rhapsody in Blue.'"

Keith smiled. "What happened?"

"He told me about George Gershwin's tragically short life, trying, I guess, to impress me with the need to gather our rosebuds while we could. And I drank my screwdrivers and ate my tuna casserole and cried like a baby, because George Gershwin died so young and because I wasn't used to vodka."

"And then?" Keith asked.

"And then he walked me home. It was 1961. People took virginity seriously in those days. He ended up studying math and physics at U. of T. Last I heard he was a high-school teacher."

"I'm too old for a change of career," he said.

"I'll bear that in mind," I said.

Dinner was wonderful, and I could feel the darkness lifting. Keith Harris was easy to talk to, and it was fun to trade stories about political battles. When we were finished, Keith said, "Do you like Metaxa? I have a bottle I brought back from Greece for a special occasion. Let's have a little and I'll put on the wisest piece of music I know."

He took Gould's 1955 recording of Goldberg out of the CD player and dropped in another CD. "This is the version of the Goldberg Gould did in 1981," Keith said.

We took our Metaxa out on the balcony. Across the park, the lights from the legislature shimmered in Wascana Lake. The air was cool and smelled of fresh-cut grass and damp earth. We sat side by side in the stillness and listened as Glenn Gould played Bach. The interpretation was very different, not brilliant and risk-taking, but mature, rich and thoughtful. It was the work of a man who had learned a few

things about life and about death. Good music to make love
to when you were closer to the end of life than the beginning. I felt the familiar stirrings of sexual desire, and moved
closer to Keith.

"Ready?" he said softly.

"I think I am," I said.

He took my hand and together we walked down the hall
to his bedroom. Suddenly, I was unsure. I walked across the
room and looked at the framed photographs on Keith's wall.
They were unmistakably pictures of the north: the sun
boiling on the horizon while the pines reached dark fingers
into the red sky; a wood grouse standing one-legged on a
piece of driftwood floating in shimmering water; a close-up
of wildflowers growing through dead leaves.

"Beautiful," I said.

Keith came and stood beside me. "Blue Heron Point," he
said. "I'm the photographer. I'm not exactly Alfred Stieglitz,
but with the north as a subject, you don't have to be. I have
a place up there. It's not much, just a cottage on the lake."

"A squeaky screen door and sand on the floor and dishes
that don't match?" I said.

Keith smiled. "And a wood stove where you can boil your
coffee and fry your eggs too hard and a woodbox filled with
old *Saturday Night*s. Best of all, it really is away from everything. Not like that palace of Lorraine's on Echo. But I guess
she had enough of the north growing up. Anyway, sand and
squeaks and all, I love it."

"Angus is going to camp at Havre Lake in July," I said.

"Good, let's take him up together, and we can stay at the
lake."

"Just like that?" I asked.

He looked at me. "Yeah. Remember George Gershwin. No
use waiting around."

"Right," I said. Keith took me in his arms, and I felt as if the broken parts of me were coming together. When he caressed my breasts and kissed the hollow of my neck, the darkness that had been hanging over me lifted.

I kissed him. "Remember that Marvin Gaye song 'Sexual Healing'?" I said.

Keith's hands slid over my hips. "I remember."

"I'm beginning to believe in it," I said.

When the telephone rang, shrill and insistent, we looked at each other.

"Damn," said Keith. "Do you want to let it ring?"

"Yes, but I'd be worried all night it was one of my kids."

Keith picked up the receiver and said hello. He listened for a while then he said, "Just keep him quiet. I'll be right there."

Keith turned to me, "My emergency, not yours. Apparently, Blaine was trying to get up and he fell. I'd better go down and have a look. Why don't you come along?"

"I don't think I feel like going anywhere," I said.

"It's just downstairs," he said.

"Downstairs here?" I asked.

"Yeah, I thought you knew. This building is sort of a family place. Lorraine owns it and she has the bottom floor. I have this. And since my father had his stroke, he and the nurse who takes care of him have stayed in the apartment at the back. It's been great, really – he has his privacy but we're close."

We walked downstairs and knocked at the door at the end of the front hall. A man in his mid-twenties wearing sweatpants and a very white T-shirt answered. He had the powerful shoulders and upper arms of someone who worked out. Keith introduced us, and the man, whose name was Sean Gilliland, shook hands with me, then turned to Keith.

"Your father got out of bed and fell," he said. "I'd bathed him and brought his bedtime snack and we watched the news together. Then I turned out the lights and came into the living room. I was doing my stretch and strengthens when I heard this crash. I went in and he was on the floor. Mr. Harris, he'd been trying to make a phone call."

Keith looked at him incredulously. "A phone call?"

Sean shook his head. "I know. But that's what he was doing. He was over by that little table with the telephone. He must have dragged himself over on the furniture. He still had the receiver in his hand when I found him."

As we passed through the living room, I glanced at the TV. The sound was turned off; on the screen, six men as muscular as Sean were silently working on their abdominal muscles.

Blaine's room was cool and dimly lit. I stayed in the doorway and Keith went to his father. The old man looked pale and shaken; even across the room I could see the ugliness of the purplish knot rising on his forehead. Keith talked to his father for a while, soothing words I couldn't hear, and Blaine seemed calm. Then he saw me.

As soon as he caught sight of me, the old man tried to push himself up to a sitting position. All the while he was pushing himself, he was trying to talk. The sounds that came out were garbled and desperate. Finally, he got out a single word, "Killdeer." As soon as he said the word, he fell back on the bed exhausted. But his eyes never left my face.

"Killdeer?" I said. "Do you mean my name, Kilbourn?"

He began to push himself up again. Sean came over to me quickly. "Would you mind staying in the other room? Mr. Harris isn't supposed to get upset."

I went into the living room. Keith came out almost immediately. He put his arms around me. "I'm going to call the doctor. Do you want to go upstairs and wait for me?"

I shook my head. "I think I'll take a cab home. The day seems to have caught up with me."

He kissed my hair. "Damn," he said. "This evening shouldn't end with your going home alone." He smiled. "Jo, if I can find a copy of 'Rhapsody in Blue,' will you give me another chance?"

"I'll bring the tuna casserole," I said. "Call me later and let me know how your father is."

Keith called the doctor and then he dialled a cab for me. While I waited for it, I watched the strong young men on the television stretch and strengthen their already perfect bodies.

When I got home, Mieka was sitting at the kitchen table in her nightgown working on her business accounts.

"Can I retire yet?" I said.

She made a face. "Not unless you have a source of income I don't know about."

"Is it going to be okay?" I asked.

Mieka smiled. "It's going to be fine. Lorraine's going to set up a line of credit for me on Monday."

"She's really good to you, isn't she?" I said.

"I don't know what I'd do without her, Mum." Mieka took off her glasses. "Are you warming to her at all? I know she's not the kind of woman you cozy up to, but you know, Mum, she hasn't had an easy life. She kind of manipulated the wedding with Greg's dad, and I think she got more than she bargained for. Alisdair had pretty well gambled away all their money by the time he died, and Lorraine had a little boy to support. She's had to work hard to get where she is."

"I didn't know that," I said. "I knew Greg was just a baby when his father died, but I always thought it was the Harris money that kept things going there."

Mieka shook her head. "All Alisdair Harris left Lorraine and Greg was that place on the lake, mortgaged to the hilt, and a lot of angry creditors. Old Mr. Harris just about went broke himself trying to pay off his son's debts. Keith tried to help, but Lorraine insisted she could do it on her own. And you know, Mum, when she was getting started in real estate, women had to be . . ." She hesitated.

"Men pleasers?" I said.

"Yeah, I guess. Lorraine still talks about having to use her womanly wiles. But to be fair to her, the kind of men you knew at the university and even in politics were more enlightened than some of the men Lorraine had to deal with. She's done very well for herself, you know."

"I know she has," I said. "And I intend to smarten up."

Mieka laughed. "See that you do. How was dinner?"

"Wonderful," I said. "Anything I need to know about around here?"

"No. The kids had three Big Macs each and fries and milkshakes, then Angus made himself a grilled cheese sandwich before he went to bed. There were a couple of phone calls for Peter. Jill called for you. She'll call tomorrow. I think that's it. Except for a prank call. Someone called and made weird noises and then dropped the receiver. Probably some meatball friend of Angus's."

"Probably," I said.

But I knew who had called, and I knew it wasn't a prank. I climbed the stairs and went into the bathroom to get ready for bed. I looked at myself in the mirror. I looked like a woman who had just about been made love to. I smiled at my reflection. Then I remembered, and I stopped smiling. What had Blaine Harris seen in my face? What was there about me that had made him drag himself along the furniture in his bedroom and risk his health to call me on the telephone?

"Killdeer," I said to my reflection. "Killdeer," and I turned away and went to bed.

CHAPTER

6

As I dressed for Christy's funeral the bedroom was dark. Since the early hours of morning, thunder had cracked and lightning had arced across the sky. Now the rain had come, steady and relentless. I smoothed the skirt of my black silk suit and checked my reflection in the mirror. The silver bracelet encircling my wrist gleamed dully – Christy's bracelet, now mine.

Three days earlier, Mieka had sent the keys to Christy's condominium to a friend in Saskatoon and asked her to go to Christy's place and choose a dress for her to be buried in. The woman had found a simple cotton dress the colour of a new fern; the price and the care instructions were still pinned to the sleeve. When Mieka brought it to the house to show me, I'd shuddered.

"Your great-grandmother always said that a green dress was bad luck."

Mieka had looked at me grimly. "I don't think Christy's luck could get much worse," she had said.

Christy wore the green dress. I dreaded seeing her at the funeral home, but it seemed to come with the territory when you were next of kin. Mieka and I drove over together the morning before the funeral. We were silent as we looked at Christy. Finally, Mieka reached over and touched the bracelet on my wrist.

"We should put this on her, I guess," Mieka said. "I never saw her without it until that last night."

"She wanted me to have it," I said.

"She did? But I thought . . ."

I turned it on my wrist so I could read the Celtic lettering. "Wandering Soul Pray For Me." In that moment, I felt the bracelet's power. Marcel Proust called these objects that are charged with independent life "Madeleine objects." Sensible people don't believe in such things, and I am a sensible woman, but from the moment I put it on, Christy Sinclair's bracelet was both a reminder and a spur.

I turned to my daughter.

"Mieka, would you mind leaving me alone with Christy for a moment?"

Mieka looked apprehensive.

"I'm all right," I said. "I just want to say goodbye."

She left, and very quickly I stepped to the casket and reached my hand under the small of Christy's back and half turned her. I pulled up her skirt. I could see the outline of the tattoo through the thin material of her panties, but still I had to know for certain. I pulled at the elastic waistband and slid Christy's underpants down. On her left buttock was the teddy bear tattoo. It was exactly the same as the tattoo I had seen on Bernice Morin the morning after she was murdered. I pulled the skirt down and turned Christy onto her back again.

"What does it mean, Christy?" I said. "What does it mean?"

We took two cars to the funeral. Peter was going with Mieka and Greg, and I was going with Jill Osiowy and Keith

Harris. When he phoned and asked what time he should pick me up, I had told him that he didn't have to be part of that sad day. His voice on the other end of the line had been matter of fact. "I'm interested in the long haul, Jo," he had said simply, and I'd thought that having Keith Harris with me for the long haul might not be a bad idea.

Planning the funeral had brought us face to face with all the unanswered questions of Christy's life. Who were the people who cared about her? Beyond a few colleagues at the biology lab, there didn't seem to be anyone. We had put a photo at the head of Christy's obituary notice in the Saskatoon and Regina papers, hoping that someone who had known her before would see it and come. But it seemed a slim hope, and we had chosen the smallest of the chapels at the funeral home to avoid the depressing symbolism of empty pews. What were her favourite flowers? Her favourite pieces of music? No one knew. Pete remembered a couple of songs she'd commented on when they'd been listening to the car radio, but they were songs for the living.

What, if anything, did Christy Sinclair believe in? She had never said. Greg went down to the library and came back with two pages of quotes about the endurance of the human spirit.

"Is there anything there we can use for a eulogy?" he asked after I finished reading them.

I shook my head.

"That's what I thought, too," he said. "My high-school coach said stuff like that when he sent us back into a game where we were really getting nailed."

"Thanks for trying," I said. "I've got an idea about something that won't sound quite so much like Vince Lombardi."

I pulled down my volume of Theodore Roethke and looked for the poem with the image of the pickerel smile that I had always connected with Christy. The poem was called "Elegy for Jane"; Roethke had written it for a student who had died from injuries when she was thrown from a horse. I copied the poem out, and it was in my purse the day I walked through the door of Helmsing's Funeral Home.

We had done our best. Still, as we filed into that tiny chapel with the empty pews and the tape of "Amazing Grace" whirring lugubriously in the background, there was no denying that Christy Sinclair's leave-taking of this world was going to be a pretty lonely affair. But as the tape changed to "Blessed Assurance," there was a stir.

Four young women had come in. Two were native, two weren't, but they all shopped at the same store: stiletto heels, stirrup pants tight as a second skin on their slender legs, nylon jackets with their names embroidered on the sleeve and crosses around their necks. They were, without exception, pretty, but their hair, gelled and curled, frizzed and sprayed, was too extravagant for their young faces, and their eyes were too wary for girls who weren't far along in puberty. They sat behind me. All during the readings I was aware of them; I could feel their presence, and I could smell the sweet heaviness of their hairspray, overpowering in the humid chapel air.

When it was time for me to read, I felt the familiar clutch of panic, but Keith smiled encouragingly and Christy's bracelet was warm around my wrist. I walked to the front of the room and took a deep breath. I had read "Elegy for Jane" many times in the past twenty-four hours. I knew it by heart. As I said the lines, I looked at Christy Sinclair's small band of mourners: at Jill Osiowy, head bowed, red hair falling forward to curtain her face; at Keith, whose eyes never left mine; at Greg, whose arm rested on my daughter's shoulder as if by his touch he could protect her; at my adult children, backs ramrod straight but sitting so close together you couldn't have passed a paper between them, reassuring one another as they always had that, no matter what, they had each other.

Behind them, the four young women listened to Roethke's words with closed faces. The final stanza of "Elegy for Jane" had always seemed to me to be heartbreakingly beautiful.

> If only I could nudge you from this sleep,
> My maimed darling, my skittery pigeon.
> Over this damp grave I speak the words of my love:
> I, with no rights in this matter.

As I recited the words, one of the girls began to cry.

She wasn't the only one. When I came to the last line of the poem, I was crying, too – for Roethke's Jane and for Christy Sinclair who had no one but me to speak the words over her grave.

The rain hadn't let up when we left the funeral chapel. There was a kind of portico outside the entranceway, and the young women were there in their thin jackets, looking up at the sky.

I went over to them. "Can we give you a lift anywhere?" I asked.

They stepped back from me as if I were an infection, but one of them, the tiny blonde who had wept during the poem, stood her ground.

"We're okay," she said.

I looked at her. Her peroxided curls were dark at the roots like Madonna's, and her skin beneath its heavy makeup had the telltale bumps of pubescence. There were streaks of mascara down her cheeks from her tears. I took a Kleenex from my bag and held it out to her.

"Your mascara has run a little," I said.

She grabbed the tissue and began scrubbing at the area under her eyes.

"Every time I wear this goddamn stuff, somebody makes me cry," she said.

"Same here," I agreed.

For a beat, the mask dropped, and she looked at me with real interest.

"Were you a friend of Christy's?" I asked.

The girl's face closed in on itself again, and she turned on her heel and stepped into the rain.

"Please, could we talk just for a moment?" I called after her.

She didn't look back. The others followed her, and I was left on the steps of the funeral home watching the four of them clip along Cornwall Street in their perilously high heels. The rain kept on coming, plastering their stirrup pants to their legs, soaking their thin jackets, bouncing impotently off the gelled curls and the hard-sprayed frizz of their elaborate hairdos. Finally, they turned a corner and vanished into the mist of the rainy city.

There are 180,000 people in Regina. Chance encounters are not unheard of here; still, running into Kim Barilko less than twenty-four hours after talking to her outside the funeral home seemed like a cosmic stretch.

I had dropped Taylor off at nursery school and come downtown to do a couple of errands. Later I was going to pick Taylor up, help Pete get organized for the trip to Swift Current, then meet Mieka and Lorraine Harris at the bridal salon for Mieka's first fitting on her wedding dress. A high-stress day.

I'd taken care of my business, and I was walking along Scarth Street toward the place I'd parked the car. The wet weather had continued. It was a grey muggy day, coast weather. There was a bridal shop on Scarth; in the gloom, its window, bright with paper apple blossoms and summer wedding gowns, was an appealing sight. I stopped to look. There was something surreal about all those mannequin brides in their virginal white. I could see my reflection in the window: a flesh-and-blood imperfect middle-aged woman in the midst of all that synthetic flawless youth. And then there was another reflection, just behind me: a young woman with the hips-forward slouch of a street kid and Madonna hair. I turned. For a split second she didn't notice me, and I was able to see her face as she looked at that fairy-tale dress. Her mouth curved with derision, but her eyes were filled with terrifying hope. I didn't want to see any more.

"Remember me?" I said. "We talked yesterday after Christy Sinclair's funeral."

She was wearing yesterday's stirrup pants and a sleeveless blouse the colour of an orange Popsicle; her lipstick was that same improbable orange, but frosted. A cross hung between her small breasts.

"I remember you," she said and she smiled. "You've got the same problem with Maybelline that I have."

There was a Dairy Queen next to the bridal shop. "Could we have a cup of coffee together – my treat?" I asked. "I'd like to talk about Christy Sinclair a little if it's okay with you."

She shrugged her thin shoulders. "Sure, I'm not going any-where. But her name was Theresa, not Christy."

"Theresa?" I said.

"Like in Terry," she said, "or the saint. If you hadn't put the picture in the paper we wouldn't have known it was her because of the wrong name." She opened her bag and pulled out the obituary. She tapped at it with an orange fingernail.

"That's Theresa," she said.

"What was her last name?" I asked.

The mask fell over her face again. "Look, I don't think I've got time for a coffee, after all."

"Can I drive you somewhere or just walk along with you?"

"It's a free country," she said, and then more kindly she added, "I have to get to the Lily Pad and help with lunch. It's my day."

"Is the Lily Pad a restaurant?"

She laughed, a short, unpleasant sound. "Yeah, it's a restaurant, a restaurant for people with no money."

"I'm sorry," I said.

"Why?" she said. "You don't have to eat there."

We both laughed, and when she began walking toward Albert Street, I fell into step with her. "My name's Joanne Kilbourn," I said.

"I'm Kim Barilko," she said.

She made good time, despite her stiletto heels.

"So," I said, "how did you know Theresa?"

"From home and then at the Lily Pad," she said. "She was going to be my mentor, but with my luck, of course, she goes and dies. I should have known better." Kim's lip curled with contempt at her gullibility.

"You're going too fast for me," I said. "Could you fill me in a little?"

"The Lily Pad is a place for runaways, street kids?" At the end of the sentence, her voice rose, and she watched my face for a sign of comprehension. When she saw what she was looking for, she continued. "They serve food and coffee and you can go there and watch TV or have a shower or just hang together. There's a lot of system stuff, crafts and counsellors and programs to help you learn a job. It's a hassle-free zone. Nobody's allowed to dick you around, not your parents, not your old man, nobody."

"Sounds good," I said.

She shrugged. "And there are mentors. Girls who have good jobs and great clothes and great lives, and they come in and talk to us and then they choose someone to kind of help along the way. Terry chose me, because she wanted to help a girl from home. Besides, she said she saw something in me."

"I can see it, too," I said. "Incidentally, how old are you?"

"Fifteen," she said.

A year older than Angus.

The Lily Pad was on Albert Street, not far from the city centre. It was an old house with the graceful lines of a building designed in the first years of the century. On the front lawn a wooden frog sunned himself on a lily pad. No words. On the grass and on the front steps, kids sat smoking. I had spent my life surrounded by children, but kids like these still tore at me. The dead eyes, the defiance, the sure knowledge that they were just putting in time before they entered their life's work as members of the permanent underclass. When I thought about what lay ahead of them, it was hard to believe we'd inched very far along the evolutionary scale.

They moved aside to let us pass as we went up the front steps, but whether we were there or not there was obviously a matter of indifference to them. Kim didn't comment about them or about anything. There was a bulletin board on the wall of the entranceway. Pinned to the top was a sign: "The Sharing Place." The board was empty. A door to what must have been the upstairs was blocked off by an old pine sideboard.

"Don't you use the upstairs?" I asked.

"No," Kim said, "they're afraid we'll set the place on fire. You know, from our unhealthy habit of smoking." She gave me a deadpan look. "When you're dealing with a dysfunctional population, you can't be too careful."

I didn't know what to say.

"That was a joke," Kim said. "Come on. I gotta get lunch started."

I followed her through a large front room filled with over-stuffed furniture that had obviously been rescued from a dozen different basements. In the corner Big Bird was singing about his neighbourhood on a large-screen TV. No one was watching. We walked down a dark hall to the kitchen. Money had been spent here. The floor shone, and the indus-trial-sized appliances were new and expensive. Kim went to the sink and washed her hands, then she took a slab of ham-burger meat from the refrigerator and threw it in an iron frying pan on the stove.

"Chili," she said. She began breaking up the meat with a fork. "I never knew anybody like Theresa in my life. She was like a person on TV, pretty and smart, and she had such great clothes, and that little red convertible of hers was so amazing." She jabbed at the still frozen centre of the ham-burger viciously. "Maybe she liked me because I admired her so much."

"There are worse reasons," I said.

The meat sizzled and Kim stirred it. A splash of grease flew up onto her Popsicle-coloured blouse.

"Shit," she said. "Shit on a stick." She looked at me sadly. "Theresa would never say anything like that. She was a lady like Julia Roberts in that movie *Pretty Woman*. I musta rented that video twenty times." Her voice fell. "Anyway, Theresa wanted to make me a lady, too."

Kim began opening tins of kidney beans and tomatoes and throwing them into the pan with the meat. She stirred the mixture with a wild, hostile energy.

"She told me she was going to teach me about clothes and hair, and we were going to talk about going back to school. She had this business and she was going to, like, train me . . ."

Behind me a voice, smooth, professionally understanding, said, "Kim, you know the rules about visitors."

The first thing I noticed about the man in the doorway was that he had the kind of unvarying mahogany tan he could have achieved only in a tanning salon. "Fake-and-bake tans," Mieka called them. In fact, he looked like a fake-and-bake kind of guy: he was about Keith's age, mid-fifties, but he was dressed like a fashion magazine's idea of a college kid, UBC sweatshirt, designer jeans, white sport socks, white cross-trainers. His hair had been professionally streaked, and whoever did it had done a better job than the hairdresser who did mine.

"No visitors in the kitchen, Kim," he said pleasantly. Then he turned his smile on me. It was as dazzling as the gold chain around his neck. "I'm sorry Kim forgot to share our rule with you."

"You run a tight ship," I said.

"We have to," he said.

Kim turned away without a word. Her face as she stirred the chili was impassive. She had withdrawn again. She was back in that detached and distant zone where nobody could dick her around. I touched her on the shoulder.

"Thanks for telling me about Theresa," I said. "I still can't get used to calling her that. I never told you my connection with her. She wanted to marry my son, and she felt very close to me. I never knew her."

Kim took a bag of chili powder from the cupboard and began shaking it into the pan. "You blew it," she said.

The man raised his eyebrows. "I think we should let Kim get on with her cooking. There are a lot of us looking forward to her famous chili. We all have our jobs here at the Lily Pad."

"What's yours?" I said.

Out of the corner of my eye, I saw Kim grin. I was glad she knew I was on her side.

His smile widened, but as he looked at me his eyes were appraising. "Why, I'm Helmut Keating, the co-ordinator," he said. "If you'd like to step into my office on your way out, I can share some information with you about how we operate here at the Lily Pad."

Behind Helmut's back, Kim carefully mouthed the word "*asshole.*" I nodded in agreement. Then I smiled at Helmut.

"Let's get in there and share," I said.

When I left, I was carrying a manila folder with some photocopied diagrams of the administrative structure of the Lily Pad and a half-dozen slick brochures to hand around to people I thought would be interested in making a contribution. "We rely on our friends," Helmut said smoothly as he walked me out the door and down the front steps.

It was a little after eleven-thirty. It was still muggy and overcast, and the kids were still sitting on the lawn smoking. None of them looked as eager to have their lives transformed as the attractive kids in the Lily Pad's four-colour brochure.

I drove to Taylor's playschool. She was waiting in the doorway with her teacher. When she saw me, she came running, and I felt a rush of pleasure. She was carrying a cardboard egg carton.

"Look," she said breathlessly. "The other kids started theirs before I came, so I was late, but teacher says it's never too late. Look at them. They all sprouted."

There were twelve bean plants in the dirt that filled the indentations.

"Do you know the story of Jack and the Beanstalk, Jo?"

"Maybe you could tell me while we plant those. If we hurry, we've got time before lunch. I thought we'd make something special. Pete's going back to his job today, remember?"

"Holding cows for the animal doctor," Taylor said seriously.

"Right," I said.

An hour later, beans planted, the kids and I were sitting down to gazpacho and warm sourdough bread. Pete had always been strong and resilient – "Peter is unflappable," his kindergarten teacher had written in a report-card comment that became a family joke. But that day as I watched him eat lunch, I wondered if there'd been too many blows. The visit to the people he and Christy knew in Saskatoon had been painful; the funeral had been worse. But it was the news that Christy had committed suicide that devastated him. He felt he was responsible, and nothing any of us said could convince him otherwise.

I didn't believe in keeping secrets from the kids. Most of the time, I thought it was best to know the truth and work from there. But as I looked at Pete across the table, pale and unnaturally quiet, I knew this wasn't most of the time. I decided not to tell him about my visit with Kim Barilko. And so we were both quiet, and I was glad Angus and Taylor were there to fill up the silences.

When Angus went back to school, Taylor went out to sit with her bean garden, and Pete and I were alone.

"I don't want to go back there," he said.

"I know," I said. "But it's the best thing. You'll be busy doing something you like, with people who didn't know Christy. And you'll be in those beautiful, beautiful hills. That's healing country down there."

He pushed his chair away from the table. "This'll put it to the test," he said grimly.

As his car turned the corner, I closed my eyes, crossed my fingers and prayed that time and distance would work their magic.

I could hear the phone ringing as soon as I went back in the house.

It was Jill. "Guess who just phoned me?" she said. "Bernice Morin's boyfriend."

"That little punk Darren Wolfe," I said.

Jill laughed. "That's a bit harsh for you, Jo."

"One of the cops who came to Judgements the morning Bernice died said it. I guess it just stuck in my mind."

"It's probably accurate enough," Jill said mildly, "but punk or not, Darren's in big trouble. He got arrested for Bernice's murder this morning. He says he's innocent, that somebody's framing him. Of course, guys like Darren are always being framed."

"How come he called you?" I asked.

"He needs money for a lawyer. He says the lawyers the court provides are either dykes or dweebs. He heard on the street that the network was working on the Little Flower case, so he's offered to give me the real story – in return for compensation, of course."

"Are you going to do it?"

"I can't," she said, "but I am going to talk to him. If he really is innocent, there are other ways to help him. Jo, I probably won't be able to get to see him till tomorrow, but I thought you might want to come along."

I thought, I don't want to do this. I don't want to step to the edge of the abyss again. Images flashed into my mind – the teddy bear tattoo on Bernice Morin's left buttock, the single entry under "Identifying Marks" in Christy's autopsy report – "left buttock, tattoo, 3 cm, bear-shaped, not recent." I knew I didn't have a choice.

"Yes," I said, "I'll come. Just let me know the time and place. I'll be there."

I hung up and walked to the kitchen window. Taylor was sitting cross-legged in her garden, looking at the place in the ground where she'd planted her beans. For a long while, I watched her. Suddenly, she looked at the window. When she saw me, her face was bright with happiness, and she jumped up and came running toward the house.

"I think they've already grown more, Jo," she said.

"We'll probably be able to have beans for supper," I said.

For a split second, she believed me, then she grinned. "Oh, Jo," she said wearily. "Another joke." She came over and put her arms around me. As I held her close, I remembered other times when it had happened just like this, times when, at the very moment when I was sure the darkness was going to swallow me, there would be a moment of pure joy. I kissed Taylor's ear.

"Come on," I said. "Time to get the bean dirt off. We have to go help some ladies sew Mieka into her wedding dress."

CHAPTER

7

When I awoke the morning after Peter left, my bedroom was filled with light and birdsong, good omens. The digital clock on my radio read six o'clock, early, but when I looked at the sun streaming in, the waking world seemed to have a lot to recommend it. I brushed my teeth, pulled on my swimsuit and went down to the pool. The dogs, ever optimistic, followed at my heels in case I decided to change course and take them for a run. I disappointed them, but it was worth it. When I dived into the pool, I felt the thrill of physical well-being, and after twenty minutes of laps, the heaviness of the day before had left my body, and I was full of hope.

It was, I decided, time to get back to work. Lost in the mountain of unpacked cartons in the garage was a box of newspaper clippings, political articles I had saved during the past year because they seemed worth thinking about again. I could start there. We were due for a federal election in the fall. I could write a book about the campaign from the provincial viewpoint. I switched from the breast stroke to the crawl. "Sky's the limit," I said. "All you need to do is start. The time is now." I pulled myself up on the side of the pool, ready to go.

Taylor was just coming out of the house. Her face was still rosy from sleep, and she was ripping off her pyjama top with one hand and trying to pull on her bathing suit with the other.

"I'm coming, Jo. Wait for me. I'll show you my dog-paddle."

She put her arms around my neck, and the ground-breaking book on the upcoming election was temporarily on hold. By seven o'clock, Angus had joined us and we were all sitting at the picnic bench in our bathing suits eating cereal. When he finished, Angus went in to watch the sports news on TV.

I turned to Taylor. "We've got time to do a little work before you go to school. Why don't you bring out your drawing stuff while I read the paper?"

She brought her sketch pad and her case of coloured pencils, always so carefully arranged and sharpened, sat down opposite me and began to draw. Today it was baseball players, and as I watched the blank page fill up with kids in baseball uniforms pitching and hitting and leaping off the page to catch a hard-hit ball, I was humbled by her ability. Even her face seemed to change when she made art. The ordinary little girl who couldn't sit still for a story or remember to flush the toilet was transformed into someone else, a disciplined person who loved her work and knew it was good. When Taylor was drawing, I could see her mother in the set of her mouth and in her stillness. It was a good feeling.

I still hadn't read the front page of the *Globe and Mail* when Jill called.

"Two things," she said. "One, we can see Darren Wolfe at nine o'clock this morning. Two . . . No, I'm not telling you about two till I see you. I want to watch your reaction."

It was a little after eight-thirty when Jill rang our front doorbell. She was wearing a white silk blouse, a navy blazer and grey slacks.

So was I.

"We look like the Bobbsey Twins," I said.

"Nah," Jill said. "One of the Bobbsey Twins was a boy. We're just fashionable – the faux prison guard look is really hot this spring."

When we turned onto the Albert Street Bridge, Jill said, "Are you ready for the big news?"

"As long as it's good," I said.

Jill laughed. "I think it is. How would you like to be one of the panellists on *Canada Today*?"

Canada Today was a new show Jill's network was trying over the summer months, nightly at seven, half an hour of national news, then half an hour of a political panel. There were five proposed panels, one from each region, one for each night.

"I thought that was all set," I said, surprised. "Wasn't there an article in the paper last week saying you were going with the presidents of the provincial parties?"

"That was last week," she said briskly. "Today the presidents are 'too narrowly partisan, too likely to be idealogues.' At least that's what the fax says. Today what we have in mind is Senator Sam Steinitz, Keith Harris, and you."

"God, Jill, let me catch my breath. That's pretty high-powered company. Am I there as the token female?"

"No, you're there as the token person with a progressive mind," she snapped. "Say yes."

"Yes," I said.

"Good," she said. "Listen, I'm going to produce the first few shows myself. The network's got big plans for this show. There's bound to be an election in the fall, and they think *Canada Today* could grab an audience. Not much of what we do here goes national, so I want to make sure this doesn't look like Aaron Slick from Punkin Crick."

"When do we start?" I said.

"June third. That's a week from Monday," she said. "Soon, I know, but you're a quick study. I'll have some specific topics for you by the weekend, but if you can't wait to get started you can spend the afternoon thinking about something general, like where you think the country should be heading."

"Whither Canada?" I said. "Hasn't that been done?"

"Not by you," Jill said.

"Okay, whither Canada it is," I said. "And Jill, thanks."

"For what?"

"For thinking of me."

"It wasn't me, Jo. When I went into my office this morning, there was your name. It had arrived miraculously, by fax."

"Miraculously from where?"

"On high," she said. "On highest. The fax came from the office of Con O'Malley himself. The president of the network."

"How would the president of NationTV know about me? Jill, doesn't this seem a bit weird to you?"

She shrugged. "Not so weird, Jo. Your publisher's in Toronto, right? He and Con were probably hoisting a few at the Boys' Club last night, and you know how these things work. This morning when somebody got the bright idea of changing the panel, your name was front and centre in Con's mind. He prides himself on being a hands-on guy. Being able to suggest a name in Saskatchewan is just the kind of thing that he'd get off on. Believe me, Jo, whatever the explanation is, it will be that simple. Now, relax and give yourself up to the pleasures of life in the fast lane of TV journalism."

We drove north along Winnipeg Street, turned right at the heavy-oil upgrader and rolled up our windows as we passed the city dump. When Jill's ancient Lincoln started bumping along the country road that took us to the Regina Correctional Centre, I tapped her on the arm.

"So this is life in the fast lane," I said.

I had been to the correctional centre before. I remembered it as a depressing and forbidding place. It still was. After we were cleared through security, a guard took us to the visitors' area. Everything about the room was uniform, drab, institutional. Everything, that is, except Darren Wolfe. He was waiting for us on the prisoner side of the Plexiglas divider, and he was one of a kind.

His blond hair was parted in the centre, and it fell almost to his waist. His eyes, eyebrows and the roots of his hair were black. A gold cross hung from his left ear. He wore black leather pants, skin tight, a black leather vest taut against his bare chest and a kind of Edwardian smoking jacket of red and black velvet.

"They let them wear their own clothes till after sentencing," Jill whispered.

"Just as well," I said. "I think Darren would be pretty lost without his plumage."

There was a speaker phone on our side of the Plexiglas, and as soon as we were all seated, Jill leaned forward and introduced me to Darren Wolfe. She said I was the mother of the woman who had found Bernice's body.

Darren looked at me without much interest. "Yeah?" he said. "That must've been a bad start to your daughter's day."

Ingratiating, saying what he thought I wanted to hear. I felt a chill.

"It was a tragedy for us all. From what my daughter said, Bernice was an interesting young woman."

"Yeah," he agreed, "she was that." He nodded his head, remembering. "She was her own worst enemy. She was just a kid when I met her, but she'd already hustled for a coupla years. That mouth a hers had got her thrown out of her last setup. They couldn't intimidate her."

I looked at the preening boy across the table from me, and my mind started to float. Bernice had gotten her prize tattoo the morning after he beat her up. She had endured three hours of agony to get a picture of unicorns etched into her upper back because unicorns were her totem; like her, they were too proud to get intimidated.

"Anyway, I didn't do her," Darren Wolfe was saying. He had turned his attention to Jill. Conversation with me was pointless; I couldn't get him a deal with the network.

He leaned forward so that his forehead was almost touching the glass divider. His mouth was sullen, and his eyes were angry. "They haven't got anything," he said. "I knocked her around a few times, but it wasn't personal. Jesus, everybody fought with that bitch. Anyway, I don't do girls." He looked quickly around the room to see who was there. Then he lowered his voice. "Look, the truth is, I haven't got any bodies."

"What?" I asked.

He looked at me, exasperated. "I haven't got any bodies." He moved closer and dropped his voice. "I've never killed anybody." Having confessed the worst, he was restored. He straightened up, and his mouth curled into arrogance. "So, Jill," he said, "I've got some things to say that you oughta hear."

For the next twenty minutes Darren Wolfe gave us a conducted tour through the world of the Little Flower murders. I felt as if I'd stepped through the looking glass. The world Darren described, casually violent, retributive, vicious, seemed in every way alien from my own. But it wasn't. The streets Darren Wolfe drove on in the course of his business day were the same streets I drove on; the street corners his girls worked were the street corners I walked past; the hotels and apartment blocks where they turned tricks were part of my landscape. By the time he finished, I was badly shaken, and he saw that.

One thing Darren Wolfe knew was women. He wanted me on his side, and he knew I wasn't. When Jill and I stood up to leave, he reached toward me, flattening his fingertips against the Plexiglas the way prisoners do in movies.

"Look," he said, "I know you think I should be all broken up about Bernice. I can live with that, but before you write me off, you've gotta understand one thing. Bernice wasn't like the kind of girls you know. Girls like Bernice, they ask for it."

"Girls like Bernice . . ." As I walked to the car, Darren Wolfe's dismissal pounded in my head. As I opened the door on the passenger side, I remembered another judgement. Hours before she died, Christy Sinclair had sounded the same chord of death, justice and dismissal: "When girls like Bernice die," she had said, her voice trembling, "it's just biological destiny . . . They're born with a gene for self-destruction."

Jill didn't say anything till we were pulling out of the prison parking lot. "Sorry you came along?" she asked.

"No," I said. "Just in a state of shock. How does a boy like that live with himself?"

"He sees himself as a businessman, Jo. Out there like the other guys, showing a little hustle, operating in accordance with the laws of supply and demand. I'll bet you a hundred dollars he sleeps like a baby."

"I'll bet his girls don't," I said. I was wearing the silver bracelet Christy had given me, and my finger traced the lines of the Celtic letters. "Wandering Soul Pray For Me."

"How do you break the cycle?" I said. "How can you make it possible for people to have good lives?" Kim Barilko's face, mascara-streaked, defiant, flashed before my eyes. "Every

time I wear this goddamn stuff, somebody makes me cry."
How many times, I thought. How many times had someone
made Kim Barilko cry?

I remembered the light in her eyes when she'd talked
about all the things Christy Sinclair was going to teach her.
Then I remembered the derisive curve of her lip as she
talked about how stupid she had been to believe anything
good could happen to her.

Fifteen seemed pretty young to be giving up on life. I
turned to Jill. "How would you like to be a mentor?" I asked.

"Yours, Jo? Finally admitting you need some guidance? I'd
be delighted. You can start by throwing out all those sensible shoes you're so fond of."

"I'll do that," I said. "But actually the person who needs
someone to be her teacher, guide and friend is a lot more
adventurous in her clothing than I am."

When I finished telling her about Kim Barilko, Jill didn't
hesitate. "I'd be honoured, Jo. I really would. But not today.
Listen, I've decided I'm going to really move on this Little
Flower case. I've tried to get Toronto to give me a budget for
this, but they say, with restraints and all, we should be doing
upbeat stories with wide audience appeal. 'Celebratory' was
the word my immediate superior used, I believe. Anyway,
give me the weekend to see if any of Darren's leads pan out.
First thing Monday morning I'll go over to the Lily Pad, and
we can get started."

"Jill, would you mind if I went over there after lunch and
talked to her? I hate to think of Kim going through the
weekend without some good news."

"Of course I don't mind. Maybe she'd like to come to my
office Monday. I could show her around and take her for lunch
in the cafeteria. Most kids get a kick out of watching the
people they've seen on TV eat their tuna fish sandwiches."

"Thanks, Jill."

"For what? Trying to redress the balance a little? Don't you think it's about time?"

I picked Taylor up at school. "Samantha's birthday party," she said as she got in the car. "It's today. Do we have a present?"

"Wrapped and on the dining room table," I said.

"What is it?"

"An onion tree. Every time Sam takes off an onion, two more will grow in its place."

Taylor looked into my face. "That's a joke, right?"

"That's a joke, right!" I said, and we both laughed.

After lunch I was in the front yard watering the geraniums when Taylor came out. She was carrying the birthday present, and she was wearing a pink party dress, her baseball shirt, baseball socks and runners.

"How would you like a mentor to advise you about your clothes?" I said.

She grinned at me.

I didn't fall for it. "T., you're going to have to change," I said. "Why didn't you wear what I put out for you?"

"Because I felt happy," she said.

It was the first time she had said that since her mother died. If I'd had a party dress and baseball socks handy, I would have worn them myself. I reached down and took her hand.

"Good enough," I said. "Let's go to Samantha's party."

After I dropped Taylor off, I drove downtown to the Lily Pad. Not much had changed. The wooden frog still sunned himself on the lawn, and the kids still smoked on the steps. When I walked past them, they looked at me incuriously through dead eyes. The front door was open and I went in. Someone had tacked up a sign on the Sharing Place: "Global

thought for the day: Have a birthday party for the world."
On the TV in the living room, Oprah was talking about relationships; no one was watching. I kept on going. The state-
of-the-art kitchen was gleaming and empty. On the counter,
what looked like twenty pounds of standing rib roast thawed
on a tray.

I was trying to decide what to do next when my friend
Helmut came in. I hadn't liked him the day before and I
didn't like him now. He was wearing a sweatshirt that said,
"Let Me Be Part of Your Dream." When he greeted me, his
smile was as dazzling as ever, but there was no mistaking
the hostility in his eyes.

I gestured toward the rib roast. "Good groceries," I said.

He moved between me and the meat. Incredibly, it seemed
as if he was trying to keep it a secret.

"Don't hide it," I said. "You deserve praise. Not many
drop-in centres for runaways serve prime rib."

"I thought I shared the rule about visitors the last time
you were here, Joanne," he said.

"You know my name," I said. "Who told you?"

The smile was even more forced. "I don't think that's
something you need to know."

"I think it would help us relate," I said. "Caring people
shouldn't have secrets from one another."

"Kim told me," he said.

Not in a million years, I thought. But I smiled at him.
"Well, Kim is the person I've come to talk to."

He gestured to the empty kitchen. "As you can see, she's
not here."

"Do you expect her back soon?"

Helmut shrugged. "The kids who come here are dysfunctional, Joanne. They aren't big planners. People come. People
go. It's called a transient population."

"What about your mentor program?" I asked.

I could see the muscles in his neck tighten, but his smile grew even wider. "That's one of our few failures. We had to abandon it. There were too many jealousies. Adolescent girls tend to be emotionally labile."

"Pretty sudden decision, wasn't it?" I said. "I'm sure Kim Barilko wasn't the only young woman who was looking forward to having a chance at a different kind of life."

Helmut Keating looked at me stonily. "We have programs here at the Lily Pad," he said, "as you would have discovered if you'd read the brochures I gave you."

"How can the programs help Kim when you don't know where she is?" I asked.

Helmut narrowed his eyes.

"Just asking," I said. "I don't think we're communicating very well here, Helmut. Maybe I'd better let you get that million-dollar roast in the oven. Is there someplace I could leave a message?"

"The Sharing Place," he said tightly.

I wrote a note to Kim, telling her that a friend of mine who worked in television was interested in meeting her, and I left my name and phone number. I pinned it right under "Have a birthday party for the world."

That night Keith called and we went to a new East Indian restaurant. We ate samosas and curried shrimp and groped at each other under the table. It was a nice evening, and it seemed to usher in a nice weekend. Saturday morning the kids and I enrolled Taylor in a summer art class at the old campus, then we went downtown and shopped for the endless items on Angus's camp list. In the afternoon, I sat on the deck and read political journals while Taylor and her friend Samantha splashed around in the pool.

Sunday evening I went to the shower Lorraine was giving

for Mieka. It was the first time I'd been inside Lorraine's Regina apartment. The floor plan was the twin of Keith's, but the decor was coolly modern – all white. The only touches of colour in the room were the silvery wrapping paper of the gifts piled high on the table beside the window, the pink of the sweetheart roses that bloomed from a crystal bowl beside the chair for the bride-to-be, and the ice-cream pastels of the dresses the guests were wearing.

It was an evening that unfolded itself impressionistically, in a series of flashes that somehow revealed the whole. The rosy pink of the cold lobster in the seafood salad was the same shade exactly as the chilled rosé Lorraine handed around in her delicately fluted glasses. Lorraine's friends, brilliantly fashionable, talked in throaty voices about new cars and old boyfriends or old cars and new boyfriends; no one seemed to care which. My daughter, who had always despaired of her looks, bloomed into beauty as she breathed in air perfumed by spring roses and listened to her friends' gently mocking talk of love.

There were other flashes, equally sharp but more unsettling: the faint shudder of distaste that ran through Lorraine Harris's body when she overheard Jill and me talking about my visit that day to the Lily Pad. Lorraine's eyes, stern behind her horn-rimmed glasses, as she laughingly warned me against raising unpleasant topics at my daughter's wedding shower. The two elegant women, friends of Lorraine's, who heard me mention Helmut Keating's name and came over to gossip about him and the Lily Pad.

"Of course, I'm on the board," said the first woman, "so I see a fair bit of Helmut. He's a bit too free with the jargon, but he works hard and the kids seem to love him. He's a very caring guy."

The second woman, who had had several glasses of rosé, roared. "And don't forget that fabulous streaking job. Now

whoever did that is an artist. I think there's a song there,"
she said. "Helmie has great hair and it's only fair 'cause he's
a very caring guy."

The first woman smiled and took her friend's arm. "Time
to say good night," she said. And they did.

And one last vignette. Just before the party broke up, there
was a knock at the door; it was Blaine Harris. I could see his
nurse, Sean, waiting in the hallway, but Blaine propelled his
own wheelchair across the room and handed Mieka a long
blue jeweller's box, tied with a white ribbon. Mieka opened
it, held the gold locket that was inside up for everyone to
see, then fastened the chain around her neck.

The old man watched intently, then made a saluting
gesture to Mieka and wheeled himself through the door into
the hall. The whole scene couldn't have taken much more
than a minute, but by the time Blaine Harris left, there
wasn't a dry eye in the room.

It was a nice moment, and as I walked home, warmed by
that memory and by other memories of the glowing party, I
decided it was time to stop worrying about the things I
couldn't change and to start cherishing the good things in
my life.

During the next week I tried. I read; I went over to the TV
station and watched tapes of politicians and press confer-
ences and pundits; I took Taylor to two art galleries to see
new exhibits; I shopped and made the final purchases on
Angus's camp list. I even bought a mother-of-the-bride dress
in aquamarine silk. Mieka was so relieved she took me out
for ice cream and a movie. It was a week in the life of a lucky
woman. And every night before I slept I could feel Christy's
bracelet burning warm on my wrist; every morning when I
stretched for the day, I could feel the bracelet's weight heavy
on my arm.

I found I made detours. I took not the shortest route between stops but the one that would take me close to the Lily Pad where I could run in and check the Sharing Place. "Have a birthday party for the world" gave way to "Wave to a bird because you cannot fly," then "Wake up early and dance for the sunrise," but there was never a message for me from Kim. Three times I went to the bridal store where I had come upon Kim by chance the day after Christy's funeral. I ached to see her. I ached to right the wrong I had done to Christy. I ached to redress the balance.

Monday, June third, I did the first television show. Keith picked me up and we drove to the studio together at five-thirty. We walked through the glass and steel lobby with pictures of the network stars suspended from the ceiling like the banners of medieval knights. A young woman, slender and fashionable in a black jumpsuit and odd socks, one pink, one turquoise, led us along corridors to an underground room where another young woman put makeup on us. She looked at Keith's solid pale-blue suit approvingly and flicked his face with a powder puff. When it was my turn, she said my makeup was pretty good. She did some deft things with eyeshadow. "Brown is always more natural looking," she whispered. She touched my earlobes with blush, then stood back and looked at me appraisingly. I had bought a new dress for the show, flowered silk, pretty as a summer garden.

"Next time," she said kindly, "try to find a solid colour. That's going to make you look like you're wearing your bedroom curtains." She looked at her watch, grinned and said, "Showtime. Knock 'em dead."

The young woman with the odd socks marched us through a corridor to the studio.

"I like your dress," Keith said.

"You'd like my bedroom," I said.

We got microphones, Jill introduced me to Sam Steinitz, who arrived breathless from the airport, and we were away. It seemed to go all right, but I was immensely relieved when it was over. When they took off the microphones, Keith turned to me and grinned. "Well, shall we go over to my place and debrief?"

We stopped at a French deli and bought crusty bread and cold cuts and a salad made of tomatoes, fresh basil and ripe Brie. Then we went to Keith's, debriefed and sat on the balcony eating dripping sandwiches, drinking wine and analyzing each other's performances. I decided I liked TV.

Keith drove me home around ten-thirty. Mieka and Greg were sitting at the kitchen table poring over the guest list. They gave me a standing ovation when I came in. I kissed Mieka and she made a face.

"Oh, why do I find myself suddenly thinking of Provence?" she said. "I don't suppose you brought leftovers."

I held up a greasy bag.

"You suppose wrong," I said. She and Greg attacked the bag like kids, and Mieka ran through the evening's messages. There were calls from old political friends, most of whom, according to Mieka, wanted to tell me what to say next time. Peter had called collect. He'd been in the middle of nowhere when the show came on, but had found a pub with a TV and made everybody watch his mother. He'd liked the show, and he said the guys in the bar thought I seemed sharp for a woman. My old friend Hilda McCourt called from Saskatoon to tell me I deferred to Keith and Sam Steinitz too much and that solid colours tended to photograph well and make the wearer look slim, but that she thought I had a future in TV. Keith and I had a final glass of wine with the kids, and by eleven-thirty, I was showered and in my nightgown. When I turned down the bedspread, I saw the picture

Taylor had left for me. It was called "Jo on TV." I was smiling and wearing my flowery dress. I looked very thin and very fashionable. When I went to tuck her in, I gave her an extra hug. That night I went to bed happy.

The next day I got a message from Kim Barilko.

CHAPTER

8

The morning of June fourth was glorious: hot, blue-skied, alive with possibilities. After I showered, I took the dogs for a run, got the kids off to school and sat down at the picnic bench with a cup of coffee. The tension of the first TV show was over; the kids were safe; the shoes I'd chosen to wear with my mother-of-the-bride dress were off being dyed. Life was under control. All I had to do was sit back and enjoy it. But I couldn't.

Half an hour later, wearing sandals, a black-and-white checked sundress and my Wandering Soul bracelet, I pulled up on the street in front of the Lily Pad. I walked up the sidewalk and made my way through the smokers on the front steps. By now they were used to me; I was as unremarkable to them as the wooden frog sunning himself on the lily pad on the front lawn. I went straight to the Sharing Place. My note was there, but there was still no answering message. As I walked to my car, I felt the familiar sting of defeat.

That's when I saw him. He was standing by my Volvo, slight, young, dressed to intimidate: sleeveless black shirt; skintight blue jeans, black hair pulled into a ponytail under a high-crowned black cowboy hat, black reflector glasses. He lit a cigarette and inhaled it lazily.

"I saw you on TV," he said. "It was on in the place where I was," he added quickly, in case he'd revealed something.

I could see myself reflected in his glasses. I seemed distorted. My forehead was huge, and my body seemed to dwindle off, caricaturelike, toward a point on the sidewalk.

"You're the one looking for Kim," he said.

My face in the shining black glass was suddenly alert.

"Yeah," I said. "I am."

"She'll meet you," he said. "Until last night she didn't believe it about you knowing someone on TV."

"Where can I find her?" I said.

"She'll find you," he said. "Tonight at the coffee shop in the bus station, ten-thirty." Then, for just a second, the tough-guy edge in his voice softened. "She's a good kid," he said. "She needs a lucky break."

I called Jill and told her the news. She sounded tired and discouraged.

"Maybe some good will come out of this after all," she said. "I'm certainly getting nowhere."

"Darren Wolfe's hot information wasn't so hot?" I said.

"Oh, it was hot, all right, at least I think it could be hot, but somebody needs to do a lot of digging, and the network is determined it isn't going to be us. I told you they were dragging their heels on this, so this morning I decided to fax Toronto all my notes from the interview with Darren. Jo, I was so sure if I just laid things out they'd see what a great story the Little Flower case is."

"And they didn't," I said.

"Twenty minutes ago I got a fax telling me in no uncertain terms that street journalism is not the network's mandate and that I'm the only regional news director who hasn't submitted plans for Canada Day coverage. Here I am sitting on one of the best stories of my life, and I have to shut everything down so I can call Eyebrow, Saskatchewan, and see what they're doing on July first."

I laughed. "I'll bet you a hundred thousand dollars they're having a softball tournament."

"No bet," she said. "Listen, Jo, see if you can shake anything loose from Kim tonight, would you? Specifically, about kids disappearing."

"You mean kids her age?"

"No, little kids."

I felt a chill. "Jill, what do you think's going on?"

"I don't know. I just get glimpses. Be careful, Jo. I'll tell you what I tell our interns from the school of journalism. Keep your eyes open, don't believe anything until you've heard it from three sources, tell only the people who need to know and always remember where the door is."

"Right," I said. I hung up and looked at my watch. It was going to be a long wait till ten-thirty. I went upstairs, made files for a box of clippings and started to organize my office. Busy work. At noon I picked up Taylor, and we drove downtown and offered to buy Mieka lunch at Mr. Tube Steak if she'd come and sit in the park with us. She did.

After lunch, Taylor and I had a swim and a nap and started to get ready for dinner. Keith was flying to Toronto that night, so I'd asked him over for an early barbecue.

Taylor and I made a potato salad and coleslaw. After she'd finished at Judgements, Mieka came by with a double chocolate cheesecake from another caterer. ("She's good, but I'm going to be better," she said, smiling, as she put the cake in the refrigerator.) Around five, Greg and Keith came over, and we barbecued chicken. It was a nice family evening. After coffee and dessert, I drove Keith to his place to pick up his bags. We walked upstairs together; when we opened the door, Keith's apartment was hot and airless.

"Air conditioner must have gone again," he said. "Do you want me to run inside and grab my bags? We can have a drink at the airport."

"Let's just sit out on your balcony," I said. "I've got some news about Kim Barilko, and I'd rather you were the only one who heard."

Keith took my hand and led me to the balcony. He was silent as I told him. When I finished, he looked at me searchingly. "Jo, are you sure you're not getting in too deep with all of this? The Hardy Boys stories are fun when you're a kid, but this sounds serious to me."

"Nancy Drew," I said.

Keith raised his eyebrows.

"For girls it was Nancy Drew," I said, "and I know it's serious, but, Keith, I can't just walk away. Kim Barilko isn't anybody's ideal fifteen-year-old, but she's funny and smart, and she deserves a chance not to be hassled by assholes."

"I take it that's a direct quote," Keith said.

"Pretty much," I said.

Suddenly there was a low moaning sound from the balcony below us. "Blaine's air conditioner must be broken, too," Keith said.

The air was split with hooting noises, and Keith smiled sadly. "Well, you are a miracle worker, Jo. Those are Blaine's approbation signs. He agrees with you. Blaine believes that Kim Barilko deserves a chance."

After I drove Keith to the airport, I came home, had a swim with the kids and got everybody settled for the night. Then I drove downtown. At ten-thirty I pulled into the parking lot opposite the bus station. Across the street at the Shrine Temple, men's laughter escaped through an open door into the hot night. The bus station was brightly lit. I went into the coffee shop, sat down at the counter and ordered iced tea. There was a Plexiglas wall between the coffee shop and the bus waiting room. I could see people sitting on benches, patient, still. Mostly they were native people or they were old. The past winter a once-famous newsman from the east had said that our city was dying, that soon the only people left in Regina would be old or native. For most of us that prospect seemed a lot more comfortable than living in a city filled with once-famous newsmen. I finished my tea and looked at the big clock over the coffee machines. It was ten forty-five.

The waitress came over and asked if I wanted a refill. She was a pretty young woman, with the dark slanted eyes some northern Cree people have. On her uniform was a button saying, "Smile, God Loves You."

I ordered another iced tea. She brought it, then picked up a damp cloth and began wiping down the counter.

"Closing time?" I said.

"I wish," she said.

The outside door opened and two young women came in. You didn't have to be a sociologist or a cop to know how they earned their living. Low-cut sweaters, high-cut skirts, bare legs, shoes with three-inch heels. The smaller of the women was holding her hand against her cheek. Without a word, the waitress scooped up some ice, dropped it in a cloth and handed it to her.

"Thanks, Albertine," the woman holding her face said. Her voice was muffled by her hand.

The other girl said, "Two Diet Cokes. Is it too late for fries?" Albertine shook her head, and the young woman with the swollen face said, "My lucky night. Two fries with gravy."

Then in the same flat voice with which she'd ordered the fries, she said to her companion, "Two blow jobs, two hand jobs and a half and half, so I'm thinking that's enough. It's too fucking hot for anybody to want to get laid, I'm going home, and if Rick says I didn't make my quota, tough. Then this suit pulls up in a Buick and we go to the Ramada, and it's cool there, and I think my fucking luck is maybe changing. A hundred, and all he wants is to do some lines of blow right off my belly, so it looks like an easy evening. Anyway, I'm lying there in the air conditioning with this pig snorting along my stomach, thinking I'll maybe get home in time to watch Letterman, when he goes berserk and starts beating the shit out of me. I got out of there, but the asshole just about caved in my face. Asshole." Then she lapsed into silence.

I got up and walked past them toward the bathroom. The one who had been talking had a pocket mirror in her hand. She was looking at her reflection with anxious eyes as she smoothed pancake makeup over the swelling line of her cheekbone.

When I came back, Albertine was bringing the Cokes and the fries and gravy – Angus's favourite, too. Up close, these girls didn't look much older than Angus, but, as I listened to their young voices trading street stories, I knew that the dates that appeared on their birth certificates were irrelevant. The morning Mieka had found Bernice Morin's body, one of the cops had given Bernice her epitaph. "She was a veteran," he had said. As I watched these girls, carefully eating French fries through lips thick with gloss, laughing at the vagaries of a world that should have been inconceivable, I thought that they were veterans, too.

Kim Barilko never showed up. I waited till midnight, then, bone weary and depressed, I gave up. I was tired of tilting at windmills. When I got home, I went upstairs to shower. After twenty minutes under the hot water, I still didn't feel clean.

The next morning was overcast – more than overcast. The skies were heavy with rain, and the air was ominously still.

When Taylor and I were leaving the house, the first drops began. Angus came out the front door just as we were getting in the car.

"Did you take out the garbage?" I asked.

He started with an excuse.

"No excuses," I said. "You better get it out quick before the rain hits."

Grumbling, he threw his books down on the porch and ran into the house. "You're my hero," I yelled, and Taylor and I drove off.

When I came back fifteen minutes later, it was raining hard. Angus's schoolbooks were still on the front porch. I went into the house, calling his name. Uneasy, I opened the door to the backyard. Angus wasn't there, and the gate that opened into the back alley was open. Angus never left that gate open. He always worried that harm would come to the dogs if they got out of our backyard. As I ran toward the gate, I felt the edge of panic.

There was a puddle just past the gate. I jumped it, but when I came down, I lost my footing in the mud and fell. In a split second, our collie, Sadie, was with me. My husband had always made jokes about Sadie. She was a beautiful animal, but not a smart one. Ian used to call her the show girl. That day the show girl was right on the money. She put her nose under my shoulder and tried to push me up. Then she barked and loped down the alley. She stopped in front of our garbage bin. Our other dog was there, and so was Angus. He was lying in the mud, moaning. I pushed myself up and went to him. His face was ashen.

"The garbage," he said, in a small, strangled voice.

"Don't worry about the garbage," I said. "What happened to you?"

Mute, he shook his head. His eyes were wide with shock. He put his arms around my neck and pulled himself up.

"Don't look in the garbage," he said.

I lifted him up and carried him into the house. He was a dead weight and he was covered in mud. I put him on the chair in the kitchen, and he sat there staring into space, holding his leg and crying. His behaviour scared me. Our kids had had their share of sports injuries, but after the first shock, they'd rallied. Angus wasn't rallying. In fact, he seemed to be sinking deeper into pain.

"I'm taking you to emergency," I said. "I think we should let a doctor have a look at you."

"Don't leave her there," he said. "We can't go to the hospital and just leave her out there."

"Leave who?" I said. "I got the dogs in. We're all okay."

"There's a girl out there in our garbage," he said. "She's dead."

I looked at him. Telling me seemed to calm him. I ran through the yard to the alley. Our city sanitation unit uses industrial waste bins, the kind a garbage truck can unload automatically. I looked into ours. On top of the garbage there was a girl. She was lying on her back. Her peroxided Madonna hair shot out like a halo around the bloody ruins of what had once been her face. Her shirt was soaked with blood, but the rain had washed one patch clean, and I could make out the original colour. Popsicle orange. I would have known it anywhere. Suddenly the air was split with the sound of screaming. Frozen, I listened until somewhere inside, I recognized the voice of the screamer as my own.

The next minutes still have a special terrible clarity for me. I ran to the house. I put on the kettle, called the doctor, and then I called the police. I called Mieka at Judgements, told her there had been a problem at home and asked her to pick Taylor up from school at lunchtime and take her somewhere. I could hear Mieka's voice, urgent, still asking questions, when I hung up the phone. The kettle boiled. I made

Angus tea with a lot of sugar and gave him two Aspirins, then I sat at the kitchen table with him until the police and our doctor came.

The police made it first. I had thought when I met Inspector Tom Zaba that he had the kind of face that was made for smiling, but when I looked at him as he came through the doorway of our kitchen that morning I thought he would never smile again. He was wearing a slicker and he was soaked with rain. Even the ends of his moustache drooped with wet. He looked ineffably sad.

When our doctor came, she took one look at Angus's leg and said he needed to be seen by an orthopedic surgeon. Inspector Zaba asked if he could talk to Angus first. She agreed.

Inspector Zaba was very gentle with Angus, and he was very gentle with me. But all the gentleness in the world couldn't undo the horror of what had happened to Kim Barilko. From my kitchen window I could see police cars driving along the rain-pounded alley, disgorging people into the muddy gravel so they could bag evidence and measure and photograph and turn the last hours of a human life into something that could be contained in a storage box. An RCMP cruiser pulled up, and I saw Constable Perry Kequahtooway get out. Outside the rain pounded on, implacable.

When I'd finished answering Inspector Zaba's questions, I stood up to go to the hospital with Angus.

Inspector Zaba stood, too. "One more question, Mrs. Kilbourn," he said. "Was Kim Barilko on her way to tell you something last night?"

"No," I said, "I was going to tell her something. There was someone I knew who wanted to help Kim make some changes in her life." I told him about the Lily Pad and the mentor program, and he wrote it down without comment.

When he'd finished, he put the cap on his pen and fixed it in his shirt pocket.

"Mrs. Kilbourn, you must have been struck by the pattern here," he said. "Two girls are murdered in less than a month, and a third young woman commits suicide. In all three instances, a member of your family is on the scene when the death is discovered. Bernice Morin dies hours after she is seen by Christy Sinclair. Two days later, Christy Sinclair dies. Kim Barilko goes to Christy Sinclair's funeral, and now she dies. There's got to be a connection."

"I know," I said dully. "I just don't know what it is. But I have to know something. Did Kim have a tattoo? A teddy bear tattoo on her left buttock?"

He looked at me hard, and in his eyes I could see the bleak knowledge of human depravity that had been in Jill Osiowy's eyes when she had shown me the photos of the Little Flower murders.

"No tattoo," he said. "But there was another trademark. Kim Barilko's tongue was split," he said simply. "Someone had slit it right from the tip to the place where it hinged at the back of her mouth."

I could feel the gorge rise in the back of my throat, and I covered my mouth with my hands.

"Why?" I said.

Inspector Tom Zaba was impassive. "The tongue thing is a street punishment for a snitch." He waited for a beat. "I'm not swaggering when I tell you this, Mrs. Kilbourn. I'm trying to impress you with the fact that these people don't have a special code for dealing with nice ladies who want to help fallen girls. If you're in their way, they'll kill you. It's that simple. I don't think either of us wants to see that. Stay away, Mrs. Kilbourn. These people play by rules a woman like you couldn't even begin to understand."

As we pulled up at the emergency ward, Inspector Zaba's warning was replaying itself in my head. Our doctor and the police officer who'd come with us to the hospital took Angus up to X-ray and I sat alone in the emergency room, waiting. I don't know how long I waited. Twice, volunteers, nice-looking women with pastel smocks and expensive perfume, came over to ask if they could get me anything, but I waved them away. My mind had gone into white space. When the orthopedic surgeon came to tell me about the extent of Angus's injury, I had trouble for a minute sorting out what he was talking about. He was an earnest young man with a quick grin and a reassuring manner. His identification tag said his name was Dr. Eric Leung.

"We've X-rayed it twice," he said. "It's a simple triangular break in the tibia." He touched the front of his leg to show me. "Angus tells me when he saw the dead girl, he started running and his toe caught on something and snapped his foot back. There's no need for surgery. You can come back with me while I put the cast on, if you like."

I followed him into the elevator.

"Angus will need the cast for about three weeks," he said. He looked at me. "Are you all right, Mrs. Kilbourn? The break could have been a lot worse. It was really a lucky break." Then, shaking his head at his joke, he stepped out of the elevator.

As I followed him down the hall, the words pounded against my consciousness. Lucky break, lucky break. The boy at the Lily Pad had dropped his guard long enough to say that Kim Barilko needed a lucky break. Now my son had one. Who made the decision about who lost and who won? As I stepped into the brightly lit cast room, I knew I didn't want to know the answer.

When Angus and I went home an hour and a half later, Mieka and Greg were waiting at the front door. Angus was still punchy from the Demerol, so Greg carried him to his bedroom, and Mieka went along to tuck him in.

I was pretty punchy myself. I was trying to decide whether I wanted a cup of tea or three fingers of bourbon when Jill Osiowy walked out of our kitchen. She was ashen, and her eyes were swollen.

"It was the girl I was supposed to be the mentor for, wasn't it?" Jill said.

I nodded.

"One of our guys lives in your neighbourhood. He took some footage of her. I couldn't believe it . . ." Jill's voice was very small and quiet. "I think you have to back off, Jo. They're starting to get close to your family now."

"I think we should both back off," I said.

Jill raked her hands through her hair. "No," she said, "I'm not giving up. If the network won't give me any help on this, I'll do it on my own time. People can't be allowed to get away with this."

I put my arms around her. "No," I said, "they can't. But, Jill, I don't want to think about any of this right now. In fact, for about twenty-four hours I don't want to think about anything."

Just then the phone rang. Jill shook her head. "Good luck with that wish," she said.

It was Peter. He'd just gotten Mieka's message to call. When he heard the news, he said he was coming home. I told him not to. He said he was coming anyway. Then Keith called from Toronto. He said he was coming back on the four o'clock flight. It was going to be a full house.

By seven-thirty everyone was sitting in the living room. Only Taylor and Angus were missing. Samantha's mother had called offering to take Taylor for the night, and Angus had eaten a bowl of Cap'n Crunch and slipped back to sleep.

It was an awkward evening. After the initial embraces and reassurances, no one knew what to do next. The wound of Kim Barilko's death was too fresh for reflection and too over- whelming to make other conversation possible. At nine, the storm knocked the power out, and I think all of us were grateful for the sense of purpose hunting down candles and flashlights gave us. Mieka and Greg took candles to the kitchen and came back a little later with a tray of sand- wiches and beer. It was reassuring to know that in a world of unspeakable horror, we could still handle the small stuff.

At eleven, the power came back on, and we watched the local news. Everyone was silent as the image of our house filled the screen. The camera lingered just long enough for the curious to know which house to stop in front of when they came looking, then there was a long shot of our back fence and our cottonwood tree, and finally, the big payoff, our garbage bin. There wasn't much information, just that there had been a murder and mutilation; that the victim, a fifteen-year-old girl, had been found in a garbage bin beside Wascana Creek in South Regina. Name was being withheld until notification, et cetera.

The next story was the storm. There were shots of trees with severed limbs and scarred trunks, of people being rescued from cars trapped in underpasses, and on the lighter side, as the news reporter said, shots of kids waving and grin- ning as they canoed down residential streets. When the news was over, I turned off the television. In the sudden silence I sat awkwardly twirling the Wandering Soul bracelet on my wrist till Mieka suggested we all go to bed.

The kids went up to shower, and Keith and I were left alone in the kitchen. I walked to the window that faced the backyard. I'd opened it that morning to let the fresh air in. It was still open; in the distance I could hear a radio playing. I stood for a moment, listening, looking at the soft fuzz of yellow the garage lights made in the rainy night. Keith came over and put his arms around me.

"I'm wondering if anything is ever going to be the same again," I said.

He pulled me closer, but he didn't answer.

It rained more that June than it had since our provincial weather bureau began record keeping, but the really bad storms began on the day of Kim Barilko's death. That night as I listened to the rain falling, implacable, unrelenting, images of Kim kept swimming up behind my eyes. Sometimes the image was of her face the day we had walked to the Lily Pad together, defiant behind the makeup mask that couldn't disguise the pubescent bumps of a child's skin. Then, horribly, there was the other face, the appalling mutilation I had seen that morning. Outside the thunder cracked and the lightning split the skies. It would have been comforting to believe the heavens were crying for Kim Barilko. It would have been comforting, but it would have been a crock.

CHAPTER

9

The letter came the last week of June. For three weeks I had made a conscious effort to pull Angus and me back into our old, safe world. The small triangular break in Angus's tibia that I had seen on the X-ray was just the tip of the iceberg. More than one fragile bone had been shattered by the grim reality of Kim Barilko's death, and the knitting together of these hidden fractures was not going to be easy.

Kim Barilko's murder didn't have much staying power as far as the media was concerned. By the time the weekend edition of the newspaper was published, the story had moved off the front page to page five; the following Monday, it had disappeared altogether.

But for me Kim would not disappear. Our last official visit from Inspector Zaba came late Friday afternoon. He had shaved his moustache, and the pale line of his lip made him look more wounded by life than ever. His news wasn't much. Forensic evidence seemed to suggest that Kim had not been killed in our alley. She had been murdered somewhere else and dumped there. There were no leads to the identity of her murderer.

"Trust me, Mrs. Kilbourn, this is not surprising in a street death," he had said. "Most of the time we don't settle these things. The Lily Pad angle was a blank, too. The board of that place is as close to an elite as you'll find in a city this size." He sounded exhausted.

When he left, he warned me again about the need to be careful. "Put this behind you, Mrs. Kilbourn. Put the experience behind you, and put the people behind you. What's done is done."

But try as I might, I could not put Kim Barilko's death behind me because there was no doubt in my mind that I was responsible for it. Keith had tried to reassure me: "Jo, you don't like it and I don't like it, but face facts. The day Kim was born a lot of things were already settled for her, and one of those things was that she wasn't going to live to a ripe old age. You know the kind of world she lived in. Violence is always the first option there. You can't hold yourself responsible for being part of her life when someone exercised that option."

"That's the third time I've heard that argument," I said. "I still don't believe it."

"Believe it," Keith said.

And I tried. I tried, because the alternative was unbearable. In those first days, I was haunted by my guilt. If I had reached out to Christy Sinclair, she wouldn't have committed suicide; if I had left Kim Barilko alone, she wouldn't have been murdered.

Saturday morning, Corporal Perry Kequahtooway came to visit. There had been a break in the weather. It was still overcast, but the rain had stopped. As soon as she got up, Taylor put on her bathing suit and went out to the backyard to run through the pools of standing water with the dogs. I took a towel, dried off the picnic bench and took my coffee outside to watch. When the dogs got tired, they flopped down near the sand pile; Taylor knelt beside them and began building a castle.

Perry Kequahtooway seemed to appear out of nowhere. Suddenly he was there at my elbow. "I rang the doorbell, but I guess you couldn't hear out back."

"I wasn't listening," I said.

He looked concerned. "I wanted to see how you were doing. After the advice I gave you when Christy Sinclair died, I feel responsible."

"Welcome to the club," I said.

He frowned. "Anyway, this is just a personal visit."

For the first time I noticed that he wasn't wearing a uniform. He was dressed in blue jeans and a sweatshirt that said, "Standing Buffalo Powwow, August 9, 10, 11, 1990."

"Can I get you some coffee?" I asked.

"That would be nice," he said.

When I came back, he and Taylor were carrying a bucket of wet gravel from the back alley.

"Is it okay to take that from city property?" I asked.

"It's a very small bucket," he said, "and I think this land used to belong to a relative of mine. You can accept it as a gift from my family to yours." He dumped the gravel carefully at the edge of Taylor's sand pile. "There's more need for it to be here anyway. Your daughter tells me that no matter how carefully she builds her castle, it keeps falling down. It needs a firmer foundation."

"I think I learned a song about that at Sunday school," I said.

He smiled. "Me, too."

Taylor, happy, smoothed the wet gravel into a base for her castle. Perry Kequahtooway and I sipped our coffee.

"I guess you're having a pretty rough time," he said.

"You guess right."

"Blaming yourself?"

"Yeah," I said, "I am. But you know I was only trying to help. I just wanted to help her have a better life."

He was silent. The sun glinted on his dark braids as he looked into the coffee cup between his hands.

"I imagine you've heard that one before," I said.

"Yeah," he said, "I have. It was at the same place where I learned the song about building my house on a firm foundation."

He reached across the table and touched my hand. "That doesn't make it wrong, you know, Mrs. Kilbourn. People have to keep trying. People have to keep trying to do right."

After he left, I tried to hold on to his words. The problem was that everyone seemed to know what was right but me. The family certainly knew. They were with Inspector Zaba. "Leave it alone," they said, and I did my best. I put the Wandering Soul bracelet in a lacquered box where I kept jewellery I didn't wear much any more, and I ignored the pang I felt when I shut the lid. I tried, in the words of the advice columns, to get on with my life. I read and I watched baseball with Angus. I talked to Greg's and Mieka's Saskatoon friends about a surprise party they wanted to hold at our house on the Canada Day weekend. I did all the right things, but I still felt as if someone had kicked me in the stomach.

The Monday morning before the long weekend Jill called and asked me to meet her in the NationTV cafeteria. After I got the kids off to school, I drove over. It was another rainy day. This rain was soft and misting. The Inuit people are said to have twenty-three words for kinds of snow; I thought by the time this spring was over, the people of our city would need at least that many words for kinds of rain. The cafeteria was empty when I arrived. I took my tea over to the window and sat looking at the patio that ran along the building. A man and a woman came out of the building and huddled under the eaves. The man was carrying a yellow slicker, and he draped it around both their shoulders. Lovers, I thought, risking the rain for a moment alone. Then they both pulled out cigarette packs and lit up.

When Jill came, I pointed to the couple. "Driven into each other's arms by the network's no-smoking regulation."

Jill glanced at them, then collapsed into the chair opposite me. "It's been seven years since you and I quit, and I still miss it. Actually, one more phone call from the powers that be, and I may start again."

"If you have a problem and you start smoking again, you have two problems," I said. "That's what they taught us in quit-smoking class, remember?"

Jill narrowed her eyes. "You know, Jo, you can be really obnoxious when you put a little effort into it." She shrugged. "Anyway, what I wanted to talk about was tonight's show. How would you feel about discussing street kids?"

"I thought that was a forbidden subject."

"No, the Little Flower case is a forbidden subject, but I don't see why you can't talk in general terms about these kids."

"As a kind of flesh-and-blood reminder of the rotting infrastructure of our cities?" I said. "That's a quote from the Montreal *Gazette.*"

She looked at me approvingly. "Yeah, that's the angle. I'm going to check with Keith and Senator Sam, but if you're game, it sounds like good television to me."

We walked out of the cafeteria together and down to Jill's office. In the hall outside the news division there was a large portrait. Jill stopped in front of it, pulled a black marking pen out of her purse and drew horns on the man in the picture.

"Childish, but it helps," Jill said.

I looked more closely at the man. He looked affluent and assured. He also looked familiar.

"Who is that?" I asked.

Jill looked surprised. "That's my boss. Your boss, too, come to think of it. That's Con O'Malley, the boss of everybody. The head of NationTV."

Jill went into her office. I stayed behind looking at Con O'Malley. He was the man in the photographs I'd seen on Lorraine Harris's desk that morning at the lake, the one reaching out to touch the flame-coloured hibiscus in Lorraine Harris's hair.

It was a small world.

That night, for the first time, our political panel generated as much light as heat. I accused Keith's party of Darwinian social policies; he accused me of believing that you can solve any problem by throwing money at it. Senator Sam Steinitz sat back with a cherubic smile, calculating the number of voters Keith and I were alienating with our intransigence.

When the red light went out, Jill was beaming. "Good show, guys," she said. "I mean that. This is what we should be doing all the time."

Afterwards, Keith walked me home through the park. "You were good tonight," he said. "Sometimes you're a little tentative, but not this time. You really tore a strip off me a couple of times."

"You seemed to handle it all right," I said.

"I've been clawed at by experts, Jo. I still have the wounds."

I slipped my arm around his waist. "Show me," I said.

"Here?" he said.

"Your place might be a little less public."

We went to Keith's. He took the phone off the hook and put on Glenn Gould's final version of the Goldberg Variations. That night when we walked down the hall to Keith's room, I didn't have any doubts. I wanted to have sex with Keith Harris. We undressed quickly and without embarrassment, and when we came together on the bed, our lovemaking was everything lovemaking should be, exciting and tender and fun. Keith was a skilled and considerate partner, and afterwards, as I lay in the dark, I felt relaxed and very happy.

"Jill and I were talking about smoking today," I said. "Right now, I wish I had a cigarette. The one after sex was always the best one."

Keith pushed himself up on his elbow. "I'll run out and get you a pack."

I kissed him. "I don't need cigarettes, I just need a distraction," I said.

"I don't have to be asked twice," he said.

And he didn't.

After I'd dressed, I went to the bureau to brush my hair. Keith was sitting on the bed putting on his shoes; I could see his reflection in the mirror.

"When I was at Nation TV this morning, I saw a picture of Con O'Malley," I said. "I didn't realize he and Lorraine were friends."

"They've been friends for years," Keith said, bending to tie a shoelace. "I think probably it's more than that. Lorraine spends a lot of time in Toronto. But she's so cagey about her life, I don't know. To be honest, I was never that interested."

"Do you think she would have asked him to hire me?" I said. "You'll have to admit I'm not exactly a national name like you and Sam."

"You will be," Keith said. "But to answer your question about Lorraine, I'd be very surprised to learn she'd recommended you to Con."

"I guess I'd be surprised, too," I said. "Lorraine never struck me as being the kind of woman who would help another woman along."

Keith came over and stood beside me. "I don't think it's that," he said. "It's just that . . ." His reflection in the mirror smiled sheepishly. "Jo, let's just let this one drop."

"Lorraine doesn't like me, does she?" I said, and I was amazed I hadn't had the insight before.

Keith looked steadily at my reflection.

"Don't worry about hurting my feelings," I said. "I really do want to know. She's going to be Mieka's mother-in-law at the end of the summer. If there's something I'm doing wrong, I should know."

Keith put his hand on my shoulder and turned me so I was facing him.

"It's nothing you're doing. Lorraine just has trouble with women like you."

"Women like me? I don't understand."

"Jo, your father was a doctor. You lived in a big house, you went to a private school, then to university, and after university you married a lawyer. You didn't have to work for things the way Lorraine did. She thinks you've had a pretty easy passage."

I was astounded. "Keith, Lorraine has so much."

"She didn't always have it," Keith said, "and I think that still makes all the difference to her."

When I got home, there was a note from Mieka. Jill had called. Kim Barilko's mother, Angie, was in town to arrange for the burial. I had told Jill I wanted to talk to her. In Mieka's careful backhand was the name of the hotel where Angie Barilko was staying. It was a downtown motor hotel that I knew by reputation called the Golden Sheaf. Most often newspaper stories about it began with the phrase, "The victim was found . . ."

I called Angie Barilko's room. When she answered, her voice was as flat as Kim's. Yes, it was tragic about Kim. Yes, Kim had had so much ahead of her. Yes, I could come over if I wanted to. We agreed to meet in an hour in the Golden Sheaf's coffee shop.

It was in the basement, and it smelled heavily of cigarette smoke and stale beer. The booths were all filled and I sat at the counter. Reflexively, I picked up the menu. The heavy wine leather cover was encased in plastic, and the plastic was sticky.

Angie Barilko had told me she'd be wearing pink; it was an unnecessary identification. I would have known her anywhere. She was Kim twenty years down the line: body bird thin, hair so dead from peroxide and back combing it looked synthetic. She was wearing a hot pink sleeveless blouse, black spandex pants that stopped at mid-calf and three-inch heels. I called her name and she came over and sat on the stool beside me. She lit a cigarette and blew a careful smoke ring in my direction.

"So you knew my girl," she said.

"No," I said, "I didn't, but I wanted to. I thought maybe you could tell me about her."

"You came to the wrong place," she said. "Me and her kind of drifted apart. She was a good kid and all, I don't mean that. It's just nobody ever handed me anything. I've had to work pretty hard just to keep myself going. Rent, food, these . . ." She held up her cigarette pack. "Christ, they really gouge you for these now."

Her first cigarette was burning in the ashtray, but she still opened the pack. "Empty," she said sadly. "Listen, I think I musta left my wallet in the room. Would you happen to have a couple of bucks on you?"

I gave her ten. She came back with cigarettes, but she didn't sit down. Unexpectedly, she smiled.

"Look," she said, "let's be up front. I haven't got a lot to say. Kim mostly stayed at her grandmother's back home."

"Where was home?" I asked.

She was suddenly alert. "You don't want to know that," she said. Then she smiled slyly. "Look, I don't want you going away mad, feeling like I didn't keep up my end of the bargain. Here's a picture of her."

She pulled out her wallet. Her subterfuge revealed, she opened her eyes in mock surprise. "Shit, it was here all along. Anyway, here she is."

In the picture, Kim was perhaps three: blonde, ponytailed, sweet. She was sitting on a man's knee and holding a beer up to his lips.

"She was a cutie, eh?" Angie said. And then to herself, not me, she said, "I wish I could remember the name of that guy." She shrugged. "Water under the bridge. Anyways, I'm taking her back to Calgary to bury. We got nobody here any more."

I went home feeling overwhelmed with sadness, but with a sense that perhaps something was ended. The week after Angie Barilko took her daughter home it seemed possible to believe that the brutal blows that had begun the morning Mieka discovered Bernice Morin's body had stopped. Lorraine and I had some nice moments together planning and shopping. She was an extraordinarily competent woman, and as I watched her tick off the tasks in Greg's and Mieka's wedding plans book, I was filled with admiration. I told her a couple of stories about my childhood that put it in a less enviable light, and I could feel her warm to me. Mieka took to calling us "the mothers," and the night Lorraine and I addressed the wedding invitations, Mieka snapped a whole roll of film of us. "For the grandchildren," she said, and Lorraine and I looked at one another and smiled.

Life seemed to be looking up for Peter, too. One night he called, sounding even less forthcoming than usual, but after a few false starts, he told me he had met a young woman. A horse trainer.

"Marriage made in heaven," Mieka said, rolling her eyes when I told her. "They can currycomb each other."

Taylor began her sketching classes. I bought her a Sunday *New York Times* that had a review of a retrospective of her mother's work, and she carried it everywhere with her for three days, then she asked for some oils so she could get started making real art.

Angus became agile with his crutches. One night when the rain stopped long enough for the league to schedule a ball game for his team, he sat in the bleachers and cheered. Then when the game was over, he ran the bases on his walking cast, laughing like a maniac all the way.

On the last morning in June I drove him down to the hospital and the orthopedic surgeon removed the cast. Unconsciously, I had established a one-to-one relationship between the healing of Angus's leg and the healing of our lives. As the cast came away and that pale, barely mended leg came into view, the symbolism was pretty breathtaking.

When we got back from the hospital, Jill Osiowy was standing at the front door. She was wearing shorts and an outsized T-shirt with the logo of *Frank* magazine on the front. Angus had brought his cast home from the hospital. It was an eerie trophy; it looked like an amputation, but Jill was enthusiastic as she examined it. Then Taylor grabbed Jill's hand and took her into the backyard to show off her bean patch. I followed along, and when Jill had finished enthusing about the beans, I said, "My turn now. I haven't got anything to show off, but I've got beer."

"You win," Jill said. "Anyway, I came because I have something for you." She handed me a letter. "Fan mail," she said. "I'll get the beer. Read your letter."

It had been opened and stamped with the network's name and the date of receipt. The notepaper was commercial, from a motel called the Northern Lights, Box 720, Havre Lake, Saskatchewan. The writing was carefully rounded, and the

writer had used a liner. It looked like the work of a conscientious grade seven student, but it wasn't.

Dear Mrs. Kilbourn,

I've written this letter twenty times and torn it up.
My husband says what's passed is passed, and usually he
is right, but sometimes it seems Fate takes a hand. I
wouldn't usually watch a show about Politics. Politics
is not for me, (no offence), but I was interested in your
topic June 3 when you talked about Street Kids. I recognized you right away. You are the woman who was
like a mother to Theresa Desjarlais. When I saw in the
paper that Theresa had passed away I thought of you but
I had forgotten your name till I saw you that night. It is
you. The picture Theresa brought me of the two of you
at Christmas was framed. It is on top of our TV, so
there's no mistake.

I know you must be very busy, but Theresa was my
friend and I want to know if she was happy before she
passed away.

This matters to me.

Sincerely
Mrs. Tom Mirasty (Beth)

Jill came back with the beer.

"I've read it, of course. Some of the mail we get isn't worth
handing along."

I looked at her. "Did you notice the address? Havre Lake.
I'm going to be driving right past there this weekend when I
take Angus to camp."

Jill sipped her beer. "I thought you'd decided that discretion was the better part of valour. I notice you're not wearing
the bracelet any more."

"Maybe it's time I put it back on," I said.

For a long time neither of us said anything. We sat and watched Taylor in her sand pile, building her elaborate city. In the days since Perry Kequahtooway visited, the castle had become a wondrous thing. When there wasn't room for one more cupola or turret, Taylor had sculpted a wall, high and protective. What was inside was worth protecting. On the grounds of her castle Taylor had created a beautiful world of looking-glass lakes and pebble staircases and tiny forests made out of cedar cuttings. When I was a child, I had dreamed of living in a place like that: a castle with a population of one where nothing could ever hurt me and no one could ever make me do things I didn't want to do. But I wasn't a child any more.

I looked at Beth Mirasty's letter. "This matters to me," she had written; I knew it mattered to me, too.

I turned to Jill. "I'm going to see her," I said. "I'm going to see Beth Mirasty. She's right. Sometimes it seems as if fate does take a hand."

Jill's brow furrowed. "Just be sure it's fate in there directing things," she said. "I've got a feeling about this one. Don't take things at face value here. For once in your life, Jo, don't assume the best."

"I'll be careful," I promised. "And you can warn me again when we tape the Canada Day show. 'A Time for Patriotism not Cynicism,' right?"

She shuddered. "Does that topic make you want to throw up, too? Anyway, taping ahead will give everybody the long weekend off, and nobody will be watching, anyway."

"Good," I said. "I'll wear that flowered dress I wore the first night. Get my money's worth."

That afternoon I drove to the liquor store to pick up the wine for Greg's and Mieka's surprise party. I was just about to pull out of the parking lot when Helmut Keating came out of the side door of the liquor store. He was close enough for me to see that he was wearing his "Let Me Be Part of Your Dream" sweatshirt, but he didn't see me. He was too busy supervising the employee who was pushing the dolly with his order on it. I watched as the two men unloaded the cases of liquor into a Jeep Cherokee, and when they went back inside, I waited. Five minutes later they came out with another load. They made four trips in all.

When Helmut pulled out of the parking lot, the only part of the Cherokee that wasn't loaded with liquor was the front seat. Whatever dream Helmut was going to be a part of was going to be a festive one. He drove north on Albert Street, turned off at the first side street past the Lily Pad, then doubled back. He pulled the Cherokee close to the back door of the Lily Pad and unloaded the liquor himself. That didn't make sense. There had been a half-dozen kids lying on the grass by the plywood frog on the front lawn, and Helmut wasn't the kind of guy who would feel he had to spare them on a hot day.

It took him half an hour to unload the liquor. When he came out of the Lily Pad for the last time he looked hot and unhappy. He got into the Cherokee and roared out of the parking lot. As he drove off, I noticed his licence plate: "ICARE," it said. I cared, too. I walked to the back door. It looked as if it had been designed to withstand a nuclear attack. The lock was the kind that was activated by a card; there was a sticker next to it that said, "SLC Security Systems." High-powered stuff for the back door of a drop-in centre for street kids.

I looked up at the old three-storey house that had been converted into the Lily Pad. There was nothing welcoming about the building from the back. There were no windows at ground level, and the windows on the upper storeys were closed off with blinds. It didn't look like a place that would give up answers easily.

The sun glinted off my Wandering Soul bracelet. I remembered Kim Barilko saying that she had known Christy Sinclair "from home and then at the Lily Pad. She was going to be my mentor." Now Kim was dead and Christy was dead.

I began to trace the incised letters on the bracelet with my fingertip. "Wandering Soul Pray For Me." "What's happening here, Christy?" I said. "What's going on?" A cat leaped from nowhere and landed at my feet with a feral scream. I ran to the car and slammed the door behind me. It was broad daylight in the city where I'd lived most of my adult life, but my heart was pounding as if I were approaching the heart of darkness.

"You're being crazy," I said, "overreacting." I locked the car doors and took deep breaths until I was calm enough to turn the key in the ignition. As I drove south along Albert Street, I tried to comfort myself with the familiar. I knew the buildings and trees on that street as intimately as I knew the back of my hand. "You're almost home," I said. "You're safe." But as I pulled into the alley behind my house, I was still shaking violently. My body knew what my mind wouldn't admit. The darkness I had felt at the Lily Pad wasn't something I could lock my doors against or drive away from. It was all around me.

Saturday night was Greg's and Mieka's surprise party. I had two jobs: to leave a key in the mailbox and to get the guests of honour out of the way. Keith offered to take us all for an early dinner at a restaurant about fifteen miles from the city. The place was called Stella's. The decor was 1950s, the music was jukebox, and the food was very good. Everything went off without a hitch.

I'd given Lorraine a key so she could welcome guests, and when we opened the front door, Mieka and Greg were met by a room filled with exuberant friends. It was a great party. Despite the fact that their wedding was two months away, Mieka and Greg were genuinely shocked – events of the past weeks had, I think, undermined their belief in happy surprises. But their friends had pulled it off, and their success made these handsome young men and women more ebullient than ever. Taylor was in her element. She loved excitement and colour and looking at people. Angus had fun, too. He was on the cusp of adolescence, sometimes a boy and sometimes a young man. That night as he helped with food and music and talked about Rocket Ismail and the Argonauts, he was a young man, and a happy one.

Lorraine was enjoying herself, too. In fact, she was so relaxed that when we found ourselves alone late in the evening, I decided to ask her if she'd been involved in getting the job for me at NationTV. Before I was even finished the question, I knew I'd made a mistake. Lorraine's smile didn't fade, but her body tensed and her grey eyes grew wary.

I tried to defuse the situation. "I'm only asking because I'm enjoying doing the show so much, and if you smoothed the way for me with Con O'Malley, I wanted to thank you."

Her manner changed. She became almost stagily coquettish. "Jo, I can't imagine how you found out about Con and me, but since you have, I'll tell you this. Our relationship has nothing to do with business. He's my gentleman friend. We have much more exciting things to talk about than NationTV when we're together. I think it's wonderful that they hired you, but the idea didn't come from me." Suddenly, her eyes were wide. "I'm not the only member of the Harris family who's friends with Con O'Malley, you know. Blaine and Keith have known him for years." She stood up and smoothed the skirt of her white linen dress. "Now, if you'll excuse me, I think I'd like to freshen my drink."

After Lorraine left, I was edgy. Her behaviour had been odd. Mieka had said once that Lorraine thought of herself as a "man's woman." If that was the role she'd been playing for me, I hadn't liked it. I poured myself a drink, but it didn't help. Since the night of their engagement party, too much had gone wrong for Greg and Mieka. They deserved a joyous, uncomplicated evening, and I was tense with the fear that my encounter with Lorraine meant they wouldn't get one. For the rest of the evening Lorraine kept her distance from me, but she held her cheek out for a kiss at the front door when she left. As I watched her walk down our front path, her hair silvery in the moonlight, I breathed a sigh of relief. From beginning to end, the evening had been flawless. I was asleep before my head hit the pillow.

In the middle of the night I was awakened by the sound of a woman crying out. I lay there in the dark, heart pounding, hoping the cry had been part of a dream. But as I listened the sound came again. It was outdoors, in the backyard. I jumped out of bed and ran to the window.

Greg and Mieka were in the pool, swimming in the moonlight. The sounds I had heard were the little shrieks Mieka made as Greg dived under her and pulled her toward him in the water. They were naked – skinny-dipping, we used to call it. I could see the pale shapes of their bodies in the dark water. I turned away and then I heard my daughter's voice. "Hey, watch this," she said. I looked out the window.

Mieka was swimming across the pool. Suddenly she disappeared under the water, then in a heartbeat, she stuck her bum up. I could see it gleaming whitely in the moonlight. Greg swam toward her and kissed the smooth white curve. Then he disappeared under the water, too. I waited till they were both above the water, safe, happy, in love. Then I turned and went back to bed. As I lay between the cool sheets, listening to the sounds of the innocent summer night, I was smiling.

Good times. There were good times ahead.

The kids and I went to the early church service the next day, and we spent the rest of the morning getting ready for our trip up north. We were all looking forward to it. Angus and Taylor had been counting the days, and now that life seemed to have smoothed out for the big kids, I was looking forward to a holiday with Keith. We hadn't exactly enjoyed smooth sailing since we met. Jill had arranged for us to do the July eighth show from the network's northern studio, about an hour's drive from where we would be staying. That meant Keith and Taylor and I were going to have ten days of sun and sand and the smell of pines.

Sunday afternoon, I met Keith at the TV studio, and we taped the Canada Day program. It went well, and the minute the technician came and took off our microphones, Keith turned to me.

"Let's go home," he said. I couldn't wait.

When we came out of the studio, the sun was shining. For the first time in a month there wasn't a cloud in sight.

"Look," I said. "Blue skies as far as the eye can see. How's that for an omen?"

Keith stopped in the middle of the sidewalk and took my hand.

"The rain is over and gone," he said. "The flowers appear on the earth; the time of the singing of birds is come, and the voice of the turtle is heard in our land. The fig tree putteth forth her green figs, and the vines with the tender grape give a good smell. Arise, my love, my fair one, and come away."

I put my arms around his neck and drew him toward me. "I wish you'd waited till we were closer to your place before you said that."

"I thought it might make you move a little faster," he murmured.

It did.

As we walked into the apartment, the phone was ringing. Keith made a face. "Should I answer it?"

I shrugged.

He crossed his fingers and picked up the receiver. I knew at once it wasn't good news. He listened for a while, then he said, "I'll be right down."

When he turned to me, his face was serious. "That was Lorraine. She wants me to come downstairs. She's decided it's time to put Blaine in a place where he can get special care."

"Did something happen?" I said.

"Nothing dramatic. I have a feeling Lorraine just took a hard look at the problem and decided to throw in the towel."

"I thought your father was doing better," I said. "Didn't you tell me that he'd put a couple of words together this week?"

"Yeah, but that was the only good news. And there's a lot of bad news. Blaine's getting just about impossible to control. Sean says as soon as he turns around, Blaine tries to get to the telephone or out the door. And he has these rages when Sean brings him back. He's terrible with Lorraine, too. Remember how he was with you that night at the lake? He's like that with her now. It's awful for Lorraine, and of course it could be fatal for my father. Sean worries that Blaine is going to get his blood pressure sky-high and have another stroke." For a moment, he stood silent, lost in thought, then he shook himself.

"Anyway, I'd better get down there. Jo, why don't you fix yourself a drink. I'll be back as soon as I can manage."

When Keith returned, he looked grim.

"So what's going to happen?" I asked.

Keith took my hands in his. "I'm not going to beat around

the bush, Jo. I can't go with you tomorrow. I'm sorrier than I can say, but this just has to be taken care of."

I pulled him close. "Damn," I said. "I was really looking forward to being with you. But I know it can't be helped. You're doing the right thing. Right now, if I could figure out a way to make you do the wrong thing, I would, but that'll pass. I know it isn't all polka dots and moonbeams at our age."

Keith poured us drinks and we took them to the balcony. Across the street in the park, some boys were playing touch football: shirts and skins. The sun was hot; the skins team would be in agony by the end of the day. Toward the lake, a crew was putting up a sound system in the bandshell for Canada Day. I thought how nice it would be to sit with Keith on a blanket in the grass, eating hot dogs and listening to the symphony.

But it wasn't going to be that kind of weekend.

I turned to Keith. "What happens next?" I asked.

He shook his head. "As usual, Lorraine has us organized. She's found a place in Minnesota that's supposed to be terrific. Out in the country, good staff-patient ratio, first-rate special care, and reliable security."

"Security?" I said, surprised.

"I told you that Blaine keeps trying to wander off."

I thought of that proud, elegant old man, and my heart sank. "What an awful thing for him," I said.

Keith looked grim. "I know. That's why Lorraine wants me to fly to Minneapolis with him."

"How soon?" I said.

"Tomorrow," he said.

"Don't you usually have to wait months for places like that?" I said.

For the first time since he'd come upstairs, Keith smiled. "People who aren't Lorraine have to wait months," he said. "But Lorraine always manages to move right to the head of the line. Anyway, this time, let's be glad she was able to pull some strings. If this place is the best thing for Blaine, then it's a case of the sooner the better." He reached over and touched my hair. "Once I get Blaine in, I can come home. If we're lucky, you and I can salvage at least part of our holiday."

"Let's hope we're lucky," I said. "Let's hope."

That night, as I sat at the kitchen table planning the route the kids and I would take to Havre Lake, hope had already given way to stoic acceptance. I'd replaced my new nightgown, silky and seductive, with the flannelette granny gown my neighbour had given me the year Angus was born. I knew that it got cold in the north when you were sleeping alone. There didn't seem to be much to look forward to except a good night's sleep and a seven-hour drive with two kids in the back seat.

Suddenly I thought of my old friend Hilda McCourt. Saskatoon wasn't far out of our way, and I was in need of a sympathetic ear. When I called her, she said she'd be delighted to have us all come for lunch. "A Canada Day menu," she said.

"Beaver soup?" I said.

"If all else fails," she said dryly. "I can assure you that one thing we will have is a bottle of single-malt Scotch. I'm looking forward to toasting our country's birthday with you, Joanne. Now, I'll let you go. You must have preparations. Drive safely. I'll look for you at twelve."

Just the sound of Hilda's voice made me feel better.

By the time I opened the windows, pulled up the blankets and turned out the lights, I was looking forward to the next day. I loved the north, and it would be fun to explore it with the kids. If all went well in Minnesota, Keith would join me, and before the end of the week, the singing of birds and the voice of the turtle would be heard in our land.

The telephone began to ring not long after I fell asleep. My danger sensors must have been off full alert, because I reached for the receiver without a second thought. The sounds I heard were barely human: angry cries and shapeless vowels. Then, very clearly, I heard the familiar word, "Killdeer," and, after a beat, two new words. "The rain," said Blaine Harris in his unused, angry voice. "The rain." Then the line went dead.

As I lay there in the dark listening to the dial tone, I was glad I was getting out of town.

CHAPTER

10

When I woke up on Canada Day the rain had started again. I turned on the radio and lay in bed, listening. The local news was a litany of cancellations: sports days, slow-pitch tournaments, Olde Tyme picnics, tractor pulls, walking tours, bed races, mud flings, parades. Everything was cancelled because of the weather. I remembered Blaine Harris's phone call the night before. "The rain," he'd said. Maybe he'd just been giving me the weather forecast.

I put on my sweats and took the dogs for a run. Greg and Mieka would take care of them while I was away. Somehow, with wedding plans and love in the air, I had the sense that the daily runs might be sporadic. We made an extra-long run: around the lake and home. It was a distance the dogs and I used to do often when we were younger, but it had been a while. By the time we got back, we were all panting and pleased with ourselves.

I fed the dogs, made coffee, showered and spent ten minutes rubbing my body with the expensive lotion Mieka had given me the Christmas before. Finally, wearing the blue dress I had worn the first night I had dinner with Keith,

I slid the bracelet on my wrist. When I felt the bracelet warm against my skin, I understood why I had called Hilda the night before. I had thought then that I needed a sympathetic ear, but that wasn't it. What I needed was advice. Every part of me that answered to the rules of logic said I should let Christy and Kim rest in peace. But life was not always ruled by logic, and Hilda McCourt was a woman who understood this. She would understand the power of the bracelet and the pull of my commitment to those dead girls. Hilda would be my final arbiter. If she thought I was wrong to keep pushing to discover the route by which Theresa Desjarlais had become Christy Sinclair, I'd give up. When I drove north, I'd stop at the Northern Lights Motel, have coffee with Beth Mirasty and tell her that her husband was right: the past was past.

When I came down, Taylor and Angus were sitting at the breakfast table, dressed, with their hair neatly combed, eating Eggos and fresh strawberries. The night before, when I had told Angus that Keith wouldn't be part of our holiday, he had started with his usual barrage of questions, but something in my face must have stopped him. He'd given me a hug and wandered off to bed. He was learning discretion, growing up.

As I looked at Taylor wearing a shirt that was right-side out and socks that matched, it was obvious that Angus had talked to her, too. The exemplary behaviour continued as we ran back and forth to the car, packing in the rain. There were no complaints from anybody about getting wet or about having to leave things behind. We hit the road early, just as the nine o'clock news came on the car radio, and no one suggested we stop for drinks or a bathroom until we drove into Chamberlain, about ninety kilometres from home. The station where we stopped gave out small Canadian flags with a gas purchase. Angus stuck his in his hat and Taylor put hers in her ponytail. They looked so patriotic that the gas station attendant gave them each a colouring book about a beaver who wanted to find the true meaning of Canada. Taylor was usually contemptuous of colouring books, but the beaver and his friends were cleverly drawn, and as we pulled away, she was already tracing the lines with her fingers, making them part of her muscle memory. The rest of the drive in the rain was quiet and companionable, and I enjoyed it.

We pulled up in front of Hilda's neat bungalow on Melrose Avenue just before noon. The Canadian flag was flying from the porch at the front of Hilda's house, a bright splash of red and white through the grey mist of rain. As Hilda opened the door and held her arms out in greeting, there was another burst of radiant colour. In her early eighties, Hilda McCourt was still a riveting figure. Today, she was wearing a jumpsuit the colour of a Flanders poppy and her hair, dyed an even more brilliant red than usual, was swept back by a red-and-white striped silk scarf.

The kids made a run for the house. Hilda stopped them at the door. "Let me have a look at you before you disappear," she said. She examined them carefully. "Well, you're obviously thriving. There's a jigsaw puzzle on the kitchen table for you. Quite a challenging one, at least for me. Harold Town's *Tower of Babble*. Taylor, your mother told me once that she thought Harold Town was splendid. Why don't you and Angus have a look and see what you think?"

As we watched the kids run down the hall, Hilda put her arm through mine. "Now, how about a little Glenfiddich to ease the traveller?"

I followed her gratefully. As we walked through to the glassed-in porch at the back of her house, I caught sight of the table set for lunch in the dining room. Red napkins carefully arranged in crystal water glasses, a white organdy tablecloth, red zinnias in a creamy earthenware pitcher.

"Lovely," I said.

"Not subtle," she said, "but I don't believe this is the year to be subtle about our country."

Hilda's back room was as individual and fine as she was. On the inside wall, there was an old horsehair chaise longue covered by a lacy afghan. At the foot of the chaise longue was a TV; at the head was a table with a good reading lamp and a stack of magazines. The current issue of *Canadian Forum* was on top. Along the wall, a trestle table held blooming plants. In the centre of the table a space had been cleared for three framed photographs: Robert Stanfield, T.C. Douglas and Pierre Trudeau.

"That's quite a triptych," I said, looking down at them.

"Two men who should have been prime minister and one who probably shouldn't have," Hilda said briskly. Then she tapped the frame of the Trudeau photo. "But what style that man had, and what fun he was."

She poured the Glenfiddich, handed me a glass and raised her own.

"To Canada," she said.

"To Canada," I said.

"Now," she said, "let's sit and watch the rain and you can tell me what brought you here."

As I felt the Scotch warming my body, I realized how much I wanted to talk.

I took off the bracelet and handed it to her. "It all began with this," I said.

She turned it carefully. "'Wandering Soul Pray For Me,'" she said. "Intriguing, but I've seen a bracelet like this before, you know. In fact, there were several of them at the duty-free shop in Belfast. The story was that monks hammered the silver by hand. Whoever did the hammering, these bracelets are costly – in more ways than one, but I presume by your face you've already discovered that. The intent, of course, is to remind the traveller that no matter how far afield she goes, the one left behind is still linked to her." She handed the bracelet back to me. "Who have you left behind, Joanne?"

In the garden a tiny pine siskin was feeding at Hilda's bird feeder. I watched until it flew away, then I turned to Hilda.

"Nobody," I said. "And that's the problem. There are two people I can't seem to leave behind no matter how hard I try."

"And you've decided to confide in me about it."

"I've decided to let you tell me what to do next," I said.

I told her everything, starting with the morning Mieka found Bernice Morin's body in the garbage can behind Judgements and ending with Beth Mirasty's letter.

When I was finished, Hilda looked at me levelly. "And your intention is to go to Havre Lake in search of Christy Sinclair?"

"I don't know," I said. "When I put it all together like this, my behaviour seems quixotic even to me. My husband used to say that there was nothing more terrifying than blind goodness loosed upon the world. You meet a lot of Don Quixotes in politics, you know. Certain they know what's best for everyone, tilting at windmills, rescuing the down-trodden whether they want to be rescued or not. I don't want to be like that, Hilda."

"And yet you can't walk away," she said.

"No," I said. "I can't walk away." I held up the bracelet. "Because of this. Because a woman gave me this bracelet and then she died. And suddenly it wasn't just a bracelet any more. Hilda, tell me honestly. Did you feel the power in this?"

"No," she said, thoughtfully, "but that doesn't mean it's not there. Your grandmother wouldn't have had any trouble putting a name to the pull you're feeling. She would have called it conscience. And she wouldn't have thought you were quixotic. She would have thought you were trying to right a wrong you did to another human being. Joanne, I've been listening carefully to you, and I know why you're so resolute about Christy Sinclair. To use a word that makes people uneasy these days, you feel that you sinned against her. A sin of omission. In your dealings with her you showed a want of *charitas*. Most often that word is translated as charity, but you have Latin, Joanne, you know the correct translation."

"Love," I said. "*Charitas* means love. Christy needed my love and I didn't give it to her." Suddenly, I was tired of the burden. I slammed the bracelet down on the table.

"Damn it, Hilda, how could I love her? She was so unlovable – the lies, the obsessions, the need. She needed so much. Every time I turned around, she was there, needing me to love her." My voice was shrill with exasperation. "How could I love her? I didn't even like her."

"According to Reinhold Niebuhr, God told us to love our enemies, not to like them," Hilda said dryly.

"Reinhold Niebuhr never knew Christy," I said.

The bracelet lay on the table in front of me, a dull circle of reproach. I picked it up and slid it on my wrist.

"It's too late, Hilda," I said. "There's nothing I can do to make it up to her now."

"It's never too late, Joanne. You know that."

"But what do I do?"

Hilda touched my hand. "You know the answer to that as well as I. You ask forgiveness, and then you try to make amends."

She held up the Glenfiddich. "Now before you begin that arduous work, would you like what the Scots call 'a drap for your soul'?"

I held out my glass. "I think my soul could use it," I said.

Lunch was good. Meat loaf, mashed potatoes, garden peas, new carrots, and, for dessert, strawberry Jell-O and real whipped cream. By the time we'd eaten and I'd rounded up the kids, the rain had stopped, and I felt ready for the drive north. Hilda walked with me to the car. We said our good-byes, then she put her hand on my arm.

"I almost forgot to tell you how splendidly you're doing on *Canada Today*. You were a little shaky at the beginning, but now you seem very assured."

"I'm feeling better about it," I said. "And Keith and Sam have been a real help."

"There seems to be a certain warmth between you and Keith Harris."

I could feel myself blush. "Is it that obvious?"

"Only to someone who knows you well," she said. "Is it serious?"

"I don't know," I said. "We've had so many outside problems to deal with. Keith was supposed to be with me today, but his father's condition is worse, so he stayed behind to take care of things."

Hilda's eyes were sad. "I'm sorry to hear that about Blaine."

"You know him?" I said, surprised. "I can't imagine you two travelling in the same circles."

"He was a great proponent of regional libraries, as, of course, am I. We were on any number of boards and committees together when the libraries were being set up."

"What was he like?" I asked. "I didn't meet him until after he'd had his stroke."

Hilda looked thoughtful. "I think Blaine Harris is the most moral man I've ever met. There's an incident I remember particularly. During the summer of 1958, we had a series of community meetings, and after one of them we had lunch at a diner in Whitewood. Later that afternoon we stopped for gas and Blaine noticed he'd received a dollar extra in change from the cashier at the diner. He drove back to Whitewood to return the money. He apologized to me for what he called our thirty-mile detour, but he said he couldn't have slept that night if he hadn't known things were set right. That's the kind of man he was, utterly fair and just."

We spent the night in Prince Albert, a small city 150 kilometres north of Saskatoon, famous for the fact that when it had the choice of being home to the province's university or a federal penitentiary, it chose the pen. In fact, the reason we were stopping in Prince Albert was the jail. Angus had seen a TV program about the prison museum, so late on the afternoon of July 1, Taylor and I were following Angus through dim rooms filled with painfully crafted weapons confiscated from hidden places in the bodies of prisoners. A celebration of Canadian ingenuity.

That night we ate dinner at a Chinese restaurant Ian and I had liked when we had campaigned in the north. Taylor ate a whole order of almond prawns and nodded off at the dinner table. We went to the motel and I switched on *Canada Today*. The warmth between Keith and me was apparent even on TV; just to see him made me lonely for him. I'd forgotten how painful physical longing could be, and after five minutes I turned the television off and took a shower.

We were all in bed by nine o'clock. The kids slipped into sleep easily. I lay in the dark, listening to the radio. There had been a contest earlier that day; people from all over Canada had been asked to call in with their renditions of our national anthem. A physics class from Halifax played ten pop bottles filled with water; four high-school principals from Saskatoon sang a barbershop harmony; a young girl from Manitoba sang in Ojibway; a Canada goose from Don Mills, Ontario, was disqualified because she was a fraud; a Vancouver group called the Raging Grannies offered a social commentary.

O Canada.

I slept well and woke up to a room filled with sunshine and fresh northern air. On impulse I called Peter. The phone rang and rang, and I was about to hang up when Peter answered, sounding breathless and happy. He had just come in – it was a beautiful morning in the southwest, hot already, and still, and he and Susan, the young woman who trained horses, had just come in from riding through the hills.

"It sounds idyllic," I said.

"It is idyllic, Mum," he said quietly. "Everything is starting to look very good again."

"And Susan is . . ."

"Susan is the best part," he said.

"Good," I said. "I love you, Peter."

"Same here, Mum."

I was hanging up when I heard his voice. "Mum, I haven't forgotten Christy."

"Neither have I," I said. Then I did hang up.

The Northern Lights Motel was just off the Hansen Lake Road. It was the kind of place I would have picked to stay in myself: a low-slung log building that housed a restaurant and a store. In the pines out back, I could see a dozen or so log cabins. On each side of the door to the restaurant, truck tires, painted white, bloomed with pink petunias. The effect was clean and cheerful. Other people must have liked the place, too; a no-vacancy sign hung on the hitching post near the entrance.

There were two people in the restaurant. A man, dressed in the newest and best from the Tilley catalogue, sat at a back booth, looking at the menu through round-lensed tortoiseshell glasses. A slender young native woman, wearing blue jeans and a dazzlingly white sleeveless cotton blouse, stood beside him, taking his order. She was a striking figure; her profile was delicate, and her hair, held back from her face by beadwork barrettes, fell shining and straight to her waist.

The kids and I sat down at the counter. There wasn't much of a demarcation between the restaurant and the store. I knew that if I ordered lake trout, the fish would have been swimming in Havre Lake twenty-four hours earlier, but if I ordered beans, the cook would walk three steps to the store and take the beans off the shelf. The wall behind the counter was filled with Polaroids of weekend fishermen squinting into the sun, holding up their prize catches: northern pike, walleye, lake trout, whitefish.

Angus grabbed my arm and pointed to a sign over the cash register: "Shower Free with Meal. Otherwise $3.50. $5.00 deposit on towels."

"That wouldn't exactly bankrupt you, would it?" I whispered.

He grinned, slid off the stool and went over to look at a display of hooks and lures. Taylor followed him.

The woman who had been taking the order came over to our table. She touched my wrist with her index finger.

"Her bracelet," she said softly. "I'm so glad you came, Mrs. Kilbourn. Just let me put in that man's order and we can talk." She turned to Angus. "If you walk down that road out there toward the lake, you'll see my son fishing on the dock. He says the jack are really biting today."

Angus shot me a pleading look.

"Half an hour," I said. "We have to get you settled in camp and get ourselves to Blue Heron Point."

He was out the door in a flash. When Beth Mirasty came back, she had a tray with a pitcher of lemonade and four glasses.

"Let's go out back where we can be quiet," she said. She smiled at Taylor. "Would you like to learn how to make wishbone dolls?" she asked softly. "My kokom's sewing today. She could teach you."

Taylor looked at her curiously. "Is Kokom your little girl?" she asked.

"Kokom is Mrs. Mirasty's grandmother," I said. "That's how you say grandmother in Cree."

The back room appeared to be the family living room. It was simply furnished, and everything in it shone. The linoleum was hard-polished and the pine furniture gleamed. I thought I would like to stay in a motel owned by Beth Mirasty. An old woman sat in a rocking chair by the window. There was a lace curtain behind her, as dazzlingly white as Beth Mirasty's blouse; the old woman was wearing a pink dress, and her white hair was carefully fixed with beadwork combs, pink and green and white. In front of her was a birch basket filled with scraps of fabric. She was sewing one of them onto a quilt on her knee.

When she heard us, the old lady looked up. She didn't smile, but there was something about her that was welcoming.

"The little one would like to know how to make wishbone dolls, Kokom," Beth said.

The old woman leaned forward and said something to Taylor. Then she pointed toward a doorway that seemed to lead into the rest of the flat. Taylor ran off where she had pointed.

"First, you need chicken bones," the old lady said to me.

After Beth introduced us and poured the lemonade, the old lady sat with her hands folded until Taylor came back with a coffee can. The old lady reached into the coffee can, took out a wishbone and handed it to Taylor. "Think about the face you want to put on the little part that sticks out at the top," she said.

In the corner was the TV. A large coloured photo of Christy and me was in a frame on top of it. I went to look closer. It was a shot of us in front of the Christmas tree. Christy was wearing a Santa Claus sweatshirt and red overalls. She was holding an old plastic angel.

I remembered the moment. We were decorating the tree, and after the picture was taken, Christy had asked me to tell her the story of how we got the angel.

I had laughed and said, "Oh, it's just one of those boring family stories."

"Tell me," she said, "please."

And so I had told her how, when Mieka was in kinder-garten, she had told her teacher that we were a Catholic family who had lost our angel, and the woman had given it to her for Christmas. And I had told her about how Angus had eaten the pasta off the jar-ring-framed picture of the dogs he had made in grade one, and about the time when Sadie was a pup and Peter had hung dog biscuits on the branches of the tree and we had come down Christmas morning to dis-cover that Sadie had knocked down the tree and eaten the dog biscuits and half the ornaments. Ordinary family stories, but Christy's yearning as I told them had been almost palpable.

Behind me, Beth Mirasty said, "She brought me that picture herself when she came home before New Year's. She was so proud of it."

The week between Christmas and New Year's. We had all planned to go skiing that week. Then, out of nowhere, Christy had announced she was going to Minneapolis with friends. When she came back, she had talked endlessly about the operas they had seen and the restaurants where they had eaten. More lies.

"She said last Christmas was the best one she'd ever had," Beth Mirasty said softly. She picked up the picture and we walked over and sat on a couch in the corner. "Theresa told me you had made her part of your family."

"What about her own family?" I asked.

Beth Mirasty seemed confused. "I thought she'd told you all that."

"No," I said, "she didn't."

Beth looked at the photo. For a long time she didn't say anything, and I had the sense that she was deciding whether to go on. Finally, she shook her head.

"I guess it doesn't matter any more," she said. "They're all passed away except Jackie. He's Theresa's brother, and he wouldn't care. He doesn't care about anything since Theresa passed on. She was all he had. The parents drank, and they fought, and they beat their kids. It was a terrible thing."

In the silence I could hear Taylor's young voice. "Kokom, can I make a dress for my doll out of this silvery cloth or is it too good?"

Kokom said something too soft and low for me to hear, but they both laughed.

I turned back to Beth Mirasty. "Did they live around here? Theresa's family?"

"In town. In a kind of shack on the outskirts. They burned it down one night when they were drinking."

"What did they do?" I said.

She shrugged. "They found another shack."

For a while we were silent again. Then Beth Mirasty said, "When I wrote to you, I said I needed to know if Theresa was happy at the last. Before her accident."

"Her accident." I had used the phrase "tragically and accidentally" to describe Christy's death in her obituary; the newspaper had never reported that Christy committed suicide. Beth Mirasty didn't know the truth. Her brown eyes were intent; I could feel the tension in her body.

I remembered that last day. Christy running across the lawn, hugging me, smelling of soap and sunshine and cotton. "I've missed this family," she had said. And later, she had stood in front of a field white with tundra swans, splitting the air with their plaintive cries as they migrated north. "If they're smart and they're lucky, they'll make it," she had said. It was best to end the movie there.

I took the photo from Beth Mirasty's hands. "Yes," I said, "Theresa was happy at the end."

Somewhere a clock struck. I looked at my watch. "I guess it's time for me to leave. I have to get my boy up to camp."

"I'll walk down to the dock with you," Beth said.

When we came through the clearing in the bush to the lake, I could feel my breath catch in my throat. Havre Lake was one of those northern lakes that is so vast it makes your mind stop. There is something anarchic about such lakes. They make their own weather and have their own intricate geography of islands and points and narrows through which they reach out into other unimaginably vast bodies of water. They exist on maps as huge, whimsically shaped expanses of nothing in the middle of the neat cartography of the places we know.

Angus and Beth's son were fishing off the dock.

When he heard me, Angus turned and held up the fingers of one hand.

"Five minutes, Mum, please, just five. There's a jack in there that's so ready to be caught," he whispered.

"Five, and that's it," I said.

Beth and I walked down to the beach and stood side by side, looking out at the horizon.

"I always feel scared when I look at these lakes," I said.

"Can't you swim?" she asked.

"Yes," I said, "but that's not good enough here, is it?"

"No," she agreed, "it's not." She pointed toward the west. "That's where you're going, Blue Heron Point. When we were growing up, the only store was over there. Then they built the hotel. Now it's a little town. Not a very nice one.

"Anyway, when we were young, that was the treat, getting in the boat once a month before freeze-up and going across the lake to the store. Theresa used to take money out of her father's pocket when he passed out, and she'd take the boat over there herself to get food for her and her brother. Sometimes when it got worse than usual at home, she'd stop on one of the islands and she and Jackie would stay there until the groceries ran out. Just sleeping on the ground. Kokom would make my dad take blankets out for them to lie on, and they'd be safe for a while. But they always had to come to shore.

"I'll never forget watching that little girl start out across the big lake with Jackie sitting beside her. Two little dots in the boat, so small, until the boat was just a dot, and then it disappeared."

I was relieved when I heard Angus shouting that he'd caught a fish. Beth Mirasty's memories of Theresa's child-hood were taking me to a place I didn't want to be.

Angus landed his jackfish, and it was a beauty. Beth offered to clean it and freeze it so we could pick it up on the way home. As we walked toward the Northern Lights Motel, Angus was ecstatic. The boys ran on ahead with the fish. I turned to Beth.

"Does Theresa's brother still live around here?"

"He lives in Blue Heron Point."

"Do you have an address?"

"Whatever pub opens first for the day." She shook her head with annoyance. "It's such a waste. He comes over here to eat sometimes if he hasn't hocked his boat to buy a bottle. When he's sober, he's as good a guide as there is. Theresa taught him. But when he's drinking, he's just another drunk. If you want to talk to him, be sure to get there in the first hour after the bar opens. Before that he's too sick with wanting it, and then after that he's just sick."

Beth stopped at the back of the motel with the boys. She sent her son inside for a knife. She said to Angus, "You might as well learn to do this now. Your mother can go and get your sister."

Taylor had a lap full of dolls. With their painted faces, their bright scraps of skirts and their wishbone legs, they were odd and very lovely.

"Dynamite dolls, T.," I said, and meant it.

Kokom said to Taylor, "In my room is a red box that had candy in it. A heart box. You can have it for your dollies."

Taylor ran off. When she was safely out of the room, I heard the old lady's voice.

"That Desjarlais girl. Let her rest in peace now. She's been wandering all her life."

I felt a chill. I turned. The old lady was sewing on her quilt again. I hadn't noticed before how badly her fingers had been gnarled by arthritis, but her needle never stopped. She didn't look up.

"The parents were no good," she said. "When she was young like your little one here, the parents used to leave her with the babies. There were two babies then. The family had a big dog, female. The kids used to play with it. One day in the spring that female dog was in season. There were wild dogs or maybe wolves. They must have smelled the female dog on that little kid. They came and tore that baby to bits. It was a terrible thing. The parents blamed Theresa. They beat her something terrible. She brought her brother and stayed with us for a while. We wanted to keep her, but they said no."

"How did she ever get away?" I said. I was really thinking aloud, but the old lady answered me. Her voice was strong and filled with anger.

"She didn't. The wild dogs got her, too. Let her rest. It doesn't matter any more."

It didn't take long to get Angus settled in at camp. As soon as he jumped out of the car, he saw two boys he had known from the summer before. They came over and grabbed his gear, and the three of them disappeared.

"Goodbye," I shouted after him.

He ran back and gave Taylor a quick hug.

"Please don't kiss me, Mum," he said under his breath.

I gave him a manly pat on the back. "See you in two weeks," I said. I took Taylor's hand. "Looks like it's just you and me against the world, kiddo. What do you want for supper?"

"Cheeseburgers," she said.

"The north is famous for its cheeseburgers," I said.

The drive into Blue Heron Point was not a pretty one. There'd been forest fires in the area the year before, and the charred trunks of trees rose spectral against the summer sky. On the rocky faces of the hills kids had spray-painted messages: "OKA NOW," "CARLA RULES," "CLASS OF 91 NO FUTUR." Blue Heron Point was the kind of northern town that exists for the people who come to fish. All the buildings faced out on the dirt road that followed the shoreline. There were two inns, a couple of motels, and, set back from the road, the Kingfisher Hotel. They all had bars, and they all had no-vacancy signs. There were two general stores with restaurants, and a liquor store.

"Which place looks best to eat, T.?" I said.

"The one with the dogs fighting outside," she said.

In fact, the food was good and plentiful: a homemade cheeseburger and a dinner plate filled with greasy, salty French fries.

After we finished, I said, "Now for the hard part, finding a place to stay. I wish I'd asked Greg's uncle if we could use his cottage."

"But you didn't," Taylor said, twirling a fry in her ketchup.

"Nope, it didn't work out," I said. "Let me go and ask at the counter what they suggest. I'm too tired to drive any more today. Besides, there's someone I want to try to find here."

I looked at my watch. Six o'clock. According to Beth's calculations, Jackie Desjarlais would have been drinking for six hours. Tomorrow would be better.

The woman at the cash register was not encouraging. It was the Tuesday after the long weekend, and a lot of people take their holidays the first two weeks in July. I paid for our lunch, thanked her and started to leave. She called me back.

"You could ask at the hotel about the fishing shacks," she said. "They're awfully small, but they're clean and they're right on the lake. Pretty views."

The man behind the desk at the hotel was huge. He was wearing a T-shirt that said, "Jackfish in Lard Makes a Fisherman Hard." When I asked about a room, he opened the registration book, ran a thick finger down the page and then grinned at me.

"You're damn lucky, lady. There's one unit left. Last empty bed in town. Twenty bucks. Pay now. The money's up front for the shacks. I've put you in number three."

The shacks were, in fact, one building, which must have been built before the province had passed its law about not building directly on lakefront property. The place was right down by the docks. It was old and had the frail, stripped-down look of wartime housing. The individual units were tiny, just one small room and a bathroom, but each unit had a small kitchen and a large window that opened onto a screened-in porch. It was obvious that they were a place to sleep for people who wanted to fish.

Taylor was enchanted. "It's like a doll's house," she said, opening the little refrigerator and pulling out an ice tray that made six cubes.

We unpacked and then we went for a swim. When we'd
changed out of our swimsuits, we sat on the dock and
watched the boats come in. A sunburned man with a tub full
of fish asked Taylor if she'd had any luck.

"Yes," she said, "I got to stay in the little house up there."
She pointed toward the shacks.

He laughed. "That makes us neighbours. I'm staying
there, too."

Nice. We had supper at the hotel, and after we ate, I decided
to call Jill Osiowy to give her the hotel's number in case there
were any changes about our July eighth show. It was almost
seven, but she was still at her office. She answered on the first
ring, and she sounded tense and distracted.

"You sound as if you could use a little down time in the
north yourself," I said.

"Sorry," she said, "but I have company. Con O'Malley and
his Corporate Choir Boys. It's been years since I've seen that
many pinstriped suits."

"You didn't mention you were having a royal visit," I said.

"I didn't know," she said. "They just arrived two hours
ago. I was editing some of the Little Flower tapes – on my
own time, of course – and my secretary called and said we'd
been invaded. I haven't the slightest idea what they're
doing here."

"Spooking you," I said.

"You've got that right," she said. "I'm spooked. CEOs are
like cops. Even when you know you haven't done anything
wrong, you'd rather they weren't around. Listen, Jo, I'd better
go. I'll call you tomorrow night."

I gave her the hotel number and hung up. Taylor and I
walked down the hill to the shacks. It was such a beautiful
night that we stayed on the dock until sunset. I looked out at
the lake and watched Taylor's small silhouette black against
the red sky and the dropping sun. How many nights had

Theresa Desjarlais stood on the shore of Havre Lake and watched as the sun dropped in the sky and the water turned to fire? Finally, when the darkness closed in on us, Taylor and I walked to our cabin.

There was just one double bed. It felt good to lie there on the cool smooth sheets with Taylor's body curled against me. Her hair smelled of heat and lake water, and I closed my eyes and remembered holding Mieka in just this way when she was small, and the boys, too, when they were little. I touched the silver circle of my bracelet and remembered Christy. "Did anyone ever hold you like this when you were little, Christy-Theresa?" I said. "Did anyone ever encircle you in close and protective arms?" And because I knew the answer, I wept.

CHAPTER

11

When the boy appeared outside the shack's screen door saying there was a phone call for me up at the Kingfisher, Taylor and I were just finishing dinner. On the table between us was a map of Havre Lake; we were planning the boat trip we were taking the next morning. It had been a good day. We'd walked the shoreline from Blue Heron Point to Hampton Narrows, an hour and a half away, and Taylor had found a piece of driftwood shaped like a bird, some fool's gold, and the torso of a Barbie doll. Serendipity.

She'd had more luck than I'd had. As soon as I knew the bars were open, I'd started checking around for Jackie Desjarlais. No one had seen him. In the last place we tried, the bartender told me Jackie had been blind drunk the night before, and if I had anything serious to say to him I'd be smart to wait until the next day.

At some level, I had been relieved. The prospect of a day without sadness or ugliness was appealing. Cut loose from responsibilities, Taylor and I had given ourselves up to the pleasures of cottage life. We went down to the beach for a swim, then we sat on blankets on the sand and let the breeze dry us off. At midafternoon, we walked to the store in Blue Heron Point and bought supplies: groceries, matches for fire starting, a bottle of sun block and a jar of blackfly repellent guaranteed to be environmentally friendly. On the way out of the store, Taylor picked up a baseball cap with the words "I'd Rather Be Fishing" written in fish across the front.

"It's to keep the sun off my head," she said. "Angus says too much sun can boil your brains."

She'd put the hat on the coat hook by the door the way Angus always did at home, and that night as we followed the boy out of the cabin, she reached up, grabbed her cap and jammed it over her hair.

"Nice hat," the boy said, and Taylor beamed. They talked about fishing all the way up to the hotel.

I went inside. The man who had checked us in was sitting on a stool behind the front desk. He handed me a message slip with a number I recognized as Jill Oziowy's.

"The lady said to call her back reverse the charges." He slid the phone across the desk to me. "I'm here to make sure those charges get reversed."

Jill sounded edgy and excited. "Things are happening, Jo," she said. "Last night when I finally got home, there was a message on my answering service. A man's voice, muffled. 'Check out the Lily Pad,' he said, and hung up. Just like in the movies. It was after midnight, and I was dead tired. Those little trolls from head office had been nipping at my heels all night, so I didn't go over to the Lily Pad till about seven this morning. Guess what? The place was closed up tighter than a drum, padlock on the front door, blinds drawn. There were two kids on the lawn by that wooden frog, but they were so pilled up I don't think they knew where they were.

"I went around and checked out the back. Same thing. Incidentally, you were right about that door, Jo, that's a serious security system. I just don't understand what it's doing there. Why would the Lily Pad people tie up that kind of money in the back door of a drop-in centre for street kids?"

"Because it's something more than a drop-in centre," I said. The manager hadn't moved from his stool. He was less than two feet away from me. As soon as my call to Jill had gone through, he'd pulled out a pair of scissors and started cleaning his nails. When I mentioned the drop-in centre, he stopped digging and looked up at me with quick and interested eyes.

I lowered my voice. "I can't talk here," I said.

"I'll talk," Jill said. "I remembered what you said about Helmut Keating taking all that liquor in on Saturday. I thought the kids on the lawn might have heard something. At first, I thought I was out of luck. Whatever drug those kids had been doing had propelled them to another dimension, but I just kept talking, and when I mentioned Helmut Keating's name, I got a reaction. One of the boys pulled himself together enough to get out a full sentence: 'They say Helmie blew town,' he said. What do you make of that, Jo?"

"Interesting," I said, and I smiled at the hotel manager. He didn't smile back.

"Keating's not in the book, but I called a friend of mine who's also into good works and she had an address for him. Jo, you wouldn't have believed his house. A big split level out on Academy Park Road."

"The dysfunctional population business must be pretty lucrative," I said.

"Right," said Jill. "But listen, Helmie's place was shut tight, blinds pulled. The neighbour was out watering her lawn and she said Helmut took off this morning, very early, in a cab. He had suitcases. That's all she knew. Jo, it's just a hunch, but I think Helmut Keating was my mystery caller. I think he's decided to blow the whistle on the Lily Pad. I'm going to make some calls to people I know at the airport and the bus station. See if I can track down our travelling man. Then I'm going back to the Lily Pad. There may be a kid there who's kept her eyes open and her brain unfried."

She swore softly. "I've lost a whole day, but there was no way around it. My new best friends from head office insisted on getting an early start. On what, I still haven't figured out. Jo, I was tracking down stuff for them all day, figures, employment records, old interviews. And whatever I got wasn't enough, they'd just send me off again. I felt like that girl in the fairy tale who had to keep spinning straw into gold, and no matter how much she spun it was never enough. What was the name of that story anyway?"

"Rumpelstiltskin," I said.

Jill laughed. "Jo, you're so well read. Anyway, after I spent the day spinning my straw, I came home and there was a threat on my machine."

The hotel manager leaned forward; he was so close I could smell his aftershave. It was artificially piny, like the little deodorant trees people hang from the rear-view mirror of cars.

"What kind of threat?" I asked.

"Just a garden-variety death threat," Jill said quietly. "I've heard worse. Anyway, that's where we are now."

"I think you should call the police," I said.

"Not yet," she said. "This one's still mine. Jo, I can feel the adrenaline. Something's coming."

"Be careful," I said. "Please, please, be careful."

I had a troubled sleep that night. I dreamed I was at the back door of the Lily Pad. I could hear a child crying inside, and I was frantic to get in. I had a card for the security system, but every time I tried to use it to open the door, the system spit the card back out at me. No matter how many ways I tried, I couldn't get the card to fit. Then Blaine Harris was there in his ponytail and his beaded moccasins. "The rain," he said urgently. "The rain," I said, and it seemed to be the right thing to say because he smiled at me and gave me an old paper dollar. I put the dollar into the card slot, and the door opened. Then I woke up.

The next morning I was up with the sun; after the puzzling dream of the night before, I was glad to see it. A car pulled into the parking lot in front of the unit next door, and that was reassuring, too. It felt good to be part of the solid world where the sun shines and people come and go. I could hear the voice of our neighbour, the sunburned man who had talked to Taylor when he came in from fishing the night we came. It was obvious that he and the man who had just arrived were old friends who met somewhere every year to fish. As I heard my neighbour and his friend exchange their bluff hearty greetings and run through the familiar litany about the condition of the roads they'd driven and how much booze they'd brought and where the fish were biting, I was smiling. Unreconstructed, unrepentant Real Men. No one needed to give these guys drums to get in touch with their inner selves.

Then the man who had just arrived lowered his voice. "So where's the hairless pussy around here?" he asked.

The sunburned man laughed. "On an island, if you can believe it. You need a fucking guide to take you there, but, sweet Jesus, it's worth it."

Beside me, Taylor, still asleep, rolled over onto her back. She muttered something, then she smiled and stretched out her arms in a gesture of animal trust.

I felt my stomach lurch, and I sat up, tense, alert to danger.

Next door, the sunburned man said, "First things first. Come on in and we'll have an eye-opener."

The screen door slammed. For the next fifteen minutes, as I sat, still and silent, I could hear the low murmur of the voices on the other side of the wall. Finally, the screen door slammed again, and I could hear the men's voices fade as they moved toward the dock. I walked onto our porch and watched until they got into the boat and started the motor. I didn't stop watching until their boat disappeared into the line that separated the blue of the sky from the blue of the lake. I hoped they would drown.

When I went in, Taylor was sitting up with the candy box full of dolls on her knees.

"We're going to the island to make breakfast," she said. "Remember, Jo? You're going to make a fire and we're going to cook bacon. I dreamed about it even."

My heart was pounding so hard I thought it would beat out of my chest. I wanted to take Taylor's hand and run.

Oblivious, Taylor arranged her dolls on the bedspread. "Kokom says on the islands you can find moss that will keep my dolls from breaking when I carry them. She says when she was a girl people used to put that moss around real babies." She looked up at me hopefully. "Jo?"

"Just trying to remember how to make a campfire, T.," I said. "Come on, let's get rolling. Get dressed and we'll pack up our food. I've already looked at the lake this morning. It's like glass. Perfect weather for a shore breakfast."

Three-quarters of an hour later, picnic cooler loaded, Thermos filled, we were fastening our life jackets. It was going to be a great day, hot and still and sun-filled, but the man at the boat rental had been cautious.

"Where you want to go is South Bay," he said. "You'll be okay there. It's close, and on that map of yours, the Xs show where the rocks are. Don't go through the narrows into the lake proper. Too much can go wrong. Hit a rock, get stuck out in the middle when a storm hits, and you and the little girl here will buy it."

I looked at my map; there were a lot of Xs, but it was reassuring, for once, to know where the dangers were.

It had been years since I'd driven a motorboat, but it wasn't a complex skill, and it felt good to put some distance between me and Blue Heron Point. As our boat cut through the shining water, Taylor's eyes were wide, taking in all the sights. When we came to the bay, I cut back the motor. There were perhaps twenty islands to choose from. They weren't the gentle islands of children's books; they were steep, with shirred rock faces that rose sharp and hostile from the water. The treeline was high on these islands, and it wasn't until you climbed to the top that you were protected by bushes and evergreens.

"You pick," I shouted to Taylor over the low hum of the motor. "Which one looks good to you?"

"Can we move closer?" she said.

"Sure," I said, and we moved slowly through the bay, checking them out.

Finally Taylor pointed to one that seemed tucked away behind the others. "That one," she said. "No one will ever find us there."

It was as if she had read my mind.

We pulled the boat up on shore and tied it to a rock. When we were sure it was secure, we climbed up the rock face in search of wood. At the top of the hill the terrain was hospitable, flat and tree-covered. The sun came through the evergreens and made shifting patterns on the moss. I was standing there admiring the view when Taylor called me.

"Look," she said. "People were here before." On a stump between two trees, someone had piled stones and made a little altar. A plastic figure of the virgin was wedged into the stones at the top. On the ground in front of the altar was a ring of stones enclosing the charred remains of a fire.

As I looked at the garish little figurine I thought of Theresa and her brother. Two children on an island. At night it must have been terrifying: the unbroken darkness of the northern sky, the birds swooping to shore, the lake black with secrets. Had Theresa built a fire? Had she found a plastic Mary like this one to mother Jackie and her through the night? So many terrors. But she was a child who was used to terrors.

"Jo? Jo, what're you thinking about?" Taylor was tugging at my hand. "Are you thinking about eating? Because I am."

"Time to make a campfire then," I said.

We built a fire on the rock, and we cooked bacon and made toast and boiled the lake water for tea. The tea tasted of twigs and smoke. After we cleaned our dishes and put out our fire, we explored the island, then we swam in the icy water. Taylor dog-paddled for a while, then she floated on her back and looked at the birds circling in the blue sky. When we got tired, we came ashore and lay in the sun on towels stretched over the rocks.

With the sun hot on my back, the warm rock under me and the sound of birdsong in the air, the tension seeped out of my body, and I drifted off to sleep. I awoke to feel my bracelet burning from the sun. Taylor was sitting on her towel, carefully arranging the moss she'd collected around her wishbone dolls.

"You were sleeping," she said with a smile.

I looked at my watch. It was twenty to twelve. By the time I got back to shore and changed, the pubs would have been open half an hour. With luck, Jackie Desjarlais would be ready to talk.

As we tied the boat to the dock in front of the shacks, I decided I'd try the Kingfisher first. That way I could check for phone messages, too. Taylor and I dropped our picnic gear at our cabin and walked up the hill to the hotel. The steps were filled with blank-faced kids smoking – Lily Pad north. When I asked if anyone had seen Jackie Desjarlais that day, they didn't even bother looking up, and as we went up the

steps, Taylor and I had to walk carefully to keep from stepping on them.

It wasn't hard to find the bar. A plastic muskellunge arced
over the doorway to a dark and cavernous room. Burned into
a block of cedar under the fish were the words "Angler's
Corner." It was only half an hour after opening, but already
the pine room deodorizer was losing out to the smells of
stale beer and cigarettes and urine. I waited for my eyes to
adjust to the darkness, then Taylor and I started across the
room. We didn't get far. I hadn't taken three steps when a
hand reached out from behind me and closed around my
upper arm.

"You can't be in here with a kid." The man behind me
was huge and menacing; they grow their bouncers big in the
north.

"I'm not staying," I said. "I'm just looking for someone."

His hand didn't relax its grip.

"I'm looking for Jackie Desjarlais," I said.

He looked at me stonily.

"Can you help me?" I said.

"If I see him, I'll tell him you're lookin'," he said, and he
started pushing me toward the door.

"Tell him I'm a friend of Theresa's," I said. "My name is
Joanne and I'm staying at the shacks down by the lake."

By the time I finished the sentence, I was out the front
door, blinking in the sunlight.

I had just started down the steps when I heard someone
call my name. I turned and I was face to face with Jackie
Desjarlais. I would have known him anywhere. He was, as
my grandmother would have said, the dead spit of his sister:
the same slight body, the same dark eyes, the same wide,
generous mouth. Except that everything that was fluid and
graceful in her had gone slack in him.

I smiled at him. "Hello, Jackie," I said.

"You know me?" he asked, surprised.

"You look so much like her," I said.

"No," he said, "she was beautiful."

Unexpectedly, his eyes filled with tears. He lit a cigarette and began to cough. He coughed so hard that he bent over double; finally, he straightened and wiped his lips and eyes.

"Fuck," he said. "These things are goin' to fuckin' kill me." For the first time he noticed Taylor. "I'm sorry," he said to her.

She moved toward him. "It's okay. My brother Angus says that, too."

Despite everything, I felt a warmth. "My brother Angus." The words sounded good.

Jackie's face seemed to open a little.

I touched his arm. "Talk to me," I said. "Tell me about Theresa. She was my son's girlfriend, but I never really got to know her."

"I know who you are," he said. "Terry showed me the Christmas pictures."

"You must have been so proud of her," I said.

He looked at me as if I was insane. "Proud?" He repeated the word uncomprehendingly.

"Proud of all she accomplished. Going to university. Putting the sadness she knew here behind her. How did she get out of here, Jackie? Tell me."

He drew deeply on his cigarette and blew a careful smoke ring. "There's only one way for girls to get out of here," he said. "I got nothin' more to say."

He opened the door to the hotel. Somewhere in that stale-aired darkness Dan Seals was singing "All That Glitters Is Not Gold." Jackie looked at Taylor. For the first time, he smiled. His smile was Theresa's smile. As his mouth curved into that familiar mocking line, my heart lurched. He reached into his pocket, pulled out a loonie and handed the coin to Taylor.

"Little Sister," he said, and he turned and walked through the door.

I guess I had known how Theresa Desjarlais became Christy Sinclair from the moment I saw the bleak sandy streets of Blue Heron Point: no businesses or offices where a young girl could work to earn enough money to get away, just hotels and bars where women's work was menial and permanent.

As Taylor and I walked down the incline from the hotel, I felt leaden. Taylor's hand was small in mine, something to hold on to. The rain started when we were halfway down the hill. Just a few drops at first, then more, closer together. By the time we reached the fishing shacks the heavens had opened, the wind had picked up, and there were whitecaps on the lake.

Taylor and I were soaked to the skin. We got inside, towelled off and changed into dry clothes. Taylor pulled down the bedspread and crawled into bed.

"I didn't sleep on the island, Jo," she said. "I had to watch."

I sat at the table by the window, listened to the rain pounding into the turbulent lake and thought about the lonely life of Christy Sinclair.

She had been a prostitute. The little girl who had been beaten by her drunken parents had used her only asset to get out. Somewhere between Blue Heron Point and the University of Saskatchewan, where Peter met her, Theresa Desjarlais had transformed herself. She'd become educated, learned how to dress, changed her name. She'd walked away from everything that made her a victim, started a new life. She'd escaped.

At least for a while. But the past was there, as permanent as the teddy bear tattoo on her left buttock, the teddy bear tattoo that was the same as Bernice Morin's. And then . . . And then what? Christy had walked into Mieka's store one afternoon, and Bernice Morin had been there. What had happened after that?

I was so deep in thought that I guess I didn't hear him knocking. Finally, frustrated and soaked to the skin, he opened the door. It was the boy who had delivered the message the night before. He was wearing a bright neon shirt and a cap like the one of Taylor's he'd admired so much.

I smiled and told him I liked his hat, but he didn't smile back. He was solemn with the importance of his message. "There's a phone call at the hotel for you. An emergency, they said, for Joanne. They sent me to get you. Quick."

I looked at Taylor sleeping, warm in her bed, and I looked at the rain outside.

I decided in a second.

I grabbed my bag, took out a five-dollar bill and handed it to the boy. "You remember Taylor. Stay with her for a while, will you? I don't want to take her out in this, and she'll be scared if she wakes up and I'm gone."

His hand shot out and grabbed the five dollars.

"I'll give you five more if you're here when I get back," I said.

"I'll be here," he said, sitting down at the kitchen table.

I grabbed my jacket. It wasn't much use against a rain that seemed torrential, but it was something. As I climbed the hill, the gravel gave way beneath my feet. It seemed I took one step forward and slid back two. The whole summer had been like that – filled with frustration, filled with rain, filled with death. I was glad to see the soft fuzz of light from the hotel through the grey. I ran across the parking lot. Incredibly, the kids were still sitting on the steps. A couple of the more sober ones were holding green plastic garbage bags over their heads as protection, but the rest were so drunk they didn't seem to realize it was raining. A girl was standing at the side of the steps vomiting. I could hear her retching as I ran past her into the hotel.

The hotel manager was wearing the shirt he'd been wearing the night Taylor and I arrived, the one that said, "Jackfish in Lard Makes a Fisherman Hard."

"There's a message for me," I said. "An emergency phone call."

"Says who?" He was smiling, enjoying his role as rustic funny man. This was going to be rich.

"The boy who brought the message last night came by the fishing shacks a few minutes ago. A little guy about ten, wearing a neon T-shirt and a new cap."

"He must've been playing a joke," the proprietor said.

"A joke?" I said.

"Yeah, a joke." His face rearranged itself into a mask of concern. "Of course, he could be a thief. These kids around here learn fast. If you've got valuables in that shack, you might be smart to hightail it back there. This hotel is not liable for anything that gets taken from a guest's room. You're warned. There's a sign on your door."

"There aren't any valuables there," I said. And then I thought of Taylor. Taylor was there.

For a split second I considered asking him to help me. Then I looked into his eyes. He wouldn't have crossed the room to save his own mother. I was on my own. I ran down the hill, slipping in the loose wet gravel, catching myself on bush branches to keep from falling. I ran and fell and picked myself up and ran again. I went as fast as I could, but it wasn't fast enough. The front door to the shack was open. There was no one at the table. There was no one in the bed.

I called her name. I called and called, but as I sank down in the chair at the kitchen table, I knew she couldn't hear me.

I ran outside and looked along the shoreline. It was deserted. I thought I saw a boat heading through the north channel, but it was raining so hard I wasn't sure. I tried to listen for the sound of a motor, but it was no use.

As I walked to the shack, I could feel the panic rising. I opened the screen door and went in. "This is how it starts," I said, and my voice echoed in the empty room. "This is how it starts."

In the mirror above the dresser, I could see myself. My hair was dark with rain, and my face was wet, but I looked like my ordinary self. I thought of the dozens of times I had seen the parents of abducted children on television. For all of them, the nightmare must have started just like this, on an ordinary day when, just for a moment, they had dropped their guard, and everything had changed forever. They had been ordinary people living anonymous lives, and then, in the blink of an eye, they were famous, their tense faces flickering across our television sets, their voices breaking as they justified themselves to the audience. "I only turned my back for a second; she was right there." "We never left him alone." "I always told him not to talk to strangers."

After the media wearied of their stories, the lost children's pictures cropped up on bus shelters and milk cartons. And I would look at the pictures of these children, faces shining, hair freshly cut for the school photographer, and tell myself this wouldn't have happened if the parents had been careful. This wouldn't have happened if the parents had been conscientious; if they had really loved their kids; if they hadn't taken chances. It was a mantra to distance myself, protect myself, and it had worked for twenty-one years.

Now, without warning, I had crossed the line that separates the lucky ones from the losers. Now I would be the one on TV, and it would be Taylor's picture that would be . . . A thought struck me, terrible, annihilating. I didn't have a picture of Taylor. She had only been with us since February. I hadn't taken her picture. I wasn't a good parent. I was negligent.

Without a picture, I could lose her forever. I could forget her face, and it would be as if she had never existed. Suddenly, finding a picture was the most important thing. There had to be one somewhere. My mind spun crazily through the possibilities. And then, I remembered.

The new bike. The morning we bought her new bike, I had taken pictures of Taylor wobbling down the driveway. I remembered looking through the view finder and noticing that the pink stripe on her safety helmet was exactly the shade of pink on her two-wheeler.

I hadn't failed her, after all. Suddenly, as if it had appeared as a reward for my diligence, I saw the postcard. It was on top of the dresser. The printing looked hurried. "Don't call the police for 24 hours and she'll be back safe." I turned it over; on the other side there was a picture of the Kingfisher Hotel, seductive under picture-book turquoise skies.

Twenty-four hours . . . I began to shake at the thought of what they could do to her in twenty-four hours. I thought about the men next door. "So where's the hairless pussy around here?" My stomach heaved, but I pushed myself up from the table and walked next door. Their car was still out back, but they could have taken her in a boat. A boat would have been the thing. They could have taken her out in the channel to the big lake, to the islands where you couldn't hear a child screaming. Their screen door was unlatched. I went onto the porch and pounded on their front door. There was no answer, but I had to be sure. I tried to smash down the door, but it was surprisingly solid. They had left the front window open an inch. Only the screen protected it, but when I tried to loosen the screen by hand, it wouldn't budge. Years of paint had stuck it firm. I went back to our place and picked up a butcher knife. I used the knife to cut through the screen and I reached in and raised the window. I crawled through onto the kitchen table. There was no one there.

Their suitcases were open on the floor. I started rummaging in them, looking for something that might help me know what had happened. The cases were filled with clothes for the fishermen. Someone had bought these things for a man who was a husband and father. ("This will be a good shirt for Dad when he goes up north.") At the bottom of the suitcases were the magazines. They were unspeakable. Think of the worst thing you know, and this was worse. The children looked as if they had been drugged. I hoped to God they had been drugged, anything so they wouldn't feel the things that were being done to their bodies, those fragile, perfect bodies.

When I looked at the magazines, I knew there was a connection between this perversion and Taylor's disappearance. And I knew something else. Everything was connected somehow to the Lily Pad. But how? As I climbed the hill to the hotel, I repeated the word, pounding it into the ground with every leaden footstep.

This time I didn't use the phone in the hotel. There was a pay phone outside the restaurant where Taylor and I had eaten that first night. I went into the restaurant and got change, then I came back out and called Jill Osiowy.

She answered on the first ring. "They've taken Taylor," I said. "They left a postcard with instructions. They say if I don't call the police, they'll bring her back safe in twenty-four hours."

"Do what they say," Jill said. Her voice was dead. "Jo, Helmut Keating called. The people who own the Lily Pad are after him. He found out something about Kim Barilko's murder, and he got greedy. He says they're going to kill him. Jo, I believe him. He wants me to get into their computer. He says if I key in the word 'teddy,' I'll get everything I need. I can stop them, Jo. I can stop those bastards."

Suddenly, Jill's voice broke. "Do you know what they did? They killed Murray and Lou. They slit their throats and dropped them in my garbage can."

There were black spots in front of my eyes, and my knees went weak. I thought I was going to pass out. I opened the door to the telephone booth and took deep breaths till the faintness passed.

All the time, Jill was talking to me. "Jo, do what they say about Taylor. Don't call the police. Don't take a chance with her."

The line went dead. For a moment my options flashed wildly through my mind. There weren't many. I thought of Jill's old tortoiseshell-cats, killed as a warning, and I knew I wasn't going to leave Taylor with those monsters for twenty-four hours.

When I walked through the door to the Angler's Corner, I was cold with anger. No one was going to hurt Taylor. Jackie Desjarlais was in the corner playing pool. I grabbed his arm and started dragging him toward the door.

"You're coming with me," I said.

"Are you crazy?" he said.

I jerked him toward me till our faces were almost touching. "Do I look crazy?" I said.

"Yeah," he said, "you do." He tried to wrench away from me.

"Someone's taken Taylor," I said, "and I think they're going to hurt her."

"Little Sister," he said.

He had been drinking, but he wasn't drunk.

"I think they've taken her somewhere in the lake. To an island. I need you to –"

"The Lily Pad," he said.

I felt as if I'd stepped through the looking glass.

His voice was dead. "The Lily Pad. That's where Theresa

was. It's a place where men can do things to kids. Theresa said it was just a business. That's how much they fucked her over. That she would think it was just a business."

"Please," I said.

"Let's go," he said. "My boat's down at the dock. You got money for gas? I drank my last five bucks."

"I've got money," I said.

When he came back, he had a gas can and a bottle of rye. His boat was a new one, fibreglass with a fifty-horsepower outboard motor. It looked sturdy. Then I looked out at the lake, and suddenly Jackie's boat seemed very small. He reached under the front and pulled out a khaki slicker.

"Put this on," he said. He opened the rye. "Take a slug."

I did. The whisky burned my throat, but it warmed and calmed me.

It took us forty-five minutes to get to the island, forty-five minutes of being pounded by the storm and my own fear. We were heading into the wind and the rain was blinding. Every time Jackie's boat slapped against the whitecaps, it shuddered as if it was about to split in two. My panic about Taylor hit in waves, overwhelming me. At one point, I looked out and I couldn't see anything: no islands, no shoreline, no line dividing earth from heaven. In that moment I felt a stab of existential terror. I was alone in the universe in a frail boat with a stranger. It was a metaphor the psalmist would have understood.

And then Jackie Desjarlais looked up and smiled at me.

"Some fun," he said.

"Yeah," I said, "some fun."

Those were the only words we spoke until the island came into view. The rain had stopped, and as we came closer to shore, I turned to Jackie.

"Shouldn't we try to keep out of sight?" I asked.

"They know the boat," he said flatly.

For a moment, I thought I'd fallen into a trap. I remembered Jill Osiowy's warning: "Don't take things at face value. For once in your life, Jo, don't assume the best."

"Everybody here works for them one way or another," Jackie was saying. "I'm one of the ones that brings the clients over." He shuddered. "And I feel like shit. Theresa always said it was a business, a service. You asked me back there how she got out of Blue Heron Point. She worked for them. She started when she was a kid. Maybe eleven. She didn't have no choice then. Our old man was a drunken son of a bitch and our mother . . ." He spat into the water. He looked at me and his eyes were dark with fury. "Our mother was no mother. A woman from town told Theresa that Social Services was going to take me and her, too, unless Theresa did something. So she did something . . ."

"She must have loved you very much," I said.

"She woulda done anything for me," he said flatly. "When she was older, they brought her into the business. They sent her down south to go to high school and look for more kids. For a couple of years she was a kind of manager at their place in Regina. She made a lotta money, bought me this boat, bought me everything. She always took care of me." His voice broke. "Fuck," he said.

We were almost ashore. He wiped his eyes with the sleeve of his jacket. I looked into my bag for a Kleenex, and there, folded neatly, forgotten, was the picture Taylor had drawn the morning after Theresa died.

I closed my eyes and remembered how Taylor had looked, running down the hill, hair tangled from sleep, laughing, eager to get the day started. And she had drawn this. I unfolded it and felt the tears come.

Frogs. Dozens of frogs, big and little, smiling and sad, dozens of frogs for Angus because I wouldn't let him take any home to the city with us.

We were almost ashore. Through the trees I could see the outline of a low building that looked like a motel. I started to fold up Taylor's frog picture. There was writing on the back of the page. The writing was familiar. I had seen it on the front of a hundred shell-pink envelopes the night Lorraine Harris and I addressed the wedding invitations. Here, in her familiar looping backhand, were the names of the players on the croquet teams the night of the engagement party.

The Jacks: Joanne, Keith, Angus, Taylor.

The Aces: Peter Kilbourn, Theresa, Mieka, Greg.

I read the names again. She had written "Theresa," not "Christy." It was impossible. That night none of us knew who Christy Sinclair really was. Except Lorraine Harris had known.

With a jolt, the boat hit the dock and Jackie jumped ashore.

For a moment, I didn't move.

Jackie Desjarlais must have seen the bewilderment in my face. He reached his hand out and pulled me ashore.

"Come on," he said gently. "It's time to go get Little Sister."

CHAPTER

12

As we moved from the dock to the shelter of the trees, I felt as if I was in a dream. As suddenly as it had begun, the wind had stopped, and there was a preternatural calm on the island. The air was dense with moisture, and as we moved toward the building, the ground was spongy beneath our feet. In the motionless air, every leaf and stone was thrown into sharp relief. It was a hushed and menacing world.

I leaned close to Jackie Desjarlais. "Where would they have her in there?" I asked. "Is there some sort of security?"

Jackie shrugged. "A guy I know says they don't need much because of being on an island. He works there nights sometimes, in case things get out of hand. But from what I've seen, during the day it's pretty much just the girls."

"Then we could go in and take Taylor," I said.

"I don't think that'd be a smart move," he said. "Let me check things out in there first." He took the flask of whisky out of his jacket pocket and held it to his lips. Then he offered it to me.

"Later," I said. "After we get her back."

He started to put the cap on the bottle, then he changed his mind. He poured some rye into his hand and patted it on his cheeks as if it was aftershave. Then he wiped his hand on the front of his shirt.

"My disguise," he said. "Nobody worries about a drunk. I oughta know." He slid the bottle carefully into the inside pocket of his jacket. "I'm gonna go in there and make a stink. It won't be the first time. Anyway, if there's security, that'll flush 'em out. At least we'll know what we're dealing with. Unless you got a different idea."

I shook my head.

"Okay," he said. "Stay outta sight till I get back. Then, if it looks good, we'll both go in."

I watched him lope across the clearing between the trees and the building; his legs were as long and as graceful as Theresa's. The sun came out, pale through the clouds. It seemed like a good omen. I walked among the trees until the Lily Pad was in my line of vision. Taylor was in there. I was sure of it.

The building looked reassuringly ordinary, like a motel or a private club. It was made of cedar, low-slung, sprawling, ranch style. There were a few windows; all were placed high, but there were skylights set into the roof, so there would have been light inside. I seemed to be standing at the side of the building. I moved around so I could see the back. There was a tennis court there, and playground equipment: a jungle gym, a swing set, a teeter-totter. I thought of someone ordering that gym set. ("No, it's not for my own children, it's for company.") The banality of evil. That's what Hannah Arendt had called her book about the men at the top of the Third Reich. The men who came here would be like those men, good to their dogs, fond of gardening, devoted fathers, even, and yet . . . I remembered the magazine photographs I had seen a little more than an hour ago, and my stomach clenched. What dark fantasies had been acted out on those swings? On that jungle gym?

A woman came from the front of the house and began walking toward the tennis court. She was pushing an industrial broom, the kind people use to sweep the water off a court after a rainstorm. Everything about the woman was shapeless: her body in its flowered cotton dress was a mass of shifting contours; her bare legs were pale and lumpy; her ankles were thick and swollen; even the way she walked, with the shambling gait of the lifelong alcoholic, lacked definition. Give this sad woman a bottle a day, and she wouldn't question anything.

Things were starting to come into focus. The elaborate security system on the back door of the Lily Pad in Regina. The locked doors to the upstairs. (Not safe, Kim had told me, the kids might smoke up there. It was a fire hazard.) But it wasn't fire the people who ran the Lily Pad were afraid of. They recruited from the street kids, lured them with the promise of a good life. ("Theresa was going to teach me about clothes and hair," Kim said, her face transformed, "and we were going to talk about going back to school. She had this business, and she was going to train me . . .")

A business. It sounded so innocent, like a bed and breakfast. I remembered the shining kitchen in the Lily Pad on Albert Street, so out of sync with the rest of that mismatched furniture scrounged from the Sally Ann. Then I remembered Helmut Keating trying to keep me from seeing a twenty-pound roast thawing in a pan on the counter. Prime rib. Nothing but the best for the Lily Pad's customers.

How many Lily Pads were there? I thought of the water lilies in the pond by our cottage when I was young. The flowers were beautiful, white and luminous, but when I looked underneath I could see they grew from thick, creeping stems that were buried in the mud at the bottom of the stagnant water. They slimed my hands when I touched them.

I heard a door slam, and Jackie came stumbling around the corner, a parody of a drunk. He picked up speed as he came toward me.

"There's nothing but the girls there. We're okay. I've been trying to come up with something. How does this sound? I go back up there and get everybody crazy and you try the doors at the back of the house. Start with the one closest to us. It's a kind of storeroom. I've delivered booze there sometimes. No one ever seems to worry much about locking it. The locks are on the side where they keep the kids."

I felt a rush of adrenaline. I wanted to find the people who had put the locks on those doors.

Jackie reached into the inside pocket of his jacket. When he pulled his hand out, he was holding a gun. "I sort of borrowed this from the guy who sold me the gas for the boat. He keeps it around in case of trouble. I figured we were more likely to have trouble today than him." He held the gun out to me. "You take it," he said. "If things get hot, just wave it around. Guns scare the shit out of people."

As I took the gun, my hand was trembling. "They scare the shit out of me," I said.

Jackie looked at me levelly. "You'll be all right," he said. He pointed to the woman sweeping the tennis courts. "As soon as she leaves, we'll go in."

It seemed like forever, and as we stood in the breathless mugginess of a July afternoon, I was half crazy with the thought of Taylor alone – or worse, not alone – in that malignant place. Jackie's gun, a dead weight in the pocket of my slicker, seemed to grow heavier as the minutes ticked by.

Finally, the woman picked up her broom and went toward the front of the house. As soon as she was out of sight, I curled my fingers around the handle of the gun and ran across the clearing. The first door at the back was metal, but it had been propped open with a wedge of wood. I opened it and found myself in a storage room. It was all very domestic and disarming. Facing me were two restaurant-size upright freezers. Next to them, in a kind of bin, were sacks of vegetables. Cartons of liquor were neatly stacked against the wall farthest from the door. There was a whole wall of canned goods. When I saw a low shelf near the front filled with tins of Spaghettios, I could feel the anger rising in my throat. I moved cautiously through the storeroom until I came to the kitchen. It was sleek and deserted.

The door was open and I could hear raised voices. One of the voices was male, demanding money, hollering obscenities. Jackie Desjarlais was putting on quite a performance.

I stood, tense, alert, trying to get a sense of the layout of the building. I moved quietly toward the voices and then at the first corridor I turned. Terrified I would make a mistake, I almost did.

She seemed to fly out of the door across from me. If she hadn't been looking toward the disturbance, Lorraine Harris would have seen me. But her mind wasn't on me. She looked preoccupied and grim. As she ran down the hall toward the trouble, her beautiful hair, knotted low on her neck, came loose. It made her look oddly girlish and vulnerable.

She had left open the door to the room she'd been in. I could see the screen of her computer. She hadn't had time to turn it off. I stepped closer. On the screen was a list of files. She had been deleting files, getting rid of evidence. Give us twenty-four hours, the note had said. Whatever these records were, they were important; I could use them as leverage to get Taylor. I tapped in the top code on the screen: spread sheets of financial records. Too complex. I tapped in the next code. More bookkeeping. I ran the list. Suddenly, I saw the code "teddy." The password Helmut Keating had told Jill to use to get into the Lily Pad computer.

The image of the teddy bear tattoo on Bernice Morin's left buttock flashed through my mind. Christy Sinclair had a teddy bear, too. I had seen it at the funeral home the night Mieka left me alone with Christy's body. The tattoos must have been a way of identifying the children as the property of the Lily Pad, a mark of possession like the brands burned into the flanks of cattle.

I typed the word *teddy*. Then I hit "Enter." The screen sprouted the kind of chart businesses use to explain their management structure. I recognized most of the names on the lower tiers: civic leaders in our towns and cities; politicians; two virulently homophobic ministers of God. The second name from the top was Lorraine Harris's. The top name was familiar, too: Con O'Malley, the president of NationTV. My boss. Jill had said the fax telling her to hire me as a panelist on *Canada Tonight* had come from his office.

O'Malley had covered all the bases. It wasn't hard to keep track of what I was doing from day to day. Lorraine was part of my family. And Jill was an employee of NationTV. When her investigation of the connection between Bernice Morin's death and the Little Flower murders hit pay dirt, Con O'Malley had bled her investigation dry by cutting off her money; then, when she persisted, he'd buried her in corporate busy work.

Busy work. That's what my job on the political panel had been. A distraction for a meddlesome woman. I looked at the management chart on the computer. Nothing was distracting me now. I hit the print key. In that quiet office, the printer seemed to roar to life, but I didn't have many options. The list had just finished printing when I felt a tug on the back of my slicker. I grabbed the gun in my pocket, and heart pounding, I turned. It was Taylor.

She was on the verge of tears, but she seemed all right. "I was beginning to get scared, Jo," she said. "Greg's mother said it was okay, but I was still getting scared."

I held her close to me. I could feel her heart beating against my chest. When I kissed the top of her head I could smell the warm, little-girl smell of her.

"No one hurt you, did they?"

She stood back, surprised. "Why would anybody hurt me?"

I ripped the sheet out of the printer and grabbed Taylor's hand. "Let's get out of here."

We started, then Taylor looked up at me. "I left my dolls," she said. She ran and picked up her candy box. By the time she came back, Lorraine Harris was standing at the door.

Lorraine was breathing hard, and there were darkening half-moons of sweat in the armpits of her cream jacket. But she was composed. Her oversized horn-rimmed glasses were lying on the table by the computer. She walked over, picked them up and put them on. It was a good look: the business-woman dealing with a crisis.

I stepped closer to her. "Hello, Lorraine," I said. "Going out of business?"

She looked quickly at the computer, at the printout in my hand, then at my face. For a time she was silent; I could almost hear the wheels turning as she decided which approach to take.

Finally, she made up her mind. "You can thank me that Taylor wasn't harmed," she said.

"Thank you?" I repeated, incredulous.

Taylor had heard her name and was looking at Lorraine with interest.

"The original plan was . . . different," Lorraine said.

There was a glassed-in space at the end of the room; it looked like a secretary's office. I pointed to it. "Taylor, why don't you go and sit in there till Lorraine and I are through talking. It'll be okay. You can see me, and I can see you."

Taylor went without question. She could feel the tension in the air.

As soon as Taylor closed the door to the office, Lorraine began to speak. Her voice was low, almost hypnotic. "The best thing for everybody would be if you just took Taylor and left. I give you my word that the business will be shut down. I'd already started to close things out. The decision came from Con O'Malley, Joanne. He won't go back on it. I'll be frank. The whole situation is just getting too hot – too many loose ends, too many people asking questions."

Her voice grew soft. "The Lily Pad is history, but our families aren't, are they? They're still making plans and thinking about the future. You have to protect them, Joanne. If you decide to be reasonable, no one will be hurt. Mieka's and Greg's wedding can be as perfect as you and I dreamed it would be. Keith's reputation won't be tarnished, and you'll have a brilliant future with the network. Sometimes, it's best just to walk away."

I felt myself being pulled into her orbit. Mieka had told me that Lorraine had taken courses in effective communication. She'd gotten her money's worth.

Lorraine touched my hand. "It will be as if the business never existed. I can erase everything."

"Including killing those girls," I said.

"I'm just management, Joanne. I don't kill anybody."

I felt laughter welling up in me. "You're just management?" I said.

"I never killed anybody," she said. "You have to believe me about that, Joanne. It wasn't me."

"Who was it, then?"

"Theresa. It was Theresa." Lorraine's grey eyes were the colour of winter ice. "They knew each other from before," she said. "Bernice had been at the Lily Pad when Theresa was in charge. Bernice was a difficult girl, a troublemaker; she didn't last. When she saw Theresa at Judgements that day, she threatened to tell Mieka the truth unless Theresa gave her money, a lot of money. Theresa panicked. She knew Bernice would keep asking for more. And she was desperately afraid Bernice would destroy her chance of being part of your family again." Lorraine covered my hand with her own. "In a way Theresa did it for you, Joanne."

I pulled my hand free of hers. "What happened to Theresa then?" I asked.

"She fell apart. She was terrified you'd find out the truth about her. And then when she saw me that night at the lake, she felt as if the walls were closing in. Of course, she knew I wouldn't expose her, but she told me it seemed as if all the ghosts of the past were rising up at once. I tried to help her. I offered to make arrangements so she could get away. I have connections."

I thought of the names on the computer print-out. They were men of power who were linked by a common sexual obsession; they were a brotherhood of pederasts.

"She could have pulled it off," Lorraine said. "She started, but she just seemed to lose her nerve. Killing Bernice did something to her. She'd tried to make what happened look like the Little Flower murders because she knew the cops don't push those investigations hard. But I think having to do it that way affected her. I'd known Theresa from the time she was ten years old, but I'd never seen her the way she was that night. She just didn't seem to have any resources left. I was going to help her. You have to believe that. But she found those pills in my bathroom and took them." Something animal and cunning flickered in her eyes. "I think she was afraid to face you, Joanne. I think she was afraid that if you found out the truth, you'd hate her."

"She killed herself because of me?" I said in a voice that didn't sound like mine. I felt myself losing ground.

"No one's without fault here," Lorraine said reasonably. "That's why it's best just to close things off without too many questions."

No one's without fault here. Her words seemed to resonate in me, touching hidden vulnerabilities. I thought of Peter. The possibility that Lorraine was right appeared at the edge of my mind. Perhaps it was best not to delve too deeply.

Then I remembered the other death. I moved closer to her. I could feel the pressure of Jackie's gun against my leg.

"And Kim Barilko?"

Lorraine twisted her hair back in a loop, then smiled at me, woman to woman. "I'll be frank, Jo. Helmut acted on his own initiative there, and he made a serious mistake. He thought it was a matter of security. He didn't know how much Theresa had told Kim and he didn't know how much Kim was about to tell you. It was a simple case of overreaction."

I knew she was lying. If Helmut had murdered Kim, he wouldn't be running from Con O'Malley and Lorraine, he'd be demanding that they protect him.

Lorraine cocked her head and gave me a winsome smile. "Don't overreact, Jo. Remember those pictures Mieka took? Remember all those shots of the two mothers addressing wedding invitations that she's saving for the grandchildren? Take Taylor back to the city now; I'll drive in tomorrow, and we can all just pick up where we left off."

I could see Lorraine's body relax. She thought she had me. She'd thought she could win, so she played her trump card. "Our kids need us," she said, and her voice was like honey. "Think of the children."

"I am," I said, sliding my hand into my pocket and curling my fingers around the handle of Jackie's gun. "I am thinking of the children. All of them. That's all I'm thinking about.

At the moment I'm thinking about the children you've got locked up here. I want them. Jackie Desjarlais and I are going to take them with us, and you're never going to touch them again. Do you hear me? You're never going to violate another child." My legs had started to shake, but my voice sounded strong. It sounded like a voice Lorraine should listen to.

I pulled the gun out and pointed it at her. "Come on," I said. "You and I are going to walk out of this room, and you're going to tell the people who work for you to bring the children to the dock. And Jackie and I are going to take them out of this cesspool. If it takes two trips, I'll wait with them. We're taking those children, and they're never coming back." My voice was rising. "Do you hear me, Lorraine? You're never going to sell another child again."

She looked at the gun, then she shrugged. "Have it your way, Joanne. I've never known how to deal with self-righteous women. You come in here like an avenging angel, sword in hand, all set to smite me down. Well, smite the fuck away. You won't be the first."

She took off her glasses and rubbed the bridge of her nose. She looked weary and wounded. "Tell me, Joanne, how do you think I got into this business? Do you think it was a career option, like deciding between being a doctor and a lawyer the way you and your friends did?"

"I don't want to hear this," I said.

Her mouth curled in derision. "Really? Well, I've decided you should hear this, Mieka's middle-class mother. Do you know how I met Con O'Malley? He bought me." She pointed in the direction of Blue Heron Point. "Over there at the Angler's Corner. My aunt was in there, drunk as usual, broke as usual. When Con came in, she offered to sell me for a bottle of beer. I was eleven years old." She looked hard at me. "What were you doing when you were eleven, Joanne? Dancing school? Pyjama parties with your friends? Con and

I had pyjama parties, till he decided I was too old. That was when he gave me a choice: go back to the Angler's Corner and be bought by anybody who had beer money or help him find some girls to replace me. Those were my career options, Joanne. Before you raise your sword, think about that. Think about how hard another woman had to work to make a good life for herself and her son. I'm not begging; I'm just asking for some consideration."

"I'll give you some consideration," I said, and I meant it. But as I walked through the Lily Pad, listening to Lorraine instruct her employees to bring the children to the docks, I kept Jackie's gun aimed at the back of her neck. No one gave me any trouble. Jackie was right. People were scared shitless of guns.

It took half an hour to get everybody down to the docks. There was a big cabin cruiser that belonged to the Lily Pad. Jackie was taking the children in that. We watched them climb on board. They were attractive and well dressed, but they seemed meek and spiritless. As they settled into their seats, I wondered if we'd been too late, if they were already beyond rescue. There were only seven of them, four girls and three boys. The woman who had cleaned off the tennis courts explained there had been a measles outbreak, and the others were quarantined in Blue Heron Point.

Two women whom Lorraine referred to as counsellors went in the boat with the children. The kids were afraid to be separated from them. Taylor and Lorraine and I were going to follow the cabin cruiser in Jackie's boat.

Finally, when everyone was in, Jackie turned and yelled to me. "Ready? I'll take it slow. Stay with me and you'll be fine."

I waved to him. Then a boy near the back of the cabin cruiser clambered over the seats to Jackie, leaned toward him and whispered something in his ear. Jackie nodded and the boy jumped out of the boat and ran to the Lily Pad. When he came back, Jackie gave me the high sign, and we began moving across the water.

Lorraine didn't speak on the trip back. Neither did Taylor. I was relieved. I didn't have any words left in me. I was grateful beyond measure that Taylor was sitting less than a metre away from me, bright and unharmed, but I had been running on adrenaline, and the adrenaline had stopped pumping. I was bone weary, and I was overwhelmed with the problems that lay ahead, what to do about Lorraine, and what would happen to the sad beaten children in the boat ahead.

As Blue Heron Point came into sight, I noticed there were people on the dock. We came closer and I saw that there were three of them. Keith was there, and Perry Kequahtooway, but the third figure was the one on whom my attention was riveted. As he recognized us in the boat, Blaine Harris raised his arm. It looked as if he was offering a benediction. I drove the boat parallel to the dock, helped Taylor out and handed the rope for mooring to Keith. Then I walked to where the old man waited in his wheelchair.

"You want to tell me something," I said.

"The rain. Killdeer," he said. Then he handed me a piece of newsprint, soft with age and handling. It was the picture of Christy Sinclair that the paper had printed at the top of her obituary. I looked at the picture, then I repeated his words.

"Lorraine killed her," I said. "Lorraine killed Christy Sinclair." His arm fell limp at his side, and he smiled at me. I looked at the boat. Lorraine was alone there; her body had folded in on itself in defeat. Perry Kequahtooway walked down the dock and held out a hand to her. He helped her out of the boat, then walked her over to a black sedan that was parked on the service road behind the shacks.

"It's over," I said to Blaine Harris, and he nodded.

Keith came and put his arm around me. I was still wearing the drab green slicker Jackie had given me. The weather had become even muggier, and the slicker acted like a sauna, trapping the hot, moist air against my T-shirt. I could feel it sticking to my skin. My runners and the ankles of my blue jeans were crusted with beach sand and muck from the island.

"Keith, I'm so dirty," I said, moving away from his arm.

"You look all right to me," he said, pulling me back. This time I didn't move away.

For a while I just stood there with his arm around me feeling tired. But I had to know. "Keith, what made you come up here?"

"My father."

"I have a friend who says Blaine's the most moral man she ever met."

Keith nodded. "He is that. I think that's why he's been going through such hell since that night at the lake. He saw something terrible happen, and he couldn't get anyone to understand what he'd seen."

I thought of the phone calls, the anguished words in the night.

Keith said, "Today when Dad and I were at the airport, waiting to get on the plane for Minneapolis, he showed me the picture of Christy he just gave you, and he tried those three words again: the rain killdeer. For the first time I put everything together. I started to ask Blaine questions. Had he seen Lorraine and Christy together that night? Had they quarrelled? Had he seen Lorraine do something to Christy? Maybe give her something to drink?" Keith sighed. "We were quite a pair: me badgering my father with all these questions, and Dad hooting away whenever I guessed right. Anyway, we did come up with a few things."

"Do you remember, Jo, that the room Dad was staying in out at the lake was Lorraine's room? The night Christy died, Dad's nurse had put him on the veranda outside the room to watch the sunset. The door to the inside was open, and Dad saw Lorraine come in and shake some kind of powder into a glass of whisky. When Christy came in, Lorraine gave her the drink. She probably told Christy it would calm her down. Christy drank the whisky. That's all we know for certain right now. But as far as I was concerned it was enough to call Perry Kequahtooway. He thought it was enough, too. That's why he came up with us."

Keith looked at the next dock. Jackie had tied up the cabin cruiser, and he and the women who worked for Lorraine were helping the children out of the boat.

"Jo, what the hell's going on here?" he asked.

I looked at this man whom I was beginning to love, and at his father, sitting in his wheelchair, looking at the lake, at peace for the first time in weeks.

"There's nothing going on that you have to know about now," I said. "It'll all be there tomorrow."

He looked at me hard. "It's bad, isn't it?"

I nodded.

"Then we should enjoy tonight," he said simply. "Are you and Taylor ready to come to the cottage?"

"The one with the squeaky screen door and the dishes that don't match and the wood box full of old *Saturday Nights*?" I said.

"The same," he said.

"My car is parked up there behind the shacks. Why don't you take Blaine up and get him settled?" I said. "I'll be right along, but there's some business I have to take care of. Could you give me five minutes?"

He smiled at me. "I told you before, Jo, I'm a patient man."

I took Taylor and we walked to the next dock and watched as Jackie made sure the big boat was safely moored. When he finished, he leaped out, graceful as a cat, and walked to the end of the dock. We followed him. The sun was dropping in the sky; as it fell, it made a path of light on the water. The fishermen's boats were heading toward shore. Time to come home.

It was Taylor who saw it first. She grabbed my hand and pointed. "Look," she said, "there's a fire over there, where we were."

At first, it was just a kind of heat shimmer in the sky above the channel, then the smoke began to rise, and the acrid smell of burning wood began to drift toward us. We watched in silence as the sky close to the water glowed red and then grew dark.

When the smoke thinned into fingers that seemed to reach into the sky, I touched Jackie's arm. "When that boy came over and talked to you in the boat before we left, what did he want?"

"Matches," Jackie said. "Matches so he could set his bed on fire."

"I'll take that drink now," I said.

The rye burned my throat, but it felt good. As I handed the bottle to Jackie, the sun glinted off the Wandering Soul bracelet. It was time. I slid the bracelet off and handed it to Jackie.

"I think she'd want you to have it," I said.

He touched the letters carefully with his forefinger, like a blind man reading Braille. Then he pulled his arm back and, in a graceful sweep, he skipped the bracelet across the water. For a heartbeat, it bounced along, flashing in the light from the dying sun; then it sank beneath the surface without a trace.

CHAPTER

13

I made one final trip to Lorraine's island. It was the morning after the fire. Taylor and I had spent the night at Keith's cabin. We had all been too tired for anything beyond bathing in the lake and collapsing into bed; sleep had come easily. The next morning, early, very early, Taylor woke me up. She'd been awakened by a scratching at the window. It was Jackie Desjarlais.

"I want to take you and Little Sister to breakfast," he whispered. "I've got something I need to talk to you about."

I looked into the bedroom with the twin beds; Keith and his father were still sleeping. Taylor, ready for adventure, had already pulled her shorts on. I wrote a note for Keith and slid it under the sugar bowl on the kitchen table, then I splashed water on my face, rinsed out my mouth and pulled on yesterday's clothes. Everything else was still in suitcases at the shacks.

We had breakfast at the café next to the hotel. When we got there, an old man was sitting on the porch watching two dogs fighting in the dirt out front. They were the same dogs who'd been fighting the day we arrived at Blue Heron Point.

When we left the restaurant, the old man was still there, and so were the dogs.

We walked down to the docks. For a while we just listened to the water lap the shore, then Jackie lit a cigarette and turned to me. "I'm going out there for a last look," he said. "I want to make sure there's nothing left of that fucker. You want to come along?"

"Yes," I said, "I think we do."

As we pushed off from land, it had seemed like a perfect day. The water was shimmering in the summer sunlight, and the sky was as cloudless and blue as the sky in the post-card Lorraine left when she abducted Taylor. But as we came through the narrows, the smell of wood smoke was heavy, and in the north a cloud, dense and malevolent, hung in the air above the island.

We moved slowly around the shoreline. We were, I think, stunned by the enormity of what had happened in the past twenty-four hours. The devastation was Biblical. The pines that had hidden the Lily Pad from prying eyes had been savaged by the fire. Stripped of needles and branches, they seemed spectral in the hazy air. The building was in ruins; nothing remained of it but a charred and smouldering skeleton. At the back, the steel door to the storage room hung crazily from its metal frame, guarding nothing. Flames had licked the playground equipment black, but it had survived, at least for a while. Unused, forgotten, it would rust and corrode; some day, in a hundred years, or a thousand, it would be gone, too.

"I can't believe that nobody even came out to the island to try to save it," I had said to Jackie as we headed back across the lake.

He had shrugged. "I think a lot of people in town were glad to see it burn. A lotta secrets in that building. A lotta things people want forgotten." Then he had turned to Taylor and smiled. "Come on, Little Sister. Time to learn how to drive a boat."

She moved to sit beside him. As she steered the boat across the shining lake, her face was flushed with pride. So was Jackie's. Once Theresa Desjarlais had taught her brother how to guide a boat through uncertain waters; now it was her brother's turn. As if he'd read my mind, Jackie Desjarlais looked up at me and yelled over the sound of the motor, "It all comes around, eh?"

"Yeah," I said, smiling back. "It all comes around."

Mieka and Greg were married in the chapel of St. Paul's Cathedral on Labour Day weekend. It was a small wedding. Hilda McCourt came down from Saskatoon, and Jill Osiowy was there to tape the ceremony for the mother who was not there. But these old friends aside, just Keith, Blaine and my children and I were sitting in the pews of that old and beautiful chapel.

In July, the papers had been filled with stories about Lorraine and Con O'Malley. At the beginning of August, the police solved the Little Flower case. When he realized that there would be no big payoff from NationTV, Darren Wolfe decided to become the police's star witness. His information was right on the money. The police moved quickly with their arrests, and the familiar picture of Con O'Malley touching the hibiscus in Lorraine's hair gave way to shots of four young pimps with smouldering eyes being escorted to and from their court appearances. As Tom Zaba had surmised, the Little Flower case was a simple matter of pimp justice. It lacked the cachet of the Harris-O'Malley case, but it pushed Lorraine's case to the back pages during the dog days of August, and we were grateful. Lorraine's story would, we knew, resurge when the trial began in early winter, but until then we all welcomed the protective cloak of a private wedding.

From the day Lorraine Harris was brought back from Blue Heron Point, Greg and Mieka had been her support and her comfort. Lorraine was being held at the correctional centre where Jill and I had visited Darren Wolfe, and Mieka and Greg hadn't missed a visiting day. They had no illusions about the horror of what she had done, but she was family, and for both of them, family was a link that was permanent.

Mieka and Greg's wedding day was a poignant one. They had learned early and publicly that marriage means caring for one another in good times and bad, and the knowledge had left its mark. As the summer sun poured through the stained-glass window, I leaned forward to look at my daughter. Under the filmy circle of her summer hat, Mieka's profile was as lovely and delicate as the face on a cameo, but there was sadness there, and there was sadness in the face of the man she loved.

The archdeacon's voice was solemn as he read from the Book of Alternative Services: "The union of man and woman in heart, body and mind is intended for their mutual comfort and help, that they may know each other with delight and tenderness in acts of love."

I thought of the seven children who had come back with us from the island to Blue Heron Point. Seven faces, pale, dead-eyed, not young, not old, not fearing, not hoping. They were in foster homes now, their futures dark and uncertain. And I thought of Bernice Morin, the veteran of the streets who believed in unicorns, and of Theresa Desjarlais standing in the field watching the tundra swans – "if they're smart and they're lucky, they'll make it" – and of Kim Barilko, her expression flickering between longing and contempt as she looked through the glass at wedding dresses that would always be for others, never for her.

"Pray for the blessing of this marriage," said the archdeacon. Beside me, Hilda McCourt, magnificent in mauve, dropped to the kneeler like a teenager. After a moment, I knelt, too. I prayed for Greg and Mieka, that their marriage would be a good one and that their lives would be happy. And then, as I had every morning that summer, I prayed for the wandering souls.

New from Gail Bowen

Fall 2004

THE LAST GOOD DAY

A Joanne Kilbourn Mystery

GAIL
BOWEN

"Gail Bowen does it all: genuine human characters, terrific plots . . .
and good, sturdy writing." – JOAN BARFOOT

A COLDER KIND OF DEATH

When the man convicted of killing her husband six years earlier is himself shot to death while exercising in a prison yard, Joanne Kilbourn is forced to relive the most horrible time of her life. And when the prisoner's menacing wife is found strangled by Joanne's scarf a few days later, Joanne is the prime suspect.

To clear her name, Joanne has to delve into some very murky party politics and tangled loyalties. Worse, she has to confront the most awful question – had her husband been cheating on her?

"A delightful blend of vicious murder, domestic interactions, and political infighting that is guaranteed to entertain." – *Quill & Quire*

"A classic Bowen, engrossing and finally, believable." – *The Mystery Review*

"A denouement filled with enough curves to satisfy any mystery fan."
– Saskatoon *StarPhoenix*

0-7710-1495-3 $9.99

A KILLING SPRING

The fates just won't ignore Joanne Kilbourn – single mom, university professor, and Canada's favourite amateur sleuth. When the head of the School of Journalism is found dead – wearing women's lingerie – it falls to Joanne to tell his new wife. And that's only the beginning of Joanne's woes. A few days later the school is vandalized and then an unattractive and unpopular student in Joanne's class goes missing. When she sets out to investigate the student's disappearance, Joanne steps unknowingly into an on-campus world of fear, deceit – and murder.

"This is the best Kilbourn yet." – *Globe and Mail*

"*A Killing Spring* is a page-turner. More than a good mystery novel, it is a good novel, driving the reader deeper into a character who grows more interesting and alive with each book." – *LOOKwest Magazine*

"Fast paced . . . and almost pure action. . . . An excellent read."
– *Saint John Telegraph-Journal*

"*A Killing Spring* stands at the head of the class as one of the year's best."
– *Edmonton Journal*

0-7710-1486-4 $7.99

VERDICT IN BLOOD

"A SEAMLESS BLEND OF HONEST EMOTION AND ARTISTRY."
- CHICAGO TRIBUNE

It's a hot Labour Day weekend in Regina, Saskatchewan, which means the annual Dragon Boat races in Wascana Park, a CFL game, family barbecues, ice cream – and tragedy. A young man is missing. And Madam Justice Justine Blackwell has been bludgeoned to death.

This is Gail Bowen's sixth novel featuring Joanne Kilbourn, one of Canada's most beloved sleuths. Teacher, friend, lover, single mother, and now grandmother, Joanne's quick intelligence and boundless compassion repeatedly get her into – and out of – trouble.

"A deeply involving novel . . . Bowen has supplied such a convincing array of details about [Joanne's] family, friends and the landscape that we slip into her life as easily as knocking on a neighbor's door." – *Publishers Weekly*

"Bless Gail Bowen, she does it all: genuine human characters, terrific plots with coherent resolutions, and good, sturdy writing."
– Joan Barfoot in the *London Free Press*

"An author in full command of her metier. Like a master chef, Gail Bowen has taken disparate elements . . . and combined them seamlessly." – *Calgary Herald*

0-7710-1489-5 $8.99

BURYING ARIEL

"A RIPPING GOOD MYSTERY."
- CATHERINE FORD, CALGARY HERALD

Joanne Kilbourn is looking forward to a relaxing weekend at the lake with her children and her new grandchild when murder once more wreaks havoc in Regina, Saskatchewan. A young colleague at the university where Joanne teaches is found stabbed to death in the basement of the library. Ariel Warren was a popular lecturer among both students and staff, and her violent death shocks – and divides – Regina's small and fractious academic community. The militant feminists insist that this is a crime only a man could have committed. They are sure they know which man, and they are out for vengeance. But Joanne has good reason to believe that they have the wrong person in their sights.

"A study in human nature craftily woven into an intriguing whodunit by one of Canada's literary treasures." – *Ottawa Citizen*

"Excellent . . ." – *National Post*

"The answer to the mystery . . . remains tantalizingly up in the air until the entirely satisfying finale." – *Toronto Star*

0-7710-1498-8 $9.99

THE GLASS COFFIN

This chilling tale about the power of the ties that bind – and sometimes blind – us, is Gail Bowen's best novel yet. Set in the world of television and film, *The Glass Coffin* explores the depth of tragedy that a camera's neutral eye can capture – and cause.

Canada's favourite sleuth, Joanne Kilbourn, is dismayed to learn the identity of the man her best friend, Jill Osiowy, is about to marry. Evan MacLeish may be a celebrated documentary filmmaker, but he has also exploited the lives – and deaths – of the two wives he lost to suicide by making acclaimed films about them. It's obvious to Joanne that this is stony ground on which to found a marriage. What is not obvious is that this ground is about to get bloodsoaked.

"The end . . . is chilling and unexpected." – *Globe and Mail*

"[*A Glass Coffin*] takes the series into a deeper dimension." – *Times-Colonist*

"Part of Bowen's magic – and her work is just that – lies not only in her richness of characters but in her knack of lacing her stories with out-of-left-field descriptives." – *Ottawa Citizen*

0-7710-1499-6 $34.99